MW00977067

Firelands

by

John G. McGill

DORRANCE PUBLISHING CO., INC.
PITTSBURGH, PENNSYLVANIA 15222

This is a work of fiction. Names, characters, places, and indicents are either the product of the author's imagination or are used fictitiously, and any resemblance to actual persons, living or dead, or locales is entirely coincidental.

ISBN # 0-8059-3995-4
Printed in the United States of America

First Printing

For information or to order additional books, please write:
Dorrance Publishing Co., Inc.
643 Smithfield Street
Pittsburgh, Pennsylvania 15222
U.S.A.

To

Mike Kreachbaum

Mike died in an avalanche in the Sierra Nevadas in the winter of 1992. He was alone in the backcountry, as usual. His body was not found until late spring. During that time, I pondered our friendship. It spanned a lifetime. He was a good man, complicated only by simplicity. He was a better friend. It was a good and true friendship. Its one great weakness was our sporadic contact. He was my wife's friend as well. I also wanted our sons to get to know him. I had promised him that I would bring them out West that summer to hike with him. Only after his funeral did these stories finally come together. Until that summer, the pieces had dogged me for several years. He was a good and true friend whom I wish my sons had known.

AUTHOR'S NOTE

The Firelands are found along the southern shore of Lake Erie in north central Ohio. They have precise boundaries, being composed of Erie and Huron counties, and additionally Danbury and Ruggles townships; but few know that.

Few also know how the Firelands came into that name. Most attribute it to the fiery sunsets and similar dawns that mark the passing of each day for its serene farms and timeless wetlands. The orange disk, glowing through the haze, is a sufficient basis for the name, but it is not. Nor is the children's story true, that the name derives from the swamp gas, ever present in the pungent breeze, periodically catching fire.

The Firelands actually draws its name from historic events during and after the American Revolutionary War. Then the treachery of Benedict Arnold and misguided punitive tactics of General Tryon brought a series of raids to Connecticut. To flush their enemy, the British burned farms, villages, and whole towns. Then, as it does today, the flames of such barbarity ignited opposition rather than suppressed it and further tempered the resolve of the insurgents.

After that revolution succeeded, in 1792 the Connecticut Assembly designated a portion of its holdings in the Northwest Territory, known as the Western Reserve, to be used to compensate some 1,800 families who were the victims of the fires. These 500,000 acres took the popular name, and remain to this day, the Firelands. That is actually how the region came to be named; but even those who know this, choose to believe that the name appropriately describes the passions of its inhabitants.

The legislative grant did not, as might be thought, trigger a mass migration. Most had reestablished themselves during the long delay in obtaining recognition of their claims. The grant was taken by most, as it was intended, in the nature of monetary compensation. Their moves, when they made them, were the calculated result of careful Yankee financial planning. They formed an association and hired surveyors in 1808 to lay out townships. Settlers first came in 1809, but slowly. Indeed, the first Connecticut settlers did not arrive in Sandusky, today a picturesque city of limestone buildings and church steeples that dominates the region, until 1817. The Connecticut Yankees left their indelible mark on the region in planning of their towns around squares and borrowing names such as Groton, New Haven, Norwalk and Oxford.

In 1848, the Germans, fleeing political upheavals of their own, began to arrive. Today, their red brick cottages punctuate the New England accent of the towns. Their farms, well-kept as one might expect, set the tone for all in the region.

Brown faces were always present in The Firelands. The first were sailors on Lake Erie frequenting the port of Sandusky and the shipyard at Huron. Even before The War Between the States, freed slaves often moved to Sandusky. Many runaway slaves, traveling towards Canada on The Underground Railroad, also decided, at some risk, to make Sandusky home. After that war, the trickle became a steady stream, continuing through the middle of this century, spurred by the prospect of high-paying union jobs in the auto industry.

There were others. Even before the Civil War, Sandusky had a well-established and distinguished Jewish community. Italians, Poles, and a variety of other East Europeans started coming in the late 1800's. In those years, Sandusky became a bustling port and manufacturing center. The farmlands became dotted with quarries and vineyards. They were heady times when fortunes were made from nothing but hard work and savvy. One vestige of those days remains in downtown Sandusky where coal from a continuing stream of trains is loaded on lake boats bound for the great steel mills. The charitable legacy of those times alone left Sandusky with half a dozen limestone churches that rival the cathedrals in most large American cities. More importantly, those churches were permanent institutions that helped cement a diverse community together.

Friends and relatives followed the initial immigrants for decades, even through the sad exodus from Hungary in 1956, then Viet Nam and Cambodia in the 1970's. Each group established its own community. Private clubs based on national origin remain popular. A careful ear still discerns strong accents in spoken English. Nevertheless, as is the American experience, the social intercourse blurred the ethnic boundaries. It is not unusual to hear an American Negro, who is the product of five or six generations in the Firelands, speak Modern American with the clipped accent of a third or fourth generation Pole.

Beyond its immigrant origins, to some extent the continuing flow of pilgrims may lend to the disposition of the Firelands. For a century tourism has been a major business in the region. There are no spectacular vistas drawing tourists to this pancake-flat region, but for Ohio's farmers and factory workers, the Firelands are the door to a weekend playground around Sandusky Bay and across the Lake Erie Islands. Every Friday night in the summer, tens of thousands of boaters and campers stream into the Firelands, only to leave again on Sunday afternoon. The amusement park at Cedar Point is the same magnet today that it was in Victorian times. This ebb and flow of as many people into and out of a region as live there certainly has an effect on the attitude of its inhabitants.

It is difficult to say when the Firelands reached its manifest destiny. That obviously depends on what one thinks that destiny is. Farming continues, but immigration for that reason alone ended before the Civil War. Ship building and lake port activity peaked at the turn of the century. The ebb of manufacturing came in the early 1970's, but the Fisher family left Norwalk for Detroit decades before. The weekend and vacation traffic continues to grow. Once, there were those who thought Sandusky would be a major city, but for a host of reasons, mostly industrial, that fate was for Cleveland, Toledo and Detroit. As it is, the Firelands is an area of primal wetlands, agriculture, and industry centering on a mature mid-sized city. It is one of those places that strikes first-time visitors as nice. Some may even have a fleeting thought of moving there, but few do. It is a place remembered. Those are the Firelands.

FIRELANDS

PROLOGUE

I know I'm over the Firelands when the shore line breaks the horizon. The drone of my engine fades away, and I watch the islands appear until I can see them all. Sandusky's steeples, Cedar Point's roller coasters, and the Marblehead Lighthouse silhouette the foreground. Looking down and west I find Bellevue. Norwalk is east, where it should be. I am back. As it always does, the weather changes. Lake effect is sometimes worse. This time it is better. It is so clear I am pulled deep into thoughts of my vista. I think I can smell the plowed fields and cut grass. I think I can hear the train whistles. I am no different than any of the other pilgrims, I keep coming back. Moments later I get busy in the landing pattern, but not too busy for one last look. When I land, I smell the cut grass over the Firelands' musk, and I hear a train whistle. It is always good to get back.

I have known Joe all my life. Molly, lovely, Molly; well, I wish I had known her better, longer. We were so young then. I first met Sandy and her husband when I was in law school. If someone asked me to list my friends, that's the list. Like anyone, I know hundreds of people, I suppose. In my line of work you meet a lot of people, but you just don't make friends. It's so structured, and everyone is playing a role and has to stick to their part to make it work. As for my clients, well, most of them have a fundamental problem with truth. They aren't exactly my kind of people.

Friendship has been on my mind a lot these days. I love my wife and kids. I can't tell you how lucky I am to have them, especially lucky that they stayed until I quit drinking. That said, I've been thinking about my friends. I know you want to hear about them, not me; so I'll get on with it. These are people that I feel close to, even though I've never been good about staying in touch. We've always been able to pick up wherever we left off.

I guess if I am going to do this right, I have to go all the way back. I grew up just outside the Firelands, explored them in my youth and left in pursuit of a career. Like so many others, I have been drawn back. No doubt that explains why I find it so intriguing that each of them also found their way to the Firelands. The Firelands have always been a safe haven for refugees; yet, I would never label my friends as refugees.

Molly was already there, and neither Joe nor Sandy was running from anything, any more than either was running towards something. I think that it can be fairly said that they were yearning for something, not seeking it. Joe and Sandy came to the Firelands by long and separate paths. Only now that I look back on their stories do I see the pull of the Firelands, and their unknowing surrender to its gravitation. Neither had to. Now, I see so clearly that their stories did not have to be; but it is equally clear that once underway, there was only one possible ending.

I.

Joe's Story

CHAPTER 1

"I don't know."

The way in which Joe said these words conveyed even more than the words themselves. He said them at least three or four times; each time in response to his mother's persistent questions; each answer more definite than the last. Finally, when impatience and the massive uncertainty of youth might have brought his voice to crack with emotion, he grew suddenly calm. Looking directly into her eyes, he said each word slowly, absolutely. Her question, "Then what are you going to do?" Her question before that, "Then where are you going to go?" Before that, "What about your scholarship?" Before that, "Why do you want to throw away a college education?"

Like many farmhouse kitchens, their's was attached to the house, with doors on opposite sides and several windows to keep the cooking heat from the rest of the house in summer. His mother was seated at the kitchen table, a flower and vegetable seed catalog laying before her. He was standing between her and the screen door through which their barn could be seen behind the house. He had just come across the room from the other door, facing the road. Coming in from the school bus, he had brought in the mail, including the seed catalog and another letter from Bowling Green about his scholarship to study agriculture. It was the first time that spring that it was warm enough to leave the doors open. The fresh country breeze through the kitchen marked the end of the long winter. He looked across the yard to the barn where he knew his father was cleaning the stalls by the periodic clumps flying through the barn door into the manure spreader parked along side the barn. "You have got to tell him." she said.

"I know."

His brother, Dieter, two years younger, had gone immediately upstairs to change out of his school clothes while Joe spoke to his mother in the kitchen. As younger brothers went, Dieter was a good one to have. He was funny, always with a twinkle in his eyes, always quick with a retort. Everyone, including Joe's friends, liked Dieter. Dieter was a C student who did not participate in sports or band, but he attended every school function. Parents and teachers took him as the congenial sort he was, but grandparents and other old timers from Attica who regularly attended the same functions recognized the boy would be one of them someday, unlike the quiet older Altznauer boy.

They looked like brothers, sharing the same germanic good looks, blond hair, blue eyes, and square faces. Both had sharp features, such as a turned up, pointed nose; thin lips; and square chin. The younger boy was a head shorter, however, and it was clear he had grown about all he ever would. He was generally regarded as his father's son, and Dieter adored the man. Joe, who looked more like his father, had his mother's disposition and intellect. Coming down the stairs, the younger brother stopped short hearing their conversation. He had intended to get out to the barn first so he could drive the tractor, but he sat down on the steps, listening to his mother turn the pages of the catalog and cry after the screen door slapped shut behind Joe.

Walking towards the barn, Joe felt different than he even had before. He drew in deep breaths of the moist April air and scanned the horizon. The fields were bright green with the winter wheat coming up, and although the woods were not fully leafed out, they were getting there. The sun was bright and warm on his face. He was relieved. She had not changed his mind. He had not swayed. The hard part was over. He knew his father would accept what he was about to tell him, but he also thought it would hurt, and he did not want to hurt him. His confidence was short-lived, for as he saw the tip if the pitch fork come out of the stall door sending another clump towards the manure spreader, his stomach grew tight with dread. It was not going to be easy, but he told himself the hardest part was over.

"Hi, Joe, how was school, short-timer?" his father said, stopping to lean on the pitch fork. He mumbled some response and asked about the pitching. His father voiced his opinions on the benefits of animal waste as fertilizer, the high cost of chemicals, the benefits of raising both animals and crops, specialization in farming, and the decline of the family farm. His father continued cleaning the stall as he polished his speech, and Joe stood back out of the way, leaning up against the wall. Across the stall, he studied the embellished pencil signature of an earlier

Altznauer written on the completion of the barn and dated August 17, 1872. As a boy he found wondrous security in that date. As a young man it conveyed an altogether different message. He looked from the date through the door and across the wheat field to the woods. From his son's lingering about in his school clothes, his father knew the boy had something to say. He kept an eye on Joe and continued to work. "Yeah, one of us has been pitching shit through this door for damn near a hundred years. Not much changes." and he stopped again to rest against the pitch fork.

"This came today." Joe said, pulling a thick envelope from where he tucked it in the waist of his white levis. "It's from B.G., final papers for me to sign. I'm not going to go."

His father didn't answer. Instead, he began pitching again. Joe tucked the envelope back in his pants and leaned against the wall. He watched his father work, studying his physique. At forty-five he was still thin. He was the same height as Joe, just over six foot. He was half bald, and what hair he had, he kept cut short. His strawberry blond hair had darkened with age, but it was cut so short, he was literally bald. His face and arms were leathery and wrinkled from the weather, but just inside his collar and above his sleeve, his skin was soft and white. Except for the years, they looked enough alike to be twins.

"You probably don't remember, but when you were six or seven, you came up to me and told me that you could tell the manure made the wheat grow better, that you could see it." He did not stop pitching, but continued to speak as he worked. "When I was riding the tractor, I used to see you sitting on the kitchen roof, clumped up in a little ball just below your bedroom window. I never told your mother, she would have had a fit. When I was a boy, I had a tree back in the woods I liked to climb, so I just let it go. Well after you said that, I went up and looked out your window. Sure enough, you could see the wheat was greener where I spread the manure. You could even see spaces between rows if I missed a spot with the shit kicker. I swear, I lived on this farm my whole life; I grew up looking out that same window; I climbed my tree a hundred times; and I have cleaned this barn and spread manure a thousand times; but I never saw that until you told me." He stopped pitching and looked over to Joe. "I always knew you'd leave."

Joe fought back tears, wounded as much by the sudden discovery that his father had known about his place on the roof as by the parental revelation. "I thought..., you're the one who pushed B.G."

"Sure I did. Every father wants his children to have it better. No one in this family ever went to college. I'm a farmer. What do I know? I read all these articles in the Ohio Farmer written by professors from O.S.U. and B.G. I know you've got a brain, so naturally I talk it up. What the hell else do I know?" He came over to his son and patted him on the shoulder, then squeezed it. "You'll do fine. Now go change. I could use some help."

Joe turned for the door with a tear running down the side of his face, when his father spoke up again. "I've been thinking about getting some chickens again. Remember when you were ten, and you talked me out of the chicken business. I figured it was time to teach you some responsibility, so I put fifty dollars in a bank account and tell you that's your capital and the chicken coop is your business. It was unbelievable, you cleaned that coop like it hadn't been since it was built. Then you come back from Attica all serious and say we have to talk. You priced paint, chicken wire, chicks, feed, the whole bit. Then you went to the grocery store with your mother and saw how much it cost to buy eggs and poultry. At goddamned ten years old you figured out that it will cost you twice as much to raise them than they can be bought for in the store. Not only do you not go into the chicken business, you talk me out of it. Can't compete with the poultry farmers, you said. Well, that old coop made a nice play house for your and Dieter, but you guys don't use it anymore. I used to like drinking a few beers on Saturday night and plucking a chicken for Sunday dinner. I'm thinking about getting some chickens again." Joe smiled and walked on back to the house.

His father raised his voice and called after him. "Tell Dieter to get out here, I need him too. You'll do fine. Just don't let those S.O.B.'s kill you in their TV war. You're an all right guy. Smarter than me that's for goddamned sure. Just don't let them kill you. They tried to kill me. They never give up. Specialization, that's how the bastards are destroying the family farm."

Joe could not have been more surprised. All of a sudden he was adrift. He had spent months brooding and preparing for a fight. His entire energy was absorbed in preparing arguments against what he perceived his parents wanted him to do, not what he wanted to do. His mind was swirling, unable to appreciate how wrong he had been and what his parents really wanted for him. He was twisting, floating, free. What he would do, he hadn't the slightest idea. He truly did not know. It was the first time he ever heard his father mention war.

CHAPTER 2

I am probably the closest thing to a best friend that Joe ever had. When we were kids, we were bosom buddies. Yet, I was more surprised than anyone when he announced that he wasn't going to college. At the time, it was a big deal, a really big deal, especially at school.

Joe was always the smartest in our class. He was number one in about everything. We were on the basketball team together, he was captain. He was big in the Future Farmers of America. He wore that blue corduroy jacket with yellow letters more than his letter jacket, even to class. Eventually, he was president of the school chapter. I can remember him going to Columbus for the FFA convention every year. I think he got elected to some statewide office, but I can't remember what it was for sure, secretary or treasurer.

The idea of Joe as a politician still tickles me. He was really very shy. Whenever a group of us would stand around, he was always a step or two back. He was always there, usually close in on the action, but always at a distance. Also, he never spoke up first. If you said something to him or asked something, he always pondered for a moment before he answered. People who didn't know him easily got the impression that he wasn't really very smart, but he was. He was just very careful about what he said, not like Dieter. Old Dieter was a total cut-up, always engaging his mouth before his brain, always caught, always in the principal's office. Not Joe, he was really big in that school. I suppose every couple of years someone like him comes through a school, someone that both students and teachers respect. That was Joe. He was the only one like that I ever knew.

Every time I drive through Attica on my way up to Lake Erie, I swing by the old high school. It's funny, but what I usually think about is graduation night in the auditorium which doubles as a gymnasium. Joe was our Valedictorian and gave a speech. I wish I could remember what he said. I can see him giving it. It wasn't long, but today I don't have a clue what he said. I do remember the murmuring in the audience when he was introduced. The Superintendent went over all his honors, which were already listed in the program. Then, when he would have announced where Joe was going to college, he said nothing. When they should have applauded, all our parents started whispering to each other that which they already knew. Joe was uncomfortable enough without having to start his speech that way. I got mad; I still do, when I think about it. I still wish I could remember what he talked about. Only three or four students from our high school went on to college each year. Who they were was understood all the way up from grade school. So it was a big deal that Joe wasn't going. I doubt that any of our parents heard or remembered what he had to say either. If it were me, I would have talked about the future and getting the hell out of Attica. Joe probably thanked everyone.

What I do remember is partying that night. We all had to put in appearances at home for cake and cookies with our parents and relatives, then ganged up for a party of our own. A bunch of us guys swung by the Altznauer place in my old car and picked up Joe. We cruised Attica, then drove over to Tiffin for a pizza at a joint at the base of the hill below the Heidelberg College campus that we used to frequent. There, we met up with more of our class. On the drive back, most of the guys and girls paired off, except for Joe. Joe rode shotgun in my car with Linda Wagenbrenner sandwiched in between us. For some reason after twelve years of school together, she started looking a lot better to me that night. I was finding parts of her to bump into with my elbow when I shifted gears; and she was tickling me, blowing in my ear. Jerry Farabaugh was in the back seat making out with Judy Clodfelter. Joe was looking out the window, looking down, watching the ditch flash by.

Back in town, Joe asked me to let him out by the drug store. It and everything else in Attica had been closed for hours. I wanted to drive him home. It was almost four miles to their farm. He said he'd rather walk. He did that all the time. He even used to jog home from track practice. In the Spring, he ran track. I played baseball. From the ball field we'd see him running home from track practice with a backpack full of his books and clothes. If it had been anyone other than Joe, we'd have had some wise remark. I can't remember his speech, but I can remember graduation night like it was yesterday.

"Come on, man, let me drive you home."

"No thanks."

"Aw, come on. It's no big deal."

"I'd rather walk."

"Well, ok, but...."

"I'd rather." and he was out of the car.

I can't remember his valedictorial address, I can't remember where we went parking with the girls that night, but I can remember his exact words. It's funny.

In my personal opinion, if Joe had had a girlfriend in Attica, he would have gone to college, come back, married her, farmed, raised a family, and I'd be stopping in to see him there today. He never had a girlfriend. Never dated. Never went to the school dances. It was amazing. He was the best looking guy in our class. The girls were always after me about him. Since I was his friend, they were always having me tell him who liked him. When the guys and I teased him, Dieter, who was always hanging around us, would rush forward to defend Joe, "Leave the fag alone!" and the little fireplug would puff out his chest and push up against whichever one of us had said it that time, looking up into our faces as if ready to take anyone on, but defied by the twinkle in his eye. Joe would wait for the guffawing to stop, then say, "I have my standards."

His standards were different than whatever Attica had to offer. I was never quite sure about his standards, for I was more than content with our girls. I never went steady, and though in a small town more did than did not, I still found enough girls free to move about with a reasonable degree of impunity. Joe just never got involved with girls. I was on the yearbook staff. I remember taking his picture with Gretchen Krendle because the two of them
had been voted "Most Likely To Succeed". Joe just about died when I pushed them closer together for the photo. It's funny the things you remember.

His parents had been an item when they went to our school. Their class picture was right over the water fountain outside the senior homeroom, so I had plenty of time to study them. Joe looked just like Mr. Altznauer, and Mrs. Altznauer was simply beautiful. There was no one in our school who could compare to her. There were a couple of pictures of Mr. and Mrs. Altznauer together in their yearbook, and I found more loose snapshots in the yearbook office. I gave them to Mrs. Altznauer one time. She was a pretty lady. She was different than the other moms. She was the same age, but wore her hair in a ponytail when our moms had beehives. She wore pants and shirts when most of the women wore print dresses and aprons. I can remember her boxing around and tickling Dieter. He would try to pull her ponytail. I would never clown around like that with my mom. Neither did Joe, for that matter. She was really hard on him, always pushing. I gave her the pictures because I liked her. I liked going over to their house.

We lived in Attica, right on the main north/south thoroughfare, two blocks north of the only stop light. The center of town is marked by the bank, drug store, and gas station. The main drag is also the state highway and just about the only easy way from Columbus to Sandusky. My parents have a nice two-story brick house built in the late 1800's. Until he sold out and retired, Dad ran a little manufacturing plant on the east side of town, just beyond the high school and across from the cemetery. His father, who emigrated from Germany, started a machine shop. My dad built it up bigger, he turned it more into a welding shop, a job shop. He still has a little machine shop, takes in odd jobs, but I doubt it makes him any money. Today his old plant keeps about fifteen on the payroll. In the sixties, however, it was much bigger. He got some small business set asides from the government. At the peak, when he got a contract to make bomb casings, there must have been fifty or sixty on his payroll. By Attica standards, Dad was a tycoon, and I was a rich kid. That meant that we had the first color TV in town, and I had a car. I paid for it myself, but I made twice minimum wage at Dad's plant.

Joe and I spent much of our adolescence lying on our backs under that 1948 Olds. I was learning about automotive mechanics as I went along, but Joe had been around farm equipment his whole life. He was quite an accomplished mechanic, even then. Long before Mr. Altznauer had put him in charge of the tool shed on the farm. Joe had that shed as clean and organized as a hospital operating room. We did the engine and brakes in my parent's garage, but after our first attempt at painting got some on my parent's Cadillac; Mr. Altznauer let us paint it out at the farm. For a three color paint job by amateurs, we did good. I learned a lot from Joe. Once, he listened to it knocking and announced my rod bearings needed replacing. We did it. Not long after that I told him the knocks were back and recruited him to help me change them out again. He listened, put on his timing light and dwell meter, and tuned my knocks away. I still can't tell a bearing knock from a timing knock, but Joe is quite a mechanic. As much time as he spent on my car, I cannot remember one instance of him ever driving it. That's just like him. He wouldn't presume to use someone else's property.

One of the many stupid things we used to do was hop bumps. That involved driving the back roads at high speeds, not the county roads, the township roads. The township roads weren't graded as level as county or state roads, so they were loaded with little hills and bends. At that time, most were still gravel, which added to our delight in drifting around corners and throwing up a dust cloud. I remember one night our junior year when we went out bump hopping with at least six guys piled into my car. Eventually we hit hard and slid sideways into a ditch. The crowd made it easy to push the car back on the road, but Joe's inspection revealed that I had smashed in the oil pan again, and it was leaking. As we nursed that crowded car back into town, I specifically remember Joe asking me about my future. He caught me off guard and my answer was about as stupid as my driving. Years later my side of that conversation would haunt me, but more recently I've been thinking about Joe's.

"What are you going to do after school?"

"O.S.U. I just hope the war doesn't end before I can get over there and kill some gooks."

"I don't know about that."

"College, killing or gooks?"

"Whatever."

Joe and I had a lot of good times in that Olds. We'd cruise around together after getting back from basketball games on the team bus. Usually, we didn't go as far as Tiffin or Bucyrus, we'd just roam up and down the back roads late at night. I'd dream out loud about finding the cheerleaders who had to be out cruising for us. Cedar Point was a regular day trip for us. Occasionally, we'd get bold and put the Olds on the ferry to South Bass Island. I loved to cruise Put-In-Bay in that car. A couple of times we went over to the sports car races at Mid-Ohio near Mansfield. Back then they allowed camping. We'd stay overnight in the in-field. I'd sleep in the front seat, Joe in the back. Same thing senior year when I drove him over to Bowling Green to check out the campus. We ate in local pizza joints and slept in the car. It was a little dicier in Columbus when he went with me to check out O.S.U. Cops ran us out twice that night, but no harm for I'm still telling the story. Joe and I cruising. I'd run on at the mouth, Joe'd listen.

I was the last one in Attica to see Joe the day he left. The Saturday morning after graduation I was waxing the Olds when he walked up our driveway wearing his backpack and lugging his dad's army duffle bag from World War II.

"What the hell?"

"Just wanted to say bye."

"What.... Where are you going?"

"Not sure. North."

"Sandusky?"

"Probably. Maybe see if I can get hired on a lake boat."

"That's it? What about the draft?"

"Well...."

"No college deferment, man."

"I'm not going to enlist. If they call me, I'll go."

"Jesus H. Christ! Joseph Altznauer leaves Attica. Holy shit, man! I can't fucking believe this!"

"Just wanted to say good-bye."

"God damn, man!" I shook his hand. "Gook luck!" He turned and started down the drive. "How can I get in touch with you?"

"Mom will have my address." he called back without breaking stride.

"Hey, Joe, let me drive you."

"No thanks, I'd rather walk."

CHAPTER 3

As he hiked north along Route 4, Joe looked at the farms in a way he never had before. He looked through the contrast of bright color on this late spring day, along the sharp blue/green horizon to the farms themselves. He saw some were pristine, some decrepit. In all he saw the passage of time. Each farm was a cluster of buildings that with a second look told much of the evolution of farming in this area.

Most had the traditional multi-purpose barns from the late 1800's with hay lofts above, horse stalls below, tack rooms, granaries, and storage space for buggies and wagons. Most of those barns had a low slung milking parlor extended out one side, although in some instances the cattle barn was separate. There were no cattle now. Scattered around each barn were a variety of smaller special purpose buildings, such as corn cribs, tool sheds, chicken coops. He saw the march of time in the use or disuse of the buildings.

Silos, added to most barns in the early 1900's, first made from concrete then later from enameled metal, were largely empty. The silos' original purpose was gone with the livestock. Those that were in use were being used to store grain. The fields north of Attica were mostly in grain: wheat, soy beans, or corn. Unlike Joe's father, few anymore kept up their fences. The ones he saw were broken down and tangled in brush. Looking about, there were frequent rolls of rusted wire, where farmers were removing them. He had read about the western feed lots, and he knew about the richness of this soil. It was too valuable for pasture. The small chicken coops he saw, like their's, were mostly abandoned in favor of the mammoth poultry barns. The old rectangular wooden and wire corn cribs were giving way to the large circular galvanized metal storage bins, which he saw on virtually every larger farm. The more prosperous farms had several connected by drying equipment and screw conveyors. For those with livestock, large rolls of hay kept outside replaced bales stored in the lofts.

Then Joe came back to the colors. He scanned every farm in sight, determining that every barn and most out buildings were painted red, trimmed in white, and had black roofs. The farm houses were painted white. On their farm, every building, including the house, was painted white with the metal roofs painted green.

As he walked along, he thought through reasons for the colors. The dark red would draw in the heat, helping keep any livestock warmer and the hay and grain dry, but so would any dark color. The white might keep the houses cool in summer. All the houses were partially hidden by trees to shade them, nature's air conditioning. Perhaps the colors came over with the Germans. Maybe someday he would get to Germany to see if his theory were true. He could ask his father, but he quickly dismissed the thought, he wouldn't have noticed. Joe knew no reason why all the buildings on their farm were white, other than it looked good.

Six miles and an hour and a half behind him, his mother still sat on the steps to their front porch. Her knees were pulled up to her chest and her arms hugged them. She did not move. She was no longer crying, but lines from her tears were still visible on her face. She was looking east along the county road to where it joined Route 4. Occasionally she saw cars and trucks moving up and down the highway. Since she had sat down there, two northbound coal trains had passed on the tracks that paralleled Route 4. When the first train came, it obscured Joe's silhouette moving up the highway. When it passed, she could not see him anymore. She sat quietly, crying, feeling more empty than he could ever know nor would ever appreciate. She wondered if his death could be any worse. Grief was a word she pondered. It was not strong enough, she thought. The breeze carried the hum of the tractor, but she did not look in its direction.

"I love you, Joe. I love you, honey." she'd said, pushing back his hair.

"You've got to get a plan together, son. If it doesn't work out, go to your back up plan." her husband said. "If all else fails, we'll still be here. The bastards are trying to destroy the family farm, but we'll be here."

Joe tried a smile, nodding yes. He didn't say anything for a long while, just looked along the county road to where it met the highway. Finally, he shook Dieter's hand and said, "Well, I've got to get going.

I'll call."

"Honey, let us drive you."

"No, I'll be working on my plan."

Across the county road to the south, Joe's father was riding the tractor, cultivating the corn. All the corn was in. In fact, it was ankle high. It was a sunny, cool Saturday morning in late May. This would be the first of several times he would cultivate the corn, breaking the soil between the rows, turning under any weeds. In six weeks the corn would be high enough to crowd out any volunteers, knee high by the Fourth of July. It made sense to him that weeding the rows until then would make the corn crop better. Cultivating was tedious and boring work, but it made sense.

Beyond him Dieter was working along the fence row with a scythe, cutting the grass that grew up and tangled in the wire. Occasionally, his father would whistle and point, and Dieter would go out into the field, pick up the stone and throw it out of the way along the fence row. Most other farmers were spraying weed killer instead of cultivating, but the cost gulled his father. Something about the clean rows and broken soil appealed to Dieter. He looked down the rows to where they came together in the distance. He smiled at the sight of the collection of crisp white buildings and bright green roofs. He could see his mother sitting on the porch. When he did he thought about the taste of ice tea. Out here, working with his dad, Joe's departure had quickly slipped from his mind.

Joe's mother finally turned to look south across the road in the direction of her husband and second son. She wondered how the cost of all the gasoline spent cultivating compared to weed killer. She wondered why he kept up fences when the only livestock they kept were a dozen steers. It was getting to be mid-morning. She should be brewing some tea to take out to them. She should be thinking about lunch for them. Instead, she thought about Joe, and started sobbing; much harder than before. She put here face down in her knees and tried to bury her moan.

Joe's father, sitting on the tractor, and looking down between his legs to the rows of new corn, didn't think of Joe, but rather, about the day they buried his father. His mother had died between Christmas and New Year's in 1944 while he was bouncing around in a tank in the Battle of the Bulge. He hadn't found out until a month later, and it never did seem real; not even three years later when he looked under his father's casket down into the grave where he could see the edge of his mother's vault. They married right after he returned from the war, and after a week in Niagara Falls, they moved in with his father. Only then did he realize how much his father had changed.

The farm had gotten rough looking, but he thought that was because he hadn't been around to help. His father had quit caring about the farm. With a woman back in the house, the older man hovered around her more than anything. Any sign of bad weather was an excuse for him to sit in the kitchen with her. He insisted on driving her to town to market. Suddenly after a year or so, they noticed he started talking about his dead wife in the present tense. Then one evening he got full of energy and recited a long list of things they had to do on the farm, including painting all the buildings. They would start the next morning; but the next morning, they found him dead in his bed.

As soon as everyone left after the burial, Joe's father had gone out to cultivate the corn. Looking across the field to the buildings, he decided that the red barn and out buildings should all be painted white like the house. The black roofs were too solemn. He would go for green. It would take time to get it done, two or three coats to cover the red, and a lot of money, but he could save other places. The old man would not approve, but even he knew it was time to paint. It was a clean break. It would make the place their's. Joe's father looked up from the ground to see the white buildings shimmering in the sunlight. He just couldn't shake the horrible feeling of his father's funeral. For him it was a more dreaded memory than the war, and he would not let himself think about the war. Joe had been born two years later, just after he finished painting the last building white. He ground his teeth together and successfully held in his tears.

Joe walked against the traffic, making no attempt to hitch a ride. Once a car slowed, its driver spoke to him through the window. It was the banker, Mr. Wirthmann. He was going to Sandusky and could give him a ride all the way. Joe was tempted, but declined. "It's a nice day. I'm in no hurry. Thanks anyway." Joe thought about money. He had saved over a thousand dollars. With part-time jobs and a scholarship, that would have put him through state school. His parents had given him a hundred dollars for graduation. That was in his wallet. He could get by on that until he found a job and got a paycheck. That was the first part of his plan.

CHAPTER 4

By mid-morning Joe had passed through Siam and was several miles north of Attica. He turned his attention from the farms to the churches. One of the things most noticed about this region, even to a casual observer, and especially to those passing through, was the churches.

Every mile or two there was another church. Each was first noticed by its steeple in the distance. All were topped with a cross. All had working bells. Each church was made from the same red brick. Some were partially obscured by shade trees. What the trees protected were small adjacent cemeteries. On the opposite of each was a gravel parking lot. Most were strikingly familiar in architecture, with the cross floor plan of the largest cathedrals in Europe, and large stained-glass windows. The locals took it for granted, and those passing through did not have time to realize, that what distinguished these churches was their size. They were too big to be country churches. Any one of them could have served the entire area, but there was one after another. That is what outsiders remembered, the sheer number of them.

Joe crossed to the east side of the highway, dropped his bags under a shade tree, and slumped to the ground, leaning back against the tree. His shoulders ached. He kept his eyes closed, not even opening them at the breeze from passing cars. After several minutes he opened them, and looked over his shoulder to the church. When he looked up the road, he could see another against the distant sky. For a time he had belonged to a Cub Scout den that met in the basement of this church.

He remembered making bookends there, plaster casts of wolf and bear heads. He joined this den in the third grade for the innocent reason that his best friend belonged to the den and incidentally this church. For reasons he did not understand, his mother was against it. He was able to ride a school bus to the church for the meetings, but his mother had to pick him up. Every time she muttered about the distance all the way home. She even complained in front of his friend, who lived in Attica, and usually caught a ride back to town with them. Of all the churches and all the denominations housed in this string of impressive churches along Route 4, all were Protestant, and most were independent. The Altznauer's were Catholic.

In the fourth grade Joe bowed to his father's suggestion that he join the den which met at their parish, Sts. Peter & Paul, a modest red brick church in town. Later, Sts. Peter & Paul Parish would build one of those non-descript, low-slung, modern churches in a field west of town. Despite the fact that they belonged to different dens, Joe and his friend helped each other build their pine wood derby racers. The race was held at the Knights of Columbus hall in Attica, with the older Boy Scouts and fathers officiating. Joe won. Waiting for his parents outside that night, Joe heard one of the boys from the den he used to belong to say to his friend, "Cheatin' fisheaters, fixed it so we couldn't win. No way!"

"Sore loser." Joe's friend replied.

In the shadow, on the other side of a bush, Joe spun the wheels of his pine wood racer against the palm of his hand. He brought it up next to his ear and listened to the wheels hum. He had polished the nail axles with emery cloth and lubricated them with graphite. No one else, not even Joe's friend who had the benefit of Joe's suggestion, had taken the time to polish their axles.

Several months later, the Boy Scouts put on their annual campfire Indian dance. It was raining, so it was held inside in the church basement at this church where his friend's den met. Joe, his friend, and the sore loser were honored to be chosen to play settlers and be tied up as captives and danced around by the Boy Scouts in their full regalia and war paint. Joe's mother took a picture of the three of them together that he still kept in a drawer.

Joe rose, put on his back pack, and slung the G.I. duffle bag over his shoulder. As he did, he noticed that the next church north was on the opposite side of the road.

"I think I've finally figured it out!" the twelve year old Joe boasted to his father as he jumped off his bike.

"What's that?"

"Why each farm is staggered on the opposite side of the road from the next."

"Now, why's that?" asked his father who had never noticed.

"Privacy and protection. See, each one more or less faces the other. That way, people can keep an eye on each other's place and still go out back and not be seen."

"Makes sense."

"I also know why each house is on a knoll."

"Why?"

"Worst soil. Knolls are rocky. The best top soil washed off them a thousand years ago. Also, you get the best view of the farm and the neighbors. If you're lucky, there might be a spring on the hill side."

"You just might be right, Joe."

"I am right. Think about it like you were the first one here and had to decide where to build. Like, why do you think most all the farms are right along the road? They could have been built right in the middle of the farms and been the same distance from all the fields."

"That might make more sense, but I don't really know, Joe."

"It's so they don"t lose good land to a long lane to the middle of the farm. Also, if you're right along the road, you don't have to worry about plowing yourself out of the snow in winter. County will take care of it for you."

"Makes sense, Joe. That makes sense."

Joe smiled and wondered if the people who built these churches were interested in keeping an eye on each other. Route 4 was as straight as an arrow, and he could see up it until it disappeared in the distance. There were enough Catholics around, but they were by no means the majority. There was St. Sebastian north of Attica and two miles east of Route 4, and even the Sorrowful Mother Shrine just off Route 4 on the Huron county line road. He wondered why none of those Catholic churches were part of the string along Route 4. Before he worked out an answer, another coal train heading north passed on the tracks that ran along the highway. For a moment he though about jumping the train, but it was too far from the road and moving too fast for him to catch.

Joe was ten the first time he saw the coal dock in Sandusky. It was a monstrous facility just to the west of downtown where trains brought up coal from southern Ohio and West Virginia. There the trains were broken down and staged for loading onto the lake boats. The freighters pulled up alongside a gigantic contraption into which the coal cars were rolled one at a time. Each car, in turn, would be lifted and turned upside down into a funnel that carried the coal onto the boats. As a dust cloud would start to rise, giant sprays of water would instantly wash it down. Watching the coal loading operation from the ferry taking his family across the bay to Cedar Point, Joe was captivated by the mechanics, the scale of the machinery, and the mammoth boats. By his reckoning, each lake boat had to be two or three times bigger than their barn. He had never imagined anything like it, and nothing at Cedar Point would intrigue him so. His little brother bounced around squealing about the amusement park and pointing to the Blue Streak. Joe did not like looking that far across the water. Looking down at it was worse. It terrified him. He couldn't swim. He studied the coal operation instead.

It was time to get serious about a plan, Joe thought. First choice, he would get on with one of the freight companies. He would become an inland sailor. He thought about seeing the lights of Chicago from the water, and going on liberty in sailor's clothes with his buddies; just like in the old movies. He admitted to himself that the water scared him, but those ships were so big, it had to be something to be on one. He wondered if they even moved in the waves. He wondered how many were on a crew. He thought of them headed across Sandusky Bay, out the channel between Cedar Point and the Marblehead Lighthouse, gliding towards unknown destinations.

The fear knotted in his stomach when he thought of being out on the lake completely surrounded by water. Plan B, maybe there were jobs at the coal dock. There had to be. The place was so big, there had to be. He searched his memory of the operation. He could not remember ever seeing a single human being as the mighty machine picked up the rail cars and poured them out onto the freighters; but there had to be lots of people working there.

Well, at least he had two plans. Now he needed to be thinking about a place to live. He had a hundred dollars. He thought he could make that last one month. By then he'd have a job and money would be coming in. He would not have to touch the thousand sitting in savings in the pillared Sutton Bank back in Attica. Soon he'd have the hundred back.

At 11:30 A.M. Joe was getting hungry. He had walked about half the thirty miles to Sandusky. Seneca County was behind him. The farms seemed smaller and poorly kept. The trees seemed shorter and tortured. The fences and ditches were suddenly derelict. He had been up this road many times, but it was different in a car and profoundly different than he now felt. He felt he had entered a foreign and forbidding land. What the hell, he thought, he was hungry. He put out his thumb. In a few minutes, a semi pulled over and gave him a ride all the way to the GM plant on the south side of Sandusky.

CHAPTER 5

The truck driver dropped Joe at the GM gate, before pulling up to the guard house where he was cleared to enter. Having grown up a thirty minute drive away, Joe was generally familiar with Sandusky. Now, however, he looked at it differently than ever before. He did not casually glance at the town as he drove through with his family or friends; nor did he study things looking for patterns as was his custom. Rather, as Joe walked, he thought only of how he was going to find a place to stay.

At that time, the GM plant was south of town. The southern edge of the city was defined by Perkins Avenue. Like similar streets in small and large cities, Perkins was a conglomeration of car lots, fast food places, discount stores, gas stations, strip centers, and other small businesses that always make you wonder how they survive. Joe spotted a Kentucky Fried Chicken on Perkins, and made a line for it. He decided to make this his big meal of the day. His box meal and drink cost 96 cents, $99 left. While he ate, he stared aimlessly out the window. He could see three car lots, and two boat dealers. He thought about lodging. He strained looking for a motel, none. He went back to watching a filthy young man with long hair and a scraggly beard pumping gas across the way. It was 1967, and he had seen such grooming on TV, but no one in Attica looked like that.

After finishing, Joe gathered up his bags and trundled across Perkins to the gas station. Joe's hippie was now inside behind the cash register lighting a cigarette. As Joe walked in, he could see black marks on the side of the cigarette from the fellow's greasy hands. Joe had a strong opinion about mechanics who were covered in grease and oil. In his mind, machines ran best when clean. Clean people were most likely to respect machinery. Slobs who neglected themselves were not likely to do any better with equipment. He concluded this fellow was not much of a mechanic before a word was spoken. The gas station attendant sized up Joe. As he did, he wiped his greasy hand on his blue jeans, that were more black with filth than blue, then combed his stringy, shoulder length hair back between his fingers.

"Hi. I'm looking for a place to stay. Got any advice?"

"I don't know, man. There's some old apartments along Columbus. What are you looking for?"

"Well, anything; a room; a place to stay until I get a job."

"I don't know man. You ought to look in the paper. There's a bunch of motels where 6 and 250 come together and over along Cleveland near the Cedar Point Causeway. Park opens next week, so they're still empty. You might find something there." Seeing Joe struggle to remember, he reached for a map, which back then gas stations gave away for free, and opened it. "We're here. Apartments here. Motels here and here."

"Thanks."

"No problem, man."

Without knowing for sure, Joe figured that apartments would require an application, credit references, and a job. He had been across the Cedar Point Causeway many times, so using the map he headed for the motels. It didn't look far on the map, but it took another half hour for him to make his way there.

What he found were several clean looking products of the 1950's. All had been spruced up for the coming tourist season. All looked beyond his means. He walked passed them and a strip shopping center, going southeast along Cleveland towards the Causeway. He passed along a nice residential section whose homes, manicured lawns and trees reminded him of Attica. With them, he lost the sense of foreboding that had crept over him that morning. He recognized the sign to the Causeway in the distance, and made out what looked to be more family motels near it. When he got about a quarter mile from them, he came across a collection of a half dozen white cottages, all sorely in need of paint. Two hand- made signs marked either side of a gravel parking lot, pock-marked with puddles. One said, "We appreciate your business." The other said, "Honest and Grateful." A neon sign hanging from the office proclaimed "Vacancy"' and a cardboard sign in the window said "Weekly & Monthly Rates". It looked good to Joe.

"Hi. How much for a room?"

The old woman got up from her over-stuffed chair which faced the counter from another room. She walked by her TV without turning it down, and stepped over the cats that did not scramble out of her way. She wore a faded print dress that buttoned up the front, and print apron over that. Despite the outward appearance of the place, the inside was well-kept. Joe felt like he was in someone's home, as indeed, he was.

"Every cottage has a double bed, TV, radio, telephone, shower, sink, hot plate, and refrigerator. Two people, $2 a night, $12 a week, $40 a month. Fresh towels and linen twice a week. Maid service daily. You from around here? You have a car?" She whistled all this through her false teeth in an accent he couldn't place. It wasn't German.

"No, ma'am. I just graduated. Came here looking for work." She did not pay any attention to Joe's life story. He had passed her background check when he called her "ma'am".

"Don't like cars spinning their tires in the gravel. Don't like loud music, TV, or parties."

"You said, two people. Any break for one person?"

"No, same rate. How long you staying?"

"Well, a week, I guess."

"I can give you Unit 2 for $10 a week, with no maid service, linen only once a week, and cash in advance."

"That will do fine."

As Joe filled in the form, twice he had to brush away a purring black cat. The key had a large plastic tag that told its user to drop it in the mail. On the other side it had the address and something that looked like postage molded in, but both were chipped and hard to make out. The cottage was clean. He unpacked most of his clothes into the dresser. He unfolded his suit and hung it on a wire hanger he found on the rack over the half-size refrigerator. The refrigerator door was open, and it was not plugged in. Joe took care of that and put water in the aluminum ice tray. He looked out the side window to the next unit, and passed it to Cleveland Avenue. As far as he could tell, he was the only one in any of the cottages. He used the toilet, then decided to take a shower. After that, he laid on the bed listening to the radio for half an hour. He hadn't been away from home for more than a few hours and only had $89 left.

Late in the afternoon, Joe got dressed again and walked back up Cleveland to the grocery store in the shopping center. He was shocked by the price of beef, and instead bought several cans of beef stew, tuna fish, and baked beans. He also bought a bag of apples, a clump of bananas, a jar of instant ice tea, and the local paper. All that came to just over $2.50, $86 left. Back in his room, Joe stirred up a glass of tea and studied the classifieds. He couldn't find anything about lake boats or the coal yard. There were dozens of clerical, mechanic, sales, and secretarial jobs; but nothing interested him. He told himself that good jobs wouldn't be in the paper anyway, and he turned his attention to apartments. One bedrooms were going for $50 to $100 per month. His cottage didn't seem like such a bad deal after all.

Later, he made dinner. The can opener he found in a drawer didn't work well, but he finally got the can of beef stew open. He made the mistake of heating it in the can, which he first realized when the label caught fire. Another problem was holding the hot can when he ate from it while watching TV. After dinner, he called home collect.

"It's an old motel, not far from the Cedar Point Causeway. The kind with cottages. Each one has a kitchenette. In fact, I just made myself dinner."

"What did you eat, honey?"

""Uh, beef stew. I had a big lunch in a restaurant."

"Joe, I just know you are not going to eat right. Whose going to cook for you?"

"I'm OK, Mom."

"It's not that far. We could be up there before...." Joe's father took the phone from his mother, and he and Joe went back over the events of Joe's day. Joe gave him the motel's name, address, and phone number. Also, Joe learned that his father and Dieter had been able to get all forty acres of the corn cultivated. When Joe's father gave the phone back to his mother, Joe heard some muffled instructions to her in his father's sternest voice.

"I love you, honey. You make sure you go to Mass tomorrow."

"I will, Mom. There's plenty of churches up here, you know."

"Honey, we could come up there for church and see you too."

"Maybe next week, Mom. I'd like to get settled first."

"I miss you. Mom's are allowed. I love you, honey."

"Yes, Mom. Mom, I...." Joe's voice cracked, and he paused to regain his composure, then changed the subject, "Tell Dieter to take it easy."

"I will. I love you, honey."

After the phone call, Joe felt like a chump. He mulled the conversation over and over. He could not understand what made him start to cry. It was getting on toward dusk. He decided to take a walk through that nice neighborhood. He did and his headache went away. He walked north through homes to the line of old factories at the water's edge. He stood watching the sunset across the bay, but about half way through it, he decided that he had better get back to the motel before dark. Home felt a million miles away, but he assured himself, he was not homesick.

CHAPTER 6

Joe usually slept in on Sunday mornings, the family went to 9:30 Mass. Sometimes, after they came home from Mass, he would go back to bed until lunch. This Sunday, Joe woke at 6:30 A.M. The TV was rasping static. He had fallen asleep with it on the night before. He turned it off. He couldn't remember falling asleep.

He opened the refrigerator and studied his apples until he remembered it was Sunday. He couldn't eat until after Communion. Looking out the front window, he saw it was barely light, but it looked like it was going to be an even more beautiful day than the one before. He found the thin telephone book and looked up churches in the yellow pages. He found three Catholic churches. Two, St. Mary's and Sts. Peter & Paul were downtown. He knew downtown from the times his parents brought Dieter and him to Cedar Point. They preferred to park downtown and take the ferry across the bay. The Causeway was quicker and cheaper. What Joe did not know was that his parents had taken the ferry on their outings as young lovers.

His parents also liked to sit among the flower gardens and fountains that surround the court house, while the boys ran and played. Joe remembered the flower beds and the large circular clock whose face is composed of plants and flowers. He also remembered how he and Dieter used to puzzle over the calendar, wondering how the plant-numbers changed every day. He remembered the gray, limestone church steeples downtown. He felt confident he could find the churches.

From the listing in the telephone book, Joe learned that the two downtown churches staggered their Masses. He was naturally inclined to attend Sts. Peter & Paul, since it bore the same name as his parish in Attica, but decided to go to the 9:30 at St. Mary's. He didn't have anything planned for the day, so there was no rush. He laid back on the bed and read the blue page history of Sandusky in the telephone book.

Then he turned on the radio, listened to Top 40 tunes and catnapped. At 8:00 A.M. Joe got back up, showered, put on his suit, and with his map in hand, headed downtown.

It was a little more than two miles from his motel to downtown. He walked on Route 6 the entire way, as it changed from Cleveland Road, to Huron, to Washington. It was a pleasant walk for him; first along the strip, then passed the nice homes, through the working class neighborhoods, into the older homes, and finally coming out in the downtown business district. He was early, so he walked by both churches. He was happy he had chosen St. Mary's, for although both churches were the largest he'd ever seen, St. Mary's appeared somewhat larger. He had no way of knowing that for long-forgotten reasons, most of the local Germans and Irish attended St. Mary's; while the Poles attended Sts. Peter & Paul; with the Italians divided between them and Holy Angels. He walked on around the court house square once before finding a bench in front. There he decided to sit and idle until Mass. After a few minutes, he noticed a pick-up truck in front of the plant calendar. A man got out, walked up to the calendar and lifted out a flat containing yesterday's numbers. He put it in the back of the truck, returned with today's numbers, and was gone in a moment. Well, Joe thought, that's how they do it. Big mystery. Why couldn't he have figured that out? He sat with his arms outstretched on the park bench, checking the big clock every few minutes. At 9:25 A.M., he headed for St. Mary's.

It was the biggest church he had ever been in. Coming up to it, the gray stone seemed to humble even the sizable red brick churches he'd passed yesterday. Inside, the dusk was accentuated by the color of the stained glass and one shaft of light. The racks of candles near the altar held his eyes as he found a pew about half way down. He kneeled to pray when he noticed an altar boy lighting the candles for High Mass. His heart sank. He slid back off the kneeler into the pew. It was a nice church, but High Mass was more than he planned. He should have known, he scolded himself. He sat back looking about. He did not know anyone. It was the usual procession of families, everyone dressed up, lots of white gloves on the women and girls. He stared down at the kneeler, listening to the creaking of the pews, the rustling of the petticoats, and the occasional cough. Then the Latin started.

Joe actually preferred the Latin Mass. All that was coming to an end. It was a favorite topic of debate for the parents after Mass, but it was going to happen. Orders were coming down. He liked Latin, because he didn't understand it. They offered Latin at his high school, but when he entered ninth grade, he, and just about everyone else, took German. For the first time, a lot of phrases that most of them had grown up with made more sense. The missals and hymn books had translations from Latin, but he had quit reading them a few years before when he satisfied himself about prayer. As usual, he took the time to determine what all the prayers he had memorized had in common. He decided there were two things, sucking up and begging. He had no use for either. Indeed, both offended him. He thought that God would feel the same. He knew enough not to share this insight with his parents. He just stuck to Latin, unless he was given prayers for Penance. Those he said so quickly, he no longer thought about what the words meant. He would kneel, but he would not suck up, he would not beg. He would not do as much to any man, much less God.

A few rows ahead was a family with two daughters. The younger one, whom he thought was about fourteen, looked back at Joe from time to time. Each time, he looked down. Next to her was her sister. Joe figured she was older by her breadth, even though the two girls were about the same height. The older sister had flaming red hair, turned under at the shoulder. Both her parents and the younger sister had dark brown hair. Joe tried to remember the business they had about genes in biology, but he could never keep it straight. He was staring absentmindedly at her hair, when he realized that she had turned to see him from the corner of her eye. Her eyes were a striking yellow-green. He saw the two sisters smile to each other, seeing that the younger had alerted the older to his gaze. A glance from their father brought the girls' attentions to the altar. Joe's eyes shot to the floor, his face flushed, and his ears burned. The next time the priest turned his back, Joe made for the door.

He reassured himself that he'd had enough church; like filling a gas tank, his was topped off. He wasn't one for prayer. The ritual bored him. Without his parents to enforce the habit, Joe was free. Joe had never carefully considered theology, but that morning he concluded that God was also outside. He assured himself that he was a good person as he scrambled down the church steps. He felt the heat of the day coming up. Besides, he had just completely humiliated himself. He remembered a diner across the square, and thinking he'd beat the after-church crowd, he headed for it. They had a 50 cent breakfast special, so he ordered that. He had enough change, so he still had $86 in cash left. While he ate, he studied the Sandusky map and decided to walk over to the coal dock.

It was about a mile west of downtown, beyond a working class neighborhood, several bars, and a warehouse district. As he got closer, he saw a freighter was being loaded. He went up to the uniformed guard at the gate and asked where he should go to apply for a job.

"Don't know. I'm just the guard. Railroad security is contracted out. You'd have to go to the office, I suppose, but I don't know where that is. There's no office here."

Joe looked into the coal yard. From this view, the machinery was obscured in the distance by lines of track and coal cars. Everything was black. It was the most desolate thing he'd ever seen. He saw a few men about, riding on switch engines and jumping off to uncouple coal cars. The men were as black with coal dust as everything else. He turned back to the guard, his eyes overcome with the rush of natural colors from the town. "Do you suppose I could go ask one of those guys?"

"No way! No how! No one but authorized personnel enter, or its my job. I got a family to feed. No way! No siree."

"Well, OK. Just thought I'd ask. I'm looking for work."

"You might try the phone book. No office here. All these guys are old timers. Takes a brain to work in a place like this. You can get killed here real quick. No one's died here in more than a year, but I've seen it. I've seen guys in two pieces. Look in the phone book."

"Thanks, I'll do that." Joe lied.

"You know, you got to be in the union. These locomotive workers are tough, and their union's tougher. They all hate my ass, think of security as management. Hell, I've got a family to feed too. They think management's killing the railroads. Management thinks the union's killing the railroads. Here I am trying to feed my family."

"Well, thanks." Joe said trying to break away from the lonely guard. Unions were a mystery to Joe. They shouldn't have been. His father was the head of Seneca county's National Farmer's Organization. Until last year, they had N.F.O. painted in ten foot green letters on the side of their barn. After the last market boycott, his mother won. Joe and Dieter got the job of painting over the letters, although a ghost of them was still visible. Holding grain was one thing, but killing calves and pouring out milk made no sense to Joe. It did to his father, who had "us and them" reduced to a science. For Joe's father, "us" was all small farmers, but Joe knew it was other farmers that would drive by and shoot at their barn. A rock through their living room window finally brought his father over to his mother's view that unless they got the letters off the barn, it was going to get burned down. The N.F.O. organizer understood. Joe had never been able to figure it out, although he tried. As it was, he associated unions with mystery and violence. He concluded the coal dock was a hell hole, and he wanted no part of it, even before he heard about unions. That only cemented it.

Walking back toward downtown, Joe came across two fellows that could only be headed for the coal dock. They both wore blue work pants, and lighter blue shirts with their first names in red script on white labels over their shirt pockets. Both were rough looking, needed shaving, but were washed and their hair was combed. Joe wrongly took them to be rail yard workers. Thinking why not, he asked them about the railroad office, after all it was only Plan B. They told him they worked on the freighter and were just coming back from church. Joe asked about getting work on a lake boat. The older of the two gestured with his thumb over his shoulder, "Skipper's right behind us. Ask him."

"Excuse me, sir. I'm interested in working on a ship. They said to ask you."

The older man did not look much different from his crew; not as rough, but just as tough. He also wore blue work pants. Unlike the others, his shirt was white and did not have a name. It was a work shirt, not a dress shirt, and was open at the collar. He was clean shaven and smelled of aftershave. "Want to go to sea?"

"Looking for work. I grew up on a farm near here. I've been looking at the freighters since I was a kid, wondering what it was like."

The captain looked over Joe's Sunday suit. Joe was suddenly aware of the coal dust on his shoes and cuffs. "You been to church?"

"Yes, sir." Joe answered tentatively.

"I always like to come in here on Sunday, especially a day like this. Sandusky's a nice town, don't you know. Holy Angels is a nice church, convenient to the coal dock. I think I might retire here someday. You married?"

"No."

"Most aren't. Not the right life for that. Ever been on a boat?"

"Just the ferry to Cedar Point."

"It's hard work and a lot of sitting around. You afraid of

work?"

"No, sir, grew up on a farm."

"Right. Well, here's the thing. I can only hire in an emergency. Our line's out of Toronto, that's where they do the hiring, but there's lots of lines. You watch the boats coming in and out of here, you'll see the names of the lines. The closest one I know from here is Cleveland. You'll need to get merchant papers from the Coast Guard. That's no big deal. Then go apply. If they hire you, you'll have to get on with the union, serve an apprenticeship and all that. Some start with the union first. It don't make much difference. You need to get over to Cleveland. You'll wait forever trying to get on here."

"Thanks."

"No never mind. Not so long ago, I walked up to a boat just like you. We all do, don't you know."

"Thanks again."

"Good luck. It's good to see a young person going to church alone. That's why I keep those two. They ain't the best, they drink too much, but they're church-goers."

Joe walked on back to the motel. Both his plans were gone. He was afraid of the water anyway, and unions seemed to be everywhere.

CHAPTER 7

By the time Joe got back to the motel and out of his suit, it was nearly noon. He wasn't hungry, but he ate a can of tuna and an apple out of boredom. He made himself a glass of instant tea and laid on the bed going through the classifieds again. $86 left. No Plan C. He had to think of something. The good jobs wouldn't be in the paper anyway. His eyes came across an ad for a yard sale. He recognized the address as being in the nice neighborhood nearby, and he resolved to make that his afternoon activity.

His feet were sore from his good shoes and his socks sweaty. The shoes were only a few weeks old. His mother had taken him to Bucyrus to buy them for graduation. They would have been for the Prom too, had he gone. He took off the socks and checked for blisters. None. He washed his socks in the sink, then decided to take a shower, since it was so convenient. He got back into his white levis and low cut tennis shoes. With a T shirt, he felt normal again. As he left for the yard sale, the morning and the demise of his plans felt like a distant memory.

He had taken to keeping the Sandusky map in his hip pocket, but he didn't need it to find the yard sale. As soon as he turned into the neighborhood, he saw a knot of cars a couple of blocks up the street. As he approached, he saw several tables piled with things, a clothes line stretched between two maples, and some furniture sitting in the grass. Two men in their Sunday suits stood on the sidewalk near their cars, smoking. The women, he took to be their wives, were poking through the things on the tables. From their bickering, Joe decided the women were sisters. He nodded to an old man sitting in a lawn chair. "My wife died. Kids moved away years ago. I'm just cleaning house. See anything you want, we'll talk price." Joe nodded again.

Joe could tell in a glance there wasn't much to interest him. He saw a ten speed bike propped against one of the maples, and assumed it belonged to someone who had ridden it to the sale. The old man called over, "That belonged to my son. We got it for him to take to college, but he brought it home, first chance. It's been in the garage for ten years. We paid $65 for it new." Joe had no intention of buying a bike, but he smiled and kept looking at the bike out of a sense of obligation to respond to the old man. "I'd take $10." Joe thought about his feet. All of a sudden, he was interested.

"Tires look rotten."

"Yeah, they're cracked, but they hold air. I pumped them up yesterday. Pump comes with it, and there's tools in that bag under the seat."

The chrome on the bike was frosted, not pitted. He could see the bike had been wiped clean in haste, for there were missed spots of dust and grime. Joe raised the back wheel and cranked the pedal. The chain jerked in three or four different places going through the derailleur. Still sitting in his lawn chair the old man said, "Chain was completely rusted stuck. I oiled it and worked with it yesterday. It's been sitting for ten years. You can get a new chain for a buck, or you can just work out the rust. Tell you what, I'll come down to $8."

"I don't know. Still have to get new tires."

"What's it worth to you?"

"$7?"

"It's yours."

Joe rode back to the motel. He worked the chain up and down through the gears. The old man had shown him how to shift. He already knew. He had never ridden a geared bike before, but some of his friends had them. He had helped work on them. The old man was right. The kinks in the chain soon disappeared. As he rode, he kept looking down at the tires, expecting them to blow. They didn't. $79 left. He had to get a job.

The old lady was sitting in front of the office in a metal chair, knitting. "I see you got some wheels." She called in her accent.

"Yes ma'am. Didn't plan to. Came across a deal."

"My name is Olschewske." She said pointing up to the broken neon sign over the "Vacancy" that hung above them. "My husband and I built this place. He was a carpenter. He built our house, then the cabins, one to a time. I waited tables until we got this business going."

"How long ago was that, ma'am... Mrs. Olschewske?"

"Too long to remember. Long before you were born. Probably before your parents." Joe smiled and cranked the pedal on the bike backwards. "There's tools, and oil, and things over in the garage if you want to use them."

"Thank you." Joe said as he hopped off the bike and walked up to the detached garage.

Like all the other buildings at the motel, it had once been painted white, though now the paint was blistered and mostly laying in chips on the ground among the weeds. Joe could tell the building had not been used as a garage in years. The grass had reclaimed the driveway up to it. Mrs. Olschewske had an 1960 Ford wagon that was parked along side the house. The garage doors swung out sideways. Joe removed the pin from the hasp and worked one door open, forcing it over the weeds. The odor of mildew stung his nose, and he moved in slowly.

The center of the garage was heaped with cardboard boxes. There were two windows on each side, so dirty that only a white haze came through. In the back was a massive work bench with a large vise and hand-crank wire brush and grinder mounted on it. Under the work bench were several tool boxes. On the right side were shelves holding dozens of paint cans, so old that the lids were rusted and the labels illegible. Carpentry tools hung on the left wall; saws, braces, planes. They were hand tools of the quality and vintage that are inherited not bought. The place was a mess, but Joe was as excited as if he'd discovered a gold mine.

"Mrs. Olschewske, do you mind if I clean out your garage? I'd like to do that for using your tools on the bike."

"Go ahead. Go ahead." She struggled up out of her chair and followed him back into the garage. She swore in a language he had never heard before when she saw her husband's clothes had rotted in the boxes. They agreed he could put all the trash at the curb. Joe cut the weeds back with a hand trimmer he found, by the time Mrs. Olschewske returned with a bucket, rags and a broom. She went back to the porch, leaving Joe with the instruction to do whatever he thought best.

Soon Joe had cleared all the obvious trash and spoiled paint from the garage. He swept the dust and cobwebs from the walls with the broom, washed the windows and shelves, then swept the floor. He found several quarts of motor oil. He wouldn't use it in an engine; but it was good enough to oil the tools, which he did. At dusk, Mrs. Olschewske inspected the result and congratulated Joe. She told him to clean up, and she'd make him dinner. After he showered, he found her waiting on the porch with dinner. He was glad she brought the food outside, for the smell of her cats gagged him.

Mrs. Olschewske talked and talked. She referred to people he had never met, people who were long dead, by their first names. She told stories of Sandusky's changes. She listed all the buildings her husband had helped construct. She bragged that he was considered the best framer along the lake. He had helped build the Blue Streak, and Cedar Point trusted only him to repair the structure. She rattled off a list of attractions he had worked on at the park. She gestured to the garage and boasted that the tools Joe had cleaned had built all those things.

When the conversation turned to Joe's employment search, Joe confessed he didn't expect to find the kind of work he wanted. "You go to Cedar Point." She ordered. "They hire hundreds of kids. You tell them Olschewske sent you. They will know the name. If they have forgotten, you tell them about the Blue Streak. They probably have forgotten, but they know good work when they see it. They kept calling Olschewske back. You get on and do for them what you did for me. They'll know."

The next morning Joe found the number for Cedar Point's personnel office in the phone book and called. He was quickly informed that all the summer jobs were filled, but told he could leave his name and address, and they would send him an application next spring. As the female voice tried to hang up, Joe asked if they had anything at all. She put him on hold, then came back saying that the only thing open was a mechanic's helper, but that usually wasn't a student job. Joe replied he wasn't a student. She asked how soon he could come in and fill out an application. Joe said he was on his way.

Joe rode his bike, hoping the tires would hold. He had been across the Causeway many times, but it seemed longer on the bike. At the parking lot, they sent him towards Personnel. There he greeted the receptionist who seemed impressed at how quickly he had arrived. He filled in the form and waited while she took it back into the office. He heard a woman's voice tell her they could skip the interview and send him out to talk to Ivan. The receptionist gave him directions.

In the maintenance shop, a few questions got him to Ivan. Ivan was bent over a pick-up truck working on the engine. The first thing Joe noticed was the Cedar Point uniform and a red shop rag sticking out of his hip pocket. "Ivan?" The stocky, forty year old came about. "They sent me over from Personnel, told me to talk to you." Ivan had a second shop rag in his hands that he was using to clean a wrench. He took the application from Joe and glanced over it, as he walked across the room to a standing desk.

"You living at Olschewske's?"

"Yes, sir."

"Place is a dump. Old Man Olschewske would turn over in his grave. You know he helped build the Blue Streak?"

"Yes. Mrs. Olschewske told me. She sent me here. Told me that good work would be recognized."

"Well, she's right about that. I wonder how old she is? I haven't seen her in years. Used to see her at church. My grandparents were friends with them. You're from Attica?"

"Yes, just graduated. I...."

"Some damn college kid was supposed to start today. He didn't show. If he shows now, he's toast. The park opens next week, and I don't need this shit. You know anything about machinery? We work on everything from trucks to golf carts, merry-go-rounds to roller coasters."

"I grew up on a farm."

"So, what have you worked on?"

"Cars, trucks, tractors, drills, combines, corn pickers, bailers; whatever needed fixing."

"Ever rebuild an engine?"

"Lots of times. We don't have a shop like this, so we do everything in place, replace rings and bearings, change out gaskets. Gas and diesel."

"Can you tune an engine?"

"My gauges and timing light are home, but sure. I tuned a lot of engines by ear before I got them."

"I work until the job is done. You got any problem with long hours?"

"I grew up on a farm."

"OK, Altznauer, you win. Here's the program. I don't hire, Personnel does; but only if I say yes." He handed the application back to Joe. "I'll call them right now. They'll hire you and give you a couple of uniforms. You be here at 7:30 A.M. tomorrow morning. If you're late, don't bother to show. I give you a week. You screw up, you're out. Make it one week, and you'll probably make it through the summer. But I won't take any crap, not even on the last day of summer."

Joe beamed. At last something had gone right for him. "Thanks. I won't let you...." Ivan reached out and shook his hand.

"I'd start you right now, but they've got forms, and I'm so goddamned mad at that college kid, I'd probably get mad at you. 7:30 A.M. tomorrow."

"Yes, sir."

"Cut the shit. It's Ivan."

Joe left without learning Ivan's last name. After waiting an hour in Personnel, he learned he had a minimum wage job with a bonus if he made it to the end of summer. He tried on uniforms until he found two that fit. The dormitories were full, but he could get on a waiting list. He filled in forms for another hour. Then he rode back to the motel to tell Mrs. Olschewske that Cedar Point still remembered her husband.

CHAPTER 8

Looking back, it was probably that Fourth of July that I began to realize that I did not know Joe as well as I thought. I had seen him once between then and graduation. He had gotten off from work in the middle of the week and rode all the way down to Attica on a bike. Cycling was not so popular then, and a ride of that distance was highly unusual by local standards. There was, however, nothing unusual about Joe doing something like that. One of the guys at the plant saw him riding through town during lunch hour and told me. That night at dinner when I told my parents I was going to go over to Altznauer's to see Joe, you would have thought I started World War III.

First, my Mom signed about how Joe broke his mother's heart by refusing to go to the Prom with Gretchen Krendle and then moving out. That was only the first volley. My Dad really got cranked up, launching into a big speech that I heard over and over that summer. The boy was throwing his life away. You had to have a college education to get anywhere. If he wanted to be a mechanic, then he should have come to work for my Dad. His father was full of shrapnel, and there would always be a place at the plant for the son of a war hero. Joe could have learned to be a machinist. Cedar Point was a playground with no future. They did not make anything. They did not add to the economy. They only took people's money for cheap thrills. In hard times, such luxuries were the first things to go. All I had said was that I was going over to see Joe. After dinner, I did.

Same old Joe. We sat on the hood of my car. Dieter leaned up against a fence post nearby. Joe asked about everyone from our class. I filled him in on all the local gossip and told him about my job. My Dad had me welding that summer. I was spot welding bomb casings in the jigs, before they went on down the line to the certified welders for seam welding. My job took no great talent, but I suppose I was learning the business. It was a couple of years before I put much thought into where those bomb casings went when they left Attica. More important to me that summer was my new found friend. He was a Heidelberg student from New York, who found a summer job at my Dad's plant through the college placement office. He was a junior, lived in a dorm, took a few classes, worked part-time in Attica, and became my ticket to meet college women. I spent most evenings that summer with that guy cruising Tiffin. Joe said he was only going to be home the one night, so he couldn't go to Tiffin; but we did arrange the Fourth of July.

Being in the recreation business, Joe had to work when everyone else was off. That meant weekends and holidays, especially the big ones like the Fourth of July, but even Joe got some time off. Joe got us passes for Cedar Point; actually, I think he got them from his boss because he didn't have enough seniority. Anyway, the plan was for us to spend the day doing the park while Joe worked, then that night we'd cruise for some girls. If memory serves me, four of us went up. Early that morning, we stopped by the old motel where Joe was living to get the passes and drive Joe over to work. The park didn't open for a couple of hours, so we did downtown Sandusky until it did.

About noon I wandered away from the guys. The lines were getting long, and I had ridden everything Cedar Point had to offer many times. I thought Joe might be free for lunch. I found the maintenance building south of the main part of the park, behind the dorms, over near the marina where the ferry lands. I remember seeing old Joe in action, just like it was yesterday. It impressed the hell out of me. I had learned enough from my Dad's plant to know the difference between the organization chart and reality. Supposedly, you went up through lead men to foremen to superintendents, but that was bunk. Everyone knew who really knew about whatever a given problem was and went straight to him. Well, there was Joe with two or three guys lined up waiting to talk to him. They were older, obviously full-time mechanics from their greasy clothes, showing him parts, asking him questions. Joe was as clean as a whistle, and making sure he stayed that way with a red shop rag in his hands. If you didn't know, you would have thought Joe was the boss. Then I noticed an older guy, leaning over a shop desk, check me out. I didn't want to get Joe in any trouble, so I got out of there. I tell you, it really surprised me. To me, Joe was always the quiet, shy type. I knew the score, and there was no mistaking the pecking order in that shop. It was a real eye-opener to see Joe in his element. Maybe

I ran on at the mouth so much, he could never get a word in edge ways.

Joe got off at 4:00 P.M., so we met up with him and took him over to his place so he could clean up. He was just as clean as us, but he wanted to shower before he got into his street clothes. While we waited for him, this crazy old lady who ran the motel kept telling us how wonderful Joe was. She gave us a big tour, showing off how Joe was scrapping and painting the cottages for her, and bragging about a bunch of antique tools in a garage where Joe kept his bike. Having spent so much time at the Altznauer's, I could see Joe's touch in the garage. It was spotless. He'd even painted the inside white and put in florescent lights. Later I learned that Joe made a deal with the old woman for free rent in return for work. I never knew Joe to be a wheeler/dealer.

That night fell into a familiar pattern, the only difference being that our hopes were higher. We had spent many evenings at Cedar Point. The basic plan was always to find a group of girls waiting in line or wherever, take them to listen to whatever band was playing, have a few beers, and end up on the beach. Back then you could buy 3.2% beer at 18, so at last we were all legal. That overcame the biggest hurdle right there, we didn't have to find someone to buy us beer. Well, the place was packed. You could barely move. We did not find any girls. That night, instead of a band, they were putting on the Miss Ohio Pageant. We watched from outside the Pavilion for awhile, but it was a bore. We drank until we were so bloated we couldn't hold anymore, and the group of us ended up walking along the beach alone. After reading the plaque about Knute Rockne developing football plays on the beach during his summer at Cedar Point, we had to try that out. I ended up in the water. It sobered me up a little. I went into the bathhouse to shower the sand off my clothes and got separated from the guys. After a while I figured out that I would have more luck finding them if I just stayed in one place, so I staked out a spot near a beer stand, and started drinking again.

I have this vague memory of a girl coming up to me and asking about Joe. For years I have tried to force the memory, but I was so drunk, I don't know. What I remember was the usual, "Does he have a girl friend? Would you fix me up with him?" Knowing me, I probably went after her myself; and knowing me, I was probably so sloppy she ran off. In my experience, single girls like that always had a fat friend stashed somewhere anyway. I much preferred to find an entire group out in the open. I don't know. I can't even say it really happened. I also remember red hair and green eyes. I can't put a face or body with the memory. I should have realized then that booze was going to be a problem. It could have been her, but that would be too much of a coincidence. I'm probably mixing up memories. At least, I keep telling myself that.

Anyway, about midnight I finally gave up and headed for the car. I stumbled into the guys at the main gate. Someone else drove my car. I vaguely remember dropping Joe at his place, but nothing else. I woke up in my car the next morning outside our house in Attica. It must have been pretty obvious to my parents just how hung-over I was, but I don't remember them saying anything. I never did see Joe again that summer. Like I said, Tiffin and the young ladies of Heidelberg were my preferred objective that summer.

Late in August, just before I left for college, I got fascinated with Attica's cemetery. It was just across from the plant, and occasionally I would see a funeral. Funerals are big deals in Attica. My parents never miss one. I don't remember what possessed me to go over there, but one afternoon I did. It gave me a whole new perspective on the town. From it, you can see about everything, the high school, my Dad's plant, the houses, the churches, the railroad tracks, the highway; just from a new and unfamiliar angle. What was familiar were the names on the tombstones.

I knew every name! I kept coming back just to make sure. I got to the point I could see the generations; I could see who begat whom. Half the names were the same as the kids in my class. Now I can see something positive in the continuity through those generations and the deep sense of community that manifests itself at the funerals. Then, however, my visits to the cemetery were the final, defining moments that made it clear to me that I had to get out of Attica. Ever since I first got my car and started roaming to other towns, I knew Attica was too small for me. That last summer, looking at the town from the cemetery, through the cemetery, I felt like I was suffocating. I couldn't wait for school to start, even if I had to leave my car at home. When my Dad would make his speech about Joe, I shrugged it off. I knew that real point was to influence me, not bash Joe. It got easier to take, for I also knew Joe had done one thing that I hadn't, and one thing that my Dad had never done. I finally saw that Joe was way out ahead of me. Joe got the hell out of Attica.

CHAPTER 9

That morning when Joe got his bike from the garage, he noticed that the patchy morning fog and hazy white sky had been suddenly replaced by heavy dew and clear blue skies. The air was cooler. It had no bite yet, but he knew that would soon follow. The leaves were still green, but a few had fallen and been blown up against the building. The grass would only have to be mowed once or twice more. The summer had slipped away again.

This Labor Day was no different than any other. The weather changed on Labor Day. That was one of the first truths that Joe was able to extract from his world. Because he only had one day a year upon which to base his observation, it took him several years to reach his conclusion. At first he linked the change to his emotions, going back to school each year, getting ready for the harvest. By the time he had become a teen, however, he knew the simple truth. The weather changed.

That morning it caught him by surprise. Of course, he knew the date, knew his job would end; but the routine of work, the excitement of daily problems, the long hours, and the puttering about for Mrs. Olschewske; kept his mind from realizing that summer was ending. Suddenly he had a knot in his stomach. It remained as he peddled across the Causeway to work. It was the Friday before Labor Day Weekend. Someone, probably Ivan, would cashier him today. He never had a regular job before this one, had never been fired, had never quit. He had mistakenly taken the job for granted and cursed himself for not having a plan in place. He felt sorry for the person who would have to tell him. That couldn't be an easy job.

As Joe clocked in, he saw Ivan already at his shop desk, looking over the day's work list and sipping his coffee. As usual, it was early, the rest wouldn't be clocking in for another fifteen minutes. "Hey, Joe, come here."

"Morning. What's on today?"

"Usual. Well, you made it through the summer. I don't ever get the time to tell someone they've done a good job. You know me, if you screw up, you know right then and there; but I never get the time. Listen, you know the park closes after this weekend. I just wanted to let you know that you've done a real good job."

"Thanks, I..."

"They'll calculate your bonus based on the hours you worked and send it to you next week. Seriously, I've seen hundreds come through here. You're the first that ever made me nervous about my job. I'm sure you've got better things to do, but if you could; I'd like you to stay on a month. This place will be a ghost town next week, but there's one hell of a lot of work to winterizing this place."

"Yes, I mean, no, I don't really have anything else. I can stay."

"Great! That will solve a multitude of problems for me. I thought you might be going to college or something. I can keep these guys busy all winter painting and fixing, but buttoning up the rides takes some brains. Do it right the first time, or fix it again later. You know the drill. It will only be a few weeks, but I need the help. What are you going to do anyway?"

"I really don't know. I like machinery. I'll just start looking."

"You won't have any trouble. I'm a sorry one to be giving advice, but here it is. You get on at one of the big plants, get in the union, they'll train you, and you'll make a good living doing the same thing for the rest of your life. You get on at some small place, they'll see your talents, and you can make your own job. Pay won't be as good, but you'll be doing what you want."

"I'll remember that. What's on today?"

Joe worked a normal shift that Friday, no overtime for the first time that summer. Over the weekend, he put in only half days. The entire life he'd made for himself turned around this job, and it was disappearing from underneath him. During the summer he had gotten to know all the guys in the shop, at least by their first names, but he wasn't after-hours friends with any of them. As for the hundreds of other young people that worked in the park, most were familiar faces, but he didn't know any of them. It might have been different if he'd lived in the dorms. There was this one girl that ran a snow cone stand. Early in the summer she had smiled at him a little longer than civility required, and he had been drawn back to buy a cone. His chest tightened when he thought of her. He had started finding excuses to walk by her stand, and he scripted conversations to have with her. Then one morning as he biked in, he saw her kiss some guy and get out of a Corvette at the main gate. His fantasy was crushed. Her red hair reminded him of the girl he had seen in church when he first came to Sandusky, and he lumped the two experiences together in his collection of humiliations. He saw them together many times that summer, he even saw them fighting, but he never again approached her. He had never learned her name.

Joe thought about her as he biked into the empty park the morning after the park closed. He stopped at the spot where she used to jump out of the Corvette and trot in through the entrance. He could see his breath. His knuckles were cold and he worked his fingers. The park was more than empty, it was still. He would probably never see her again. No doubt, she had gone off to some college and was eagerly starting a new life. He had never seen the park closed before. He didn't like it. The nervous energy that filled the shop all summer was gone. As they rolled their tools from ride to ride, he started thinking of himself as an undertaker. He hadn't felt like this since his last few weeks in high school. He put in the time, but he really wanted out.

He had fixed just about everything for Mrs. Olschewske that needed fixing, and for the first time, he had weekends off. The first Saturday he biked out on Catawba to the point where the ferry leaves for South Bass Island. He watched the ferry come and go, but felt no desire to take it. The next day, he went back to Catawba then all the way out to the end of Marblehead. He went up in the lighthouse. It was a perfect day to be there. The clear cool days made for long vistas. Sandusky, south across the bay, was as picturesque a view as Joe had ever seen. The commercial buildings along the waterfront were backed by the court house clock tower and church steeples. The coaling operation seemed an insignificant appendage on the right side of downtown. He looked across the channel to Cedar Point. On any summer day, he might have heard the carnival music and roller coastering shrieks carried across the water, but now he heard only the breeze. He could see how strong the breeze was from the white steam plume eight miles east, over in Huron. Looking north to Kelley's Island, he could clearly see its victorian mansions. There were a stubborn few sailing, fishing, and pleasure boating; but nothing like in the summer. Joe took a chill and headed for Sandusky. It took him an hour and a half to get back.

"Are you sure you won't stay? I don't know how I'm going to get on without you."

"No ma'am. You've been more than fair to me. The place is in good shape. You got on fine before I came along. Summer's over."

"I know, I know, but you really made a difference. This place is just hanging on with me. With all the motels, no one wants to stay in a place like this. I just get the overflow."

"Yes, ma'am."

"You're right. You shouldn't spend the winter alone with an old woman like me. You need to be around young people."

"I'll be around. I'll stop by to see you. I'm only moving into an old apartment house over on Columbus, The Willdred, maybe you know it."

"Know it? I knew Willdred! He wouldn't let anyone but Olschewske frame it up. Olschewske did all the woodwork and cabinetry too."

"I'll have you over. I got a good deal, two bedrooms and a kitchen. It's pretty much furnished, and it will be nice to have a full kitchen. I'm going to use the second bedroom as a workshop for the bike."

"They're lucky to get a tenant like you."

"Thanks, but I don't know. I just think if you don't take care of what you have, then you don't deserve to have it." Joe heard himself repeating his father.

"You come by and see me."

Joe moved out of Olschewske's Motor Court with little more ceremony than he arrived. Mrs. Olschewske drove Joe and his things over in her old station wagon. He hadn't ridden with her before, and wished he had not accepted her generosity then. He tried to find the nerve to tell her she shouldn't be driving anymore. Even if he had found the nerve, she never gave him the opportunity. The ride over was crowded with her non-stop commentary on everything they passed. In the old building, she leveled all the criticism that could have been said of her motel a few months before. On the way back, she promised curtains and pestered Joe with questions of color and interior decoration. Joe finally got away from her and biked back to his new home. The first things he missed were the radio, telephone, and TV.

Joe's attraction to the Willdred was immediate. It was a

handsome building. Although incongruous with the two story frame houses that surrounded it, it was an addition to, not a detraction from the neighborhood. It was built at a time when there were bigger things in mind for the area than frame houses. It was a three story building of sand tone brick, much like Joe's high school in Attica, with sandstone slabs marking floor lines, and all built up from a cut limestone foundation. The center entrance was framed by two large columns that support porches on the second and third floors. The apartments on either side had bay windows. A militaristic cornice was laid in relief in the top courses of brick over the building name.

Joe was able to get a large apartment for only $50 a month because it was in the basement. It had a bed and rag tag collection of furniture which found their way into the basement when left behind by upstairs tenants. The interior walls were plastered and painted, but the exterior walls were cut stone. It had windows, but they were small, higher than eye level inside, looking out at ground level. The furnace, water tank, laundry, and storage rooms were across the hall. Other than the small coin laundry, the basement was cool, dark, and musky. He had the landlord's permission to keep his bike inside and to use one bedroom as a workshop. He looked forward to setting it up and to bringing up some of his own tools from Attica.

As always, money was on Joe's mind. When he took the apartment, he had yet to line up a new job. To get the apartment, he had given Ivan and the lady at his Sandusky bank as references. He still had $1,000 in the Sutton Bank in Attica, but had also saved another $1,000 in an account in Sandusky over the summer. His handyman deal with Mrs. Olschewske made food his only expense. He never reasoned through his compulsion to save, nor his finances beyond immediate expenses. Those he calculated constantly. He did not take the advice of the lady at the local bank who tried to get him to set up a checking account and apply for a credit card. They didn't pay interest on the checking accounts, and he paid cash for everything. He had never counted on the bonus from Cedar Point, and even though he'd had it for two weeks, he had not deposited or cashed the check. He knew if he put it in savings, it would never come out. He was debating whether to buy a car or a quality bike with his bonus.

Joe had found a bike shop early in the summer that carried more than street bikes for kids. Over time he had replaced the brakes, chain, and derailleur; but his was still a steel bike, with a cast crank, and chrome plated wheels and handlebars. At the bike shop he picked up cycling magazines. He studied them and spent hours inspecting the professionally posed photographs of alloy bikes and their components. These machines were the most sophisticated that Joe had ever encountered. Having grown up with heavy farm equipment, and working daily with the even heavier machinery at the amusement park; the highly refined light designs of bicycles that had evolved over generations of engineering became Joe's obsession. Although Joe didn't own one, and the shop didn't carry such bikes; they had catalogs which Joe also borrowed and studied. On his second night in his new place, listening to the transistor radio he had just purchased, and feeling more alone than ever before, Joe decided. The next day he ordered a quality touring bike, with front and rear racks, three piece crank, toe clips, and eighteen speeds.

He had worked and saved. Maybe he'd take some time off. When his bike came in, maybe he would ride down to Columbus and visit his friend at O.S.U. He spent his evenings listening to the radio, studying road maps, and contemplating advertising pictures of the $250 bike he'd ordered. Whenever he thought of the price, he cringed. He could have bought a decent used car for that price. He reassured himself, he could bike any place he needed to go. It was good exercise. As for the places he wanted to go, he much preferred to be out in the open. He enjoyed the countryside. He enjoyed the solitude. It made him feel good. Although all his evenings that summer had been passed in work at the motel or in thoughts of the next day's tasks, now his cycling fantasies crowded out any thought of work. In the mornings, he drug off to his last few days at the park. He daydreamed about cycling.

CHAPTER 10

"Hey, Joe, have you lined anything up yet?" Ivan asked as Joe clocked out for the last time.

"No, I really haven't been looking. I'm thinking about taking some time off."

"Yeah. It's been a long summer. Reason I asked, one of my drinking buddies works over at Falloni's. He said they're looking."

"Falloni's?"

"Falloni Marine, right across the bay. They're about a half mile from the other end of the Causeway, passed Venetian Marine, you know, the old black water tower, not as far down as Cross Bay."

"Oh yeah. I know right where they are."

"They get busy this time of year, taking boats out of the water and laying them up for winter. They spend the winter rebuilding engines, redecorating cabins, and doing hull repairs. In the summer, they sell gas and keep 'em running. If you're interested, I can make a call."

"Yeah, sure. I was going to take some time, but I got to have a job."

"Wait here." Joe stood in the door looking across the bay to Falloni's sign next to the old red brick factory and it's landmark water tower. He scanned west to the silhouette of downtown Sandusky in the late September afternoon sun. Ivan returned. "OK, here's the deal. I just called my buddy. He asked and Falloni said for you to come on over."

"Gee, thanks."

"You don't have the job yet. I told them you do good work, but Falloni doesn't listen to anybody. You've got to prove yourself. His old man started the business in the thirties. He never learned English very well, and always had Peter translate for him. Peter Falloni is the man you ask for. He's a couple of years older than me. He's been around boats his whole life. You can't bullshit him, so don't try."

"Thanks again."

"No problem. Don't be a stranger." Ivan shook his hand.

As Joe climbed off his bike in front of Falloni's, he realized why he did not recognize the name. The only sign was on the bay side of the building. The entrance on First Street was neglected and obscured by overgrowth. Although Joe had ridden down this street daily since he moved into his apartment, he hadn't taken note of the business. From outer appearances, he began to doubt if it would be his kind of place.

Mr. Falloni was waiting just inside, making small talk with a girl at the counter. He wore nice clothes; shiny shoes, casual slacks, a long-sleeved white shirt open at the collar, with a gold bracelet and necklace showing. He was short, carried a small pot belly, and looked to be about fifty. He had an unlit cigar in his mouth when he wasn't holding it out to study it. "You the kid from Cedar Point? Follow me." He led Joe down a corridor into a large office with a sofa, coffee table, chairs, desk and book shelves. The office reeked of cigar smoke and was filthy. The desk was covered six inches deep in paper. The shelves were crammed with boating magazines, catalogs, and family pictures. Leaning back in his high chair, he looked over the desk to Joe, "One of the guys told me that Ivan says you're a good worker. You know anything about boats?"

"No, sir. I grew up on a farm. Cedar Point is the only job I ever had."

"Don't worry about that. Not much to know. If they leak, they sink." Joe wasn't sure if he was supposed to laugh. "Listen, kid, I'll only say this once. I built this business on trust. My old man started it, but I built it up. It ain't much, but we do the best work on the lake. People come here because they trust us. If we don't do the work right, we do it again for free. People trust that. People trust me. I hire people if I trust them. I keep people who I trust can do it right the first time. Without trust, the whole thing falls apart. I run a business. I know this place is a dump, but fancy digs don't make us money. I'd rather pay good people and let them take some of it home. I come here in the morning to make money. So do the people that work for me. If you put in a good day's work, at the end of the day you don't owe me anything; and after I pay you, I don't owe you anything. It's a fair trade."

"Yes, sir." Joe agreed tentatively.

"I got a son your age, Petey. He's going to Notre Dame this year." Mr. Falloni gestured with his cigar towards one of the photographs showing him, a portly woman, several girls, and a young man slightly taller than Mr. Falloni. He stared at it for a moment, then turned back to Joe. "Starting pay is $3.50 an hour. You'll do whatever needs to be done. We don't have job descriptions and organization charts around here. If you can't figure out who your boss is, then I'll fire you and him both. I don't pay for that shit. We get real busy this time of year. I need someone right now. Can you start Monday?"

"Yes, sir." Joe beamed.

"7:30 Monday morning." Mr. Falloni stood. Joe did likewise. "I've known Ivan since he was a little kid. I trust him. Now listen, you remember what I said, and we'll never have a problem. Don't be late."

Peddling home, Joe couldn't believe it. When he figured that $3.50 an hour was more than $7,000 a year, he gave out a hoot, congratulating himself that it was as much as college graduates made. He thought about calling Ivan to thank him, but the thought reminded him that he knew nothing about Ivan, where he lived, whether he was married, if he had kids, nothing outside the shop. Instead, Joe resolved to go by the park sometime and thank him. He went over Mr. Falloni's speech several times. He liked it. Still, the place could use some fixing up. They may do the best work on the lake, people may know it, but he wouldn't have known by looking at the place; his first reaction was that Falloni had no pride. Anyway, the money was great. Things were falling into place. Nonetheless, when Joe went into his apartment, the place seemed more gloomy than ever.

He thought about going back out for dinner, but eating alone in a public place was something he'd worn out months before. Even the thought of it depressed him. He threw together a quick meal. As he finished, he turned to look at his portable radio. It was time to buy a TV. With his new found prosperity, he could afford it. He'd get a phone installed. He didn't have anyone to call, but it would be convenient if his family needed to reach him. He might even get a car, maybe a truck. Maybe not. He'd better be careful. He unfolded a map and started thinking about where he could go over the weekend. He didn't have anything else to do, and the weather looked good. After he decided, he fiddled with his bike, wiped it down, checked the brakes and spokes, then oiled the chain and derailleur. About 9:00 P.M., he went to bed. He turned off the radio and laid in the dark. He listened to the traffic and watched the passing lights as they made shapes on his ceiling. He felt more alone than he had since he first left home. He wanted to go home, but that would be defeat.

The next morning, Joe biked over to Catawba. He wore long underwear with gym shorts over them, his high school sweat shirt, a stocking hat, and brown cotton gloves. They kept the chill off him, yet still let the perspiration dry. He wanted to order the knit clothes he saw in the cycling magazines, but they were too expensive for his thrifty ways. The weather was just as he had expected, a crisp clear autumn day. Waiting for the ferry at Catawba Point, he noticed the wind was up, and with it, the waves. Shallow Lake Erie is notorious for the dramatic effect of even moderate weather. The ferry was big enough to plow through about anything, but the three foot waves sent spray back from the bow over the cars and passengers as it came in from South Bass Island.

Despite his earlier aspirations, Joe hadn't been on a boat all summer. As much as anything, his decision to go to the Islands was a test. He wanted to see about the water. He had crossed on the ferry more than once with his friends, but he usually stayed in the car listening to the radio. Today, he planned to walk around the ferry, to really see what it was like. Although the cars were lined up with about a two hour wait, Joe got on the first ferry, for bikers could squeeze in anywhere. He found a place for his bike, but stayed inside on the main deck watching the crew cast off. As Catawba Point grew smaller behind them, he moved out into the sunlight and up to a gate on the side of the ferry. His stomach was tight and his breathing shallow. He took hold of the top of the gate and cautiously looked over into the water. No sooner than he did, a wave crashed, soaking him with cold water. He screamed in fright. Several others yelled and laughed. Under that cover, Joe retreated back into the boat. He went up the stairs into the cabin where he found a spot on a bench. The sun through a window warmed him. He looked north to South Bass Island. From his vantage point, it was a bright green line above the water. He could seen the old lime kiln where they would land and Perry's Monument beyond it.

South Bass is generally considered the first in the string of islands that cross the western end of Lake Erie. Technically, Catawba Point is not part of the mainland, it too is an island; and Kelleys, which is directly north of the mouth of Sandusky Bay, is further south; but

South Bass is easier to get to and more populated. Of all the islands, it is the only one with what you could call a real town, Put-In-Bay, and the monument is a tourist attraction. The island is shaped something like an hour glass. Put-In-Bay is at the top of the lower half, and the monument is on the isthmus where the two parts nearly pinch in two. The monument is a single 300 foot doric column made from pink granite. The column supports a square observation deck and giant bronze urn that rises another fifty feet.

Officially titled "Perry's Victory and International Peace Memorial", it is many things to many people. It marks a decisive American victory over the British in a naval engagement in the War of 1812. A fortuitous shift of wind and some quick thinking by young Oliver Hazard Perry gave the Americans not only the day, but control of the lake. Perry's note to General William Henry Harrison, "We have met the enemy, and they are ours." is something memorized by every school child in Ohio. Shortly after, General Harrison also defeated the British on land, killing the great Tecumseh whose Indian confederation allied against the Americans was the lynch-pin of the British strategy. The revolution had driven the British from the East Coast, and this war forced them to stay up in Canada whose border is an imaginary line between the islands only a few miles north of the monument. For students of Ohio history, it is a memorial to war dead and victory. For Canadians and diplomats, it marks a peaceful border. For boaters, it is the largest light house on the lake.

His fear still there, but checked; Joe realized he was never going to be a sailor. He forced himself not to look down to the waves. He kept his gaze out on the horizon. He focused on the monument and studied it. He assured himself that the ferries ran back and forth all day, every day. They'd make it this time. He could get through it. Soon they landed, and he biked on up to town. He dried in the sun and wind. He was surprised at the number of people in town. Apparently, the fair weather had attracted others like him. There were the usual yachts and sailboats moored in the harbor, and dozens of power boats docked at the marina. Those people pretty much stayed close to their boats. The bars were already filling up. Every time Joe had come out, the town seemed a little seedier than the time before. The presence of so many in worn blue jeans, tie-dyed shirts and long stringy hair convinced Joe that Put-In-Bay was in decay. In Joe's estimate, the whole place could use a couple coats of paint. With the money in his shoe, he bought a pitcher of beer and half a chicken from the barbecue next to the Round House Bar. He wouldn't have wanted to eat alone in the crowd, even if it weren't so rough looking. He walked across to the park. There he found a comfortable spot under a tree where he ate and nursed the beer while he studied the Lonz Winery across on Middle Bass Island and watched the boats come and go.

When Joe woke, it was nearly 3:00 P.M. He muttered and swore at himself. Rather than go up the monument, he resolved to ride around the island to clear his head. He did that for an hour, then caught the ferry. He still had another 15 miles to ride when he got back across on the ferry. It was dusk when he got home. He ate a can of tuna fish and went to bed listening to the radio. He slept late the next morning, and woke hung over from too much sleep, not the beer. He thought about going to church, he hadn't been all summer, but dismissed it with a frown. Somehow he was getting along just fine without that nonsense. He stayed for a long time in the shower where he decided he would get a TV. He wasn't sure what he should wear to work the next day, so he'd also look at some work clothes. He got to the discount store before it opened and sat waiting on the curb for an hour. He bought a 12" black and white for $50, and a matching set of khaki work shirt and slacks for $10. He rode them home balanced on his handle bars. The entire way he scolded himself at how stupid it was. The thought of losing $50 in shattered glass, disgusted him.

He spent the afternoon lying on his worn out sofa watching the new tube. He wanted beer, but it was Sunday and there were Blue Laws. He resolved that he would keep beer on hand. He thought about tuning his bike, but the sofa was more comfortable. He dozed, waking the last time a little after 10:00 P.M. When he woke he remembered he had been so excited the night before he started at Cedar Point that he had lain awake half the night. Now he thought casually about his new job. The money was going to be great, but the work couldn't be as challenging as the machinery at the park. Whatever, he'd wake at the usual time, and put in a good day's work. He had no doubt that he would put in as good or even a better day than anyone else at Falloni's. He had learned that much about himself that summer. He relieved himself and fell into bed. The TV was still on in the other room.

CHAPTER 11

"Hey, kid, nice clothes." Joe flushed at Mr. Falloni's greeting. "Follow me." They went down the corridor, passed the owner's office, the parts counter, and out into the warehouse. It was poorly lit with large boats supported in cradles lined up along either wall. Several workers were milling about a shop desk, sipping cups of coffee. One man, half seated on a stool, was shuffling papers and motioning directions at them. It was much like the beginning of each day working for Ivan, except that Cedar Point's shop was pristine and the workers uniformed. Mr. Falloni nodded to each man who looked his way and led Joe outside.

Behind the warehouse was a large gravel yard leading to the waterfront. There was a concrete wharf, leftover from a time when this had been a factory, shipping and receiving by lake boats. At the wharf, three men in their twenties were taking orders from another who looked to be about the same age as Mr. Falloni. They were positioning a large traveling lift over a slip, preparing to take a 38 foot Hatteras out of the water. There were several other similar yachts docked along the wharf, and at least a dozen in cradles in the year. "Red, this is... Hey, kid, what's your name?" Joe answered. "Red, this is Joe... whatever. Ivan sent him over. Joe, you tell the girl up front how to spell your name sometime this week so she gets it right on your check. Friday's payday. Beer and checks at the close of business Friday."

"Sir, is there anything else I should do?"

"I don't even care if she misspells your name. That's between you and your bank. No, we don't have forms and all that horseshit. We're in the business of taking care of boats, not filling neat little files full of paper."

"Should I clock in?"

"Do you believe this guy!" Listen, kid, Red will keep track of your time. Lynette will make out your check. I tell her how much. You work. OK? Red, be gentle." Mr. Falloni walked off inspecting his cigar.

"Come on, Joe" Red said. "Hope you don't mind getting those new clothes dirty."

In the middle of the following week, Joe's new bike arrived. He had taken to stopping at the bike shop on his way home every evening. That night he learned the UPS had delivered it just moments earlier. Joe and the bike mechanic opened the box and exchanged compliments as they inspected the parts. The mechanic assembled the bike the next day. Joe paid the balance. After closing the shop, the mechanic gave Joe a ride home, with Joe's two bikes in the back of his pick-up. It was early October, and the sun had set before Joe finished his snack and changed into his riding clothes. The darkness couldn't keep him off the new bike. Before turning the crank twice, he was absolutely amazed at the difference. As he cranked and worked up through the gears, the most he heard was a hiss and click. There was no grainy sound from any bearing or chatter from the derailleur. He thought he could even feel the frame flex slightly when he stood to pump. This was a real bike, his other a toy.

He headed east out Route 6. Because it was dark and cold, he decided to turn back when he got to the airport. Coming back into town, a police car flashed its lights and motioned him over. Joe contritely accepted the lecture about dark clothes, reflectors, and lights. The cop told him Sandusky had an ordinance about lights, and he'd have to give him a summons if he saw him out without a light again. Business out of the way, the policemen asked if Joe belonged to the local riding club. The policeman and his wife did. He wrote a name and number on the back of his business card. Joe already had them from the bike shop, but didn't say anything. Soon the two were squatting down on their haunches, inspecting the bike in the headlights of the police car.

Joe continued to ride his old bike to work, saving the touring bike for weekends. The following Saturday, he rode home. The week after that, he did an out and back to Vermillion. After those two rides, he took it back to the bike shop for the free tuning that came with the new bike. The head of the local club happened to be in the shop and after admiring the machine, persuaded Joe to join the local group that Saturday for a "century", a one hundred mile ride south through Norwalk to Mansfield then over to Bucyrus and back north to Sandusky.

It was a humbling experience for Joe. He had the best bike, but he quickly saw that all the riders had spent as much on clothes and gear as on their bikes. Worse, by half way, he could no longer keep up with them. For the next hour, he kept them in sight, but he finally gave up on that, and rode into Sandusky alone at dusk.

At noon on the Wednesday before Thanksgiving, Mr. Falloni came out to announce that he'd just tapped a keg of beer. Anyone who wanted to keep working could, but anyone who wanted to meet with him in his office was welcome. Other than one-for-the-road on paydays, Joe hadn't had more than an occasional beer in front of his TV since his trip to Put-In-Bay. He was quickly drunk. Being the new kid, he smiled off the teasing, especially about his clothes. The newness had long since been washed out of his khaki's, and he'd even bought a second set. Somehow, he always managed to stay clean in contrast to his motley coworkers. Mr. Falloni, bought bailed rags from Goodwill, but after trying them, Joe found them lacking. He bought his own red shop rags from an auto parts store, and his trademark became the one hanging from his hip pocket. Joe had progressed from yard work to rebuilding diesels after he prevailed on Red to let him work on one.

About 4:30 P.M. Mr. Falloni's son, Petey, arrived. Mr. Falloni stood next to the keg with his arm around Petey. Lynette periodically found excuses to touch Petey's arm. After ten minutes or so, the knot that formed around Petey loosened. Petey filled a beer for himself and came over to Joe, "Hi, I'm Pete Falloni." Joe introduced himself, and they shook hands. "You'll never hear it from my old man, but he thinks you're great. Really. When I call home from school, he always gives me a report on the business and raves about the new kid."

"Thanks. He's quite a guy. They broke the mold. You should know that we all get regular updates about you. Heard about how well you did on mid-terms and some swanky society girl from Chicago."

"Sounds just like the old man." He wasn't at all what Joe expected, not a pampered rich kid. He seemed like a nice enough guy. He was definitely a cut above the guys who worked in the shop, but he didn't act that way. The guys were starting to leave, so Joe excused himself. He thanked Mr. Falloni, collected his bike from the warehouse, strapped his light to his calf, and wobbled out across the gravel. Dizzy, he stopped in front to take a few breaths. He watched Pete come out and climb into a Corvette. It was the same Corvette. Joe was sure of it.

"I'll be goddamned." Joe said under his breath. After Pete

drove off, Joe got back up on his bike. The ride home was his first one drunk. He found it invigorating. The cold did not bother him in the slightest. Lucky for Joe, he did not sideswipe any of the parked cars that flashed passed in a blur of color. From time to time he laughed at himself. "I'll be goddamned. I thought Attica was a small town."

CHAPTER 12

Since Falloni's was going to be closed Friday, Joe had planned to ride his new bike home and stay for the holiday weekend. The next morning he woke late, hung over. Looking out his window the sky was grey, and he thought he saw a snow flurry. He called home for a ride. Within an hour, Dieter was there to get him. On the way to the farm, they talked about Dieter's activities; school, the county fair, and the farm. Dieter had been elected secretary of FFA. The harvest had gone well. They compared bushels per acre yields to previous years. Joe fell silent, not sharing his guilt. It was the first harvest of his life that he hadn't helped bring in. Worse, until this conversation, he hadn't even thought about it. As they approached the farm, he could see his absence had not changed the place, but he contemplated how the work went, split two ways instead of three. It was an unintended consequence of his departure that he had never even considered.

They entered the farmhouse just before noon. It was warm and full of the smells of Thanksgiving dinner. His face was puffy and his nose ran. When his mother fawned over him, she predicted he was getting a cold. His father got him outside for a walk before he had a chance to take off his coat. They inspected the equipment. After getting the crops in, his Dad had shifted over to winter work. He was in the process of rebuilding the corn picker. There wasn't much wrong with it, just the usual, broken teeth on the shear, broken and loose bolts, dents in the points.

His father complained about the early winter and talked of plans to put up an insulated metal building which they could heat to work on the equipment. Joe commiserated, telling his father about the unheated warehouse in which he worked, and how they used gas lanterns and flashlights to see what they were doing. Joe quickly followed that with a note about his good pay. The amount dumbfounded his father. Most years on the farm they hadn't made that much, even though they'd been able to keep the debt low and raise a family. As he went off into his speech, Joe could see it was not jealousy, just that his father had discovered another manner in which they were destroying the family farm by stealing the young men.

The family around the table at mid-afternoon was a repeat of a ritual so firmly established that none thought it could or ever would be otherwise. They all over ate. As was the custom, Dieter and Joe had to clean the dishes. In the living room his father read the paper, and his mother darned. Dieter wanted to put a football game on TV, but they insisted on an old movie. When the phone rang about dusk, Joe, who normally would have jumped to answer, hesitated. It did not seem his place to answer their phone. His father never answered it, Dieter was upstairs, and his mother grumbled as she got up from her sewing. It was Joe's friend who was going to college at O.S.U. He wanted to go for a ride, but Joe didn't think he should go out that night. Instead, they planned that his friend should come by in the morning.

Joe's mother watched from her kitchen window as Joe and his friend raised the hood of his old car and chatted with each other. In the distance Dieter and Joe's father were experimenting with a new tool for cleaning the fence rows, a circular blade on the opposite end of a long aluminum tube from a small gas engine. Joe had earlier taken one look at it and concluded it was dangerous. His mother had a snapshot of Joe and his friend taken on the first day of school in 1955. She beamed at the memory of it, and the handsome young men that they'd become. Joe came in to announce that they were going for a drive.

They drove over to Tiffin, his friend boasting of his summer conquests at Heidelberg. In their usual manner, Joe's friend rambled on. He hadn't driven his car since leaving for school. Freshmen weren't allowed cars, and on the gigantic campus, student parking was miles from everything. He had put too much work into it to leave it on the street, so it sat in his parents' garage in Attica. He couldn't believe how empty Heidelberg was; he should have known, everyone would go home for the holiday. He planned to major in business, but was thinking more about history or political science. He didn't know what he'd do with a degree like that; he didn't want to teach. Joe would never believe the action at O.S.U. There were great places to hang out on High Street. There were even two bars on High Street named Heidelberg, North Berg and South Berg. The reference launched a plan to drive down to

Columbus on the excuse of showing Joe the campus, they'd party, stay overnight in his dorm room, and come home the next day.

Joe waited in the car while his friend cleared it with his parents, and Joe did the same when they got back to the farm. Dieter and his father listened from the kitchen table where they were eating turkey sandwiches. Joe's mother quickly approved, well aware she lacked the authority to disapprove, but touched by Joe's deference to her wishes. Although she didn't say it, Joe knew she still held the hope he'd go to college. She would be thinking that a college visit might turn his head. Joe refused her offer to make lunch for them, bounded upstairs to put an overnight bag together, then left. They bought lunch at a hamburger joint in Bucyrus, and his friend procured a case of beer because it would be cheaper there than in Columbus. The minute they got out of town, they cracked open their first beer using the church key dangling on a cord from the radio knob on the dash.

While the scale was grander, they found the O.S.U. campus as empty as Heidelberg. After boldly parking in a faculty lot near the dorm, they put the beer in the trunk of the Olds, each taking one in their coat pockets. They ran into a campus policeman in the lobby of the dorm. He told them the dorm was nearly empty, but raised no objection to their staying overnight. A few minutes later they were back out on the campus. They looped the quadrangle, started drinking the beer they carried at Mirror Lake, and then went all the way passed Horseshoe Stadium to the river where they finished the cans. They went back to the dorm to warm up, each taking two more beers from the car. Beer in the dorms was strictly forbidden. All that meant to them was that they must remember to take the empty cans to a trash bin outside.

They listened to records on the roommate's stereo while lying on the bunk beds. His friend recalled memorable drunks from the fall. As usual, Joe responded, but did not volunteer. He never spoke of his life in Sandusky. He preferred his apartment to the dorm. He had more room, more things, more freedom. He made more than most school teachers. He started to see that he had less and less in common with his friend, except that they were friends. He loved to be with him. He loved to listen to the bullshit. Joe nodded off, only to wake to the sound of his friend swearing about the beer he'd spilled. Laughing off the trouble he might get into, they decided it was time for dinner.

They retrieved more beer from the car which they drank on their way across campus. They ate in a pizza parlor on High Street, then retired to the North Berg where they drank beer by the pitcher and ate popcorn for a couple of hours. There was a reasonable number of people in the bar, but it was empty by normal standards. When it was clear that they were not going to find any girls, Joe's friend laid out two proposals, a porno theater further up High Street, or the South Berg where there were surely coeds. Joe was tempted by the porno theater; but afraid of how his friend might taunt him, he chose the bar.

The long walk in the brisk air did not sober either of them. Although they could have sat just about anywhere they wanted, Joe's friend led him down into the basement, where they searched for his friend's name on the ceiling. It was a long-standing tradition to autograph the ceiling with the smoke from a match or candle. They never found his name, but after another pitcher; both signed the ceiling. They ordered their last pitcher, which they forced themselves to finish by chugging contests, then headed back to the dorm. Coming up out of the basement reminded Joe of his apartment. He missed it. They stumbled and laughed their way back to the dorm, getting another six pack out of the car on the way. They each started another beer in the room. Joe wished he were not there.

Joe woke with a headache so terrible that he felt he couldn't open his eyes or move his head. He was still in his clothes and finally had to give into his bladder. He climbed slowly out of the bed, being careful not to disturb his friend, and made his way to the restroom at the end of the hall. It was fully half way through his urination before he noticed the smell of vomit. He looked around to see it all over the floor around one of the toilets. He tried, but couldn't remember making the mess. Back in the room, he found his friend had vomit down his sweater. Joe woke him. They both muttered alot and showered. His friend did a half-way job of cleaning the mess. He assured Joe that it was no big deal, dismissing it as an everyday occurrence in the dorms. Joe wasn't so sure. He only wanted to get home, home to Sandusky.

Joe slept most of the way to Attica. When dropped at the farm, Joe declined the opportunity to share the left over beer. The thought made him sick. His mother had many questions, but he shrugged them off, "Not my kind of place. Too big." He slept most of the afternoon. He tried to get a ride home that Saturday, telling his mother that she could shop in Sandusky. She would not hear of it. They finally agreed the family would run him up after church in the morning. His mother attached great significance to attending church as a family, and his father wanted to eat out in Sandusky. Joe's cold was much worse.

CHAPTER 13

The weekend after Thanksgiving, Joe went on a ride with the local club. He had officially joined it at the bike shop one day when asked if he wanted to be a member. He'd answered yes, gave his address, and was told he was on their mailing list. There were no dues. He had never as yet been to an official meeting, but he understood that they met in a neighborhood bar once every month or so. They had loosely organized rides at least once a month. Also, whenever there was a big ride in Toledo, Cleveland, Columbus, or the like, several would go to it as a group. That Saturday, a half dozen of them gathered at the bike shop for an out and back to Marblehead. Joe had accumulated a modest amount of gear, although he was not yet as colorful as his companions. He wore black lycra shorts with a padded leather crotch over his long underwear and tightly woven red nylon turtleneck sweater. He didn't own a helmet yet, but had padded gloves. Standing around afterwards, Joe noticed a "best offer" for sale sign in the window of the shop mechanic's pick-up.

Knowing the mechanic was a fastidious sort, and having ridden in the truck, Joe went looking for him. "I see your truck's for sale."

"Yeah, I'm getting a van."

"What do you want for it?"

"It's in real good shape. I did the rod bearings, rings, and valves. There's no rust at all. I'd like to get $400."

"Tires are bald. Does the bike rack stay with it?"

"Most people wouldn't appreciate that. Built it myself. It holds four bikes. $350 and you can have the bike rack."

"Would you take $300 if I left the rack?"

""$350's more than fair."

"I know, but I don't have it. You keep the rack."

"Oh, you can have it. When can you get the money?"

"Title clear?"

"Sure. Monday?"

"Yeah, if you could pick me up from work at noon, I can go to the bank with you." And so Joe acquired a motor vehicle. While he loved to cycle, it was getting bitter cold. The few times he'd biked to work in the snow, he slipped and slid all the way. From then on, he drove to work.

There was another change in Joe's life between Thanksgiving and Christmas. He accepted an invitation to stop for a beer after work with some of the guys. Two or three times a week he was asked, and he always invented an excuse. After their customary beer with Mr. Falloni on Friday afternoon, he was showing one of the guys how the bikes hooked into the rack in the back of his pick-up; when several others came out. He was easily caught up in their plans, and followed them to a cement block building on the edge of town, on a street he'd never been on before. Inside, a wood stove heated the room and lent its aroma to that of cigarette smoke and beer spilled on the concrete floor. It was a perfect place for his companions, but Joe didn't fit. He was too clean cut and stood out. He kept up with the rounds, nodding and smiling, but not talking until 7:00 P.M., when he made an excuse and left.

He had planned a solitary ride that Saturday morning, but it was snowing. He went Christmas shopping instead. He found a wicker sewing basket for his mother. He came across a ceramic figurine of an old man cutting a log with a cross-cut, and bought it for Mrs. Olschewske. He stopped in a little restaurant downtown for lunch. He had a hot dog, and for the first time ever, a beer with his lunch. After lunch, he drove over to Sears to get tools for Dieter and his father. On the way, he inspected every bar he passed, wondering about its clientele.

That night, he put on his wool slacks, sweater, and school shoes and went to a bar downtown. It was basically empty when he arrived. He sat at the bar. There was a nice restaurant two doors down, and it became apparent to him from the well-dressed older couples who seemed to be coming in after dinner, that the place was a little high-brow for him. He finished his third beer just when a piano player started singing, paid his bill, and went home. There he had a beer while watching TV.

After an hour, he went back out. He cruised around Sandusky, ending up on the familiar motel strip. He had never been into any of the bars there. It seemed like the largest number of cars were in front of the bowling alley, so he went there. There were a few couples his age bowling, but everyone in the bar was at least his parents' age. He had one beer, then left. As he went to his truck, a twin engine aircraft passed low overhead and began to turn for landing at Griffing Field. The cold air was so dense, and the engines sounded so close, that Joe's first reaction was to duck. He drove out Cleveland Road to the airport. From the parking lot he saw a figure take two canvas bags from a van and load them into the plane. Another figure fueled the plane from a pump on the ground. Joe stayed watching until the place took off, then he went home. There he had another beer before going to bed.

The following Tuesday morning, Mr. Falloni called Joe into his office. Other than paydays and the Thanksgiving party, Joe was never called into the office. Even worse, Mr. Falloni closed the door. "Joe, sit down. Relax." After settling into his own chair, Mr. Falloni continued. "When you started, I told you that I have succeeded because I built this place on trust. I know that because I tell everybody that. Seriously, I don't know how many of them really understand me, but I want to make sure you do. I really believe it." Joe wondered if Mr. Falloni had been drinking, then realized his slur was only the result of the cigar in his mouth. "I know it's a business, and you know I work for money. You do too. That's why I have to pay you guys. We all work for money. The business, though, money just goes through it. It comes in, it goes out. It lubricates the place. Any good and lasting business is built on trust. The only thing that we really sell is our promise to do a good job. People pay for our promise. They trust us to deliver."

Mr. Falloni noticed Joe looking over his shoulder to a new photograph on the clustered bookshelf. He turned to look at it himself. It was a picture of his son in a tuxedo and a beautiful girl in a formal. She had a long thin neck and her dark hair up with ringlets hanging down. "That's Petey and his new girl. She's Faulk's kid, you know, the car dealer in Norwalk. I've known him for years. Can you believe it? I send my kid over to Notre Dame, and he meets a local girl. Pretty ain't she? I haven't met her yet, but Petey says he'll bring her home at Christmas. Anyway, back to business."

"You got more on the ball than these guys around here. Ivan was right. That's why I trust him. My problem is, I've got good men who have worked here for years. They were doing good by me years ago, and they'll be doing good by me years from now. They're the kind of guys you can trust, or they wouldn't have lasted with me. You see,

I just can't bring in a new guy and push them aside." Joe was a little befuddled. He had long before reconciled the things he didn't like about Falloni's with his paycheck. He concluded he was about to be fired. "What I'm saying is that I don't want you to get discouraged or impatient. I want you to know that you have been recognized. I know that you could probably run the shop, but hell, Red's been here twenty years. I've got to recognize that too. You're doing a fine job. I want to keep you here because you're the kind of guy I can trust to build the next twenty years of this business." He paused, opened the center drawer of his desk, and handed Joe a check for $300. Joe's mouth fell open. "We don't pay Christmas bonuses around here, and I don't want anyone else to know you got this. You know we close for two weeks over the holidays, and no one makes any money then, not even me. It's not a bonus, it's not vacation pay. Just think of it as recognition, a token of my trust."

"Thanks, I can't...."

"This is between us. You do a good job. You put in a good day's work, and you're entitled to a fair day's wage. You don't owe me anything, and I don't owe you anything. I just need to make sure we trust each other."

"Yes, Mr. Falloni. Yes, sir." Joe shook his hand.

"Now get back to work."

That Friday was more than payday. It was the day they closed the place for Christmas. Mr. Falloni had a keg in his office and gave everyone large canned hams. Joe got high, but not drunk. He talked to Red and Lynette more than anyone else. He noticed Lynette had a habit of touching him from time to time as she talked. He didn't know anything about her, not even her last name. He assumed she was single from the Mustang she drove. She was a couple of years older than him, but he couldn't guess her age. She was nice and took care of her appearance, but just a little too much. To most of the guys in the shop she was a goddess with whom they wouldn't dare flirt. To Joe, her features were too round, too ordinary; much like the farm girls in Attica. As he chatted with her, he realized she had to know about his check. His face flushed.

Mr. Falloni took the lead in breaking up the party. He lectured everyone about driving safely, telling them he didn't want any accidents this time of year and wishing everyone happy holidays. In the parking lot, Lynette asked Joe if he'd like to stop by a particular bar with her over on Milan near where there was talk of building a mall. The bar had fried cheese and mushrooms that they could make into a meal. Joe concluded that Lynette was single and noted the bar might be to his liking. He knew where it was, but he gave Lynette one of his usual excuses. He went home and had a few more beers lying on the sofa. Lynette spent the night at the bar, unsuccessfully trying to get picked up.

CHAPTER 14

Joe woke Saturday, still unsure what he was going to do with himself during Falloni's shutdown. The weather made a bike trip out of the question. It had been an early winter, and it was apparently going to be hard. The temperature rarely got up into the thirties. On the brightest days, the sky was grey. More often, it was overcast with low ceilings. Every few days, there were two or three inches of snow that blew off in the howling winds to long, low drifts, leaving great sections of the frozen ground exposed.

He didn't want to go home to the farm for the two weeks. There would be work there that he could help with, there always was on a farm; but he didn't want to go there. He felt guilty about not going and tried to think through the reasons. It was not because his mother worried after him, nor was it his father's economics and politics. It was simply that he felt out of place. That was the way he felt on Thanksgiving. He was not anxious to feel that way again. He resolved to go to the farm for a day or two over Christmas, but not yet. Still, he had to find some way to fill his time.

He turned his TV on, flipped through the cartoons, then turned it off. He went into the second bedroom that he had made into a bicycle shop to putter with his bikes. He had installed hooks in the ceiling, and both bikes bung upside down from them. He had built shelves from crating lumber he scavenged from work and bricks from a pile near an abandoned factory. On them, he kept his growing collection of cycling-related tools, lubricants, and parts. In the center of the room was a work stand he'd purchased from the bike shop when they had gotten a better one for their mechanic. It wobbled a little to much for a mechanic who worked on bikes all the time, but it was more than adequate for Joe's light use. Looking over the hanging bikes, he realized that there was nothing to be done to them that he hadn't already done. A blast of wind hummed through the window frame around the ground level window and brought Joe's attention to the stone wall.

Since the heat had been on, the basement had dried out and had lost most of its musty smell. Studying the wall, Joe took note of how clean the cut blocks of limestone were. He could still see clean chisel marks. There wasn't a trace of mildew. He tried to reconcile that with the prior dampness and concluded the other side of the building might be wet or moisture might be coming up through the floor. When he looked around to the interior walls, they suddenly seemed dingy and marked. Except for the stone exterior wall, the entire apartment had been painted a flat white a few tenants earlier. Joe decided to paint the apartment. His landlord couldn't possibly mind, it would be an improvement.

Joe went out to a discount store and bought yellow paint for his kitchen and a light blue for his bathroom. It was his intention to paint the entire apartment, but a twinge from his thriftiness prevented him from buying more than he would use that day. He also bought a couple of brushes, a roller, and a pan. He deliberately went out of his way to drive passed the bar Lynette mentioned. It was new and had an expensive sign. There were already a few cars in front. Joe picked up a twelve-pack at a drive through and opened one in the truck on his way back. He sipped it at a stop light as he absentmindedly counted the headlights of a funeral procession going the opposite direction. At home, he started painting in the bath, then put a coat on the kitchen. Later that afternoon, he put a second coat in the bath. He was about to start the second coat in the kitchen when he realized that it was past dinner time, and he was dizzy from the fumes. In fact, he was drunk from the beer he'd been drinking all afternoon. He admired his work and decided that he'd treat himself to dinner out.

By the time he cleaned the brushes, rollers and himself, it was 7:30 P.M. Going to his truck, he was surprised to find a bright night with stars and a full moon. He kicked at the powdery strands of snow that drifted across the sidewalk, and deliberately slid along the patches of ice. He stopped in a family restaurant that was empty except for a few regulars sitting at the counter. The dinner trade had gone, and the after-the-basketball-game crowd was yet to come. He bought a paper and sat down in a booth. Only when the waitress came, did he realize that he wasn't hungry; indeed, he was bloated from the beer. He ordered a cup of coffee and an order of french fries. The coffee habit had been recently acquired at work. He scanned the news as he waited for his order, then began to work the paper from the back forwards as he munched down the fries.

He felt as if he'd suddenly fallen, falling weightless and dizzy, when he saw Mrs. Olshewske's name in the obituaries. She had died on Wednesday from natural causes. There had been visiting hours the night before and a funeral Mass that morning at Sts. Peter & Paul. Joe no longer had any peripheral vision. He read the notice again and again. No survivors. Did she have any friends? He couldn't think of any he knew. Shit. She was already buried. He visualized a grave side service that desolate morning. In it, he stared at clumps of earth pick-axed from frozen ground. In them, he could see crystals of ice shimmering in the half light. He heard the priest's monotone. When he tried to make out the words, he lost his reverie and realized that he was in the restaurant. He looked about and forced himself to take several deep breaths. He finished the coffee in a gulp, but left the fries.

He sat in the truck, staring down at the steering wheel until he took a chill and realized that his breath had frozen on the windshield. He started the engine and continued to sit waiting for the heat and the defroster. When the windshield was clear enough to drive, he started for the bar.

He caught a red light heading south out Milan. In the distance to his right, he recognized the entrance to the Oakland Cemetery. He had been by it many times before, not giving it much thought. It bordered Pipe Creek, had gentle rolling hills, trees, many large stones, and mausoleums. Limestone was plentiful, and Sandusky's prosperous past was reflected there. He drove directly into the cemetery, idling slowly about until he spotted a fresh grave. He had no way of knowing Mrs. Olschewske had been buried across town in the Calvary Catholic Cemetery.

He left his engine running and walked over to it. The moon was so bright he could easily read markers, but this grave had none. He pulled off his glove and touched the mound. The clumps were hard, but loose; he pushed down slightly and his hand sank into them. He jerked his hand out in fear, realizing it was, indeed, a fresh grave. It had to be her's. He stepped back, still looking down. One side of the mound had a shadow from the moonlight. He looked around, then tried to recall her face as he looked back to the grave. He couldn't. A gust caught him, and he put his hands up to his ears. They were burning. He went back to the truck, then left. Driving out, he thought that maybe he should go to church in the morning and offer the Mass up to her. Then he realized that he hadn't prayed at her grave.

It didn't seem right to him to pray in the truck, and the thought of church slipped away as he drove on south passed the Soldiers' and Sailors' Home. The parking lot at the bar was full. Joe drove around the lot twice to make sure Lynette's Mustang wasn't there. He parked in the frozen field just beyond the lot, next to several other cars. Before getting out of his truck, Joe looked at his wrist watch. It was 9:30 P.M. Saturday night, the place should be jumping.

CHAPTER 15

Inside, Joe quickly saw that it wasn't the kind of bar that jumped. There was a large square bar in the center of the room with cocktail tables and chairs around the edge of the room. They were mostly taken. Joe ambled around the room. On one wall were a hallway to restrooms and a swinging door to the kitchen. On the opposite side was an opening to a second room which had a dozen stuffed chairs scattered about the room. There was a fireplace in one corner of that room with a small sofa in front of it. Both rooms were decorated with old photographs of local interest.

Joe continued to circle the bar until he found a section of several empty stools. He took one in the center. Joe ordered a draft, which the bartender got after he carded him. Waiting for the beer, Joe thought of the Christmas gift he had gotten for Mrs. Olschewske. What was he going to do with it? He didn't want to take it back. He didn't want to keep it. He couldn't give it to someone else. Should he throw it away? What a thing to be thinking about! Joe turned around on the stool and took gulps from the mug as he scanned the room.

It was most definitely his kind of place; a bar for pick-ups, tables for conversation, and the fireplace for intimacy. There was no dancing, which was fine, for he did not know how. He realized that he was younger than most of the crowd, but it was clearly a singles bar. The more Joe looked, the more he liked it. He didn't know, but he imagined that this was the classiest place in town. He finished the beer and was turning back to order another when he saw her.

The red-head from Cedar Point was sitting on the opposite side of the bar, directly across from him. He quickly looked away. Maybe he was mistaken. The bartender stepped in between them and took Joe's order. When he stepped away, Joe shot a second glance in her direction. Yes, it was her. It looked like she was alone. There were people on the stools beside her, but they were ignoring her. She was staring at her mug. Joe paid for his beer, then forced himself to look up to the lighted glasses hanging overhead. Then he stared at the racks of liquor bottles in the center of the bar. How in the hell was he going to handle this? He drew in a deep breath and raised his eyes over the bottles to her.

She was still looking down, but now someone was standing beside her, talking directly into her ear. Joe lifted his beer and looked about. Just his luck, too late. He looked back to confirm his fear. It was Pete Falloni pulling away from her hair. She was shaking her head no. He was persuading, nodding his head repeatedly toward the fireplace room. She took her beer and went with him. Joe chugged his beer and raised the empty mug to the bartender. He drank the next one more slowly, making ring patterns on the bar with its condensation. The bartender brought another mug before Joe ordered it. Joe was starting to feel woozy and looked across the bar only to focus his eyes in the distance. She was back. She cleaned the corner of one eye with her finger and immediately ordered a drink. Joe looked more closely to see if she was crying. She wasn't, as far as he could tell. She might be mad, Joe thought. He remembered more than one morning when she'd slammed the Corvette door and stomped into the park. "Joe! How the hell are you?" Joe jumped at the slap of a hand on his shoulder.

"Fine." he said extending his hand to Pete.

"I just got back from school. You come here much?"

"Actually, this is the first time." Joe suppressed a belch under his breath and realized how badly he needed to relieve himself.

"Nice place. Listen, I've got to get home. You know, first night back and all that. The Old Man will have a fit if I stay out late. Maybe I'll see you here again."

"Yeah, sure thing. Merry Christmas. Give your Dad my best."

"I'll do that." Joe watched Pete look beyond him and across the bar. Pete made no move to leave. "You from around here?"

"I grew up on a farm near Attica."

"That little town about half way to Bucyrus?"

"Yeah."

"Going home for Christmas?"

"Yeah."

"You have a good one. I've got to go."

"Merry Christmas." Joe turned back to his drink and saw her look quickly away from him. I just can't believe this, he thought as he took another gulp, caught in a crossfire. He deliberately left the mug half full to save his place at the bar and went to the restroom. As he came out of the men's room, she was going into the women's. Joe looked down to the floor and turned sideways to pass her. He had almost made it when she spoke.

"You're Joe from Cedar Point, right?"

"Hi. I mean, yes." He stammered, not sure if he should extend his hand. "Yeah, I remember you."

"Molly Brennan." Joe missed her name, wondering how she knew his. "I've never seen you here before."

"First time."

"Really. This is a great place. I come here every time I come home." Joe looked a little puzzled, and she answered. "I'm in college at Bowling Green."

"No kidding? I almost went there."

"Where do you go?"

"No place. I mean, I didn't go to college. I came up here after graduation and stayed."

"I'm sorry, Joe." She smiled. "I've got to get in here. Nice to see you again." Joe nodded then blushed. She disappeared into the women's room.

Now what was he going to do? How could he keep this going? He reclaimed his bar stool and finished his beer as he studied her seat across the way. There were still people sitting on either side of her stool. There wasn't room for him to move over there. When the bartender brought another mug, Joe quickly finished the one he had and paid for the new one. She still hadn't come back. Maybe she wouldn't. Joe turned on the stool to survey the room. She was a step and a half away, coming up to him. He looked directly into her face. Now he could feel his ears flaming. She smiled broadly and gave her head a little shake to straighten the hair on her shoulders. Joe noticed that she kept her head tilted a little back, probably because she wasn't very tall and spent her life looking up at others. He already knew about that porpoise-like smile.

"You going to be here a while? Mind if I join you?" She left for her beer before Joe could answer. He watched her walk around the bar. She had on ski pants, fleece-lined boots, and a sweater. The sweater was snugged in against her waist by a wide belt. It was still true. She was Joe's essence of woman. It not only excited him to look at her, but it also gave him comfort. To him, she was alluring, wholesome, and maternal. He had thought all this before and made no sense of it. He had only his mother as a model, and she was nothing like his mother. She wasn't nearly as tall as his mother, nor were they built remotely alike. His mother was lean and athletic. She had wide shoulders and hips, indeed, her rear protruded well beyond normal proportion. Any disproportion was lost on Joe. He had been attracted directly by her, not by way of comparison. He knew he had little knowledge of females. He could at least think through religion, and machines he completely understood, but he had never been able to make sense of females. He was terrified and happy at the same time. She was coming back with her beer. Well, here goes nothing.

"Why don't we go in there." He suggested. "It's more quiet, and the fire...."

"Sure."

They found two wing-backed chairs diagonally from the fire. She leaned back in her's and closed her eyes. It gave Joe his first chance to study her face at close range. Her nose was narrow and her skin clear. She had blond fuzz on the side of her face, and some, but much less, over her lips. Her eyebrows were the same auburn as her hair, but her eyelashes were white. She opened her eyes and asked, "So, you know Peter?"

Joe cleared his throat. "I work for his Dad."

"You do? No more Cedar Point?"

"Actually, I liked it there. I liked the work; but, you know, it closes."

"Ivan keeps a crew year round."

"You know Ivan?"

"His brother lives a couple of doors from us. His brother and my Dad and Mom were in the same high school class. Mr. Falloni was also in the same class."

Joe was reminded of Attica, but didn't want to talk about it. "Ivan's a good guy."

"Yeah, I love his kids. I babysat for them today. They had to go to a funeral. Melody, his wife, didn't want the kids to go. I personally think they should. It's part of life. Got to face it all, but I need the money, and it's not for me to say."

Joe didn't answer. His mind was crowded with many thoughts, then all of a sudden, it was clear. He was suddenly at ease. He looked at her as he might an old friend. "How did you know my name?"

She laid her hand over her breast then pulled it back and tapped her finger close to her shoulder, "You did have it sewn on your shirt all summer,..." Joe fought to recall her name, "...and Ivan teased me about you all the time."

"I don't believe that!"

"He did. He kept volunteering to fix us up."

"I just can't believe this." Joe drew in a breath of courage. "I would have given anything to...."

"One time when I fell out with Peter, I almost,.... You remember the Fourth of July?" Joe nodded. "I saw you going around with some guys. I followed you all over that park, but kept losing you. Finally, I went up to this one guy, but he was so out of it, I...."

That would be my good buddy,...."

"Guess it wasn't meant to be." Joe's heart sank. "So, you work at Falloni's now?"

"Yeah. I do what needs to be done. Pay's great."

"Peter ever say anything about me?"

"I only met him once before tonight. No."

"Doesn't matter. We are officially 'just friends'. Doesn't matter. I was sick of the fighting anyway. We broke up."

"I know."

"I thought he never said anything?"

"He didn't. Mr. Falloni has a picture in his office..." Joe tried to stop, but couldn't "...of Pete and another girl."

"Oh that's just great!" She moaned, looking up to the ceiling and gritting her teeth. Joe could see tears sliding down the side of her face.

"Listen, I'm sorry. I've had too much to drink."

"Not your problem."

"You two go together long?"

"Steady since junior year; but really since 7th grade. Jesus!"

"I'm sorry."

Joe watched her cry for a moment, then looked to the fire. He didn't notice when she had stopped crying. They both sat quietly watching the fire for several minutes.

"I lived with her last summer." Joe said.

"Whose that?"

"Mrs. Olschewske."

"Who?"

"The lady that died. The funeral today."

"I'm sorry."

"I didn't even know she died until tonight. I saw it in the paper." They each sipped from their drinks and stared again into the fire. Joe balanced his elbow on the chair and rubbed his forehead. His hand quivered. Without looking up he said, "I just bought her a Christmas gift, now I don't know what to...." his voice cracked, and he quickly cleared his throat. She looked directly at him. Aware she was watching, and when he couldn't pretend any longer, he wiped his eyes. "I'm sorry, this isn't one of my better nights." She leaned across and rubbed the top of his hand with her's.

"Come on." She said, slapping his hand and standing. "Time to go home."

They got their coats and went outside together. Joe asked her where she was parked and walked her to the family station wagon. She quickly got in and closed the door. She rolled down the window and called after Joe who had turned to walk away. "Hey, I'm going to be home for two weeks. Maybe I'll see you again." Joe raised his hand to wave. He smiled and searched for some way to say yes, but she rolled her window up before he got it out. The entire drive home, he cursed himself. He still didn't know her name.

CHAPTER 16

Joe prayed. He prayed for the immortal soul of Mrs. Olschewske. He prayed for himself, for forgiveness for not being a better friend to her and a better son to his parents. In the front of St. Mary's, the High Mass droned on in Latin. Joe, alone in the back pew, ignored it. He was lost in his prayer. He did not stand, kneel, beat his breast, or do any of the ritual when he should have. He stayed on his knees, hunched over the pew in front of him throughout the service.

Lying in bed that morning he pondered the problem of Mrs. Olschewske and her Christmas gift. He had decided that he would go to church for her. He felt compelled to do something. He didn't know what else he could do. He reexamined his conclusions about prayer to the extent that he allowed that praying for someone else would not be groveling. He was never quite sure what was accomplished by offering up a Mass, but he would do that for her. He might even say a Rosary for her if there were time. There should be. He wasn't going to go to Confession. He had never liked confessing his sins. He hadn't reached formal conclusions yet, but it seemed to him that if he did something wrong, he should bear the consequences. Confession made it awfully easy for a lot of bums, he thought.

Except for the Sunday after Thanksgiving with his family, he had not attended Mass since coming to Sandusky. His suit, which he had not worn in months, felt strange when he put it on. It had been loose on him, now it felt snug. He had gained a little weight; he told himself it was muscle. Looking up out the window, he concluded it was going to snow again. He did not own a dress coat, so he wore his green corduroy school coat over his suit. Forgetting that Mrs. Olschewske was a member of Sts. Peter & Paul, he went instinctively to St. Mary's where he attended Mass the day after arriving in Sandusky.

Driving downtown, Joe felt good that he was doing this. He

knew that as time passed he would think less and less of Mrs. Olschewske. He owed her something. This would do nicely, he concluded. He went over his plan for prayer, the appropriate salutation, praise, supplication, the request for her eternal reward. He would throw in the Rosary during Mass, provided he still paid attention to what was going on. That seemed important to him, for if he was going to ask for credit for both the Mass and the Rosary, then both should be given equal dignity.

Events did not follow Joe's plan. By the time he finally found a parking place two blocks away, Mass had started. He stopped at the first pew in the back of the impressive church and opened his prayer. Soon, he was reliving the summer, literally day by day, first leaving home, then his evening conversations with the old woman. He could picture her face and hear her voice. He recalled her great pride for her husband's work and gave thanks for his assumption that they would now be reunited forever. When he prayed, however, more of his prayers were for his own conduct, past and future, than for Mrs. Olschewske. He came to his senses when he noticed that the crowd was shuffling out of the church.

Coming outside, he gathered his coat collar at his neck. It was now sunny and the sky turquoise. He smiled at the day but was startled to hear his name, "Joe! Hey, Joe! Come here." A few feet away the red head was standing with her family. His stomach turned. There was no way out. She wore a navy blue coat, like her mother and sister; but unlike them, she wore no kerchief over her hair. Her father wore a light suit and no coat. His belly protruded through the suit coat that no longer fit. He kept his hands in his pockets as he bounded for warmth. As Joe walked up to them, she greeted him with a broad smile, "Joe, these are my parents, and my sister, Maggie." Joe smiled at them all and extended his hand to the man.

"Kelly Brennan." Her father said. Joe marked the name several times in his memory.

"Joe Altznauer."

"Joe, worked at Cedar Point for Ivan last summer. Now he works at Falloni's"

"Ivan's a good guy." Her father said. "You could learn a lot from him."

"Yes, sir. I was really lucky to get that job, just sort of stumbled into it." Joe thought of Mrs. Olschewske.

"We've known Ivan since he was a boy, went to high school with his brother." Mrs. Brennan added. "He has a lovely wife and family. Mary Margaret babysits for them." Joe made another mental note. Just then another couple walked up and got the Brennan's attention.

"It's nice to meet you." Mr. Brennan nodded at Joe, and the couple moved over to speak with their friends.

"Well, I see you got home safely." She said.

"Yeah, you too. Looks like it's going to be a nice day."

"Yeah."

"You going to be in town over Christmas?"

"No, I mean, I'm going home for a couple of days, but I'll be around." Joe stumbled, remembering that she would be home from school for two weeks. "So how do you like Bowling Green?"

"I really like it. I have a good roommate. It's so different from high school. The campus is huge, seems like I spend forever walking, but I love it. You should come over sometime, I could show you around."

"Yeah, I'd like that."

"Molly." Her sister called, motioning impatiently for her to follow. "We've got to go."

Molly. Molly. Molly. Joe repeated her name in his mind.

"Well, I've got to go."

Desperate with fear, Joe gathered his courage, "Listen, maybe we could get together when I get back?"

She smiled without hesitation, "OK, call me." Molly bounded off down the church steps.

Joe stayed at the top of the steps watching her walk down the street with her family. Mary Margaret "Molly" Brennan, he said to himself over and over, Molly. Not only did he have her name, but they had a date, sort of.

The first thing Joe did when he got home was write down her name. He also wrote, "Father-Kelly, Sister-Maggie". Then he went through the telephone book, found her father's name, and wrote down the address and number. He knew the street and from the number concluded that she lived only four or five blocks away. His heart pounded and he wanted to immediately go by her home. He thought better of it and changed into old clothes for painting. That day, Joe put the second coat of yellow on his kitchen. He wanted to drink when he worked, but he didn't He wasn't sure of his evening plans yet and felt he should stay sober.

At mid-afternoon, after cleaning up, he went back to the discount store and bought two more gallons of paint, light green for his living room, and a sandstone for his bedroom. He wasn't yet sure what color he wanted to paint his work room. On the way back, he drove past her house. It was a narrow two story wood house with a short wall and fence only a few feet from the front porch. It looked just like every other house crowded along this and every other street for several blocks in any direction. The station wagon was parked on the street. There was one large window next to the door on the front porch. The drapes were pulled, but light glowed behind them. They were probably watching TV. He drove on down the street, confident no one had seen him.

Back in his apartment, Joe painted his living room. The entire time he thought only about her. He had a can of beer with his can of tuna fish for dinner. During the meal he concluded he should call her. He figured they were probably having dinner, so he'd wait until 7:00 P.M. to call. While he waited, he deliberately restrained from another beer. He idled about, checking the paint and watching the news, waiting. Seeing it was 7:00 P.M., his chest tightened. He got another beer and had half of it while he studied the piece of paper on which he wrote her name.

He finally overcame his dread and dialed the numbers. "Hi, uh, Maggie, this is Joe Altznauer, is Molly there?"

"Hang on." He heard her sing out "Molly. It's Joe." She yelled over the sound of the TV.

"Hello."

"Hi, Molly. Joe." His courage drained as he spoke.

"How you doing?"

"Fine. Uh, I'll be getting back the day after Christmas, and, uh, I wanted to know if you'd like to go to a movie or something on Thursday or Friday?"

"Sure! That would be great." Joe sucked in the breath that he had exhaled and had not been able to redraw. "Why don't you call when you get back. I should be home all day."

"OK, fine."

"Well, what have you been up to all day?" She asked. Joe slipped comfortably into a recitation of his day. He told of painting his apartment. She asked much about it, knowing right where it was. She'd like to see it sometime. She wished she could have a place of her own and told him of how the students at B.G. grouped together to rent houses. She asked Joe if he had a lot of parties and had a lot of friends over. Joe laughed but never answered.

"Listen, I'm really afraid to ask this, I don't want you to think I'm weird? It would be a favor." Joe interrupted the cadence of their banter.

"What? What is it?" She asked, suddenly serious.

"You know when I talked about Mrs. Olschewske last night?"

"Yes, the lady that died."

"See, I got her this figurine. It made me think of her busband, the way she described him. I guess, the way I imagined him. I don't feel right about keeping it. I can't take it back. I just wondered if you would take it, kind of in her name. I don't want you to think, you know, I don't want you to think that I'm out of line giving you a Christmas gift when we just met; and I don't want you to think I'd give you someone else's gift, I just...."

"Yes."

"It would be a real favor. I want to give it so someone who would appreciate...I mean, I think that she would have liked you. I'd like to think that she was something like you when she was young. If you could just hold it."

"I said, yes."

"Great! Thanks. You can pass it along to your grandchildren someday."

"Joe?"

"Yeah?"

"You are the weirdest guy I've ever met. You are seriously different." She laughed.

"Will you still go out with me?"

"Call and see. Bye."

That night Joe put the second coat of paint on his living room and got happily drunk as he did.

CHAPTER 17

Joe's Christmas at home went much like Thanksgiving. With his newly acquired truck, he was not dependant upon anyone for transportation, so he had more freedom in timing his return. He chose to arrive mid-afternoon Christmas Eve. That would allow sufficient daylight to show-off his truck and to walk the farm with his father and Dieter, before dinner, TV, and midnight Mass. During the early part of the week, he had finished painting his apartment. He finally chose pewter for the workroom, and also painted his shelving the same color. Despite the cold, he washed his truck at a 25 cent spray car wash and waxed it in the lot behind the apartment house. He cleaned the interior and hung a scented paper pine tree from the rear view mirror. Each time he went out, he hoped to run into Molly and found it convenient to drive by her house. He didn't so much as catch a glimpse of her. He wondered how she was spending her days. It wasn't until the afternoon of Christmas Day that he realized that he was aching for her.

Midnight Mass, gifts the next morning, and the heavy breakfast went as they had his entire life. They frittered away the late morning with their gifts. As his mother made lunch, the men walked the farm. Outside, it was a day much like any other this time of year. The sky was a slate grey, backlight by an unseen sun. It did not snow, but there were traces of snow against the buildings, along the fences, and under the trees. The ground was frozen and crunched as they walked.

Joe enjoyed the hour or so more than the gifts. They inspected the tension on every wire fence they crossed, getting the same lecture from their father that they had since youth. "Go through gates, not over them. If you have to climb, climb at a post." The winter wheat got up six inches before it froze, amazing them. They talked about soybeans, giving Dieter a chance to bait his father about the Japanese. Catching a wink from Dieter, Joe backed out of the conversation and let it run.

Dieter was a master, nudging his father's speech this way and that, bringing it to a crescendo on the soil bank. "If the government would quit subsidizing the corporate farms and buying off the little guys with the same program and just let go of the markets; and if the farmers would all get together on selling; then everyone would be better off. But they don't want us to be better off. The big guys own the politicians, and they want to squeeze out the family farmers." Joe took note that he didn't mention the N.F.O when he concluded, "The law ought to protect the market, not rig it. We could learn a lot from the unions."

Without purposefully doing it, by clearing agribusiness from his father's mind, Dieter had given the lunch table conversation over to his mother. She was most interested in Joe's activities and was relentless in her inquiries. She wanted to know everything about Falloni's. Joe, sensitive to his father's struggle with the land, deliberately avoided his salary and bonus, but did recall the substance of his private conversation with the owner. She mocked disapproval of his cycling, among other things, finding it inconsistent with the climate; but many of her questions included references to the statements and opinions of friends and neighbors to whom she had been talking about bicycling; which Joe took as an admission that she was proud of him and had been bragging. Late in the meal she asked if Joe had found a girl. He protested her prying but did admit that he was taking a girl from B.G. to the movies later that week. He cringed at the exposure of his flank, but his mother did not pursue it. Instead, she picked up on the reference to Bowling Green and started in on him about going to college. The only other statement his mother made was to the effect that maybe the girl could talk sense into him. It might work out for the best, Joe thought, the disclosure of a girl might influence his mother not to resist his early return to Sandusky.

Later that afternoon his friend from O.S.U. dropped in. They poked through the gifts, then watched a Tarzan movie with his father and Dieter. As usual, Dieter did more talking than Joe. When his friend left, Joe followed him outside. There his friend asked Joe to come to Columbus for New Year's Eve, promising more action than Thanksgiving. Joe declined, saying that he didn't think he could live through another tour in Columbus. For no reason other than to balance the thought, Joe suggested that a quiet New Year's in Sandusky might be more appropriate. Immediately his friend seized upon it, asking if Joe would mind him staying overnight. They could hang out; he needed to rest up before going back; college life was killing him. It sounded good to Joe, and their plan was laid.

As he drove back to Sandusky the next morning, New Year's Eve was the last thing on Joe's mind. He thought only of her. On the way in town, he bought a few groceries and a newspaper. He opened the paper to the listing of the few movie theaters in Sandusky and studied them as he drove. He made his regular swing by her house on the way to his apartment. The freshly painted apartment seemed much brighter than he remembered. He put his gifts away and made himself some lunch. He would call her after lunch. He ate the lunch standing by the sink, working over a script for his call. When he called at 1:00 P.M., he was not quite as nervous as the first time; but when she answered, it took him by surprise and caught his breath.

"Hi, Molly. It's Joe."

"Hi. Did you have a good Christmas?"

"Yes, went home to the farm."

"You're a farmboy! I didn't know that. I guess, I should have known."

"Gee thanks. What's wrong with being a farmboy?"

"Nothing. You're nice. You've got manners. These guys around here all act like hoods, like that should impress someone. Where's the farm?"

"Attica."

"I don't know where that is."

They talked through the location of Attica, the farm, the generations of Altznauer's, that Joe's parents were high school sweethearts, that he had a younger brother, that Joe had broken family tradition by leaving the farm, and that things at home were more than a little uncomfortable.

"So you move a half hour from home and get a good job? What a rebel! What about the Altznauer that left Germany and came here? Now that's a big deal."

Joe paused, getting much more from her words than she intended. "Well, uh, would you like to go to the movies?"

"If we hurry, maybe we can catch a matinee."

Before Joe knew what he was doing, he was in his truck on the way to her house. He had thought that if she would still go, it would be the following night, or that night if she were bored. He had grabbed the paper on the way out. Not until he saw her standing on her porch, did he remember his grooming. Then it was too late. He probably still had tuna fish on his breath. She had no more time than him. As he slowed, she walked into the street and jumped into the truck. She sat sideways, leaning back against the passenger door with her right arm resting on the dash. She watched Joe as he drove. She found from the paper that the only matinee was the musical, Camelot. There weren't choices. Joe would have suggested the musical, even if there had been another choice. Molly agreed. They shared a bag of popcorn. Joe held it and was self-conscious about how he ate when he saw the care with which she ate. She had long finger nails painted white.

Driving back to her house at dusk, Joe took Arthur's case. Guinevere might have been more understanding of his responsibility and burden. Lancelot was supposed to be Arthur's friend. Molly placed no blame on Lancelot, his actions were as pure as his love. It was love, that was all. She found Guinevere no more at fault than Lancelot. Maybe not, Joe opined. Guinevere might have contained herself. Lancelot might have exercised some restraint. Arthur deserved better. Molly countered that Arthur might have shown her a little more affection. Arthur was not free of blame. There was plenty of blame to go around. It was all because of love. Joe stuck with Arthur as a victim. She concluded, "How can there be any sin in sincerely?" Joe did not respond. "Which one would you rather be?"

Joe paused a moment, then smiled at her, "Lancelot. He got the girl."

Joe stopped in front of her house, but before he could say anything, she urged him inside. He stopped inside the front door. She crossed the living room to put her coat in a closet under the narrow stairs. Maggie, in rollers, was lying on the sofa watching TV. She acknowledged him but continued to work her bubble gum. Molly took him through the dining room into the kitchen. It was much like the farm, linoleum floor, chrome furniture with plastic padded seats, and formica table tops and counters. Mrs. Brennan asked about the movie. Molly jumped up on the counter. Joe shuffled nervously, still in his coat. Noticing his coat, Mrs. Brennan got two long-necked beer bottles from the refrigerator and asked Joe to take them to her husband in the garage.

Following her instructions, Joe went out the back door and walked across the small yard. There was a small, free standing garage that opened on the alley. A man door faced the yard. Through the window of that door, Joe could see Mr. Brennan leaning over the engine, silhouetted by a trouble light. The station wagon was half in the garage, half in the alley. There was too much stored in the garage for the car to fit. As Joe opened the door, Mr. Brennan turned to him. "Mrs. Brennan asked me to bring these to you."

"Thanks. You drink?"

"Sure."

"Then have one. You're skinny, but this stuff will catch up with you." He patted his belly. "You know, they talk about beer on a hot summer day, but it'll warm you too. It's colder than a well digger's ass out here." He tipped the beer toward Joe and took a slug.

"What's the problem?"

"It's a real pisser. It turned a little slow this morning, so I decided to clean the cables. Now the goddamned thing won't even crank. Battery's got plenty of juice." Joe sipped from the beer as he looked over Mr. Brennan's shoulder. He was built like Dieter, short and stout. He could see that Molly had his features, and Maggie her mother's thinner lines. "I thought the starter solenoid might be froze, so I fooled with it, cleaned all the connections while I was down there. I tried to jump the starter, but it's not getting any juice. It's got me. I was about ready to start fussing with the voltage regulator."

Joe took another sip, then tapped Mr. Brennan on the shoulder with the bottle. "There's your problem." Joe pointed to a small wire between the coil and distributor hanging loose.

"I'll be goddamned!"

Joe snapped the wire back on its terminal, "There, start it up." The car started immediately. Mr. Brennan swore in chains. "You probably just bumped it when you were working. At least now all the connections are clean. That helps a lot this time of year." Mr. Brennan swore some more, but laughed as he did.

"You staying for dinner?"

"No, sir. I was just dropping off Molly."

"Come on, let me buy you dinner." They pulled the station wagon around to the front of the house. As they walked up the steps to the front porch, Mr. Brennan slapped Joe on the shoulder, jostled him, and cussed more about how he would have lost his fingers to frost bite if it weren't for Joe. Inside, he went immediately for the kitchen where Joe saw the refrigerator held more beer than food. He boasted to the women about Joe's skill, and cracked open two more, handing one to Joe. "I've asked Joe to stay for dinner. If it's a problem, he and I can go to the Shamrock." Joe felt like he was shrinking. Mrs. Brennan kept a poker face as she looked to Molly. Molly signaled with a slight smile.

"Of course, you're welcome, Joe. I'll set another place."

"Come on in here, Joe. We've got to talk."

"Kelly, he's Molly's guest."

He waived off the scolding and pulled Joe back into the living room. There he turned off the TV and sat Joe in his wife's chair. He slumped into his own chair and complained about how complicated automotive electrical systems were getting. Joe agreed, but said it was still only a process of elimination; it might take a few more steps, but there were only so many things that could possibly go wrong. Mr. Brennan was a few beers up on Joe and had a few more before dinner. Joe kept pace, but was inhibited beyond his normal restraint by the surroundings. As they sat down to dinner, Mr. Brennan inquired into Joe's employment situation. Mrs. Brennan, her tone escalating, warned him that Joe's pay was none of his business.

"I know that. Hell, I've known Falloni most of my life. He's a good guy, likes to think he's tough, but that's all front. I think he treats his men good. I'm just trying to make sure. My friend, Joe, here, is a good man. He deserves a fair wage."

"Mr. Falloni pays well. Sometimes I think he pays more than he should for the work. The work's not that difficult, not nearly as complicated as the shop at Cedar Point."

"Now you listen up. You work with your hands. You have skills. Just because you don't think something is difficult, that don't mean it ain't. You're a skilled mechanic. There's dignity in that. You should be proud. What's it worth? It's worth what someone will pay you to do it. Falloni's no dope. Those rich bastards pay him big to take care of their toys. It's worth a lot to them, and you're worth a lot to him."

"You sound like Mr. Falloni."

"Talk's cheap, kid. Only thing that counts is in your paycheck. Do you have any benefits: sick pay, vacation pay, health insurance, life insurance?"

"No, but...."

"You don't, and you won't ever. Falloni thinks big, but he ain't big enough to offer his men that life. You ought to think about getting on at Ford. We've got a good contract. It'll only get better in the future. You'd have more than good pay, you'd have full benefits and a job for life. They ain't gonna stop making cars. Hell, with what you have on the ball, you could go all the way. You get into the apprenticeship, you could be in maintenance, or even better, a tool and die maker. I do OK on the line, but those guys, they keep the machines going. Without them, the whole damn thing stops."

"Kelly, let the boy eat."

"Joe, you think about it. You're young, you got to be planning for the future. It's a good deal. It ain't no accident either. Hank The Duce is no different than Falloni. He always paid good, but that doesn't mean that's what the work is really worth. You got to push a little to find that out. You get on, and you get the benefit of what we earned in past strikes. The union'll take care of you."

"Kelly, save it for the union hall. Really, let the young man be."

"Dad's a steward for the U.A.W." Molly explained.

"Mr. Brennan, do you know anything about the N.F.O.?" Joe asked. He didn't, but did shortly. Joe talked about holding crops from market, pouring milk, and killing calves. Mr. Brennan shook his head, damning the waste, but agreeing with the need.

"It's the same as a strike. There's no way to make sense out of it in the short run. You can't make back what you lose. You've got to take the long view. You make it better for those that come after. You hang together and hang tough. It's the only way a little guy stands a chance against the big boys."

Until he looked in Mrs. Brennan's face, Joe felt good about the dinner. All his father's ranting had paid off. He held his own with a union steward. Mrs. Brennan was furious. As far as she was concerned, dinner was ruined. "Damn you, Kelly Brennan! You never were, and you never will be anything but shanty Irish. Molly brings her young man home, and you make a spectacle of yourself."

"Joe understands. Don't you, Joe?" Mr. Brennan gestured with his silverware, and Joe saw that his eyes were glazed. "Women just won't understand that work is all a man is. When you start valuing labor, you're pricing human dignity." He made a dramatic sweep with his arm, which pulled him off his chair onto the floor. He didn't even try to get up. He laughed and started singing an Irish song to himself. Mrs. Brennan apologized to Joe, and asked for his help. Molly and Joe half carried Mr. Brennan upstairs to bed. Mrs. Brennan followed, muttering. Mrs. Brennan was taking off his shoes and socks when Molly and Joe left the room. Joe distinctly heard him sing a refrain, "How can there be any sin in sincerely."

Downstairs, Joe got his coat, and Molly walked him out without her's. She followed Joe around to the driver's side of the truck. As he got in their eyes met, and they both burst out laughing. As the laughter subsided, Joe pulled the door shut, then rolled the window down. "I'm really sorry. I shouldn't have stayed. Please tell your mother I'm sorry."

"Forget it. He'll be hungover on the line tomorrow, lying to everybody about showing Falloni's best mechanic how to fix an engine." She reached through the window and stroked his cheek with the back of her fingers. "Thanks." She smiled. He continued to feel her touch for hours.

CHAPTER 18

Joe was startled from his sleep by the phone the next morning. He rarely got calls, and when he did, only from home. "You're still sleeping?" Molly chided. "Dad's already gone to work."

"I stayed up late watching TV."

"Bad habit. You'll turn night into day."

"Yeah." He cleared his throat. "What are you doing today?"

"Nothing. It's sunny out. Would you like to go for a ride?"

"Yeah, sure."

"Where?"

"I don't... how about Marblehead. We ride out there a lot." He didn't explain the "we", and she didn't ask. "The lighthouse might be open."

"Fine."

"When?"

"I'm ready to go right now."

"It's 7:30 A.M. Well, give me a little while. I'll be over as soon as I get dressed."

"Don't eat, we've got leftovers."

When Joe walked up on the porch, he heard, then saw, that Mrs. Brennan was vacuuming the living room. He rang the door bell, but she didn't hear. He opened the screen door and tapped on the glass. She still didn't hear. A moment later she was startled when she saw him. "Come in, Joe. I'm sorry about last night. He'll never learn."

"Nothing to be sorry for. I was drinking too. I need to apologize for spoiling your meal."

She smiled and led him to the kitchen. Joe could not possibly know that Mrs. Brennan was thinking about Peter Falloni, and how after all those years, he had never come into her house. The only time Peter even got close was when he picked Molly up for the Junior and Senior

Proms. He'd knocked at the front door and stayed on the porch as she came down. Then they'd walked around the side of the house to take pictures in the back yard. Surely, she thought, it must have been him. He would have been welcome. Well, maybe. His Corvette cost about as much as her home, but it would have been a better life for Molly. Molly was sitting at the kitchen table listening to a Cleveland station.

"Too bad for you, I ate the last bacon. Want some cereal?"

"Do you have any bread?" Joe continued to stand.

Molly got up and went towards the toaster. "Sit down."

"I'd rather just have a couple of pieces of bread, not toast."

"Plain bread? Your choice."

"Milk?" Joe asked nervously.

He wanted to dip his bread in his milk, but he limited himself to taking bites which he held in his mouth until he could take in a drink of milk. He ate without speaking. Molly sat opposite him, leaning on her elbow, alternatively watching him and tapping her finger nails to the music as she hummed.

"Do you know how to dance?"

Joe's face shot red. "No."

"That's OK. Maggie and I will teach you." She continued to move with the music.

He quickly finished the rest. "Ready?"

"Mom!" She called upstairs. "We're going out for a ride."

"You be back before lunch."

On the drive to Marblehead, Molly learned about Joe's cycling. She kidded him about going out in tights, then got serious and told him that there were lots of cyclists at B.G. He already knew that, explaining that the bike shop posted most rides and kept entry forms. She was shocked when he told her how much his bike cost. Periodically, as they drove further into the marshes, she repeated that she couldn't believe he rode that far. He told her it was nothing, that they sometimes did 100 miles in a day. She couldn't fathom it and wondered how he ever got interested in it. He did not have an explanation that satisfied her. When Route 2 followed the railroad across the bay, they saw that the west end of the bay was frozen, and most, but not all of the main bay. The channel and waterfront along downtown was still open.

When they got to the lighthouse, they found it locked. They walked on down to the rocks and picked their way along until they found a place to sit. It was so sunny that both squinted. They looked across the channel to Cedar Point. Joe asked if she was going to work there again the coming summer. She thought she would, she had every summer since sophomore year. She found a stick and poked at her shoes. Joe took small stones and threw them. Some hit the ice near the shore and bounced. Others disappeared into the waves of the channel. After a while, Joe turned and looked south across the bay to survey the courthouse clock tower framed by the church steeples of downtown Sandusky.

"It's pretty." He said. She didn't respond. "Those stone churches are something. If you look close at how they're built; well, they really knew what they were doing. There isn't anything else in town built that good."

"I don't believe in God. Do you?"

Joe was dumbfounded, not by the topic as much as how she had ambushed him with it. The topic was most definitely not part of his everyday conversation; in fact, his only previous introduction to the idea of non-belief was from priests speaking from the altar. Until this moment, however, he simply accepted that everyone believed. Everyone he knew did, that is, as far as he knew, He was well-acquainted with the fact that there were many denominations from the different churches in Attica, but he had never carefully worked through their differences, let alone get to a consideration of the premise upon which they were all founded. Everyone believed in God. He had never considered the contrary, never thought it through. Despite his careful and critical analysis of his church and most of its rituals, his theology had not progressed to a close consideration of the existence of God. It may never have without her question. He wouldn't have imagined anyone he knew thinking such thoughts, much less this girl. Off guard and stumbling through his thoughts, he searched for something to say. He wanted to acknowledge that he also often thought differently from those around him, that he hadn't considered her question before, that it didn't shock or scare him, that he was overjoyed to find someone like this girl would consider anything beyond the moment. He finally said, "I don't know."

"I saw you praying in church last Sunday. You looked like a first class believer."

"Yeah, well, that was the first time I went to church in months. I really don't like to go. I have better things to do with my time. I only went then because I wanted to do something for Mrs. Olschewske. Even that didn't work. I mostly daydreamed."

"Didn't look that way to me. Looked like some pretty serious prayer."

"Maybe. I'm not much for begging. I'm not good at it." Joe threw another stone. "Damn. I forgot the figurine, Mrs. Olschewske's gift." They sat quietly looking across the water. After a moment, Joe continued. "If you don't believe in God, then why do you go to church?"

"Simple. I love it. I like the candles. I like to dress up. I like to see the families together. I like the incense. I like the Latin. I like the music. I like the shadows. I like the smell. You know, those churches are really built. I absolutely love to go to church!"

"I don't."

"Come on, I'm freezing."

For the first time, Joe followed her to the side of the truck and opened the door for her. As she turned to get in, he leaned forward to kiss her. He lost his nerve at the last second, but she was already leaning into him. It was soft and quick. Neither reached up nor touched the other. Only their lips met. When Joe came around and got in, Molly scooted into the center of the seat and nestled up against him. Neither spoke all the way back to her house.

CHAPTER 19

I can honestly tell you that I fell in love with Molly Brennan within minutes of meeting her, deeply and profoundly in love. I loved to look at her. I loved to talk to her. I loved just being near her. If it's not obvious, I still get a twinge just thinking about her. I don't think I'll ever get over her. Of course, you never knew her. It's so difficult to describe her. Beautiful and gorgeous are close, but a little too sophisticated. That conveys the wrong image of her personality. You might say she was cute and perky, but those words don't begin to do her justice. The thing was, you could not separate her appearance from her emotions. She was pure happy or pure sad. I guess she was the purest person I ever met. She captivated me. That red hair and those green eyes got everyone's attention, but it was so much more that held you. She had an air. Her face always rested in a little smile. You could never tell at first that she wasn't happy, but when she was happy or laughed...well, you had to see her. She was attractive and captivating in the most primal sense of those words. She attracted, and she captured. I fell in love. My problem was that she was Joe's girl.

That's what really got me. Who would ever have expected Joe to come up with someone like her. Joe was my best friend. We were closer than brothers. It just never seemed fair. I never did get it straight how they met. Like I said before, I have this vague memory of a red head at Cedar Point the summer before, but I don't know. I was so bombed, it's embarrassing now to think about it. I never did get around to asking Molly or Joe about it. I have a lot of memories a little out of sequence, that's why I didn't, I guess. Anyway, after my behavior on that Fourth of July, and then Thanksgiving, I took a pledge to behave myself New Year's Eve. That's why I went up to Sandusky to see Joe. I could count on him to be tame, and if I did get out of hand, I could trust him to lock me up somewhere.

I drove up to Sandusky after lunch on New Year's Eve. It was easy to find Joe's apartment. The building was frayed around the edges, but Joe had fixed up his apartment. Of course, when you're a college kid living in a dorm, almost anything looks good; but Joe's place really had the feel of home. It wasn't like that little motel he lived in the summer before. That place was nice, but his apartment was very comfortable. He showed off this fancy bike he had. He had a stand he could put it in for working on it. He showed me how that worked, and we fooled around with that for awhile. He had a collection of cycling magazines which I scanned. He also had a scrap book in which he kept the pin-on numbers he got from the rides he had entered. I had come in with a case of beer, and was already working on one when Joe told me he'd been working on plans for the evening.

Let me tell you, was I ever surprised. I thought we were going to sit around, drink beer and watch TV. Joe told me he had been dating a local girl, and she was working on a friend of her's to accompany me that evening. Naturally, no one wants to admit that they want a blind date, so I had to protest; just as I assume my counterpart did also. The negotiations took place by phone until early evening. The phone kept ringing, and Joe kept answering questions about me and what we might do that evening. I caved in quickly, but the girl was a bit more discriminating. She wanted it understood that it was not an official date, that we were going out as a group, and that she would not, under any circumstances, come to Joe's apartment. Then there was a big deal about where we would pick her up. She wanted to meet us somewhere, but her mother wouldn't let her have the family car. She didn't want us to come to her house. Finally, it was resolved that she would stay over with Joe's girl, and we would pick them both up there. Knowing that I had a date, I laid off the beer and watched TV.

Joe and I hung at his place. We scrounged up a meal, then showered and dressed. We went over to his girl's house about 8:00 P.M. Girls' homes were always a little dicey for me, but not for Joe. Her mother answered the door and ushered us in like long, lost friends. Her father and sister were sitting in the living room watching TV. Her father was sucking on a bottle of beer. The little sister, wasn't that little and was very good looking. Now that I think of it, as crazy as I was for Molly, I should have pursued the sister. Anyway, her mother brought us a couple of beers and put us on the sofa. Joe and the father were like two old buddies. He talked about his work and pestered Joe about getting a better job. Like anybody talking to Joe, the discussion got around to engines. It seemed like forever before the girls came down.

I had never met Molly and had no idea who was supposed to go with which girl. I don't remember exactly how it went, but I am sure I probably screwed it up royally. Like I said before, I simply fell head over heels for Molly. Whatever was said, I am sure Molly handled it well. I don't remember her greeting Joe in any special way, but it was quickly apparent who was who. Today, I can't remember the other girl's name. She was very nice. If you think about it, any friend of Molly's had to be. Some might say she was prettier than Molly. She was taller, thinner, and had dark, shoulder-length hair. They both wore those tight ski pants that were popular then. It was bitter cold that night.

We finished the beer and took my Olds, since Joe's truck wouldn't accommodate two couples. Joe gave directions from the back seat. Molly recited this long history of her and her friend. I remember the friend was going to a Catholic school somewhere, maybe John Carroll in Cleveland. Joe never was much for small talk, so I did the reciprocating and gave everyone the scoop on Attica and O.S.U. We went to a bar on the edge of town. It was a really nice place. They had a deal where you paid on the way in and got drinks and finger food all night. I think it was $5.00 each. That was a lot of money then. They stamped us for 3.2% beer only, and the evening began.

There was a side room with a fireplace where we were lucky enough to find seats. They had a disc jockey playing records and running contests in the main room. There was a small area cleared for dancing. After a few beers, I was up to my usual jovial self. Things seemed to be going great until all of a sudden I noticed that Joe and Molly were gone, and I was alone with the girl. She said they were dancing. Dancing! Joe dancing? That I had to see. I came around the corner, and there he was. I simply could not believe it. Joe was doing the Watusi and the Mashed Potatoes, not simple stuff like the Twist. My date didn't want to dance. She had actually been quiet most of the night, until then.

Then all she wanted to do was go on about how wonderful Molly and Joe were together. She driveled out something about an old boyfriend that everyone thought she would marry, but it got to be on-again, off-again; then all of a sudden Joe was in the picture. As far as she knew, it had only been going on a few weeks. She did know that Molly's father and mother were crazy about Joe. I finally got her to slow dance. When we did, I looked at Molly and Joe; and well, it was pretty obvious there was no hope for me. It was just one of those scenes you always remember and never forget. They were looking directly into each others eyes, no blinking, no kissing, no smiling. I wish I would have thought more about her sister back then. Maybe those qualities ran in the family.

There's another thing I remember about that night. Joe was off getting us another round. I don't know what I was talking about, but it must have been brilliant bullshit, for Molly laughed and laughed. When she finally calmed down, she touched my knee and said, "You're a lovable bag of wind." Boy, did she have my number. Of course, I don't know how much Joe had primed her for me; and these days, I don't know how many of my adversaries would call me lovable. It was just one of those things you remember; fondly, I must say, coming from Molly.

At midnight, there was the usual balloon popping and kissing, although if I recall, I gave my date a hug and got a peck on the cheek. I was probably pretty far gone by then. That or it's just the twenty-five years since then. We did go bowling after that. I suppose we were out until 2:00 A.M. I don't remember driving the girls home. Joe probably did. If he did, that would have put me in the back seat with the other girl. I can't imagine her going for that. Hopefully, for her sake, I just passed out. I really don't remember. It wouldn't be like Joe to drive my car. It's a wonder any of us are alive today. The one thing I do remember, and I remember this very clearly, the Aurora Borealis was out that night. You don't see them very often in Ohio. It was a totally clear night. There were a million stars. Both before and after the bowling, we stood together and watched the glow. If fact, I haven't seen it since. I wonder whatever became of that girl.

Back at Joe's apartment, we had one last beer. I teased Joe that he and Molly looked pretty serious. He wouldn't answer. Naturally, I told him that Molly was the most endearing female I had ever encountered, and if he weren't interested, that I considered her fair game. No doubt, I confessed my own love for her. I couldn't have kept that a secret. I remember him saying, "I'm not stupid, you know." The thing is, I don't know if he was acknowledging my description of her, or my love for her. Whatever he was referring to, it was as if he took it for granted. I did tell him that if I couldn't have her, I wanted to be in the wedding. The next morning we woke in our clothes; Joe on the sofa, and me sprawled in a chair. I limped home that afternoon, and went back to college the next day.

CHAPTER 20

The mail boxes just inside the main entrance to The Willdred became Joe's first stop on the way in from work every day. Throughout the fall he had not checked his box more than once a week. When he did he found only junk mail and the regular phone bill. Now he got something from Molly every day. It started with a long letter just after her New Year's return to school. The subject was Peter Falloni. After getting through her schedule and the tedium of being back, she wrote him that there were many things she had to tell him, was afraid to, and thought it would be better once and for all in a letter.

It hurt Joe to read it. His first and enduring reaction to the letter was pain, not jealously. He thought about her all the time. During the day at work, whenever he noticed the time, he wondered what she was doing. When he looked up at the weather, he wondered if it were the same where she was. When he ate at the picnic table in the lunch room with his co-workers, he thought about her having lunch with her friends. He didn't want to think about her and anyone else, let alone his boss's son, but he read it. He read it over and over. He searched for special meanings in individual words, for signals in phrases.

She had gone with Peter since junior high school. They had come up through Catholic elementary school together. She could remember him in kindergarten. He went on to St. Mary's Central Catholic High. Despite her mother's protests about academics and discipline, her father insisted she attend Sandusky High School. He though it more democratic and would give her more opportunity and choices. She thought it was to get her away from Peter. They remained a regular couple. They were a couple that people took for granted. They did everything together.

Peter would never have been big enough for football nor tall enough for basketball at Sandusky High; but at St. Mary's, he lettered in every sport. He was best in track and always placed in the state finals. She went to all his meets. Peter had been on student council, was the president of the senior class, and the valedictorian. Because of his coaxing, she ran for class secretary at S.H.S. and lost. She played flute in band. Most of her friends, boys and girls, were from band. Peter thought that was OK for girls but made fun of the guys in band. She loved to play her flute, and missed band. For awhile she volunteered as a candy-striper at the hospital, but she hated to be around sick people, especially sick children. She also needed to make money, so she got a part-time job in a drug store. Peter thought it was beneath her.

He also didn't like her working at Cedar Point. He thought she could get a better job, but she concluded that he didn't like the fact that she was meeting all the young people that worked in the park. From the time Peter got a car, he drove her to school and work, on the excuse of not liking her walking alone. Everyone expected them to get married. They probably would have, but she couldn't take the fighting. For at least a year, she thought it was her fault. Then she saw that he started every fight, and that they all began in his criticism of something about her. She couldn't take him running her life.

She thought she loved him. She was convinced she did. Now she knew better. She always called him Peter, even though everyone called him Petey, and he called himself Pete. That was just how wrong she'd been. Since she met Joe, she saw just how different, better, things could be. She considered herself lucky that things had gone as they did. She signed the letter "Fondly,"

The letter was several pages long. Sometimes Joe wouldn't read it, he would just shuffle through the pages taking note of the large loops and frilly style of her handwriting. It couldn't be more different from his, which was small, tight, and sharp. Each time he read the letter, it stung all over again. Try as he might, he could not bring himself to concentrate on the hopeful end of the letter. After a few beers, he wrote back, sitting at his kitchen table. He wrote in pencil on lined notebook paper. Things were back in the groove. The town was empty, the weather gray, work was OK. He was glad she had written. It probably wasn't easy. He had never dated anyone before. He missed her. He labored over the closing, studying her's. Finally, he came up with "Thinking only of you,". He didn't have any envelopes, so he ran downtown during lunch the next day and bought a package, and got stamps from the Post Office. He sent the letter without re-reading it. It was barely a page long.

Molly wrote long letters two or three times a week; but she sent something, a postcard, a picture from a magazine, everyday. When she wrote long letters, they were about the future. She wanted to be a teacher. She loved children. Joe's letter mostly responded to her's, although she learned much by implication of the his life on a farm and school in a small town. Unlike her, Joe was content with what he was doing. He liked his work, but did not boast about it. Occasionally, he would see something in the local paper that he thought would interest her, and he cut it out and sent it to her.

Molly came home at the end of January with a plan she and her friends had concocted. There was a big Valentine's Dance at the school every year. It wasn't officially formal, but everyone dressed. Most girls wore their Prom dresses, but Molly and her mother were going to make her a new dress. In fact, they spent most of Saturday morning shopping for a pattern and fabric. She had already checked into tuxedo rentals for Joe. He could pick it up in Sandusky Friday night and return it Monday. She knew three other girls who had boyfriends coming, so the four of them could share a motel room for the night. There was no resisting Molly, and although he never said yes, Joe nodded and was swept along in the plan.

Joe stopped by the bike shop once or twice during January and February, just to stay in touch, but he had no interest in biking in the cold and snow. His truck barely had time to heat up on the way to work, but he appreciated even that by comparison to riding a bike. On the Saturday of the formal, he drove his truck over to Bowling Green. It was an enjoyable drive through the flat farm country of mostly prosperous grain farms. He was able to park close to Molly's dorm, and she was waiting in the lobby for him. He was typically stiff, but she hugged and kissed him on the lips. She explained the rules. No men in the dorms. He could call up for her. They could stay on the first floor where she showed him the TV lounge and rec room, but he had to sign in and out at the desk to be there. She walked him all over the campus, taking him into her classrooms, the library, and the student union. There, at lunch, they met the other guys with Molly's friends. Joe did not even try to remember names.

All three were attending other schools. Invariably the question was "So where do you go to school?" or a slight variation with the same question embedded, "So what's your major?" Joe never got comfortable with his answers, although he forced himself to be resolute and terse in response. "I work on yachts in Sandusky." There were never any follow-on questions. One of the guys was studying engineering, another math; so they paired off. The third, who had chin length hair, never said what he was studying, but he carried a book of poetry and talked only politics. They checked into their motel room and then returned to the girls dorm for an afternoon of ping-pong. Joe did play, but he took every opportunity to sit with Molly. That was difficult for she was good at the game and spent most of the time playing. As he watched her playing, he suddenly concluded that he was in love with her.

The girls ran them off at 4:00 P.M. The political poet rode back to the motel with Joe. They bought a twelve pack and each had one as they rode. Joe almost started to hit it off with the fellow, but back in the room, the poet insisted they not play the TV. It was bourgeois pablum, a phrase that conveyed no meaning to Joe other than the arrogance of its speaker. He turned on an FM radio station, and read most of a poem aloud, before the other two threw pillows at him. Joe took the whole scene in from a chair where he sat nursing a beer. He could put up with anything for one night. The scientists were children and the poet a jerk, but he would live through it. What could those girls possibly see in these guys. They didn't seem that different from Molly. God, he missed her.

The young men took turns in the shower and joked as they got a little buzz on from the beer. The brisk evening air cleared their heads when they returned to the dorm to pick up their girls. They waited around the lobby for another half hour before the girls came down. In an instant Joe saw that the other girls were nothing like Molly. They all had their hair up and wore full length dresses. Their's were fluffy, Molly's straight. The dress she and her mother made had a classic Grecian look. It was made from a soft, shiny, off-white cloth that hung over her shoulders and down like a sheet. Bumps of her nipples showed through the cloth, forcing Joe to deliberately look up to her eyes. She beamed and bussed him on the cheek, telling him how handsome he was. He wanted to tell her she was beautiful, but couldn't find the right words. He had done the right thing, he told himself, when he followed the florists suggestion and got a wrist corsage.

The group made its way across campus to the gymnasium wearing winter coats that did not match their formal clothes. The girls shrieked about the cold through their light shoes, and the guys responded with denigrating remarks about women's fashions and pretended that they were bored. Joe's mouth fell open at the size of the gym. He had seen it only from the outside, the seats seemed to go up forever. The basketball floor had been covered with a heavy paper that was taped together at the seams. Rectangular tables for dinner filled half the floor, and beyond them was an open space for dancing with an orchestra under the backboard. On either side of the dance floor, were open bars serving 3.2% beer in plastic cups. The guys left the girls at the tables long enough to get drinks.

Were it not for the beer, the dinner would have been much more uncomfortable for Joe. It was filled with talk of campus comparisons, sports, majors, job prospects, graduate schools, and politics. Joe quickly gulped his drinks, and lead forays to the bar, each time coming back with his hands full. He lost track of how much Molly was drinking. She couldn't possibly be keeping up with him, but it seemed she was. He was now sure he loved her, but too drunk to think through the problem of telling her and getting her response. Finally, the meal ended and the dancing started. Joe had learned his lessons in the Brennan living room well. They barely left the dance floor that night, and then only for the rest rooms and a quick drink. He found that if he held her close enough, her loose breast cradled into his right elbow. He got a chill when he felt it move, but not as much as when she reached up on her toes and kissed his ear. Mostly, she simply laid her head sideways on his chest. They stayed until the last dance.

The girls who hadn't gone to the dance had set up hot chocolate and cookies in the lobby of the dorm. The guys idled there for a time with their dates. Joe and Molly quickly went out side where they made out with Joe leaning his back against the building. When the other three came out, they collected Joe and took him back to the motel. The next morning Joe got up first, no doubt because of his work routine. He showered, packed and left while the others still slept. Molly quickly responded to his call from the lobby, and they drove around town in his truck with Molly's head resting on his shoulder, until they agreed on a short order place for breakfast. Even during breakfast they didn't speak much. She had a lot of studying to do, he should be getting back. They kissed in the truck when he dropped her in front of the dorm. He touched his finger to the tear that leaked down the side of her face, but he didn't tell her that he loved her.

CHAPTER 21

Dieter gave Joe a plastic label maker for Christmas. It was the perfect gift for Joe. It made a conspicuous change in his apartment, most prominently in his work room. Joe had cleaned and saved food cans. Into these he sorted miscellaneous bolts, nuts, washers, and other bicycle parts. Joe labeled each can by its contents. The labels were different colors depending upon the type of part, for example, bolts were red, washers yellow, and nuts green. Each label was placed precisely at the same height on each can, so that when the dozens of them were lined up on the shelves, there was an overwhelming sense of order. Joe also labeled the edges of the shelves with the generic category of the contents of the cans on them. He had brought most of his personal tools up from the farm, they were labeled as were his tool boxes and the shelves upon which they rested.

If Joe couldn't find something to do on one of his bikes, he would often sit on the floor in the work room drinking a beer and contemplating improvements to the organization. In this manner he had decided to build a work bench from 2 x 4's and plywood he bought new from a lumber yard. He painted it the same grey as the shelves and walls. Not long after, he mounted two peg board squares on the wall to hang his most frequently used hand tools. He painted these white, because he liked the contrast. His work shop had come a long way, and he was pleased with it. As was his custom, he ended most evenings at his kitchen table responding to the latest mail from Molly.

Once he had tried to write to her about the joy he took in mechanics. He had a recurring memory of tightening a nut on a fine threaded bolt when he was no more than five or six years old. It was as deep and personal an experience for Joe as for the born again; so much so, that he had never talked to anyone about it. It didn't look well when written, so he crossed it out, and his letter became a draft. Instead he wrote her about fixing broken toys, and taking apart ones that weren't broken. He progressed to unwinding the thin wire on the electromagnets in the small battery driven motors in toys. He rewound them, and they still worked. He used various parts from broken toys and coat hanger wire and made his own two brush motors. He took his father's burned out electric drill apart, bought wire and rewound it by hand. It worked. He wrote about showing the drill off for his father, but when he read it, it sounded corny and he crossed through it also.

There were other steps along the way that he liked to recall, taking watches apart and trying to get them back together. He succeeded once, but had a cup full of parts left over. He had appointed himself the master of finding burned out tubes in the TV and radio, but when transistors came along, there was no further need. He had yet to figure transistors out, but he like to look at the circuit boards and compare them to the diagrams printed on labels inside the appliances. One of his favorite discoveries was the wire donut that circled the neck of the back of the picture tube of the TV. By twisting it, he could cock the picture diagonally on the screen or even flip it upside down. His family eventually tired of his pranks. He couldn't find a way to start to write these memories or fit them together for her in a way that made sense to him. How could he ever explain the satisfaction he found in a thin film of oil on clean machined steel. Eventually, he gave up and contented himself with a short note about the weather, work, and their next visit.

At the bike shop he noticed an entry form for a century ride that started in Bowling Green the last weekend of March. It was a perfect excuse, so he sent off the entry with a money order. He still refused to get a checking account. He knew he was way out of shape, especially for one hundred miles; and even though the weather was cold and damp, he started riding everyday. He rode his old bike to work and back. He laid off the beer in the evenings, and started longer and longer rides at night. At first ten miles, made his legs and rump sore. Soon he was out until 10:00 P.M., doing 20 to 30 mile rides. One weekend he rode to the farm and back. The next to Mansfield. The last, to Bay Village in the suburbs of Cleveland. He felt good, but all his riding was alone, none in competition. He didn't know anyone going to this ride, and really didn't want to be stuck with club members.

When he picked Molly up at her dorm that morning, he felt absurdly dressed when he came into the lobby in his tights. After reading the cycling magazines, he had ordered Italian rather than French from a catalog; but the difference was not something Molly could discern. Driving over he had felt proud of his attire, but when Molly came down with a couple of friends, he felt naked. She put one arm around his neck and kissed his cheek. If he didn't mind, her friends would come to the start to cheer him on. After a little lecture about the bike which stood in the rack in the back of the truck, Joe got the girls situated. As usual, there were only about twenty cyclists. They were staged on a side street just off the main drag. A start/finish banner had been hung over the main street in downtown. Joe checked in, got his bike inspected, and returned to the girls who were waiting around the truck. Except for Molly, none resisted the temptation to display their boredom. Molly was wearing Joe's new helmet, which he had also ordered by mail. He took it from her, and pressed the label he had put inside the brow to make sure it wasn't coming loose. Someone on a bullhorn told them to move out to the start line. Again, they kissed; then Molly and the girls followed him to the line. They stayed on the sidewalk while Joe found a place in the back of the pack. As he peddled under the banner he yelled that he'd meet her back here at 3:00 P.M.

The ride went west to Defiance, then northeast to Toledo, looped through downtown, and then came straight back south to Bowling Green. Joe passed several people during the first few miles, eventually matching up with two other's holding his pace. One was a 50 year old doctor from Columbus, the other a zoology graduate student from B.G. They talked intermittently until the outskirts of Toledo, when Joe's condition caught up with him. He couldn't hold their pace and fell back from them. He had a banana in the back pouch of his shirt, but they offered cut bananas and oranges at the twenty mile tables, so he ate those instead. He had no trouble following the map they had issued each rider. During the early afternoon, a few riders passed him. He hoped there were riders behind him. He wasn't sure. He hadn't counted.

He got back to Bowling Green a half hour later than he expected. As he sprinted alone under the banner, the only person he recognized was Molly, bouncing to keep warm, not to cheer. She did wave and smile. She congratulated him, but he thought he found in her tone an indication that she did not understand his hobby. She watched his bike as he checked out and visited the men's room of a corner gas station. Only there did it occur to him that he stunk and had no clothes to change into nor any place to shower. Back in the truck, he apologized to Molly.

"We can still get a bite somewhere." she said.

"I can't go in anywhere like this."

"You can."

"No. I don't know what I was thinking. I should have gotten a motel room and stayed over."

"Maybe next time." Joe wound on through the quiet streets contemplating the possibilities of having a motel room to himself. Would she? How would he ask? He had to tell her he loved her. He wanted to. He wanted to make love to her. "Spring break's in a couple of weeks. I'll be in Sandusky for 10 days. I'm really looking forward to the time with you." Again Joe weighed her words.

"Yeah. It'll be fun. We can spend a day at Put-In-Bay if you'd like."

"I'd like that."

When he pulled up in front of the dorm, Joe remembered and opened the glove compartment. He took out a box the size of two fists wrapped in Christmas paper and gave it to Molly.

"What is it?"

"Mrs. Olschewske's gift. Remember? I keep forgetting to give it to you."

"Joe. It's lovely. I'll keep it forever. I love it."

"It's kind of embarrassing."

"No, it's wonderful. I'll never forget that night we first met. Then you asking me about this. Joe, you're so sweet." She put the figurine back in its box, sat the box on the floor, and then turned to put both arms around Joe's neck and quite deliberately kissed him. Joe worried about his breath, then satisfied himself at the taste of the orange he'd just eaten. He felt grimy.

"Listen, I smell like a barnyard." he said trying to pull back.

She wouldn't let him, and only a breath from his lips, she smiled into his eyes, "I haven't noticed." and she kissed him again.

Joe started cooperating. Eventually, he slid one hand inside her jacket. He cupped his hand over her breast, waiting for her to move back. She didn't. He gently massaged her. They kissed on and on. She ran her fingers back and forth along his stomach, inside the elastic waist of his tights. Joe lowered his free hand and spread his fingers across the top of her thigh. She kissed him softer and longer than before, then sighed, pulling away.

"Hmmmm." She smiled looking at his lips then into his eyes. "I can't wait until Spring Break."

They talked more about what they might do together over the holiday. She tried again to get him to go to dinner with her. He shook it off. Finally, she got out of the truck, still holding his hand and leaning in. He wanted desperately to tell her. He gave himself the excuse of his motley condition and the fact that he was in the truck. It should be special, better than this anyway.

"God, I'm going to miss you."

"Me too."

She let go of his hand and closed the door. She stood on the curb watching as he drove away. The days were getting longer.

CHAPTER 22

On Friday morning Joe biked to work along his normal route. As usual, he passed a heavy-set brown-skinned woman walking her small son to school. It was their custom to say hello. This morning she shouted, "You can't keep us down forever!" In the few days before Molly came home, Joe, like everyone, was never out of listening range from a radio, and when near a TV, he sat transfixed before it. Martin Luther King's assassination set America's cities on fire. In Sandusky, as the initial shock wore off, rapid action by churches and community leaders diffused much of what might have been; however, the days did not pass without incident. The local Negroes who were always more disposed to sitting on their stoops and gathering on street corners, now had more than their daily fare to share. Neighborhoods changed quickly in the small city, and when the light-skinned passengers of cars would quickly roll up their windows and lock the doors at the sight of a brown face, or even run a red light rather than sit near three or four people conversing; jeers followed, fists were shaken, gestures made, rocks and bottles thrown. The police responded, but when they did, entire neighborhoods came out on their porches. All of this profoundly troubled Joe. The images on TV reminded him of those he had also seen of bombed out Europe in World War II, which when seen growing up among crisp white buildings on a quiet grain farm was something ancient, far away, and so horrible that even his father would not talk of it. Joe was wounded and befuddled by the woman's jeer. He had done nothing to her. The hell with it, he thought, Molly would be home that night.

Her birthday was the following week. She would be nineteen. He had secretly conferred with Maggie about what he might get her, but he didn't feel right about clothes or jewelry. Maggie had cavalierly suggested a car, which put Joe in mind of a bike. He found a used ladies touring bike at the bike shop for $150. He bought it and spent every evening rebuilding it. He stripped the frame and spray painted it the same color as his good bike. He cleaned and reassembled the components, and put two new tires on the bike. It looked like new. He knew it was better than new. When he was half way through the project, he called Maggie to see if she thought Molly would like it. She told him that Molly had never been very athletic or outdoorsy, and her hesitation caused a knot in his chest. Well, he thought, at least she'd know what it's like to ride a good bike. If she doesn't like it, it won't be the bike's fault.

Molly called Joe within a few minutes of getting home with her parents. They made little excursions of picking her up. Her father and mother would drive over after he got off work, pick her up, and have dinner in a family restaurant in Bowling Green. Joe was waiting when she called at 8:00 P.M. Her father wouldn't let her go out because of the assassination. Joe was welcome to come over, but only if he would not sit and drink with her father. Within minutes, Joe was on his old bike peddling the four blocks to her house. He rode, not because he was trying to stay in shape, nor because he wanted to prove anything to Mr. Brennan, the brown woman, or himself. He rode because it was a beautiful spring evening. He had all the windows to his apartment open. The sky was clear and full of stars. The air tasted cool and fulfilling. He loved Molly. He went for his bike instinctively.

Molly was waiting in the front porch swing when he rode up. He leaned his bike against the low wall by the sidewalk and sat down beside her. She kissed his neck between his ear and chin. "You smell good." she said.

"It's good to see you." They held hands and swung back and forth. They talked about the riots. Joe told her about the woman who yelled at him. Molly had sarcastic stories from B.G. about student groups that had demanded soul food be served in the cafeterias. Neither had anything in their backgrounds that prepared them to do more than trivialize the reasons for the unrest. When they finished with current events, they sat quietly. After a few minutes Molly said, "I took my flute back after Christmas vacation. I've been playing it."

"Play it for me."

"No. No, that would be embarrassing."

"Common on. Please. I'd love to hear you."

"Maybe sometime. On nights like this, I go out in the courtyard of the dorm and play."

"I love nights like this."

They talked about what they would do during her break. Joe had to work, but they had evenings and weekends. He hadn't entered any rides. She complained about that, telling him she liked to watch him. He asked if she wanted to go out to Put-In-Bay the following morning. She went inside to ask her father if he thought that would be safe and returned with his permission. They stayed in the swing until almost 11:00 P.M., when her father came out with a beer in his hand. It was getting late, Joe shouldn't be out on the streets after curfew. Joe said goodnight and went for his bike.

"Jesus H. Christ, Joe! You're riding a bike! Let me drive you home."

"I'll be fine. It's a beautiful night. I know a cop."

"Joe, you better wake up and see what's going on. I work with some of these people. I know. They've had it. They're organizing. Hell, we got together and cut Hank The Duce down to size more than once. You can't beat organization. These people are not organizing against one man. They are organizing against us!"

"I'll be fine. Don't worry. I never did anyone wrong."

"Joe, you ain't got a fucking clue! Excuse my french, honey. You ride fast, and you lock your door."

"Good night, Mr. Brennan. Pick you up at 8:00, Molly."

The next morning Joe showed up in his truck, with two bikes in the rack, his good bike and the gift bike for Molly. He wore casual biking clothes, khaki touring shorts and a turtle neck sweater. Molly wore school clothes; slacks, a blouse, and sweater tied around her neck. She had her hair in a pony tail. She took her day pack, telling Joe she packed a lunch for them. When she asked about the second bike, Joe told her he had rebuilt it for the bike shop, giving the impression that he was going to sell it. They drove over to Catawba Point and caught the ferry for South Bass Island. They parked the bikes deep inside the ferry, and Joe led Molly upstairs, never letting on about his fear of water. It was a perfect spring day. There wasn't a cloud in the sky, and the lake was as smooth as glass. From a distance the trees on the island seemed mostly brown, put when they got close, they could see the new leaves were out.

They rode directly to town, although they did stop briefly to watch a small plane land at the airport. Molly got the shifting right away. She laughed in the process. She said she liked the bike. Along the way, people were mowing their grass for the first time, and its smell was in the air. Perry's Monument wasn't open yet, nor were many of the shops. They walked the marina, looking at the few boats that had ventured out. They decided to ride back south through the vineyards to the state park and then come back to town after lunch. The state park had once been the grounds of Hotel Victory, a victorian resort built in the 1890's, complete with its own dock, gardens, pool and trolley. It burned in 1919. Now, a campground sat amid the ruins. They circled through the campground, stopping to explore the old pool. It was built on the hillside, below the ruins of the hotel. The shallow end was cut into the limestone, and the deep end extended above the surface. A concrete deck surrounded the pool, supported by posts along the deep end. They parked their bikes under the deck, and made their way through the trees and vines around to the shallow end. Later, they walked their bikes across from the pool to a shale bluff overlooking the old dock. Joe sat, leaning against a tree. Molly leaned against Joe with his arms around her.

"I brought my flute."

"Great. Please, play for me."

Molly assembled the silver instrument from its small case and sat up cross-legged. Joe smiled at her during the first song. She closed her eyes during the second, and he settled back against the tree looking west across the water. During the third he closed his eyes also and only listened to her dreamy interlude. During the forth he nodded off, startled when she stopped. "God, I'm sorry. That's hypnotic. You are really good! How come you never played for me before? You should be in a band or orchestra. Why don't you do that?

"Oh, I'm not that good. Since I started playing again, I think I feel better about things. It's my therapy. I'm content to play for myself."

"What about me? I love it."

"...and you."

"Molly, I think I love you."

"I know. I love you too." She laid the flute aside, and they kissed. They laid on their sides kissing and petting for a long time. Finally, Molly sat up and looked across the water. Joe propped himself on one arm and played with the grass. "Joe, I didn't know I could feel this way. I had no idea."

"I know."

She broke her flute down and put it away while Joe got out the sandwiches she made. They ate, then biked back into town. He followed her through the shops. They got ice cream cones and ate them in the park. They were attracted by the sound of musket fire from the mock platoon marching near the monument, and rode over to it. They went up on top. It was an incredibly clear day. North, they could see beyond Pelee Island to the Canadian shore. West they could see the stacks in Monroe, Michigan. They could easily see the Marblehead Lighthouse and the cable cars, roller coasters, and spire at Cedar Point. The lake was punctuated by a growing number of white sails. Joe leaned back against the stone wall, she leaned against him.

"I'm afraid of heights." She said.

"Me too." After a moment he said, "I'm also afraid of water."

"Really? Water? We came over here on a boat."

"Tell me about it."

As they put the bikes back into Joe's truck in the ferry parking lot, Joe asked her if she liked the bike. She did. She didn't think she would ever ride like Joe, but it was fun. He told her it was her birthday gift. She hit him playfully then tickled him, telling him that he had ruined her birthday. Driving back to Sandusky, they talked about the evening and the next day. There was no way her father would let her go out at night. Joe could come over and watch TV, her father would enjoy the company. Joe asked her if she would like to see the farm. She cringed inside, but turned to him and kissed his neck. "Sure."

CHAPTER 23

Driving south down Route 4, Molly and Joe surveyed the serene and unchanging country side. The winter wheat was already knee high. Although it had been a hard winter and wet spring, the last few weeks were dry enough that many of the farmers had started plowing for their corn, oats, and soy beans. It was impossible for either of them to comprehend that every major American city was burning. That was what the TV said. Saturday night had been the worst rioting so far. That morning, Molly had gone to Mass with her family. Her mother had asked her to invite Joe along, but Molly dodged by saying that Joe was a big boy and could take care of himself. Joe had done a quick twenty miles instead, following Route 6 east along the lake. He picked Molly up late that morning. The night before he had called home, after getting back from the island and before going over to Molly's.

"No, Mom, nothing is wrong. Everything's fine. I was wondering if you guys are doing anything special tomorrow?"

"Nothing special. Chicken dinner at noon. Your father put a couple dozen back in the old coop. You coming down?"

"Thought I would. Do you mind if I bring a guest?"

"Of course not. Who?"

"It's the girl I've been seeing. Molly." Joe hated this conversation.

"Tell me more, Joe. You can't just walk in without giving us the scoop."

"No scoop, Mom. She's from Sandusky. She worked at Cedar Point last summer. She goes to Bowling Green. She's home on Spring Break. Her father is paranoid about the riots and won't let her do anything up here, so I came up with a drive in the country."

"Sounds like her father watches after her. Does she come from a good family?"

"Yes, Mom."

"What does her father do?"

"He works at the Ford Plant. He has for years. He married his high school sweetheart. She keeps the house. They have two daughters. Molly's the oldest. They're Catholic. They go to church every Sunday. Anything else?"

"What's their name?"

"Brennan. Mary Margaret Brennan."

"Joe. That's Irish, Joe."

"I know. Tell Dad Mr. Brennan drinks beer and is a union steward. We should get there right around noon. Mom, don't do anything special." Joe knew he had just set off a frantic evening of house cleaning. Dieter would kill him.

Joe did a lap around Attica, showing Molly his friend's house, his church, and his high school. From the athletic field he pointed southwest across the bottom of town towards their farm. He drove her through the cemetery, where there were several Altznauer's. His parents already had their plot and tombstone complete with their names and birth dates. The other date was blank. The grave tickled Dieter. He had taken a picture of his parents standing stiff on either side of the stone. He kept the photo stuck into the mirror in his bedroom. Joe seemed to be making some point, but Molly wasn't sure what it was. Joe took Molly into the drug store that sits diagonally from the bank at the Attica's only stop light. They had a coke while Joe explained that this was "the spot" for the high school kids. Molly noted the time, not wanting to be late. They rushed the drinks. Joe had dressed casually. Molly still wore the bright spring dress that she had worn to church. Joe thought it was a little too dressy for walking around the farm, but didn't say anything.

When they pulled in from the county road, Dieter came out to greet them. Banter was Dieter's domain, and he quickly took the edge off Molly's nerves. Joe's parents waited on the stoop, just outside the kitchen door. They were smiling. Mr. Altznauer had his arm around his wife's waist, she had her arms folded, but both were smiling. Molly was taken by how much Joe looked like his father and how much his father and mother looked like each other. Dieter shared the facial resemblance, but not the long, lean build. The kitchen was open to the spring breeze but smelled of fried chicken. Their timing was perfect. Dinner would be ready in a few minutes. Joe expected to sit with his father and Dieter in the living room, while his mother sat the food out; but instead she took Molly off on a tour of the farmhouse, with an instruction for Joe and Dieter to set the table. When they returned, they were talking about sewing. Molly had admitted to making her dress which Mrs. Altznauer had admired. Joe could see that the major tests had been passed. He did not know that his mother had shown Molly all his awards, letters, and trophies.

Dinner went well, except that his mother dominated the conversation. The more familiar she got with Molly, the chattier she became. Mr. Altznauer, Dieter, and Joe looked at each other. It was a strange new world for them. This was a men's house. Serious things like their work, farm equipment, the weather, crops, grain markets and the economy were discussed at this table. Things had gotten totally out of control, faster than any of them would have ever expected possible. Mrs. Altznauer extracted a report on Bowling Green and learned that Molly wanted to be an elementary teacher. She brought Joe into the conversation informing Molly about his scholarship. Joe's face flushed. He had not told Molly about that. She went on about what a good farmer Joe would make, but farming was big business, and no one stood a chance anymore without a college education. She came right out and asked Molly if she could get Joe to go to school. Joe started to intercede, but his father came in louder.

"Will you leave the boy alone. He's finding his own way. Everyone has to. He brings this lovely girl here, and you start nagging. Let me tell you something, you're lucky there wasn't anyone like her in our class, or you might not be sitting here today." He winked at Molly. "I wouldn't wish farming on anyone. They're out to destroy the family farm...." and the table conversation got back to normal. Dieter lit up and prodded his grumbling father this way and that. Molly was surprised at how much it was like her family's table.

After dinner, Molly and Joe did the dishes. Then he walked her through the various buildings. He was particularly interested in the chickens, explaining to her that the coop had been his and Dieter's club house. A coal train passed in the distance headed north. Molly said she had always wondered where they came from. She had never been on a farm before. It was so peaceful. Joe showed her the tool shed. She saw him in it. They kissed for a few moments there. Later, they watched an old Tarzan movie with his parents, then went out on the front porch for a time. His parents took the swing, Molly and Joe leaned against the banister. More than once Molly looked from the view to Joe, then his parents, and back again. She never knew the advantage he had on her, seeing her at home, until she saw him in his. Now they were equal. Mrs. Altznauer had no doubt that the two were in love.

"I want to see your apartment." Molly demanded as they drove back into Sandusky.

Joe protested a little, warning about her father catching them. Joe's heart raced. He hadn't planned for anything like this. She was one endless surprise. He loved her.

They parked in back, but he walked her around front and through the main entrance. He showed her the mail box where he got her letters, then led her down the hall to the back steps into the basement. Since the heat was off, the basement had regained it's moist scent. That and the poor lighting in the hall made Molly think that the place was thoroughly depressing, but she said nothing to Joe. In stark contrast, she found his apartment light and airy. He had left the windows open that morning, and he bragged about the paint job. She went quickly about inspecting everything. She surveyed his bedroom from the doorway. He had not made the bed that morning, although he usually did. Some clothes were lying about, he apologized. The bathroom was clean. She teased him about the labels in his work room, where she toyed with her birthday bike that was hanging from the ceiling. Joe came up behind her, but she went quickly through the living room and into the kitchen. It too was clean. She opened the refrigerator seeing as much beer as food and took a can. She found a can opener in a drawer and took a long drink from the can.

"I don't think it's right that you live alone."

"What? I like it here. I've really fixed this place up. You should have seen it. It used to be as dark as the hall."

"That's not what I'm talking about. I can't stand the thought of you coming here alone at night. You should be around people. Don't you miss your family."

"Sure, a little. But don't you when you're at school?"

"It's not the same. I'm around people. I have a roommate."

"I work with people all day long. I come home, change, ride, write you, go to bed. It's not a bad life."

"I don't like thinking of you here alone."

"When I'm alone, I think of you." Joe kissed her and held her more tightly than he ever had.

She wiggled away, took another drink from the beer, then handed it to Joe. "Finish it. We've got to get going. Mom expects us for dinner."

"Another meal?"

"I still don't like you here alone."

CHAPTER 24

Although they ached for each other, the Spring went quickly. Molly's studies kept her busy, and she started rehearsing with the orchestra. She was as good as anyone except the first chair, but they accepted members by audition only in the Fall and didn't even allow challenges among members that late in the season. Recognizing her skill, she was permitted to rehearse with them, and that gave her great satisfaction. Joe was busy at work, getting all the laid-up boats into the water and running again. He drank less and rode more. In fact, he entered a formal ride or race almost every weekend. One Saturday he rode all the way to Bowling Green alone. It took him most of the morning to get there. He made overtures about getting a motel room and staying over, but Molly did not respond. They got carry-out Chinese, and she played the flute for him. He got back that evening. Soon, her term was over, and she was home. That summer, they were inseparable.

A few weeks before she returned, Joe started focusing on what he should do about Pete Falloni. He too would be returning for the summer. It couldn't be avoided. He strained for gossip about Pete, but couldn't learn much more than he already knew. He was his father's pet. He didn't like to work with his hands, so Joe had nothing to worry about, he would stay in the office like he always did. The only time Joe would ever see him was when he came out to take work orders from boat owners or show them the finished work. Joe needed more and concluded he had no other alternative. Standing in the door wiping his hands with a shop rag, Joe asked, "Mr. Falloni, may I speak with you?"

"Sure, Joe." Joe stepped inside and uncomfortably closed the door behind himself. Mr. Falloni's tone became serious. "What is it, Joe? You're not going to quit are you? You need a raise?"

"No. You're very generous. I like the work. This is

embarrassing. I need your advice."

"I don't know how good it will be, but go ahead, shoot."

"Is your son still going with that girl from Norwalk?"

"Petey?" He turned to look at the photograph of the couple. "Yeah, their tight. Why do you ask?"

"I'm going with Molly Brennan."

"I see. Listen, Joe, I learned a long time ago not to get involved in matters of the heart. I can see why you're concerned. As far as I know, that's ancient history. You know they went together for a long time?"

"Yes, sir."

"It's none of my business, but I never did think that their dispositions were suited for each other. You know, cats and dogs. Now me and my Mrs., we have a stormy and tempestuous marriage, but we both love to yell. You know her father, Kelly?"

"Yes, sir."

"I went to school with him. We went our separate ways. I keep hearing about him from the Ford guys at the country club. He's a trouble-maker. Molly's a lovely girl, but two different worlds, you know." He licked his cigar.

"Yes, sir. Do you think I should talk to Pete?"

"Speaking as the owner of this business, not Dear Abbie, yes. Hopefully, Petey will run this place some day, and you'll be here to help him. Just get this out in the open quick, and that should be the end of it.

"Thanks, Mr. Falloni."

"Get back to work and make us some money."

Pete Falloni did come to work that summer. His second day back, Joe saw him giving the girl from the photograph a tour. She was about an inch taller than Pete, wore her hair in a bun on the back of her neck, and looked more elegant than the photograph. All the guys in the yard talked about her the rest of the day. A few days later Joe caught Pete in the parking lot after work. "Hey, Pete, got a minute?" Joe trotted up, pausing to catch his breath and feeling his face flush. "I, uh, I wanted to let you know that I'm going with Molly Brennan. You know, I didn't want you to..."

Pete finished opening the Corvette door, and turned back to Joe, "Don't worry about it. She and I, well, it was high school stuff. Long past."

"I didn't want it to be a problem."

"Don't worry, man. I wish you two the best." Joe smiled. Pete started the sports car and spun the tires in the gravel as he drove off.

Molly not only got back on at Cedar Point, she got the day shift, and was promoted to lead person in a refreshment stand. Occasionally, if they needed an extra person in the evening, she jumped at the overtime. One such night towards the end of June, Joe found Molly in her uniform standing at his apartment door when he came back in from his ride. He said hello and asked her what was up. She smiled, hugged, then kissed him, but never answered. Inside, he protested her affection with his sweaty condition and smelly clothes. She continued to smile and led him into the shower. Joe couldn't believe it was happening, but did not again protest. They undressed each other, pausing to kiss and touch as they did. They washed each other in the shower. Joe, inexperienced in such matters, was barely able to contain himself in his pleasure and discovery. Molly took the lead in moderating the progress of events.

She turned the shower off, and they frolicked with the only towel Joe had. She took Joe's hand, collected her purse from the living room, and led him into the bedroom. Operating on instinct only, Joe made moves that he thought he was supposed to. Molly redirected many of his attempts, and without words guided him along. A fleeting question passed through his thoughts when she did, and he reciprocated actions that were not instinctive for him. A few moments later she climbed out of the bed and returned with a condom from her purse. He should have had them, he thought. He was glad she did. He took comfort knowing that she must have been having the same thoughts that obsessed him. She did not fumble at all when she put the condom on him, and again that question flashed through his mind. It was lost in yet one more discovery. After, they laid under the sheet, with her head resting on his chest. Joe told himself he could never ask. He already knew the answer.

"I love you."

"I love you."

That Saturday night, they went to a movie, then returned to Joe's apartment to make love again. This time Joe had a box of condoms in his night stand. They showered after. They dressed and got two beers. They laid sideways on Joe's lumpy sofa, watched TV and nursed the drinks. After finishing her drink, Molly rolled over on top of Joe.

"Do you like children?"

"Kids? Yeah, sure."

"Well?"

"Well, what?"

"Well, do you want to have children."

"Yeah, sure. Someday. I really haven't thought about it."

"Why not?"

"I don't know."

"How could you not think about children?"

"Because I'm a guy, I guess."

"That's no answer. That's the kind of answer these guys around here would give." Joe knew who she was talking about.

"Yes, I want children, a lot of children. Two is not enough. I always wished there had been more kids in our family. There should be boys and girls, not just boys or girls. I think there should be at least two of each."

"How many altogether?"

"I don't know. At least four, maybe six or eight."

"Now, that's an answer."

"What about you, do you want children?"

"Oh yes! Four, six, maybe eight. Boys and girls."

During the week, they planned the following weekend around their love making. Saturday morning they rode to Huron and back on the bikes. Molly kept her bike at Joe's apartment. He wanted to make love when she walked over that morning, but she put him off until they got back. That afternoon, he helped her father tune the station wagon and had several beers in the process. They told her parents they were going to a movie, but went back to Joe's place instead.

"Do you think that we'll ever get married?" she asked, wrapped up with Joe in a blanket on his living room floor.

"There will never be anyone else."

"When?"

"When do you want to get married?"

"I love you so much."

"What about Bowling Green?"

"I want to be a teacher, but I hate the thought of going back."

"I'll still be here."

"I love you."

CHAPTER 25

Joe and Molly went to the farm at least once a month that summer, usually for Sunday dinner. His father had a rooster in with the hens, and there were soon more chicks than the coop could support. At first they tried to sell chicks, then they took to giving them away. Everyone told Joe's father to get rid of the rooster, or at least separate him. The only response anyone ever got was that he liked hearing the cock crow in the morning. Once Joe took the bikes, and he and Molly rode into Attica and back. Fifteen miles was Molly's working limit, and Joe never pushed it. Sometimes Joe would help outside with a project that took an extra hand; but most times, he, Dieter and his father walked the farm. His mother worked through the family albums with Molly and her drawers full of dress patterns. She gave Molly a couple of bib-aprons she'd made that Molly liked to wear when she helped in the kitchen. She put aside the wisdom about the Irish that had been handed down through her family. Her own daughter couldn't have pleased her more than Molly. She knew that for the love birds it was a matter of when, not if.

Joe and Molly were also an accepted part of life in the Brennan household. Indeed, their names rarely came up separately; it was always, "Joe and Molly this." or "Joe and Molly that." Molly's mother did find more than one occasion to get her alone to obtain an additional assurance that Molly would finish school. One Sunday, her parents came to the start of a ride that Joe's club sponsored. Because they were the hosts, Joe was busy before the start; but he also rode, leaving with the back of the pack. Later, Molly's father came back downtown for the finish. With Molly off serving cut oranges, he told Joe how important Molly's education was to her. They had never really pushed college, but she had wanted it all through school. Saving his best argument for last, he told Joe that she would always have her education to fall back on if anything ever happened to Joe. Joe nodded without responding, touched by the assumption in the statement.

Joe and Molly could never agree on who asked who or even when they decided, but he was determined that she should have an engagement ring before she went back to school. After shopping for one together, Molly wanted no part of it; it was too expensive. That brought on Joe's disclosure of his finances. He had $4,000; $1,000 in the bank in Attica, and $3,000 in Sandusky, both earning interest while he slept. He was saving half his wages, and would have more if it weren't for his expensive habits. Molly could not believe it. She knew her parents lived from paycheck to paycheck, and that without her summer job, she couldn't even afford state school. He had it all figured out, $500 for a ring, $500 for the wedding, $500 for the honeymoon, and enough left to furnish a place and get a car. There was time and he could save a lot more before they needed it. Staggered by his savings, Molly gave in. On a Saturday in mid-August they bought a half carat diamond and then made love in Joe's apartment.

That night they came in on her parents and Maggie watching TV to make their announcement. Molly held out her hand, wiggling her fingers, as they walked in. Her parents looked to each other and back when Molly cut off the unstated question, "No date, but we're engaged." Maggie stayed on the floor watching the TV while her parents hugged Molly and took the couple to the dining room table. Coming back from the kitchen with four beers, her father handed them out and made a toast before sitting.

"To love. Ain't it great?" They all laughed. "Joe, I couldn't order up a better son-in-law, but you'll pardon my saying, you two have a lot of details to iron out. Molly's in college, and three years is a long time."

"Daddy!"

"I've been with your mother twenty years, this place may not be Fairlane, but things don't happen by accident. You have to make them happen. Joe, if you got on at the plant, you could almost finish your apprenticeship by the time Molly gets out of college. You've got to be thinking about benefits, health coverage."

"Kelly, there's plenty of time for that later. Show us the ring, dear."

The following morning they went to the farm for dinner and to make the same announcement. Molly insisted that Joe take her down early, so she could go to church with his family in Attica. Joe took her directly to the church. They were a little early and his parents a little late, so they went inside together as soon as his family arrived. His mother, kneeling beside Molly, saw the ring during Mass. She reached over and covered Molly's folded hands with her own and smiled to her as her own eyes filled with tears. Joe missed the moment, he was busy staring at a statue of the Blessed Virgin wondering how anyone anywhere could ever be stupid enough to believe that tears could flow from a statute's eyes. He caught up quickly after Mass, when he came outside to find his mother introducing Molly to the priest as "Joe's fiancee" and asking if he knew the priests at her parish in Sandusky. Falling back two steps, Joe blushed and told Dieter and his father that they were engaged, no date. His father put one hand on Joe's shoulder and shook him with a smile, "She's a good woman."

Back at the farmhouse, the two women disappeared into his mother's sewing room. The door was closed, and though the men could not understand any of the words, the talk was constant. They heard the talk and the periodic laughter, and went about the business of making chicken dinner. Contrary to his custom of drinking only on Saturday nights, Joe's father opened three beers. Dieter hesitated, smiling at Joe. "Go ahead, Dieter, you're old enough. Joe here's about ready to go over the ridge. Enjoy life while you can." They talked mostly about cooking. Dieter fried the chicken, his father took care of the mashed potatoes, and Joe sat the table. When they got to a settled moment, they again noticed the muffled talking of the women in the other room. Unknown to them, Joe's mother was refining her plan to help Molly's mother make the wedding dress.

"I've had considerable time to reflect on this." Joe's father started, studying the label on the beer bottle. "I've concluded that the ideal situation is three houses in a compound. The women and men each get one to spend the days in without having to listen to the other, and at night they sleep together in the third. All the benefits, none of the burdens." Neither boy had a response. After a moment, Dieter asked if either of them had paid any attention to the political conventions. It had the desired effect on Joe's father. "Did you hear what those lying bastards are saying about the Department of Agriculture? Well, let me tell you, it's the same old thing. They just can't stop rigging the market. They keep coming up with new ways to do it, but it's the same old thing. I'd sell this place and give every penny to the first politician who promises to make the market fair." Thereafter, Dieter kept him on the roll.

The meal went smoothly. Little more was said about the engagement. Dieter was going to be a junior. He was thinking about college. If he went, he'd study ag. When asked about her studies, Molly said she was going to try out for the orchestra. Joe explained she played the flute. His mother advised that she could teach music too. Joe liked the beer with the meal. He laughed more easily at Dieter, and saw more and more humor in his father's speeches. Since the men did the cooking, Joe's mother and Molly did the dishes. The men had one last beer on the front porch before Joe and Molly left.

Molly raved about Joe's mother all the way home. She was wonderful. She loved Joe. Joe was so lucky. Joe didn't appreciate her. She wouldn't tolerate Joe's behavior from her own sons. They went by Joe's apartment for him to change out of his suit, but ended up making love.

CHAPTER 26

I showed up at Joe's apartment one evening in August, 1968. It took awhile to raise him. I heard voices, then the TV, and then Joe came to the door. Molly was on the sofa. It didn't take a rocket scientist to figure out that I had caught them in the act. I hadn't seen either of them since New Year's. Things had quite obviously progressed. I had a little trouble finding his apartment, but then Sandusky isn't that big. I wandered around until I matched the building that I remembered with his truck. I was on my way back from Chicago. I would have gone straight home, but I was stoned, and didn't want to deal with my parents. I brought a twelve pack as a deposit on hospitality.

That was my political summer. I guess you could say that my political phase was after beer and marijuana and before hash. I went over to Chicago that summer on the excuse of the Democratic Convention. There were a lot of people there, but it seems to me that there is a direct relationship between the years that have passed and the number of people with Chicago stories. I hope I don't bore you with mine. Mine's true.

I came home from school that summer and worked in my Dad's shop like I had since I was sixteen. We were still cranking out bomb casings. I got a promotion, my job was QC, quality control. I got a clip board and government forms to fill out. Mostly, I looked at welds all day long. At first, I was shy about rejecting work, but the government inspector came by once a week to check up on me. Then I figured out that the welders didn't mind the rejections. Other than the forms for the government, no one in the shop kept track of who screwed up. They got paid by the hour, so it was just more work for them. I finally figured out that the government was looking for a 5% rejection rate, and that's exactly what they got. One time the inspector even told me I was being a little too tough. You could tell he was proud of his pupil. By the time I saw the casings, they had been from one end of the shop to the other, and almost every one had picked up some kind of message written inside in chalk or crayon. I don't know why I remember these two: "Party time!" and "I'm sorry, I've got a family too." I spent most of that summer helping make bombs, yet I made little connection between that and politics. That was still to come.

I had discovered grass that Spring. I was much more interested in that than war. I had a student deferment, so the war was something very remote to me. I really didn't appreciate the significance of LBJ stepping aside that Spring. My hair was still short when I got home from school, but I let it go that summer because most of the guys in the shop had long hair. My parents hassled me a lot about it. I had a friend from school who lived in Evanston. He called and invited me to come over for the convention, he promised the biggest party I would ever attend. I knew he had grass, and I didn't. I had worked for over two months, school was about to start, so I convinced my parents I needed a vacation. I really did need to get out of there, so I drove the Olds on over to Chicago. They had a nice house with a pool in the backyard. My friend lived in a small apartment over the garage. We did dope, listened to music, laid out by the pool, and took the El downtown every day. We walked around, listened to the bands, and scored more dope. We were in the crowd and looked scruffy, but you couldn't honestly say we were protestors. We were tourists, just taking it all in. We weren't there the night of the beatings. We spent that evening getting stoned and listening to records on my friend's stereo. We saw it all on TV the next morning when his mother made us breakfast. We had no further interest in going downtown, and she wouldn't let us anyway. That's probably the most truthful Chicago story you'll ever hear.

I laid that all out for Joe and Molly. They were a little put off by the dope, and wouldn't take any, but they didn't mind me smoking, I guess. They drank beer. We put the TV on some evangelical and turned the sound off, Molly tuned in a Cleveland radio station. She danced alone for awhile, then Joe danced with her. As you know, Joe was always wound a little tight, but Molly was a party person. She knocked them back just as fast as we did. I have no idea where she put them. It's great to think of those two dancing. Wish it had been me. Anyway, they were slow dancing, with Joe's back to me. They came around and Molly smiled at me, showing off the ring. "I knew it. I knew it. I knew it." I chanted for a long time, lost in the drugs. Eventually, the song ended, and I stumbled up to congratulate them. I was pretty far gone, but I do remember prodding them into a group hug, something I picked up in Chicago.

I soon learned that Molly planned to finish college, and, no doubt, expressed my opinion that three years was a long time to wait. If I was as wasted as I remember, I probably stepped on Joe's toes a little, and wondered out loud if I still might have a chance. I remember warning him about the draft, there was no deferment for marriage anymore, even a baby wouldn't keep you out. He just blew it off. We must have kept talking about the war. The most amazing thing I remember was when I asked him what his father did in World War II. He didn't know. I told him that my Dad said his father was a hero. That was all news to Joe. Of course, in my condition, it didn't sink too far in that night, just enough to remember. I've thought about that more and more over the years.

What did sink in was another of Molly's observations. Again, she scored a direct hit. I must have been railing with the slogans I'd picked up in Chicago. Anyway, I clearly remember her boredom. She repeatedly left and wandered around the apartment. The last time she came back with a round of beer and laid it on the line for me, "If you really want to change the world, have kids, and raise them right." I can see her. I can hear her voice. I was probably thirty before I understood. She was only nineteen then.

Later Molly produced a flute and played along with an easy listening station. That did it for me. I think it was then that I gave in to my jealousy of Joe. After all, he had a regular life, a home, and Molly. Joe was way out ahead of me. I passed out listening to her. I didn't wake up the next day until almost noon. I showered, shaved, and washed my clothes in the laundry across the hall. I went out and had a hamburger for lunch, and then I bought a case of 3.2% for Joe. I left a note and went on down the road to Attica.

CHAPTER 27

Molly made the orchestra, second chair. She was self-conscious about how her high school marching band instrument compared to the others in the orchestra. She felt she could never be first chair without a better flute. She talked to her fellow musicians about theirs. She found time to visit the local music store which only carried band instruments, but could special order the quality she wanted. They also gave her the names of several pawn shops in Toledo. It didn't matter anyway, she knew she could never afford what she wanted and still make tuition, room and board. She never discussed the subject with her parents or Joe. Merely getting the formal clothes she needed was enough of an expense. Her mother made a full length black skirt for her and also an elegant sequined black gown. She bought a white silk blouse and shoes. Her parents brought the clothes and Joe over to Bowling Green the afternoon of her first performance. Her mother and Maggie helped with some last minute fitting adjustments in the dorm. Mr. Brennan and Joe walked the campus, looking as out of place within their Sunday suits as they felt on the campus. They had dinner in the usual family restaurant, and came back for coffee after the performance. Molly beamed and rambled happily about the winter performance season and her education classes. She was glad Freshman year was behind her. Joe was characteristically quiet, but Molly sensed more.

They continued to correspond constantly, but not everyday. In the mail, Molly proposed that Joe come alone to another performance, bring the bikes and stay over in a motel. Although Molly had come home once, they hadn't had an opportunity to make love since she returned to school after Labor Day. He checked into the motel before going to the dorm for Molly. They left his truck near the dorm, and rode only around town, circling the campus, and going up and down the quiet streets in the residential neighborhoods. While Joe loaded the bikes back into the truck rack, and locked them in place, Molly went into the dorm and returned with her formal wrapped in plastic, and a small overnight bag. Inside the motel, they kissed, but she had her period and did not want to make love. They showered together, and once again Joe suppressed his urge to ask where she learned the things she did. Later, he helped her put up her hair. They talked and laughed. She stayed over with him that night for the first time. They drank a six pack in bed watching TV. He held her all through the night as they slept like spoons in a drawer. She kept chewing gum beside the bed and woke Joe by pushing a piece into his mouth that she held between her teeth. They petted for some time and showered together again. They rode the bikes out to breakfast then around the town again. She cried a little when she kissed Joe good-bye after lunch.

Mr. Brennan showed up at Joe's apartment with a twelve pack of malt liquor one Friday night in early October. Joe gave him a quick tour of the place, taking time to explain the crank set from his good bike upon which he had been working. He told Mr. Brennan that most people pack too much white grease into the bearings, too much of a good thing. Mr. Brennan acted like he was interested, but quickly got Joe to the small kitchen table and down to business. He produced two booklets from his hip pocket, one was their union contract with Ford and the other was the benefits booklet.

He started with the union contract, thumbing through the pages and explaining as he went along. He passed quickly through the definition of the bargaining unit. That was not a big deal anymore. Janitors and maintenance workers were in now, so everyone but security was covered. That's how the coloreds first got in the union. He grumbled something about subcontracting-out which Joe did not totally understand when they went over the description of unit work. The grievance process was long and involved with several steps that intrigued Joe. He was completely unaware that the company couldn't fire someone without a reason, just cause. Mr. Brennan could not resist the opportunity, "Falloni, can." Going over the section on job classifications and descriptions, he told Joe there were lists in the back of the book which he could read later. He explained the seniority provisions gave old-timers priority in bidding for better jobs and protected them in layoffs. They were the last to go except for union officers, who had super seniority. Joe asked if that applied to him as a union steward. It did. Joe questioned the fairness of that. "Well, without it, Hank The

Duce can clean out the union leadership whenever he wants, and the bastards will do anything to break the union." Joe diplomatically held his thoughts about the union leaders negotiating a special deal for themselves. The wage scales were another exhibit in the book, and the benefits section just generally described contribution amounts that would be made to pay for the benefits in the other booklet. The paid vacation and sick leave amazed Joe. If he didn't come to work, he didn't get paid. These guys got paid for not working.

Flipping though the benefits book, Mr. Brennan explained that disability insurance paid on top of Workman's Compensation if you got hurt on the job, or even if you didn't. Joe knew he had Workman's Comp at Falloni's, but he had never before understood what it was for. Life insurance went to your family if you died on or off the job. Health insurance was absolutely necessary, the goddamned doctors were going to own the country before they finished. "You know, when I was a kid, before the war, doctors were just like anyone else. They didn't cruise around in fancy fucking German cars. They could at least drive Cadillacs, Lincolns, or Imperials. The bastards. That's not why we fought the fucking war." He left the subject with special emphasis for Joe to read it. He knew Joe had no coverage, so he didn't push it further. He went on at length about the pension fund. He was especially proud of it. Not only would he retire at 60% of his wage forever, but all the money that the company put aside for that was managed by the union. The union was the one a working man had to look to for protection, not the company. "Everybody gets old. What the hell are you going to do, keep working until you die? You look through these. Let me know if you have questions."

"I've got one right now. How come these are printed in such small booklets? They're hard to read."

"My boy, that is one of the most important victories of the movement. The contract is made to fit in the working man's pocket. When the bastards start pushing, all you have to do is pull out the contract. I've backed down many a foreman just by waving the contract."

They adjourned to the sofa and watched the TV for awhile. Joe was not used to high powered beer, much less malt liquor, and had a hard time staying awake. Joe learned that Mr. Brennan had walked over, so when he left, Joe walked back with him trying to sober up in the cool night air. Joe carried the remnants of the twelve pack which

Mr. Brennan had refused to take. Joe didn't want to be tempted to drink the stuff and pressed it on him when they got to his house. He tried to persuade Joe to come in for another, but Joe went on back to his apartment. Within half an hour Joe fell asleep reading the maternity benefits section of the health coverage.

"Mr. Falloni, do you have a minute?"

"God, I hope you don't want more advice for the lovelorn."

"No, sir. I, uh, I got a job over at Ford Plastic. Molly's dad sort of persuaded me. I got an apprenticeship in maintenance. I'll be working on all the machinery. I have to go to class at night."

"Sounds like this is something you've thought through."

"Yes, sir."

"Joe, if there were any way I could persuade you, more money..."

"Actually, sir, I'll make less at first, but, you know, with benefits and seniority...."

"Joe, you know, I think only the best of you. You'd have a place here as long as I'm in business."

"I appreciate that, sir. I've been thinking about the $300 you gave me, I could pay it back."

"Joe. You've earned every penny I ever gave you, and I've paid you every penny you ever earned here. You don't owe me anything."

"Thank you, sir."

"Joe, you've got to do what's right for you. You just remember, if you ever get tired of that big business bullshit, you talk to me. You got that?"

"Yes, sir."

"You'll always be welcome here. I didn't build this place up alone. I have to have good people."

"Thanks."

"Joe, you don't need to go back to work. I'll pay you through the end of the week. Get on out of here. Take a couple of days. Besides, you know how it is, when someone quits, they really quit twice, once when they decide and again when they actually leave. It's bad on morale for the others. You understand?"

Joe said he did, but he left feeling as if he'd been fired. Mr. Falloni walked him to the front door. He never went back into the shop or said good-bye to the guys. That afternoon, he rode his bike the fifty miles over to Bowling Green. After checking into the motel and showering, he sat in the lobby of Molly's dorm for two hours waiting for her. When she first saw him she shrieked with laughter. They had sex both before and after dinner.

CHAPTER 28

Joe drove down to the farm alone for Thanksgiving dinner. He stayed all day, but not overnight. Molly was home for Thanksgiving, his parents understood. Molly also had Thanksgiving dinner alone with her family. That night, after seeing a movie and stopping by Joe's apartment on the way home, she told Joe that she never wanted to be separated from him like that again. He had felt uncomfortable without her, but she was absolutely strident on the subject. They should be together on such special days. Joe enjoyed holidays as much as anyone, but was curious at the emphasis she seemed to place on them. He accepted her plan to split Christmas day between their families.

Once his mother got a hold of Molly's Christmas idea, Joe was little more than a passenger on their train. Joe and Molly came down to the farm the afternoon of Christmas Eve. The women prepared a large meal. His mother would not allow TV that night, nor beer, because they were going to midnight Mass. Instead they played Christmas songs on the hi fi, and his mother brought out the family photograph albums. Most of the evening his mother and Molly sat beside each other on the couch going through the photos. Joe flipped through a large stack of Ohio Farmer's and chatted with his father and Dieter about crop yields. Later Joe spent over an hour at the kitchen table showing them the union contract. His father had never before seen anything like it. He was befuddled with the length and specificity. From time to time he muttered about now understanding why strikes drug on and why cars had never been as good as they were before the war, everyone was spending all their time fussing with fine print. His mother only had to hear that the apprenticeship required school to be satisfied. She didn't stay to hear Joe explain what he had learned about gear ratios to his father and Dieter. All three took paper and pencil and worked calculations. Joe explained that there was gearing in the plant machinery that made automotive transmissions look simple.

It was a High Mass with a procession and incense. Joe watched Molly throughout the ritual, especially noting the dramatic and exaggerated manner in which she crossed herself and performed her "mea culpas". His mother did also, seeing profound devotion, where Joe was perplexed by what seemed to him to be hypocrisy. Joe spent most of the service trying to reconcile his mother's thinking with her beliefs. She had granted everyone in the car her dispensation from the fasting rule, implicitly ordering them to receive Communion despite the large meal they'd just shared. It was Christmas, she said, some things are more important. Dieter teased her about granting things that were not her's to give, and asked her repeatedly about what penance she thought appropriate for various sins. He might start going to her for Confession. Joe's mother warned Dieter about sacrilege. Joe's father stayed out of the conversation. Molly agreed with his mother. Joe sat silent. He never talked about such matters with his parents, but he worked the subject of convenient obedience over pretty thoroughly during the service.

His mother made a big production out of Molly sleeping in his bedroom. She made the couch into a bed for Joe, complete with a pressed cotton sheet over the cushions. Once she got Joe tucked in, she sat on the coffee table talking to him in hushed tones. She loved Molly. Joe could do no better. After she left, Joe thought about Molly in the full length flannel night gown she had come out of the bathroom wearing. He had never seen her in night clothes before, and it excited him. He thought briefly about sneaking into the bedroom, but the house was too small. He knew that from years of listening to his parents. It didn't snow that night, but the wind blew steadily. Joe could hear it outside in the trees. Joe went to sleep thinking about Molly.

The next morning followed routine; the heavy breakfast and the opening of gifts. Molly had picked out the gift they got his mother. He bought hand tools for his father and Dieter. They had done the same for him. His mother got Joe clothes and Molly a hand-carved rosary. Molly gave Joe a sweater. Joe put off giving his gift to Molly. Just before lunch, Joe and Molly packed off to Sandusky for a similar session with her family.

There they had a large meal, and after cleaning up from that, they launched into the postponed opening of gifts. At the Brennan's, beer was flowing. Everyone, including Maggie, drank. Mr. and Mrs.

Brennan gave Joe a two-wheeled tool box cart. Joe loved it. All the guys in maintenance had them. Mr. Brennan knew that, knew all about the swagger of the maintenance jocks as they made their way through the plant to resuscitate down machines. He had tried to get off the line and into maintenance, but he never made it. A trouble-maker never would. The machines were too important. At least that's what he told himself.

When the gift giving tapered off, Joe produced his gift for Molly. At first she was shocked, then angry at the expense. No one in the orchestra had as fine a flute. How did he know? Joe never answered that, but he immediately explained that it was gold plated, not gold. He bought it in Cleveland. If she didn't like it, they could trade it for whatever she wanted. She would never trade it. No one had a flute as nice. She laughed. She cried. She hugged Joe. She played it. When she did, Joe winked at Maggie from time to time. Maggie enjoyed the beer as much as anything.

Joe and Molly spent New Year's Eve on the couch in his apartment, that is up until 11:30 P.M. when they walked over to her house to watch the ball come down with her parents. Mr. Brennan was three sheets to the wind when he greeted them. "I hope you two have been behaving yourselves!" he laughed as he opened the door and then headed for the kitchen to get them beer. Her mother protested, but Joe was actually relieved that her parents were making correct assumptions. At midnight, he kissed Molly in front of them for the first time. Mrs. Brennan kissed Joe on the cheek. There was at least a foot of snow on the ground, but it was a clear, crisp night. Molly stepped out on the porch without a coat just to say good-night to Joe.

"How come you won't ever answer me?"

"What do you want me to say. I have no control over the draft?"

"What are you going to do if they draft you?"

"I don't have a deferment, and they haven't called so far."

"I don't want you to go."

"I don't have much choice."

"Canada is only fifteen miles across the water. They make cars in Canada too."

"I can't do that."

"You won't do that. Everyone who lives in this country came from somewhere else."

"I can't."

"I love you. I don't want you to die." She started crying and nestled up to him to stay warm.

"I could enlist. Everyone who enlists goes to Germany."

"You don't know that for sure. Once they get you, they could send you anywhere."

"I could be out by the time you finish college."

"You could be dead."

"You don't usually look at the worst side of everything."

"Don't you see, there is no up side."

"Germany's not so bad. No Germany, no Altznauer's. You could come with me."

"You can't make a joke of this, Joe. If you knew the truth, the first Altznauer probably came here to get out of a German draft."

He held her for a moment, but didn't say anything. They kissed. She stood on the porch, watching as he crunched along the sidewalk until he was a silhouette under a distant street lamp.

Throughout the long months of January and February she wrote letters on the subject. She had visited an off-campus draft counselling office several times. She sent him brochures. She sent him a diocesan publication she picked up at the Newman Center on the Catholic Church's teachings that purported to reconcile the Fifth Commandment with just war. It was written with Hitler in mind, but Molly saw only the reverse side; that was, the unstated responsibility of Catholics in unjust wars. She even had a Vatican II pamphlet about conscience, that mentioned the Nurenberg trials as an example. She also found a Jesuit pamphlet on selective conscientious objection at a table an anti-war group periodically sat up near the student union. Joe looked them over, but never read them.

The thought of killing someone did not particularly bother Joe. He could think of a lot of people who deserved to die. Who should die, well, there were a lot of better minds than his to decide that. He didn't like what he knew of Viet Nam. It seemed awfully far away and insignificant, but there must be good reasons. He didn't want to kill anyone, but if he had to, he could. He had hunted, and he had helped butcher farm animals. He didn't think killing a human would be that much different. He never told Molly any of that. In fact, he didn't respond to any of what she wrote him until she ended one letter saying that if he really loved her, he would face the issue.

To that he wrote a short note, "Because of you, I started thinking about God. I believe there is a God. I think something more than an accident started everything. I believe that. I also think that God left the rest of it to us. As far as I've been able to see, churches and everything connected to them, including prayer, are a cruel joke. It's our world. God gave it to us. We have to accept the responsibility. The big fish eat the little fish. If the good people don't stand up to the bad, we may as well give up. There are bad people. There are people who do not deserve to live. I know you do not agree. I know you are very religious, in your own way; and your way is very different from mine. Religious objection to war begins with belief in a God who commands you not to kill. Mine doesn't. I am not a hypocrite nor a liar. I cannot do that, even for you. I love you."

Molly never pressed the subject again. Just before Easter she wrote Joe what she had learned about the coming lottery. There wouldn't be any more deferments; not for students, nor teachers, nor anyone. That was good for Joe because it made the draft pool bigger. The bad part was everyone would get a number, including Joe. Depending upon the luck of the draw, low numbers would be called first. She never wrote or spoke of it again. She knew she had only one option left before he might be taken from her. If he wouldn't do anything, she had no choice.

"Let's get married." she said after a long silence sitting in Joe's truck as they drove through the grain fields in northern Ohio. He had driven over to Bowling Green to pick her up for Spring Break.

"Sure. What else is new?"

"I mean, let's do it."

"Now? What about school?"

"They don't throw you out of school for being married."

"You mean you would stay at Bowling Green?"

"I could. There are other school's. I could take classes at the community college in Sandusky." She lied, she knew it was only a two year school. "You could get a job in Toledo, and I could day hop at Bowling Green. I could go to another school. There's a way to do this. We can work it out."

"What about the orchestra?"

"I can work that out."

"What if I get drafted?"

"I finish school while you're gone. I might even go to Germany with you. Don't you love me?"

"Yes, you know I love you." Joe took a deep breath. "OK, let's do it. When?"

"I'll finish out this year. We can get married in June."

That evening they had a very similar conversation with her parents. They were not pleased about the vagueness of the school plan, but were very happy about the marriage. A much less tense version of the same discussion took place at the Altznauer table on Easter Sunday after Mass.

Events quickly overtook Joe. He did not protest a church wedding. He knew how important such rituals were for Molly, and he also looked on it as his gift to the combined parents. They met with a priest at St. Mary's the following Tuesday evening. They could skip the classes because they were both Catholic. If the wedding was in late June there was still time to announce the bands the requisite number of times. At that time of year they often did three weddings on a Saturday, two in the morning, one in the early afternoon. They could still do it if the early afternoon was OK. It was. After that, Joe stepped out of the planning. Mrs. Altznauer drove up and met Molly and her mother for the first time. They spent a day pattern shopping. It took one more trip before Molly decided on her dress; two before the bride's maids and the mothers. Mrs. Altznauer drove up two days a week after that to help with the sewing. She always took work back with her. Joe didn't see Molly much that vacation, but he got her into his apartment every time he could. He spent her birthday getting drunk with her father while Molly and her mother worked over the invitation lists at the kitchen table. Joe's only contribution was to tell them to talk to his mother about the Altznauer list. Lying in bed with Molly one night, it occurred to him that they should have a nicer place to live and a better vehicle than his truck.

CHAPTER 29

There were only three weeks left before the wedding when Molly got home from school. A general level of intensity was building that Joe did not like. When Molly discovered that Joe had not yet rented the tuxedos, she dressed him down unmercifully. The reason for Joe's delay was that his friend from O.S.U. was still in school and couldn't get up for a fitting. Joe had checked with the shop and knew he could get them on one week's notice. As far as he was concerned, he had plenty of time. He didn't explain any of that to Molly. He stood looking at her with her fists clenched at her sides, her feet planted, and her flushed face cocked up to his. She reminded him of Dieter, but there was no humor to be found in her scolding. He tried, but could not, hear the words she was saying. When the tone of her scolding tapered, he reassured her that he had the task in hand. That Saturday, his friend drove up with Dieter. Ivan and Joe were sharing a beer in his apartment when they arrived. After another with the new arrivals, they went to be fitted. The next two weekends after that, Joe did something he had not done during the two years since he left home, he went to the farm, worked and stayed overnight. He never explained the reason. His parents thought he was getting nostalgic. In fact, he was avoiding Molly.

Every afternoon when Joe got home from work, they ran endless errands; and every day they spent more money. Joe walked around feeling like he had a tight band around his chest as he watched much of his savings disappear. Every day Molly had another list. They found a two bedroom apartment in the Eureka, a four-story, red brick, U-shaped building a few blocks further south on Columbus Street. They got an end apartment on the top floor that had a door out to a small balcony just big enough to stand on, but not big enough for chairs. The master bedroom looked down on the courtyard. They were just high enough to see over the tops of the trees, which gave them a view of water towers, church steeples, and on clear days, Cedar Point. They both signed the lease. Molly signed "Mary M. Brennan Altznauer" and smiled at Joe.

The apartment had to be furnished. They collected some things from their families, but Molly wanted a new bedroom suite, living room furniture and a dinette. Not only did furniture shopping bore Joe, the prices shocked him. Over Joe's protests, they opened a joint checking account and ordered checks with their married name and new address. Joe didn't even try to resist when the lady in the bank suggested they sign an application for credit cards. She would fill it out later. Joe found a five year old, four-door, Ford sedan that was acceptable to Molly. He bought it directly from the owner for $500. Her father had convinced him of the logic of driving cars built by their employer. He had it titled in both their names. He and her father spent several evenings working on the engine, then Joe sent it out for a $29 paint job. That was delayed two days after the car went in for Molly kept changing her mind about the color. When his Sandusky account got down to $2,000 dollars, Joe had a long harsh talk with Molly. The result was that they went to one furniture store and applied for credit. A week later they were approved with a limit of $1,500. Joe told Molly over and over that she did not have to spend the limit, but beyond that, he did not participate further in the furniture shopping. The idea of debt gnawed at him.

About the only light moment the two shared during this time was Molly's report of her mother's handling of the visit to the gynecologist. She had never been to one before, although she had her appendix removed in the ninth grade and had an internal examination then. She assured Joe, that everything was fine and in working order. She did not tell Joe that she had declined the doctor's offer to discuss birth control. Her mother had collected several pamphlets from the waiting room at the doctor's office and had several more from church. She took Molly out for coffee and tried to discuss them all with her. Molly felt a little guilty about playing with her mother's serious attempts, but couldn't stop laughing as she recalled her mother's instruction, "...and rhythm is the only acceptable method in the eyes of the Holy Mother Church." The pamphlet from the church had a six month calendar grid that her mother tried and failed to force Molly to complete. When her mother got mad and started lecturing in a whisper between tightly clenched teeth about how important this was to her honeymoon, Molly told her she would do it later. Joe asked several times if anyone overheard them. Molly never answered, instead she laughed as she recollected additional details of her mother's embarrassing duty.

The last Sunday on the farm, Joe went for a bike ride when the family went to church. It was a little tense with his mother who did not accept his glib remark that he was going to inspect the cathedral that God built. Instead, she extracted a promise from him that he would go the 5:30 P.M. Mass in Sandusky later that day. Joe rode south to Bucyrus on the county roads that parallel Route 4. He hadn't been riding more than once or twice a week since Molly got home. He was amazed at how quickly he had gotten out of shape. His muscles were fine, but his wind was lacking. Including the loop around Bucyrus, he figured he had done about 35 miles. When he got back to the farm, his mother was putting lunch on the table. Even though it was Sunday, since it was such a nice day, his father was planning to cultivate the corn that afternoon. Dieter was going to go over the hay bailer and make sure it was working. Joe thought about cycling back to Sandusky, but that meant he would have to find a way to get his truck back. His mother would love the excuse to visit the Brennans, but Joe dismissed the thought of an afternoon of listening to the women and then having to listen to it all a second time as he drove his mother back to Attica. He showered after lunch and gathered his things together. He kissed his mother good-bye. She said they'd see him Friday at the rehearsal. Driving out, he waved to Dieter and his father. He spent the afternoon alone in his apartment going over the bikes.

CHAPTER 30

I was in Joe and Molly's wedding. When Joe asked, he was a little embarrassed, explaining that Dieter would be his best man. Hell, I was honored just to be asked. Some Polish guy that Joe had worked for and I were the ushers. Molly's sister was the maid of honor. We teased Dieter about her, but she was a little too classy for him. The Pole's wife and the girl I had gone out with that time on New Year's Eve completed the wedding party. I'll be damned, I just can't remember her name. Nice girl. I'm sure she had even less use for me at the wedding than she did earlier. By then, I had a pony tail and beard. It was a great wedding. Molly's fingerprints were all over it.

The rehearsal was at the church on the Friday evening before the wedding. It was one of those big stone churches in downtown Sandusky. The rehearsal didn't last long, no more than ten minutes. After that, we all walked through the downtown gardens to the Cedar Point Ferry. They had it arranged for the ferry to take us across the bay as a group to this fancy fish place at the Cedar Point Marina. I had no idea the restaurant was there. They had the tables arranged in a large T-shaped with the wedding party across the top and the families down the stem. It was a nice view across the bay with the setting sun. Molly's Dad was really pounding the drinks down. Mr. Altznauer was sitting across from him. Dieter tried to get served, but they wouldn't. I got pretty well lit, but I noticed that neither Joe nor Molly was drinking. In fact, they spent most of the dinner leaning toward and talking softly to each other like the rest of us weren't there. On the way back to the ferry, I made a play for the New Year's girl and got shot down. On the ferry, I invited the Polish guy to the bachelor party.

Dieter and I had helped Joe move his things over to their new apartment that afternoon. Joe's parents went back to Attica after the dinner, but Dieter stayed over. The plan was that he and I would stay in the Joe's old apartment, and Joe would stay over in the new one. Dieter left the party arrangements to me. I had never been to a bachelor party and really didn't know what was expected. It was a good thing I didn't, for I can't imagine Joe going along. Anyway, after we got out of the good clothes, we went to a bowling alley for about an hour. Again, they wouldn't serve Dieter, so we headed on back to the apartment. As far as I remember, it was a good time. We teased Joe and got drunk. Joe still didn't drink anything, which only gave us more to tease him about. He could be real serious about things, and he had no intention of being hung over at his wedding. Of course, we explained to him that he was whipped. Joe caught me rolling a joint in the kitchen and told me to cool it in front of the others. I understood. Later I found some excuse and went out to my car. There I did a cube of hash in my traveling pipe. It was way too much dope for one person. I missed my bong. I burned my throat smoking it and was hoarse for days. I vaguely recall going back in and drinking a lot more to soothe my throat. When Joe's friend left about midnight, Joe did too. Dieter and I kept drinking, I guess. When I woke up the next morning I was still in a chair, and Dieter was on the couch. Neither one of us made it to the bedroom.

As you know, in my opinion, Molly was about the prettiest girl I'd ever seen. She was an absolutely gorgeous and radiant bride. They always say that, but it was true. She had some of her friends from B.G., a string quartet, playing in the church up until the processional; then the organ came in. That organ just about lifted everyone out of their seats. It was all very impressive. I was surprised at how many people came. Just about everyone I knew from Attica was there, including my parents. The bride's side had a few more people, but not that many. The church was about half full, and it's a really big church.

They had a horse and buggy pick up Joe and Molly in front of the church and take them for a ride around downtown and through the old homes while everyone moved into the church social hall for the reception. There the string quartet played again. When Molly and Joe got back, they collected the wedding party and families for pictures. Dieter and I slipped out and decorated their car. The rest of the afternoon was pretty tame. Joe and Molly danced once. Everyone applauded, but no one else danced. It broke up after an hour and a half or so when Joe and Molly left. Everyone I knew went home to Attica. I helped Joe's friend get Molly's dad home. He had been doing some serious partying before the ceremony. Her mother was furious, to say the least. I stayed over again at Joe's. I told my parents I had some things to take care of for Joe. The apartment was furnished and empty, who would care? I spent the evening alone, getting stoned.

I still have one of those little cards they give to people at weddings with their names and the date. I would give anything for one of the wedding pictures of Molly and Joe. We were so young. Never before or since have I seen Joe so happy. Molly, I'd like to have any picture of her. She was beautiful. It was a great day. God, they were beautiful. I need to ask Mrs. Altznauer for a picture sometime.

CHAPTER 31

With all the decisions that their wedding involved, the easiest for Molly and Joe was the honeymoon. Both of their parents had gone to Niagara Falls. Growing up with those stories, that is where they decided to go. They drove east out of Sandusky taking Route 6 along the Lake Erie towards Cleveland. They took their new car. Joe was a little concerned about it making the distance. He wasn't familiar with it and had only done superficial work on the engine. He didn't say anything about that to Molly, nor did he tell her that he wished they had brought the bikes. Instead, he pointed out things along the way that he had noticed on his bike trips. It was a sunny afternoon and from time to time when they caught glimpses of the lake, they could see a horizon lined with white sails. Late in the afternoon they checked into the City Plaza, an elegant old hotel just off Public Square in downtown Cleveland. They were both nervous when they did, not because of their youth or the coming honeymoon, but because of their inexperience in lavish places with marble pillars, oriental rugs, and potted palms.

Once they got rid of the bell boy they were quickly about the business of undressing each other. After a few moments Joe broke away to get a condom. When he returned, Molly said, "Don't use that."

"Why not? You want to get...."

"We're married now."

"So?"

"God's plan."

"Come on, Molly. I know your little secret about God." She pulled him closer. "I think this has more to do with Molly's plan."

"I want a baby. I want your baby."

"I knew it. I knew it all along. What about school?"

"Don't you want children anymore?"

"Yes, but what about you. What about your plans?"

"I have the rest of my life for that. Who knows how long I'll have you in this crazy world."

"Molly."

"I love you. I want you."

Joe surrendered.

They spent the week at Niagara Falls on the Canadian side. Neither had been out of Ohio before, so they made a point of stopping to walk on Pennsylvania and New York. Joe had learned that Molly could not read a map when they drove into Cleveland, so to avoid more snapping at each other, he made sure she drove through Buffalo and up to Niagara Falls. He read the maps and gave directions. They were both put off by the stench of the industrial air pollution as they drove through Buffalo. It made them nauseous. Soon they crossed over into Canada and found their motel.

They did the rim that afternoon. That night they walked the shops. After a time, Joe stayed on the sidewalk while Molly searched for trinkets to take back to family and friends. The next morning they went up the new observation tower to look down on the Falls. They talked about taking the boat, but never got to it. They talked about driving up to Toronto, but never got to that either. They stayed up late watching old movies on TV. They idled in bed in the mornings, not getting out for breakfast until mid-morning. Towards the end of the week, they barely left the motel.

They spent most of the day lying by the pool and reading. When they got hot, they jumped in the water to cool down. Molly tried to teach Joe to swim, but he was a poor student. In fact, he was embarrassed and deliberately avoided the lessons. He stayed in the shallow end, marveling at her flips and pikes off the diving board. She was a powerful swimmer, but cut through the water with little splashing. She was good at flip turns. Each lap, Joe tried to catch her. Occasionally, she let him. They would start kissing and retire to their room. It was a quiet, idyllic week. By week's end they were tanned and used to their lazy routine. They hated to leave, but drove all the way home in one day. They wouldn't learn for another month that Molly was already pregnant.

CHAPTER 32

Married life brought the usual adjustments and compromises that were only slightly exaggerated my Molly's pregnancy. Their sexual activity before the marriage took some of the edge off the changes on that front.

Joe went immediately back to work at the plant. In addition to working a normal shift, he had apprenticeship classes from 7:00 to 9:30 P.M. on Tuesday and Thursday evenings. Then during the August shutdown, when everyone but maintenance went on vacation, even greater demands were placed on Joe's time. He worked late every night and every weekend. Since it was temporary and the overtime was helpful, neither he nor Molly complained. Joe's drinking became limited to a Friday night ritual with Molly's father. Joe's biking was also limited and ritualized to a Sunday morning ride down to the farm in which Molly drove the pick-up truck and met his family at Mass. Joe did not attend Mass. No one discussed it. The first few times he rode down and back, then he simply loaded the bike and came home in the truck with Molly.

Molly's pregnancy was easy as such things go. She had some early morning sickness, but it was mild and soon passed. Despite the fact that she gained weight more quickly than she should have, and earned warnings from her OB-GYN, she did not show the weight. Her build of wide shoulders and hips coupled with a narrow waist allowed most of the gain to disappear in the middle. Indeed, at four months, she barely looked pregnant. Both her own and Joe's mother teased her that she was built to carry babies. At first, it embarrassed Joe; but Molly loved to hear it. She immediately suspended her love for beer, and refused any drugs, even those suggested by the doctor. She did sign up for one class at the community college on Tuesday and Thursday evenings, not so much to further her education as to offset Joe's similar absence for classes those nights. There she caught up with some high school friends; however, her marriage and pregnancy placed her in the role of mother hen, confidant and advisor; rather than bar hopping companion.

The quickening in late October brought a major transformation in Molly. She began to relish maternity clothes that emphasized her abdomen. The only topic of any conversation that held her attention was one that centered on the baby. To her thinking, this included the war in Viet Nam. She also became an outspoken advocate of Lamaze, which then was just beginning to become popular in the big cities. With the support of her doctor's nurse, they got him to agree to let Joe in the delivery room; but he did that only after meeting Joe twice; and then, only when he learned of Joe's participation in calving on the farm. The nurse went to a seminar in Cleveland and returned to start the first Lamaze class for the doctor's patients after the holidays. Joe and Molly were in it. About the same time Molly changed her wardrobe, she also starting wearing her hair differently. She stopped getting it trimmed at shoulder length, and she started wearing it in a high pony-tail or in a low bun on the back of her neck. The effect of her alternative looks was wholesomeness and maturity, rather than youth and sophistication.

It only took a little of Molly's prodding to get Joe to approach their landlord about breaking the lease. No one retreated to the language in the lease. Joe simply stated Molly's pregnancy and the need for more space as the reason. The landlady agreed, and providing she could re-rent the apartment within one month, also agreed to return their security deposit. That, she later did. They found a small house for rent for $150 per month and took it. It was still in town, actually closer in than their apartment, about a half-mile to the northeast. It was further from her parent's, but that was not a factor in the selection. It was a late 1940's frame house, one story, slab on grade, and a detached garage.

The cottage sat on a larger lot than her parent's house and thus had more front and back yard. The house, however, was much smaller than her parent's. There was no front porch, just a concrete pad at the front door. The front door entered the living room. The dining room and kitchen were to the left. Two bedrooms separated by a bath were across the back of the house. There was a door from the kitchen out into a fenced backyard. Molly was particularly attracted to the fenced yard for her future toddler. Joe was particularly attracted to the garage. Within two weeks of moving in, Joe had painted the interior of the garage, installed better lighting, and sat up his bike shop.

Both Molly and Joe felt older and somehow more married now that they were in a house. Molly's made dinner for Joe's family their first Sunday in the new house. She fried chicken as a special concession to his father. The following Sunday, they had her family over for dinner. They spent Thanksgiving day with Molly's family. After work the next day, they went to the farm for the weekend. It was the first time they slept in the same bed in his parent's house, something of more awkward significance to Joe and Molly than to his parents or Dieter. Joe's mother spent much of Saturday giving Molly photographs of Joe from the family albums. Joe helped his father and Dieter put new rings in the old John Deere.

The first draft lottery was held just before the Christmas holidays. Joe and Molly sat quietly late one evening and listened to it on the radio. Molly wrote down each number and each birthday. Joe's number was 248. It was high enough that, for all practical purposes, Joe had been exempted from military service. Joe closed his eyes and sighed. He was relieved, but he had a well-developed contingency plan that included living with Molly and the baby on any duty except Southeast Asia. He let that thinking drift calmly away. Molly, however, squealed and danced about. She was overjoyed, and made no secret of it. She had become outspoken on the unpopular subject and regularly embarrassed Joe, family, and friends. With the personal urgency of her politics removed, she embarked upon the happiest holiday season of her life.

Joe and Molly spent Christmas Eve alone in their new house. Alone, they quietly opened their gifts that evening. Their gifts to each other were modest. Molly got Joe some metric box wrenches that he had asked for, and Joe got Molly a gold crucifix on a neck chain that she had asked for. Their big gift was the crib and nursery furniture that they went out and bought together two days before. Joe paid cash. Except for their initial furniture purchase, they had no debt. Joe had them on a cash basis, and they were saving. Joe nursed a few beers through the evening. They spent much of it in the nursery. Joe sat on the floor leaning up against the wall. Molly folded and refolded the blankets, sheets, and other such items they had acquired for the baby. When Joe urged her to bed, she turned off the colored light on the baby's dresser and said, "Can you imagine how wonderful next Christmas is going to be with the baby?" Standing in the dark room, they kissed, and Joe gently stroked the sides of her belly. Joe looked passed Molly, out the window to the falling snow. When he felt the baby move, he closed his eyes and drew in a deep breath of the scent of Molly's hair. They spent Christmas morning with her parents and Christmas afternoon with his. They never did make it to church.

At 1:30 A.M. on Monday, March 2, 1970, Maureen Altznauer was born after an unusually short first labor and natural delivery in which her father assisted. She weighed 7 pounds 4 ounces and was 19 inches long. She was mostly bald, but had a strawberry blond fuzz. She inherited the light skin of both her parents, and her features were such a uniform mix of Molly and Joe that both families claimed them. The hospital stay was uneventful. On the first pleasant day of what promised to me a beautiful Spring, they brought their baby home. They had her baptized the following Sunday after the 9:30 A.M. High Mass at St. Mary's. Dieter and Maggie were her godparents. It was the first time they took Maureen out since bringing her home from the hospital.

Molly nursed Maureen. At work, Joe constantly thought about them. He spent hours in the evenings simply holding Maureen. She was an easy baby who started sleeping through the night at six weeks old. Molly's mother tried to keep the baby on their first anniversary in order to let the couple have a quiet night together. She pulled Molly aside and whispered that she wouldn't have to worry about getting pregnant as long as she breast fed the baby. Joe and Molly, however, took Maureen to a family restaurant and spent their anniversary dinner cooing at the baby. They were both comfortable in their domesticity.

CHAPTER 33

Their descent into hell began with a low grade fever. Molly talked to the pediatrician's office Friday afternoon. Given the symptoms, the nurse recommended an over-the-counter medicine and made an appointment for the following Tuesday morning with the proviso that Molly call and cancel if the baby got better. Even with the syrup, Maureen was fussy and slightly warm all through the Fourth of July weekend. Like most mothers, Molly had become quite proficient in treating mild ailments, but the watery glaze over Maureen's green eyes troubled her. She kept the 10:00 A.M. appointment.

The nurse did the preliminaries, interviewed Molly, took Maureen's temperature, and made notes on a printed form. Waiting for the doctor, Molly played with Maureen on the examining table, kissing her stomach and blowing in her ear. Maureen smiled and cooed. Usually, she would have giggled. The doctor, Dr. Clancy, had been Molly's doctor when she was a child. He was a distinguished man of sixty with thick grey hair that was carefully trimmed and precisely parted. He always wore a suit and bow tie. In the office, he wore a white lab coat. He went immediately to work on Maureen, looking in her ears, down her throat, and felt her neck and abdomen as he exchanged pleasantries with Molly. "This is an absolutely beautiful child, Molly. Yes you are. Yes you are." He gently pushed into her upper abdomen one more time before he put the diaper back in place. "When you were her age, I thought you were the prettiest baby I would ever see. I was wrong. Look, her hair's a brighter red than yours." He explained that he thought she was probably fighting off some bug that was going around, but he wanted to take a little blood. Molly helped hold her when the nurse came in and stuck Maureen's heel. Ten minutes later the doctor returned, "Molly, I don't like what I see, but you can't tell much from one drop. I want to take some more and send it to the lab."

"What do you mean. What's wrong?"

"Now don't you stew. You know me. I just want to make sure our little lovely only has a flu bug. Now this is not going to be fun baby, Maureen. Here, Mom, you help, and we'll get this done just as quick as we can." Maureen shrieked and fought as Molly and the nurse held her down. Dr. Clancy filled a small vile from her arm. "There, all done. I'll have a report back from the lab first thing in the morning. Can you be here this time tomorrow?" Molly nodded. "Good. We won't do anything different tonight. Just keep her comfortable. We'll talk tomorrow." He kissed Maureen, then patted Molly on the side of the arm.

Back at the doctor's office the next morning, the receptionist escorted Molly and Maureen directly into the doctor's personal office without any wait in the reception room. With Maureen in her lap, Molly inspected his office from a wing-back chair in front of his desk. She had been in the office before, but only once or twice in her life. It was quite a contrast from the toy-filled reception area, the sterile examination rooms, and the cluttered file room. It looked more like a study in someone's home; bookshelves, a stereo, family pictures, walnut desk, two leather chairs and a sofa. "Good morning, ladies. Here let me hold her." Maureen fussed at first, but cozied up to him quickly. When she did, he took her around behind his desk and sat down in his high-backed chair. He played with Maureen for a moment, ignoring Molly.

After a time, Molly asked, "What did the lab say?"

"Molly, it's not good. I don't want to upset you. There will be plenty of time later for all this to sink in. We'll take this one step at a time." Molly's eyes widened in terror and her lower lip trembled. Dr. Clancy came around his desk with Maureen, and sat of the front of his desk holding Maureen. "Listen, calm down. I want you to listen carefully to me. Maureen is a sick little girl. I am going to make sure that she gets the best treatment possible. You are going to have to get used to many changes very quickly, but you are going to have to be strong for Maureen." Molly buried her face in her hands and sobbed. Dr. Clancy walked around the room with Maureen, bouncing her and talking softly to her. After a few minutes, Molly regained her composure.

"What is it?" She asked softly. He came back behind his desk and opened the file laying there. He went down a list reading words she had never heard before, putting a number with each one. Some were good, some were average, some concerned him, some were bad. The one word she did understand was leukemia. When he finally said it, she froze and ground her teeth together. Tears streamed down the sides of her face.

"Molly, this doesn't have to be a death sentence. There are new treatments. Break throughs are being made everyday. We have a lot to do for Maureen, but right now the most important is to be strong. I don't want you to drive, can I call someone to come get you. I also want to give you something." She refused the prescription for herself, and she gave him her mother's phone number. She sat numbly staring at Maureen in Dr. Clancy's lap as he talked to her mother on the phone. She heard the word leukemia again.

After work, as Joe drove up the street he noticed the Brennan's station wagon in front of their house. He found his mother-in-law sitting on the living room sofa. The drapes were closed, and the lights were off. Joe also noticed that the TV was not on. It was only as she told him that Molly and Maureen were taking a nap together that he saw she had been crying. She took him into bedroom where Molly was asleep on top of the double bed beside Maureen. Her mother gently woke Molly. Molly looked up, then immediately to Maureen. Her mother whispered that she would stay with Maureen. Molly led Joe back out of the darkened room.

In the living room Molly turned and started to talk, but when her eyes met Joe's, she shuddered into a sob. Joe put his arms around her, and he held her silently as spasms racked through her body. Joe, still with no definite knowledge, also began to cry from the contagion of the circumstance. He fought his tears by tightly closing his eyes. All he could see was Maureen lying on a patchwork quilt in the shade of a tree on the farm that past weekend. Then he felt Maureen lying on his chest and holding his shirt in little fists that night as she screamed at the fireworks they watched as the rockets were launched out over Sandusky Bay. Molly regained her composure and told Joe that they had to go talk to Dr. Clancy. His stomach tightened. He thought he would vomit when he heard leukemia. Her voice cracked when she said it. She covered her mouth and cried.

Within half an hour they were back in Dr. Clancy's private office. They sat side by side in the wing-backed chairs, silently facing the empty desk. Joe had heard many adoring stories, but he had never met Dr. Clancy before. They shook hands. "You're a lucky man. You spend your days with the two prettiest ladies I know." Joe did not respond. He instructed them to move to the sofa, and he slid one of the wing-backed chairs in front of them for himself. "Joe, I told Molly to bring you in because right now the two of you are my biggest concern. You two have to be terrified. I know that only a little of what I say will stick, so I'll be brief." Joe took Molly's hand. "Maureen has leukemia. There are several kinds of leukemia, actually it is just a label for a group of diseases. What they have in common is that the leukocytes, the white cells in the blood, multiply out of control. When cells multiply like that, it's sometimes called cancer. When I was your age, we thought leukemia was simply cancer of the blood. Now we know it's not that simple. There are several kinds of leukemia, and we have successful treatments for many of them. I have identified the problem, now we need to get Maureen to a specialist, a hematologist. That's a blood doctor. He will do more tests, identify the leukemia, and set up a treatment program. I've already talked to Dr. Kleinfelt, and I sent copies of Maureen's file over to him. He wants us to put Maureen in the hospital tomorrow. Molly, you should take her to Admissions tomorrow morning about 10:00 A.M. They'll be expecting you. After some tests, he will meet with us late tomorrow afternoon. Molly, they'll let you stay with Maureen in the hospital. Joe you go ahead and go to work. You can come to the hospital after work. This is going to be a long haul. It is any parent's worst nightmare. I wouldn't wish it on anyone. It's real, and we're going to deal with it. As all this settles in, I am sure you'll have questions. When you do, ask. Don't hesitate to ask."

Molly drew in a breath, "Is she going to die?"

"I don't know. Ten years ago, fifteen years ago, the answer would have been yes. Today, there are treatments. You got her in here early. That's good. The sooner you catch these things, the higher the success rate. Once Kleinfelt identifies exactly what we're fighting, he can tell us the chances. If you don't understand anything he says, you ask me. This is a very serious situation. Right now, we have a jump on it, and that's the way I want to keep it. OK?"

Molly let go of Joe's hand to wipe her eyes. When she did Joe looked down to see his hands trembling. He folded his hands together to stop them.

CHAPTER 34

Dr. Kleinfelt led Dr. Clancy, Molly, and Joe down the hall from Maureen's room to a sitting area at the end of the hall. A candy striper stayed in the room to play with Maureen. There were two cribs, two rocking chairs, and two single beds for the mothers. The other mother had more experience with this terror and unsuccessfully tried to talk to Molly. The other father had arrived just a few minutes after Joe. Both babies were Dr. Kleinfelt's patients. When he came in with Dr. Clancy, he recognized the familiar tension and took them down the hall.

They stood as he spoke. He spoke without looking up from the clipboard in his hand. They had rerun the initial tests. He quickly read down the list and gave the matching numbers as if Joe and Molly understood. The second test confirmed the first. The numbers were close, slightly worse. Standard deviation might explain that. They had proceeded to run a battery of more sophisticated tests. He had a verbal report and would have a written report tomorrow. He told them it was definitely some long phrase that began with "acute" and ended in "leukemia". There was an accepted treatment with a good prospect of success. They would do one more test before beginning the treatment, just to be double sure they were treating the right thing.

Dr. Clancy asked questions for Molly and Joe's benefit. The tube would be left in Maureen so that they could draw blood and administer the chemotherapy without additional sticks. Assuming the best, they were looking at two weeks in the hospital, then weekly office visits and blood tests. If it didn't work, they had other options, other treatments with more severe side effects. Sometimes one treatment would work when another wouldn't. They were going to follow the conventional wisdom first, and progress to other options only if they had to. She was a strong, otherwise healthy baby. That was good, for the treatments would make her sick. She would be nauseous, run a fever.

She would probably lose her hair. They were getting an early start. That was good. He refused to put numbers to her chances or length to her time. If she made it to her first birthday, there was a good chance she'd make it to her fourth. They needed to focus on what was in front of them, not the horizon. It looked like they could save her spleen. Neither Joe nor Molly knew what a spleen was, what it did, or why it was at risk; but they did not ask. Dr. Kleinfelt left them with Dr. Clancy. He went over everything for them a second time.

Joe stopped by the hospital every morning before work and came to the hospital every afternoon directly from work. When Joe arrived, Molly went home for a couple of hours, then stopped at her parents for dinner. Joe ate the dinner the hospital brought to the room for Molly. Molly's parents alternated evening visits with Joe's parents. Maureen did lose her hair. She burned with fever. The first few days she cried weakly, after that she whimpered if left alone in her crib. When they held and rocked her, she would stare at them through her glassy eyes without whimpering. They came to understand that the treatment was poison. They were killing the cancer with poison. The trick was to kill the cancer, then stop the poison before it killed Maureen. At night, Molly brought the crib up against the bed so that she slept face to face with Maureen. Joe slept alone at home. He fell asleep thinking about holding and rocking Maureen. He did not remember his dreams.

Dr. Kleinfelt was satisfied with the initial treatment and released Maureen at the end of the second week. The grandmothers concluded that the doctor released Maureen on the strength of her crying. It had grown quickly. The attention had completely spoiled the little beauty, she protested loudly when left alone for an instant. The fever subsided. She smiled again. They took her home. Molly took her to Dr. Kleinfelt's office every Monday morning for a blood test. Maureen quickly associated the trips with the pain, crying loudly the entire car trip to the office, fighting to stay in the car. Kleinfelt's office called the results over to Dr. Clancy's office, and one of the nurses there called Molly by mid-morning with the numbers. Molly kept the weekly numbers in a ruled ledger. Joe graphed the two that he had learned were the most important. One was improving, one was holding without change. Two months passed. Then one Monday morning they called to tell Molly to take Maureen back to the hospital.

This time Molly and Joe were the parents experienced in terror. Nevertheless, they had no help for the other young couple and their baby. This time the regime lasted an entire month. Everything was as it was before except that Maureen was even more sick. She had constant dry heaves. They fed her intravenously, so she did not lose weight, but she suffered horribly. Finally, the treatments were lessened, the fever left, the heaving stopped, the crying strengthened. Once again Maureen was sent home. Once again the weekly blood tests were taken. Joe and Molly had Thanksgiving at home with Maureen. They made brief, terse telephone calls to their families. Six weeks passed. Then one morning the call came to schedule an appointment for Joe and Molly to meet with Dr. Kleinfelt that evening.

His office was cluttered. One wall was covered with diplomas and certificates. There were stacks of magazines and journals on his desk. There were books on shelves. There were books stacked on chairs. There were books stacked on the floor. Joe read the diplomas. Molly looked about for family pictures. There were none. He entered briskly. As they knew, the first treatment had not worked. It stopped the progress of the disease for a time, but ultimately failed. The same was true of the more aggressive second treatment. He had one more thing he felt comfortable trying in the hospital in Sandusky. It would be classified as experimental. It would be rough on Maureen. It might work. It was a last ditch effort. There was one other thing he could recommend, a bone marrow transplant. If the patient survived the procedure, the long term survival rates were much higher. It was experimental. Only a few hospitals did it. Different hospitals, different doctors, did it differently. He could recommend a hospital in Cleveland or Columbus. If it were his child, he would take her to the University Hospital in Columbus. They nodded yes without discussion. He would make calls in the morning. There might be a waiting list. They would have to locate a donor. He drew blood from each of them for that purpose. Insurance wouldn't cover it all. They should talk to the Personnel Department at Ford. They should call his office in the morning. His nurse would coordinate everything.

His nurse told Molly over and over how lucky they were. There was a sudden opening at O.S.U. She did not say another baby had died. It was their's if they could get Maureen to Columbus the next day. The blood test showed Molly was a compatible donor. The nurse had already given O.S.U. all the insurance information. O.S.U. estimated that as much as $50,000 of the cost would not be covered by insurance. Although $50,000 would otherwise have been a staggering fortune to

Molly, she did not even flinch at the number. The nurse told her that O.S.U. would admit her on the basis of the insurance, providing she immediately applied for a federal grant and a state assistance program. They had the forms. Joe took two days off work, and they headed for Columbus. Molly's father and mother also drove down with a woman from the union hall who had experience with health claims. Maureen was quickly admitted and assigned to an isolation room on the tenth floor of the new red brick cube of a hospital that sat along the Olentangy River just south of the football stadium. Molly was also taken aside for tests. Joe and the union lady filled in forms for several hours.

That night a battery of doctors came up to Joe and Molly in the corridor outside Maureen's room. Her room was actually a single room divided in two. Maureen was in the smaller inner room, crying from her crib. The outer room had a special air conditioner filtering the air going into the room, scrub facilities, and a gowning area. Everyone who went in put on a full gown, shoe covers, cap, mask, and gloves. The oldest doctor, an Indian wearing a turbine, spoke. They proposed to push down the cancer and wipe out Maureen's immune system with chemicals and radiation. They would do minor surgery in the morning to install a catheter directly into her chest. It would be used to introduce drugs and medicine. She would have to stay in complete isolation. Then they would extract bone marrow from Molly's hip. They would push a big needle directly into her bone. It was uncomfortable and she would be sore, little more. They would inject the bone marrow into Maureen. It would find its way into her bones and start manufacturing healthy blood. The first hurdle was getting the transplant to take. If it did, then the next hurdle was reintroducing her to germs and building up her resistance. It would take six weeks to two months. They were gone as quickly as they came. They ate with Molly's parents and the union lady in the basement cafeteria, who then left for Sandusky. Joe and Molly found a motel on Olentangy Boulevard. Everything was swirling around them. Neither could sleep, but neither touched or spoke to the other.

The next morning the nurses showed Molly how to scrub and dress. Maureen went wild when she came into the room. She screamed whenever Molly tried to put her down. Molly ended up holding her until she fell asleep from the shot they gave her for the surgery. When they took Maureen out for the surgery, they put a surgical mask over her tiny face. Molly waited. Joe went to Admissions, and they sent him to a garden apartment complex that rented to the families of patients on a daily basis. Molly might have made a different choice, but Joe took a two bedroom unit that four people shared. There were already three other mothers there with children in University Hospital. There were four twin beds, a living room, and small kitchen. The other women were already at the hospital. The property manager explained that most of the guests left early in the morning, ate out, and only slept in the units. Joe checked out of the motel and returned to the hospital.

When he got there he found Molly pressed up against the glass of the door of the outer room. Maureen was inside, lying naked, her arms and legs strapped down to a plastic shell. There was a large brown stain on her chest and a brown tube coming from it. There was a stainless steel fitting on the end of the tube. There was also a nurse in the room who sat at a small table filling in forms. They stood there for two hours. Finally, at the 3:00 P.M. shift change, the nurse who came out told them that Maureen would be sleeping for several more hours and that they should go out for a while. Joe took Molly to the apartment complex. They left her bag there and drove through the large homes in Upper Arlington. Neither spoke. They went quickly back to the hospital. The soldiers at the checkpoint recognized them and motioned them through. Since the Kent State killings that May, the O.S.U. campus had been sealed off by the National Guard. Admissions issued them passes for that purpose. Both were so numb that neither felt intimidated by the jeeps, helmets, guns, and bayonets.

They skipped dinner and returned to their posts outside Maureen's door. She still slept. The nurse inside motioned to a phone on the wall in the outer room. Molly picked it up and the nurse told her that everything was fine, Molly was resting comfortably. She was partly sleeping off the anesthetic, partly reacting to the treatments that had already begun, and was mildly sedated. Joe's parents arrived about 7:30 P.M. They visited for an hour at the end of the hall. They watched Maureen sleep for half an hour, then they all left. Joe's parents followed Joe and Molly to the apartment. They waited while Joe and Molly went in. The other mothers were sitting quietly watching TV. There were introductions, but no conversation. Joe kissed Molly on the cheek and told her he'd be back down by noon the following day.

They got back to the farm about midnight. Joe stayed the night. The next morning, Dieter drove him on up to Sandusky. Dieter went to the refrigerator for a beer, but found none. Joe quickly went through the mail and packed a small bag. He called a Columbus telephone number that his mother had given him. It was his high school friend's apartment near O.S.U. Joe really didn't want to call; he especially did not want to explain the circumstances, but he did. His friend was still sleeping when he called. Sure Joe could crash at his apartment. It was easy to find. He gave Joe the address, it was a side street just north of the campus across Lane Avenue. Parking would be a problem. If Joe had a parking place at the hospital, he would be better to walk or ride a bike. He checked to make sure Joe had a pass, and warned Joe not to mouth off to the N.G. Joe loaded his good bike into the truck and headed for Columbus.

Once again a dismal routine settled over the lives of the young couple. Molly spent every day standing in the door of Maureen's room. She left only to visit the restroom, or to go to the cafeteria. Depending on Maureen's disposition, usually, but not always, they let her gown and go into her room for an hour during the evening. She went back to the apartment after visiting hours. The other mothers never talked. They watched TV and went to bed. The next day was the same as the one before. Joe came down Friday afternoon after work. He and Molly nodded hello and goody-bye. They did not kiss or touch. Their only conversation was Molly's report of Maureen's condition. Joe stayed as long as they were allowed, saw Molly to her car, and biked to his friend's apartment. Inevitably, as he progressed across the campus, he was stopped three or four times by the National Guard. His friend and his roommates usually had a party going, but Joe wouldn't take a drink. He knew he made them uncomfortable, so he went quickly into the bedroom. He always left in the mornings before they woke up. The transplant was performed in the middle of the second week. It hurt Molly more than they said it would. She gritted and pictured a healthy Maureen. She was left with a large bruise on her left hip. By Joe's return that weekend, she was no longer limping. They spent that Christmas in the hospital. There were no gifts. Maureen was not even allowed a stuffed animal.

Within a week they were telling them that it looked like the transplant had taken. They gave Molly the numbers daily. She did not have to write them down or see them to understand their significance. Joe did not have to graph them for her. She had learned. They were getting better, slowly, steadily. Now the focus shifted to her immune system. Gradually, they would reintroduce her to all the evils of the world. Steroids and rich feedings gave little Maureen a moon face and a dark fuzz of facial hair. Molly was now such a part of the hospital routine that she spent as much time in Maureen's room as the nurses. She gowned and helped them without waiting for prompting. Joe was hesitant to enter. The fourth and fifth weekends, he stayed in the door while Molly brought Maureen up to the glass. She recognized him and touched a pudgy finger to the glass near his nose. The sixth weekend, with Molly's guidance, he scrubbed and dressed and went into his daughter's room. He rocked her for over an hour. As he did, Molly laid her hand on his shoulder. It was the first time they had touched in almost two months.

The following week, the barriers started coming down. Those who entered wore surgical masks but no longer scrubbed and gowned. Molly started through a succession of fevers and runny noses. The doctors promised a rapid succession of mild illnesses as she picked up bugs and built up a resistance to them. The seventh week she was taken from the isolation room and moved into an ordinary hospital room with another child. Molly was allowed to stay in that room and moved out of the apartment. Molly decorated the room with Valentine's hearts and balloons. They looked forward to taking Molly home at the end of the coming eighth week, but that Wednesday Maureen was set back by a strain of herpes, chicken pox.

She was consumed in a fever. They moved her back into an isolation room, not for isolation, but for intensive care. Molly slept on a couch at the end of the hall. Friday morning, the nurses could not wake Maureen. Molly heard them say mild coma. She did not call Joe, because she knew he was coming that afternoon. At noon, Maureen was connected to a respirator. When Joe arrived, a remarkable red sunset cast its glow through the room. Like the day the horror first began, Molly started to explain, but her voice broke. This time, however, she was beyond tears. Joe turned and surveyed the room, again knowing, but not knowing. As it darkened outside, the softly lit room was colored by the glow of the various instruments connected to Maureen. The periodic click and hiss of the respirator and the electronic beeps of the various monitors were not hidden by the soft music that the nurses played in a well intended but futile effort toward that end. Maureen was once again naked, spread-eagle and strapped down on a plastic shell. The respirator dominated her face. There were three different drip monitors controlling drugs into the catheter in her chest. Another tube emerged from her groin and drained into a small bag hanging at the side of her bed. Wires were taped to her chest and head and ran to separate machines. Joe watched her little chest inflate then collapse, inflate then collapse, inflate the collapse.

They stood in the dark on either side of her for hours. Nurses continued to come and go. At all times there was at least one nurse checking the equipment, gathering data, taking the strip charts from the machines and putting them into a binder. Joe studied the respirator until he mastered its simple control, breaths per minute. He looked at the dials, he noted the gauges, he counted the cycles. He was not able to make sense of the cardiac monitor. Even more confusing were the brain wave tests taken at the top of every hour. At 10:00 P.M. the turbined doctor reappeared. They had not seen him in weeks. This time he was alone. He spent several minutes examining Maureen and then gathered up the records and the nurse and went out to the nurses' station where they went over the records together. He came back with the nurse and motioned Joe and Molly into the hall. He looked at them and simply shook his head back and forth. "She's already gone. The machines are keeping her alive. The virus got her. I'm sorry. We were so close." A tremor took hold of Molly. Joe pushed up against her, but he did not put his arm around her. Instead, he put his arm out to steady himself against the wall. "Say good-bye. I'll come back later and take care of the equipment."

They re-entered the room slowly, revolted by the hideous exposure of their child and dreading the unknown path they trod into darkness. Joe leaned over one side, gently stroking Maureen's cheek with the back of his forefinger. Molly knelt on the other side and hummed lullabies into Maureen's ear. Several times she moved closer and kissed her cheek. Joe laid his hand softly on Maureen's shoulder and upper arm. Later, the doctor returned. They stepped back into the doorway. He gently flipped the master switch on the respirator. The hissing and clicking stopped. A moment later a buzzing came from another machine. He quickly flipped another switch and stopped that sound. He turned and nodded to them.

Molly backed into the hall shrieking at the top of her lungs. Several nurses rushed up to her, surrounded her, and walked her down the hall to the sitting area. Joe slumped up against the wall, slid down it, and sat on the floor quietly sobbing. Inside, the doctor continued to remove the equipment. A nurse moved each piece back as he did. He loosened the straps, and covered her with one of the diapers that they had used to place below her. When he came out of the room, he carried all the charts to the nurses' station and sent a nurse to assist Joe. He scolded himself for doing it in front of the family. That was a mistake. He would not do that again. He wrote down the time of death at 10:36 P.M.

Maureen Altznauer died of complications from a bone marrow transplant, chicken pox, on Monday, February 15, 1971; the day after her first Valentine's Day, two weeks before her first birthday. She never walked. Had she lived, today she would be older than her mother was when she died.

CHAPTER 35

Their grief and the funeral might have brought Molly and Joe back together. During the calling hours, however, they stood apart nodding stunned acceptance of the words offered them. Joe mostly stood with Dieter and his father. When not with them, he listened quietly to his friend from O.S.U. They alternated between the back of the room and the cold night air outside the doorway. It snowed everyday that week, but that night there were stars. Molly was kept in a protective ring of women, her mother and sister, Joe's mother, and friends. The viewing room was briefly closed, and then everyone was invited back in by Father O'Shaungnessy who led the rosary. Molly used the carved beads that Joe's mother had given her as a present. Joe stayed outside. Afterwards the priest spoke briefly with Molly then sought Joe.

"Joe, may I have a word with you?" Joe looked to him without speaking. "Joe, Molly is drawing great strength from her devotion. You know how devout she has always been. Thank heaven the Church is able to give to her some little part of what she has given it." Joe continued to stare blankly at the priest. "Joe, Molly tells me that your faith is much stronger than her's. Your faith can help you through this. Could we go inside and talk?"

"Priest, do your job and stay the hell away from me!"

"Joe, open up to your faith. Don't turn away, not now." Joe stormed off into the night.

But for the flowers surrounding it, the little casket was almost lost in the front of the large church. The weather broke. It was a sunny morning with at least a foot of accumulated snow. During the funeral Mass, Joe sat beside Molly. He sat, stood, and kneeled at all the appropriate times, but he did not hear any of the ceremony or the eulogy. He had absentmindedly picked up a holy card lying in the pew. It had a picture of some saint on the front and a prayer printed on the back. In fine print below the prayer was the promise of a 120 day indulgence. Joe's mind, his old mind, started working on the 120 days. If a soul was beyond time and space, then where was heaven and hell? How could they be considered as a place? How could a soul go there? Go anywhere? Purgatory, somewhere in between. That was rich. Say this prayer and your soul will get 120 days off its time in purgatory. What time? She is beyond all that now. No longer of this world. Beyond space. Beyond time. Maureen. Little Maureen. God, I love you, Maureen.

Joe felt a hand on his shoulder. It was Molly's hand. He was on his knees. He pulled his hands back from his face and squinted in the light, not able to focus. The Mass had ended. Everyone was standing. The priest was standing just above the casket. Joe wiped the tears from his eyes, and struggled to his feet, unfolding his length before all who had watched him pray.

That night Joe lay awake looking at the shadows on the ceiling. Molly, in her customary position, was lying on her side along the far edge of the bed with her back turned to him. Joe ached. He cried from time to time but suppressed any sound. He remembered seeing Mrs. Olschewske's grave that morning at the Calvary Catholic Cemetery, and realized for the first time that he had been in the wrong cemetery the night he thought he visited her grave, the first night he talked to Molly. He loved Molly. Molly lay completely still, too still to be sleeping. He listened to her breath, it was too shallow for her to be asleep. After an hour, he slid over against her, working one arm under her head and the other over her side. He wriggled until the full length of his body fit up against the line of her back and legs. He had not been this close to her since the summer before. She made no sound, nor responded in any way. He wanted to say something. He wanted to say he loved her. He wanted to say he loved Maureen. He wanted to say he was sorry. He wanted to help her. He had no words. Her warmth, her scent filled his emptiness. He felt much better just lying with her. He listened to her breathing, and it put him to sleep. Molly never slept that night. She stared at the curtains across the room.

CHAPTER 36

Naturally, I went to the baby's funeral. It was one long ordeal. During her treatment at University Hospital, Joe had stayed in my apartment whenever he came to Columbus. I didn't know what to say to him. I looked in on Molly a couple of times a week, but she didn't have anything to say to me. I went to the funeral because I couldn't stay away. For years, whenever I thought about that funeral, I felt like a real jerk; the way I ran on and talked to Joe about the old times. God, what a time and place for that! Joe stayed close to me. Molly seemed to be giving me the evil eye, staring at me. I deserved it. She certainly deserved better.

Molly's continuing stare bothered me. At first I thought it might be drugs. I certainly was familiar with that look. Fortunately, by that time I was pretty much out of them myself. I had cleaned up, put in my law school applications, and was just waiting for the responses. I studied her vacuous look. Maybe the drugs would help her. Thanks heavens I was off them. How did I ever function? When I got close enough to see that her pupils were not dilated and there was no jaundice, I realized that it wasn't drugs. Something was very wrong. More than that little child had died.

Molly functioned. To everyone's surprise, she took over at the cemetery. The pallbearers were her father, Joe's father, Dieter, and I. At the cemetery, Molly changed that. She wanted no one but Joe and herself. When she got worked up about something, there was no stopping her. You should have heard her about the war, but that was before any of this. There was a brief attempt to persuade her; first her father, then her mother, then the priest. Joe didn't say anything, he just went along with her directions. They each took a side of the little casket and, facing each other, shuffled along sideways through the snow to the grave. I worried that they would slip and fall. I remember Joe looking down at the flowers on the casket. I will never forget Molly staring at Joe. Molly never took her eyes off Joe the whole time they carried their daughter to her grave. Joe looked down at the flowers not back at Molly.

It was miserable experience. I tried to do what I could for Joe. I wish I could have done something for Molly. What can you do? I hate funerals.

CHAPTER 37

Life may go on, but those who live it are forever changed. Joe went back to work. Molly stayed home. Neither had much concept of what the other did during the day.

During their ordeal, Joe's work at Ford Sandusky Plastics had been a diversion for him. It occupied him with something other than Maureen's plight and demanded his attention at least during the day. It had been a helpful distraction. After the funeral, he saw the plant with a fresh perspective. It was like beginning an old job anew. He felt like a long-lost traveler returning home. He took comfort in wheeling his tool box down the long aisles marked by the painted yellow stripes among the massive presses. When he first came to work here, everything was new and completely outside his rural experience, but the size of the presses impressed him more than anything. At first, he could not comprehend how it took a machine the size of a room to make a part smaller than his hand. Now size and the products made were the last thing that occurred to Joe. He took in the sights, sounds, and smells.

The operators knew a lot about the machines, and could coax much from them before they called maintenance. As Joe approached the machines that he had been called to fix, he would have the operators run several cycles. He would circle the machine listening for grinds and knocks, smelling the air for the scent of hot oil or burnt vinyl, and touching it here and there to see if there were vibration or hot spots. It was the perfect job for Joe. He had been recruited by his father-in-law and had come to work for benefits and security. He stayed because it was a place of order. The machines were lined up and bolted down. Their operators had little fenced work stations. Painted aisles controlled the human and cart traffic. Work uniforms differed by work assignment. Raw materials came in one end, finished product went out the other. You knew where you stood. Everything and everybody had a place, and

Joe fit. Joe was happy to be back. He could work here forever.

Molly had not had the benefit of any diversion during Maureen's illness. Molly had lived it. Molly had often told herself during that time that one merciful thing was that despite Maureen's suffering, the baby did not understand her illness. She might hurt, but she wasn't afraid. Her mother could give her comfort. The child's brief life had not been burdened with fear. Molly had carried that load, not thinking it a burden until now, after the funeral. Everyone was getting on with life, going back to work. No one was looking back. Molly now felt the weight of her burden, and it angered her. There had been only one thing in life she abhorred, dying children; and life gave her a dying child. She ground her teeth working over her pain and the injustice as she did her house work. She turned the little house into a show piece. Every morning she made their bed, vacuumed the carpet, swept the kitchen. She made curtains. She painted. Her mother came by for lunch once or twice a week, each time offering to help her with Maureen's room when the time was right. Molly kept the door to that room closed. In the afternoon's she played the soap operas on the TV in the living room, but she sat in an overstuffed chair from which she watched the closed door to Maureen's room or looked up the quiet street. When Joe came home, she would start dinner and stay in the kitchen to avoid him.

"Why don't you practice your flute."

"I don't feel like it."

"You could play for me."

"Right."

"Why don't you sign up for a class."

"It's the middle of the term."

"You could work something out, you used to talk about independent study projects for the professors."

"You could leave me alone."

Thereafter they would return to their meals and not speak to each other until a similar exchange the following evening. Molly would clean up after dinner. Joe would go out to the garage and putter for a couple of hours. A few times a week he went for solitary night rides. Molly also avoided the garage for she assumed Joe would urge her to ride with him. In fact, Joe had bought a stereo kit and was building it for Molly's birthday. Although he had turned the garage into a clean room, it was not heated. Joe fought the spring chill with an electric heater aimed at his legs and a piece of cardboard that he stood on to the insulate his feet from the concrete floor. A few times he thought of revealing the project and asking her to help, but he knew she would take no interest in electronics, and would not tolerate bringing the work into the house. Molly took to nursing a beer or two before going to bed. Joe, without any conscious decision, stopped drinking altogether. When he fell asleep at night, always holding Molly after an initial separation, he looked forward to going back to work in the morning. Molly got so she could only sleep after he put his arms around her, but it still took an hour or more.

Joe drove Molly's father to work since he had to drive near the Brennan's coming and going. He was thus exposed to union business on a daily basis. He heard the usual railing against the Company, but got a more even-handed report of the negotiating sessions in which his father-in-law had actually participated. When they worked on the job classifications and work rules, the area stewards had been invited into the bargaining room. From what he heard, Joe developed a sense that wages were not a big issue. He thought strikes were about wages, and thus he assumed that the whole matter would simply run its course. The only issue that was loudly discussed was management's request to liberalize job classifications by including one new paragraph on temporary work assignments. This would give allow management the flexibility to be able to make temporary work assignments outside job classifications to keep people busy. He recognized some logic in that. He still flushed in the memory of getting dressed down after work by a steward for taking work from a janitor. Joe's infraction had been to pick up a broom and sweep the maintenance room one afternoon when he was not busy.

Strike fever caught Joe unaware. He first realized its presence the Friday afternoon before the strike vote. The membership had rejected a proposed contract the week before, but kept working. Management refused to change its position. Now they were going to vote to strike. Fifteen minutes before the buzzer, word spread among all the maintenance men that they were to take their personal tools home with them. It would be an act of solidarity. It would show them how serious the men were. Joe thought it a small stunt, but he had close to $1,000 in tools. He had no intention of risking them. It wasn't until he looked back at the plant from loading his tools in his truck that the gravity of the act occurred to him. He felt he had quit. Joe cast his secret ballot against a strike, Joe and 34 others.

Hundreds wanted and got a strike. Joe got an assignment to man the picket line in the middle of the night, mostly because he had little seniority, but partly because he could not be counted on to be boisterous on the line during the day. The slogans and the chanting bothered Joe. He liked to work. Joe wanted to work. It was that simple. For Joe, it was not pay, nor job classifications, nor work rules. It was not the $17,000 in uninsured medical bills that he was paying off at $75 a month, nor the $2,000 funeral bill at $50 a month. He simply wanted to work. He could not stand the idea of being idle. He, however, found himself idling outside the plant gate late at night, contemplating a plant full of idle equipment. Joe concluded it was wrong. He did not fit anymore. He tried to talk to his father-in-law the next afternoon, but that was a failure. He did not show up for his assigned watch the next night.

"Joe! It's good to see you! How the hell have you been? Sorry about your baby. We came by the funeral home, but you were talking to someone." Mr. Falloni waved Joe into a chair and returned behind his desk. "You wouldn't know it, but we lost a little boy. He was between Petey and the girls. They took his tonsils out at six years old, and he bled to death overnight. Enough of my problems, I just wanted to let you know that you're not alone. Someday you'll be my age looking back. It will still hurt, but don't let this stop you. You're young. You have more kids. It's the only reason for living. Listen to me. What brings you by."

"You probably know about the strike."

"Hard not to. Tell me, have you had enough of big business?"

"Actually, I like working at Ford. I've learned a lot. I'm in the apprenticeship program. As far as I'm concerned, everything's fine."

"But you're on the street?"

"Not by choice. All I want to do is work. The plant's closed. Who knows when it will reopen?"

"These things come and go, you know that, Joe. A couple of weeks or a couple of months, it will end. It will end, and things will go back to normal. A few years from now you won't even remember it."

"No, that's not it. I work for a living. I can't stop working. If I didn't like the conditions, I'd just leave and find something better. I can't stop working. I can't have my work dependent upon what other people think."

"Well, Joe, any big plant is going to have a union. Listen, you know we're busy getting boats in the water this time of year. We can always use an extra hand. You can work here temporarily, then, when the strike ends, you can decide what you want to do."

"No, if I was going to stay with the union, I'd stay on the line. I've got to decide if I ever want to work in a place like that. I really like the work, but.... I was wondering if I did decide to leave Ford, would you take me back?"

"Full time?"

"Permanently."

"Of course I would. I'd have to shuffle things a little, but I do that everyday. A good business is nothing other than a collection of good people. You know what I think about you, Joe. There's always a place for you here."

"Let me talk to Molly. I'll call you tomorrow." Joe rose, then motioned to the fading picture of Pete and his date. "How is Pete?"

"He's graduating at the end of May. They're getting married in June, then it's off to Philadelphia. He's going to get a Master's in business at the Wharton School of Business. Ever hear of it?"

"No sir."

"Me either, but all I do is run a successful business. You be sure to call."

"Thanks, Mr. Falloni. I'll call."

Molly was furious. She called her father, and she sat with him and Joe at her kitchen table until 2:00 A.M. that morning. She served the drinks. She matched her father beer for beer. Joe drank Coke, and was animated by the caffeine. The debate cleared Joe's thinking and brought him to a decision. In the end, Joe agreed that the only way things would ever change for the better was with the union. He had received the benefits of previous battles. All the benefits, the good wage, the medical insurance, the apprenticeship classes, all that was won by the union. He admitted that it was his turn to fight; but Joe was a worker, not a fighter. He only wanted to work. He was not up to the fight. He was sorry. He saw it wasn't ethical to take the benefits and not shoulder the burden, so he was quitting Ford and resigning from the union. He was going back to work for Falloni. Molly was livid. That night she shook off Joe's arms when he went to hold her and ordered him back to the other side of the bed. It was the first emotion she had directed at him in a very long time.

CHAPTER 38

That is when the fighting started, if it could be called fighting. Typically, Joe would do something other than what Molly expected or not do something she wanted. She would start in on him. He would explain, but offer no excuse. She would unleash a second, more impassioned volley. He would walk away. As he did, she would shout invectives after him. The pattern became so predictable, that to Joe, it became part of a daily routine which he ignored. When he came home from work, he knew what would be in store; and he knew he could do nothing right. If he forgot to stop and get a loaf of bread, she unloaded on him. If he got the bread, it would be the wrong brand. On the other hand, for Molly, the incidents were cumulative; honing the edge of her impatience and anger. When Joe retreated to his work in the garage or to his bike rides, she simply added that to her list of complaints, and started with it when he returned, amplified by the few drinks she would have in the interim.

In bed, however, nothing changed. They would both quietly get in from opposite sides of the bed, read for a while, then turn off their lights. After a few moments, Joe would work his way up against Molly's back and wrap his arms around her. There was no sex. Occasionally, one or the other of them would try to recall the last time, but that effort was always lost in a flood of pain at the memory of Maureen. Then they slept. The next morning they would wake in each other's arms. Holding Molly strengthened Joe. He had no appreciation for her struggle. Joe would leave for work, without having any significant conversation with Molly. When he came home later in the day, it began again.

The first break in this routine came on a beautiful late spring afternoon, a Friday afternoon, the week before Memorial Day. When Joe came in from work, Molly greeted him at the front door. She stopped him in the door, put both arms around his head and kissed him passionately. With his lunch box in one hand, and the mail in the other, he broke away from her and pushed inside. She had closed the curtains, and lit several candles. The telephone was off the hook, and soft music was playing on the radio.

"You've been drinking."

"I had a couple getting ready for you. Here, have a beer."

"No thanks. What's the deal?"

"What do you mean? Can't you see?"

"I was planning on a bike ride."

"I thought we could have a drink and talk."

"I'm sweaty. I need to shower."

"We could shower."

"Right."

"You don't have a romantic bone left in your body."

"I've been working all day. I'm dirty and tired."

"I thought we could drive over to Port Clinton. We could walk along the beach, have dinner in one of the restaurants, and go dancing in one of the honky-tonks."

"I want to go for a bike ride, maybe tomorrow."

"Tomorrow the town will be full of pilgrims. Come on. We haven't done anything together in...."

"Not tonight."

"What the hell is your problem?" Joe did not respond, but walked silently into the bedroom where he took off his work clothes. Molly went to the kitchen and got herself another beer. She came back, but stood in the small hall just outside the bedroom. Joe slipped past her on his way to the bathroom. He closed that door behind himself. She snarled at the door, "I did all this for you. I spent the whole afternoon getting ready. You dirty bastard." Joe made no response and proceeded to take a quick shower. Molly finished her beer, got another, and resumed her watch before he came out wrapped in a towel.

"Molly, you just can't turn this marriage on and off like a light switch."

"You could take me out to dinner. Why the hell is that such a big deal?"

"We can go tomorrow night."

"We can go tonight. No pressure. You don't have to make love to me."

"What's that supposed to mean?"

"You know exactly what it means. You can't get it up anymore...can't get it up." Joe gritted his teeth and walked away from her into the bedroom where he started putting on his biking clothes. Molly followed, shrieking. "Can't get it up! Can't get it up!" Joe came to her with tears in his eyes.

"Molly, I'm sorry. I don't know what to say, what to do. I can't undo what's done. I can't make it all better. I love you. I'm still here. I have never felt closer to you than when we hold each other at night."

Molly was suddenly calm and spoke to herself in a monotone. "You don't love anybody but yourself. You don't have a minute for anyone or anything but your machines. You don't know how to love a human being." She turned away from Joe, much as he would from her, and went into the kitchen. She returned with a six pack. "I'm going for a drive."

"You shouldn't drive. Molly, don't go." She continued to the front door and opened it. "Molly, I have no idea what you want. Is this the way it got with Falloni? Did you ruin that too? I just don't know how to deal with you."

Molly looked at Joe for a long moment, then said in her most peaceful voice, "Don't worry, Joe, you don't have to deal with me."

Joe stood in the door as Molly walked down the sidewalk to where Joe's truck and her car were parked on the street. She calmly got in the car and started it. Before she put it in gear, she leaned forward and looked back to Joe. She smiled and waved good-bye. He stood solemn, not responding. She drove away. Back inside, he immediately began to worry about her. He put down the urge to follow her, and convinced himself that she would shortly return. He abandoned the bicycle ride, and changed out of his riding clothes. He continued to stand watch at the front window waiting for her return. When she didn't, he wanted to go looking for her, but he did not know where to begin. He continued to wait.

Within fifteen minutes of leaving Joe, Molly was passing the marshes west of Sandusky, starting across the causeway on Route 4 that crosses the bay and goes on towards Catawba Island and Port Clinton. She had not drunk any of the beer that sat beside her on the front seat. She had kept the window down, and the fresh evening air sobered her and lifted her hair.

Earlier that day, Molly had gone to St. Mary's, paid for a candle, and said a rosary. Then she went to Calvary Cemetery and prayed again on Maureen's grave. On her way home, she stopped to visit her mother and stayed until her sister came home from school. Driving along, Molly pulled her carved rosary from her purse. She wound it around her right wrist and held the crucifix in her left hand with the beads draping across the top of the steering wheel.

Molly took in several deep breaths and reached down and tightened her seat belt. She floored the accelerator and moved into the passing lane. When the car would go no faster, she cut the wheels sharply to the right. The car skidded sideways across the right lane. It turned up on the driver's side as it slid across the shoulder and down the stone rip rap. The car continued to roll, and hit the water roof first, wheels up. The water was only four feet deep. The wheels and drive train were above the water. Molly drowned before the wheels quit spinning.

Joe's first reaction to the Highway Patrol car that pulled up in front of the house was relief. Waiting for Molly, he had tried to eat, but could not. He even opened a beer, but ended up pouring it down the sink. Joe did not wait for the patrolman to come to the door, he went outside. When he saw no one else in the car, he thought she might be lying in the back seat. Maybe they busted her for drunk driving, and she was in jail. Joe met the officer half way on the sidewalk.

"Sir, are you related to Mary Margaret Altznauer?"

"Yes, I'm her husband."

"Sir, could we go inside for a moment?"

"What is it? What's wrong?"

"There's been an accident, sir."

"Molly? Is she OK?"

"I'm sorry."

"What? She's all right. She's not...."

"I'm sorry, sir. It's a tragedy; a young woman, her whole life ahead of her, so much to live for. This job never gets any easier. I'm so sorry. May I call anyone for you?" Joe stood mute. "Please, sir, let me take you inside. There must be someone we can call."

"What happened?"

"Single car accident. She went off the Route 4 Causeway at a high rate of speed and landed upside down in the bay. Her seat belt was fastened. There was no sign of injury. We still have men at the site investigating. I think she drowned."

"No injury?"

"None visible. I'm sorry, sir. I'm so sorry. Please let me call someone." Joe made no move except to look off towards the sunset. "Sir, I need to tell you that in these single car accidents there may be a suspicion of suicide. After we complete our report, and the coroner completes his report, you might get a visit from the county sheriff. If you find a note or anything like that, you should let them know. Most likely, she was driving too fast and just lost control; hit a pot hole, looked away for an instant, something like that. There was an unopened six pack in the car, so it doesn't look like drinking. She was holding religious beads. Maybe they distracted her. Do you know where she was going?"

"Said she was going for a drive. She wanted me to go to Port Clinton with her."

"Guess she was going there." Joe's knees suddenly buckled, but the officer caught him. "Please, sir, let me take you inside." The officer walked Joe up to the house. As he did he spoke softly. "I know it's little consolation, but I am sure she did not suffer. The impact probably knocked her out. I think she went peacefully. I don't think she suffered."

Joe slumped into Molly's chair in the living room and gave the officer the telephone numbers of his and Molly's parents. He balanced his elbows on the arms of the chair and cradled his chin. He listened to the officer make the calls. Already the agony he would never share tore at him. Did he drive her to it? Would she have killed him too? When he heard the officer talk about suffering, he sobbed into his hands.

CHAPTER 39

I went to Molly's funeral too. I was a pallbearer. I.... Excuse me. I'm sorry. You'd think that after twenty years I could hold my composure. I just wish that things could have been different. She was so young. I wish that I could have done something, anything. God, all I can think of is her lying among flowers. I can't begin to tell you how beautiful...peaceful.... I'm sorry. Excuse me.

II.

Sandy's Story

CHAPTER 1

"This is what I want."

Sandy said each word in a measured staccato, as if each was a sentence of its own. Each time she said them, saying them hardened her resolve. She said them to her mother. Her mother was both critical and pleading, "You had four years to find a husband." "If you want a profession, why not a nurturing one like medicine." "Why law school?" "Everything about lawyers is antagonistic, confrontational." "You were never like that."

Like many of the parlors in Grosse Pointe, theirs looked out across a manicured yard with mature trees and a winding drive. Lake St. Clair could not be seen from the house, but was clearly visible from the lower yard and street. Her mother was seated in a tufted leather chair, a woman's magazine laying in her lap. Sandy stood across an oriental carpet next to the full length draperies. She had just taken a cab home from Marygrove College in northwest Detroit, in order to have dinner with her parents and discuss her graduate school plans. The smell of roast permeated the house as did miscellaneous sounds from the kitchen where their cook was preparing dinner. Sandy looked across the yard. It was already twilight, the winter sun setting in late afternoon. She watched her father turn into the driveway in his Imperial. He always came home early on Wednesday, having spent the afternoon at The Club. "We'll see if your father agrees." Her mother warned.

"It is not his decision."

Sandy left the parlor going out into the long central hall. It, like the entire house, had finished oak floors with oriental rugs and potted plants. She walked past the oil paintings without taking note of them, and bounded up the formal stairs. She grabbed the banister at the stained glass window on the landing, using it to boost her jump up the last few steps to the upper hall. Until this day, she would have limited such rambunctious behavior to the back servants' staircase as her mother had drilled into her over the years, but now she felt strong and defiant. She was wearing the plaid wool dress and cotton blouse that was once the required uniform at her school. Most still wore it. She wanted to change before dinner. She changed in her room which was a busy collection of pinks, reflecting the tastes of her mother's decorator and nothing of Sandy. Today, as on all visits, she found new clothes hanging in the walk-in closet that her mother had purchased for her. She chose a simple red dress with a white collar and cuffs. It fit.

Sandy was an only child. Physically, she resembled her mother. Both had slight frames, light complexions, blue eyes, and were natural blonds. Sandy, however, was several inches taller than her mother, although she did not appear to be tall because of her thinness. Sandy wore her shoulder length blond hair swept straight back as did her mother and others of their social station. Sandy habitually wore large gold earrings, but beyond that, she refused additional jewelry and any make-up. She washed her face and studied her complexion in the mirror. She then sprayed herself with perfume. It was a self-indulgence that she knew she abused. She wiggled in the dress, satisfied it hung well. It was going to be easy, she told herself, the hardest part was over.

"Hello, dear, how is school? Are you resisting senioritis?" her father asked, looking up from the Wall Street Journal spread before him on the desk in his library. She kissed him on the cheek, close enough to his mouth that she felt the bristle of his mustache. He commented favorably on her fragrance, but it did not mask the odor of scotch on him. As Sandy walked to a wing-back chair facing the desk, he took a sip from the cocktail glass sitting on his desk. He was a dapper man who wore expensive blue suits and oiled his dark hair for a crisp part. Sandy surveyed the stacks of leather bound books that surrounded him on every wall of this room.

As a child, she thought that he had read all of the classics he collected. When not at The Club, or at work, he could always be found in this library nursing a scotch, smoking his pipe, and reading the WSJ or one of his books. Now she knew he had not read them all, and she also knew the library for what it was, his sanctuary. The rest of the house reflected her mother. His office at Chrysler in Highland Park and its bland 1950's furnishings reflected the spartan corporate culture. There he was one of dozens of house counsel. His specialty in mergers and acquisitions gave him some measure of prominence, for it meant almost daily contact with Lynn Townsend who had quickly transformed Chrysler into a multinational conglomerate. Townsend, the accountant, however, was careful not to disturb Chrysler's austere image beyond his own long sideburns. Within Chrysler, her father was a known man, but he was still one face in a massive organization. At The Club where there were fewer faces, he was one of the boys. In their dining room, he was her mother's husband. In this library, he was himself.

"Your mother tells me you want to go to law school."

"I took the LSAT last fall. I'm getting ready to fill out applications. I thought you might help with references."

"Of course, I will; but references from your professors will go further. How did you do on the LSAT?"

"98th percentile."

"Good heavens! Congratulations. You know that means you can go wherever you want. Despite what they say, the test scores are the first cut. Even if it wasn't, with your grades and extracurriculars, you would be competitive anywhere. With that score, well, the decision is yours. You know I'm a Harvard man, but I don't think that they will hold that against you at Yale. Coming from Marygrove, you might feel more comfortable at a Catholic school like Georgetown. Where do you want to go, honey?"

Before Sandy could answer, her mother entered and summoned them to the dining room for dinner. It was late in the dinner before the conversation got back to Sandy's future. "Did you talk her out of this nonsense?" her mother asked.

"No, dear. She's at the top of her class, she's won all sorts of honors, she's scored just about as high as humanly possible on the law school admission test, and she wants to go to law school. When we hire young lawyers at the office, that's exactly the background we look for."

"I should have known you two would conspire. This is just because you are a lawyer."

"It is not. I did not follow my father, and there is little I can do for Sandy. You know as well as I do how this town works. Nepotism is a kiss of death. My Dad was in the second tier at GM. American, Chrysler, and Ford recruited me; GM wouldn't even interview me; and I knew better than to try."

"Yes, dear, we've heard it a thousand times. You're a lawyer. Now admit that you've unduly influenced your little darling."

"I have not."

"Mother, this is what I want."

"I will not have it. Women are not suited to be lawyers. If you become a lawyer, it will limit your opportunities. I suppose you want to go away to some east coast school."

"It would be an honor, but I haven't put in any applications yet."

"You will spend years preparing for a career for which you are not suited. You may say you want it, but you will live to rue the day you ruined your life." She tossed her linen on the table and stormed from the room.

Sandy and her father were used to the theatrics. Until she cleared the room, neither reacted. When she was gone, they both smiled, and her father winked. They knew it signaled her mother's surrender. After dessert, Sandy collected her school clothes, said goodbye to her mother through her bedroom door, and her father drove her back to Marygrove. For most of the drive, they did not talk. Finally, her father spoke. "Honey, there is a big difference between you and I. You have the fire. I don't. Never did."

"What do you mean?"

"I did well in school. It was hard not to do that with good parents pushing and the finest schools. I do very well as a lawyer. But honestly, it is not something that I ever truly wanted. I went to law school because I got out of college and didn't know what else to do. I knew I couldn't follow my father, and all my friends were going to law school. That's the simple truth. If you truly want something, you are much farther ahead than you can imagine. Someday, you will look back and see that."

"You say that, but you are at the top. You whisper in the ear of one of the most powerful business leaders in the world."

"That's exactly right. I whisper, step back, and blend into the furniture. I'm really no different than the other servants. I've read more and have a specialized vocabulary."

"Daddy."

"I'm not being cynical. It's just the way it is. I'm not complaining. We have a good life. I'm content. You are different, that's all."

"Harvard is not known for mediocrity."

"You are missing the point. Since you were a little girl, you moved right to the center of the action, whether it was in a field hockey game, or school, or whatever. I remember once when we had a dinner party, you were about ten; no, you would have been eleven because it was the election year, 1960. Your mother dressed you up and paraded you in for an introduction before dinner. A few minutes later, I found you in the library umpiring an argument between two drunks over Nixon and Kennedy. You dismissed the missile gap and economic issues and urged that the best test of the men was a close reading of their positions on the Nuremberg trials. Who knows where you got that. Those old boys still inquire after you at The Club."

"Daddy."

"Don't miss the point. People like me walk into a room and hold back to survey and critique. You go for the action. People like me end up talking to each other about people like you. We may love you or hate you, but we talk about you. People like you make things happen. In all of Chrysler there are maybe six people who make things happen. That, my dear, is the first tier. The same is true at Ford or GM, or, for that matter, the United States government."

"Do you think I would make a good lawyer?"

"Honey, that is your decision. If you want the first tier, it is yours. I have always known that you would excel at whatever you do in life." He turned the car into the campus entrance and rolled to a stop under the leafless trees in front of the liberal arts building. "You may think that your mother is overprotective, but let me tell you something; if you think you are ambitious, you should take a hard look at her life."

Sandy leaned across and kissed him on the cheek. "Thanks, Daddy, I love you."

"Sandy, for your mother's sake, you might consider a law school close to home. I will never admit to saying it, but you can get just as good a legal education at Michigan or Notre Dame as at my alma mater."

Standing under the clock of the elegant Tudor Gothic building, Sandy watched him drive off through the mounds of snow. She took in a deep breath of the bitter cold air. It invigorated her.

CHAPTER 2

When her parents had dropped her off at Marygrove to begin her freshman year in September, 1967; the exhilaration Sandy felt was born of trepidation. Now it flowed from conquest. She strode proudly down the corridor of the Madame Cadillac Hall. The clap of her steps on the oak floor echoed and put her in mind of that first busy day, when her parents helped her with her luggage along this same hall. She took in the scent of a fire from one of the terra cotta fireplaces in Denk-Chapman Hall. She recalled the first time she smelled it during a tour after her admissions interview. She made her way around a corner and into the adjacent Florent Gillet Residence Hall. She exchanged pleasantries with Sister Mary Paul while signing back in. She passed the suite she previously shared. When she closed the door to her private room, she heard her mother's voice. "Sandy, you'll be happy here. This is perfect for you. The world is crazy. There are values here. You will get a good education. You will meet the right kind of people."

She had rushed her parents out on the excuse of being late for an orientation seminar, kissing them good-bye on the steps to the entrance of the residence hall. Her father had been silent during the drive over, throughout the unpacking, and continuing through the drive back to Grosse Pointe. He had left the parting advice to his wife, but he had quietly placed his business card on the desk in Sandy's room, hoping she might take the hint to call him.

To that point, Sandy's admission to the small, prestigious school was the crowning accomplishment of her mother's life. In her mother's view, Sandy was perfectly positioned for the future. It was far from an accident. It was the result of a subtle lobbying campaign that spanned years. From Sandy's junior year forward, her mother had worked around the advice of guidance counselors at Detroit's elite University-Liggett School who were nudging Sandy east. There, Sandy was at the top of her class. There was also the problem of her father, who was active in the Detroit Harvard Club and assumed Sandy would go to Radcliff. Her mother had taken the tack of encouraging Sandy to consider every school that was mentioned. They wrote for catalogs and discussed them. Her mother's device was to talk about each in comparison to Marygrove. The average test scores were higher, lower or the same. The library had more, less or the same number of volumes. Her mother found excuses to drive her by the Marygrove campus. How could any school match the architecture or private dormitory suites. She advised Sandy to look for that during her other campus visits.

Throughout, Sandy thought that her mother had only one object, keeping her close to home. Sandy put that aside, for somewhere along the way she had become genuinely attracted to Marygrove on its own merits. Unbeknown to her mother, Sandy was most attracted by its bragging tradition that it molded independent women for leadership. Her mother knew of the claim, but dismissed it as inconsistent with a religious girls' school. Instead, her mother was reassured by the hovering IHM's, the Sisters, Servants of the Immaculate Heart of Mary, and her knowledge of the family backgrounds of most of the students. In that, her mother's trust was misplaced. It would take Sandy years to appreciate just how thoroughly the philosophy permeated the institution, and how perfectly that philosophy suited her.

On her mother's part, keeping Sandy close to home was more related to the auto industry than family ties. Neither Sandy nor her father appreciated that. Her mother would never admit it; and among her peers, she never had to, for it was understood. She wanted her daughter to move up, to find a man who would make it to the first tier. Her mother felt that no man could do that in Detroit without the right woman, bred and trained for the role. They were second generation, second tier. Although her husband did not have the disposition to move higher, her mother believed that it was her own background that held him back. She looked rich, and no different than any of the other mothers who dripped in jewelry and wore white gloves and fur coats to drop their children off at school before they flocked into The Grosse Pointe Club to play bridge; but her mother's background was not what one supposed.

She had grown up on a farm outside Wichita, Kansas, one of seven children in a family of German extraction. Their farm was not in the worst of the Dust Bowl, but it could not support the family. They were able to keep it because her father got on as an aircraft worker at Beech. Mr. Beech hired him because he believed that a farmer would have a strong work ethic. Mrs. Beech kept the books and brought him his paycheck each week. Her brothers worked the land after school, and her father farmed until late at night. It was never clear to her if her father had been drafted into World War II or had enlisted. In either event, there was a family story that Mr. Beech was somehow involved. Her father ended up in the Army Air Corps assigned as an inspector of the bombers Ford built at Willow Run. She carried vivid memories of riding from Kansas to Michigan in the back of a pick-up. Her oldest sister married and stayed in Wichita. Her two older brothers both went into the Navy. The farm was rented out. The rest of the family crowded into a small rented house in Ypsilanti.

In Michigan, she did not return to high school. Instead, she got on the line at Willow Run, spending three years mounting plexiglas windscreens in B-24's. For the last two years of the war, she went to business school at night. That led directly to a secretarial job at Willow Run when production started winding down in 1945. After that, she campaigned for and eventually got a transfer to Ford HQ in Dearborn. There she spent three more years, first in a typing pool, then as a secretary. At the end of the war, her father, mother and her younger brother and sisters returned to the farm in Wichita. Her father took the lessons of Willow Run back to Beech. She felt that Wichita held little for her in comparison to the excitement of young men returning to post-war Detroit. Her parents were not happy with her choice, but she ended any discussion in the blunt statement that she could and would support herself. She took an apartment in Garden City with two other secretaries.

Sandy's mother and father met in the front office at Willow Run during the summer of 1945. She had recently transferred in from the line. He had a summer job as a mail boy. In the morning he pushed a cart to deliver the mail; in the afternoon he was a runner for the engineering department, constantly carrying drawings out into the plant. His father at GM had made a few calls and quickly gotten him the job at Ford. It was part of the unwritten code of cross-pollenization that all the automakers honored. Such jobs were typically held for the sons of executives. These jobs were a crash course in the organization of large industrial plants and corporate culture for one inclined to pay attention to what surrounded the menial tasks. He had just graduated from Harvard, and had gone straight into the Army after four years of R.O.T.C. He had been sworn in as an officer, and forever listed himself as "Lt., U.S. Army" on his resume; but he was never issued a uniform, and he had been sent home two weeks after VE Day. His father arranged the summer job, and he scrambled an application to Harvard Law. He returned to Boston that fall, but before he did, he had fallen in love with the petite blond farm girl/aircraft worker/secretary.

They were married at a country church in Kansas in August, 1948. She had wanted a June wedding, but he spent the summer cramming for the Michigan Bar at the end of July. Among his first assignments for Chrysler, as he waited for the results of the bar exam, he was to monitor the U.A.W.'s involvement in the 1948 election campaign. He invited his pretty young wife to accompany him to observe Truman address a Labor Day Rally in downtown Detroit. Afterwards, during their picnic, she told him she was pregnant. The excitement of this news merged with his impression of the huge political rally, and carried over into the tone of the memo he wrote the next day at the office. He wrote a memo predicting Truman's victory. Other similar memos, all comparing the massive crowds along Truman's whistle stop campaign to Dewey's staid after-dinner speeches to contributors, were noticed and branded absurd. After the election, however, they were remembered as insightful and prophetic. His career leapt forward. Later strategies for labor negotiations were built around his memos about the idealism of the Reuther brothers. It was only natural that the big egos, absorbed in their own reflections, would come to rely on his observations and insights of their counterparts. He was well on his way to becoming a high priest of the big deals. Their first and only child, Sandra Lee Cook, was born the following Spring.

In Sandy's youth, her mother took her for extended summer visits to her grandparents' farm in Kansas. Her grandfather, then a foreman for Beech, always took them on plant tours. On those occasions, Sandy was wonder struck at the conversation between her mother and grandfather. It was like listening to her uncles talk to him about farming. They spoke easily in a language she did not understand. She would always remember the rows of planes in the plant; and when she recalled them, it was always flavored with a sense of some wonderful mystery that her mother and grandfather shared in a time long before she was born. Sandy also recalled how Mrs. Beech, who wore the same heavy bracelets, earrings, and necklaces as her mother, always took time to speak directly to her and always remembered her name. Her grandfather told her that Mrs. Beech ran the operation, and although she did not believe him, what she saw confirmed it. This memory also carried an embedded mystery of how an elegantly dressed woman came to give orders to men.

Sandy had not grown up thinking of herself as privileged or rich. Without siblings, she was drawn to her cousins. She was the same age as two of the girls in Kansas, and for a time she thought of them as sisters. She wrote them frequently until high school. Gradually, she stopped liking the visits to Kansas. It wasn't that her relatives' homes were ordinary and small, but that they all seemed so complacent. They seemed satisfied with little, when to her it seemed so easy to want and to get more. Any of them could be like Mrs. Beech, but none of them ever would be. Sandy was more at home in the circles within which they moved in Detroit. She preferred the pool at The Club and power boating with her friends to sitting in Kansas kitchens hearing the tired stories again. By the time Sandy got to college, she no longer kept up with her relatives and declined her mother's invitations to accompany her to Kansas. The truth was, her mother did not like to go either, but it was easier to go there than to try to make them comfortable in Grosse Pointe.

The truth also was that they were not rich. By the time her father paid the jumbo mortgage, the servants' salaries, the fees at The Club, and Sandy's private school tuition; they were left living from paycheck to paycheck. There was an inheritance from his father, but that was never discussed in detail in front of Sandy. She knew that it involved annual visits to a lawyer and accountant, and was only lightly referred to as her father's safety net if he ever got caught by one of the recurrent waves of reorganization that swept through the automakers. They may have looked and acted rich, and they certainly enjoyed all the privileges Detroit had to offer; but like the vast majority of the Motor City, they also were only a paycheck away.

Through a friend, Sandy's mother made sure her photograph and the news that she was graduating summa cum laude from Marygrove got into the Free Press and also The Club's newsletter. She would have preferred a wedding announcement to the closing note that Sandy would attend law school at The University of Michigan. At least, Sandy would be close to Detroit.

Throughout the graduation exercise, Sandy's father blushed and could not have suppressed his proud smile had he tried. Listening to the speeches, he thought only of how quickly she had grown to be a woman, a beautiful woman. Now when he looked at her, he could not help but think of his wife in her youth. Her mother sat quietly thinking of her own years on the Liberator line at Willow Run. Although Sandy frequently asked about that time, her mother avoided answering. What Sandy knew, she got in small pieces from her grandfather and her cousins when she was young. Her mother knew exactly how far she had come from Kansas, never forgot it, and had no intention of jeopardizing anything by Sandy's loose talk to her friends. Her mother started thinking ahead. She would have to work with this law school business. It was a hurdle, not a barrier. She could handle it. With Sandy in Ann Arbor, they could still have Sunday dinner with her at The Club. There was always the chance that Sandy could meet some nice young man also having dinner with his family. She reminded herself to call the law school for a student directory. There might be an opportunity there.

CHAPTER 3

I noticed Sandy on the first day of law school, Torts I. She was below in the second row center of the amphitheater-style classroom. I settled in ten rows above as a natural back-bencher. I had spent enough time in school to have learned that those first few days were the time you found friends that would stay with you for the duration. The guys in the back row were easy acquaintances and fast friends.

There was no doubt that she was the most attractive female in the room, and so far as I had seen, in the law school. My first reaction was that she had class. There was no substantial difference in her clothes from anyone else. Just about everyone wore canvas shoes, jeans, and sweat shirts. There was, however, a material difference. She wore designer jeans. Her sweat shirt bore no logo. Every time she turned, I noticed the earrings, large gold lumps. They looked expensive. Had I known how expensive, I might have moved down closer. Sorry, I'm really not that cynical. As it was, I found her pretty and a pleasure to view; but I can't recall ever being attracted to her.

I don't think it was the socio-economic/cultural thing, although she was clearly from a different world than I. Knowing me, it was the fact that she was one of those down front types. They always rushed into a classroom as the last class left to stake out close seats; always asked a lot of questions; always had glib responses, even if they didn't know the answers. They all seemed so very genuinely interested in learning. Up in the nose bleed section, we looked on that as brown nosing. We only wanted to know what would be on the exam. Different worlds.

A few days later I saw her up coming out of an apartment across from mine up in Northwood. Those are apartments run by the university on the North Campus. I had lived off campus at O.S.U, but going into Ann Arbor cold, it seemed logical to move back into student housing until I got to know the place. Fact was, I lucked into a quiet roommate, and financially, you really couldn't beat the deal. With the shuttle buses running back and forth to the Central Campus, there was no reason to live downtown unless you wanted to be closer to the action. Ann Arbor is fundamentally different than Columbus. There, OSU is an enclave, surrounded by a busy city. Although both schools are Big Ten giants, Ann Arbor is a college town. Truth was, I liked Ann Arbor a little more. Nice town, no troops. I was as content on the North Campus as I had been off-campus in Columbus, and I spent the next three years there. Anyway, I saw her at Northwood, and on the buses a couple of times, but I didn't meet her until a few weeks into the term. By then people and things had pretty much settled into place.

I was sitting in the snack bar of the Law Quadrangle with a couple of my buddies, killing some time before class. Football season was underway, and as I recall, I was taking some ribbing from the guys about OSU Michigan and Ohio State have this rivalry; anyway, my friends at OSU hassled me about going to Michigan, and the same always occurred when anyone at Blue discovered that I had graduated from Ohio State. Sandy came away from the counter juggling her books, taking care not to spill a large cup of coffee, and looking for a place to sit. None of us knew her, but she came right over and asked if she could join us. After introductions, she asked what we thought of Hoffman, the Torts Professor. That was the end of the football discussion. Truth was, we were all so dumbfounded that she recognized us from class that we grunted lame answers, pro and con. There was a lull after that, then she shifted right over to politics. I think its fair to say that most of my buddies, like myself, were so absorbed in trying to keep their noses out of the water in law school, that politics was about the last thing on their minds. Sandy went ahead against the silence, opining that the Democrats should nominate a Washington, D.C. insider, like a senator, someone who could claim foreign relations experience. No governor would do. Nixon had gotten the peace vote in 1968, with his "secret plan", but he had failed to keep Viet Nam Lyndon's legacy. Now it was Nixon's war. The Democrats could use that against him. They had to nominate a major Senator with a conservative background. There was another silence as we looked at each other. Then she looked me directly in the eye, "What do you think?"

I doubt if Sandy realized it, but in that instant, she became my friend. She really wanted to know. Realizing that I might have an opinion that meant something to somebody was a new experience for me, and one that I liked. About the only specific questions that ever came from my circle of friends was if I had any copies of prior exams, where the party would be, and who was going to pay for the beer. She continued to probe my thinking while the others watched. I quickly realized that a mild disagreement with her fueled the discussion, so I went that route. I told her that Nixon was going down regardless. The Democrats should find a party man who was "presidential", but neither the candidate nor the Democrats would dare oppose the war. Most people liked the war, it reminded them of the good old days of WWII. Those that didn't would never admit it because of all the dead. It worked. She went on for half an hour, testing the specifics of my opinion from different directions, trying to harmonize my thinking with hers, trying to convince me she was right, openly admitting that I might just be right. When it came time to go to class, we left Sandy down front and settled up in the crow's nest. Naturally, my guys kidded me about hitting it off with her. I liked that too, but they were wrong. I knew she wasn't interested in me on the male/female level. The same was true with me. That spark just wasn't there. She did, however, impress the hell out of me. Maybe I was wrong about the down front crowd. Maybe not. Maybe she was just different than the rest of them.

Looking back, I can now see how that was a very intense time for me. Sandy was like a safe harbor in a storm. Michigan is a good law school. I was lucky to get in, and it was difficult for me to keep up. Although I hung with the same type of crowd that I did in college, my partying was more restrained. It was an occasional diversion, not an every night thing. Thank heavens for that, my liver got a reprieve for a couple of years. Most of my time was devoted to the pressure of the academic work, but much of it went to my National Guard duties.

That is a whole other story, but suffice it to say, that's how I disposed of my patriotic chore. I got a low number in the lottery, leaving me with the same few choices that were available to all male members of my generation: wait and get drafted, enlist in something, Canada, and conscientious objection. Anything other than acquiescing to the draft required quick action. Because of that pressure, the next time I got stopped by the NG on the OSU campus, I asked about the Guard and ended up getting a big sales pitch. If I did it right, I could stay in school, and never do much more than go camping with friends. Even the troops on the OSU campus were on a two week rotation, so getting activated was not a realistic consideration. I got really bummed when Joe's baby died, and later when Molly...; anyway, I came close to letting the draft run its course; but I finally went with the Guard. In fact, I was so busy with enrolling, finding a unit, attending basic then summer camp, and finally moving to Ann Arbor that, except for Molly's funeral, the summer after college I had no contact with Joe. I should have found time. I even avoided Attica. I may not have been an anti-war protestor, but I had no intention of helping to make more bombs. Anyway, I got into a Toledo unit, so one weekend a month I drove down for NG duty. Most other weekends I studied a little harder than everyone else. Since I lived up on the North Campus, and my apartment was a quiet place to study, I wasn't a fixture in the law library like so many others. Except for my roommate, my back row buddies, and Sandy, I never met many of my fellow law students, didn't have time, and didn't really care.

You know, there was another instance that fall that I remember about Sandy. One day I lost track of time studying, and the bus was slow in traffic. I rushed up for class, half out of breath. Luckily, I was early, the other class was still in session. Sandy was talking with a cluster of her friends. They were poised in their usual spot, waiting to spring into the classroom and grab the seats they thought that everyone wanted. She saw me and motioned me over. "I need to know what you think about something. I'm on the Student Bar Association, ABA Liaison Committee. We're meeting this afternoon. Is there anything you think we should be doing for law students?"

"Yeah, right. How about making law school easier? How about getting me a job if I live through this torture?"

"You're not the first to mention that. You see, we do have valuable input with the ABA on uniform standards for the on-campus interviewing and job offer process."

"What's that mean?"

"That things like on-campus interviews be held everywhere at a designated time, that deadlines be set on notification of summer clerkships and job offers so that you can plan your life."

"Sounds good to me. Yeah, tell your committee that I'm all for anything that helps me make sense of my life."

"Thanks. If you think of anything else, let me know. I'm really interested in hearing what you think. I can make it an agenda item." Had it been anyone else, I would have muttered about putting it where the sun doesn't shine; but it was Sandy. Before I had time to think that through, she continued. "We were just talking about whether law school is just another trade school or an intellectual pursuit. What do you think?"

That was Sandy.

CHAPTER 4

The University of Michigan Student Bar Association / American Bar Association Liaison Committee held its second meeting during the fall 1971 term in one of the several elegant conference rooms in the Law Quadrangle. The paneled room was furnished with leather chairs and focused on a fireplace on the south wall. Five of the six committee members attended. Sandy was the only first year member. The committee gathered at one end of the room. Except for a large red headed fellow sitting next to the fire reading a paper, there was no one else in the room. Sandy had not seen him before. She took him to be an associate professor not just because he wore a coat and tie, but because his coat was rumpled corduroy and his slacks khaki. He seemed to ignore their proceedings. Sandy duly reported on the student concerns she had heard. Their chairman reminded everyone to attend the speeches by the delegate candidates scheduled for 7:30 P.M. that evening in the same room. Sandy had planned on going back to her apartment, but she decided to stay at the Law Quadrangle and study, grab a sandwich, and attend the session.

Sandy was a joiner with a long list of extracurricular activities in college. During law school orientation, she made the rounds of the tables staffed by the various student organizations, and decided to get involved only in the Student Bar. In her opinion, there were only two groups that carried any real weight, the Student Bar and Law Review. Law Review was an academic honor by invitation only, leaving the Student Bar. Unlike college politics, the Student Bar was connected to the world outside the university. Belonging to it made Sandy feel that she was part of the profession.

Sandy returned to the conference room a few minutes before the meeting. She recognized the President of the Student Bar Association, a second year student who spoke at her first committee meeting, and two other students from her committee. There were about a dozen others in attendance. A small group whom she took to be the core leadership stood talking near the fireplace. Among them was the red head whom she had seen earlier. Standing, he was well over six feet, half a head taller than anyone in the room. He was fleshy, not the slightest bit athletic, but not fat either. Within the group, he spoke, the others listened. Sandy found a chair close to the front. The President called the meeting to order.

He explained that the meeting was intended to introduce the candidates who were running to be student delegate to the ABA He described the position as involving travel for committee work, and also the opportunity to attend seminars, to observe the ABA House of Delegates, and to attend the ABA convention the following summer. He also explained that the cost of the travel was borne by the Student Bar, and that the position was long regarded as the final position for students who had contributed their time and efforts to the Student Bar throughout law school. He said that he was pleased to say all the current candidates were distinguished members of the Student Bar, and recited their individual laurels as he introduced each in turn. The red head had an engineering degree from General Motors Institute and been last year's president.

Sandy took notes during the speeches. The first speaker was a disheavled anti-war activist who railed against the war without once connecting it to the Student Bar. The next speaker was an articulate black who promised to use the position to advocate social justice, in general; and more scholarship money for blacks, in particular. The third was a short, plump girl who wore wire rim glasses and advocated protection of the environment. She wanted the ABA House of Delegates to adopt a resolution in favor of a tougher Clean Air Act, speaking of the automakers as an enemy. The last, the red head, agreed that all those issues were important and should be raised at the appropriate times, but promised to carry specific proposals to a committee which was writing uniform standards for the interviewing and hiring process since that would directly and immediately benefit the members of the Student Bar. In the small room, the applause for each was polite and equal. After, Sandy deliberately stood to the side of the group clustered around the red head, waiting to meet him.

"Hi, I'm Sandy Cook, first year. I'm on the Liaison Committee."

"Right. I saw you here this afternoon. If you haven't figured it out, this room is the hang-out for the Student Bar. I find it more comfortable here than the library, although whenever I'm running I work the library for votes." He paused and looked into Sandy's smile, "I'm sorry, Daryl Dobbins. That was Sandy, right."

"Yes, Sandy Cook." She shook his hand.

"I'd appreciate your vote, Sandy."

"The students I've talked to are very concerned about standards for the hiring process."

"I heard you say that this afternoon. It's a traditional issue. Maybe we can make some changes."

"I think that most students will vote for you on that basis alone. You wouldn't get the weirdo vote anyway. It doesn't look like you have any serious opposition."

"Don't talk down my constituents. Most law students could care less about the Student Bar. Those that think about it see it as a place to make connections with firms. They join for that or some other kooky reason. Kooks or not, one man, one vote."

"Real politik."

"You a poli-sci major?"

"No, liberal arts."

"Where?"

"Marygrove. Ever hear of it?"

"Marygrove? Sure. That's where all the auto execs sent their daughters, right? Your father an auto exec?"

"Lawyer for Chrysler."

"Close enough. I went to GMI. Everyone there dreams of the first tier and the beautiful daughters at Marygrove."

"How'd you like GMI?"

"Actually, I didn't. Flint's a nice town, the campus is modern, it's a great education for the money, and I had an academic scholarship; but five years is a long time. I did get much better grades there than here, but this is what I want. I haven't got a clue what I going to do with an industrial engineering degree and a concentration in systems design. I also sat for the PE before law school, but I can't imagine practicing engineering, not now. I never thought I'd I like the law as much as I do. I only saw a good living. I really love it. You'd just never know it from my grades."

"Do you want to join one of the automakers?"

"With my grades, you've got to be kidding. They wouldn't have me. I would like to get on with a firm in Detroit, though; more money, plateau sooner. It's just these damn grades." He noticed someone else waiting and smiled to him over Sandy's shoulder. "Listen, it was good to meet you."

"Nice meeting you." They shook hands again.

"Remember, vote for Daryl." He smiled and slipped by her, reaching out for the next extended hand.

Sandy watched him for a moment, until she realized that she was starring. This was great. This was exactly what she wanted.

CHAPTER 5

The next time I saw Sandy was in the hall before a morning class. She saw me coming and motioned me over.

"Are you a member of the Student Bar?"

"I don't think so. Is it something that you have to join?"

"No, you don't have to join, but you should. You'll get ABA publications and start making valuable connections."

"Is this another front with phoney offices for the resumes of student politicos?"

"You're a cynic."

"Isn't that one of the qualifications?"

"The Student Bar can directly help you by injecting some fairness and certainty into the hiring process."

"I remember hearing this before."

"It's true. It can. There are a bunch of weirdos running for Student Bar offices, and there are a couple of good people. The good guys need your vote."

"I give up. How do I join?" Sandy retrieved a folded application from the back of her contracts case book. "Hey, this costs ten bucks!"

"Money well spent. Just fill that out and put it in the student mail to me. Don't forget or you won't be able to vote."

"Vote? I knew this was about politicos."

"Don't be cynical. Join and vote for Daryl."

"Daryl?"

"Daryl Dobbins. He's a good guy. Someday you can say you knew him when. Vote for Daryl. Tell your friends. Vote for Daryl." She laughed and sang it as she sauntered off down the hall.

That was how I came to know of Daryl Dobbins. Once I learned his name, I started seeing it everywhere. There was no mistaking a big man on campus. He was a regular in the law school paper, and also frequently quoted in the university paper. My theory is that those people write about each other, then sit back and count how many times they see their names in print. I'm serious. Anyway, I was very busy. I had better things to do, but I did join, and I did start getting the ABA publications. I also voted for Daryl. The others were seriously whacked.

CHAPTER 6

Waiting for her father, Sandy stood outside, protected from the rain by a covered walk that ran between two of the modern buildings in Northwood. He and her mother had brought her over in August, but they had not been back since. The residential buildings scattered along the curved streets looked much the same, and she was afraid her father would not find her's. From his long standing habit of picking her up at Marygrove on Friday evenings, she knew he would leave his office at 5:00 P.M. She came outside at 6:15 to watch for him. She had two bags, the smaller an expensive overnight bag with toiletries, but no clothes. There were plenty at home. The larger was a backpack, straining to contain the heavy load of case books. She bounced back and forth against the evening chill. She watched the succession of headlights reflecting off the wet pavement. Finally, she saw him and waved. In an instant she was inside the Imperial, and they were on their way home.

"This car's a couple of years old. Isn't it about time for a new one."

"Yes, but I like it. Each year they get smaller, lighter. Who knows how much longer you'll even be able to get a car like this. I like it. I think I'll hang on to it for a while. Tell me about school."

Sandy started with her courses, they were hard but she was keeping up. For the first time in her life she was studying something that she could see had an immediate, practical application. She liked it. She liked class. She liked the stress of responding. She could see the strain getting to others, but not her. Still, she thought the case method was a huge waste of time. They were struggling to extract the substance of each course from hundreds of cases, when the essence could be outlined in half an hour. You could even buy such outlines in the book store. She was nervous about having her grade for the entire term riding on one final exam, but she felt she knew the material. Her roommate was OK, shy. She was from Chicago. Her father was a CPA. Their classes were at different times, so they didn't see much of each other, except by chance in the Quad or late at night in the apartment. She was active in the Student Bar and was making friends there. She was surprised by the diversity. Almost one fourth of her class was female, ten per cent were black. Even the white males came in dozens of flavors. After being filtered through so much education, she had expected that the law students would be more alike. Her father nodded and smiled, but did not respond. Before Sandy had time to finish, they were pulling up the drive in Grosse Pointe.

Her mother was waiting inside the side door. Sandy left her bags there. Their cook was busy setting the dinner out as they came straight into the dining room. Her mother had a scotch waiting beside her father's plate. Sitting down in this room between her well-dressed mother and father, Sandy felt out of place in jeans. As she scooted her chair in, she lightly passed her hand over her hair to assure it was in place.

"Tell us, Sandy, have you met any nice young men?"

"Mother."

"I'm serious. Surely, there are nice young men in law school."

"Mother, I am not in law school to find a husband."

"I know that, dear. I am only inquiring after your social life. Law students are allowed that, are they not?"

"I am very busy with my studies. I also have committee work for the Student Bar Association."

"That is what I was asking. Does the Student Bar ever have parties? Your father used to write me about all the mixers he did not attend in fidelity to me."

"Mother, there is more to life. I am very busy. That is why I haven't come home weekends."

"Sandy, I remember a case we had in Contracts, I've forgotten the name, but it was a warranty claim against a surgeon for a defective skin graft. The poor fellow was left with hair growing in the palm of his hand. We called it the "hairy hand" case. Do they still teach that?"

"Hawkins v. McGee, holding for the plaintiff, but limiting damages against the surgeon. Contract damages, not pain and suffering, were awarded on the basis of an express warranty. The case teaches that contractual remedies are not an adequate alternative to tort for plaintiffs in medical malpractice cases, and suggests viable contractual defenses for defendants."

"Good for you. I remember now. Twenty five years later, but I remember. How about Hadley v. Baxendale? Have you read it?"

"Damages for breach of contract are limited to those reasonably foreseeable at the time of the contract."

"Jacobs & Young v. Kent? Now that one, I still use from time to time."

"The flexible standard of substantial performance."

Her mother finished her meal without looking up from her plate. Sandy and her father ignored her and continued to play legal trivia. They moved from contracts to torts. This time they talked about proximity and reasonably foreseeable victims. He wanted to compare her edition of Prosser to the one from his law school days. He still had all his law school books in the library. Much had changed. The hairy hand surgeon would no longer get off so lightly. After dinner, Sandy went upstairs to bathe on the excuse of still being chilled. She lounged in the bath for more than an hour, then went directly to bed.

The next morning, when Sandy came down for breakfast, she found her mother having coffee alone in the kitchen. Sandy poured herself a cup and sat down with her.

"When did you start drinking coffee?"

"I couldn't keep up without it. I've gotten to crave the taste."

"It's an acquired taste. When it starts tasting good, you're hooked."

"I guess."

"Your father's already gone to the office. He'll be back for lunch. What are your plans?"

"Study. Study. Study." There was a silence. Sandy refilled her coffee cup. "I guess I'll get started."

As Sandy went through the kitchen door, her mother called after her, "I only want what's best for you."

Sandy brought her books down to her father's library. She had so much reading, she did not know how she would finish it all. She determined to follow a rotation, spending an hour each on Contracts, Property, and Torts, before beginning again. At each change in the rotation, she emerged from the library long enough to relieve herself and get another mug of coffee. At noon her mother came into the library and asked her to look out the window. Sandy did and saw her father standing beside a new, economy-sized Plymouth.

"Well, what do you think?" Sandy did not react, her eyes were still bleary from the law books. "It's for you, dear." Sandy hugged her mother then kissed her cheek. She trotted from the library and joined her father outside. She circled the car a few times, expressing her disbelief and thanks. He urged her into the driver's seat, and they went for a ride, leaving her mother standing in the side door.

"This will make life so much easier. I won't have to rely on buses. I can take a drive in the country if I want to. I can come home without inconveniencing you."

"Your mother thought that maybe you would come home more often if you could drive yourself over for a few hours. You get a break, we get to see you, and you can stay on top of your studies."

"So why didn't you say anything. Why the surprise?"

"Why not?" They cruised among the mansions for several minutes before he continued. "Actually, I forgot about my executive choice this year. I got a memo a couple of weeks ago reminding me of my options and the deadline. You need transportation more than I need a new luxury car. I talked it over with your mother and here we are. I hope you like the color. She chose it."

"I do. I love it. This is perfect. You couldn't have done anything better. This is going to change my life."

As they pulled into the drive, her father cleared his throat. "Sandy, your mother loves you. She only wants you to be happy."

After lunch in the kitchen, which her mother made, Sandy gathered her books from the library. Her father volunteered the room to her, but she refused, knowing his habit to spend Saturday afternoon reading and drinking. After another three hours of study, she came downstairs. Her father was asleep on the sofa in the library. She took her mother for a ride. They drove north along Lake St. Clair through Grosse Pointe Farms and Grosse Pointe Shores. Neither spoke. When they got back, her father was still asleep. Their cook came in for two hours on Saturday just to make the evening meal, and walked up from the bus stop three blocks away shortly after they returned. Sandy and her mother dressed for dinner. That evening, they sat quietly together watching TV. After the Jackie Gleason Show, Sandy went to her room where she fell asleep reviewing her notes. She kept her notes on yellow legal tablets for the obvious reason.

The next morning Sandy woke, showered, and returned to her studies wearing a long terry cloth robe. After an hour she dressed and came down to her parents at their customary stations at the kitchen table where they shared the Sunday paper. Shortly after they left to attend high mass at 10:00 A.M. They took their traditional pew off on the right side. Sandy spent much of the mass absentmindedly starring at the stained glass window to her right. At the base of the window a brass plate proclaimed: "Presented by the Cook Family". Sandy tried to calculate when her parents had donated the window. There was never a time that she could not remember sitting beside their window. She remembered a snapshot of her mother and father standing beside the window with the artist. She was not in the photo, so maybe it was before she was born. She would dig out the photo and see if it were dated. It was not likely they donated the window before she was born. They didn't have that kind of money then, although it would be like her mother to establish them with the Church first. She could ask her mother. After mass, Sandy slipped her hand into her mother's. They walked out arm in arm. Sandy forgot to ask.

From Church, they drove directly to The Club. Henry, the doorman, made over Sandy, having not seen her for nearly two months. He complimented her parents, and called for James to take their coats. They stopped at half a dozen tables to exchange greetings as they made their way to their own. Throughout their meal, others stopped at their table. Scattered about the room were young families with meticulously dressed children, old couples, and large tables seating three generations. There wasn't a single other person Sandy's age, although there was much talk of sons in college and graduate school by those they greeted. Usually, the mothers promised to exchange the addresses of their children so they could correspond. Sandy was used to getting those from her mother, but she never wrote, and she never received any correspondence.

Near the end of the meal, Sandy thanked her parents again for the car. Her mother smiled but did not respond beyond that. Her father reminded Sandy that it was a responsibility and warned her not to loan it out. He paused, then told her that she was a woman and soon to be a professional. Somehow that had slipped passed him until her mother reminded him that Sandy was nearly as old as her mother had been when they married. At Sandy's age, they had been through a war, and her mother had worked for six years. It was appropriate that a professional woman should not have to rely on others for transportation, but it was also a privilege that Sandy should not abuse. Sandy nodded, studying her mother each time her mother looked away.

That afternoon Sandy drove herself back to Ann Arbor in the new car. It was an adventure for her, more so even than her initial move over for law school. Every Sunday after that, it became her custom to drive over to Grosse Pointe for mass and dinner at The Club. She would meet her parents at the house for coffee, then follow them in her car. She always left directly from The Club. She got back to her apartment by 3:00 P.M., changed, and was down at the Law Quad by 4:00 P.M. The arrangement proved to everyone's liking.

CHAPTER 7

One Thursday morning in early November Sandy went to the Student Bar's conference room to study between classes. She had begun spending more and more time there. Stepping from the bustling hall into the quiet paneled room, was like stepping out of the present into a timeless oasis. She found that the cases she read in the comfort of this room seemed to be more studies in human nature than legal posturing. Similar cases read in her apartment, the law library, or the snack bar were always colored by the manic frenzy of preparing to respond in class and defend her interpretations. Here she recognized that her studies were calm and efficient. For that reason, it had become her venue of choice. Whenever she entered, she had a quick memory of her father.

Rarely were there ever more than a few other students in the room. This morning Daryl Dobbins was the only other person. He was sitting next to the fire, reading a newspaper. Sandy unpacked her books at the other end of the room. As she started to sit down, Daryl folded the paper in his lap and said good morning. Sandy smiled, stood back up, and went to him. She stood looking down on him.

"How've you been?"

"Oh fine, I guess. It's offer letter season. So far, I'm not doing very well. Of the six firms on my short list, I've gotten three 'nice knowing you's' this week. Listen, I never got to thank you for your help in the ABA Student Delegate election. I'm flying over to Chicago this afternoon for a meeting tomorrow. It's an all-expense-paid distraction that I really need right now."

"I thought first year was bad. Whenever I look at you guys holding your breath, or think about the bar exam, I'm not so sure."

"It doesn't get any better. You just get used to it." Daryl folded the paper again and laid it on the table at his side. He looked around the room, then back to Sandy. "I really love this place. I'm going to miss it."

"I know. When I come in here, I feel like...I feel like I'm part of it; centuries of tradition."

"You're right. I know that feeling. Getting these rejections has cut like a knife. I've been thinking a lot about why I came here. I really want it. I really want to be a lawyer. Now its getting down to whether or not the profession wants me."

"You'll do fine. I do know what you mean. I want it too. My mother doesn't understand. My father says he does, but I'm not so sure."

"He's a lawyer, right?"

"Yes, but he says he never really wanted it. I think he understands. He calls it 'the fire', says I've got it."

"I think he's probably right. I thought I had it." Daryl looked from her to the fireplace. "So here we are. Everyone out there is scurrying to get it. We hide in here convinced that we've already got it. If you've got it, how does anyone else know that? How do you get recognition?" Sandy stood silently, also looking into the fire. Daryl stood. She barely reached his shoulders. He was twice her bulk. Fully extended, he looked down on the top of her head. "I'm sorry for the heavy duty rap. It's the damn letters. I do like talking to you. I really haven't talked to anyone like this since my Colonel in Nam."

"You were in Viet Nam?!."

"Another life. I've got a class."

"Your Colonel?"

"A great man. Without him I wouldn't be standing here. Sine qua non. It's a long story. Class." Sandy walked along beside him as he made for the door.

"How old are you anyway?"

"Twenty-seven. I got my draft notice my fifth year at GMI, '66. I worked a deal to enlist for the same two years with the Marines. Then I got all fired up, became an officer, and extended my obligation. I ended up in logistics, supply. Anyway, I spent a year in Thailand, got to be an aide to a Colonel, spent thirty days in Japan, then went back for a tour with him in Nam. Like every officer, I handled a few court marshals. That's where I got the bug. My Colonel recommended law school."

"The timing doesn't work. You're third year here. If you extended your obligation...there's not enough time."

"Like I said, it's a long story, and I'm late." Sandy stood looking directly at him, her demeanor demanding more of an answer. "Listen, a lot of things happened over there. My Colonel kept me in line. That's part of it, the brotherhood. On my own, I'd probably be running a bar in Bangkok right now, if not dead. Instead, I'm here on the GI Bill. He helped me get an honorable discharge as a conscientious objector, early out. I want this so bad I can taste it, and I owe him." They stood at the door looking directly into each others eyes.

"I understand."

"If you do, then you're the only one around here I've ever met who does. This place is full of children."

"I do." Sandy felt an urge to touch his arm and started to, but he turned for the door knob before she made contact. Half way through the door, he turned back to her.

"Listen, I'm not normally this intense. A lot of things are piling up on me right now. We're having a party at our house Saturday night. Would you like to come by?"

"Sure."

He scribbled the address and his phone number on a legal tablet, tore off the sheet, and handed it to her. "It's only a few blocks from here, over off Packard. I get back tomorrow night. I'll be around here all day Saturday. If I don't see you, just come over about 8:00 P.M."

Sandy settled back into her chair. Her heart was racing. She looked down the length of the room to the fireplace and did not open her books. She had never spoken so personally with anyone. More than that, she had a date, sort of. She had never been on a date. She could feel her heart. In high school, her grades made her remote, and she made herself aloof. At Marygrove, there wasn't much opportunity, and she avoided it. She put off her mother only by hanging with a group at The Club and boating with them. She took in a deep breath to calm herself. This wasn't a date. It was just a house party. It would be like boating with her friends, a group thing. She wondered about the war. Until this conversation it was little more than background noise for her. Her exposure to it was limited to TV news and petition tables around campus. It was not an issue high on the agenda at Marygrove, for no one there faced the draft. Instead, their social consciences had been directed at Detroit's inner city problems. She knew that war had shaped her parents and all their friends. Now this war pushed Daryl out of the pack, made him seem older, more mature, and closer to the mystery of her parents and the generation that ran things. Later that day, she drove by Daryl's house on her way home.

Driving to Detroit Metro that afternoon, Daryl tried to work off a knot in his chest. He went over and over his conversation with Sandy. Why in the hell had he told her so much? Even his roommates didn't know as much. He didn't care who knew. He wasn't hiding anything. He didn't care who she told. He just didn't like to talk about it. His resume showed his honorable discharge, not the reason. What in the world was it about her that made him spill his guts? She was pretty. He never thought he had a chance with a girl that looked like her. She was smart. You could tell within minutes of speaking to her. She seemed to draw him out, but he couldn't recall much questioning. When he realized that he had wanted to talk to her, to tell her, to keep talking to her; the embarrassment he felt shifted to excitement at the thought of the party. It would be a good evening, not just a routine drunk. He took a chill and his thoughts returned to the traffic. There was a heater in his MG Midget, but it only scalded his ankles. He could feel a cold draft up his pant legs. He could see his breath. Still, he liked the car. When friends saw him climbing into it, they teased that he wore the car and that he weighed more than it.

Walking among the business travelers in Metro, Daryl's thoughts returned to his career. He was jealous of all of them for they were established, had positions, places to go, families waiting at home. Carrying a briefcase and overnight bag, he did not look that much different than any of them; only his sports coat and slacks suggested he was a student. He carried his blue suit for the meetings tomorrow. During the short flight, he reviewed the materials they had sent. He knew the meetings would be perfunctory. It was the first for the new delegates. They were all staying at the Palmer House, and most of the meetings would be there. Several speakers were scheduled in the morning. After a break they were to get a tour of ABA headquarters before a luncheon. In the afternoon, they could attend organization meetings of the smaller committees they wished to join. It was scheduled to end at 4:00 P.M., giving him time to get back to O'Hare for his 6:00 P.M. flight.

He took a bus from the airport into the Loop. There were half a dozen others bound for the Palmer House. None looked like law students. On the way in he marveled at the skyline. He fancied that the parking garages might be higher than the tallest building in Detroit. He passed through a moment of self-congratulations, telling himself he had come a long way from Battle Creek, the son of an auto mechanic and school teacher. Then he thought about his career prospects. He desperately wanted to play in the big league. He did not have the money or patience to start a plaintiffs' practice. His prospects of getting in a big firm were dimming. Hell, he should have realized he never had a chance. He hadn't even bought a casebook or hornbook since his first term. He was not about to play that game, not when he could buy outlines in the book store. Fifteen minutes preparation for class made a lot more sense than ten hours. Anyone who played that game was a sucker, but then they made law review and got in the big firms. He wondered exactly when he changed. He had been an honor student at GMI.

He liked the lobby of the Palmer House with its marble, oriental rugs, and potted palms as much as the Student Bar conference room. After getting his room, he bought a paper and had dinner alone at a coffee shop in the lower level. Instead of returning to his room, he found a soft chair near the piano in the lobby. He sat there nursing beer after beer. Within an hour he spotted a group that looked like they were there for the same purpose. He took his beer and went over to them. They were. He introduced himself and shook all their hands. He liked meeting people. He did more than greet each one, he repeated their names and asked background questions. Within minutes, everyone in the group was listening to his opinions. He got very drunk, and came to the first meeting in the morning with a headache. He individually greeted each of the fellows from the night before, repeating their names and wishing them well. He deliberately left them behind and found new people to sit with. Throughout the day, with each break he took a new seat and made more friends. Coming back from lunch he passed a man who was on his way into another meeting room. They smiled at each other and nodded, each seemed to recognize the other, but Daryl couldn't place him.

That evening on the plane Daryl found himself across the aisle from the same fellow. Daryl saw he wore a Marine ring. Daryl also determined he was a lawyer from the documents he was busy reviewing and the yellow legal tablet on which he made notes. The fellow stopped working during the takeoff roll. After they were airborne, Daryl caught his attention. "Hi, Daryl Dobbins. Didn't I see you today at the Palmer House."

"Right. Frank Sloan. I thought I recognized you."

"I see you're a Marine." Daryl said gesturing at the ring. The fact that Daryl spoke in the present tense told much to Sloan. Others did their duty and recalled having been in the service. Marines were always Marines. Daryl did not wear the ring, but had taken his coat off before sitting and had rolled up his shirt sleeves exposing the tatoo on his forearm. Sloan took note of the tatoo and responded.

"Where did you serve, Marine?"

"Thailand, Nam, '66, '67 and '68."

"I finished my active in 1965. Did one tour in country, but I guess we missed each other."

"I see you're a lawyer." Daryl motioned at the papers.

"Yeah. Came over for a seminar today. I'm with Campbell Short in Detroit."

"Campbell Short! I clerked there last summer."

"You're kidding. Well, that explains it. I knew I recognized you. I'm in Mergers & Acquisitions. I don't recall you spending anytime with us."

"I didn't. I got rotated through Environmental, Immigration, Labor, and Litigation. I spent most of the summer in Litigation."

"Is that what you want, litigation?"

"It seems to fit, but I'm keeping my options open."

"Have you got an offer yet?"

"Still waiting."

"I know what you're going through. It doesn't get any better. I just made partner after five years of hell. The partnership committee put me through a wrath of bullshit interviews and evaluations after all that. All I can say is hang tough, Marine."

They compared backgrounds, colleges, law school, duty. Sloan had studied mechanical engineering, then gone to law school hoping to become a patent lawyer. He entered the Marines after law school when a recruiter lit his fire. He had been a JAG, did military attache embassy duty in Europe, and finished up prosecuting court marshals in Viet Nam. He thought he wanted litigation, but the only opening his first season was in corporate documents, so that is where he went and stayed. There was no way out now. He said he didn't mind. Daryl told him about being in Chicago as a student delegate to the ABA and his past political offices. Sloan did not seem to care. After a pause, Daryl returned to the Marines, talking about his service in logistics.

"Logistics, you ever come across Colonel Braun, world's greatest living logistician."

"I was his aide."

"I'll be damned, small world. I got to know him when I was handling court marshals. You know the drill, drinking and fighting. He always came and stood up for his men. He never testified. He just stood at attention in the back of the room. You know, as a prosecutor you want to win; but he always conveyed to the panel that they're findings were irrelevant. There was no mistaking that one way or the other, he was going to take care of the errant. His men respected him. That's where I picked up the logistician business, used to hear them say it."

"I owe him a lot. If not for him, I would never have gone to law school."

"Good man. Wish I'd known him better."

The plane landed. On the concourse Daryl saw that Sloan was hard muscled, ever a Marine. Daryl felt self-conscious about his weight. He was forty pounds heavier than when he was active and still gaining. He had no more use for exercise than study, and he loved beer. He did straighten to attention and return the vigorous handshake when they parted. Too bad he hadn't met Sloan that summer. Too late now. He ought to write Colonel Braun. He needed to do something about the heater in the MG. Sandy was really pretty.

CHAPTER 8

Daryl spent most of Saturday in the conference room. Whenever he left, he looked for Sandy. She was in the stacks of the library. It had been two and a half years since Daryl had been in the stacks. Then he had a research paper for Legal Bibliography and could find no way around the library work. Sandy was in the library because she had made a connection on Friday that intellectually stimulated her. She was going to the full text of cases that were abbreviated in her casebooks to see if her thinking was born out in the footnotes. It was, time and again, with each case she checked.

It came to her while reading a case in the conference room the day before. In itself, it did not seem so profound a realization. To anyone other than a law student trying to dig out of the countless details of hundreds of cases, it is simple. It could easily be told, but in law school it was guarded like a religious truth. It was simple, it ruled everything legal. Most students didn't get it. For them, it was dished out their final year in their Remedies class which pulled all the subjects together. It was the standard of reasonableness. All contract issues turned on what was reasonably foreseeable by the parties to the contract at the time of their contract. Recovery in tort came down to conduct limited by reasonably foreseeable harm to others, and damages were limited by the same standard. Technical details might control the property issues taught in class, but modern statutes assured that details were reasonably interpreted. The Supreme Court really didn't care what the constitution said, they did what they felt was reasonably necessary to keep the peace.

Sandy had stumbled upon the great truth and realized it. She had grasped the central organizing principle of the law. Further, she was on the verge of discovering the second great truth; that is, when the law failed to provide redress; there was an alternative in equity. When reason alone was not enough, the courts would retreat to conscience, and do what was fair. This was what the legend above the Supreme Court, "Equal Justice Under Law" was all about. Barely two months into law school, Sandy had found what the case method was designed to hide. Too many of her peers stumbled on in the darkness.

Daryl, for example, intuitively used what he called "the right thing" to control his examination answers. He used buzz words from the outlines to flesh up his result-oriented answers. His work pleased him, but it rarely got him more than an average grade. He reached the correct conclusions, and he felt the underlying rationale; but he never truly understood the subjects, nor knew why when he was right. Both Daryl and Sandy did have it, but on profoundly different terms. She came to it through intellectual analysis; he by gut reaction.

Twice on Saturday she checked the conference room for Daryl. Each time, she narrowly missed him. Late that afternoon, he caught a glimpse of her driving north up South State Street as he walked the other direction toward the house he shared with several other law students. Back in her apartment Sandy tried to share the truth with her roommate, but she didn't get it. They shared a light meal, and their discussions turned to the evening. Her roommate had a date. She also knew this was Sandy's first night out. When Sandy appeared in an expensive dress, her roommate sent her back to tone it down. She came out in plaid wool skirt, knee socks, and a sweater that was very much in keeping with the season.

Sandy parked just down the block from the Victorian frame house. Parking spaces were much easier to come by on a weekend night, than during the week. She could hear the music from the house as she walked up the sidewalk. When the President of the Student Bar greeted her at the door, she learned he was one of Daryl's roommates. The hall and living room were crowded. She recognized most of the people, but did not see Daryl. She saw a girl from her Torts class, and they were quickly in a discussion of the nuances of Cardoza's opinion in Palsgraf. Neither realized that Daryl had come up to them and was listening until he placed a hand on the shoulder of each. His face was already flushed with the beer and his eyes were glassy.

"Ladies, I hate to burst your bubble, but the amount of insurance coverage controls who recovers, not all that flowery language about zones of duty and proximate causation." He spilled a little beer on Sandy's friend, and they laughed as he stumbled out an apology. He led them into the kitchen where a keg of beer sat in a tub of ice and got them some in plastic cups. He chatted with them for a few minutes until another roommate came up to the keg. Daryl introduced him to Sandy's friend, then steered Sandy through a swinging door into a pantry that connected the kitchen with the dining room. There was another crowd in the dining room, so he stopped to speak with her in the pantry. "I see you didn't have any trouble finding the place."

"This is really convenient. I gather you walk to class. How was the trip to Chicago?"

"Fine. The hotel was great. The ABA offices were much bigger than I imagined. It was just a large collection of students. I met a lot of people from all over the country, but beyond that it was just another committee meeting. On the way home I did meet a lawyer from the firm I clerked for last summer. A fellow Marine."

"Think it will help?"

"No, too late for that."

"I got two more letters today. So far five out of the final six have shot me down."

"That's too bad. Were any from the firm where you clerked?"

"No."

"Well, there's still hope. If you don't mind me asking, and tell me if you don't want to answer, but why do you talk like you're still a Marine? Isn't that inconsistent with being a conscientious objector?" Daryl finished the beer in his German stein as she asked, then looked into the empty mug.

"I started drinking before the party, so I apologize in advance for anything I do or say. Please, stay here a minute while I get another round. Do you need any? OK, stay here. Don't leave. OK?" In a moment Daryl came back into the pantry, sipping foam off the top of his mug. "You know about Semper Fidelis?" Sandy nodded. "Here's how it works; it's not what they preach; but every Marine knows it. They put out that we're faithful to country, family, and the Corps in that order, and that sounds right and good. Well, we're faithful to each other. The Corps replaces family. If you have a wife and kids, they become part of the Corps. Country is irrelevant. That's only orders. There are good orders and bad orders. Marines stick together either way. It's a brotherhood."

"And you still think of yourself as a Marine?"

"I am a Marine."

"Do you think of yourself as a conscientious objector?"

"I am a Marine who adheres to the Catholic religion. I don't accept the just war business. I had a Marine priest who organized his life around that fact that God was always on our side. We used to go round and round. I go along with the Vatican II stand on conscience. I saw things that I cannot reconcile with my conscience or my understanding of the Church's teachings. I was part of a meticulously organized, expertly run, highly efficient and methodical killing machine. I just could not see that as God's plan for man. For those reasons, the Marines honorably discharged me from active duty. I'm a Marine, not a conscientious objector."

"I cannot imagine other Marines wanting anything to do with you, other than maybe to kick in your teeth."

"Well, you don't understand. I am a Marine. I did everything I was supposed to do, when I was supposed to do it. I kept the faith. When my conscience and religion started getting in the way, I talked to the proper people and filled in the proper forms. That Marine chaplain and my Colonel were more help to me than you can ever imagine, on every level, personal, professional, and spiritual. When I was discharged, I was saluted and I saluted back." Sandy shook her head. Daryl smiled. "Semper Fi. If I had run off, they'd have found me. We called it the Big Green, but the jungle wasn't that big. They'd have found me. If they brought me back, and that's a big if; I'd still be in a cell. There was no reason to run off, not from the Corps. I don't know a single Marine who hasn't felt something of what I felt. They understood. They respect honor. I did not dishonor the Marines nor myself. I honored them, and they honored me. No Marine would kick out the teeth of an honorable man. God, I love the Corps."

"You were cut from whole cloth."

"I wish you'd tell that to my parents. They don't talk to me. To them I'm a coward and a traitor."

"You want me to believe that a pacifist is a Marine, and parents who raise a devote son reject him for his faith?"

"Yeah, it goes something like that."

"It's a crazy world." Daryl touched his stein to her plastic cup, and they shared a toast.

"What about you? What's your story?"

"Nothing so mysterious. I'm an only child. You know my father is a lawyer for Chrysler, mergers and acquisitions. My mother maintains the social front. I was sent to the best schools in Detroit, University-Liggett and Marygrove. They want nothing but the best for me. I want to be a lawyer. They, at least my mother, thinks it will limit my choice of men. I want this so bad I can taste it."

"I know."

They spent the next two hours in the pantry. Others, making their way from the dining room to the kitchen squeezed past them and forced them together. Once, Sandy felt his breath on the side of her face and experienced an immediate bolt of longing. They talked mostly about school, the graduating senior giving advice on subjects and professors. Sandy wanted to know about law review, but Daryl dismissed it as a collection of elite snobs. Although he didn't say anything, when she brought up the subject, he thought of his summer in Campbell Short's library with the other clerks, all of whom were law review. They churned out flowing research memos, why he struggled with the indices. Sandy made excuses after her third beer, and Daryl walked her out to her car. He was very drunk and swayed as he stood in a cloud of his own breath watching her drive off into the night.

CHAPTER 9

Each member of Campbell Short's hiring committee received Frank Sloan's memo on Daryl Dobbins by mid-morning the following Monday. Sloan had dictated the memo while driving home from the airport Friday night. He had it, and a dozen other memos and letters, typed during his normal Saturday hours; and he signed it Monday morning. Daryl now had what every aspiring associate needed, a sponsor. Sloan's motives were simple. Now that he was a partner he could exercise a small degree of influence, and he intended to test it. The firm was full of nerds and wimps, whose presence was an irritant and embarrassment. If he was going to spend his career in the firm, he intended to influence its character. Dobbins was a Marine. That alone was enough of a reason, but there was more. He admired Colonel Braun. Any young man who had worked with Braun would have learned the fine points of character. Of course, none of that was in the memo. The memo merely recited the facts. Sloan had met Dobbins on an airplane and had a good discussion. The committee might not know that after his clerkship at Campbell Short, Dobbins had been elected an ABA student delegate. Sloan knew nothing of his grades, class standing, nor research and writing skills; but he suspected a diamond in the rough. Dobbins gave him the impression that Campbell Short would be his first choice.

The last item was a slight exaggeration. It was based upon Daryl's statement that he was keeping his options open. Sloan's interpretation was that Dobbins was most likely desperate and would take anything. What Sloan wanted was an offer. Dobbins himself was only slightly more than incidental. Sloan knew the firm was more likely to make offers that were certain to be accepted. Also, his memo deliberately did not mention any department or specialization. Sloan's own department had only one opening, which two other partners, the department chairman and the third most senior lawyer, had built a fence around to hold a Princeton magna and third generation lawyer. Sloan was not yet in a position to mentor anyone into a specific position, but a generalized sponsorship would be an appropriate test of his clout; and who knew, maybe he could help a fellow Marine.

Just before noon, the chairman of the hiring committee, C. Ellington Hale, IV, called Sloan to report on the status of Daryl Dobbins. The first wave of offer letters had gone out a week ago Friday. Dobbins had not been made an offer, nor had he been sent a rejection. The consensus was that, legally speaking, he was a light weight. His excellent academics at GMI, his military service, and his social skills were considered to have enough potential value for the firm, that he had not immediately been sent a rejection. His name was in the pool for the second round of offers to be made after learning which candidates would decline first round offers. If he were to be made an offer, it would have been in an "appropriate" department. Sloan understood that to mean a position with low visibility and low intellectual content. Hale went on to say that he had quickly polled the rest of the committee. They were in agreement that Dobbins should be extended an offer immediately, prior to the second round. Sloan did not thank him, but did say he was confident that the committee would not be disappointed. He hung up, unable to suppress the sweet smile of satisfaction. He had more clout than he thought. A few minutes later Sloan looked up from the asset purchase agreement he was drafting and out the window. He scolded himself in the realization that now he owed the hiring chairman and each member of the hiring committee.

Daryl did not have a class until 1:30 P.M. on Thursday, so he stayed around the house that morning to get the mail. He heard the mailman's steps on the wooden porch and retrieved the mail before the letter carrier was back to the sidewalk along the street. This was it. There was a letter from Campbell Short. It was thin and could only be one page. Daryl immediately concluded it was a rejection, like the others. His last hope was gone. He did not open it. He slid it into the inside pocket of his sports coat and gathered his notes. If he was looking at the end of his high powered legal career, he would do it the right way.

Fifteen minutes later he was in the conference room at the Law Quad warming himself at the fire. On the walk over, he had some non-specific thoughts about his alternatives. With his engineering background, he might still pursue patent law or finagle his way into the law department of a mid-size manufacturing corporation. It was a beautiful sunny day, and the sunshine diverted his thoughts. He settled into the leather chair next to the fire and watched it for a few minutes until he gathered his nerve. When he read the letter a hoop could be heard down the hall above the noise of the crowd.

"On behalf of Campbell Short I am pleased to extend.... Given current staffing, the offer is limited to a position in the Insolvency Department (formerly Bankruptcy), where you will report to.... The starting salary is $25,000...a signing bonus of $2,500...usual benefits, such as.... We hope you decide to join the more than seven hundred distinguished members of the bar who have been part of Campbell Short's 110 year tradition of service. Of course, you understand that all offers are contingent upon successful completion of law school and successful bar results upon first examination. Please reply in writing within...." He could not remember C. Ellington Hale, IV, and really didn't give a damn. It was party time.

Sandy found Daryl in the hall outside the snack bar about 4:00 P.M. that afternoon. He was loud and drunk. The circle around him was laughing. She quickly discovered his good news; nonetheless, Sandy felt that his conduct put him at risk. She suggested they go to the conference room more than once. Finally, she took his hand, leading him in that direction, and asking him for details. He was unable to communicate any. In the conference room, he collapsed into his favorite chair. He offered her the wrinkled letter that dozens of law students, half a dozen bartenders, and several total strangers had read. As she read it, he dozed off. She put the letter in his pocket and studied for an hour while he snored. When another student came into the room, she woke him and walked him home. At a stop sign he started to wander into the traffic. Sandy took his hand to keep him at her side. This time, she put her fingers between his.

At the house, his roommates had two cases of beer and a small collection of friends waiting. Sandy slipped into the background as another circle formed around Daryl. The president of the student bar pressed a beer on her. She sipped and watched, smiling. When Daryl got through the story and started the letter around the room, he saw Sandy and went to her. He put his arm around her and announced that she was his guardian angel, protecting him for the greater good of Campbell Short. Emboldened by the applause for Sandy, he kissed her on the lips, then stumbled across the room for a beer. Within fifteen minutes he was asleep on the sofa while the party continued around him. Sandy wrote "Congratulations" and her name and phone number on a yellow legal pad. She folded the note, put it in his coat pocket, and left. No one noticed.

Sandy woke to the ring of the phone beside her bed at 6:00 A.M. the following morning. As usual, she found she had slept on an open casebook. She recognized Daryl's voice.

"I'm really sorry. It's just...."

"No need to apologize, I ...."

"Whatever I did, whatever I said, I'm sorry. I had too much to drink."

"No problem, really."

"Well, I'm sorry. What I do remember is embarrassing."

"You don't remember?"

"Bits and pieces. I remember you at school, then walking, then at the house. Listen, it was the booze. That's not to say, I don't enjoy your company. I'm sorry if I embarrassed you. I embarrassed myself."

"No need to apologize. It was fun watching you celebrate. You're up early aren't you?"

"That's the problem with drinking during the day. I slept right through the party here."

"How do you feel?"

"Bad."

"I wish there was something I could do?"

"Forgive me."

"Forgiven."

"Good. I'm glad. I'd really like to go out with you. I thought I might have blown it."

"I'd like that."

"Great."

"When?"

"You are really something. You should think about litigation. Great interrogation."

"When?"

CHAPTER 10

Daryl took Sandy out to dinner that Saturday night. After the party Thursday, he gave himself Friday off. He walked over to the Law Quad only to rustle up some drinking buddies. He ran into Sandy in the conference room. There they agreed upon the particulars of their date. She gave him her address and directions. They would eat downtown then catch a movie. She wasn't interested in partying with his friends that afternoon. He left with his friends, and she returned to the stacks. Daryl and his audience did pitchers in a student bar on East Huron until he ran out of money. That was about 8:00 P.M. They had drunk their way right through dinner, but all were so bloated that none noticed. They left the bar together, but as they made their through downtown and along the edge of campus, one after another peeled off in their own directions. Daryl walked the last few blocks alone. He was too drunk for the crisp air to sober him, but it did wake him. He was also too drunk to care about talking to anyone or watching TV at the house, so he went to bed. He laid awake for awhile, wanting to call Sandy. He stopped himself. He was afraid that his drinking might make the wrong impression. Soon, he was asleep. He slept in the next morning.

Saturday, Daryl hoped that he might run into Sandy at the Law Quad. He got there mid-morning, and made the rounds looking for her. He checked the empty classrooms, the halls, and the snack bar before giving up and going to the conference room. He did not check the library stacks, where she was. He read the paper by the fireplace and then scanned a commercial outline for his Labor Law course. While such outlines were available for most of the courses, they were not for the more specialized elective courses that third year students usually took. That was the situation in his Creditors' Rights class. Fortunately, he had a friend who had taken the course last term and even participated in a study group. He had offered to sell Daryl their outline for $25.

Daryl was pleased when that friend came into the conference room. It was getting well into the term, and without books or a commercial outline, Daryl was flying blind. He reminded his friend of the promise. Soon they left for the friend's apartment. Daryl came back to the conference room where he looked through the outline then chatted with several second year students. He left for home at dusk.

Sandy left the Law Quad shortly after lunch. She spent the early afternoon sorting through her clothes. Although the date was hours away, her face was flushed and her ears burned red. Her roommate sensed Sandy's excitement. Sandy never confessed to her that this was her first date, and her roommate did not guess it. She thought that Sandy's tension was because Dobbins was a big man on campus and had an offer. To her, those raised the date above the level of an informal grad student Saturday night. She did try to get Sandy to do something with her hair, but that ended in Sandy rolling hers. Later, Sandy studied her notes for a few hours, then bathed and dressed.

Sandy's roommate greeted Daryl, placed him on the sofa, then excused herself with the instruction that Daryl was to answer the door. She was expecting her date, a graduate student in architecture. Sitting alone, Daryl surveyed the living room that continued into a dining area and open kitchen. It was easy to see women lived here. There were little touches everywhere, dried flowers, pictures on the walls, dishes washed and in a drainer; all this distinguished the inhabitants from those with whom he shared a house. Daryl was amused by the contrast. The architecture student arrived a few minutes later. He was Daryl's first architect. Daryl tried not to be too obvious as he took stock of the snake skin cowboy boots, silk clothes, lacquered fingernails, and pony tail. Daryl looked for beer in the refrigerator. There was only wine. Daryl avoided wine. The architect searched for a long stemmed wine glass for himself. While he did, Daryl went to the stereo and set upon finding a different radio station. The architect put the wine back when he could not find a satisfactory glass. Daryl smiled. Sandy came out first, then her roommate. During the banter, Daryl helped Sandy into her coat. As he did, he noticed her perfume, then pulled in a deep breath of the fragrance. It intoxicated him. He wanted to wrap his arms around her and kiss her neck. He stepped back, wanting to compliment her for how she looked and smelled, but he couldn't find the right words. The two couples walked out together and left in separate cars.

Daryl warned Sandy about the MG as they walked up to it. She had never ridden in a sports car. He opened the passenger door and helped her down into the car. While she waited for him to come around, she came to the quick conclusion that this son of an auto mechanic and alumni of GMI took no interest in cars. It was old and dirty. When Daryl got in, the situation was immediately intimate. His wide shoulders pressed well into her side of the car. Sandy held her legs together and pushed them against the door, still Daryl extended far enough over the edges of his bucket seat to be sitting tightly against her hip. For practical purposes they were separated only by the gear shift, but his movements in shifting made them even more familiar. Sitting at a stop light, Daryl worked the shifter through the gears. Trying to make herself more comfortable, Sandy adjusted herself and laid her hand on top of Daryl's. Looking ahead, he smiled, then asked if she liked Chinese. They ate at a Chinese restaurant on East Liberty just around the corner from the downtown business district.

During the meal he apologized again for his behavior Thursday. It was the beer. He had completely given up on getting into a big firm. Somewhere along the line he had forgotten what he knew going in, they wanted academics and law review, he had only his demeanor and politics. Last summer he had realized how out of place he was among the other clerks in Campbell Short's library; nonetheless, he held on to his delusion. Now he was in. He made it. He was riding high. Sandy asked if he thought he could take the long hours and hard work. Daryl avoided the question saying only that he had gotten through the front door and was out of the cold. She asked if he had planned for a career in bankruptcy, if he had taken extra courses in accounting and business. He laughed. She didn't understand. He had no illusions about that. He had no interest in bankruptcy. He had not expressed any such interest to Campbell Short. He had not been given any assignments in the area. His opinion was that they had an open slot, their first choice turned them down, and they didn't have anyone else interested. Sandy asked if he thought the fellow he ran into in Chicago might have played a hand in it. Daryl said no, but made a mental note to write Sloan a letter. He would not say thanks, for he wasn't sure. He would say he just got an offer and looked forward to working at Campbell Short. If Sloan had helped, that would cover it. If not, it was still appropriate.

Sandy was careful not to disclose her dismay. She had thought she understood this fellow. She thought she recognized the same ambition in him. She was finding out quickly how wrong her impressions had been. How could he or anyone come to law school, much less get most of the way through it, without having a specific career path in mind. How could he be so indifferent to a career in a particular field of the law. She made one of the elements of her studies the discovery of what fields she found most stimulating so that she could pursue one in practice. She tried to form a question to that end that would not offend him, but before she could, he returned to her question on the work load. He knew it would be difficult. He would be competing with the brightest, but they weren't necessarily the best. He couldn't wait to get in practice. He saw practice as the manipulation of power. Sandy started to say something about justice, but he cut her off. One thing was for sure. His income potential in a big firm was four or five times higher than anywhere else. He would work harder than anyone else. He wasn't going to let that kind of opportunity slip through his fingers. It was clear to Sandy that Daryl Dobbins was one who saw law school as a trade school, not an intellectual pursuit.

After a pause he asked Sandy what kind of practice she looked forward to. She had no answer. She said she liked all the first year courses. She was still feeling her way along. From what she saw of her father's work, he was either entertaining businessmen or drafting documents. Neither was her idea of practicing law. She wanted to work in the law. She loved the books, their smell, the stilted language, the struggle for logical reasoning. Every opinion, even the ones with which she disagreed, sought to set forth their reasoning in a rational, persuasive, and compelling form. Given the binding nature of legal precedent, she could think of nothing more exciting than the challenge that the only way to change the law was to find some fault in the careful logic of prior precedents.

Daryl told her that she had been seduced by the case method. The legal changes that made a difference were made by politicians. He reminded her that constitutions, statutes, and regulations set forth modern society's rules in infinite detail. Cases were important only when there was a close question of interpreting those rules. Rule number one was to read the rules. Law school missed that entirely. If that was not enough, the cases they taught were not really cases, they were opinions of appellate courts. Those opinions indicated little of the underlying disputes, many of which might have gone on for years before anyone ever sought out a lawyer. Then there was the little matter of pre-trial discovery, posturing, and trial. You could make a good living in the law and never take up an appeal. For that matter, you could make a better living doing deals and never going to any court. In his opinion, teaching law by the case method was like teaching medicine by limiting the students to autopsy reports. He bragged that he had not read a case in two years. Even in his writing at Campbell Short, he cited cases that the reference books indicated supported what he wanted to support, but he never read them nor digested their logic. He saw judges as result-oriented politicians. They would find the logic to do what they wanted to do. That's why they had graduate lawyers for their law clerks, all of whom were law review. The system generated rough justice, and the intellectuals could fill the law libraries with tidy logic.

Although Sandy had explored the trade school issue, much of what he said was new to her. Most of it rang true. All was grounded in his bluntly pragmatic outlook. Still, much of it offended her; for all she really knew of the law was her father's library, the stacks, the language, the logic. She put aside what offended her because she wanted to know more of this view. She drew him out with her inimicable questioning, "Do you really think...? Are you sure, what about...? Have you ever considered that...?" Daryl was used to keeping the attention of a group. Sandy made it easy for his speeches to go on and on. They kept ordering more tea and talking. They missed the movie, so they agreed to stay in the restaurant.

There was little of legal education that they did not consider. Daryl came squarely down on the side that law school was a empty tradition that taught vocabulary and library skills that were largely irrelevant to practicing law, but had the benefit of keeping immature students out of the marketplace for a few years. Sandy was not so sure. She didn't think so. When they noticed that they were the only ones left in the restaurant, Daryl paid, and they left. By then Sandy was again convinced that his perspective and ambition set him apart and made him appropriate for her. Daryl was convinced that, although she was an academic, she was genuinely interested in what he had to say. He hoped he hadn't bored her. She was so pretty, he couldn't believe his good fortune. He had never been out alone with a girl before.

It was snowing when they left. The snow was so deep that the doors to the MG scrapped arcs in the snow. Daryl deliberately slid the car a few times on the way back to Northwood. He laughed. It scared Sandy, but she did not complain. He walked her to her door. He asked if she would be around school the next day. She told him about her

Sunday ritual with her family, but said she would be back by the late afternoon. He said he would probably be in the conference room late Sunday. If she wanted, she could come by, and they could get a bite to eat. Sandy agreed with her smile and eyes. She did not speak. He leaned down. Before he could kiss her, she rose on her toes and kissed his cheek. He smelled her perfume again. This time he told her that he loved the fragrance.

CHAPTER 11

Sandy met Daryl Sunday afternoon. They ate together in the snack bar. Thereafter, they shared a meal at least once a day, usually lunch or dinner. More often than not, it was a sandwich in the snack bar. Occasionally, they got subs or chinese and took it to Daryl's house. At least once a week Sandy made dinner for them in her apartment. She had never cooked and approached the task as her education had trained her, in the library. Other than the time with Daryl, searching for recipes was her only diversion from study. She enjoyed it and put more and more time into it. At first she made Daryl responsible for the wine, but when he came with wine for her and a six pack for himself, she added wine selection to her shopping. She insisted he have wine with the meal, although he drank beer before and after. She also insisted on picking him up and taking him home in her car. She used the excuse of her own need to do library work or his drinking; he never opposed it, and he understood the real reason was either his car or his driving.

Neither had a class the Wednesday afternoon before Thanksgiving. It was an unusually sunny afternoon, and Daryl invited her for a drive in the country in his car before she left for home. Soon they were speeding over secondary roads in the rolling countryside northeast of Ann Arbor. He charged the curves. No longer so inhibited, Sandy scolded him when the rear tires broke loose, and they drifted through one curve. He slowed. A few miles later they crossed the Huron River just north of where the Honey joins it. He turned around and went back to park off the end of the bridge where they could see down the stream. Within moments they were in each others arms, ignoring the tight quarters and their heavy coats. Until this afternoon, their petting had been limited to a few minutes at his house or her apartment, always when they were about to part. Now they went further. After twenty minutes, Sandy pulled back and wiggled around until her back rested against his side. As they looked down the river, she asked about his Thanksgiving plans and was shocked at the response.

"How can you not go home for Thanksgiving? Your parents aren't more than an hour away!"

"It's easy. I'm not welcome."

"I don't believe that."

"I'm not."

"What are you going to do?"

"I'll get drunk tonight, sleep in, watch the parades and football, get a pizza, and get drunk again. It will be a quiet day."

"That's terrible! No one should be alone on Thanksgiving. What did you do last year?"

"Same thing. Listen, I haven't been home in years. It's no big deal."

"It's wrong. If you haven't been home, how do you know that you're not welcome?"

"When I was applying for my discharge, still in Nam, I got separate letters from both my parents which made their position crystal clear. One even said that it would be easier for them if I had been killed."

"Who said that, your father? A mother would never say that."

"It doesn't matter. I got the message."

"I don't. What's the message?"

"They are ashamed. I am a source of embarrassment. If I am not around, they do not have to be reminded of their failure."

"Failure? My god, you're deeply religious, an honors graduate of GMI, a Marine officer, a prominent law student, and now you've gotten an offer from the most prestigious law firm in the state. They must be so proud, they could burst."

"Not likely. I doubt if they even know where I am."

"You can't be serious! They don't know you're in law school?"

"Nope."

"This is wrong. You have got to make it right."

"Honor thy father and mother."

"Give me a break."

"I'm serious. I learned a long time ago that the best way to play the game is by the rules. I did not write the rules."

"You are a total and complete hard head."

"Thank you. As a Marine, I take that as a compliment."

"There will never be a wedding unless you invite your family."

Daryl turned back from the river and kissed her softly. During the drive back to Ann Arbor neither spoke. She kissed him before she got out at her apartment.

Thanksgiving dinner in Grosse Pointe was a predictably sedate affair. Their cook arrived early and prepared an elaborate meal. As was the custom on this day, and also Christmas and New Year's, she made two meals, taking one home for her family. Sandy spent the morning studying in her room. Against the smells permeating the house, she could hear the muffled sound of her mother watching TV. She assumed her father was in his library. She dressed just before noon, picking out a new blue dress from her closet. She found her parents in the library where her mother was having a glass of wine while her father nursed a Scotch. Her mother poured a glass for Sandy. Her father spoke first, "How go the studies?"

"Tedious with a capital t."

"You'll do fine. Just don't lose sight of the forest for the trees. Cases are intended to illustrate the principles. Learn the principles, not the cases. You can't possibly memorize the facts of hundreds of cases. Draw out the essential principles. There are not that many. Too many law students miss the bait and get caught in the trap."

"So I've heard."

"Tell us, Sandy, have you met any young men?"

"Mother."

"Well, there are four males to every female, and that only considers the law school, not the other graduate schools, nor the faculty."

"Will there never be a respite?"

"I am only concerned for your future. You will do fine with your studies. I am not so sure about your personal life. If you don't get it organized soon, someone may have to step in and help."

"May? Mother, you've been up to no good for years."

"I only want what is best for you."

"Mother, I can take care of myself. For your information, I have been seeing someone."

Her mother looked directly into Sandy's eyes. Her's was a perfect poker face. Then she looked to her husband and smiled, then back to Sandy. "Is he a law student? Tell us more."

"Yes he's a law student, third year."

"Well...."

"I met him through the Student Bar. He was president last year. This year he's the ABA delegate. I'm on the ABA liaison committee."

"A politician?" Her father asked.

"Only Student Bar, no other offices."

"Law review?"

"No."

"How are his grades?"

"I really don't know. He clerked for Campbell Short, got an offer, and has accepted."

"Campbell Short." her father repeated in an approving tone. He nodded to her mother, although he did not have to. She was well aware of the firm. The husbands of several of her friends were partners. Her father thought of asking more, but restrained himself. If he did, he would disclose everyone he knew at the firm, and she would order him not to say anything. This way he was free to make inquiries. He had just that week started document negotiations with one of the young partners in Campbell Short's Mergers & Acquisitions department for an asset purchase of a vinyl manufacturing company in northern Ohio that Chrysler was acquiring. He had a ready opportunity to make some discreet inquiries.

"Tell us about his people." her mother urged.

"Mother, I don't know. He's a nice guy. I've gone out with him a few times. Most of the time I study."

Sunday afternoon, Sandy drove directly to Daryl's house. She found him there alone. None of his roommates were back yet. He had been drinking and watching football on TV. She noticed he smelled of beer, but she did not taste it when they kissed. He was not drunk, but he was loose enough to urge her to his bedroom. She went upstairs with him, just to see his room, she said. When she did, she was appalled.

"This is disgusting! How can you live like this?"

"I get along fine."

"When is the last time you washed those sheets, or even made that bed. Surely the Marines did not tolerate such squalor."

"What difference does it make now?"

"It makes a big difference to me. Dogs live better than this. Your bed looks like a nest. What a turn off!" She wiggled away from him and went back down stairs. She got herself a beer from the kitchen and returned to him in the living room. Daryl had already resumed his place on the sofa.

"I didn't know you were coming."

She snuggled up against him on the sofa. Not long after his roommates started returning. At 6:00 P.M. they pooled their funds and ordered a couple of pizzas.

The following Friday night, they returned to the Chinese restaurant where they had gone on their first date. This time, the discussion was not about law school nor the legal profession.

"Tell me about your other girl friends?"

"My girl friends?"

"Yes, I want to know everything, names, dates, places. Have you ever been in love?"

"There isn't anything to know."

"Come on."

"I'm serious."

"OK, we'll start with the big issue and work back. Have you ever been in love?"

"Only from afar. I've had my eye on a couple of girls over the years, but I never had the nerve to ask them out. They were pretty, like you. I do have my standards."

"Thank you, but get back to the point. Is your answer that you have not been in love?"

"Correct. That is my answer."

"OK, then tell me about the type of girls you have dated."

"I haven't dated."

"OK, then tell me about the girl you dated."

"I haven't dated."

"No one?"

"Never."

"Not in the Marines, nor college, nor high school?"

"Never."

"But you're so popular?"

"I've been waiting for you."

"Are you telling me the truth?"

"Nothing but."

"That's awfully hard to believe."

"Well, it's true. I've spent a lot of years getting drunk with a lot of smelly guys who do nothing but talk about girls. What about you? Turn about is fair play."

"There's nothing to tell."

"College, high school?"

"Nothing. No one."

"Never?"

"Never."

"Maybe we do have something in common."

The Friday morning before Christmas break, Sandy found Daryl in his favorite fireside chair in the conference room. There were several others in the room, so neither made any overt display of affection. After several minutes of chatting, Sandy bent over and whispered in his ear. He looked up into her eyes. She stood up and smiled back. They left the Law Quad together and drove to Northwood in Sandy's car. Inside her apartment, Daryl realized that what he thought was spontaneity had been premeditated. Sandy went directly to the refrigerator for wine. Two wine glasses were waiting on the kitchen table and the blinds were drawn. He turned on the stereo. She explained that her roommate had left for Chicago that morning. They drank quickly and laughed nervously. They kissed for several moments in the kitchen, then she led him into her room.

The undressing was awkward, but both were silently surprised at how comfortable and natural each felt in front of the other. The sex went quickly. Daryl was more disappointed than Sandy. He was sure that he had performed poorly. What each would remember most was the time they laid in each others arms after. Later they got up and showered together. That brought them back into the bed. This time it was slower, better. It was obvious that Sandy took more pleasure this time. They napped afterwards. She drove him back to his house at dusk on her way home to Grosse Pointe. Daryl told her to wait and ran into the house. He came out carrying a Christmas gift and came around to her side of the car. He leaned in her window.

"Merry Christmas. I love you."

"I love you. Merry Christmas."

They kissed. Sandy got out of the car and went to the trunk. She handed him a small wrapped package. They stood in the street and hugged and kissed.

"I do love you."

"I love you too."

Neither waited for Christmas to open their gifts. Daryl opened his as soon as he got inside after she left. It was a gavel. Sandy opened her's at a stop light. It was a glass paper weight with etched scales of justice. Both were pleased at the other's perceptions.

CHAPTER 12

Sandy woke the next morning in the warmth and familiarity of her childhood bed. Within an instant, a wave of dread washed over her. She was convinced that she must be pregnant. How could she have been so stupid? How could she? She counted forward. Daryl would be busy with the bar exam this summer. The wedding would have to be before or after the bar exam. They would elope. She could not stand the embarrassment of being a pregnant bride. Her mother would die. What would this do to Daryl's prospects in Campbell Short? What about her own? This was not what she wanted. She had never seriously considered children, a family. She had never excluded it either, it had been something distant, remote. Now it was upon her. She was scared and trembled. What a mess! What had she just done with her life?

Daryl woke that morning with a feeling of contentment and fulfillment that he had never before known. He sprang out of his bed. After showering, he set upon cleaning his room. While the bedding was in the washer, he straightened and vacuumed the room. When he made the bed, he bounced a coin on it. When he rolled his socks and underwear, he tested them by throwing them against the wall. He organized the contents of his drawers and closet. It was noon when he finished the room. He spent the afternoon on the kitchen. Over the next two weeks he worked every room in the house. When there was nothing left to do, he bought paint and painted his bedroom. Then he painted the entrance hall and living room. Putting the paint away in the basement, he discovered its neglect and thoroughly cleaned it.

Sandy called him the first Sunday evening, and every other day thereafter. She did not tell him. She charged the calls to her apartment phone. She did not want her mother's oversight. The calls elevated Daryl, and that was reflected in his voice. Sandy was not so. Her tone was flat, her comments clipped. Everything about her side of the conversation was restrained. At first Daryl took it to be the result of her calling from home, perhaps she was concerned someone would overhear. Then he began to think that maybe she was having second thoughts about him, after all he had not performed well, he was overweight, she was so beautiful. In every call Daryl told her that he loved her. She never said it. Her voice during the call on Christmas was so stressed, he was convinced that it was over. Yet, he reminded himself, she called him. Maybe that was just to preempt the embarrassment of him calling her home. Suddenly, the day after Christmas Sandy called when he did not expect it. A range of tone had returned to her voice. She told him that she missed him, that she loved him.

Convinced that her period had ended, Sandy resolved to return to Ann Arbor New Year's Day. It was two days earlier than she had planned. Her mother protested. They were to have dinner at The Club. Sandy explained she was nervous about her studies. She wanted to get back to the law library. She drove directly to Daryl's house where she found him making himself a salad for lunch. Everything was a surprise to her, the condition of the house, his appearance. He had limited his drinking to the evenings. His face was not flushed, his eyes were not puffy. He took her on a tour of the house, bragging at each stop along the way. The tour took them to his bedroom.

"Well, what do you think?"

"Maybe there is some Marine left in you."

He took her in his arms and kissed her. When that escalated, she grabbed his hand and stopped him.

"Do you have anything?"

"What?"

"Protection."

"No. I thought that you...I assumed you were on the pill or something. Women are supposed to take care of these things."

"I'm Catholic."

"I know that. So am I."

"I can't."

"But I can? What's the logic in that?" When she did not answer, he continued. "Listen, I don't buy this birth control business. I've seen too many kids born to die young after a life of horror. I don't care what the Church says. They say its OK to take a life in war, but not OK to plan for something as important as a human life. They say its OK to follow your conscience if it is inspired by faith, but then they tell you what you have to learn from your faith. Well, I know my conscience. This is OK with me. I'll take care of it."

"You shouldn't have assumed. I thought I was pregnant."

"I'm sorry. I love you. I should have taken care of it before."

"Please do."

"Listen, this is OK with me. I just want to ask something, not start a fight."

"What?"

"You really think its a sin?"

"Yes."

"A mortal sin?"

"Yes."

"Eternity?"

"Yes."

"If you believe all that, and if you love me, how can you ask me to go to Hell for you?"

"You bastard." Tears ran down her cheeks. "I love you. Please do this for me."

"I will. No sin here. I don't buy that crap. I'll take care of it."

"When?"

She kissed him again and again. He tasted her tears. Soon they were in his bed. They made love in ways that did not require her protection.

CHAPTER 13

During the winter and spring of 1972, Sandy and Daryl became established as a couple. Except for their separate classes, they were constant companions. When one had a class and the other was free, the free one could be found waiting in the hall outside the other's class. They had their own booth in the snack bar. The fireplace chair opposite Daryl's in the Student Bar lounge was widely regarded as her's. Daryl, still a boisterous drinker, was no longer a fixture next to party kegs. They were still highly visible at student parties, but left together before the real serious partying got started. Sandy was so frequently at Daryl's house that his roommates began to regard her as one of themselves, although she never spent the night. Likewise, Sandy's roommate became quite familiar and informal with Daryl. When first term grades were posted, Sandy's reputation as an academic was fixed. Although the posting of the grades was anonymous by student I.D. number, word spread. She was sure to be invited to law review. Those who knew them both considered her intellect as a compliment to Daryl's personality.

Sandy was more at ease with her work second term. As a parting senior with a job, Daryl had even less incentive to apply himself, and did not. He made two more trips to Chicago for ABA meetings. He also went to Detroit a few times, once for a lunch meeting with members of Campbell Short. This was neither required nor expected. It was pure Daryl, and he could not help himself. After receiving the offer, he had written upbeat letters acknowledging the offer and his gratitude to Sloan, Hale and every other member of the hiring committee, and every lawyer in the Insolvency Department; but he did not formally accept the offer at that time. He then called the firm administrator for advice on acceptance procedure. She advised a letter from him to Mr. Hale was enough. Then he called Hale's secretary to say he was going to be in Detroit and would like to drop by with his acceptance letter. After a pause, she returned to the line with a invitation to lunch with Hale and Melvin Goldfarb, the chairman of the Insolvency Department and the firm's grand old man of bankruptcy.

When the day and time came, Daryl discreetly left the letter with the secretary, whom he knew from the prior summer, and was ushered into Hale's office for the first time. Hale was priggish but pleasant. He warned Daryl to enjoy the comparative leisure of law school and the bar refresher before the real work started. Then they toured the firm on the way to the Insolvency Department two floors down. Goldfarb dominated the lunch with discussion. He was loud and chewed with his mouth open. He was also prone to spilling food on himself. Hale was quite obviously distressed with Goldfarb, and Daryl was challenged to play up to both at the same time. In Daryl's opinion, the luncheon went well.

Back at the firm, Daryl and Goldfarb returned to the department offices, leaving Hale on the elevator. Despite having spent the summer there, Daryl had never been in this department and did not know anyone. Goldfarb introduced him to everyone. Daryl struggled to remember the names of the secretaries and paralegals. He had already memorized the names of the lawyers from the Martindale-Hubbell directory at the law school library. Daryl's first impression of the department was that it was a boiler room operation. This group stood in stark contrast to the rest of the firm, where decorum ruled. There was even a rule that coats must be worn in the halls. Here, rolled-up sleeves on wrinkled shirts were the uniform of the day. The level of nervous energy was high. The support staff scurried about with armloads of paper. Every lawyer's office was a mess. There was paper everywhere. Most offices had stacks of banker's boxes against each wall and expandable files lined up across the floors. Goldfarb's office was the worst of all. The top of his desk was at least one foot below the surface of the paper. Nothing Goldfarb said, nor anything Daryl saw, indicated who worked for whom. Daryl liked the energy level, was at home with the clutter, but was troubled by the seeming lack of a chain of command. After a few interruptions, Goldfarb wished Daryl well on the bar exam and said they'd look for him the first of August.

On another occasion, Daryl came to the offices to pick up some materials the office administration had gathered on housing. She helped summer clerks and associates find apartments. He had shared a two bedroom apartment on the second floor of a nearby building with another clerk the prior summer. The administrator had arranged that. During this visit, Daryl went to each floor and reintroduced himself to each receptionist. He also called upon the law librarian. Finally, he stopped by Frank Sloan's office. Sloan's secretary knew Daryl's name and was very cheery to him. She explained that Sloan was in a meeting, but she was sure he would want to be interrupted. She had him wait in Sloan's office. It could not have been more different from the yellow wall paper and fluorescent lights of the Insolvency group. The walls were paneled with built-in bookcases. The floor was wood with two oriental rugs. The desk was mahogany. The chairs leather. Framed photographs of a young family were prominent on the shelves and desk. Likewise, Marine memorabilia was everywhere. A chrome plated bayonet lay on the desk, apparently a letter opener. There was a view to the east across the Detroit River to Windsor, Ontario. When he entered, Sloan surprised Daryl, who had his back to the door looking out the window.

They exchanged pleasantries. Sloan then told Daryl that coincidentally his name had just come up in his meeting. Daryl looked quizzical, and Sloan went on to explain that they were in the process of closing a Chrysler acquisition of a manufacturing plant in Sandusky, Ohio. The Chrysler team was in a conference room waiting on the delivery of some additional accounting documents. Their most senior lawyer had brought Daryl's name up with the notation that he was a friend of his daughter. Sloan teased Daryl that he had reluctantly told the man the sad truth, but seeing that Daryl did not understand the joke, he quickly reassured him that he had only said good things. He offered to introduce them, but Daryl explained that Sandy, his girl friend, the daughter, was arranging a meal for that purpose. Sloan nodded understanding, then expressed his optimism about Daryl's joining the firm. He couldn't wait for Daryl to get on board. He needed some help kicking ass.

Several days later Daryl received two letters, one from Hale acknowledging Daryl's acceptance and welcoming him to the firm, the other from the office administrator which contained a check for $2,500, the signing bonus, and a commitment that he would go on the payroll June 1 even though he would not be expected in the office until August 1. Daryl was dumbfounded. He had been counting on the signing bonus to pay for the bar refresher and living expenses until he got established. All of a sudden, he was established. He thought about buying a new car, but that was moving a little too quickly. He deposited the check before he went to class, to get it earning interest. He was going to like having money.

Initially, Sandy's plan was to bring Daryl along on her Sunday visit home. She reasoned that his church attendance would alleviate some of her mother's concerns, and dinner at The Club would be formal enough to limit the awkwardness of the first meeting. She also thought that Daryl needed to see the window in the Church and The Club to round out his understanding of her background. Finally, the need to return to Ann Arbor would give them an easy excuse to leave. With his new found prosperity, Daryl proposed a modification to the plan. He would get a hotel room in Detroit. They could escape there and make an adventure of it. Sandy resisted, although she didn't explain it to Daryl, she felt their affair in Ann Arbor went unnoticed by the world, but if they did anything in Detroit, they were sure to get caught. Daryl modified his plan to a weekend trip for apartment hunting. Ultimately, it was so close to Spring break that the free time became a factor. When Sandy brought her mother in on the planning, she wanted to have Daryl for dinner at home on a Saturday night. She felt it would be less formal and more comfortable for all. There was no persuading her to the contrary.

As usual, Sandy went home the Friday night before the holiday. Daryl came over the next morning and checked into a classical old downtown hotel. Sandy informed her parents that she and Daryl would spend the afternoon looking for apartments, and did nothing to correct their misunderstanding that he would be returning to Ann Arbor after the dinner. She drove downtown to meet him. She called him from the lobby, and was quickly in his room making love. After, they showered and had lunch in the hotel restaurant. During lunch, Daryl showed her the information on apartments that the firm administrator had given him. He was undecided on whether he should find something close and convenient, or out west so he would be closer to her in Ann Arbor. After lunch they drove around downtown and along the river. Sandy took him northwest to Marygrove. She took him into the Liberal Arts building. He immediately picked up the scent from the fireplaces. Then they went out and sat under a tree. He laid on his back with his head in her lap. She looked down stroking his hair. It was a sunny spring day, the buds were just starting to appear, and the ground was cool. They drove back to the hotel and made love again. At dusk, Sandy left him with written directions to her parent's home.

The house was so far back from the street that Daryl decided to pull up the driveway. He parked along side of the house and walked around to the front door. Sandy's father was waiting him there. He had a scotch in his hand and took Daryl into the library. Daryl asked for a beer, explaining that he would be driving.

"I heard I just missed you at Campbell Short a couple of weeks ago."

"I was there for a meeting."

"So Sloan said. I was there for a closing. Sloan's a good man. They could use a few more like him."

"Yes sir."

"He speaks highly of you."

"Considering the source, I take that as an honor."

"He says you were in the Marines, as they say, at different times together."

"Yes sir, we know some of the same people. There was this one colonel, in particular,...."

Sandy and her mother came in together. Sandy stayed back, when she introduced her mother. Daryl shook her hand and while still holding it became uncomfortable at how he should greet Sandy. They smiled at each other, but did not touch. Daryl returned his attention to her mother. He was struck at her diminutive size. Her hand was almost frail, it was so slender. She looked much like Sandy, they had the same blond hair, the same hairstyle. Sandy was a head taller than her, and did not wear any makeup beyond lipstick. They both wore large earrings, but her mother also wore heavy necklaces and bracelets. From Sandy's perspective Daryl looked like a large bear of a man next to her mother. She was struck, first at how small her mother was, then at how large Daryl was. He was twice as thick as her father and several inches taller. Sandy's father was the polished corporate lawyer he had expected, but he had not expected her mother to be....elegant. He had expected common stock from a Kansas farm, people like his family.

Soon they were seated at the dining room table. Sandy's parents sat at either end. Sandy and Daryl were opposite each other. The cook poured wine. Daryl sipped it, he still did not like it. Sandy's father returned the discussion to the military.

"I was in the Army, briefly, at the end of World War II. I was in R.O.T.C. during the war, and went directly upon graduation in '45. I was winding up and the war was winding down, so I never really saw active duty. I gather you did."

"Yes sir. Two tours in Southeast Asia."

"Well, I don't know if you will be able to help me, but I simply cannot understand these protestors. I don't know about this war, I trust our leaders know what they're doing. I'll tell you, these protestors befuddle me. Do they think that they're the first ever to be asked to fight and die for something they don't understand? Are they that ignorant of history, of power and politics? Are they just selfish? Is it the drugs?"

Sandy froze. She wanted to stop the conversation, but was at a loss for something to say to change the subject. Her mother intervened.

"Dear, you are not going to ruin my dinner with a political discussion. You two can argue later in the library."

"I want to know. I have been trying to make sense out of all this, and I just can't. Daryl was there. Maybe someone who has actually been there can explain this to me."

"Yes sir, I was there; but I don't know what to say. The only war I know is this war. I can't imagine that this war is really much different from any other."

"See, that's my point. If that's true, then what's with these kids? When I got out of school, I was eager to serve. I was scared, but I was actually disappointed when I didn't get to go."

"Well, sir, I went and stayed. I'd have to agree with the protestors, it's not right. It can't be. I can't believe that such killing and destruction could ever be justified."

"I understand that Viet Nam is a little backwards country and its hard to see its significance. What do you do about a Hitler? Pearl Harbor? They started it, we had no choice."

"Like I said, this is the only war I know. The only answer I have for you is what I was taught, 'Two wrongs don't make a right'."

"That is compelling, but the world is sometimes a much crueler place than that for which we prepare our children."

"Sir, everything I saw is consistent with your statement."

"If the rabble would just quit protesting, we could get this thing over with and get back to business."

"I don't know about that. They are loud and offensive. Obviously, I am not one of them. I do say, that if you tune out the screaming and listen to what they are saying, really listen; they're close, if not right on."

"Right on! I get sick when I hear that. We've had enough of a taste of that right here in Detroit. I don't know if this city will ever recover from the '68 riots. The industry is decentralizing for a lot of reasons, and although everyone talks about revitalizing Detroit, I can't begin to tell you how many meetings I've been in where these racial riots get added into the equation. Right after the unions, it's race. Now if you throw in the anti-war mobs, no one in their right minds would invest in a big city. Industry is moving to small cities and the South. The old cities are war zones. I'm concerned we might be headed for civil war."

"Once again I agree with you. I am only telling you to listen to the adversary. Surely, as a lawyer, you...."

"I can't believe that you, a Marine, are telling me you are against this war."

"Yes sir, this and any war."

There was a long silence as Daryl and Sandy's father looked directly into each other's eyes. Each was taking the measure of a man. Daryl was well practiced in this from the military; Sandy's father from years at bargaining tables. The women could not tell it, but these men liked each other and had just become friends. Sandy's mother interrupted.

"Daryl, Sandy may not have told you, but I spent three years during the war at Willow Run. At the time I was proud. It was so exciting to be young and to be a part of it. After the war when we started seeing the pictures of the destruction, not just the death camps, but the destruction, the cities that we destroyed; it made me sick. I had nightmares. I still do when I see the old pictures. Now on TV I see these jets dropping bombs on the jungle. It can't be right."

Everyone fell silent. Sandy, the great prompter, could think of nothing to say. Everyone busied themselves with their food. Everyone had learned a great deal about the others. Sandy, for example, had no idea that her father was a racist or that her mother was a latent pacifist. She knew about Daryl's beliefs, but had never before seen him so diplomatically maneuver from a hot seat. They all noted Sandy's silence. She was sitting this one out. Daryl was a little miffed that she took no apparent interest in what he saw as the single most important issue in history.

After a few minutes Sandy turned the discussion to Daryl's apartment hunting. There was no discussion of Campbell Short. Her parents had already shared what her father had learned about Daryl, and they knew the firm. He was probably going to take something close in, to accommodate the long hours. They hadn't found anything that day. Daryl might be coming back Sunday afternoon to look again. Her father bemoaned the decline of Detroit. Uptown, downtown, it was all decaying. Daryl would be well-advised to be careful. If was going to live intown, then he should consider getting a gun. Sitting at the table, Daryl actually paused to consider it. He was no stranger to arms. He had never himself killed another human, but he knew how, and he knew he could. With his training, he knew he could do it quickly and easily, as a reaction, with little or no thought. That is what convinced him he should apply for conscientious objector status. He knew he could kill, and he did not want to. It was wrong. No, he wouldn't get a gun, but he might join the Y, get in shape, get back into Judo. He ought to do that. It was dangerous in the real world. Sandy worried that the discussion was still too tense, but reassured herself that the worst was out of the way. The next time they met, they would all be friends.

Sunday, after lunch at The Club, Sandy changed and rushed downtown to meet Daryl. He had taken the room for an additional day and had a bottle of wine brought to the room for her. He drank beer. He had been drinking before she got there. She sat in the side chair, reviewing the night before, as she quickly drank three glasses. Daryl stood looking out the window. In conclusion, she thought it had gone very well. She could not have planned it any better. Her mother had never even thought to ask about his family. Daryl pressed her for a position on the war. She had none. She loved him. He came up to her, and she rose to him. They kissed and fondled each other through their clothes. There were no buildings opposite the hotel, and they left the curtains open when they made love. She stayed until dusk. The next morning Daryl signed a lease on a one bedroom apartment only four blocks from the office. It was much higher in the same building where he had stayed the summer before. The materials the office administrator gave him indicated that at least a half dozen Campbell Short associates chose that building each year.

CHAPTER 14

Sandy had never been employed. Her school days had always been filled with study and extracurriculars, her summers with swimming and boating. Knowing that summer clerkships for law students are just as indispensable to a legal career as law school itself, Sandy spent much of her Spring seeking advice on the subject. Daryl was first and adamant. First year law students should not clerk. They did not know enough of the law. A weak performance might cost a critical second year clerkship or at least taint a resume with a poor reference. It simply wasn't worth the risk. He had, wisely in his opinion, spent his first summer in an office job for the university. The Law Student Placement Office disagreed. They claimed that law firms knew the difference between first and second year students, that assignments would be tailored to skill levels, that many non-clerk support positions were available (like, librarians, messengers, and paralegals), and that experience working in a law office would give any student a leg-up on the hostile world of second year clerking. One of Sandy's acquaintances mentioned that he was going to be a volunteer in the political campaign that summer. She discussed it with her father who thought it a fabulous idea. Nixon was sure to get re-elected, and she could make invaluable contacts. He made some phone calls.

The end of her first year of law school was upon Sandy before she knew it. Again she distinguished herself in her exams. She knew that she now had a lock on law review. She stayed an extra week in Ann Arbor to attend Daryl's graduation. It was an idyllic time for both. Their days were filled with drives in the country, picnics, and love making. She had come to crave their times together. She no longer struggled with inhibition and guilt, but she also no longer felt as intense during. Now she wanted and longed for him. During was a time of warmth and intimacy. After, she would begin to hunger for the next time, which was never as satisfying, but which, in turn, increased her further desire. They also spoke for hours on end on every subject imaginable, but it always came around to Daryl's family. Sandy was relentless on the subject. She wanted him to reconcile and found the graduation ceremony the perfect occasion. Each time she brought it up, they ended up fighting. She cried. She pleaded. She cajoled. He would simply not agree. She would bring up another subject, yet it too would eventually return to his family.

Daryl found the graduation exercise a memorable pleasure beyond his expectation. Weeks before, he had been measured for a robe along with his classmates. His first sight of the robes was an hour before the ceremony. The robes had rows of velvet sewn into them. He remembered that his college robe did not. As they were herded into lines, he could see that the faculty and administration had even fancier robes, but the law school's were among the finest. Clearly, they were more impressive than the undergraduates. He liked the distinction. It appealed to his sense of order and hierarchy. He missed wearing a uniform. He had not felt so proudly conspicuous since the first time he wore dress in the Marines. Waiting in line, he and his friends signed each other's programs. He looked for Sandy, but never saw her in the huge stadium. He ignored the speeches, instead he stroked the velvet and looked about, waving to friends and acquaintances. Sandy listened to each speech carefully. She disagreed with the main speaker and silently argued with him.

Afterwards, she waited almost two hours for Daryl. It took her forty-five minutes to find him in the parking lot, and then she stood aside from the circle he was commanding. She told herself that this might be the last time he would see most of them, but her impatience won. She critically studied his gestures and started mimicking him. She rolled her hand over exposing the palm as he constantly did. She mouthed the words she saw him saying. She knew his lines before he said them. She was not disappointed about his family, she was mad. It didn't matter to her that they would have been as faceless as her in this crowd. She was furious.

That afternoon Daryl and his friends held a reception with a keg at their house. At any one time there were about twenty people attending. Throughout the afternoon at least a hundred stopped by. Daryl got quickly drunk, but noting the hour and Sandy's presence, he tapered off and gradually sobered. To the extent he and Sandy found themselves in the same room, it was only by coincidence. She greeted everyone she knew, but Daryl was working the crowd. Eventually, she went up to his room, and looked through his old sports magazines. She wanted him. She wanted sex. She wanted to touch herself, but would not. Eventually, she fell asleep. She woke at dusk, coming down to find Daryl and his roommates in the living room reminiscing over their law school experience. They were all moving out in the morning. Again, she felt misplaced, and went into the kitchen to attend to the dishes.

That night they ate Chinese in the same restaurant that they had many times before. They did not talk, except about the food. Daryl had not initially ordered any beer, but half way through the meal he did. He drank several as quickly as the waitress brought them. It did not make him any more talkative. With each drink, Sandy got more angry. She drove him back to his house and kept both hands of the steering wheel when he kissed her cheek. She told him to call her when he got settled in his apartment. She spent the evening packing the remainder of her things for the summer at home.

Sandy drove herself home the next morning. She deliberately did not drive by Daryl's house, and she timed her arrival in Detroit to miss the rush hour. Her mother helped her unpack, and they went out to lunch together at The Club. Sandy came back that afternoon to lay out in the sun. Daryl rented a van for the day to move his possessions into his new apartment. He had used a fair share of his signing bonus to buy furniture for his apartment from a large discount store in Livonia. He also used the van to pick that up during the day. It was dusk when he got back to Ann Arbor. He dropped off the van, walked across the campus one last time, inspected the empty house, and then drove his MG to his new home in Detroit. When he got to his apartment, he wanted to call Sandy, but he did not yet have a phone. He could have gone out to a pay phone, but instead he started into a twelve pack, listened to music and looked out the twelfth floor window at the city lights.

Sandy met her father for lunch in an Italian restaurant downtown. The only place she could find to park was three blocks from the restaurant, and the walk scared her. Both were early and took a nice table before the lunch crowd. Her father told the host his name and that he expected a gentleman would join them. Over their ice tea he reviewed with Sandy what he had already told her the evening before. She masked her impatience for she liked the careful and stylized way in which he spoke. He had contacted Chrysler's governmental affairs people, they used to be hidden in the law department, now they had their own box on the organizational charts. They suggested Willie Sturtz. He was the state coordinator of the Nixon campaign. He was originally from Michigan, and was back from Washington on assignment. He had managed two congressional and one senatorial campaign before going to work for Romney in 1967. He had made the transition to Nixon after the Republican convention in 1968. He had spent three of the last four years in the Commerce Department. He was a pro across the board, but fund raising was his specialty. He was not part of the state party apparatus, but that was not a problem. He knew them all and got along well. They had the titles. They liked hearing his campaign stories. He called the shots. Just as her father finished, a well-dressed young man came up to their table.

He was her father's twin in everything but years. They were both slender, the same height, wore their dark hair short, oiled, and with a clean part, and also wore dark blue suits, white shirts and red ties. Sandy was surprised. She had expected a middle-aged, overweight, rough talking drunk, who would blow cigar smoke in her face. This fellow looked like something from a men's fashion magazine. He apologized for being late. He explained his days went long into the night. He had slept in and just finished his run. He liked the loop around Belle Isle Park. Her father warned him that the park was a rough place for someone with his complexion. He ignored the remark and smiled at Sandy. She wondered what Daryl would look like if he lost weight. Sturtz got right down to business. He told her he understood that she was a law student with excellent academics who was interested in working in the campaign. She nodded. He told her the hours would be long, the work tedious, and best of all, no pay. She nodded again. He told her she was hired.

For the first time, she spoke, asking if that was it, wasn't he interested in knowing her specific skills and experience. He wasn't, there wasn't time. There was work waiting. There was work for her to do. If she did it well, she would be rewarded with more work. If she did not, there was still work for her, just less, and further from the action. Sandy was taken back by the bluntness, but she remembered his specific words. They ordered, then he returned to her father's earlier warnings. He knew downtown was rough. He had taken a small furnished apartment for the summer near Grand Circus Park, just a few blocks away. The change for the worse just in the ten years he had been in and out of Detroit was sad. Still, he doubted that anyone would want to mug a runner. Her father asked about his background, and they spent the meal discussing Romney's strategies. It was a safe topic, old news. He knew people liked hearing an insider's view. Not once during the lunch did they discuss the Nixon campaign. As they finished, he urged Sandy to come with him to the office to get started. She had not expected it and immediately made an excuse. She could start in the morning. He pressed her to at least stop in and see the office. She agreed. Her father lingered to pay the bill, and they left.

The campaign office was two blocks from the restaurant and another two blocks from her car. It was an old store front. Sturtz explained that it had been a shoe store. A painted banner was tied across the front of the building. He unlocked the front door. There was no one in the building. In the front were several tables with old typewriters. He explained it was for mailing lists. Someday somebody would computerize that. For now, they did it by hand. He asked if she could type. The next group of tables was covered with telephones. Taped on the tables beside each phone was the text of the standard pitch and canned answers to the most common evasive responses. Fund raising, he explained. She should get to know the pitch. Towards the back were three desks. Two were for men whose names she did not catch, one was finance, the other media. The third desk was for Mary Jane, their secretary, she usually got in around noon. He gestured to the only office and said "Mine." They walked passed it and through the old store room full of printed literature and yard signs. He opened the back door to show her a potholed gravel parking area for half a dozen cars. He told her she could park there. Back inside, he took her into his office and found a door key for her in his desk. He suggested she come in early in the morning when no one else was around. She nodded. The phone rang. He told her he'd have Mary Jane leave her a list of things to do, and he answered the phone. Sandy's heart raced on the walk back to the car, not from fear of the neighborhood, but from anticipation. She circled Daryl's apartment building. It had underground parking, so she could not tell if he were there. She thought about going in, but she did not.

Daryl dressed and paid a courtesy call to Campbell Short that morning. He started on the lower floor with Goldfarb in the Insolvency Department. They spoke briefly about the bar refresher and the bar exam. Goldfarb warned him to take it seriously, that anyone could fail it. Daryl stopped on each floor and greeted each receptionist. He also stopped in the mail room and told the mail boy who he was and that he may be getting mail. He confirmed Daryl's identity from a typed list posted on a corkboard next to the pigeon holes. He also showed Daryl his name had already been added under one of the slots. Daryl smiled. He stopped in on the librarian on his way to the office administrator. He gave her his new address, which was the real purpose of his visit. He wanted to make sure those paychecks found their way to him. Sloan got off an elevator as Daryl waited for one down. He warned Daryl to take the bar seriously, that anyone could fail it. He suggested Daryl might come to the office and study in a library. It lent discipline to the effort. Daryl liked the idea.

That afternoon, he scanned through the bar refresher outlines. They were concise. He liked them. He wished he'd had them during law school. Combined, they were six inches thick. The refresher course started the following evening, four hours a night from 6:30 to 10:30 P.M, Monday through Thursday nights, and a practice exam on Friday nights. He reasoned that six weeks of the course meant only one inch of outlines a week. That wasn't so bad. He could spend each morning at the office reviewing previous outlines, and each afternoon learning the one for that evening. Saturday and Sunday he could review the week's work. There was one week off before the exam. That would do nicely for cumulative review. The more he thought about it, it wouldn't be so bad. He thought about giving himself weekends off, but then he remembered the warnings. Anyone could fail. He would have plenty of time to screw off later. He promised himself not to waste one moment on anything other than bar preparation. The next morning he dressed and went to Campbell Short with his outlines. He staked out a carrel in the library as his own. He introduced himself to that year's flock of clerks who were just beginning their summer in the library. To them, he was something of a celebrity. He called Sandy's house that afternoon and had a pleasant, though measured, chat with her mother. He left the number that the phone company had given him for his apartment, even though it would not be connected until the end of the week.

Sandy had a difficult time sleeping. She laid awake working through arguments with Daryl, thinking about sex. The real reason she couldn't sleep was her excitement over the job. She woke the next morning before her alarm. She found a bright red dress and wore it. She left the house before her father had even come down for breakfast and got downtown easily before the traffic. She parked behind the store front, and hurried inside. She inspected the office to make sure no one else was there, and found an envelope with her name on it laying on top of the secretarial desk. First, she could type mailing labels for Niles, the list from the state party was in one of the notebooks in the labels area. Second, the papers would come in around 10:00 A.M. She should read them and clip articles about anything she thought important, and everything that related directly to either the Democrat or Republican national campaigns, also she should be sure to clip the top corner of the page showing the paper name and page number and staple it to the article. Finally, she should answer the phones.

Sandy did not do much typing because of the phones. There was no switchboard, the calls rang directly into the desks, pulling her from one to the other. Most of the calls went to the media desk. A few were printers saying that their orders were ready and telling her the exact amount of the check to bring when they picked them up. A few were TV stations giving time slots, prices, and reminding that they must have checks 24 hours before air time. Most were from radio stations saying that they had received the tapes, but that they would not be played until they got their money. When asked questions, she looked for answers, but found the desk drawers locked. Sandy made careful notes and rewrote them after the calls. Once the phone in Sturtz's office rang. It was someone from Washington who needed the name of a heavy contributor from Traverse City. His desk drawers were unlocked, and she started looking. She found a green notebook with a large dollar sign written on the front cover. Inside were two alphabetical lists, the first by last name, the second by city. She gave the five names listed under Traverse City. The person on the other end also asked for Sandy's name.

Sandy was relieved when Mary Jane came in just before lunch. She wasn't at all disappointed that the typing had not gotten done. They had high school kids and housewives that could do that. The clipping was important. It had to be done everyday. She showed Sandy how they photocopied each story, as many times as there were different topics in it, and the notebooks in which the stories were filed. Sandy described all the media calls. Mary Jane frowned giving Sandy no room to doubt that their media man was a problem. Mary Jane congratulated her for finding the answer to Washington's question. Willie would not be in today, he was traveling with "the candidate" during stops in Lansing and Traverse City. She knew there was to be a reception on a yacht in Traverse City. No doubt someone was going to get stroked. Sandy had done good. Sandy responded saying it was a good thing that Willie didn't lock his desk. Mary Jane smiled and nodded, then frowned when she looked to the locked media desk.

The two women worked right through lunch. By the early afternoon, the volunteers started drifting in. Sandy watched Mary Jane give the teenagers typing assignments, and when Mary Jane got busy on the phone, she took over the supervision. She did the clipping when not answering questions from the typists. An older crowd started arriving after 5:00 P.M. They were mostly downtown office workers, both men and women, who came in for the dinner time telephone work. Most brought sandwiches and drinks. Sandy had not eaten breakfast nor lunch and was very hungry. She didn't want to, but Mary Jane urged her to make some calls. She told her she would never know anything about politics or religion until she learned to beg for money. After several calls, Sandy was do longer inhibited by the task. She had quickly grasped the essence of the script, and spoke naturally, without reading it. Soon each call was a challenge. Whenever anyone scored, they rang a bell. Sandy's parents were waiting for her when she got home at 9:00 P.M. They sat at the kitchen table listening intently to her excited stories as she ate. Once again she couldn't sleep. It was only then, lying in bed, that she realized she had not thought about Daryl all day.

CHAPTER 15

That Saturday night, Daryl and Sandy went out for dinner and a movie. His telephone was installed that Friday afternoon. When he came home from the office to change into less formal clothes for the bar refresher, he found the phone working and called her home. Her mother gave him the number of the Nixon office. He reached her there and made the date. He told her about studying at the firm library and not getting home from the bar refresher until 11:00 P.M. each night. She told him how busy she was at the campaign office. Daryl wanted to say how much he missed her, but from her monotone, he concluded he was still fallen from grace. Sandy wanted to hear an apology or at least that he loved her. When she did not, she was angry again. She was going to be busy in the campaign all day Saturday. He could study. She did suggest the date. They caught up with each others activities during the meal. Daryl did not drink. They held hands during the movie. He pulled into the driveway and up alongside the house. She kissed him on the check and got out of the car without words.

Sandy called Daryl Sunday morning just as she was leaving for Church with her parents. There was a range to her voice, and he took the cue. She suggested a picnic, along the river or in one of the parks. He told her not to make anything, but just come to his place. They could get some carry-out. Sandy called again when she got back from lunch with her parents at The Club. They agreed she should drive on down to his apartment. They could walk from there. She had not been up to his apartment. Although he had not hung anything on the walls, the furniture was new and she approved. She found it much more acceptable than his house in Ann Arbor. She liked the view to the southeast across Capitol Park to the office buildings and river. She pointed out where her office was, only three blocks away. They talked of having lunch together during the week. It was a sunny afternoon.

They bought a Sunday paper at a corner drug store, and submarine sandwiches in the only shop they could find open. They found a tree in Capitol Park and had lunch. Daryl glanced through the paper then cat-napped. Sandy read the paper, then started kissing him. They went back to his apartment.

Daryl's appetite for sex was much the same as his appetite for food and drink. He liked it all. Moderation was difficult. He continued to experiment. This afternoon he was learning clearly what he already suspected, that Sandy had defined a narrow range of what she liked. She did not direct him to it, rather, she censured him when he did not find it. She would grab a wandering hand and remove it, but not place it anywhere else. She would say no, but not yes. More than once when she did this, he flashed mad and wanted to stop, but then his urgings overcame his frustration. He retreated to his prior experience of what she allowed, telling himself that it was not, after all, so bad. She would not participate when he paused for the condom, but she welcomed him back. Sandy, concentrated on her memory of prior times, working for a similar feeling. Looking back, not forward, her disappointment continued, increasing again this time from the last. She showered after. Daryl stayed in bed. On other occasions she had resisted him in the shower. He did not feel like another struggle. She left at dusk. He called her at her office from Campbell Short's library the next morning. They were only two blocks apart. The monotone had returned to her voice. She would be working through lunch.

They did meet for lunch later that week. Daryl, dressed in one of the new suits he had acquired for the office, made the brief walk from Campbell Short to the Nixon office. He met Mary Jane and Willie Sturtz. They were both complimentary of Sandy. She demurred and called Daryl the politician. She told them he was president of the Student Bar and an ABA delegate. She could see Willie taking special note of the remark, although Daryl missed it. Daryl bragged about her grades. When the door to the street closed behind the young couple, Mary Jane and Willie agreed that they were well-matched. Daryl and Sandy walked down the street holding hands. After they bought sandwiches, she held him by the arm as he carried the sack. They found a bench outside. Sandy talked the entire time, telling him everything she knew about Sturtz. He was easy to work with. Although he was abrupt, she did not mind his work assignments. She was disappointed that he did not talk about strategy or even tactics with her, although she knew that he did to others on the phone. Their interaction was limited to specific tasks. They met for lunch like this a few additional times during the summer, but not often. He called her every morning at her office, but she usually could not take lunch. The following weekend they both put aside the pouting, and confessed their love for one another. Their Saturday nights and Sunday afternoons became a ritual.

One afternoon late the following week, Willie took Maury Bernard, their media man, into his office and closed the door. From the look Mary Jane gave her, Sandy knew that it was show down time. Bernard was a young account executive from McMurough, James & Ashton, a prestige advertising agency in Bloomfield Hills. He was "on loan" from the agency. His time was billed to their Ford account, with Ford's approval. Aside from the messages embedded in Mary Jane's looks, Sandy had quickly formed her own low opinion of him. He had a habit of touching her when they spoke and brushing against her when they passed. She did not like him. The longer Willie kept him behind the closed door, the closer Sandy and Mary Jane hovered. After an hour an a half, they came out together laughing as if they had just shared a joke. They shook hands. Willie told him to hurry, that he was expected. Maury went directly to his desk and started collecting his personal things. As he did, Willie asked Sandy to come into his office. He closed the door behind her.

"You're our new media coordinator."

Sandy stammered, "I don't have any background or experience."

"You've been covering for that bum since the first day you got here. Before that Mary Jane carried him."

"I wouldn't know where to begin."

"You passed the beginning a couple of weeks ago. You're in it up to you knees right now."

"I just don't think I...."

"Sandy, I told you the first day I met you that the reward for good work was more work. This is a political campaign. There is a beginning, middle, and end. Things have to get done on time. We can't fiddle around. I don't have the time to train anyone, or the inclination to do it if I had the time. We're all in well over our heads. Capable people stay on top. Once you know how to swim, it really doesn't matter how deep the water is. You're smart. You're reliable. You get things done. If I didn't think you could do it better than Bernard, he'd still have the job."

"You sure seemed to part as friends."

"He's worthless, and he doesn't even know it. He left here thinking he got a promotion. We've moved him out to the western suburbs. He thinks he's going to inject life into the faltering campaign of a congressional candidate. The truth is that it's a throw-away campaign in a working class district. There hasn't been a Republican elected in it since before Ford invented the Model T. Even the candidate, a young lawyer, knows he's going to lose. He only agreed to run to get his name known and develop his legal practice."

"Bernard doesn't know any of that?"

"Listen, he got a dream assignment. You work here for gratis. He was on full salary. He could have parleyed this into something big. Instead, he slept in, drank his lunches, and moved on every pretty young volunteer who came through the front door. He had a chance at the big time, and he blew it. Nixon is going to win big. When the young lawyer loses, a few people like me are going to say it was Bernard's fault that he slipped off the coattails. His political career that never was, never will be. He will go back to the ad agency. After the holidays, he will be fired. They will say its a staff cut-back. The real reason will be his drinking and philandering on company time. He will never understand why. McMurough, James & Ashton pushed him off on us for that reason and because it was gravy for them to have the meter running full time on their least productive salesman. Ford now knows that. The staff cut-back will be real because Ford will be significantly trimming back the amount of work they send to McMurough, James & Ashton. It's a done deal. I made all the calls myself."

"That's how it's done?"

"That's how it's done." There was a pause, and he smiled at Sandy. "You can do his job a thousand times better than him on his best day. You can do my job better than me."

"I'll try not to let you down."

"You won't."

The second week of July, Nixon flew in for a speech to the Detroit Economic Club. Willie gave Mary Jane and Sandy a choice. They could stand in the back of the room and listen to the speech, or they could accompany him to the airport where he had a meeting with two of his superiors on Air Force One. They went with Willie. On the plane, Willie introduced both women to the men who were waiting for him. He complimented them in his introductions. Although Mary Jane did not know either man, one said he had heard good things about her from Maurice Stans. She blushed. He also told her that if she ever got tried of working with Willie to give him a call. He went and got the co-pilot who gave Mary Jane and Sandy a tour of the aircraft while the men settled in the conference room. When the co-pilot mentioned that they were flying west that afternoon for brief stops in Kansas City, Topeka, and Wichita; Sandy launched into the story about her mother at Willow Run, her mechanic grandfather, and Mrs. Beech. The Lieutenant Colonel was a partner in a Beech Bonanza and stayed with the women for lunch. He knew of Mrs. Beech by reputation, and was fascinated with Sandy's recollections.

The President and his entourage boarded at 1:30 P.M. He knew Willie and greeted him by name. Willie introduced Sandy and Mary Jane. The entire time, a photographer took pictures. Only one was posed. Nixon gave the instructions of where to stand and when to smile. As they left the plane, the co-pilot handed Mary Jane and Sandy a vinyl portfolio with the presidential seal molded into the side. Inside were a brochure about the plane, a writing tablet and ball-point pen labeled Air Force One, and a photograph of the plane autographed by the crew. He asked Sandy for her grandfather's name, saying that they landed in many of places, and one never knew. He wrote it down, as well as Sandy's. They stood on the ramp until the departing jet could no longer be seen.

Riding back to the office with Willie, each kept their own thoughts. Sandy congratulated herself. She was in the circle. She had been near it for the last several weeks and not even recognized it. Today, for a little while, she was there. She loved it. This was where she belonged. It was only when they got back into the downtown traffic that Sandy noticed Willie. She was sitting in the back seat, and after studying the lines of his perfect haircut, she began to wonder what he had discussed on the plane. She wondered if it was grand strategy for the remainder of the campaign in Michigan, or petty pay backs. She extended the Maury Bernard scenario in her mind to the point that the Nixon administration would do something to zap Ford for sponsoring Bernard's brief and undistinguished presence in their campaign. She chided herself that her daydream was taking it too far, but then she thought over events that she knew were sure to result from his fumbling of the printing of bumper stickers and yard signs, and placements of 15 second radio spots. She turned her thinking to the positive side, wondering for a moment how competence was rewarded. Was it just as easy to get noticed and brought into the circle? She starred at the back and side of Willie's head, wondering what he knew that she did not. He really was handsome. He lived in the circle.

There were more volunteers than usual in the storefront, no doubt the result of the President's visit. Many of the regulars had either been at the luncheon or had waited outside. Everyone had a story, but none topped the souvenirs from Air Force One. Willie listened politely and after several minutes slipped away into his office to make calls. Shortly after 5:00 P.M. he surprised Sandy and Mary Jane by inviting them for a drink and dinner. They walked to an after-work bar two blocks away. Sandy had white wine, Mary Jane had whiskey, and Willie had mineral water. He said he wanted to run later. They ended up having four rounds, during which they relived the Air Force One visit. As the discussion progressed, Sandy learned that Mary Jane and Willie had worked together in the Department of Commerce, and on two other campaigns before that. They debated restaurants and after agreeing, walked back to the office for their cars. They met again at the restaurant. The dinner went long and the women were getting so drunk, that halfway through the meal, Willie gave up on his run and ordered a scotch. He was thin and by his own admission not much of a drinker. Soon he was as drunk as them. Mary Jane pressed for a continuation of the party, but Willie said he had an important meeting at 10:30 P.M. When she discovered that the meeting was in Willie's apartment, she invited them there. Willie reluctantly agreed. He had a half gallon of wine at home, but nothing else. They followed him to his apartment.

Sandy was surprised that Willie's apartment was two buildings down from Daryl's. Willie had inside parking, so she and Mary Jane found separate spots on the street. They met him in the lobby. Willie apologized about the apartment, he was only camping there. The women toured the one bedroom unit as he got them wine. Despite the cheap furniture and worn carpet, Sandy was struck at how the towels in the bathroom were neatly folded and at the order apparent through the open door of his closet. The clothes progressed across the rail from blue suits, to white shirts, to red ties. All neatly spaced. Three pair of very shiny shoes were on the floor. Back in the living room, Mary Jane settled into a chair, Sandy sat on the sofa, and Willie leaned up against the wall next to the window. Mary Jane was very drunk. She talked about Washington. She loved the city, but her work was boring. She lived for the campaigns. She was sad that soon this one would be over.

She did not look forward to going back. If only. Willie agreed. After her second glass, Mary Jane decided she'd better head home while she could still see straight. She acted as if she expected Sandy to leave with her, and it seemed that Sandy started to, but then Sandy said she'd have just one more.

After Mary Jane left, Sandy got her wine glass and stood close to Willie as he filed it. She smiled at him. He nervously looked away and took the empty wine bottle into the kitchen. Sandy took in a deep breath, hoping to relax the tightness in her stomach and hoping that her own nerves did not show. She took a large gulp from the glass and followed him into the kitchen. He was just coming out, and they clumsily bumped into each other. The wine splashed on both of them. Sandy grabbed a towel and wiped his tie, then her own bosom. Catching his eye, she dropped the towel and pressed herself up against him.

Coming home early from the bar refresher, Daryl thought he saw Sandy's car on the street. After he parked inside, he walked back out to see that it was her car. It was only two weeks from the bar exam, and the classes were tapering. He was home an hour earlier than usual. She must be waiting inside for him. He would surprise her surprise. When he got to his apartment, however, she was not there. He called the lobby desk and learned that no one had left a message for him. He got himself a beer and went out on the balcony to look down on her car.

When Sandy started to put her arms around Willie, he stiffened. She knew immediately she had crossed the line. She was ashamed. She couldn't believe she had made a play for her boss. She had never done anything like this. How stupid could she be. Once she got her breath, she told him all that. He told her not to worry, they all had too much to drink. She apologized. He said he had to get ready for his meeting. She got her purse and opened the apartment door to find herself interrupting a man who was just about to knock. She apologized to him also and said good night to Willie. He told her he'd see her at the office. She looked back toward the apartment from the elevator wondering what sort of power meeting Willie was involved in this late at night. He never talked about his work. What a fool she was.

Daryl was on his third beer when he noticed her coming down the sidewalk. There was no mistaking her. Her gold earrings caught the light from a street lamp. He recognized that familiar gesture in which she tilted and shook her head as she passed her hand over it to pull back her hair. Still he thought that he was watching her in the act of surprising him. He thought that perhaps she had walked up to the corner store for soft drinks or something. He could hear her steps and almost called out to her, but he noticed her gait. Had she been drinking? He started to get excited. He wanted to hold her. He missed her. They hadn't made love in several weeks. He loved her. Looking at her excited him. She was beautiful. He had never told her that. He would. He would tonight. His stomach tightened when she left the sidewalk and walked around to the driver's side of her car. She unlocked the door and opened it. As she started to get in she looked up and saw him on his balcony looking down. She continued to get in the car, but hesitated leaving one leg out of the car. Daryl could see her hands on the steering wheel. After a moment, she pulled in her leg and reached out for the door. Daryl thought he would faint as he watched her drive off.

He drank until he passed out on his sofa. He woke from habit at the usual time, and dressed for Campbell Short. In the law library, he starred at his outlines. What in the world was happening? He loved her. He knew that. She was so perfect. She was smart. She was pretty. He thought she loved him. He should have known from the beginning that it wouldn't work. She had more class than he ever would. She could do better than him. Apparently, she had. He was no good at sex. He knew he did not please her. She deserved better. Who could it be? The librarian told him he had a call. It was Sandy. She wanted to talk, right away, not on the phone, it couldn't wait. Could he come to his apartment? Daryl dreaded the encounter. This was the end, and he hadn't even seen it coming. God, he loved her. He was just a big dumb Marine. What did he expect? He fought back tears. The few blocks seemed miles. She was waiting in the lobby. They did not greet or touch. They did not talk on the elevator ride or in the hall. Inside his apartment, she turned to him. When their eyes met, she started to cry. He did not look away from her eyes, even though he also cried. "I love you." she said. "I love you. I will never love anyone else."

He took her in his arms and held her. After a moment they kissed. Each tasted the salt of the others tears. They made love. He walked her back to the Nixon office and then returned to his outlines where he left them in the law library. He never asked, and she never explained the evening before. He suspected much more than had happened, but he was as always, satisfied with the result and not concerned at how it was obtained. She did love him. Now he was sure. That was enough.

CHAPTER 16

When Sandy got back to the office, she found Willie there. It was unusually early for him. She went straight into his office.

"I'm sorry."

"Nothing to be sorry for."

"I am. I'm not like...."

"I don't know what you're talking about. We all had too much to drink. Fortunately, we all got home safely." He smiled at her. She smiled back, relieved. She started to leave, but stopped when he spoke, "Sandy, you're a quick study. We haven't really had to teach you anything. There is one lesson I've learned about working in an office. Keep work at the office and your personal life at home. Anything else is a ticket to disaster."

"Understood."

Willie, spent the rest of the morning on the phone. After an hour, he closed his door. When Mary Jane arrived, she complained of a hang over and asked about Sandy. Sandy asked her to go to lunch, which they had never done before. At a sandwich shop down the block, Sandy confessed her impropriety.

"Is that all?"

"Isn't that enough?"

"I have worked with Willie for eight years. You are not the first to make a fool out of yourself over him."

"Is he married, does he date?"

"Willie?"

"I feel so bad. I never thought about his life. He handled it well."

"That's Willie."

"Does he have someone?"

"No, well, not really, just me."

"Oh my God, I can't believe what I've...."

"It's not what you think. Well, once maybe. I made your move look amateur by comparison. You know Willie, he handled it well."

"I'm sorry."

"I've worked with him every day for over eight years. I don't ever want to be with anyone else."

"And your not...."

"No." Mary Jane played with her food and looked around the room. "Willie is the best there is. He has earned what he has. He should be on the White House staff. Maybe this term..... Anyway, there's big things in store for him. I won't let anything interfere with that."

"I don't understand."

"Do you like him?"

"Yes, do you think I would have done this if I didn't."

"I mean as a friend."

"Sure."

"I'm talking politics. Are you loyal? Would you ever no anything to hurt him?"

"Of course not."

"Then promise me that somewhere down the line at a fund raiser or rally, you let on to someone that you had an affair with him. You'll get the chance, believe me. It will help Willie."

"What the hell are you talking about?"

"I love him. I protect him." Her voice cracked and she wiped a tear from the corner of her eye. "He's gay. I will never leave him. When I think it's needed, I create suspicions about us. I cover for him. He doesn't deserve what would happen if I didn't."

"Does he know?"

"I don't know. Maybe. It doesn't matter. I love him." She gathered her composure. "You can't breathe a word of this to anyone, ever. I have never told this to anyone. You have to promise me."

"You can trust me."

Two days later Mary Jane, Sandy, and Willie received large envelopes from the White House with autographed copies of the photograph of them on Air Force One with Nixon. There was also a brief letter thanking them for their work. Until he saw the photograph, Daryl had not believed her. Her father was also impressed, but her mother was most of all. The following morning she took it from

Sandy's room and carried it to her bridge game at The Club. As she explained it, Sandy was second in command of Nixon's Michigan campaign. She would have to leave the campaign to go back to law school, but she would probably be spending more time in Detroit this year. Her fellow was an associate at Campbell Short. The following week Sandy got a handwritten letter from Mrs. Beech. Air Force One had landed at the Factory Field. She had learned Sandy was a law student and making a name for herself in politics. She was proud of her. She could do anything she wanted. She should find time to come to Kansas and visit her grandfather. When she did, she must come to the factory for a visit. She should also give her best to her mother. Sandy's mother also carried that letter to the bridge game.

Sandy had dinner with Daryl every night during the three day bar exam. She was taken at how relaxed he was, especially after the first day. She recognized an easy air in him that she had not seen since she first met him. He was confident he was going to pass and that his position at Campbell Short was secure. Sandy noted that he did not mention that he would be a lawyer, a member of the bar. That is what would be going through her mind if she were in his place. Daryl mocked some of his peers. She wouldn't believe it, there were people who brought casebooks and hornbooks to the bar exams and studied from them on every break. He laughed that some people would never get it, but that was fine. Everyone who failed pushed him one notch higher in the heap. The outlines were the key. It was going well.

It did not go so well the following Monday morning. Daryl appeared outside Goldfarb's office. Goldfarb was surprised and distracted by his own work. He gave Daryl the impression that he had forgotten he would be joining their department. Goldfarb turned him over to Fell, a junior partner. Daryl spoke with Fell for about half an hour. Fell described the department. Everyone had their own cases. There would not be any staff meetings or the like. They did not function as a team. The only distinction was that the senior lawyers got the bigger cases. If an associate needed help, he could ask, but that wasn't done. If an associate got in trouble, a partner would review the file. That had never happened in his seven years with the firm. Daryl would be billing his time, and billable hours were important, but it wasn't like the other departments; their fees were limited and approved by the Bankruptcy Court. The most important thing was to close cases. That's when the firm got paid. The revenue he generated would be carefully tracked. Billable hours was an important statistic on any associate, but the critical number was fees collected. Keller took Daryl to a smaller office and passed him off to Edwards, a senior associate. Daryl got a similar orientation from Edwards. He then took Daryl further down the hall to a small, windowless office between two secretarial work stations. There he introduced Daryl to Diana McClure. Hiller, last year's new associate, and Daryl would share her. She was nineteen and taking paralegal courses at night. Daryl liked seeing his name on the plaque next to the door. He called Sandy from his new office, but cut the call off when Diana appeared in his door. She pointed to the five banker's boxes stacked up against his wall. The week before they had held a garbage collection. Everyone gave their old dog cases to Daryl. Daryl nodded and smiled, indicating that he was familiar with such drill.

"I don't know the first thing about bankruptcy."

"You will before this is over. The first order of business is getting out letters to the clients, two letters for each file, one to be signed by the parting lawyer, one from you. You write both."

From that day forward Daryl disappeared into the bowels of Campbell Short. He left his apartment at 6:30 A.M. and rarely got back before midnight. He spoke with Sandy several times each day by phone, but Saturday nights and Sundays were their only times together. Sandy was also putting in six day weeks on the campaign. Nixon came back to town the third Saturday in August for a golf game with a crowd from the first tier at the Big Three. It was Sandy's last day before returning to school. She did not get to see Nixon again, her assignment was to get Bob Hope to the golf course. He was appearing at the Ohio State Fair, and she chartered an executive jet to bring him up to stroke the deep pockets with Nixon. She rode in the limo with him from Detroit City Airport and was very serious about her assignment of reviewing the list attending. He interrupted her, making jokes and ignoring her briefing. It seemed he knew most of the names, but she persisted.

Willie had ridden over with Nixon. He met Sandy in the parking lot and they commandeered a limo to take them back downtown. He took Sandy and Mary Jane to an elegant restaurant for a farewell luncheon for Sandy. He carried the conversation, recalling the initial luncheon with her father, Sandy's eagerness to present her resume, and his disinterest. Mary Jane understood. He recalled the Bernard experience. He and Mary Jane exchanged a half dozen other names, all new to Sandy, who had come and gone the same way in this and other campaigns. He complimented Sandy for a job well done. He made a weak effort at cajoling her not to leave, telling her that it may be her only presidential campaign and that the law school would still be there when it was over. Sandy thanked them both for the summer and assured them that what she really wanted was to be a lawyer. Nixon could win without her.

On Sunday, Daryl came up to Grosse Pointe for church and lunch with Sandy's family. As Sandy's mother and father followed them up for Communion, she imagined their wedding in this church. During lunch, her father ran through the list of names he knew at Campbell Short. Daryl knew most of the names but not the individuals. Her father did not know any of the names in Daryl's department. Daryl asked about the organization of Chrysler's law department, and the two men were off on a management discussion that bored Sandy. Her mother chatted with her about her packing. Sandy's father could not believe that Campbell Short's bankruptcy group was horizontal, without oversight or controls. Daryl assured him that as far as he knew most other departments in the firm were not organized that way, but insisted it was true. Even Goldfarb, the chairman, paid no attention to case assignments. His secretary divied them out by size. When they exhausted that subject, they started speaking of the ABA Her father urged Daryl to stay active and participate. He found his own participation in the Antitrust and Business Law Sections was invaluable. Daryl expressed doubt that ABA work could do much for his situation at Campbell Short, but her father reminded him never to underestimate the value of who he knew. Daryl liked the sound of that and remembered it.

Back at their home, Daryl helped load Sandy's car. He followed her over to Ann Arbor in his car. She had gotten back in Northwood, a different apartment, but the same roommate. Her roommate would not be coming in from Chicago until that evening. After unpacking, they made love. Driving back to Detroit, Daryl thought only of his files. Sandy went grocery shopping and worried about getting registered for the classes she wanted and the long lines in the student bookstore.

CHAPTER 17

I spent the summer of 1972 working in the re-election campaign of Richard Milhouse Nixon. That was an experience. My Dad was tight with our local congressman, and he recommended the position. It was in the Nixon office in Columbus. They had similar offices in Cincinnati and Cleveland, but they needed people in Columbus. Dad's company was still making bombs in Attica. I just couldn't do that anymore. I told him I needed to be moving into my legal career, but I couldn't find anything, not as a first year student with mediocre grades. Fortunately, this political thing came through. I didn't get paid, but I was able to get a job tending bar at the South Berg, six hours a night, six nights a week. I crashed with some of my old buddies who had a rental house on Neil Avenue. Naturally, I didn't go around bragging about being in Chicago in 1968. Actually, it was a good summer. I learned a lot. It never ceases to amaze me how much you can learn in a menial position if you pay attention. That applied not only to the campaign but also bar tending. By the way, I may have worked for Nixon, but I voted for McGovern. Over the years, that has worked out well. There is a benefit to being on both sides of an issue, but it can be a high wire act.

I did go back to Attica for the Fourth of July and stopped there on the way back to Ann Arbor before Labor Day. Anyone I knew in town was married and starting families. Most were gone. I asked about Joe. What I learned came from his mother through mine. They would run into each other from time to time at the bank, the grocery, store or the post office. I could have gone out to the farm for a visit. Dieter would have given me a straight report. I didn't. By the same token, I could have called Joe or even gone a little out of the way to stop in Sandusky on the way to school. I didn't. From what I heard, he was OK. He was still working on boats. He had gotten quiet again, like he was in high school. Same old Joe, she said. I didn't quite buy that.

Law school was a much easier life second year. By then everyone had their place, including me and my buddies up in the back row. I ran into Sandy from time to time in the hall or snack bar. I can't say we were friends, just friendly. We were long passed a fork in the road. She was in with the Student Bar crowd first year. They had a conference room where they all hung out. I spent three years in the Law Quad and never once saw the inside of that room. Sandy ran for Student Bar president that year. I voted for her. She won. There were a lot of jokes at the time about keeping it in the family, because of Daryl. She also made law review. I knew that because I saw her name posted on the bulletin board on the list of invitees. I was stupid enough to be looking for my name. We all have our dreams. Well, once she made law review, I didn't see much more of her. Law review had its own offices which I was also never inside. I'd see her around. Maybe once a month we talked briefly. I always enjoyed talking to Sandy.

CHAPTER 18

As one of the pool of Notes and Comments Editors, Sandy chaffed at the responsibility given her. She was to check citations. That meant making sure the footnoted names of cases were abbreviated and punctuated in accordance with Harvard's standards. What gave Harvard the right? What made the third year student that supervised her work think that he could lecture her because one of her penciled corrections to a footnote was not in accordance with proofreader's standards. It could be understood by anyone looking at it. Still she let it all pass. The first time she sat down at the conference table in the law review offices she knew what she wanted. She wanted to sit at the head of the table, she wanted to be Editor-In-Chief. She was President of the Student Bar Association, and she found that she liked the head of the table. She could put up with the pettiness to get there. The petty could never qualify for the position, although there seemed to be some mystery surrounding it. Supposedly, the best student got the job; but only if the student participated in law review. Then there was measure taken of the level of participation. Then there was measure taken of the quality of performance. She would never again deviate from the Harvard or the proofreader's standards. Her grades made her a contender. The rest was politics. Daryl would love this.

Daryl had quickly found that of the three prongs of his background, an engineering degree in industrial systems design, the Marines, and law school; law school had done the least to prepare him for his career as a bankruptcy lawyer. The tangible part of his work manifested itself in filling out forms. Most of the lawyers regarded forms work as beneath them. They felt that forms inhibited their thinking and discourse on the great legal principles to summary information presented in an unimaginative and rigid form. They usually deferred such tasks to their secretaries. Not Daryl. His legacy from the

Marines was an abiding appreciation for forms, not just for their organization and uniformity, but for their underlying purpose; to treat everyone the same. Rules and forms had recognized and protected his special conscience. Daryl learned bankruptcy law by learning the forms. It didn't matter to him how a statute or rule read, or how the cases interpreted them, it only mattered how all that manifested itself on the standard forms. If he had to read a rule, he read it with a form at hand so he could understand its application. By mid-September, Daryl had worked through all the backlog dumped upon him. He closed half, because they were ready and only neglected. The others he had moved ahead. He left his files clean and orderly. Anyone could pick one up and in a few minutes understand it. That was not the way he found them.

Having progressed, largely through the clerical skills he learned in the Marines, Daryl found himself with increasing amounts of time. He could comfortably address his work in eight hours, but no one else did. Because of that, he asked for and got a disproportionate number of small cases. In that manner, he continued to work the same hours as his peers. Still, he grew progressively disgruntled. He looked around and saw that all the lawyers were doing exactly the same work. The numbers in their cases may be different, bigger than those in his cases, but the work was the same. Each lawyer did it differently. Each worked independently with his secretary, but the work was the same. Their system was no system. Daryl could not help but draw upon his training in industrial systems design. The department cried for division of labor and controls. He went to Goldfarb who listened impatiently. He claimed to have heard it all before. Campbell Short had been doing things this way for decades. As far as he knew, they always worked this way. He came up through this system and prospered. He saw no reason to change anything. Daryl asked if he could at least get a mag card machine for his secretary so they could fill out the forms faster. Goldfarb refused. Office equipment decisions were made by the Administration Committee and had to be approved by the Executive Committee.

Daryl's secretary, Diana, had started in the firm's Mag Card Center, the contemporary name for a typing pool. The new name resulted from the upgraded equipment they used. It was essentially the first generation of word processing equipment, combining an electric typewriter with documents stored on a magnetic strip painted on the traditional paper punch cards. The Mag Card Center shared the other half of the lowest floor of Campbell Short's offices with the Insolvency Department. There were a dozen noisy machines in the open room, and a supervisor who controlled the flow of long documents that came in from the secretaries. Each partner had a secretary. There were two secretaries per associate. Secretaries had conventional electric typewriters with no memory. It was through Diana that Daryl learned about the power of mag card machines. She took him on a tour of the center. Diana described that with one of the machines she could do in a day what now took her a week on a typewriter.

After he struck out with Goldfarb, Daryl cultivated the supervisor of the Mag Card Center. He learned that they kept one machine in reserve and usually acquired one or two new machines a year. This year they were going to trade in two for newer models. Daryl then went to the office administrator. She refused his proposition to assign the reserve machine to his secretary as a demonstration project. She also refused his proposition to keep one of the trade-ins for a similar use. She did not have the authority. He asked how much credit the firm got for the trade-ins. When he learned it was $500, he offered to buy one with his own money for $600. She agreed in the name of the firm's greater good, but also told him that any consequences of his breach of firm operational procedures and especially the disruption of secretarial morale would be his alone. She was convinced that he was one of those associates who would no longer be with the firm by Spring. By early November, Daryl and Diana were processing five times more small bankruptcies than any other associate.

With his new found time, Daryl sat upon righting another wrong. More than once he had been forced to research and brief issues in his cases. The summer clerks were no longer available for the task. Before he went to the law library, he asked around the department to see if anyone else had previously dealt with the issues. He encountered two barriers. No one wanted to take the time to dig through their files, and everyone reminded him that the need to research and write increased legitimate billable hours. Since all major typing projects went through the Mag Card Center, Daryl found what he needed there and not the law library. He made an arrangement with the mag card supervisor to get duplicate cards of all the bankruptcy related research memos and briefs. He and Diana organized that into their own desk drawer law library.

Limited now by Goldfarb's secretary who refused to assign him any more cases, Daryl turned his free time to the court. Rather than use the firm's runner's to file documents at the Bankruptcy Court, Daryl started carrying his own. Inevitably, Daryl ingratiated himself with the counter clerks. He idled with them telling jokes, talking about the weather. They started sharing their coffee pot with him, which made him a familiar figure behind the counter. Eventually, he got to know the staffs of the Bankruptcy Judge and Referees. Whenever the Judge caught sight of Daryl, he would invite him into his chambers. The Judge was a football fan also. The Referees were less friendly with Daryl, but still social. They were less secure in their positions and suspected that Daryl might be politicking for one of their jobs.

Just before Thanksgiving the Associate Performance Review Committee noticed a significant discrepancy between Goldfarb's lackluster memo about Daryl Dobbins and some of their statistics. Consistent with Goldfarb's memo, Dobbins' total billable hours were slightly less than the average for associates in the Insolvency Department, and significantly lower than the firm average. On the other hand, Dobbins' caseload was 527% higher than the average department associate. He was closing cases at a rate 1,143% higher than the average department associate. His billable hours per case was only 19% of the average department associate, but he generated 617% more fees collected by the firm than the average department associate. He was working less and making more than anyone else. The office administrator, who presented the numbers, suggested that the answer might be the mag card machine she had let him have. The committee chairman called Goldfarb. Later that day the Performance Review Committee met with the Executive Committee. Goldfarb and the office administrator attended by invitation. When she disclosed that Daryl had paid for the mag card with his own money, the chairman of the executive committee went wild. A three month associate had generated more revenue than any two partners in the department, and the firm was charging him to do it! Heads should roll. He scowled at Goldfarb who sat in silence.

Later that week the Administration Committee authorized the office administrator to hire a consultant to study the firm's use of the Mag Card Center, the possibility of improving the interface between the Mag Card Center and the secretaries, and the possibility of integrating mag card machines into select departments with special needs, provided that it would not disrupt secretarial morale. Also, and coincidentally, the chairman of the Executive Committee found himself seated next to the

Bankruptcy Judge at a Bar Association luncheon. The Judge asked after Daryl Dobbins. He was an impressive young man. That afternoon, and on his own authority, the chairman had a $1,200 check prepared for Daryl. He called Daryl into his office, and they had a long talk.

Sandy continued to come home on Sunday's. Daryl also attended church and dinner with her family. Daryl dismissed any detailed question into his work, with a general response about the low life of associates and billable hours. That left the focus of their discussions on Sandy. Her academic endeavors seemed easier this year. She was content to limit herself to her casebooks, hornbooks, and class notes. She no longer did independent research in the law library. She needed that time for law review. It was tedious, and she did not like most of the people involved in it. The Student Bar was almost recreation for her. She attended all the meetings, but as President, there was not much more to do. The committees did all the work. The Sunday after the election she wondered what would happen to her friends Mary Jane and Willie, now that Nixon had won. She had called the office, but the phones were disconnected. She had their addresses in Washington, she would write. Daryl made a mental note to write to his colonel. He had been meaning to for years. That Sunday, Sandy stopped at Daryl's apartment before going back to Ann Arbor. They alternated such visits. Daryl would come to Ann Arbor Saturday afternoon and stay with her for dinner. If he did not, she would come by his apartment that Sunday.

Daryl had Thanksgiving dinner with Sandy's family. It was during that meal that her mother inquired about his family. Sandy cringed, she had never explained the situation to her mother. Daryl cleared his throat before he spoke.

"I am not in communication with my family."

Sandy's mother looked to her father, then Sandy. "I'm sorry, I don't understand."

"It's not complicated, really. I applied for conscientious objector status and was honorably discharged from the Marines. They could not accept that and informed me not to contact them again."

There was a long silence, then Sandy's mother continued. "But that was years ago. You surely can't still...."

"It was their choice. I am honoring their wishes."

Sandy broke in. "Daryl grew up in Battle Creek. His mother teaches school. His father's a mechanic."

Sandy's father spoke. "Daryl, I am sure they are proud of you.

Any parent would be. I don't agree with you, but I admire your stand. It's this war, tearing the country apart, tearing families apart."

There was a pause for Daryl to respond. He did not. The remainder of the meal passed in silence. After the meal, Daryl was anxious to watch football, but they did not watch football in Sandy's house. After an hour of fiddling about, Daryl suggested to Sandy that they go for a drive. They drove north along the water in Daryl's MG, and parked in a lot at Jefferson Beech. It was cold and gray. They watched a shaft of blue rain a mile out on Lake St. Clair. Daryl spoke first.

"Do you think we will ever get married?"

"Yes."

"Kids?"

"Yes."

They sat for an hour watching the weather and not talking.

CHAPTER 19

Sandy came home for the holidays the weekend before Christmas. Daryl reluctantly agreed to go Christmas shopping with her. He wanted to shop downtown, so that if it got boring he could easily break away to the office or his apartment. Sandy summoned him north, and they went to the Eastland Shopping Center in Harper Woods. Periodically, he asked what she wanted for Christmas. She would not answer. He followed her about dutifully for a few hours, but his impatience was apparent and growing. Sandy suggested he get a drink and wait for her on a bench opposite a jewelry store. He finished the coffee just as she came up to him.

"Come here, there's something I want to show you." he said, leading her to one of several small windows showcasing jewelry. "Do you want to get married?"

"Yes." She dropped her packages and kissed him.

"Come on, if we're going to get engaged, let's do it right."

They went inside and spent half of what Daryl had saved on a two carat diamond. Back at her house she took Daryl into her father's library where, Daryl, uncharacteristically joined him in a Scotch. While he did, Sandy went and got her mother. Just as the women entered the library, Sandy said that they had an announcement to make. She came across to Daryl and slipped her hand around the arm in which he held his drink. Her parents looked to them, knowing, yet waiting to hear. Daryl said that they were engaged. Sandy said no date. She showed off her ring. Her parents wanted to take them to The Club for dinner, but Daryl wasn't dressed. They agreed that their usual Sunday excursion would now have that special purpose. They had several more drinks in the library, then Sandy left to dress for the dinner reservations she said they had downtown. When she returned, Daryl was finishing his fifth Scotch and laughing with her father. She decided that they would leave his car, and she would drive him downtown.

Daryl slept during the ride to his apartment, but the shower woke and sobered him. When he stepped out, he found Sandy disrobed and waiting for him. She started to dry him with a towel, but their kissing interrupted. They went to his bedroom where they made love in the sheets that stuck to them because they were damp from the water on Daryl. After, Daryl nodded off from the alcohol until Sandy woke him. She did not want to go out and asked if that were OK. He agreed, and closed his eyes again. She left the bed long enough to order a pizza. When she returned, she straightened the covers and crawled back in to initiate another encounter. A half an hour later both scrambled out of bed and into their clothes when the pizza man came. Later Daryl walked her down to her car. She came back the next morning to take him to church and to retrieve his car.

That Monday, Sandy had a follow-up interview for a summer clerkship with Wheate, Cornfeld, Racine and Rock. She had signed up for and attended ten on-campus interviews in early November. That was the first step of the formal recruiting process by law firms. Because of Daryl, she chose to interview with only Detroit firms. Also because of Daryl, she did not interview with Campbell Short. Of the ten firms she interviewed, she was truly interested in only the three or four largest. Campbell Short would have been on that list, but for the Daryl conflict. Even if it were on the list, Wheate Cornfeld would have still been her first choice. They were an established firm, well into their second decade when Campbell Short had been formed in the Civil War by two enterprising young lawyers who wanted to cash in on the big business of war bonds.

The on-campus interviewers were typically partners from the firms who had attended Michigan. They volunteered for the duty because the autumn day in Ann Arbor was one of sweet nostalgia for them. Because it cost them a day of billable time, they grumbled about the thankless duty around the office. They were uniformly poor at interviewing, spending most of the allotted fifteen minutes describing themselves and their firms rather than reviewing the students' credentials. Always in the last few minutes of the interview, they would scan down the student's resume and make a few quick notes on it. From Sandy's perspective, she saw her career was riding on superficial consideration and cavalier notes, but she was wrong. Objective criterion such as her L.S.A.T. score, her grade average, law review, extracurriculars, and most importantly her class standing would be weighed by a committee that she would never meet.

The initial interviewer was there merely for the all important "smell test", that is, a quick sense of the compatibility of the student with the firm's culture. Everyone understood that to be a test of dress, bearing, and general demeanor. Still a few students would regularly show up in jeans and get into political arguments with the interviewers. Years later they would still be bragging from their small suburban offices of how they first took on the silk-stocking lawyers. Also known, but not discussed, was that the initial interview was for the purpose of determining age, race, religion, sex and national origin. In this the alumnae partner was all powerful, for all any had to do was trash the resume of a student who did not meet their subjective standards. Of twenty on-campus interviews, maybe four resumes went back to the committee. Still, with recruiters visiting law schools across the country, that left the committees with dozens of resumes for each clerkship. Second interviews were not customary, but Sandy lived in Detroit, and it was convenient. The second interview was presented to her by the initial interviewer who called it a need to impress one partner who had hesitations about her. In fact, Wheate Cornfeld wanted her, and the true purpose of the second interview was to rush Sandy. Both Daryl and her father suspected as much. She couldn't have looked any better on paper or in person. Still, she approached the interview as if she had to sell herself.

The partner who spoke with her in Ann Arbor greeted her and gave her a forty-five minute tour of the offices. He pointed into the offices of department heads and gave their names. When they weren't on the phone or in conference, he introduced her to them. He then escorted her passed a secretary and into a large corner office. Inside was an emaciated, chain-smoking woman in a blue business suit seated behind a large desk. Sandy's tour guide slipped away, leaving Sandy alone and wondering why this woman might be her detractor. Elizabeth Cromwell came around her desk and sat next to Sandy in one of the two chairs that faced her desk. There was no paper on her desk, nor anywhere in the office, yet it was quickly apparent she knew all the details of Sandy's resume. They chatted through Sandy's background then she told Sandy that she was a tax lawyer, estate planning. She was the firm's first female partner. She then went into a long discourse on how there were no barriers for advancement in the firm, other than excellence. That alone was the only reason there were not more women and minorities in the firm. She repeatedly assured Sandy that she could succeed in the firm. After an hour she took Sandy to a private club on the top floor of the building for lunch. There, four middle-aged men were waiting for them. They were the department chairmen from Business Organizations, Litigation, Securities, and the chairman of the Hiring Committee. Each talked about the nature of their work, and the Hiring Chairman ended the meal asking Sandy if she would like to meet privately with any particular department.

Sandy had expected a one hour interview. She was unprepared for the long session, and though it exhilarated her, she was overwhelmed and exhausted. She walked to Daryl's apartment, where she laid down on his bed and rested. After a half hour she called him. She already knew what the session meant. She was in. Still, it sounded good coming from Daryl. She took off her suit and napped until 4:30 P.M. Then she dressed and walked over to Campbell Short where she met Daryl. He introduced her to Diana and others about as his fiance. They went out for dinner. Afterwards, he walked her to the parking garage where she had left her car, then went back to the office. It was also good to hear it from her father. She was in.

Sandy went directly to Daryl's apartment the Friday afternoon that marked the beginning of their Spring Break. Since the holidays, she was not content to see him only on Saturday night or Sunday with her parents, and had taken to sneaking into Detroit to spend the night with him. As far as her parents knew, she had to stay in Ann Arbor for some law review work on Saturday, and would be home Sunday. She showered before she called Daryl. Because it was Friday, he left the office early. They made love, then dressed and went out to the Italian restaurant that had become Sandy's favorite. She was nervous about walking back after dark, but Daryl assured her that he thought no one ever bothered him because of his size. Still, she thought it would be safer to have a place farther out. The comfort and security would offset the commute. They spent most of the evening on the sofa watching TV. When the news came on at 11:00 P.M., Sandy started kissing him, and they retired to the bedroom. After breakfast the next morning she rejoined Daryl on the sofa. He was watching cartoons. It maddened her, and she deliberately interrupted him.

"Let's get married." She urged.

"What else is new?"

"I mean it. Let's get married."

"When?"

"As soon as school is out. I've been thinking about it. There is no reason not to. That gives us two months to get ready. Mother can arrange the wedding. We can take two weeks to honeymoon. I can live here with you during my clerkship."

"You can live here with me during your clerkship anyway."

"I won't do that. Don't ask me."

"OK, let's do it."

"Are you sure?"

"You're the one that needs to be sure. You've still got another year of school and the bar exam."

"I've already thought about that. We will get an apartment out west. I commute to school; you commute to work. We split the difference. As for the bar exam, I'll have you and your outlines."

"It's OK with me, if it's OK with you."

"It's OK with me."

CHAPTER 20

Their wedding was the first Saturday in June. Initially, Sandy's mother was against it. She wanted Sandy to finish law school first. Sandy countered that preparing for the bar exam the following summer was not the best circumstance in which to start a marriage. Her mother suggested that they wait until after the bar exam. Although Sandy never accused her of it, she thought that her mother's only objection was her limitation to two months for planning the wedding. It never occurred to Sandy that her mother might actually be concerned that Sandy was jeopardizing law school. Her father seemed happy, and took no overt roll except for the periodic mediation of arguments between Sandy and her mother.

The only serious prospective impediment to Sandy's will was the priest, but their evening meeting with him went well. Monsignor O'Kiernan had known Sandy's parents since he was first assigned to their parish in the early 1950's. He had heard Sandy's First Confession and served her First Communion. The Church was available because of a cancellation. That was always for the best. He advised them that they should never be too proud to call it off. What God put together, let no man.... He was willing to accept Sandy's Christian Marriage class at Marygrove as an acceptable substitute for the pre-cana classes. He ignored Daryl when he volunteered that he had never attended a Catholic school. Later he gave Daryl the paperback text from the classes. They were both Catholic and over twenty-one, so most of his usual lecture was not needed. Technically, they should have ninety days to read the bands three times, but since it was early April and the Sunday before the wedding was June First, he could read the announcement once in the three intervening months. That satisfied him. It also satisfied Daryl. He liked this priest. He thought like a lawyer. He blessed them before they left the Rectory. On the steps outside, Sandy reached up to take the lace off her hair. As she did, Daryl swept her up in his arms, kissed her, and hugged her after the kiss. Sandy always remembered that as their most romantic moment.

The rehearsal dinner was held at The Club. Daryl was determined to avoid a traditional bachelor party and succeeded with the help of Sandy's father. He reserved a private room at The Club for Daryl. The rehearsal dinner was scheduled from 8:00 to 9:30 P.M. and the bachelor party from 9:30 to 11:00 P.M. Daryl's guests simply moved across the hall from the dinner to the bachelor party. Although it was difficult to tell, Daryl had lost twenty pounds for the wedding, and he had no intention of loosening his discipline the night before. The bachelor party was, therefore, a sedate affair that even the open bar did not breach. The guests broke into two large groups, Daryl's friends from law school and his associates from work. The only partner invited was Frank Sloan. Daryl asked him mostly because his colonel, now Major General Braun, had agreed to be Daryl's best man. Daryl had started corresponding with him the fall before. After a few letters, he called him. By February, they were speaking at least once a week. If one didn't call, the other would. They never talked about their work or personal lives. They simply chatted about current events. The General had not hesitated when Daryl asked him.

Daryl flew him and his wife in from Washington and took a cab to meet them at the airport. To his surprise, Willie Sturtz and Mary Jane were on the same flight. They had not gotten into the White House and were back in the Department of Commerce. He had known that politicos such as himself would not have an important roll in a second term, and it was just as well he didn't get a White House job, for his peers were scrambling to distance themselves from Nixon for other reasons. He was hoping for a senatorial campaign assignment in the off-year elections. The General, doing a year at the Pentagon, was quickly in conversation with Willie. During the rehearsal dinner, Willie at first refused Daryl's invitation to stay for the bachelor party on the excuse of needing to accompany Mary Jane back to their hotel; but Sandy's parents intervened with their offer to drive her and the General's wife. Willie, The General, and Frank Sloan stood together near the bar, aside from the two groups. Daryl circulated until the party ended promptly at 11:00 P.M.

The ushers were instructed to balance those attending on both sides of the church, so it was not apparent that Daryl's family had not been invited. Monsignor O'Kiernan's vestments were more striking than Daryl had expected. When the organ sounded the first chord of the processional, Sandy was startled, muffled a shriek, then laughed. The bridesmaids were cousins from Kansas with whom Sandy was barely acquainted and knew mostly from her mother's dinner table reports. Her maid of honor was her roommate from law school. Selecting all of them had been Sandy's worst challenge, and almost brought her to favor eloping. She had discovered that she had no friends. It had never occurred to her. She knew dozens and dozens of people from her various activities, but they were acquaintances, not friends. She had Daryl. Daryl had friends. Her mother saved the day with her cousins; and her roommate was a logical, easy choice.

Her father was more dapper than ever. He wore his formal clothes as comfortably as he might wear old clothes in the yard, but, of course, he did not do yard work. Sandy thought that more people might be looking at him than her. She had powdered her face, but wore no other makeup. Her mother had given her new earrings. She smiled at her mother, whom everyone said looked more like her sister than mother. The weight of the train tugged at her balance and made her self-conscious. More than anything, she wanted to be done with the ceremony and off with Daryl. The red cumberbund on The General's formal uniform caught her eye. Half way down the aisle her eyes finally met Daryl's, and she did not look away after that. Daryl smiled and made no move to wipe away the tear that slid down the side of his face.

They honeymooned in Jackson Hole, Wyoming. It was Daryl's idea. Actually, it was Daryl's idea of a compromise. Sandy had wanted to fly to Europe, to see mountains and the coast of France. Daryl wanted a Caribbean Island. They both gave up water, Sandy got the mountains, and Daryl got a long cross country drive in the MG. Even he knew that was a mistake by the second day. His little car was either hot or cold, depending on the weather. It leaked in the rain, and was so noisy that they had to yell to each other. Leaving the wedding reception in it with their suitcases on the luggage rack was an adventure which continued to Ann Arbor where they spent the first night in an old downtown hotel. The second day into Chicago was tedious. The third day across Iowa into Omaha was an ordeal, which continued the fourth day into Cheyenne. The excitement returned the last day on the way into Jackson Hole.

They finally saw mountains and trees after the seemingly endless prairie. They stayed in town for the next two days. On the first, they never ventured further than the motel pool and restaurant. The next day they did the shops. The following day they went on a white water rafting trip that they booked in town. They took a long drive along the Grand Tetons the next. They spent another quiet day in town. During it they discussed selling the MG and flying home, but ultimately agreed upon a different route back and leaving early. The next morning they left for Cheyenne where they spent the night. Then they dropped down to Denver where they spent two nights in the Brown Palace. During that time, they deliberately stayed away from the car, limiting their exploration of the city to the places they could walk, such as the Civic Center, the Capitol, and Larimer Square. Then it was east across Kansas. Since Sandy had just seen all her relatives at the wedding, she did not want to stop to see them, but she did direct Daryl passed her grandparent's farm, and the Beech factory. They drove until after dark and stopped outside Kansas City. The last day, they rose early and drove again until late that night to get back to Detroit. When they got to Daryl's apartment, both wished that they were still on the road, but did not admit it to each other.

Daryl went to the office the following morning. Sandy did not report for her summer clerkship at Wheate, Cornfeld, Racine & Rock until the following week. She postponed calling her mother until the middle of the next morning. She felt uncomfortable in talking to her, as if the trip had somehow made her a different person. She felt no different, but she knew that she was supposed to be, for now she was a married woman. If she had not changed, certainly her mother's reaction to her would be different. Since Sandy's car was still in Grosse Pointe, her mother came by the apartment to pick her up. They had lunch at The Club, then went to the house to go through Sandy's clothes. There wasn't room in Daryl's apartment for more than a small portion of her clothes. Sandy started for the darker dresses. Her mother was concerned that Sandy dress appropriately for the office. She had not bought her any new suits, but she had been out looking during their honeymoon. That afternoon she took Sandy out to try them on, and she bought Sandy three new suits. Her mother also had the scoop on the private lives and eccentricities of half a dozen of the partners at Wheate, Cornfeld; all gained from their wives, all of potential value to Sandy, in her mother's opinion.

Sandy liked the summer clerkship. After an hour with the

chairman of the hiring committee during which he outlined the program for the summer, she found herself in a litigation partner's office with two associates. It was the kick-off meeting on a new products liability case they were defending for the insurer of the pool manufacturer. A four year old had drowned in an above-ground, backyard swimming pool. He had gotten stuck on the filter intake either because of its force or his own exploration of it. In any event he was revived, but he was severely brain damaged and would never walk or talk, much less feed or dress himself. The liability exposure was enormous. They could not afford to go to trial. Their task was to slow the discovery process by technical objections and motions, during which they would research even the most remote defense theories for use in negotiations with the Plaintiff's lawyer. The delays should make them anxious to settle, the technical defenses should whittle down their number. Because there would be no trial, the partner's role would be supervisory, except for the settlement negotiations. The senior associate would coordinate all work, would have signature authority on pleadings, and would personally handle depositions. The junior associate would draft pleadings and motions, handle document productions, and attend depositions as second chair. Sandy would draft research memoranda. She was off to the law library an hour later to determine if and to what extent blame could be shifted to the parents for not having the pool fenced as required by local ordinance and by not keeping a closer watch over their son.

Two weeks later she was given the task of a fifty state "Blue Sky" memo in connection with a securities offering. That was part of a ritual in securities work and within the firm. In it, the details of the offering had to be checked for compliance with the securities laws in all fifty states. The senior associates and partner who prepared the offering knew the answer before the work was undertaken because they were well-versed in the law and had drafted compliance into the documents. Nevertheless, an opinion letter assuring compliance would be required of the firm, and it was the firm's policy to have contemporaneous research of the specifics of the offering in the file to support the opinion letter. It was considered billable gravy for the firm and a good experience for the clerk or associate who drew the duty.

After that she got what she considered her most intriguing and challenging assignment from the Real Property department, for which she never found the answer she sought. A major client had bought two farms and built a factory. In the deal, the county abandoned an old road, which was now under the floor in the middle of the factory. Under old surveyor's conventions, the adjacent farmers actually owned the land to the middle of the road, and the county took an easement; however, for some reason long forgotten, the surveyors measured to one foot from the center of the road, leaving a two foot strip of no-man's-land. The firm had handled the land assemblage, and no one, including the county and the new surveyors discovered the problem. Later a new computer program installed by the county real estate tax people, discovered the land and after the appropriate notices in the paper, the two foot swath, along with hundreds of others, was sold by sheriff's auction to a local real estate lawyer who was a solo practitioner. Sandy was given to understand that she was to find any law under any theory that could exculpate their valued client, and also, the firm in a potential malpractice claim. She researched and wrote a half dozen different memos, all coming back to the same conclusion; the sliver of land may have gone unnoticed, but it was there to be known; the law may have gone unnoticed, but it was there to be known; the sale to the lawyer may have gone unnoticed, but it was there to be known; she concluded the lawyer had good title. While she felt a failure, the lawyers to which she reported were satisfied with her work, and reported as much in their "reaction memos" which, unknown to Sandy, went back to the hiring committee with a copy of every research memo she drafted.

After the real estate project, Sandy did two estate tax memos for Elizabeth Cromwell. Lawyer Cromwell had noticed a footnote in a recent Circuit Court of Appeals case that indicated if certain language in a trust had been drafted differently then a tax might have been avoided. Sandy was instructed to gather every case that would remotely support the footnote. Since the Circuit Court was binding precedent for them unless and until the U.S. Supreme Court ruled otherwise, Sandy's second assignment was to discover any indication of how the Supreme Court had or might handle the issue. Sandy knew that she was under scrutiny, worked late for several weeks, and re-wrote her memos several times before presenting her findings. Ms. Cromwell was pleased. Sandy gained more satisfaction from her reaction than any of the other projects. Although Sandy did not know it, her work was the basis of a new paragraph that would henceforth be included in all trusts drafted by the firm. In addition, letters went out to over two hundred clients suggesting changes to their estate plans. Two thirds of them responded, resulting in their having state-of-the-art plans, and the firm gaining significant additional revenue.

In addition to the long days of quiet research and writing, there were constant social obligations on the summer clerks. Monday, Tuesday, and Wednesday they were invited to lunch by the associates. Thursday and Fridays, the partners would take the clerks to lunch, one on one. Sandy knew that the partner lunches were for the purpose of evaluation and suspected that the associate lunches were also. In truth, some were, some weren't. All associates wrote memos to the hiring committee voicing their opinions on clerks, some after an individual luncheon and the rest in summary at the end of the summer. Some of the partners did also, but most did not. If a partner was particularly impressed with a clerk, he or she simply picked up the phone and called the chairman of the hiring committee. If not, the silence was usually fatal. There were also two outings for the clerks during the summer. They were invited to the firm picnic on the Fourth of July weekend, which everyone in the firm and their families attended; and later a dinner cruise on the Detroit River the second week in August, attended by all clerks and only those lawyers who chose to go. Sitting on the boat, Sandy noticed that her's was the only table at which three partners were sitting. In some instances there were tables with four clerks and no lawyers. She was beginning to feel confident about the summer.

Sandy left the clerkship one week earlier than she had initially planned, because she was at a breaking point between research projects, and because she wanted to have some time before school to get settled into the new apartment that she and Daryl had found. On her last day, she was taken to lunch by the chairman of the hiring committee, Elizabeth Cromwell, and the office administrator. The discussion during the meal was light and pleasant. As they finished their food, the hiring committee chairman described the firm's commitment to honor the ABA standards on the hiring process; accordingly, Sandy would have to wait like everyone else for her letter. Then he winked, and Elizabeth Cromwell and the office administrator smiled. They all shook her hand and without restraint expressed their hope that she would choose to join the firm. Daryl took her to dinner that night to celebrate her success. It would be the last time they would make love in his apartment. That weekend they moved to the garden apartment they had found in Redford Township. It was a three bedroom. They planned to use the extra bedrooms as a guest room and study. The unit had two levels, with a patio outside the ground level and a balcony from the master bedroom.

It overlooked the Rouge, south of its confluence with the Upper Rouge, just west of River Rouge Park, and just outside the Detroit city limits. From there, Sandy would commute to Ann Arbor and Daryl to downtown. The summer had been exciting, and Sandy liked eating breakfast with Daryl and walking to work; but she liked the new apartment more and was more excited about getting back to school. To facilitate his commute, Daryl sold the old MG and bought a new Triumph.

CHAPTER 21

Sandy felt at home sitting at the head of the conference table in the law review offices. In the ordinary course, whatever that was, she had been selected Editor-In-Chief. She was even more comfortable in the position than she had imagined. What she had not imagined was the nature of the demands upon her. The position took much less time than she thought, much less than her cite checking as a Notes and Comments Editor, and much less than her presidency of the Student Bar Association. It wasn't the time nor the decision making that stressed her, it was the constant beseeching by her fellow students. They pressed their ambitions not only in the law review offices, but wherever they found her; in the halls, in the snack bar, in the rest room, and by phone calls late at night to her apartment. They pressed even after she had decided against them.

What everyone wanted was a by-line. Sandy had thought that she would avoid the struggle by deciding that there would be no student articles that year. They had received more manuscripts from established legal scholars than they could publish. That decision only placed more competition on the student-drafted comments and notes published in the back of each issue. Everyone wanted a comment more than a note, and everyone wanted their name on their work. Sandy understood the pressure on the students competing for positions in the large law firms, but with her own position secure she was less sympathetic. She decided that the names of the authors of comments would be footnoted on the first page of the comment rather than at the end, and notes would continue to be anonymous. The struggle continued, and got worse when various comments and notes were rejected. After her own summer of researching real legal problems, she had no further personal desire to expound on the hypothetical; and had decided before the term began, and before she was named Editor-In-Chief, that she would not write a comment or note. Also, the time saved would be a concession to marriage. From her view, the more desperate the lobbying became, the more pathetic she found it. Her stomach tightened even at a casual thought about law review. She wanted to sit at the head of the table, but she came to dread it. The responsibility was one that she was not capable of leaving in the office. She spent most of her commute each day either working over arguments past or preparing for arguments anticipated. Her studies, on the other hand, proceeded at an easy, comfortable pace.

Late in October she received the letter from Wheate, Cornfeld, Racine & Rock that she expected. It was delivered a week ahead of the ABA standards. A deniable, unsigned handwritten note on a small slip of paper enclosed in the envelope promised an additional $1,000 signing bonus if accepted immediately, before the offers of the other firms went out. The salary offer was $5,000 a year more than Daryl made, but all the other terms were similar; successful completion of law school and passing the bar exam on the first attempt. Sitting at the kitchen table in their apartment and watching the shadows grow from the trees which were now passed their peak color, Sandy opened a bottle of wine and toasted herself. She did not start dinner, nor remember to call Daryl and ask him to bring in Chinese. Halfway through the bottle, she did call her mother.

"Oh, honey, I'm so happy for you. I can't tell you how proud I am of you."

"I seem to remember you trying to talk me out of law school."

"Sandy, that's ancient history. I only wanted what was best for you."

"I really wanted this."

"That's just like you. You went after it, and you got it. I can't wait to tell your father. Why don't you and Daryl come over tonight."

"No thanks. It's already late. He hates to do anything that we haven't planned in advance."

"Congratulations. This is really for the best. You will make a good lawyer. You're suited for it."

"Thank you."

"You're welcome dear, but don't thank me. You got what you wanted."

"Mother...."

"Yes dear?"

"I love you."

"I love you too dear. I'm very proud of you."

Sandy had finished the bottle by the time Daryl arrived. He found her resting her head on the table. He kissed her on the side of her face. When she raised up, he saw the letter. He wanted to take her out to celebrate, but she wouldn't go. They agreed upon a pizza, for which Daryl called after getting himself a beer. Sandy opened another bottle of wine and took a glass into the bathroom where she drew a bath. When the pizza came, Daryl found her napping in the bath, with the glass of wine balanced on the edge of the tub. He bent over and kissed her on the lips. She woke, wrapped her arms around his head, and kissed him for a long time. He eventually pulled back, complaining about his tie, which had dipped into the water. Standing, she gulped the wine. She posed for him, and he stepped closer to hold her. Soon, they were in the bedroom. Sandy rarely drank more than a glass or two of wine. She was drunk. They had never made love when she was drunk. She was aggressive and much less inhibited. Afterwards Daryl was troubled. Something didn't seem right.

The pizza was cold by the time they got to it. As they ate it, Sandy worked quickly into the second bottle of wine. Daryl threw down several beers and quickly caught up with and then passed her inebriation. He had gained back every pound he lost for the wedding and then some. It was the beer. She complained to him about law review. He complained to her about the office. They decided that they needed to get away. Daryl justified it as a celebration of her job offer. Sandy called it a second honeymoon. They debated various destinations, mostly small towns on the coast, before finally agreeing on Mackinac Island. It was a long drive, but he would take off Friday. They would spend Friday and Saturday night on the island, and drive back Sunday. Daryl would get reservations through the office. This time Daryl was the aggressor. He coaxed her into the bedroom. They kissed for several minutes. During a lapse, Sandy fell asleep. Daryl decided not to wake her and went for another beer.

When they got out of the Triumph at the ferry dock in Mackinaw City, both were stiff and tired. It was a big improvement over the MG, but six hours and three hundred miles was still trying. It was a cold, gray day. Daryl had never been to Mackinac Island or even the area. He marveled at the bridge. Sandy had been up once with her parents in the summer 1957 when they opened the bridge. They drove back and forth across the bridge, then took the ferry to Mackinac Island. They stayed at the Grand Hotel, which was what she suggested to Daryl. Diana had found a weekend package deal at The Island House, which included the ferry, so Daryl took it instead. He liked the idea that it was closer in town. When he learned that it pre-dated the Civil War, he knew Sandy would like it. Coming aboard the ferry, the captain joked that they should have crossed the bridge and gotten a ferry from St. Ignace. Sandy smiled, not understanding. Daryl thought it was because St. Ignace was closer, but he was stuck with the package arrangements. The reason for the captain's comment was the weather. There was a 20 knot headwind and three foot waves. Their crossing lasted for a pounding hour and a half. By comparison, the ride up in the Triumph seemed a cake walk.

It was dusk when they got to the harbor. They took a horse drawn carriage to the hotel, where they learned checking in that this was the last weekend of their season. They spent only a few minutes in the room before heading for the dining room. Both were hungry and wanted a drink. Again, Daryl drank beer; Sandy wine. After dinner they went to the lounge where they drank until nearly 10:00 P.M. Back in the room, they kissed and showered together; but in bed, they fell asleep. Both were hung over the next morning, but that passed with breakfast and several cups of coffee in the dining room.

It was a sunny day, and they decided to go for a bike ride that morning just in case the weather changed. They could do the shops that afternoon, even if it rained or snowed. Using a map from the hotel and the bikes that were part of their package, they rimmed the island. They hit all the usual points, Nicolet Monument at Arch Rock, and Sugar Loaf. Both liked the many unnamed ravines, natural bridges and strange rock formations more. They scolded each other for forgetting a camera. They ended their bike tour at Fort Mackinac just before noon. There they ate hot dogs. They did not tour through the many buildings, rather they stood in the sun looking down on the harbor. They got back to the hotel at 1:30 P.M. and decided a drink would be just the thing to cure their chill. They went to the lounge rather than their room. There they drank the afternoon away, reminiscing about how they met, law school, and the people they knew. They had never done that before.

When they undressed to change for dinner they were quickly distracted with each other. Sandy, plainly drunk, lead Daryl into the shower, then quickly out. Daryl still had the sense he was taking advantage of her, but it did not stop him. To the extent he needed to salve his conscience, he reminded himself that she was initiating everything. When he pulled away to get a condom, she held him.

"Don't do that."

"Come on, it's no big deal."

"Don't wear it."

"Sandy, it's not your problem. No sin."

"That's not what I mean. I want you to feel me...like the first time. It has to feel better for you."

"I am not complaining."

"There, that's better."

They dressed for dinner and spent another evening in the lounge. They made love again late that night. By then both were slovenly drunk. Daryl made no effort to get a condom. Once again they were hung over. They both ordered large meals, but neither ate more than a few bites. Daryl's face was flushed. Sandy's eyes were bloodshot and puffy. Sandy vomited in the head on the ferry ride. Daryl was nauseous, but held it down by pacing up and down the aisle between the seats in the cabin of the ferry. On the drive home they talked about catching an evening Mass, but when they got to their apartment, they ate and went directly to bed.

Sandy accepted Wheate Cornfeld's offer in time to assure the additional payment. When she started law school the ABA hiring guidelines had seemed an admirable thing, easing the plight of the graduating students by uniformity and deadlines. Now she saw them in another light; if the firms adhered to the guidelines, they lessened the price competition among themselves for the top students by essentially making it a sealed bid process. She noted that almost in passing, and with no judgment one way or the other. A year before she would have been enraged and eloquent on the subject. Now she was cool, dispassionate and objective. She did not realize it, but her legal education was complete. She was also content to accept the additional stipend. Wheate Cornfeld had shown themselves to be flexible, as all good lawyers are, able to adapt to any rules and to continue to play within the rules; provided the interpretation is not too literal; and with lawyers, there is always a proviso. She also got busy with a law review deadline and did not notice that she had missed her period until two weeks later.

It was the morning sickness that made her remember, but she

was preparing for finals and forced herself not to think about it. Ultimately, she went to her gynecologist and confirmed what she knew but would not admit. She was pregnant, at least six weeks along. He prescribed something for the nausea, but advised that saltine crackers before getting out of bed in the morning were likely just as effective. She did not fill the prescription, nor tell Daryl. She struggled through her finals, over-preparing much like she had her first year. Although she doubted herself, her grades were the same as always, top of the class. Through the holidays she kept trying to find the right time to tell Daryl, but never did. She thought about asking her mother for advice, but did not. She wanted the baby, but felt she was disappointing everyone.

Events overtook her on New Year's Day. They went to Mass and The Club for brunch with her parents, then returned to her parents house. That afternoon, her father read in his library, while Daryl watched football. Her mother helped the cook in the kitchen, so she could get off to join her own family. Sandy wandered from one to the other, then decided to nap in her old room. The wetness woke her. When she saw the blood through her clothes and all over the bedspread she was terrified. She called for her mother, then fainted. Sandy did not regain consciousness until early that evening in the hospital. Her mother called an ambulance and her doctor. Daryl could barely be restrained during the wait. He wanted to put her in the car and drive to the hospital. Her mother finally ordered him from the room. She took off Sandy's clothes, cleaned her, and diapered her with a bath towel. She dressed Sandy in a robe just as the ambulance arrived.

Her parents and Daryl kept a silent vigil, first outside the emergency room, then later, after they decided to admit her, in the third floor waiting room. Daryl took care of the paperwork after the emergency room physician told them she had stabilized from the fluids and medicine they were giving her. She had lost a great deal of blood and would have to stay in the hospital, but her pressure was good, and he was not calling for whole blood yet. Two hours later, her gynecologist, Dr. Winchester, whom neither Daryl nor her mother had ever met, came to the waiting room to speak with them after examining her.

"Sandy's awake now. She's groggy, not from anything we've given her, just the situation. In my experience, we need to be careful what we say to her. She needs plenty of rest and sleep and as little stress as humanly possible."

"What's wrong?" her mother asked.

"She hemorrhaged. You knew that. She is still bleeding, but it has subsided to the point we are not concerned. Most likely she will spontaneously abort, probably before morning. If not, we will have to intercede. It was a very serious hemorrhage. Sandy is not in jeopardy now, but I am sure that she will lose the baby." There was a long silence, during which they all looked to each other. Dr. Winchester never realized that none of them knew she was pregnant. "You can go in to see her. Just comfort her. Don't try to keep her awake. I'll be back first thing in the morning."

Her parents stayed until visiting hours ended. Daryl spent the night on the chair in her room. They were true to the doctor's instruction, their only communications were to comfort and reassure her. She slept most of the evening. The few times she woke, she would call to whoever was closest to her, "My baby, how's my baby? I'm so sorry. It's my fault. I did too much. How's my baby?" Then she would drift back off to sleep.

Daryl found Dr. Winchester just completing his examination of Sandy when he came back from the cafeteria the next morning. They shook hands. Daryl went to Sandy, and stroked her cheek with the back of his finger. The doctor wrote for several minutes on the chart, then hung it on her bed.

"Sandy, you are still bleeding. I thought you would abort during the night. At this point, I don't recommend waiting any longer. I want to do a D & C. We'll keep you here a few days, and you will be as good as new."

"What about my baby?"

"Sandy, this is nature's way of telling us the fetus in defective. Even if it wasn't, at this point it has to be severely damaged. We are only working with what nature intended."

"You are talking about an abortion."

"Sandy, I am talking about your health. If we do the D & C, you will be back on your feet in a week. There should be no reason whatsoever to stop you from getting pregnant again. If we do nothing, you will continue to lose blood, you run the risk of infection, and at some point, when you are weaker, you will spontaneously abort anyway."

"I will not have an abortion."

"Sandy, I am treating you, not the fetus. Your placenta has

detached from your uterus, that is the source of the bleeding. The blood flow to the fetus has been compromised. Even assuming that the fetus was perfect, which I do not, but even assuming that, in all likelihood, the fetus is damaged."

"Do you know that for a fact?"

"Of course not. In my experience, I believe it to be true. At the least I would expect serious brain damage. If you went to term you might deliver a perfectly formed baby that is little more than a vegetable. More likely, the damage will effect development, for example, no limbs or withered limbs; no brain or only a portion of a brain. Most likely, the damage was already there, and your body is spontaneously rejecting it."

"I will not have an abortion."

Dr. Winchester patted her on the shoulder then nodded to Daryl. He walked for the door. There he turned and spoke, "Sandy, you rest. You think it over. I will have the resident give you his opinion. If you want another doctor, just say so. I think you should talk to another doctor."

"I will not kill my baby."

"Sandy, it's only a matter of time. I'm a Catholic. If you were my wife, I would...."

"I will not."

He nodded and left. Daryl and Sandy looked at each other. Her eyes told him of her absolute resolve, but they told him nothing more about this pregnancy. He knew that there was nothing he could do when her mind was set. As she drifted off to sleep, he slumped back into the chair. His stomach was in knots. He felt as if the weight of the world was descending upon him. He had still never talked with his wife about their child.

CHAPTER 22

The last time I can remember seeing Sandy in law school was the fall of our last year. I am sure I must have seen her in the halls and at the snack bar, but the last time I remember was at a party that fall. The party was in one of those big victorian houses just south of the Central Campus. To tell you the truth, today I can't remember whose house it was, or how I happened to be invited. I do remember that when I got there, the party was going strong. I got a drink and surveyed the crowd. Daryl Dobbins was there. He always held court to a circle of admirers, but to that gathering of insecure graduating law students, he was the conquering hero returned. I spotted Sandy off to the side talking one on one with various people that I recognized as part of her crowd. I knew that she was Editor-In-Chief of the law review. That was a big deal. In fact, to my way of thinking, that was the top of the heap. I would have expected to find some geek or other emotional cripple in that position, but Sandy wasn't like that. When I noticed that she was free, I made my way over to her.

I'm sure we talked about the usual. There were only two significant topics of conversation for third year law students, job prospects and the bar exam. At the time, I felt comfortable, although I had no good reason to be secure. I had clerked in the U.S. Attorney's office in Columbus that summer. My grades were OK, but not big firm OK. I wasn't law review, in fact, I had no extracurriculars whatsoever. I did the on-campus interviewing, but got no where. The U.S. Attorney's office was the result of telephone calls to some of the people I met working in the Nixon campaign the year before. If I am honest with myself, my research and writing was probably pretty shabby. I remember that during my clerkship I decided to reinvent the research memo into a one page synopsis. This kid was not into close analysis of judicial suggestions. I would simply make a summary statement of the pro position and list the case names adopting it; then state the con and string cite the case names taking it. I attached photocopies of the cases in alphabetical order with tabs separating them and the relevant language highlighted in yellow. It seemed to me an efficient reference. My superiors could draw their own conclusions. No one ever rejected my work, but then government offices are not exactly pressure cookers. I finished the summer without an offer, but then they didn't give offers in the fall. They made offers in the spring, just before graduation. Like I said, I felt confident because of the political connection. I had resumes out, but that did not generate any offers. I banked everything on the political connection.

Sandy had three offers in writing and expected three more, in other words, a sweep. She was planning to go with a big firm in Detroit where she had clerked. She liked it. I remember her saying that her biggest surprise was that she found more freedom in the big organization, there were more options for her to choose from. She wasn't sure what she wanted to do, but there was no hurry. I told her that I wanted criminal law. In fact, that was true. I never thought about anything other than criminal law before or during law school. Criminal practice was my definition of being a lawyer. All the rest were selling out. It was also true that criminal law was all that was available to me. We were well into the conversation before I figured out that she and Daryl had gotten married. I can't remember how it came up, she must have mentioned something about the summer or their apartment. That's it, I asked her if she were still living in Northwood. Anyway, I was surprised and told her I didn't believe it. She showed me her ring. Then I tried to dig my way out with congratulations. She was gracious. Then I remember saying, "It makes sense. It really makes sense." Boy, that was a dumb thing to say, but I remember her agreeing.

I also remember talking about politics. She ran off a list of names of people that I might know from the 1972 campaign. Of course, I didn't know any of them. The only people I knew were in Ohio. We each had a Bob Hope story. She had actually gotten on Air Force One. I only saw Nixon once from about fifty yards away at Port Columbus. She claimed to have an autographed photo with him. I believe she did. It was just like her to get closer in than me. I think we must have talked for more than an hour. I do remember drinking a lot. I also remember Daryl coming over towards the end. I congratulated him. He was in a hurry to leave. He looked at his watch and talked about their drive. I had no one else holding me at the party, so I walked out with them. I remember standing on the sidewalk and shaking hands good night with each of them. It was very formal.

Like I said before, I really don't remember seeing Sandy at school after that. I made a special point of looking for her at graduation, but I never found her. Someone told me she was pregnant and having a rough time of it, but I dismissed that as gossip. To me Sandy was far from the maternal type. I saw her as a partner in a big law firm or the head of some government agency. As far as I can recall, that party was the last time I saw her in law school. I remember that night like it was yesterday.

After I left Sandy and Daryl, I bar hopped my way through downtown until I found a couple of undergraduate girls. Both were drunker than me, and I was drunker than I like to recall. I remember that both were from Kalamazoo. They snuck me into their dorm. I tell you, I did some crazy things, stupid really. It's easy to write it off to the booze, but I know better than that now. I remember one of them getting madder than hell when I...., well, after everything else we had done, it didn't seem like a big deal. I thought she had flipped, so I beat a hasty retreat. I think she just sobered up enough to realize what was going on. I suppose that the booze was no more an excuse for them than me. We all act on our guilt differently. I wonder if they ever figured that out. I wonder where they are now. The sad part is, if I had the chance, I'd probably do it all over again. Lucky for me, I've learned how to avoid such opportunities.

CHAPTER 23

Sandy buckled down and went to work on her pregnancy. While still in the hospital, she developed a list of OB-GYN's with the help of the nurses, and her mother's friends. As her doctor recommended, she got a confirming opinion not only from the resident, but also from the obstetrician she selected. Nevertheless, she refused the abortion. She never discussed the decision with Daryl, and he never brought it up. Unlike her, he spent the balance of the pregnancy in a continuing state of dread at the prospect of a deformed and disabled child. He was distracted at work, and lost weight, although it was always difficult to see the loss on his frame. Sandy never once visualized what might be. She focused her efforts on sustaining the pregnancy to term.

Also while still in the hospital, she called the law school registrar and explained her situation. She was informed that there would be no problem in finishing her studies the following year. She contacted the law review advisor who assured her she would get recognition for her efforts, but that they would have to name a new Editor-In-Chief. She spoke with the chairman of Wheate Cornfeld's hiring committee. He also assured her that they would keep a place waiting. She called Elizabeth Cromwell, who reassured her that she could have it all. After a week in the hospital, Sandy's doctor discharged her with another unpleasant lecture, including a warning that she was likely to be back in the hospital, instructions on how to handle the inevitable spontaneous abortion, and strict orders for a sedentary lifestyle if there was to be any hope of getting to term.

Sandy controlled her behavior beyond what her doctor expected. She went to bed early and rose late. She did little more than walk slowly to the sofa where she read and watched TV. When she read, she read books on pregnancy and pediatrics which her mother brought her. Her mother came by every day to make her lunch and start a dinner.

Daryl would set the table and serve the meal when he came home. On his part, Daryl stopped working late at the office. He came home early every day; and although he carried work home, he rarely did much of it. He spent his evenings doing housework and shopping. Sandy lifted nothing heavier than a book, and Daryl willingly volunteered whatever she needed. She was more pleased with his attention than she ever told him, his ministrations filled a gap left by her not being in school. She had never before realized how deeply he loved her. He was so absorbed in the trauma that he usually laid awake beside her for thoughtless hours. Sandy filled out and looked rested and serene. Daryl drank very little, but took on deep, dark circles under his eyes, and looked generally consumed.

She returned to her original doctor for one more visit, but two weeks after that made an appointment with the second doctor she had consulted in the hospital. Sandy found him less strident in bleak predictions and more supportive of her will. Her mother drove her to the doctor's, and in the weeks when she did not have an appointment, her mother would take her on a drive about the city. They never stopped for a meal or to go shopping. On the weekends, Daryl would do the same. He took her to church on Sunday and then to her parents for breakfast. Their cook would have it waiting. Her mother regularly brought up a subject in the presence of the two lawyer husbands that she never did alone with Sandy.

"What are you going to do about law school, dear?"

"First things first."

"You could be using this time to study. Couldn't you get credit for work at home?"

"I don't have a law library at home, and I have other things on my mind right now."

"I hate to see you lose what you worked so hard to get."

"I haven't lost anything, Mother. The schedule has just slipped a little."

"If you break stride, it will not be easy to get back to where you were. You'll see."

"I'll worry about that later."

"You should be thinking about it now."

"I'll cross that bridge when I come to it."

Throughout the exchange, Sandy's mother would look to the men for support. They kept their eyes on their food.

From time to time Sandy would spot. When she found that she had, she immediately consigned herself to bed for several days. At seven months, her new doctor told her he was truly amazed that she had made it, that the baby's heart was strong, and that even if the baby came prematurely, they should be able keep it alive. Sandy began to plan the birth, and enrolled in a Lamaze class the doctor's office recommended. The doctor himself, in light of her history, wanted to schedule a caesarian. Sandy resisted. She wanted to try for a natural birth. He warned her that it was not likely to happen. Nevertheless, he advocated the classes so that both she and Daryl could learn more about the process. Every Wednesday night for the next six weeks, they attended the classes at a conference room in the hospital.

The last class was the week before the Fourth of July weekend. They got a tour of the obstetrical floor and the nursery. The clear plastic containers holding perfectly formed babies captivated Sandy and further stressed Daryl. They were given pre-admission forms to take home for completion. That evening, Daryl filled them out under Sandy's guidance. When finished, he packed a suitcase as she instructed.

On Sunday, July 15, 1973, Robert Daryl Dobbins was born by caesarian section after a seventeen hour labor that failed to progress. Although the fetal monitor indicated that the baby was not in distress, Sandy's vital signs began to fail. Without conferring with her or Daryl, her doctor ordered the procedure. Daryl, already gowned, was asked to wait outside. Daryl was amazed at how quickly a nurse appeared in the window of the door holding up a baby. He was long and skinny at 23 inches and 7 pounds, 3 ounces. Unlike either parent, the baby had dark black hair, a full head of it, like Sandy's father. For that reason, they would later give the baby his first name. Daryl did not want his son to be branded with the implications of being a "junior", so it was a convenient circumstance which mitigated Sandy's plan to name a boy after his father. More than an hour later the doctor came out with a full report for Daryl. The baby was fine, perfect. Daryl felt the tension he had lived with drain away. Sandy's uterus was not. They left it, but he had serious reservations. They would take it one step at a time. She had general anesthesia and would sleep most of the day. Daryl spent that time in the window of the nursery. The next morning the doctor found Daryl in the room with Sandy. She was nursing the baby.

"Well Sandy, you got your way."

"I knew it all along."

"It just goes to show you the limitations of medicine. Even when something is 99% certain, there is always the 1%. There is always hope. You've been blessed. He's a beautiful child."

"Thank you."

"As for you, young lady, it's another matter. Your uterus is a mess. I have never seen anything like it. If I can be blunt, it looked more like an old shoe than healthy tissue. There is more scar tissue than anything else. There is evidence of infection. We left it, because of your age and because this little fellow somehow thrived; but as I told your husband, it was a difficult decision. It does not look good."

"I can have more children?"

"It's way too soon to be thinking about that. We will be watching you carefully to see how it heals. The nurses will be checking you every two hours, so don't mind them. I want them to. Your uterus does not look good to me, but you've proven me wrong once before. Any other questions? Good. I'll be back this time tomorrow."

Again the next morning Daryl came by the hospital before going into the office. When he arrived, he discovered the baby was not with Sandy nor in the nursery. After a moment of terror, he found the pediatrician had him in a room off the nursery performing the circumcision. It was only when he heard his son shriek that he thought to question the procedure. No one had consulted him. Sandy must have decided it when she contacted the pediatrician. He meant to question her, but when he returned to the room, he noticed how poor she looked. Her skin was ashen. Although she smiled and spoke, she was weak. Within a few minutes, the OB-GYN was there. He checked the dressing on the incision and the nature of the blood on her pad. Daryl stood back and out of the way. He felt uncomfortable merely being present during the personal attention to his wife, but that was soon lost in the tension he drew from the doctor's manner. The doctor opened the chart and made notes before speaking.

"Sandy, the chart shows that your uterus is not healing. In fact, the flow is much heavier than it should be. This is serious. I recommend that we take the uterus. We will leave the ovaries, they're healthy."

Sandy looked to him and started to respond, but drifted off into unconsciousness. He leaned over her, lifted each eyelid and shined a penlight into her eyes. He quickly took her blood pressure, then called the nurses station on the intercom. As he took her pulse he spoke to

Daryl.

"This is very serious. Her vitals are down. I want to do surgery to remove the uterus right now. Will you approve it?"

"What if you just leave it? She wants children."

"She's bleeding to death. That uterus is beyond repair. I should have taken it when I had the chance."

"Sure. Whatever you say. You're the doctor."

Just then two nurses came to the room. He gave them several instructions. One of them called for an orderly. As he left he told Daryl not to worry, but not to leave the hospital. The nurses would have forms. He could visit with his son. Suddenly Daryl found himself overcome with the old sense of dread, now even more foreboding than it had been during the pregnancy. The surgery went well and quickly. Sandy was out of recovery and back in her room just after lunch. Two days later she was out of bed and walking to the nursery for Bobby. Her milk came with no problems, and Bobby's navel and circumcision healed nicely. He was a sound sleeper. The nurses kidded that it was the result of Sandy's anesthesia. She knew it was. She had gotten a book and several pamphlets on nursing from the La Leche League. They stayed in the hospital for a total of ten days. On the morning Daryl brought them home from the hospital, Sandy's classmates were sitting down to take the Michigan Bar Exam.

CHAPTER 24

Soon after arriving at home, young Robert Daryl Dobbins proved his will. He never slept more than two hours, and his mother was up around the clock tending to him. Whether or not his extended sleep in the hospital was attributable to his mother's double dose of anesthesia, the hospital episode was soon a distant memory. Sandy nursed him on demand and hurried to his crib at the slightest whimper. Often she stood over his crib gazing at him as he slept. Daryl picked up the gentle hints of Sandy's mother that she was spoiling the baby, and armed with passages from two different child-rearing books, he confronted Sandy and urged her to get the baby on a schedule and to resist the temptation of immediately rushing to him at the slightest fussing. Sandy lashed back, surprising Daryl with the severity of her tone. Men, their rigid schedules and mindless discipline had made a mess of the world. Her child was going to be raised as nature intended. Babies were helpless and given only limited means to express their needs. She fully intended to meet his needs. She, not Daryl, got up in the middle of the night to feed him. Daryl had no standing whatsoever to tell her how to nurse and nurture her child. By the time Bobby was six weeks old, he was totally in control of the household.

Daryl never again confronted Sandy on her child-rearing, except for an occasional sarcastic remark said with a smile. Nevertheless, he silently brooded about the man his son would become. He saw the world as a harsh place, with the little order there was imposed by human discipline. This imposition of order should, but rarely was, directed toward the common good. Those with benevolent iron-wills maintained order for the rest to enjoy and protected them from the threat of equally iron-willed despots. It was a view one would expect of a Marine. It was a view seriously at odds with that of his wife, who had come to deeply believe that a new and wonderful world might emerge with a generation structured only by natural instinct. Daryl and Sandy never talked about these issues, but each debated the other in their daydreams. He saw human instinct as base, selfish, and if not directed toward higher ideals and left to its own compulsions, would descend into chaos. Sandy was convinced that if civilization and society did not impose so many burdens corrupting its members, that the world could be a true Garden of Eden.

The unspoken flared a little when Bobby was seven months old and just beginning to crawl. Daryl came home with a play pen. Sandy objected to it as a prison. Daryl found it protection against the child wandering into things he should not and creating a space of his own for him to rule. Daryl relied upon the proof that when he put Bobby down in the middle of the living room floor he would sit up and cry, but if put in the play pen he would immediately begin to play with his toys. On her part, Sandy relied upon equal proof that the child screamed to get out of the play pen. The disagreement consisted of a series of running barbs that never progressed to the level of an argument. Actions spoke louder than words. Sandy never put the child in the play pen. Daryl would in the evenings when he sat down beside him to read the paper. There was no resolution, for in time, Bobby learned how to climb out of the play pen when he was bored with it. He also made it known by his screams that he preferred the play pen to his crib for his naps. He also learned how to climb into it.

Sandy went to her first La Leche League meeting when Bobby was two months old. It was her first time out alone without the baby. At the evening meeting she knew immediately that it was to her liking when she saw that she was the only mother who had not brought her child. Most found an occasion to nurse their babies during the meeting. Henceforth, Tuesday nights became her and Bobby's night out. Sandy got more than dietary and behavioral advice, her new world view was ratified at each meetings. She made new acquaintances, and often two or three would collect in a family restaurant after the meetings to continue their discussions. What had originally been intended to be Sandy's night out, became Daryl's night to work late at the office. Sandy was elected Secretary of the club after four months. The following year, she was elected President.

Daryl had pressed Sandy to return to law school that fall after Bobby was born. She refused, reasoning that he was only two months old and needed her, and more persuasively that the classes she missed were offered in the spring. She successfully put him off, but her mother did not drop the subject. At least once a week she asked Sandy a question that assumed she would return to school, such as, what she was going to do about child care, would she use a day care center close to home or in Ann Arbor, would she continue to nurse, and the like. Sandy developed a custom of acknowledging the questions without answering them.

That fall, between Thanksgiving and Christmas, Elizabeth Cromwell invited Sandy down to Wheate Cornfeld. Sandy arrived a half hour before lunch. Elizabeth toured her about, stopping to exchange pleasantries with whatever partners they found in their offices. All inquired about the baby, Sandy's completion of law school, and offered individualized warnings about the bar exam. Sandy beamed in her responses about her son, and gave well-rehearsed, non-responsive acknowledgements on any question related to her legal career. Sandy actually thought that she was handling the situation well, but she was not giving due credit to lawyerly skill of listening to and analyzing answers while moving on with unrelated questions. Her answers were accepted in the polite desk-side conversations, but at lunch Elizabeth Cromwell got quickly to the point.

"If you are not going to pursue your career, then why did you come in today? You are just making it that much harder for the next woman to get in the firm."

"Who said I am giving up a legal career?"

"Come on, Sandy! You think we were standing behind the door when the brains were passed out? You may as well have posted a notice at all the coffee stations."

Sandy looked directly into Elizabeth's eyes for an instant. She was dumbfounded. She was suddenly embarrassed and looked down to her food. When she looked up, Elizabeth was lighting a cigarillo. Sandy did not see the same woman she had just looked away from. Elizabeth was no longer an admired role model, but rather, a withered cynic who had denied her femininity in a hopeless attempt to play with the boys in a men's game. She missed Bobby. She wanted to get up and get away from this person as quickly as possible, but she forced herself to be polite. "I'm sorry you feel that way. I certainly have not decided...."

"Sandy."

"I did want it. You probably know how much I wanted it.

Things change. Priorities. It's just not what I want anymore."

"You should finish law school and take the bar. At least finish law school. You can take the bar later. That baby will grow up."

"That's a lifetime from now."

"Don't be so sure. Don't burn bridges behind you. You're life is more than this child."

"How would you know?"

"I have three children. My baby boy is a sophomore in high school. My daughter is a freshman at Smith. The oldest would have been 26. He died in Viet Nam."

"I'm sorry, I had no idea."

"Because I'm a middle-aged woman lawyer, you assume I'm a spinster; but you also assume that the men in the office have families. You don't need to apologize. I understand more than you think. Men are expected to have lives outside their careers, women are not. It's up to you, not me. For your information I started law school when my youngest started first grade, and it took me five years after that to finish. You're only a few months from the finish line."

Sandy searched her memory to recall a family photograph in Elizabeth's office. All the men had them. If she is a crusading feminist, then why did she hide her family. "It's just not what I want anymore."

"It may not be what you want now. You yourself said, things change."

Unknown to Sandy, Ms. Cromwell called Daryl, and they had lunch two weeks later. She and Daryl agreed upon a campaign to persuade Sandy. Daryl truly tried to be diplomatic, but failed. His first attempt at a discussion evolved into an argument. A later attempt more quickly descended into the same with a crescendo that he could not possibly understand what it was like to be a mother. He slipped and disclosed his confidant when he said that Elizabeth Cromwell did. Later arguments were ignited merely by any reference to law school. Sandy had no intention of returning. In the early arguments she reasoned her decision giving restructured priorities. Later, she did not bother. It was simply not what she wanted. Surprisingly, to Sandy, only her father accepted that.

When Bobby was two, Sandy began to learn about Montessori from her associates in the La Leche League. Most were enrolling their toddlers in the program and were as enthusiastic about it as they were about nursing. Sandy started to study the pamphlets and progressed to books on Maria Montessori's method. In sum, it was a proven and highly successful educational method that was built around the individual, not the group. In an open, and apparently undisciplined classroom that reacted to the spontaneous interests of the child, each child worked with materials in an area that interested it until his or her interests changed, then the child was encouraged to follow that interest. She observed at three different schools and found three and four year olds reading and doing cube roots. It was consistent with Sandy's world view, and she had to have it for Bobby. There were two conditions precedant, Bobby had to be weaned and potty trained before he would be admitted. Neither would be easy.

Without Daryl's intervention, Sandy would have failed at both. On the nursing, Sandy had increased the intervals and decreased the session times; but at two and a half, he would walk up and insist. One week Daryl spoke every night about an outing that weekend with Bobby. Finally, that Saturday morning as they prepared to leave, Daryl casually informed Bobby that he was a big boy, they would eat out and Mommy would not be there for nursing. They toured Daryl's office, walked along the river front, and had fast food. After lunch they drove out to the suburbs and watched a Disney movie. After that they bought Sandy a small gift. Bobby never again demanded a breast. Three months later, after a succession of accidents, Daryl started taking Bobby into the bathroom. They had contests to see who could finish urinating the fastest. He would wait outside the door when Bobby sat on the seat. It worked.

Bobby started Montessori the September after his third birthday. Three months later Sandy was appointed to fill a vacancy on the Board of Trustees when a family was transferred out of town. The following spring she was reelected. The year after that, she ran for and was elected President. Daryl went to the annual picnic, but stayed on the sidelines. Soon after the beginning of Bobby's second year, when he was four, he begged Daryl to come to the classroom to observe. Daryl was shocked. He knew better than to challenge Sandy, but after little more than a few minutes, he concluded that what was boasted of as self-discipline was no discipline. There were no rows of desks, no teacher at the front of the room. The children excelled and progressed at an unbelievably accelerated rate, but he wondered where would they ever fit into society? How would they ever fit in? The world was not so kind as a Montessori classroom, eager to meet the passing whims of its inhabitants. Daryl was sick. His son was being molded to be a misfit, a precocious misfit. He felt totally helpless. He did not want to fight, and he saw no way to discuss the matter without a fight.

Later that fall, they bought their first home. Sandy had grown comfortable in their garden apartment and built a life in its environs. Daryl wanted a house, and won Sandy over on the promise of a fenced yard for Bobby. In fact, Daryl wanted to move far enough from the Montessori school that the inconvenience would ultimately free his son from it. They found a very nice three-bedroom home in Grosse Pointe Shores. It dated from the 1920's and needed fixing, but both Daryl and Sandy had ideas. Neither looked on it as their final home. Both wanted Grosse Pointe, but that also was something that they did not talk about. Their starter house was five minutes north of her parents. Both Sandy and her parents were pleased at the convenience. Throughout the time that they had lived in Redmond Township, they attended her parents' parish. Now they could join. Daryl resisted her parents' suggestions to join their Club, but he was pleased to be close to Jefferson Beach. He regularly took Bobby on outings to the marina there. They walked up and down looking at the boats. Daryl wanted one. After a month of commuting to the old Montessori school, Sandy withdrew Bobby and resigned her office. There were two other Montessori schools much closer to their new home. She chose the more expensive, better equipped one. Soon she was doing committee work and planning her run for office.

CHAPTER 25

In the early summer of 1976, Sandy's political past caught up with her. Willie Sturtz was a regional coordinator for Gerald Ford's presidential campaign. The state campaign chairmen of a dozen midwestern states reported to him, and he to the national chairman. He had survived the Nixon resignation unscathed and managed a senatorial race in 1974. He had earned this new position, and deserved it. It also fit well because he was a Michigan native as was the President. Mary Jane was still his assistant. They made Detroit their base of operations because of the Michigan connection. It was a small example of the classic way in which politicians reward their home districts. They spend money there. Mary Jane was given the task of locating Sandy. Willie wanted her on their staff full-time. He was willing to pay fifty percent more than whatever she made as a lawyer. He shrugged that it couldn't be that much. Mary Jane finally found her through Daryl. They agreed to rendezvous for lunch at Willie's favorite Italian restaurant.

Willie hadn't changed. He was pleasant and chatted about Sandy's marriage and child, although Mary Jane kept the conversation moving. No, she hadn't finished law school or taken the bar. Her mother was watching the little one. At a seemingly inappropriate moment, Willie shifted subjects and got down to business. Sandy was the most qualified person he knew for the position. Law school and bar exams were irrelevant. She was organized, had initiative, and was not afraid of hard work. He wanted her to be Michigan state campaign chair. Sandy flushed. She was flattered and surprised, but before she knew what she was saying, she was running out a long list of reasons why she could not possibly take the job. Willie was used to politely putting off people who maneuvered for positions, not cajoling the disinterested, and he was quickly impatient. He laid out the responsibilities, the long hours and the need to get started on building an organization immediately. He mentioned the convention as a plumb. Sandy still refused. He told her they would pay her $10,000 a month, $60,000 for the campaign. She was staggered, silently comparing that to Daryl's salary. Still, she refused.

Sandy offered to volunteer part-time at whatever they wanted her to do when her son started school that September. She could come to the office while he was in school. Willie ever so graciously truncated their luncheon. His mind was busy on Alternate Plan B. They parted with promises of getting together during the summer, but they never did. That night Daryl urged her to take the job. She never told him about the money. In the fall, when she volunteered, she became Mary Jane's junior secretary. She handled her overflow. She never got any independent projects of her own. Still she found it interesting and exciting, but she rarely caught more than a glimpse of Willie. She provided a valuable service, but she was not on the inside. After the election, she missed the routine of dressing and going downtown every day, but she quickly returned to her familiar habits. Daryl took her, Mary Jane and Willie out to dinner the week after the election. They had closed the office and were headed back to Washington.

"What will you do now?" Daryl asked.

"Look for work. This had to happen eventually. I just didn't think it would happen this year." Willie mused.

Sandy, in her old prompting manner came in, "Really, you didn't expect to lose? Didn't you think Watergate would carry over, especially after the pardon?"

"Sure, but that was surmountable. We have our own polls. We saw ourselves getting behind. In my opinion, we could have won; should have won."

"Vox populi." Mary Jane said, hoisting her glass in a toast. She was drunk.

Sandy smiled and turned back to Willie, "So why didn't you win?"

"In my opinion, the campaign was mismanaged. We were too complacent going in, and did not react quickly enough along the way. I guarantee you that years from now the pros will be using this election as an example, saying that Ford lost, Carter did not win. We lost at the front line. Our managers were just not up to it. You see, Sandy, its partially your fault. We needed people like you. We needed you." He smiled at her and tipped his glass toward her. "A toast for what might have been. Mary Jane and I could have gotten into the White House, you could have been the Administrator of some sub-cabinet agency. Now we're all unemployed. A toast to those who land on their feet."

They all drank heavily and stayed late. They said good-bye on the street in front of the restaurant, bouncing on their feet in the cold while they did. Willie and Mary Jane walked home together to their temporary apartments. Daryl drove Sandy in the used Porsche he'd recently acquired. He drove fast. It scared and angered Sandy, but she did not complain. After Daryl tired of fast starts and power shifting, he spoke, thinking that he was complimenting her. "See what you could accomplish if you went to work. But for you, the presidency. For want of the nail, the shoe was lost."

"Go to hell."

"I love you too."

"I am doing what I want. I am raising a child. I happen to think that is the most important thing anyone can do."

"I was only trying to say that you have alternatives that most people don't. You are very intelligent and talented."

"You were trying to run my life."

"Oh, the hell with it. It's real easy for you isn't it. I go off to work every morning. I sell myself in little slices all day long doing work that I hate. That's fine, I don't mind that. I'm a man. I meet my responsibilities. I like the money. I know my limits. But I am a glorified clerk. I fill in forms. You could be so much more than me and choose not to. That's fine too. Just don't tell me that I'm trying to run your life when I compliment you."

"You want me to finish law school. You want me to take the bar. You want me to practice. You want. You want. You want. It is not what I want."

"Screw it. You do what you want. You always have. I don't get to do what I want. That's fine. I am not capable of doing what I want anyway. That makes me an average working stiff. You are capable of anything and choose nothing. That makes you stupid. For the first time I see it. You are the smartest dumb person I know."

"Go to hell."

"Meet you there, bitch." Daryl drove even harder.

So began another of many episodes, both before and after this one, in which Daryl and Sandy co-habituated, but put their marriage aside. When they spoke, it was only to arrange their mutual schedules.

They slept in the same bed, but went to lengths not to touch. If they passed close in a hall, they each pulled back just an inch further than they otherwise would. They avoided eye contact. After a week or two, they would reverse the flow, just as subtly. They would catch each other's eyes in furtive glances. They would touch ever so briefly in passing. They slept more casually and closer. Then one night they would brush their teeth before going to bed. Their white flag. It was always the last contest of wills to see who would make the first move. Usually, both would doze off, but within half an hour someone woke and soon they were touching, kissing, and making love.

The partners at Campbell Short held an annual retreat the first weekend in February each year at a lodge outside Traverse City. Some would come early or stay late and do some skiing, but Saturday and Sunday were long days spent reviewing committee reports, departmental reports, financial statements, projections, and strategic plans. Saturday night was traditionally a roaring private party, but those with their own agendas knew this to be the one night of the year that deals were cut. Those individuals moderated their behavior and met in small groups scattered throughout the lodge. The chairman of the executive committee was always on his best behavior Saturday nights. He was the target of much lobbying, and tonight one of the many arrangements he sought on his own was two department heads to sponsor Daryl Dobbins for partnership.

The only written rule on admission to the partnership was two-thirds approval by those partners attending the annual meeting, at which a majority was a quorum. There was, however, more than a century of tradition. There was, as might be expected, a partnership screening committee. Until 1970, a partnership was a certainty for any associate who was still with the firm after five years. Then a reform took place. A cadre of "staff counsel" was created. They were senior lawyers who did good work, but who did not attract new cases or clients. Until they brought in business, they would never be partners, but they were retained as workhorses and paid more than associates. Also, the minimum service before partnership was raised to seven years. After clearing the partnership screening committee, the department chairmen for the departments in which the candidates worked traditionally nominated their senior associates for partnership the last thing Sunday afternoon, and they were approved by acclamation. In the matter of Daryl Dobbins, he did not clear the screening committee because he had only been with the firm five years. Worse, Lawyer Goldfarb, Insolvency Department chairman, had no intention of ever nominating him under any circumstances. That Daryl had upstaged his boss was firm lore, and often retold as new secretaries were acquainted with their mag card machines.

There had been an instance in 1947 when an intransigent department chairman was circumvented by an alliance of the heads of two other departments. The chairman of the executive committee had been an associate then, remembered the story, and used it as precedent. The chairman of the administration committee, also chairman of the Estate and Personal Taxation Department, was an avid supporter of Dobbins based upon the numbers. The management reports reflected that 35% of the seventeen lawyer Insolvency Department's fees collected were attributable to an associate, Daryl Dobbins. No partner in the firm generated that high a percentage of a department's revenue. By his personal labor, Daryl generated 11.3% of the department's collections, that is, he brought in as much as any two other lawyers. When that was combined to the work that he spun off to other lawyers, he brought the firm as much as six other lawyers, or any two other partners. Noted was the fact that Lawyer Goldfarb generated 8.6% of the department's billings in contrast to Dobbin's 35%. Last year, by virtue of a partner's coronary, Frank Sloan had become chairman of the Mergers & Acquisitions Department. Thus, the coalition was completed. All agreed that if they did not act, Dobbins would jump ship with the work and the best associates. Goldfarb could stay or go as he saw fit. Sunday afternoon, Sloan made the nomination, seconded by the others who led a round of applause. When it subsided, all eyes turned to Goldfarb. He flushed and hesitated, but begrudgingly joined the second. Back in Detroit that evening, Sloan called Daryl and arranged a breakfast meeting in a downtown hotel. The next morning he presented the good news and also friendly advice not to cross Goldfarb; there was no need to, for the first strong wind that came along would blow Goldfarb away.

At the end of the quarter when Daryl got his first partnership distribution check, he was flabbergasted. He knew that the partners' incomes were big, but until he saw the check, the numbers were never real. The check was for $21,500, on top of the $24,000 he had drawn during the first three months. At this rate he was going to make $180,000 that year, more than three times the $50,000 he was making as a senior associate. Of course, the numbers depended upon results, and there was the mysterious formula by which everyone's share was calculated. He never tried to decipher the formula, but he did understand its principal factors were work performed, work generated, committee service, and years of service with the firm. As a partner he had an equal vote in all partnership matters, but no two partners were compensated equally. That came out of the formula, and he liked this formula. The new level of income gave him the confidence that he could take more time for professional service, so he increased his bar activities. He had long been a member of the American Bar Association's Business Law Section. Now he joined the Construction Industry Forum Committee because so many of the bankrupt businesses he represented were contractors. Indeed, that is where he got most of his new cases. Word spread among the contractors. He had already been invited to speak before meetings of both the local chapters of the union Associated General Contractors and the non-union Associated Builders and Contractors. In early April, he bought Sandy a Volvo wagon, which immediately marked them as other than an automaker family. In late April, he paid cash for a 21' powerboat with a cuddy cabin and 225 hp inboard V8 engine. He also got a slip for it at a marina in Jefferson Beach.

The blustery wind and waves kept them off Lake St. Clair most of that spring, but every weekend he bundled up Sandy and Bobby and cruised down the Detroit River, passed downtown, under the Ambassador Bridge, passed the steel mills at River Rouge, around Fighting Island, and back up the Canadian side of the river. One Saturday in late May, they picked up Sandy's parents at the Grosse Pointe Club marina. Daryl's growing prosperity was apparent to both her parents. Indeed, Sandy's father assumed that a partner in a big firm had to make more than he did at Chrysler. Had he known Daryl made twice what he did, even he would have been shocked. He sat on the left behind the windshield nursing the scotch Daryl served. Bobby knelt behind the wheel with Daryl standing at his side. In the back, Sandy and her mother sat in opposite corners sipping white wine from plastic cups.

"Sandy, you should be proud of Daryl. He has really made something of himself." Sandy nodded and smiled. "No one would have thought he was big firm material, but he made it. Bobby's a wonderful child. Daryl's good with him. You wouldn't have expected that either with him estranged from his own family. You're lucky, Sandy."

"And...?"

"Nothing, I'm just happy for you. When you were growing up, I was never sure what would become of you. You were well down the road to being a career woman and spinster."

"Mother, you are so out of touch."

"You are lucky to have a beautiful family and a prosperous life."

"None of this is an accident."

"Are you so sure of that? Most women get whatever life gives them. Didn't you give up your legal career that way."

"Damn it, mother, I did not give it up. I chose this life. This is what I want."

"I only want you to be happy, dear."

That fall, Bobby Dobbins was enrolled in the first grade of the University-Liggett School. Sandy considered keeping him in Montessori, but the combined pressure of her parents and Daryl, and her own comfort with her alma mater brought her to enroll him there. On parent's night the first week in October, Daryl was concerned to find that Bobby's classroom did not have the desks in rows, but was reassured later when they spoke with his teacher. She professed experience in "normalizing" Montessori children. She promised that by the third grade he would be moving at the same pace as the others. Daryl was furious that it would take two years to deprogram his son. Sandy was pleased that he was two years ahead of his peers, saddened at the thought of him being held back until they caught up, and frustrated at the prospect of how much he might never learn. Still, it was a wonderful school. She hadn't turned out so bad.

CHAPTER 26

I had a very unusual and engaging conversation with Sandy in an unlikely place in December, 1978. We met in a sky box in the Superdome in New Orleans and spent an hour and a half getting drunk and looking down on the state championship high school football game. I came very close to falling in love. I got very drunk. I leaned in so close to her face to hear her speaking over the crowd that I can still remember her breath on my face. She was quite a woman. If not love, the old friendship was still there with a touch more attraction, at least for me. I was drunk enough to think that it was for her too. Hell, her husband was in the room. That shows you what booze does to the brain. I can't remember exactly how we parted, but I do remember the hangover the next morning. I need to tell you how we came to be in New Orleans.

I did get on with the U.S. Attorney's office in Columbus. I started out handling the paperwork on the sales of seized property. Most people think of that as the exotic cars and airplanes of drug dealers. There is a lot of that, but just as often it's farm, factory, or office equipment; or buildings, houses, or land. It was a gigantic paper shuffle, making sure that every form was filled in correctly, filed and published on time. It was not work that required legal scholarship, and I, no doubt, got the assignment because of my poor performance as a law clerk. I considered it the bottom of the barrel and most of the other young lawyers on the staff treated me in that manner. At least I had a job.

Ironically, that job led to everything else. I got good at the paperwork; in fact, I found it a challenge to dig through and make sense out of the files that came my way. Oh, the quiet joys of government service. Anyway, one of the agents in an IRS seizure had blown the grab, but the agency really wanted to stick it to the bad guy. It was a high profile case against a prominent real estate developer, so a couple other lawyers in the office got first crack at the case. After a quick look, no one wanted it. No one wants a loser. I ended up with it. Judge Oversteel, an aged Roosevelt appointee, had been a contrary and crotchety young man, and by the time I started appearing before him, was a terror to be avoided like the plague. He read the papers, didn't like the bad guy, and was agreeable to signing whatever I pushed in front of him. We won. Saved the agent's butt. Six months later, the IRS agent insisted on my being assigned as liaison to a large tax fraud case they were working. I found it fascinating. It was like finding an entire secret population, that I had no idea even existed, living on the same planet. Those people started most cases by lifestyle surveillance. They snuck around following their targets to see if they lived beyond the income reported on tax returns. How you got to be a target is another story. Anyway, it was the computer jocks and accountants that fascinated me. They tapped into all kinds of data; banking, credit card, telephone, any kind of electronic records. The accountants then wadded in to make sense of it. They call themselves, forensic accountants. I was supposed to make sure their summaries and conclusions were supported by the underlying documents so we could get them in evidence. In short, I was along for the ride. I second chaired that trial. We won. Henceforth, I was the designated tax fraud expert in the office.

I spent two and a half years as a prosecutor. I liked it and would still be there day except for politics. I got flushed when the Carter crowd came in 1977. Before that I handled some pretty big cases; mostly tax fraud, but also a few bank and corporate embezzlers. Those cases always bothered me. Usually, the bank or the corporation had discovered the bad guy by their own internal audits. They pretty much handed the cases to us. The thing was, after enough of them I saw the pattern. They were all clerks or managers of clerks, and the amounts they took were thousands or tens of thousands. Our tax cases were regularly hundreds of thousands or millions. Well, you can't help but think that the banks and corporations were making examples out of the little people, while the big ones slipped away. I can't say they were covering their own tracks; more likely, they were afraid of what a really big scandal would do to the price of their stock. It always bothered me. In the tax cases, once we got rolling, it didn't really matter whose toes got stepped on. No one likes to pay taxes, but most people do. Our work was supported by the instinctive reaction that the good citizens pay more than they should to offset what the cheats don't pay. Naturally, my interest followed the big dollars into the bigger tax cases.

During those years I developed a pretty cushy lifestyle. I leased a cottage in German Village, which is an enclave of red brick houses on narrow brick streets about a mile south of downtown Columbus. The federal court and my office were just north of downtown, perched on the banks of the Scioto River that winds through the city. Actually, the Scioto isn't much more than creek, but it's all Columbus has to work with. Anyway, my entire life was confined to that tract bounded by the federal building and German Village and included all the bars in between. I also liked that life, and grew complacent; however, when I was summarily cashiered by the new U.S. Attorney, things changed quickly. I hadn't saved a penny. I had no prospects. Most of my compadres got swallowed up by the bigger firms for insurance defense work and a lifetime of depositions. A few got on with the smaller criminal defense and personal injury boutiques. I could not scare up anything. I sold my BMW, but only cleared a month's rent. When it got to the point of not having rent money, I broke down and borrowed from my parents. I rented space in one of those office suites places for the credibility of a business address and scrounged for cases. When I look back, I can't believe some of the things I did; but then when you're desperate, you do what you have to do. I didn't just leave my cards in bars and restaurants; I went through the Franklin County Court and Columbus Municipal Court buildings, introduced myself to judges, and asked for indigent appointments. I got a few, but they were a lot of work with little reward. Next, I started through the phone book calling other lawyers, introducing myself, telling them that I was just starting practice, and begging for referrals. All were polite, reminisced about their own early days, and got rid of me. A few came through, but they were just jettisoning their own dead wood. Somehow, I hung on. I did traffic tickets, divorces, wills, real estate closings, anything for anybody. Most of the time, I hadn't a clue as to all the legal ramifications of what I was doing. Malpractice insurance was something for those who could afford it, not me. Then one day Roosevelt Thomas showed up at my office with two body guards.

The Carter administration was seen as more friendly to labor than its predecessors, but to demonstrate balance, they undertook a crack-down on union corruption. Roosevelt Thomas was a self-made man. He had come from no where to head the largest construction union in Central Ohio, The Laborers. It's membership was almost exclusively Negro, and they typically performed the unskilled jobs at construction sites that were not claimed by the other higher paid and lily-white building trades unions. Roosevelt had everyone after him, all at once. There were federal prosecutions with innumerable counts for violations of the anti-trust laws, the labor laws, the racketeering laws, and also for tax evasion. There were state prosecutions for theft. I couldn't possibly keep up with all the cases, so we assembled a team of two other lawyers, three investigators, and four accountants. Even that group was puny by comparison to the resources of the DOJ, DOL, FBI, IRS, and the rest of the alphabet soup. Well, to make a long story short, Roosevelt was acquitted on all but a few lessers in the state cases. He paid me with cash. Once again for the sake of balance, the government turned its attention to the local contractor's and started a half-dozen anti-trust, racketeering, and tax prosecutions for bid-rigging, bribery, kick-backs, and tax evasion. All of a sudden I was very busy. I felt compelled to learn more about the construction industry and decided to attend a two day seminar put on by the ABA Construction Industry Forum Committee in New Orleans. I still don't know how Roosevelt found me or why he chose me. Someday when I have more time I'd like to tell you about him. What a great guy!

It wasn't until I looked over the brochure describing the seminar on the plane ride to New Orleans that I realized that Daryl Dobbins was one of the speakers. He was speaking on The Bankruptcy Reform Act of 1978. All I knew about the new law was that it was going to elevate the Bankruptcy Referees to the level of federal judges. I looked on it as a way for Carter to reward his friends. I never visualized Daryl Dobbins as a bankruptcy lawyer, but it made perfect sense to me that he should show up as a speaker at an ABA function. Some things just don't change. I got to the hotel at about 9:00 P.M. that night. The seminar was in The Fairmont, a swanky old hotel a couple of blocks outside the French Quarter and a couple of blocks from the Superdome in the other direction. I went back down to the lobby bar as soon as I got my bag to my room, hoping I might run into Daryl. He was not to be found, so I had a couple of drinks and quietly recalled my law school days. About 11:00 P.M. I decided to take a walk.

I went over to the French Quarter and walked the length of Bourbon Street. Let me tell you, for a young fellow from Columbus,

Ohio, that was an experience. I stopped outside a few bars and listened to the jazz, but each time I did four or five street walkers would circle around me and start urging their services upon me. Remembering it now is really amusing. Competition is a wonderful thing. They were all criticizing each other's attributes and talents, bidding their prices down, and speculating about my attributes. About the third time that happened, I got over my shyness and had entertaining conversations with them. I didn't utilize their services that night, not because I'm above that; actually in some circumstances, I think it makes a lot of sense. No entanglements. The reason was, they were all brown-skinned. I thought my work with Roosevelt had cured me of that prejudice, but I had never made it with a Negro girl. That night I had a blonde in mind. I started searching for one and even asked the other girls for help. The only white girl I found was fat and really trashy looking, so I gave up. One tall and elegant negress walked with me for two blocks trying to convince me, but I resisted. Maybe I shouldn't have. Who knows? I did go into a porno theater for about twenty minutes, but I was sobering up and that got boring. I closed the lobby bar in the Fairmont at 1:00 A.M. and got to the seminar late the next morning. No Daryl in sight.

The next evening one of the large law firms in New Orleans sponsored a reception in their sky box at the Superdome. I didn't know anyone at the seminar, nor did I make any friends. The seminar was really dry. Nearly all the subjects involved contracts and civil litigation which was not exactly my forte. Daryl was scheduled to be the first speaker Saturday morning. When I didn't see him Friday, I assumed that he would fly in just for his speech. After him was a lecture on bid-rigging, so I had that to look forward to. After the seminar on Friday afternoon, I pondered my options, the hotel, Bourbon Street, and the reception. I really didn't want to get stuck with the seminar lawyers, but it seemed the best choice because it promised an open bar. I showered then walked on over to the Superdome just at sunset. I spent the first half hour getting a quick buzz and trying to get away from a short, Italian county attorney from Massachusetts who had sat beside me all day. I don't think I would have ever shaken him had I not seen Sandy standing alone by the window looking down on the field. My heart raced. It was the same Sandy, gold earrings and all, nothing but class. She hadn't seen me. I scanned the room and saw Daryl dominating a group thirty feet from her.

"Hello, Sandy." I took her hand.

"I can't believe it! It's good to see you! You here for the seminar? God, it's a small world!"

"I guess it is. I didn't realize Daryl was a speaker until I got here yesterday. I looked for him today, but never saw him."

"We just flew in this afternoon. This is supposed to be a second honeymoon for us. Daryl travels all the time, but this is a first for me. It's the first time I've ever been away from my son."

"You have a son?"

"Oh yes, he's five now and in the second grade."

"That's young for the second grade isn't it?"

"He went to pre-school, and we were able to get a few rules bent."

"I would think that with two lawyers for parents, rules would not get in the way."

"I never finished."

"You know, I heard you were pregnant, but I didn't believe it. The word was you were having a tough time. I looked for you at graduation. I don't keep up with anyone from law school. Do you?"

"No, just Daryl's partners."

"So you two stayed in Detroit."

"Yes, and you?"

"Columbus. It seems the nuts don't fall far from the tree."

"Yes."

"Remember a party in Ann Arbor, at some house our third year. I met you there. In fact, it was a lot like this. Daryl holding court." We both looked at him for a minute.

"Yes, I remember that."

"The years have been kind to you."

"Thank you. Tell me about your practice."

I did, but we talked about a lot more than that. We had both gone to our ten year high school reunions the year before and come out of them philosophical. She couldn't believe that I wasn't married. She teased me with hints of stories that circulated in law school about me and various girls. I almost told her about the two that last night I had seen her, but I stopped myself. Kiss and tell was never my thing. I painted a picture about life as a bachelor; working late, getting drunk, going home alone, going camping alone. I could see it was getting her sympathy, she hummed her condolences and touched me a few times. Oh, what might have been!

Eventually, Daryl came over to collect Sandy. They had to leave for a dinner with the chairman of the forum committee. He invited me along, but I begged off. We promised to look for each other at breakfast in the hotel. I had a few more drinks, then headed for Bourbon street. Later that night, I found that tall girl from the night before and lost the last vestige of that prejudice. I slept through breakfast the next morning and got to Daryl's presentation when he was half finished. Sandy was no where to be seen. I checked out during the noon break, and left a note and my business card for Sandy. After the last lecture, I grabbed my bags and headed straight for the airport. New Orleans is a great town, but every time I think of it, I feel a twinge of decadence. I would have done it. I know I would. I would have taken her right from under his nose, if I could have. I'd still like to think she was willing, but I know better. Booze. The damn booze.

CHAPTER 27

Over the next several years Sandy and Daryl's life settled into a comfortable and prosperous routine. The summer before Bobby entered the fourth grade, 1980, they finally found the house they wanted in Grosse Point. It was three blocks further south of her parents and one block further inland, but among the stately homes, it did not seem close. The house was Georgian, built of orange-red brick, and distinguished by four white pillars along the front. There was a circular drive that came up to the portico and circled a fountain in the front yard. Along the street there were two entrances opening through an iron bar fence, that spanned brick posts. Daryl immediately wanted to install electrically controlled gates, but he never got around to it. The home was of the same vintage as her parents, but half again as large. There was a detached garage behind the house, also built of brick and mirroring the architecture of the main house, with servants quarters above the three car garage. It was reached by a spur off the main drive that looped around behind the house. There were six bedrooms on the second floor. Sandy and Daryl took the master bedroom along the front of the house. Bobby took a large bedroom along the back of the house that looked down on the back yard. They also made another of the bedrooms into a playroom for him. The house was large enough, and the walls thick enough, that when he had the TV on in his playroom, they could not hear it in their bedroom.

Sandy had long been a stalwart member of the elementary PTA at the University-Liggett School. She had been elected Treasurer the year before. This year she was President. In that regard, she spent much of her evenings on the telephone or drafting the group's newsletter. The house was so much bigger than their previous home, that Sandy, when not engaged in her volunteer work, spent much of her time decorating. She decorated the three unused bedrooms on the second floor more elegantly than the rooms they used, for their rooms got the old furniture. The fancy rooms were collectively referred to as the guest rooms, but they never had any guests stay in them. There was a library downstairs that Daryl converted into a home office. There were built-in bookshelves, much like those in her parents' house, but Daryl did not collect books. He put framed photographs, nautical brick-a-brac, and stacks of boating catalogs and magazines on the shelves. He had a separate telephone line installed just for his office, but it saw no more use than the desk. There was a TV in the far corner with two overstuffed chairs facing it. Daryl often watched TV there with Bobby. More often, he went to Bobby's playroom and laid on the floor with him watching TV there. Most often, Bobby was asleep before Daryl got home.

Daryl adhered to a schedule in which he left the house at 7:30 A.M. and rarely returned before 9:00 P.M. Most of every morning was spent dictating responses to the day's mail. Lunches were most often two hour affairs with current or prospective clients, although at least twice a week he tried to have lunch one-on-one with the young lawyers in the department. Daryl had long since passed 280 pounds. The thought of breaking 300 was unacceptable to him. He therefore had joined an exercise club downtown. After attending to his own cases in the afternoons, every day at 4:00 P.M. he went for exercise. He started by merely walking laps around the indoor track, and progressed up into light free weights and swimming. He did not lose any weight, but he felt better. The real problem was that when he finished exercising, he ate out and had a couple of drinks. After that he went back to the office and spent two quiet hours reviewing the work of others. Towards the end of his evening office hours, he would have another scotch, then drive home to several more.

Sandy abhorred the odor of alcohol on Daryl, but never communicated that to him. In fact, she kiddingly told him and others that the secret to their marriage was Daryl's drinking. He was a happy go lucky drunk and his manner was contagious. Occasionally, he would encounter a belligerent or surly drinker and soon they would be laughing or even singing. Daryl drank every day, but usually got drunk only on the weekends. Still the odor of alcohol was his odor. His appetite for sex was as strong and undisciplined as his appetites for food and drink. His method of moderating it was drink. When he felt the urge, but knew through the innumerable little signals husbands and wives have, that

Sandy was not interested; he simply drank heavily and passed out. He usually made it to bed, but it was not unusual for him to spend a night on the sofa in his clothes. On those occasions, Sandy did not wake him to come to bed. It was his odor of alcohol.

When Daryl sensed Sandy's mood was receptive, he drank a little less. She was habitually heavily perfumed, but on such nights, she also sprayed their pillows. Daryl liked fragrances as much as everything else. He liked her perfumes on any occasion, and he recognized one particular scent as her signal for sex as much as her brushing her teeth. She avoided kissing his mouth. She developed a habit of turning her head and pulling in deeps breaths of scented pillow through her nose. This was just one small part of the marital ritual they evolved that had become increasingly mechanical. In the mornings, it gnawed at Daryl that he did not know what to do to stimulate and satisfy her. When he had a little more than normal to drink, he would sometimes ask. She never answered. He promptly fell off into the alcohol stupor after. Sandy laid awake staring at the ceiling and listening to the sounds of the night. The odor of alcohol nauseated her. She hated it. She could not separate it from Daryl. When she thought, as she did more frequently, that she hated him, she would lie awake crying. She muffled her cries so as not to wake him, but a bomb would not wake him. He drank, he smelled, he snored. She lay awake alone.

Sandy continued her flirtation with party politics. She volunteered in a local congressional campaign in 1980. She did telephone solicitation from her home during the primary campaign that spring; then after school started that fall, she put in a couple of hours each day at the store front campaign office. She got a letter from Mary Jane. She was on staff with the Republican National Committee in Washington. Willie was living in Los Angeles and doing political consulting out of the offices of an advertising agency there. She did not offer any more than that. From it, however, Sandy inferred that the long-standing team had been broken. She meant to write a long letter to Mary Jane, and after a fair amount of time passed, she intended to call. Ultimately, she sent her a Christmas card in which she asked for Willie's address. Mary Jane did not respond.

That winter, Daryl determined that it was time for a bigger boat. He gave Bobby the assignment of reading the advertisements in the back of the boating magazines and also the Sunday paper. On mild weekend days, they made the rounds of the marinas and yacht brokers looking for the "for sale" signs. They did the boat show downtown that spring, and even got Sandy to come with them. He was after a sport fisherman. He didn't fish, but he liked the idea of drinking under the sun on the business end of a fishing boat. After climbing through several, he decided that he had to have a Hatteras. The prices of new boats were beyond Daryl's budget, but not his means.

His income was well over $200,000 per year and growing. He was diverting more than half that, after the home and life-style expenses, into a stock portfolio. He had tried to get Sandy to manage their finances for he knew she would be better at it than him, but she refused. It was his money, he earned it. Indeed, the entire episode, which included many arguments, had resulted in Sandy setting up separate checking and savings accounts for herself. Her resolution was that Daryl would pay the mortgage, taxes, and insurance; she would pay the household expenses. Whenever she needed money to pay bills, she asked. He called the bank and had it transferred into her account. He did not understand or agree with her logic, and several months later when he took notice of the size of his portfolio, he started doubling the amount she asked for. He would transfer the amount she requested into her checking account; and, without her knowledge, transfer an equal amount into her savings. From time to time he would urge her to invest in something, but she simply ignored him. He would scold her that money was a responsibility. She would tell him to take it back. He regularly backed off before it got to an argument. He simply did not understand her, and she was not about to offer an explanation.

Still Daryl could not bring himself to invade the amount he set aside for investment for his own pleasure. The result was that they kept the Bayliner for another year. By the following winter every yacht broker between Chicago and Cleveland knew that Daryl was in the market. Finally, a used 38' Hatteras sport fisherman found its way into the hands of a Toledo dealer from an estate. Daryl and Bobby drove down the weekend before Christmas and inspected the boat. It was in a cradle and shrink wrapped. From a ladder on the frozen ground they climbed through a zipper door in the plastic. Even the musty odor inside did not put him off. He wanted this boat, and tried not to act that way. They came back twice more with Sandy. Whenever he asked her opinion, she would not respond beyond telling him that it was his thing. Silently, she brooded that the boat cost almost as much as their home. Daryl put in his first offer in February. They went back and forth for several weeks. Finally, they signed a contract contingent on a survey and sea trials. Everything was in good order, and what was not was attended to. In mid-April 1981, Daryl became the proud owner of his first yacht. Although nearly twice the size of his previous boat, it fit the slip he rented, so he brought it back to Jefferson Beach and kept it there. The following month he sold enough stock to pay off the balance of their home mortgage. Then he recorded a quitclaim deed transferring his interest in the house to Sandy. It was his intent to give it to her as a Mother's Day gift.

They left for their first overnight cruise in the new boat the Friday afternoon before Mother's Day. Sandy spent the early afternoon packing food and clothes and took Bobby directly from school to the marina. Daryl took off early and met them there. Daryl promised Sandy creature comforts, and by comparison the previous boat seemed little more than a runabout on which they picnicked. The new boat had a galley with a double basin sink, a four burner stove, a full size oven, and a large refrigerator. Bobby and Daryl had spent the previous weekend cleaning and puttering on the boat, but Sandy was shocked and disgusted to find mold growing in the refrigerator. As they got underway, Sandy was already busy down in the galley cleaning the appliances and muttering under her breath. Across from the galley was a small room with over and under bunks. Forward were the head and captain's quarters with its own head. Up the stairs aft was the lounge and behind it the fishing platform. Up a ladder was the flying bridge from which Bobby and Daryl captained their progress.

Aside from his image of the craft, one practical reason Daryl wanted to boat was that sport fishermen as a class were faster than cabin class yachts. Even with the twin screws and gas driven V-8's, however, they seemed to plod at half the speed of their previous boat. Daryl quickly trimmed back his plan to a more realistic destination. They made the north end of lake St. Clair in two hours. Daryl started to go down to ask Sandy if she minded anchoring out, but then knowing better, stopped himself and started searching the charts for marinas. Because they still had plenty of light, he decided to explore the Clinton River. They passed several places near the mouth where he concluded they could comfortably spend the night, and continued west passed Selfridge Air Force Base into downtown Mount Clemens. Daryl did not feel comfortable going under the bridges even though he had enough clearance, and he turned back east just before the first one. Sandy came up on the bridge just as he turned back. Bobby, who was quite pleased with his ability to read their charts, pointed out the Macomb County Court House to her.

At dusk they tied up at a marina just inside the channel from Anchor Bay. Sandy had dinner on the table in the lounge when Daryl got back from registering. She also had quite a lecture for them about cleanliness. She did not intend to be their cook and maid. Daryl tried to defuse her anger with a reminder that he thought she liked being a homemaker and had, indeed, refused his standing offer to hire domestics. It did not work. In addition to the work required by the sorry state in which she found the appliances, she had spent the balance of the afternoon washing all the dishes and the cupboards. She would cook, but the men were going to wash dishes and make the beds. After dinner, while the men worked, she sat in a folding chair on the deck, bundled against the chill, drinking a glass of white wine and watching the military aircraft coming and going from the nearby base.

When she came inside, Daryl and Bobby were laying on the floor of the lounge watching TV. Sandy curled up on the sofa. Periodically, Daryl made statements about how wonderful the boat was and what a great life they had. Sandy sipped wine through the evening. At 9:00 P.M., Daryl started drinking scotch. He put Bobby in the lower bunk after he fell asleep on the floor at 10:30 P.M. After the 11:00 P.M. news, Daryl and Sandy went to bed. The pie-shaped bed in the bow forced their feet to touch, and they were soon petting. After several minutes when Daryl noticed that Sandy's interest did not seem to progress, he rolled over on his back and sighed.

"I'm sorry, I must have had to much to drink."

"Come on. Don't mind me. I'm just not used to this bed, the boat. It smells musty in here. Everything needs to be scrubbed. Come on. Don't stop."

Daryl tried to stop himself, for he knew how it would end; but as usual, his appetite prevailed. When he finished, he passed out. He woke the next morning to a lecture. Sandy and Bobby had already eaten. He was wasting the day. She wanted the sheets to wash in the marina's laundromat while he got dressed and fed. She came back aboard and belittled him more about watching cartoons with Bobby when there was so much work to be done, including his own breakfast dishes which he had left behind. He deliberately remained on the floor with Bobby until she left for the laundry. Then he lumbered up, did the dishes, and took a shower. He and Bobby made the beds when Sandy returned with the clean sheets. She also returned with a sack of cleaning materials and air fresheners she bought at the marina store.

They finally got underway at 10:00 A.M, cruising east across Anchor Bay to catch the North Channel of the St. Clair River. Sandy served cold sandwiches on the bridge for lunch. Other than that, she remained below, and they did not see her until they made Port Huron in the middle of the afternoon. Daryl surveyed each marina they passed, looking for a nice place to spend the evening. Bobby went below and brought Sandy back. The only good looking marinas were on the Canadian side. Daryl did not feel like fussing with Customs, so he proposed that they go out into Lake Huron just to say they'd been there and head back south. There being no objection, they did that. Coming back down the St. Clair River between Port Huron and Sarnia, they took on gas at a fuel dock on the U.S. side. They stopped for the night at a marina on Harsens Island off the North Channel. By then Sandy had the interior of the boat cleaned to her satisfaction and sweet smelling, but when Daryl complimented her, she grumbled.

Daryl grabbed a bottle of scotch and sat outside drinking from it while he watched the sun set. Bobby helped Sandy make dinner. Daryl drank through dinner and kept drinking in front of the TV. He fell asleep on the floor where Sandy left him. He woke at 5:00 A.M., showered, and put together a Mother's Day breakfast for Sandy. He woke Bobby and had him serve it to her in bed. A few minutes later he came in with his cup of coffee. Sandy asked how he felt with a sarcastic edge in her tone. Before he could answer, she asked if he was enjoying his new toy. He turned and walked out, promising himself that he would die before she found out about the house. He went outside where he finished his coffee. He pulled a handwritten letter from his pocket and read over it. Then he tore the letter he had written to her about her choices, their son, and his love into little pieces that he dropped overboard. He was convinced that he did not deserve her treatment. He did not go back inside, and Sandy did not come out. They cruised back up the North Channel, then caught the South Channel because Daryl liked to look at the homes along Big Muscamoot Bay. When they cleared the channel, he headed straight southwest across Lake St. Clair for Jefferson Beach. Sandy took Bobby home in her car. Daryl stayed on the boat to putter and drink.

CHAPTER 28

Physically, Sandy and Daryl had always been something of an odd couple. She was of average to tall height for a woman, but slender and refined. Daryl hovered almost a foot taller, spilling out of his rumbled clothes. For a number of years his frame disguised his weight, but no longer. He fought to keep it below 300 pounds. Sandy weighed little more than one-third of him, but with each year after her thirtieth birthday, she also gained weight. In the fall of 1982 Sandy had become so self-conscious about her weight gain, that she refused to attend the Marine Birthday Ball.

Each year, Frank Sloan attempted to persuade Daryl and Sandy to accompany him and his wife to the Birthday Ball, an annual affair at which the Corps celebrates its founding. Daryl had attended several during his active duty. They were formal galas that typically included bag pipes, chromed swords, visiting dignitaries, a giant cake, recognition of the oldest and youngest Marines present, and dancing into the early morning. At the second one he attended, Daryl was surprised to find himself the youngest Marine. The oldest was in a wheel chair. Both were saluted with great ceremony by the visiting general, who, as he formally lowered his salute, suddenly lunged into Daryl to knock him off balance. This too was tradition for which Daryl was prepared. He had to take a step to keep his balance, but recovered smoothly, never out of attention and holding his salute all the while. The crowd laughed and cheered. Each year Daryl wanted to go to the ball, and each year he made an excuse. He felt he had lost the right. It was the same reason he did not wear a Marine ring.

"So Marine, what is your excuse going to be this year? I wish you would come. We could have a great time."

Daryl got up from his desk and closed the door to his office. "Frank, I should have told you years ago. I was discharged as a conscientious objector."

"Honorable?"

"Of course."

"Then what the hell's your problem? It's a party."

"I just wouldn't feel right."

"General Braun's your friend, he was in your wedding, and you don't feel right about coming to our party."

"Something like that."

"For christ's sake, Braun is going to speak to all the balls on closed circuit TV."

"No kidding?"

"The Commandant always does."

"Well, OK. Let me talk to Sandy."

After a day of shopping for a formal, however, Sandy refused to go. She was now forty pounds heavier than she had been at her wedding and twenty-five pounds heavier than when she carried Bobby. She found gowns that disguised it, but she did not like them. Daryl cajoled her, but to no effect. She refused. They argued. She refused. After a week of trying, he finally went to Sloan's office. After the decade lacking candor, he resolved to be forthright. His face was flushed, it usually was from the booze and the weight, but this time it was even redder in embarrassment. Sandy thought she had a weight problem. She would not go. Sloan acted as if he understood.

Sandy also made excuses when Willie Sturtz called to have lunch with her. As usual Sandy was volunteering in a congressional race, and had worked for the Reagan campaign in 1980. Willie had joined the Reagan group in California in 1977 as a strategic planner and followed them into a small office in the basement of the White House. Public relations for a sitting president was not to his liking, and after little more than a year in that role, he finagled a move to the Republican National Committee where he rejoined Mary Jane. Now they travelled around the country putting on how-to seminars for prospective candidates in the slow times, and during the season, they came in for two to three day consulting sessions with troubled campaigns. Willie had deliberately scheduled six hours between connecting flights at Metro so he could meet Sandy. She initially agreed, but the day before, she called him back to say she had the flu. She did not. Willie quickly called a few locals to meet him. There was always work to be done.

Daryl had the boat pulled and shrink wrapped late that October.

It was in far better shape when they laid it up than it had been when he bought it. Much of the credit went to Sandy. Their Mother's Day dispute passed in the ordinary course. Although she did not spend every weekend on the boat as Daryl did, she did make several weekend trips during the summer. They thoroughly explored Lake St. Clair, and made tentative trips out into Lake Huron. Often they simply cruised up and down the Detroit River and stayed on the boat overnight at the marina. In late June, Sandy had the carpets steam cleaned and had the captain's quarters and lounge wall papered. She also bought new bedding. In August she prepared a candle-lit dinner party for her parents. Daryl cruised south down the river while she cooked and her parents had cocktails with him. He anchored for dinner just off the channel between the southern tip of Fighting Island and Turkey Island. Cruising back passed the downtown lights, Daryl realized that Sandy would be much happier with a cabin class yacht that had more room for dining. In the back of his mind, he started shopping; although he felt he was not in a position to buy a bigger, more expensive boat. Before they shrink wrapped the boat, Daryl had a name painted on the stern, "Chapter 11".

Daryl's practice was bankruptcy for construction contractors, but within it, he had developed a sub-specialty. He had become a master of liquidating reorganizations under Chapter 11. The simple view of bankruptcy is that a debtor is protected while its financial affairs are either liquidated and distributed to its creditors, or reorganized and kept alive so that the creditors get a more favorable pay-out. Under bankruptcy reform, lawyers, as is their custom, found a way in which to interpret and apply the words into a seemingly nonsensical result; thus, the liquidating reorganization. A hard look at the result does lend some sense to the double talk. In it, the business is reorganized under the control of its principals who continue their salaries and benefits during the reorganization. After they have picked the bones clean, the business is liquidated. Of course, to obtain court approval for the reorganization, it had to be demonstrated that the reorganization holds more potential benefit for the creditors than an immediate liquidation. Potential is the kind of word around which lawyers can build a practice, and Daryl did. It was not a practice without controversy, for many bankruptcy lawyers found it ethically lacking. The work Daryl generated for the firm increased even more. Against all the statistics associated with Daryl, Chairman Goldfarb commenced a whispering campaign.

In Goldfarb's view the issue was clear, money or morality. He found the liquidating reorganization unethical and its practice a corruption that tainted the firm. The Dobbin's view was that the law was not chiseled in stone but written into the surface of a moving stream. The law continually changed to adapt to contemporary economic and social conditions. He was doing nothing more or less than zealously representing debtors with the most recent developments in the law. As lawyers, they had all taken an oath to do that. They were advocates, not judges; and as inappropriate as it was for a lawyer to sit in judgment of its client, if that was to be done, the judgment should be made on the basis of the law, not personal morality. The practice was within the bounds of the law. Throughout, neither Goldfarb nor Dobbins spoke to each other or openly defended themselves outside closed committee sessions. The debate, however, permeated the firm. Everyone from the messengers to the executive committee members had opinions and expressed them at the coffee stations and in the halls. Daryl relished the politics. Goldfarb retreated into his office and brooded.

Department chairmen in the firm were partners like any others. All partners were theoretically equal. Compensation was calculated off various factors, including service to the firm. Thus, department chairmen were financially rewarded for their service. The problem for the firm, however, was the power historically exercised by department chairmen and the deference traditionally given them. They were, in fact, more equal. There was no precedent in the history of the firm for any lawyer defying a department chairman. If a chairman did not like a particular type of case, those cases were simply referred and not accepted. Indeed, criminal defense was generally regarded as particularly distasteful for the firm; but they were a regular occurrence for the firm's large corporate clients with anti-trust, environmental, securities, and tax matters. The firm resolved the touchy subject by associating solo practitioners and boutiques that would handle the individual criminal cases without coveting the firm's clients. There were those who saw that approach as a compromise solution to the civil war in the Insolvency Department. No one wanted the dispute to make it to the annual retreat, there was too much other business to consider to be distracted by a philosophical debate. Pressure came to bear on the executive committee to resolve the matter, once and for all. They did.

It was never publicly or privately disclosed exactly who made what decisions or when they were made. It was all handled swiftly and confidentially. That was no small feat given the number of people involved and their animosities. When it was concluded, they all had self-congratulation in common, for they had pulled it off. At a few minutes before the close of business on a Friday afternoon a memo was distributed to everyone in the firm by the chairman of the executive committee. Lawyer Goldfarb, three other partners, eight associates, and nine secretaries were leaving the firm to establish their own bankruptcy boutique. Saturday morning the movers came in to move them out. Saturday night partners' offices were cleaned, painted and papered. Sunday afternoon, all the offices in the Insolvency Department were shuffled. Monday morning a second memo was distributed. Bernard Weinstock was the new chairman of the Insolvency Department which now consisted of four partners and twelve associates. Weinstock never knew that Daryl had been offered the chairmanship and refused because of Weinstock's seniority. Daryl never knew that the firm paid the cost of moving Goldfarb's group, including one year's rent for their new space. Three month's later, Daryl was pleased to see a 25% increase in his distribution check. He scolded himself that if he'd known how much of a drag the carrying overhead of Goldfarb and his dead wood had been, he'd have made a move years before. He complimented himself at the automation and efficiency of his department. If the formula held, he would make $250,000 that year. He just might be able to swing a bigger boat. He started looking. A year later, when the firm stopped paying Goldfarb's office rent, Daryl's take home pay got another boost.

Daryl found his next boat in a most unlikely manner. A local nightclub owner was in the throws of a divorce from his 23 year old wife. He had two objects in the divorce, to save his business and chisel the wife. His estranged wife was now living on their 46' Trojan with twin diesels. The boat was in his name, but he agreed she could live on it until the divorce was final. She expected to get the boat and more in the divorce. Shortly after she filed for divorce, the cash flow of the night club fell off dramatically. The divorce lawyer recommended a bankruptcy specialist. Daryl suggested a liquidating reorganization to maximize flexibility. A week later when he saw the schedule of assets, he recognized the name of the boat. It was berthed at his marina. It was scheduled for a third less than what he thought was its fair market value. He asked the night club owner about it and learned that his plan was to quickly sell the boat, run the wife off it, and use the proceeds to pay operating expenses of his club which was going down the tubes. Once the divorce was complete, and his club bankrupt, he was planning to open a new club with a different format. Daryl did not ask where he would get the money for the new club.

Daryl said he'd buy the boat for the scheduled price, and the night club owner put out his hand with a smile. Daryl told him he could not be his lawyer if he bought the boat. That was fine with him, he only wanted to sell the boat. Daryl picked up the phone and called a yacht broker. He thought he could sell Daryl's Hatteras within sixty to ninety days for $50,000 less than what Daryl proposed to pay on the new boat. The second call was to his broker. They would lend him the balance against his securities, $1 loan for every $2 of stock collateral. They could wire the money to his bank that afternoon, the paperwork would follow. All Daryl had to do was come up with $50,000 cash. He had stashed that much in savings from the Goldfarb bonus. He made one more call to his bank and had it transferred into his checking account. He wrote a check to the night club owner, got Diana to run down a printed sales contract, and within twenty minutes the paperwork was complete. He temporarily owned two boats, but what a deal. On the way home that night, he decided against "Chapter 11, II". He would call her the "Sandy Shores".

Everything associated with the deal clicked neatly into place. The new bankruptcy lawyer had to get a court order to get the wife off the boat, but that happened in three weeks. She took one of the three color TV's and some stereo equipment that she should not have, but Daryl did not mind. It only took a couple of hours to walk their possessions down the marina from the Chapter 11 to the Sandy Shores. He had the name repainted the day after the wife left. Two weeks later, the Chapter 11 was sold to a glass executive from Toledo. He repaid the brokerage house loan. Most importantly, Sandy loved the new boat. It was as comfortable as a home. Although Sandy did not know it, it was larger than the house in which Daryl grew up. The stern was enclosed, but the side panels could be removed if one desired. The enclosed deck was carpeted and contained wicker furniture. It opened off the lounge which was furnished like a comfortable den with a pull-out sofa and color TV. The engine room was in the center of the boat, accessed through a hatch in the lounge floor. Ahead of the lounge was the dining table that seated eight. Beyond it was the galley, twice the size of that on the Chapter 11. Opposite the galley was the interior bridge. There was a flying bridge above, accessed by a ladder on the rear deck. The flying bridge was covered with a canvas enclosure. A life boat hung on davits over the stern. The captains's quarters were aft of the engines below the rear deck. It contained a queen size bed and had its own head and shower. The forward stateroom also had its own head and shower and contained a double bed. Each stateroom had TV and stereo equipment, as well as an intercom.

It was really too much boat for Daryl and Bobby to handle, especially docking. Sandy broke her tradition, and finally came outside to help them in that process, for it took Daryl's lightest touch on the bridge and hands on both the bow and stern to dock her. They repeated their familiar excursions on the Detroit River and around Lake St. Clair, gaining confidence with each voyage. They planned their longest voyage yet to begin Memorial Day weekend 1984. They would return to Mackinac Island. The Sandy Shores did not cruise as fast as they were used to in the Hatteras, and it took them four days just to get to the Straights. They made Port Huron the first day, Port Austin the second, Presque Isle the third, and Mackinac Island the fourth. They were long days, but the weather held. Daryl called the office from the marinas each day, and ultimately had to extend his vacation because he underestimated their speed. Also, they got weathered in at Mackinac for three days. Bobby spent most of those days exploring the island on one of the three bikes they kept aboard. Daryl and Sandy revisited most of the places they had years before. The second night in port, Daryl moderated his drinking and Sandy perfumed the bed.

"Do you think we should tell Bobby?" Daryl asked, holding Sandy in his arms.

"What?"

"That he got his start here."

"You can't be serious?"

"Sure, why not?"

"You can't be certain."

"Oh yes I can. Don't you remember. You...."

"Don't touch me there."

"I only wanted...."

"Don't."

"I'm going up for a drink."

"I'm sorry that I'm fat. I'm sorry that I'm not pretty for you. I'm sorry that I'm not good for you."

"Give me a break. We both know that it's me who is the disappointment. Do you want a drink?" She didn't answer. "The stars are out. I'll be on the bridge."

That night Daryl began what became his regular custom. On clear nights he did it even in port at Jefferson Beach. He went up on the flying bridge, put back the canvas sun screen, opened a sleeping bag on the deck, and drank himself to sleep under the stars. Below, Sandy got up and made herself a sandwich. She took a bag of potato chips and a can of Coke back down to the Captain's Quarters. The late eating kept her awake. She rarely got to sleep any more before 2:00 or 3:00 A.M. She still rose at normal times, and gained dark, puffy circles under her eyes.

CHAPTER 29

The next time I saw Sandy was the Fourth of July weekend, 1985. I took my oldest son up to South Bass Island for a father-son campout. Tammy and I married in 1979. She was a court reporter for Judge Gallo on the Franklin County Common Pleas Court. I met her just after I went out on my own. We dated on and off for three years. It was, and is, a stormy and tempestuous relationship; which I admit is mostly, but not exclusively, my fault. Now that I don't drink, it's easier to throw some blame her way. She is two years older than me and had been supporting herself for a decade before we met. Since we both lived in German Village, we kept running into each other at the bars, the Big Bear grocery, and Schiller Park. We were going to stay in German Village, and both of us were going to keep working. That was the plan.

A year after our marriage, Number One Son was born. Number Two Son came along eighteen months later, and Number Three Son two years after that. Tammy never went back to work. Just before number two was born we moved to Pickerington, a suburb east of Columbus. Tammy grew up there when it was a farm town. She felt more comfortable with the schools there. Anyway, when I was single I went camping a lot alone. That had gotten put aside with marriage and the kids. For a hobby I had started flying lessons down at the Fairfield County Airport near Lancaster. I still didn't have my license, and Tammy constantly fought me about it. Anyway, that summer I decided to get back to camping for a hobby. I started by taking my oldest son, Klaus, up to South Bass Island. We stopped in Attica and had dinner with my parents, then caught the last ferry from Catawba Point. We camped in the state park. We got a nice site on top of a thirty foot shale bluff near the Hotel Victory ruins. The next morning we drove into town. We were walking on the municipal marina looking at the yachts when I heard a familiar voice call my name.

At first, I couldn't place the voice. I stopped and looked around, then started walking again. She called again. I saw her waving from the fantail of one of the biggest boats there. I still didn't recognize her. I mean no disrespect, but she was a grotesque caricature of her former self. She had to weigh over two hundred pounds, maybe two fifty. I studied the obese woman trying to connect a name. Then I noticed the name of the boat, Sandy Shores. I looked closer, the blond hair, the earrings were the same. Everything else about her was hideously bloated. I truly could have walked right passed her and not recognized her. She acknowledged when I tentatively said her name. Soon we were aboard, sitting on the deck furniture catching up.

"What brings you to Put-In-Bay?"

"I grew up in a small town near here. Klaus and I are camping on the southwest side of the island, a little quality time. Klaus, this is Mrs. Dobbins." He smiled and fidgeted. "I went to law school with her and her husband. Nice boat."

"Daryl's folly. He started with a speed boat. They have gotten progressively bigger. We spend just about every weekend aboard. We discovered Put-In-Bay last summer. We come in here about once a month."

"Where is Daryl?"

"Oh, he's below swearing at one of the engines. He'll be out soon. He had trouble with it all the way down, then about fifteen minutes out, it died. We came in on one engine. There he is."

I saw Daryl's head appear from a hatch in the floor in the salon. He didn't look much different; a little heavier, a little older. He was drenched in sweat. I went inside and greeted him. I offered my name, just in case he had forgotten. Behind him, a dark haired teenager climbed up the ladder from the engine room. He was wearing a swimming suit, finely muscled, and also perspiring heavily.

"Good to see you. Engine problems, its hotter than hell down there. This is my son, Bob. Bob, get us some ice tea. Thanks." We went out on the deck where Sandy had Klaus in her lap and was telling him about Perry's battle. "Sorry, I'm such a mess. How's Columbus?"

We made light conversation and finished the tea. The boys sat and listened. During a lull, Bob spoke up and asked Sandy if he could go swimming. She asked me if Klaus could join him. Naturally, Klaus lit up like a Christmas tree. We found a life jacket for him, and he went in wearing his shorts. Klaus was generally shy, but he made up to Bob quickly. Within minutes they were jumping off the bow. Later, Bob talked Klaus into jumping off the roof over the rear deck. The first time they held hands and went together. Bob was quite a swimmer. From what I could see, he was also quite a diver, he did swans, jack-knifes, and flips. When he hit the water, he barely made a splash. After a while Daryl excused himself saying that he had to find someone to work on his engine, and he left the boat. Sandy and I sat watching the boys and chatting. Daryl came back about a half hour later, he spoke to Sandy.

"I hope you're not in a hurry to get home. There isn't anyone on this island that can work on the engine before next Tuesday."

"Can't we go home on one engine, and get it fixed in Detroit. We came in on one engine."

"No dear, we can't."

"Did you call a place named Falloni's in Sandusky? I went to high school with their head mechanic. Service is supposed to be their big thing."

"Do you know if they work on diesels. Not just anyone can work on a diesel engine."

"This guy was working on diesel tractors on his father's farm when he was no older than Klaus. We spent half our youth lying under cars."

I went with Daryl to a pay phone on shore at the base of the marina. I called Falloni's and asked for Joe. In a instant, we were speaking. I apologized for not staying in touch and explained the situation. He asked to talk to Daryl. Daryl went through the history. On their trip down from Detroit, the starboard engine simply stopped running. He fought it to get it started. It would run perfectly for a time, then it would die again. Finally, it wouldn't start. He ran the battery down trying to start it that morning. Daryl told him that they would like to leave for Detroit Monday. He thanked Joe and handed the phone back to me. Joe told me that he was getting off at noon anyway, so he'd catch the ferry and bring his tools. He estimated he'd get to Put-In-Bay by 2:00 P.M. I invited Daryl and Sandy to lunch, but she wouldn't hear of it. She said that cooking was the only thing she did well anymore, gave Daryl a look, and disappeared inside. Daryl said it was a little early, but asked if I'd like a drink. While he was inside getting them, the boys finally came out of the water. Klaus was after Bob to take him to the old carrousel. Bob said he didn't mind. Daryl approved. I gave them a twenty, and Daryl and I watched them walk down the marina together.

"Your son is a nice young man."

"Wish I could take the credit. Genetically, he is his grandfather, Sandy's father. Intellectually, he's her son. He is smart, but as stubborn as they come. We're really lucky, he's a good kid. No trouble. He swims. He's a competitive swimmer."

"That would explain the muscles."

"He never wins, but he never quits."

"I hope my sons turn out as well."

"I hope this whole generation turns out better than us. What a mess we are. Ready for another?"

I am not about to make excuses for my drinking, but a cold beer on a muggy July day is one thing, scotch another. I was drinking beer. Daryl was drinking scotch. It was before lunch, and he was knocking back the scotch like it was ice water. We had a couple more and were laughing at each other before Sandy came out with the food. Somehow she had come up with homemade soup, a platter of lunch meats and cheeses, and three different kinds of bread. She drank white wine. We were nearly finished eating when the boys returned. They were fast friends, even with the age difference. They hurried a sandwich, got some more money from me and headed back to a video game parlor just across De Rivera Park. We watched them run across the park. Sandy produced an apple pie. I have no idea where the time went, we were still sitting drinking and talking when I saw a new pick-up truck stop along the waterfront park near the base of the marina. Joe got out. He came carrying two tools boxes. I hurried down the marina to greet him.

Joe was the best man in my wedding, but I had only seen him two or three times since then. We really tied one on the night before my wedding. I didn't have a bachelor party. I just took Joe out and showed him the finer points of the various bars in German Village. He was driving and staying in a downtown hotel. He dropped me back at my place about 11:00 P.M., but from what I gathered the next day, he kept going until the early hours. I remember kidding him about being a country boy in the big city. He was still pretty much in the bag during the wedding, but he rallied afterwards when the bar opened at our reception. I will say that Joe seemed to stay in shape. I don't think that he kept up the biking, it was more likely that he simply inherited the slender build of both his parents. Even though he was thin, his eyes were puffy and his face usually flushed. He was a drinker, but who was I to criticize. People that live in glass houses.... My Mom kept me posted on Joe with what she picked up through the local grapevine; and I assume Mrs. Altznauer did likewise for Joe. When I was in Attica, my mom always knew when Joe was also home. When he was, I'd call, then drive over to the farm. That was about the extent of our contact. Daryl and I were drunk, and Sandy was high when Joe came aboard.

"Joe, I'd like you to meet the Dobbins, Daryl and Sandy. I went to law school with them. Daryl's the skipper with a broken engine." Joe smiled, but still holding his tool boxes, did not shake hands.

"Like a drink?" Daryl asked.

"Let's see about this engine first."

Daryl and Joe disappeared down the hatch. I sat with Sandy on the deck. When she finished her drink, she asked if I'd like to go for a walk. She made a beeline for the liquor store across from the old wooden water tower. It was leaking, and I was hot enough and drunk enough to take pleasure standing in the sprinkle that came down from it until she pulled me on. She bought twelve bottles of the local island wine. I carried it for her, suspecting that was why she wanted me to come. The work sobered me. I remember the sweat rolling down the side of Sandy's face. The heat was killing her. That kind of weight can't be healthy. On the way back to the marina, she got herself a large vanilla cone at the Dairy Queen. We found Joe at the back of his pick-up.

"The magneto is crapped up. Once I get it cleaned out, she'll run like new." Daryl walked up with a fresh drink and looked over Joe's shoulder. "You could have this replaced the next time you have the boat in, but that's not necessary. It's just a little corrosion from the moisture."

"This guy's great!" Daryl announced. "Saved our ass."

Daryl followed Sandy and I back aboard. Soon Joe came back with the cleaned part. Daryl and I followed him down the ladder into the engine room with our drinks. It was sweltering down there. I remember looking at Joe in his fresh khakis wondering why only Daryl and I seemed to be perspiring in the heat. Within a few minutes Joe had finished reinstalling the magneto.

"Ready to try to start her?"

"Not yet, Skipper." Joe switched batteries, so the fresh one was connected to the ailing engine, then he starting tracing wires. He found a broken wire, and pointed it out to Daryl. "It couldn't possibly have run with that wire broken. That's the ignition circuit."

"I'm telling you it ran yesterday, and it cranked this morning. We must have kicked it when we were down in here this morning." Joe kept inspecting things as if following a mental checklist. Daryl spoke again. "I've really got to thank you for introducing me to Joe. It's easy to see I'm in the presence of a master."

"Thanks, but its a pretty easy job. An engine is a closed universe. Problems are solved by a simple process of elimination."

"That's what I tell the young lawyers in the office. You break the big problem into little pieces and deal with them one at a time. They never learn. Most of them go all the way through law school and still don't know their ass from a hole in the ground. They could learn a lot from a guy like you."

Joe looked to me and smiled. "She'll start now, Skipper."

"Sure?"

"Sure." Joe connected a set of wires with alligator clips to the electrical system, and pushed a button on one of the leads. The engine cranked and fired immediately. It idled smoothly. "Let's go get some air."

Joe and Daryl went up on the flying bridge so that Joe could watch the gauges. I stopped in the galley where Sandy was busy making hors d'oeuvres, just long enough to get another beer for myself and one for Joe. I joined the men up on the bridge. Joe was showing Daryl how to operate the Loran. Daryl cussed the thing as impossible, and said he was about to buy a new model that was more user-friendly. Joe told him to save his money. In a year or two they would be down to a reasonable price and would be easier to program. Part of the problem was the mid-continent gap from the radio towers, that was not the receiver's fault. Everyone complained about their Loran on Lake Erie. It would get better soon. They got coordinates off a chart and Joe showed Daryl how to enter them. Daryl protested that Joe wasn't doing it the way the book said, but it worked. Joe finished the beer and went back to the engine room to switch the batteries back. Daryl was still playing with the Loran like a kid on Christmas when Joe returned. He couldn't believe how easy it was to enter waypoints. He cursed the instructions and praised Joe. Joe had him start both engines, and they ran them for about five minutes until Joe was satisfied both batteries were charged.

"How much do I owe you?"

"It's $45 an hour for one hour." Daryl started to reach for his wallet. "You just give me your address. The office will send you a bill."

"$45 bucks for coming all the way out here?"

"An hour's an hour. Service only, didn't need any parts."

"Here take this for your trouble. This is for you not the company." Daryl pushed a twenty towards Joe.

"Naw, I can't take that. It's a nice day. I got to see my old friend. I will have another beer, if you don't mind."

"I wish I could find someone in Detroit like you."

"Falloni, Old Man Falloni, treats people right. He charges fair and stands behind our work. If you have any trouble getting home, don't pay the bill. Just write a note on the invoice and say what happened. If you pay, and it doesn't work, we make it right. Company policy. If we can't fix it, he doesn't want your money."

Daryl was impressed. We had another beer, and Joe went over the Loran one more time. Then Daryl and I walked him back to his truck with his tools. The boys were still out, so I told Daryl to hang on to Klaus if they came back to the boat. Daryl said good-bye, and Joe and I went over to the Round House. We got a pitcher of beer and sat outside at a picnic table. It had turned into a beautiful afternoon. The harbor was full of boats. The horizon on either side of Middle Bass Island was dotted with sails. The park and street were full of pilgrims, mostly drunk or getting there. As always, the carrousel music filled the air.

Joe asked about married life. I talked about the boys. He asked about Tammy. He really didn't know her, so I went through her history. She could be demanding, but I deserved most of what I got, and I knew I was lucky to have her. I wanted to ask about him, if he had a girl. I wanted to asked about Molly, if he thought about what might have been, if his daughter hadn't, if Molly hadn't, if they would have had more kids, if they would have made it. I didn't. We just sat and watched the world go by. Joe finished a long gulp of beer and said that the porno theaters and massage parlors in Columbus were probably hurting since my marriage. It was a strange remark. I laughed it off, but I didn't forget it. For one thing, Joe would have no way of knowing that about me. I never talked to him about such things, or went catting with him or anyone else for that matter. At first, I took his statement as an indication of how well we knew each other. To a large degree, I still feel that way today. He had me pegged. The other thing about that statement, though, was that it answered the questions I wanted to ask. I learned how Joe was filling the void in his life.

We saw Bob and Klaus walk by and yelled to them. They were broke again. I told Klaus it was time for dinner. He whined, but agreed to stay. I invited Bob to have dinner with us. He acted like he wanted to but said he'd have to asked his parents. He ran over to the boat and was back within five minutes. We each got a half chicken and ear of corn at the barbecue. Joe and I finished another pitcher of beer, the boys got a pitcher of Coke. At twilight Joe said he had to get going. We said our farewells at his truck. Klaus and I got back to the state park just at sunset. The tent and our gear were all in place. It was a picture book scene watching the sun go down across the lake from that bluff.

The next day we explored the hotel ruins. Klaus was all over the old swimming pool. He found a grape vine hanging down from a tree and swung from the deck out over the leaf filled pool. I got down in the empty pool and caught him when he jumped. We played miniature golf and went up to the observation deck on Perry's Monument. Late that afternoon, we went by the Sandy Shores. Daryl and Sandy were sitting on the deck drinking. Bob was inside watching a Tarzan movie. I had a couple of drinks with them while the boys swam. Later Klaus and I went back to the Round House again for another barbecue chicken dinner. When in Rome.... We broke camp the next morning and caught an early ferry to avoid the crowds. We stopped for lunch at my parents'. Until recently, that was the last time I saw Sandy.

CHAPTER 30

Bob Dobbins was a determined competitor. He first swam competitively when he was eight years old. Daryl and Sandy took a limited membership at The Grosse Pointe Club for access to the swimming pool. Sandy remembered her own summers there and wanted it for him. She envisioned lessons and someplace for him to go on summer days. Soon, he was on the club swim team and bragged that he was much better than he was. His grandfather frequently came to watch practice. He could see the pool from the veranda off the bar. Sandy's father also never missed a meet. Bob quickly picked up the physique that swimmers do, but he was naturally so thin and tall, that the rounded shoulders and hump back were not what you noticed. You noticed the thickened chest and tight waist. Bob, he became Bob that same summer he started swimming when he ordered his parents to stop calling him Bobby, was strong and cut the water smoothly, but he had a defective stroke that no coach was ever able to cure. When he swam free style, he whipped from side to side. He looked something like a shark, but his sidewise motion cost him forward speed. Although he thought that free was his best stroke, his times told another story. He did not like breast, but swam it often. He could never master the butterfly. His events were increasingly limited to relays. He was a loyal team member. The coaches liked him and looked to him to bolster team spirit.

Soon, Sandy was involved. She started as a lane timer at their meets. She bought her own clipboard and stopwatch. She kept a notebook of statistics on Bob. His second season, she worked the scoring table. The few times Daryl could break away from the office to come to the daytime meets, he recognized the cleverness behind the file card system that allowed those who worked the table to make order out of what seemed mass confusion, but he also recognized that it was a system that cried out for a computer. When Bob wasn't swimming, he walked up and down the edge of the pool shouting encouragement at his teammates, or he ran cards from the officials' table to the lane timers and back; pink cards for the girls, blue for the boys. Sandy assumed the title of team mother his third season at The Club. She organized the team picnic at the end of the summer.

Beginning in the seventh grade, Bob started swimming on the school team. The coaches there faced the same dilemma. His stroke was beyond repair. His times were abysmal. Yet, his spirit was such, and the others liked him so much, that cutting him was unthinkable. Finally, they found his nitch his freshman year. A dive coach noticed him clowning around on the board with some friends before a preseason practice. Two weeks later the coach called Sandy to recommend private diving lessons. He was excited, the boy had real potential. That season, and thereafter, Bob was a major contributor to the team's scores. Where 3's and 4's were typical high school diving scores, Bob rarely came in with any thing lower than 6's, and occasional 8's. Adjusting that for the degree of difficulty, which is standard practice, his complex dives carried many a meet for the team. Sandy kept a notebook of his scores for each season. She also kept statistics on his major competitors. Daryl came to the evening and weekend meets. The state championships were an annual overnight outing which both his parents and grandparents attended. Each summer his grandparents paid the cost of the two week swim camp at Mission Bay in Boca Raton, Florida, where Bob worked on his dives. They drove him down, stayed in a nearby motel, and sat in the grandstands watching all day.

Sandy did not gain from Bob's athletic example, she did not exercise at all. Indeed, she came to his meets with a shopping bag of junk food; ostensibly for the team, but she ate most of it. She no longer even tried to diet. She paid a yearly visit to her gynecologist, and each year he scolded her about her weight, but otherwise gave her a clean bill of health. The year Bob started high school, she had a recurrent urinary tract infection. The gynecologist referred her to a urologist. He performed a minor procedure in his office, which he hoped would solve the problem. He told her that her weight might be a contributing factor. She complained about an upset stomach, and he referred her to an internist. The internist also scolded her about her weight, and gave her a pamphlet outlining a diet. He also recommended several diet books. He thought he heard a little abnormality in her heart, and referred her to a cardiologist. The cardiologist diagnosed mitral valve prolapse. It was common in women. If it became painful, he would give her something. Until then, he was more concerned about her weight. Each year a card came from the offices of the four doctors. Each year Sandy dutifully made the rounds. Each year they warned her about her weight. Each year she weighed more than the year before. She attributed it to anxiety, she was a nervous eater.

Daryl had essentially built his position at Campbell Short by staying current with the latest office technology. As he told it, he was just lazy and naturally gravitated toward the easy way of doing things. In 1987, he discovered scanners and laser printers, and quickly realized a whole new method of bankruptcy practice was at hand. He had succeeded in breaking the firm away from dedicated word processing equipment in favor of personal computers in 1985. His knowledge of personal computers started with a Christmas gift for Bob. Once again he tried the committee route, then went out and bought a desk-top for Diana with his own money. It gave them the power to crunch numbers as well as type. That was a day in the life for the Insolvency Department. Word spread from their department. The administrative committee hired a consultant. Soon PC's began appearing throughout the firm and secretaries and paralegals disappeared for week-long training sessions.

When Diana got the more powerful model that became the firm standard, Daryl took the one he initially bought for Diana into his office. Everyday he made an additional discovery. Soon he and Diana had their computers networked, and they put together three programs, a data base manager, an accounting package based on a spread sheet, and word processor, so that they could jump from one to the other and generate everything they needed in a case. Daryl started talking with his partner, the department chairman, Weinstock. Three years before they had worked together and produced a reference titled, Weinstock and Dobbins on Bankruptcy. It was a two volume set. Weinstock and a team of the law review types produced the text of the first volume from the department's library of research memos that Daryl had started years before. Daryl and Diana pulled the second volume of standard forms from their forms files.

Just as they had produced the standard treatise, Daryl urged that they could now set the practice standard with a software package for bankruptcy attorneys. It would be great PR for Campbell Short, and if they didn't do it, someone else would. Weinstock was convinced when

Daryl showed him how they could scan financial statements into the computer and how the laser printer could reproduce the official bankruptcy forms with the information blanks completed. Daryl handled the license negotiations with the software houses whose programs their system used. After their book publisher refused the opportunity to market the software system in connection with their books, in 1988 they signed with a software house that commenced a direct mail campaign to bankruptcy lawyers across the country. It was marketed as the Weinstock-Dobbins System, but everyone who used it called it the Campbell Short Software. The firm got the royalties. Daryl split the origination credit equally with Weinstock.

Daryl's efforts on the book and software system, in addition to his regular practice, kept him at the firm late most nights. He was one of the few partners who kept associates' hours. Unlike the associates, he did pamper himself. He continued his exercise break in the afternoon. At his desk in the evening, he routinely put away a half a fifth of scotch. He kept the bottle in plain view as he worked. The firm had a policy about liquor in the offices, that would have resulted in discharge if any associate engaged in Daryl's conduct; but Daryl was a partner, and more, the revenue statistics made him untouchable. It was about 7:30 P.M. one such night when Daryl got a call on his private line from a Dr. Stairs, who identified himself as Sandy's internist. She was fine. He was in the emergency room at Holy Cross with her. He understood their son was at a swim meet. He didn't want Sandy to drive, Daryl should come by in about an hour to drive her home.

"Slow down, doctor, what is going on?"

"Sandy came into my office this afternoon with a fever and intestinal complaints. As you know, I noticed some arrhythmia in the past and referred her to a cardiologist. I have also noted her anxiety. Her cardiogram is now 80, that's higher than it should be. I'd like her to come back to the office tomorrow for blood work. The only question now is the level of digitalis. It's all fairly straight forward at this point. She probably could drive herself home."

"I'm sorry, you're losing me. Sandy came in with a fever, and now you're in the emergency room with her. What happened?"

"We were discussing her anxiety. She said that you would never approve of psychiatric treatment and got into a very emotional state She demonstrated a contemporaneous arrhythmia. Her heart raced. I brought her over here. We have determined it is an atrial fibrillation, not ventral. Ventral is worse. We have it under control with digitalis. She needs psychiatric help."

"First, you have caught me way off guard. I had no idea about any of this. I don't know where she gets this business that I must approve of her doctors. I don't approve of any of the other doctors on her list. I don't even know their names. What difference would one more doctor make? She is making me her excuse."

"Her attribution to you would be consistent with the condition I believe she has, but I am not capable of an accurate diagnosis?"

"What does that mean?"

"I believe she is deeply depressed. The episode I witnessed today borders on a classic panic attack. She needs to see a psychiatrist for an accurate diagnosis and treatment."

"Can you recommend a psychiatrist?"

"Yes, John Bowars. His office is in the same building as mine. I know him. I know his work. You should call him first thing in the morning and tell him I said it is urgent."

"I have never told her not to see a psychiatrist. We have never discussed the subject. I don't know where she gets that. Have you told her that you want her to see this Dr. Bowars? What does she say? Shouldn't she agree or at least acknowledge that she needs the help before I go making an appointment for her?"

"I don't think you appreciate what I am saying. She is deeply depressed. She is incapable of making a decision. I will call Bowars."

"Doctor, I'm sorry, you have caught me by surprise. It's hard for this to sink in. She seemed fine this morning. We went on a cruise last weekend. She seemed fine then. She gets a little flu and then wham, she's in the hospital for her heart and you say its a psychiatric problem. Have you conferred with her cardiologist?"

"I am capable of administering and monitoring a digitalis regime."

"Couldn't all this be the result of her weight. That weight can't be good for her heart. Maybe she's depressed because of her weight."

"Her weight is the primary indicator of her depression. We seem to disagree on whether its the chicken or the egg. At this point, it does not make much difference. She needs a psychiatrist. I am not a marriage counselor. I am not a psychologist. I am not a psychiatrist. I am not a hospital. I am an internist administering a didg regime and referring a patient for what I reasonably believe to be indicated treatment."

"I will do whatever you want me to do."

"I have gotten fond of Sandy. I want to see her cured."

"Do you want me to come and pick her up?"

"I think that would be best."

Daryl picked her up an hour later. On the way up to Holy Cross Hospital, he remembered he had left his bottle of scotch out on his desk. He thought briefly of the comments that would be raised in the morning, then he thought the hell with it. He also noticed he was sober. He found Sandy sitting in a plastic chair in the waiting area outside the emergency room. She was embarrassed, but otherwise looked and acted perfectly normal to him. She said the doctor had left. Chicken shit, Daryl thought to himself. He wanted to stop on the way home for Chinese carry-out. Sandy wanted pizza. When they got home, she ordered the pizza and set the table. They ate the pizza with little discussion. Later when Bob called, Daryl drove out to pick him up. He told Bob that his mother had the flu. Her heart had flared up, and she ended up in the emergency room. Now she was taking medicine for her heart and everything would be fine. When they got home, Sandy had prepared a meal for Bob. Daryl slept late the next morning and ate breakfast with Sandy. They drove over to Dr. Stairs' office together to get her car. She went inside for the blood test. Early that afternoon she had her first session with Dr. Bowars. She saw him weekly for the next six months, then monthly after that. When they changed to monthly sessions, he enrolled her in one of his weekly group sessions. Also, when at the end of the six months she mentioned she was still gaining weight, he recommended a nutritionist, who was a registered nurse. Sandy started weekly visits with her.

Daryl resumed his routine. Bob had another successful diving season. Other than attending Bob's meets, Sandy's time was spent shopping, cooking, and visiting doctors. She no longer belonged to any volunteer organizations. She had not volunteered in a political campaign since she got heavy.

CHAPTER 31

Bob started college at Harvard in the fall of 1989. Where he would go was really never much of an issue. Daryl urged him to read through a guide to colleges he bought and to think about the type of career he wanted. Beyond that, his role was limited to saying that they were lucky to be able to afford whatever Bob wanted. Sandy was much more insistent. She was determined that he go Ivy League. Bob had placed in the National Championships held at Emory University in Atlanta. Coming from Detroit, he liked the mild winter with buds already peaking out in February, the modern nautatorium, and the white marble buildings on campus. Sandy would not tolerate a southern school. He never understood her opposition to what he considered an elite and prestigious school, but he did not share her images of sheet-covered men on horseback. Ultimately, Bob's application to Emory was tolerated as a "safety school".

Sandy's father was the true force behind the scenes. He often picked Bob up from swim practice and had dinner with him on the way home. He spoke nostalgically of his years at Harvard. Bob contrasted that with his parents' stories of the tumult of the 1960's. Sandy's father also spoke of how much he drew in his career from the basic liberal arts education. He had not been spoon fed information, he had been taught to think. He also made friendships that lasted decades. Bob did not know that his grandfather made several telephone calls. He made sure the development office, to whom he had sent contributions for forty- five years, knew that his grandson was applying. He made sure the athletic department was aware that a nationally ranked diver was applying. He made sure the local Harvard Club assigned someone to rush Bob. Daryl tried, but could never get Bob to commit to any career objective. The Harvard diving coach saw to it that an acceptance letter went to Bob a month before the usual mass mailing.

Daryl and Sandy drove Bob over to Boston to begin his first year. Daryl still owned a Porsche which he drove to work, and Sandy drove a Mercedes Sports Coupe. They also owned a Lincoln Continental which they used for church and trips. Its size was a concession to their own. With everything that Bob took to college, the Lincoln was tightly packed. They made it a two day trip going over. None of them had ever seen Niagara Falls, so they stopped there the first night. Daryl was more interested in the Welland Canal, and spoke of cruising into Lake Ontario the following summer, but Sandy would not agree to driving out to inspect the canal. They talked about the countryside. Bob filled them with stories he had heard from Sandy's father about going off to Boston alone by train and attending college during the War. Sandy was not familiar with the stories. They made Boston the following afternoon. Their hotel was across the Charles in downtown Boston. They drove around Cambridge that evening, and walked the campus. Daryl took video. Sandy avoided the camera, and Bob made fun of him. Checking in the next morning went quickly. After meeting his roommate and the roommate's family, they lingered about for an hour. Bob had an orientation meeting at 11:00 A.M. Daryl made videos of the farewell hugs and Bob walking off across the campus. Both Daryl and Sandy recognized the emotion in each other, but neither cried.

Neither did they speak much as they drove west across Massachusetts. When they did, they recalled the beginning of their own college years, or they asked each other if Bob had remembered to pack this and that. For reasons he did not explain, Daryl was insistent upon seeing Fort Ticonderoga. Sandy agreed. They diverted off the Interstate, but it got late in the afternoon, and he abandoned the plan. They stopped overnight in Lake George. The town and the countryside reminded them both of Mackinac Island, although they did not share that with each other. They stayed in a bed & breakfast and had dinner at an inn across the street. They had sex that night for the first time in a long time. Each took more pleasure from the shared joke that the others in the old house might hear them, than they did from the act itself.

They left early the next morning. Soon they were back on the Interstate. When Daryl drove, Sandy sat in the middle of the front seat next to him. Daryl put his arm around her. They almost stopped again east of Cleveland, but agreed to press on. They got home just after 8:00 P.M. No sooner were they unpacked, than they each wished that they had stayed over on the road. Daryl went to his library, opened mail, and started drinking. Sandy made them sandwiches in the kitchen.

The following Sunday morning before church, Daryl asked Sandy to trim his hair. It was a lingering vestige of their early marriage. From the earliest, Sandy began the ritual by lecturing Daryl that he was cheap and could afford a barber. Daryl began with instructions that he only wanted a trim and not a haircut. He took off his T-shirt and got down on his knees in front of their bathroom sink. His red hair had thinned and yellowed. There wasn't enough to justify a barber. He looked at his pasty skin and flaccid trunk. He looked at Sandy in her robe. They were a pair. They should get in shape. He winced from a cut as Sandy stepped back from him. He looked into the mirror and protested the chunk she had taken from his hair. He ignored the small trickle of blood. Sandy's face flushed and she started laughing. He scolded her that it was not funny, and demanded she do something to fix it. She laughed all the harder, tears rolled down her cheeks. He swore and demanded she fix it. He couldn't go out looking like this. Sandy told him to fix it himself and tossed the scissors on the countertop. Daryl was furious and started to rise, but as his eyes met Sandy's, he was disarmed by her look. She was laughing hysterically, crying, but her eyes were wide open, wild. He was suddenly afraid of her. She returned to their bedroom and dressed, laughing sporadically and talking to herself as she did. He stayed in the bathroom and tried to fix his hair.

They rode to church in the Lincoln without talking. On the way Daryl thought back to the first conversation he had with Dr. Stairs. Years had passed. What was that psychiatrist and group doing to her. He had never seen her this way. She was on a half dozen different drugs for who knew what. Maybe it was one of the drugs, or the mix of drugs. He wondered if each doctor knew what the other prescribed. It was more serious than her weight, but they couldn't even get her to lose a few pounds. Twice along the way, Sandy laughed spontaneously when she noticed his hair. He got angry again and growled that it wasn't funny.

They joined her parents who were already in the pew next to their window. After a few minutes of prayer, Daryl left them to go to Confession. As he waited in line, he tried to recall the last time that Sandy had gone to Confession. Later, when Sandy stayed in the pew while he and her parents went to Communion, he tried to recall the last time that Sandy had received Communion. As they drove home from brunch at The Club with her parents, he tried to recall the last time they had sex. He forgot about the incident in Lake George. He couldn't remember the last time. Sandy told him that she did not think her parents had noticed his hair. A few minutes after that she started laughing again, and laughed so hard that tears came.

A month later Daryl was indulging in his long-standing fondness for a warm bath. He had an oversize tub with water jets installed in their bath for this purpose. He gave the excuse of a pampering a bad back, but he knew that his back pain emanated from his swollen liver. Still the hot baths were soothing. He lifted a wet wash cloth draped over his face when he realized that Sandy was standing over him.

"You don't talk to me. You don't touch me. This is not a marriage."

"Lighten up, I'm taking a bath."

"You do not have a clue what's going on."

"I'm taking a bath."

"You won't do a thing about it."

"What exactly am I supposed to do lying naked in a hot bath? Is this your idea of a joke? I couldn't be more helpless. You show up from nowhere accusing, attacking. I know an ambush when I see one." He wiped the perspiration from his face, and his eyes met her's. They were wide, wild. For the first time, he admitted to himself that this was mental illness. He fought to control his temper. "Sandy, I have no idea of what is going on with you. I love you. I want to be married to you. We have a son, a life."

"This is no life. It's all your fault. You do nothing to change. I will not live like this. I do not want to."

"Change what? I love you. I love our life. I have worked hard for all this. I have done everything that was expected of me. Don't forget, you chose this life. You wanted it."

"You don't even have a clue."

"I don't deserve this. I have done nothing to deserve this."

"You are totally selfish. You always were. You always get what you want. It is always your practice, your boat, not me. It is never me. It is whatever you want. You want to go to Fort Ticonderoga so we drive to hell and back for nothing. It is never me." Sandy yelled.

"We did not go to Fort Ticonderoga. I had a wonderful time in Lake George with my wife, whom I love." Daryl cried and made no attempt to disguise his tears. "You wanted this life. You came from

Grosse Pointe, I came from Battle Creek. Surprise, surprise, we live in Grosse Pointe. I have kept my end of the bargain. It's supposed to be 50/50. I have more sins than I want to confess, but by anybody's measure, I have put up more than half."

"You can't twist it around with words. You have done nothing for this marriage. You have ruined this marriage!"

Sandy stepped back from the tub. At the sink she rinsed her face with cold water. She combed her hair and perfumed herself. She turned toward Daryl, who was studying her from the tub, and playfully squirted an atomizer of perfume in his direction. She strutted out of the bath smiling. Daryl laid in the water unable to hold any thought, past, present, or future.

The weekend after Thanksgiving, Sandy came up behind Daryl as he was sitting alone in one of the overstuffed chairs in his library. The TV was on, but he ignored it. He had been drinking for several hours. Several boating magazines were scattered on the floor next to the chair where he had dropped them. He was looking through a set of snap shots from the week before when Bob had flown home for the holiday. Sandy opened up on him before he realized she was even in the room.

"You can't hide from me forever."

"Sandy, I am tired of this. I love you. I will do whatever you want me to do, but I can't, I won't take this. I don't deserve it."

"You selfish bastard. You can't make this my fault. You decide."

"This is another ambush. I have done nothing to deserve this."

"Oh sure! I clean for you. I cook for you. I wash for you. I pick up your dirty underwear! You hide at your office and drink. When you're not on your precious boat drinking, you're drinking in here and thinking about the damn boat."

"I work hard, every day, all day. I paid for this house and every thing in it, and the boat, with money that I earned. I come home every night. I always have. Do you think other men do? You better do a little reality check. I come home to you, even when I don't want to."

"Don't act like you've done me any favors. I have put up with more than most women would."

"I have kept my part of bargain, and I intend to keep doing it."

"You do what you want."

"I will do what you want. You have to say it. I will not make it easy for you. I love you. I want to be married to you." Again, he started crying.

"You don't even know what a normal marriage is. This is not a marriage. You are the most selfish, self-absorbed person I have ever met."

"Look in the mirror, bitch. You chose to hide from the world. You engage everything on your terms. You pamper yourself. When you are unhappy, you make me the bad guy. It is not true. You can lie to yourself all you want, but someday you have to face the truth."

"I will not continue to live like this."

"Sandy, please. I love you. I want to be married. We have a good life. You are risking everything. You better be very careful. You will destroy this. When you finally realize what you have done, it will be too late."

"What I have done! That's rich. This is your fault. You are full of disappointment, anger, and hate. You are a hateful person. You need help. You should see someone. You won't do anything to change. You never have. You never will."

"You assume I want to change. I like this life. I know my limits. I lead a moral life. I will not ask you to forgive my weaknesses. I meet my responsibilities. I keep my obligations. I have nothing to apologize for on that score."

"You are a stinking drunk. I am not an obligation. You will not seek help."

"So tell me, what's all the help done for you? You have spent tens of thousands of dollars on doctors. That money could have fed your average third world country for a year. You tell me. What has changed, years of analysis, but what has changed. I'll tell you, money changes hands. They pander to your neurosis. You are not a psychotic. You are no crazier than anybody else."

"We all need help, but you're too proud to ask for it."

"I don't want help. I want to live my life, the way I want to live my life."

"You've got to resolve the situation with your parents."

"Where the hell did that come from? Give it a rest. You always have to point a finger of blame. That's not why I drink. I drink because I drink. It isn't complicated. It doesn't take a fancy psychiatrist or group to explain anyone's life. The reasons don't matter anymore. We are what we are. What on earth would contacting my family after twenty years do except make everyone uncomfortable and dredge up pain that people buried long ago?"

"You have to resolve it."

"It was resolved, by time."

"You will never be happy until...."

"Who is happy? Are you? Is that why you sit around with a bunch of whiners every week? Do you tell each other you are happy? I doubt it. You can't find enough unhappiness in your own lives, so you start working over each other. When that's not enough, you probably sit around and work over me. Isn't that the way it is? I'd like to know."

"You should come to group. You could use the help."

"You're the example. Look what they've done for you. Five medical doctors, one certified nutritionist, and four years of group. You're no different. They can give you chemicals, they can cut on you, they can talk to you and hold your hand; but they can't change you. Only you can do that. It's got to come from inside. A priest and a little prayer would do more for you than all the chemicals and shrinks in world. You are not crazy. They are pandering to your normal insecurities. They have made you worse by keeping you down wallowing in your problems."

"You have no idea what you are saying."

"When is the last time you went to Confession or Communion? When is the last time you prayed?"

"When is the last time you touched your wife?"

"It is not all my fault. Everything that is wrong in this world does not have a cause outside of you. Look at yourself. You make choices. You can make mistakes. You have, just like me. Everyone lives with that. I love you. I don't understand why you don't listen to that."

"If you loved me, you wouldn't drink."

"Now who doesn't have a clue? It's all inside, Sandy. 'Oz never gave nothing to the Tin Man that he didn't already have.' You look inside. Afraid you might see what you really are, a spoiled brat, a self-indulgent cow?"

"You leave my house!"

"Don't do this Sandy. Please! I love you."

"You bastard, you don't love anyone but yourself. Leave my house." She slammed the door as she left the study.

Daryl turned off the TV and finished the bottle of scotch. An hour later, Sandy opened the door long enough to push through a suitcase of his clothes. Daryl spent the next week on the boat, then got a furnished apartment in town. Sandy sent a letter to the office advising him that the locks had been changed and that he was not welcome at the house for Christmas. She would have Bob call him when he got in from school. Daryl continued to transfer money into her accounts as he always had.

CHAPTER 32

Sandy later came to mark a day in mid-February 1990, as the breakpoint in her life, not her separation from Daryl. On that day she had just finished running some errands after the monthly session with her psychiatrist. She was driving east on McNichols Road near Detroit City Airport when she noticed a billboard filled with the image of a high-wing light plane coming towards her. "Learn to Fly" the sign said, nothing more. She was sitting at a light, and she stared absentmindedly at the sign. It was getting close to lunch. As she made her way back to Grosse Pointe, she thought about dropping in on her mother for lunch, but then she didn't want to get another lecture about Daryl. She decided on fast food and diverted her course.

The altered route took her by their church. As she approached, she noticed a few parishioners going in for noon Mass. On impulse she stopped and went inside. It was ten minutes before Mass, so she went to the front of the Church, put a five dollar bill in the box and lit a candle. She kneeled before the statue of the Virgin and started a Rosary. She did not have her beads or even know exactly what drawer she had left them in. She counted the prayers on her fingers. The shuffle of the priest entering the confessional caught her attention, and she lost count. She got up and went to the confessional. She told the priest that she could not recall how long ago her last confession had been, maybe ten years. Later, he interrupted her confession because they were delaying the Mass. He told her to go ahead and receive Communion, but to come back after the Mass. She did.

At home Sandy ignored the mail. She sat on a stool in the kitchen staring at the refrigerator. She had liked the sacrament of Penance much more as a child. Then, it had been tidy and predictable. Certain sins resulted in a certain number of prayers. It suited her sense of order. The only open issue was the comparison of the priests. They were usually close in the number of prayers that they assigned, but not always. Her acceptance of the Vatican II changes was begrudging at best. After forty-five minutes of spilling out her most guarded thoughts, something at which she had become well-practiced from the therapy and the group; she felt she had gotten nothing of value. What in the hell was she supposed to do with an instruction to do good to those you have hurt, start with yourself, and go forward into life on new terms, those you know God has set forth for you. Her eyes came to rest on the yellow page telephone directory. She went to it, forgetting that she had not eaten lunch.

She spent the next hour calling flight schools and feverishly taking notes. After that, she reorganized her notes into a matrix, showing the name of each flight school and a summary of the critical information, the cost, the time involved. She could begin at any one of them immediately, weather permitting. She decided to drive back to the airport to talk to them in person and to look at their operations and aircraft. She went to the Cessna facility first, because it had a large lighted sign that she saw driving in. A young woman at the counter turned her over to a flight instructor who was sitting in the reception area reading a flying magazine. He gave her a tour of the facility. There were two conference-size classrooms, four small rooms for viewing training tapes, and several carrels with telephones for weather briefings and flight plans. He took her out on the flight line. They had five 152's and seven 172's. All were on the ground because of the fog. The 152 was the primary trainer that she would start in, but he had her sit in a 172 with him because it was roomier. When he took the gust lock off the controls, Sandy felt a rush of excitement when she moved the yoke back and forth. Back inside he showed her the textbook and other training materials. He finished by giving her a rate sheet showing three options, hourly, block time, or lump sum package price. As she left, he winked at the receptionist and waddled after Sandy with his arms extended and his cheeks puffed out.

Sandy drove around the airport looking at the buildings in search of the Piper school. It turned out to be an oversize room in one of the old hangers. There was a counter just inside the door and a desk covered with magazines behind it. A thin man, about fifty years old who wore a cheap toupee, greeted her. He remembered her from the phone. He invited her around the counter, and she sat down beside the disheveled desk. She noticed that he had taken to crushing his cigarettes on the desk top and tossing them into a mound under which you could see the corners of an ashtray. She did not like him from the first, but they spoke for more than an hour. He emphasized that he was the flight school, she would not be rotated through a half dozen of the young gypsy flight instructors that hovered around the larger flight schools. Also, he would not try to sell her an airplane. The other schools started as dealerships and ran flight schools to sell new planes. Now that no one was manufacturing light planes, they pushed the flight school business, but they still made money brokering used planes. Why wasn't anyone manufacturing airplanes? Lawyers. She nodded. When she asked to see the trainer, he stood and pointed out the back window. It was a four place single that appeared well kept. He made no move to take her out to see it. He used an FAA publication for a text book. Everything else they would talk about before and after her lessons. He did not have a price list. He told her that he would rent her the four place plane for the same price Cessna charged for a two place trainer, and that his instructor rates were the same as their's even though he had logged 10,000 hours. She thanked him and said she'd call back. As she left, he told her that she would learn to fly, and she would love it. Sandy did not like him, but she liked his attitude.

At the Beech operation, everything had an upscale appearance. The facility was newer. The carpet clean. The furniture modern. It was no more than one-third the size of the Cessna operation. The receptionist pushed a button on the phone and spoke into her headset. Soon, a short stocky thirty-five year old man appeared. He, like the others, wore tan dress slacks, a white shirt and tie, and a cloth jacket. The uniform, Sandy thought. He took her back to his office. Along the way he pointed out the conference room and a small room with a TV and VCR for training tapes. She was now proficient with the questions, and they spoke for no more than ten minutes. He took her out to their flight line. They had four planes, two Skippers, a Musketeer, and a Debonair/F33 retractable. The two place Skippers were the primary trainers. She liked the look of the low wing and T-tail. He opened the cockpit and helped Sandy up on the wing. She had difficultly stepping up on the wing. He grabbed her foot when she started to put it down on a no step area and made a joke.

Once she had settled into the left seat, he came around and worked himself down in beside her. She silently compared the lack of space to the four place Cessna she had just been in. He kidded her that flying was an intimate experience, and suggested they move their seats so their shoulders were staggered. He personally did not like the T-tail because the elevator was above the prop wash. That made for mushy controls at low airspeeds, but he reassured her, when she learned to fly this plane, she could fly anything. Again she got a rush when she felt the controls. He told her that both Skippers were as new as they come, they were built in 1981, the year Beech halted production. Sandy knowingly mentioned lawyers. He agreed with a frown. Holding the controls, Sandy told him her grandfather worked for Beech. He said that with serial numbers they could trace the planes back, if her grandfather could tell her years and models he worked on, they might have one of the planes he built. Climbing out of the plane, Sandy told him that her grandfather was long dead, but that when she was young, she had met Mrs. Beech. She made an appointment for a demonstration ride the next morning.

The instructor had Sandy sit in the left seat. He told her what he was going to say and explained why before he started the radio work. During the taxi he had her follow along with her feet as he steered with the rudder pedals. The takeoff seemed long, even to Sandy. He mentioned that she would be learning about weight and balance. It was never to be taken for granted, but they were OK. They departed Runway 7 and flew directly east over Grosse Point. He turned north at the river and flew along the shore. Sandy spotted The Club, her home, her parent's home, and the marinas at Jefferson Beach. He turned back for the airport and told Sandy she had the aircraft. He followed that with instructions causing her to make gentle banks and to lower and raise the noise. Soon he was back on the radio, they entered the pattern and landed back on the same runway. Inside, they sat down for a debriefing, then Sandy watched the first video that welcomed her to the program and reviewed a flight much like the one she had just taken. At home that night she read three chapters, read them again making notes, and then made a one page outline of the dozens of pages of notes. It worked for Daryl.

Sandy's lessons progressed quickly. She went to the airport everyday for the tapes and progressive tests, even if the weather was not above minimums. She flew three to four hours a week. They generally flew north to a local practice area over the countryside northwest of Rochester Hills. Because of the season, they typically flew between two and three thousand feet above ground level, one thousand feet below a solid ceiling. Each lesson built slowly upon the last. They started with ground reference doing S's along roads, and turns about points using intersections. Those progressed into figure 8's along the roads, then across the roads. Finally, they did 8's about pylons using two barns about a mile apart. It became a regular progression. After the ground reference, they added slow flight to the repertoire; clearing turns, carburetor heat, power back, full flaps, wings level, power to hold altitude. After that came steep turns with the horizon knifing into the dash and real G's pushing them down in their seats. She felt as if she had something in common with the astronauts. Sandy did well, and progressed to stalls the second week. He had her set up slow flight, then demonstrated the power off stall by bringing the nose up until it broke. Sandy did not appreciate his skill. She brought the nose up more quickly than him and over-controlled the recovery. He let her develop a quarter spin before he took the controls and talked her through the recovery. Her heart raced from what appeared to her to be a vertical dive, but she laughed and calmed down. They did six more after that. Sandy mastered the approach to landing stalls that day. They did some more ground reference, and then moved up to power on stalls. Sandy knew what was coming. She liked losing the horizon as they pulled the nose up. When the plane broke, she recovered instantly. With ground reference, takeoff and departure stalls, and approach to landing stalls under her belt, they started touch and go landings at Macomb.

It wasn't until the third week of her training that Sandy learned she would have to pass a physical before she could solo. None of her regular doctors were authorized to give the government physical, so she acquired yet another doctor. The receptionist at the flight school gave her a name with a wink and a nod, indicating that this doctor passed everyone. The examination took much longer than Sandy anticipated. The questionnaire they gave her took her half an hour to complete, and she had to ask for additional paper to list her doctors, her medicines, and explain her treatments. When the physical examination began, Sandy attempted to link the various inspections to capabilities requisite for flight, but except for the eyes, could not. She was left sitting in an examination room for another twenty minutes before the doctor returned. When he did he told her that he had spoken with both her cardiologist and psychiatrist. It had been several years since the cardiac episode, there had been no recurrence and both attributed it to psychological factors for which she had been successfully treated. He was also concerned about her weight, not just the obesity but also her recent weight loss. She assured him it was a deliberate diet. He made notes and urged her to keep losing. He told her he was going to pass her, but not until the other doctors confirmed the substance of their conversations by letters to him. She could expect her Third Class Medical Certificate in the mail within two weeks. She got it, as well as a letter from the Manager of the Aeromedical Certification Branch at the FAA in Oklahoma City noting that while she was eligible for a third class medical certificate, in light of her medical history, she was advised to make herself familiar with other regulations relating to medical deficiencies that prohibit operation of an aircraft in the presence of any new or adverse changes in her condition. For the first time, Sandy was troubled by her collection of physicians. She wondered how long this was going to follow her. On the other hand, she gained respect for the FAA.

She soloed the day after she showed her instructor the medical certificate. It is an event long in tradition and good-natured ceremony. Sandy was presented a Beech T-shirt to wear during her flight. Her instructor made one takeoff and landing with her, then got out while she made three touch and go's on her own. He stood outside watching and listening to a hand-held. After her last landing, the tower congratulated her. Inside, her instructor wrote the date on the back of her T-shirt with a felt tip marker and then cut a semi-circle out the lower back. Her tail feathers were thus clipped and added to a dozen others posted on a bulletin board. They went back outside and took snapshots of her and the plane together. Despite the ceremony, Sandy found the flight anti-climatic. She was actually more at ease without her instructor sitting beside her commenting upon every move. She spoke with him before and after each flight, but for the next several weeks, she flew alone. Each time she repeated the ground reference maneuvers and practiced the stall series. For her long cross-country, she followed Interstate 75 up to Clare, where she landed, refueled and got her log book signed. Then she flew southwest to Kalamazoo. It was her first experience at a field with air carrier operations. The radio work was no different, but her self-esteem grew immeasurably when she waited for a airline captain to finish his transmission so she could broadcast. To the tower she was just another plane in the sky. She was one of them. She was part of the club. Flying home along Interstate 94, she flew over Battle Creek. For the first time since she had begun her lessons, she grew relaxed and flew without thinking about flying, much like others drive a car. She thought of Daryl.

On the last weekend in April, Daryl was startled when Sandy climbed up on the flying bridge. It had been a mild winter. He put the Sandy Shores back in the water early. This Saturday he was installing a new Loran in the dash. Instructions and hand tools were scattered about. He struggled up from where he was lying on his back, leaving wires hanging down from behind the dash.

"Sandy, you look great! It's good to see you. How much weight have you lost? You look good, healthy."

"Seventy five pounds, so far. You look good too."

"Me? Yeah, I've, ah...., I've been sober since Christmas. Say, you should be careful about losing that weight too fast."

"So I've heard. I talk to Bob once a week. He never writes."

"Yeah, I call him too. I see your parents at Church."

"I know."

"Don't you go to church anymore?"

"You'd be proud of me. I go to 7:00 A.M. Mass every morning, Sunday's too, that's why you don't see me. I've been taking flying lessons. That's where I go Sunday's."

"You like it?"

"Do I ever! If only I had done this twenty years ago. The most amazing thing is that I find it more intellectually challenging than law school. I had no idea how much you had to learn, a lot of math. I'll tell you though, when you're up there alone, well...."

"Yeah."

"I never understood about you and the water. I'm sorry."

"That's OK."

"Listen, I've been thinking. I think it's time...."

"I knew that all we needed was time."

"Daryl. It's time we got a divorce."

"Oh God, Sandy, no! Please!" Daryl trembled and cried. He turned his back to her, steadied himself against the dash, then wiped the tears from his face. "I'm sorry. Sobriety is a bitch."

"You'll make it. You drank because you drank. Now you don't."

"Sandy, can't we wait. We have almost twenty years, half our lives."

"It's time. Don't make this worse than it has to be. We will still have the twenty years, and we'll always have Bob. You make up a list of lawyers. Send me their biographies from Martindale-Hubbell. I'll pick first, you pick second, like the old thing of having one kid cut the cake and the other choosing the pieces. There's no need to fight."

"Please, Sandy."

"You know as well as I, that it's too late. We can't turn back the clock."

"I'm sober."

"It's not that. That was never it, really. I'm so proud of you. You'll make it. This is what I want."

"Damn it, Sandy."

"Daryl?"

"Yes?"

"May I keep your name?"

"Oh God, Sandy. Please don't do this." He sat down sobbing. She rested her hand on his shoulder for a moment, then left.

CHAPTER 33

By the time Bob got home from his freshman year at Harvard, his parents' separation was old news, nonetheless it was uncomfortable for him. He kept ahead of the awkwardness by circulating among the house he grew up in, his grandparents' home, and his father's boat. His grandfather had helped him get a summer job at Ford, except that now summer jobs were called internships. Bob had expected to be little more than a clerk and was pleasantly surprised. He quickly figured out that the internships were extended job interviews during which the company was taking a closer look at him; nevertheless, he was given responsible work. His summer was divided into three segments of three weeks each. First, he would rotate through Government Affairs, then Advertising, and finally Production Planning. The first and last were among the three he had cavalierly chosen from a list, the second was assigned to him. In each, he was given work that involved reviewing documents, organizing files, preparing summaries, and on occasion, writing a memo stating an opinion or recommendation. On those occasions the massive corporate staff of the automaker was not delegating its destiny to a summer intern, but rather, using him as a sounding board for the ideas of others, before they went up the line. Bob had never visualized a career for himself with one of the automakers, but the contrast of responsible work to idle study was seductive.

Work that summer went quickly for Bob, but not the evenings. Evenings were a diplomatic ordeal. His father was obsessed with tinkering on the boat. His father never mentioned his mother, and Bob took any mention of her as taboo. On the other hand, his grandparents became Daryl's advocates and campaigned to restore the marriage. They made continuous attempts to posture Bob as a mediator, a role he successfully avoided. His mother did speak casually about his father when the opportunity presented itself, but he found her a new person that he did not know, and had great difficulty relating to her, even though he liked what he saw.

Sandy had lost 115 pounds, half her weight. Bob had to force himself not to stare at her. She had acquired a completely new wardrobe. He always knew her to wear dresses, now she wore slacks and expensive blouses. Most often, her look played off the aviation stereotype, with tan slacks, a light blouse and a tie or scarf. On cool days, she wore a leather flight jacket. He looked to find some trace of the plump matron whom he had kissed good-bye the prior fall. Instead he saw a slender women who could easily pass for ten years younger than she was. Indeed, when Bob saw her sitting and studying her flight manuals, which she did every night at the kitchen table, he was reminded most of his female classmates. Even her hair, which she still wore pulled straight back and shoulder length, no longer seemed prim and out of fashion. In general, Sandy looked and was athletic, casual, and energetic. During the spring she had progressed from long walks through Grosse Pointe with hand weights, to jogging, then aerobics. Now she was swimming daily at The Club. The change, however, was much more than physical.

She was vibrant in a way he had never known her to be. He wondered if she had been this way when she was young. He wondered if the woman she became was the result of the years or the mileage. He wondered what life would do to him. He hoped it would be kind as it seemed to be to his mother. With the weight loss, she had also jettisoned the psychiatrist, her group, her cardiologist, and the nutritionist. All considered her their personal success. The gynecologist and internist only wanted to see her annually, and the urologist only if there were some specific problem. Sandy continued to go to Mass every day, usually on her way to the airport. Bob wondered if in the end her revived interest in the Church would forestall a divorce. He did not know that his mother was also going to the same confessor weekly. In the confessional, the priest continued to counsel her to make amends and move toward the good, but he was adamant about divorce. Sandy did not tell the priest or her son that she had concluded the good of her family, her husband, and herself were inconsistent with marriage. Mostly when Sandy and Bob talked, it was about his job or airplanes. Airplanes did not interest Bob, but he found his mother interesting.

Sandy took the FAA Private Pilot written examination the week before Bob got home. Despite the urgings of her instructor, she delayed taking it because of her own insecurity even though she regularly made near perfect scores on the course quizzes and practice exams. She only took it when she did because she wanted to be able to fly Bob when he got home, and that required a license. As a student pilot she had gotten used to soloing across the Southern Peninsula with only an occasional check ride with her instructor. She had piled up three times the hours most students did before getting a license, all because of her delay in taking the test. When the score came in the mail, she was disappointed that she scored 95. She was expecting 100. She scheduled a review flight with her instructor and then the final, official check ride with an FAA designated examiner.

From her perspective, the flight did not go well. The examiner was well passed 70 years old and nearly deaf from years in noisy, light planes. His vocabulary was slightly different from that of her instructor, and she repeatedly asked for clarification of his instructions. After virtually every maneuver she demonstrated, he took the controls and showed her a slightly different version. An hour into the flight, she began to regard the experience as another lesson; she was sure that she had failed. On the ground, he took her into a small conference room for a debriefing and additional questioning of her aeronautical knowledge. Then he told her to wait. He went outside and started filling out a form at the counter. She watched him from her peripheral vision. Finally, he returned and handed a small piece of paper to her and shook her hand. She did not look immediately at the temporary license. She got lost in the twinkle of the old man's eyes. She had her ticket. A moment later her instructor and the receptionist came in with the instant camera. Before the examiner left, he complimented Sandy on her stall recoveries. They went outside and took more pictures of her next to the little Skipper. The receptionist pinned one photograph on the bulletin board with pictures of the other students who had made it. She took the rest home. Driving away from the airport, Sandy turned on rock music and sang along when she wasn't lost in the bliss of congratulating herself.

Sandy got to Church early enough before Mass the next morning to go to confession. Once inside, however, she decided against confession. She ratified her decision, paid to light a candle, and then offered a rosary and the Mass for any pain it caused. At Detroit City the winds were westerly, and she departed Runway 33 as instructed. Nothing was different than any of the previous dozens of solo flights she had made, however, everything felt different. Now she was a pilot.

She couldn't wait for an opportunity to say that. As she went north, skirting around Selfridge ANGB, she thought of the years of fumbling an answer at cocktail parties when asked, "What do you do?" Now she would say, "I am a pilot." North of the Selfridge airspace, she turned northeast and overflew Port Huron. She remembered the first boat trip there with Daryl and Bob. When she got back to Detroit City, she found that neither Skipper would be available that evening when she planned to take Bob for a ride. Her instructor suggested the four place Musketeer 23, reassuring her that the transition from the Skipper was easy. Both had time. Fifteen minutes later they were airborne. They went back to the local practice area and put the plane through the paces, ground reference drills, steep turns, slow flight, and stalls. In general, Sandy found the plane felt slightly more sluggish than the Skipper, but more responsive in slow flight. She was quickly comfortable with it. The second day of her licensed status, Sandy's instructor made an entry in her logbook checking her out for both the Model 19 and 23 Musketeers. He told her she had bragging rights to three aircraft. That evening she retraced the morning flight to Port Huron with Bob. They landed just after sunset on Runway 15. He was more impressed with her checklist work and radio communications than with the flying. He had never imagined how much was involved in flying an aircraft. Still, it was a great way to see a sunset.

Sandy called Daryl at work the next morning. She called from a pay phone on the flight line. He had the list of lawyers. He was sorry he had delayed getting it to her. He would have a courier take it to the house right away. She told him that the delay was no problem. She had used the time to think things through. She told him that she was sorry. She did not want to hurt him. She had hurt him enough. She never wanted to hurt him. They had come close to killing each other. She could see no other way out. He would be fine. He would stay sober. She would stay healthy. They were both better off since the separation. They would be better off this way. Daryl kept trying to break into Sandy's speech, but couldn't. When she finished by saying that she loved him, he choked up and could not speak. She quickly said she would contact one of the lawyers on the list immediately, that she was planning a trip that would take her out of town for a few weeks and hung up. That afternoon she studied the photocopied Martindale Hubbell biographies of the six lawyers Daryl picked. She chose a lawyer in Bloomfield Hills whose name she recognized from law school. He had graduated the year after Daryl, the year before she would have. She was able to cajole an appointment for the next morning on the excuse of travel.

From the elegant decor and low energy level in the offices, she concluded that there must be money in an upscale divorce practice. When he saw her, he remembered her. He said he had followed Daryl's career with interest. She returned the compliment by telling him that Daryl had included him on a list of six highly regarded divorce lawyers from which she got the first pick. He was intrigued at their procedure and laughed that he thought he had seen everything. Sandy got right to business. She wanted the divorce as quickly as possible. He should not hesitate to call Daryl for the name of his lawyer. She wanted only to continue the $5,000 per month that Daryl put in her checkbook until she got established in her career, then for every dollar she made more than $5,000 per month, Daryl's payment could be reduced. He started to ask about property, and Sandy cut him off saying Daryl took care of all that. She also wanted her son's education through graduate school to be guaranteed. She did not react when he brought up the $200 per hour, $20,000 minimum fee. He quickly added that the wife's fees were usually paid by the husband. Within thirty minutes Sandy was out of the office and on her way to her morning flight. She went to noon Mass on the way home. She stayed after the Mass to say a rosary.

CHAPTER 34

With great ceremony, at 3:00 P.M. the following Sunday afternoon, Sandy departed on her trip. As usual, she rose early, went to 7:00 A.M. Mass and then the airport. She did not attend church or brunch with her parents, Bob, and Daryl. At brunch, she and her trip were the main topic of conversation. Only towards the end of the meal did Daryl announce that they were proceeding with the divorce. Her mother cried. Bob was not surprised, but caught in the contagion of his grandmother's tears, he ground his teeth together to hold back his own. Bob and Sandy's parents got to Detroit City at 2:30 P.M. They found Sandy inside on the telephone. Bob gave them a quick tour while Sandy finished filing her flight plan. Outside, they found the plane loaded with Sandy's flight bag full of charts and two small bags. When Sandy came up to them she saw her mother had been crying. Sandy wrongly assumed it was because her mother did not approve of the trip. Sandy told them she would call every night, and restated her instruction that Bob check the house every other day and her insistence that he not live there alone. Her father said they were excited about having a young person back in their house and told her to be careful. Sandy hugged everyone and climbed into the small plane. They backed up when she started the engine, and stood together while she taxied away. Bob took them inside where they listened to the tower communications on a radio. When they heard Sandy's voice say she was rolling, they crowded to the window to watch her takeoff.

Sandy could not remember exactly when or how she had gotten the idea for the trip, but once the seed was planted, she was determined it had to be. It was a force that drove her obsession with flying. She would takeoff and fly where her whim directed and the weather permitted. Business was off at the flight school, so they were eager to lease her one of the Skippers. She would have preferred the bigger

Musketeer, but since she was going solo, she could not justify the higher cost for space considerations. She did not mind flying the slower trainer. After considerable discussion, they agreed to rent her the Skipper on the basis of engine hours flown, with a minimum rent of 12.5 hours a week and a maximum rent of 20 hours per week. Sandy felt she was going to get the best of that bargain. When she took off, she did not know exactly how far her travels would take her, but California was not out of the question. Because she got a late start, she did not get far the first day. She bought fuel and tied down for the night at Ross Field near Benton Harbor and stayed at a motel three miles from the field. The motel sent their courtesy car to pick her up. She read while she soaked in the bath, ate alone in the restaurant, ran the TV with the sound off, called her parents, called for weather, and read herself to sleep with the TV still running. In the morning, she filed her flight plan from the motel and hung around the field only long enough to chat with the local airport bums. It was a regime that was instantly comfortable, and she repeated it over and over.

Within forty-five minutes of her departure the next morning, Sandy radioed Flight Service and amended her flight plan. She had initially planned to head southwest towards Kansas, but while circling Notre Dame University she decided she would fly south to see Kentucky. She had never been there and that was what this trip was supposed to be about. She made a mid-morning fuel stop and another longer stop that included lunch at an airport counter in the early afternoon. She stopped for the night at Henderson, Kentucky after spending fifteen minutes zig-zagging along the Ohio River. The next morning she stuck to her plan and followed the Ohio River to Cairo. There she circled the confluence with the Mississippi, repeatedly crossing back and forth over the great river. She followed Route 60 across southern Missouri to Springfield. She stopped there for the day, even though it was only mid-afternoon when she arrived. She stayed in a motel with a pool and swam laps.

The weather continued to hold, and the fourth day she easily made Wichita. She landed at the Beech Factory field for two reasons, her own sentimental journey and to take the Skipper home. The lineboy encouraged her to visit the factory, but she was frazzled from the complexity of the airspace, there were half a dozen airports within a few miles, and she wanted to get closer to the city for a motel. After taking off she did make one circuit in the pattern without landing, just to look down on the factory and remember. She kept her eye on traffic out of the Cessna factory field, and sat down at Wichita/Maize five minutes later. From the rush of cold up her back as she climbed out of the aircraft she realized that she was perspiring from the workload. The motel lobby was decorated with aeronautical memorabilia and the restaurant menu named its dishes after locally manufactured planes. Sandy had planned to visit relatives, but after looking up names and phone numbers in her room that evening, she decided not to call anyone. There was too much to explain. Also, she wanted to get away from Wichita. She had come to the nerve center of general aviation, only to have her nerves overwhelmed. She would much rather be tied down at some small town field and stay in a Mom & Pop motel. All she wanted was out. She was much relieved to leave the Wichita airspace behind the next morning.

From Wichita she flew southwest for Amarillo, Texas. She had never been to Texas. She deliberately landed in Boise City, Oklahoma because she had never set foot in Oklahoma either. She liked Amarillo. The countryside was different than she expected, there were hills and it was early enough in the summer that they were still green. She skirted around Amarillo International and landed at Tradewind. To her, Amarillo seemed as big as Wichita, although it wasn't; but she found it distinctly more relaxed. She took a cab from her motel to a Japanese steak house and a mall after that. The next morning she got an early start and headed northwest for Colorado.

Her sixth night out she stayed over in a small motel on the prairie near Las Animas, Colorado. Saturday morning she raced north hoping to miss some incoming weather. She stayed far enough east of the front range to avoid the traffic from Colorado Springs and Denver, but was close enough to study both cities. For the first time, she wished she had brought a camera. Her progress seemed slow and tedious measured against the massifs of Pike's Peak, Mt. Evans, and Long's Peak which she saw until she crossed over into Wyoming. She landed in Cheyenne just long enough to get fuel and make a log book entry that she had been there. She circled the Capital building, then followed Route 85 most of the way northeast to Scottsbluff, Nebraska. She landed at Hellig Field with flashes of lightning visible in the thunderstorms coming in from the west. Her weather luck had run out. It stormed heavily all Saturday night and drizzled throughout the next two days.

After early Mass, Sandy spent Sunday morning at the airport cafe hanger-talking with the airport bums. Then she holed up in her motel room. Lacking anything better to do, Monday morning she decided to call her lawyer. He reported progress. He had spoken with Daryl and also the lawyer Daryl hired. Sandy's stomach tightened when she learned Daryl had a female lawyer. She tried to recall her biography. Sandy's lawyer had worked with her on several cases and found her prompt but tough. She was already insisting on drafting the documents. He did think that Sandy would like their proposal.

"Here's the deal. They will put 10% of all the assets in an irrevocable trust for your son to be used for his education and support. Your father will be trustee, and if he dies, you and Daryl are co-trustees. After college he can draw down the trust to help him buy a house or start a business. He gets half of it free and clear at age 26 and the rest at 30. As for the rest of the property, you two split it right down the middle, 50/50; actually that would be 45/45 when you account for your son's trust."

"What about the $5,000 per month?"

"Oh yeah, there's no problem with that. In fact, Daryl will pay that for the rest of your life with annual increases for inflation, no decreases, and no adjustment for your earnings."

"Even though I get half the property?"

"He wants it that way. Oh, another thing, which is typical. He would like both of you to execute new wills after the divorce leaving everything to the trust for your son."

"That's fine, but I don't have much."

"You know, I get the impression that you haven't paid very much attention to your financial affairs."

"Daryl did that. We have the house, cars, his boat. He has some stocks. He put money in my checking account, and I paid the bills."

"They faxed me a schedule of assets Friday afternoon together with bank statements, brokerage statements, boat title, car titles, and the deed. I think that you may be surprised. The total comes to $2,935,650.00." He waited for Sandy to respond. She said nothing. "You've already got $578,000 in your savings account and a dozen CD's, plus the house is free and clear and is in your name alone. They valued it at $650,000. Do you think that's high? Sounds OK to me for Grosse Pointe."

"I don't understand. I don't know anything about accounts in my name. And the house, I remember when we bought it, we both signed.

It's in both our names. We have a mortgage. Daryl pays it."

"Paid it off years ago. I'm looking at the deed right now, quitclaim from Daryl to you in 1981. She thought you might not know about that or the cash. Every time he transferred money into your checkbook, he put a like amount in your savings or CD's. I'm looking at the statements right now, $578,000." He heard Sandy start crying. He waited a minute for her to regain her composure, but she did not. "Listen, this is going to be an easy one. Usually we have to fight to find out what the assets are. They've opened their kimono. Almost everything that you will get is already in your name, plus you get the support. I'm sure he's good for it. I don't see this kind of behavior very often. Looks like a good guy to me."

"I'm sorry. Please excuse me. Yes, it sounds good. Proceed. I'll get back to you." Sandy hung up. She closed the drapes to the motel room and laid on the bed most of the rest of the day. She tried to think of nothing, but kept thinking of Daryl. When she did, she cried.

The weather broke Tuesday. She found a lot of water in the fuel and even after draining it out worried about it. She ran the engine for ten minutes before takeoff. She left the nagging pain of her divorce behind on takeoff. She flew north because she wanted to see Mount Rushmore. From the air it was smaller than she expected. She stayed over that night in Pierre, South Dakota. On the following days she worked east, making over night stops in Mankato, Minnesota; Rochester, Wisconsin; and Sault Saint Marie, Michigan. Her pain returned when she first saw the Mackinac Bridge as she flew south across the Upper Peninsula. She diverted east and circled Mackinac Island. On an impulse she landed on the island and topped off the tanks even though she did not need fuel. The pain lessened as she followed Interstate 75 south and made another fuel stop in Bay City. There she called her parents to let them know she was coming home. She landed at Detroit City two hours later. Both her parents and Bob were there to greet and congratulate her. She was a pilot. She had over a hundred hours in her logbook. For an instant she wished that Daryl were there, but that passed.

CHAPTER 35

The next morning Sandy sat quietly at the kitchen table watching Bob rush his breakfast. They had come home together after dinner with her parents in a restaurant near the airport. Although Sandy had spoken with them daily, most of the meal was spent in her report of the adventure. Her father beamed. Her mother frowned and stared away. She told them she was tired of travel and ready to stay home for awhile. At home that evening, however, she was struck by the quiet and size of her house. Once it had been their dream. The furniture, every empty room, every shadow reminded her of other times. Now her home was a mausoleum holding memories of another life. It even put a melancholy edge on the memories of the happy times. She had not been home an hour after unpacking when she began to feel like she was suffocating. She well knew the ins and outs of anxiety attacks and sought to control herself by regulating her breathing. She had to get out of the house. She went out on the back patio. She looked at the stars and wished she were flying. She wished she were swimming laps in a motel pool or soaking in a strange tub. She knew it was time. The decision was no more difficult that any of the others. She rationalized it by concluding that the house was too big for one person and a sometime visitor home from college. The thought of the effort it took to clean the house cemented her resolve.

"Bob, would you mind if I sold the house?"

"You're really going to do it?"

"It's only a building. You're never home anyway. Even in the summer, you don't do much more than sleep here."

"I'm not talking about the house. The divorce."

"Yes."

"He doesn't want to divorce you."

"I know."

"Then why can't you work something out?" Sandy shook her head and looked away. "You shouldn't just throw away twenty years. You shouldn't do that."

"It's not that simple. We are both still your parents. We both love you. This is not your problem."

"It is! Why can't you see that?" His voice cracked and he looked down. "I just want us to be happy. The way it used to be."

"We weren't happy. You were a kid wrapped up in yourself. Look at your father. For the first time in your life he is sober. Look at me. It wasn't the way you remember, but I'm glad you remember it that way."

"Don't you love him?"

"Yes, but not the way a wife should."

"I just can't believe this whole thing."

"So what do you say?"

"What?"

"The house?"

"Do whatever the hell you want!" He stormed towards the door.

"It's what I want."

Sandy picked up the dishes and watched him pull out of the garage through the window over the sink. A few minutes later she was on her way to Mass. After Mass, she drove to her bank. She waited in her car for a half hour until the branch opened. Inside she went to the woman seated at a desk in the lobby and asked if she could get a listing of all her accounts and balances. Sandy told her that her personal records were too jumbled to organize, that she was starting fresh. The branch manager fought not to show her disdain for yet another pampered Grosse Pointe wife. The interest in Sandy's accounts was as much as the banker earned. She worked eight hours a day for the same dollars, but this woman could not be bothered to keep track of a few pieces of paper. A few moments later Sandy left with a printout and friendly smile from the banker. She sat in the car and studied it. She actually had more than the lawyer reported. He must have been working off older statements and perhaps Daryl's most recent deposit had not been included. In any event, she had $593,010.80 in cash, sprinkled among her checking and savings accounts, and a dozen $25,000 certificates of deposit with staggered maturities. She wanted to talk to Daryl, but with lawyers involved, that seemed inappropriate. Maybe they could have lunch. No, someday when it was all over, she would sit down and talk to him. She needed to tell him that he was a decent man. She could never remember saying exactly those words to him. No one may ever have told him. Maybe the Commandant, but probably not. She knew they would mean more to him than anything else she might ever say or do. He was a simple and quiet man of honor. Somewhere along the line she had lost touch with his most basic quality. She thought of them as a young couple. She had been lucky.

Pulling out of the bank, she noticed a drug store across the street. She pulled up to it and went inside. She bought a simple card with flowers on the outside and nothing inside. She sat in the car for several minutes trying to find exactly the right words. Every time she started to compose them in her mind, the simple thought became a paragraph. She edited it, and started again. Finally, she balanced the envelope of the dash and addressed it to his office. After that she wrote the card. "Daryl, I finally understand. Things are as simple as you always said. You have done what you set out to do. You have been good. You are a good man." She signed it: "Love, Sandy". She got back out of the car and dropped it in a mailbox just down the sidewalk.

From a telephone booth at the airport she called her lawyer. He informed her that he had spoken with Daryl's lawyer about approving the essence of the deal. He was waiting for her to draft the documents. Sandy told him there would be one change, she wanted to sell the house and divide the proceeds in accordance with the formula. The lawyer said that should be no problem. Sandy stepped away from the phone booth and breathed in a deep breath of the morning air. The worst was over. Now she could move forward.

Inside the Beech operation her instructor and the receptionist crowded around with some others to hear her stories. When she finished and the group broke up, she asked her instructor how she might go about buying an airplane. He smiled and told her to subscribe to Trade-A-Plane to get a feel for the prices and to keep renting and flying different planes in the meantime. When she was ready, and if she wanted Beech, they could help her find one. They took a ten percent commission on brokered sales, but he thought their contacts and ability to screen out lemons was worth it. He also told her that she could talk to the other broker/dealers or buy direct. In her mind Sandy was committed to Beech and likewise determined to deal with the people she knew, but she did not tell him that. He went on to suggest that she start working on her instrument rating. She would never truly appreciate the value of an aircraft until she cut herself free of the bounds of weather. They adjourned into his office where they spent the next hour going over the requirements and costs of the various progressive ratings. He was selling the next rung on the ladder, an instrument rating; but Sandy was most interested in a commercial pilot license. For the first time, she spoke of what she wanted all along.

Both the instrument rating and the commercial license required hours. Sandy would have flown every day that weather permitted anyway, but working with those goals, she had an additional incentive to build hours. The flight school's Musketeer had a full IFR panel, so she spent most every week day flying it. Once or twice a week her instructor went along. She spent most of those flights under the hood, an uncomfortable plastic shield that limited her vision to the instrument panel. This time her instructor got her to get the IFR written examination out of the way early in her training. She scored 97. As time passed he arranged to rent other aircraft to accommodate Sandy's search for a plane of her own. He checked her out in Debonair/F33 with retractable gear. She quickly got over the feeling of having no feet underneath her and was soon addicted to the increased airspeed. She refused to fly a Bonanza 35 with the infamous V tail because of all the articles in the aviation magazines, but she did get checked out in a Bonanza A36TC. After sitting in the cockpit of a visiting Duchess, a light twin engine, she pushed for a multi-engine rating. Her instructor told her to get one at a time, and promised that the rating would be there for her when she finished her instrument training. On weekends she often got Bob to go for a flight. He went as a concession to her, not because he shared her enthusiasm. Once her father came along with Bob. After the flight he announced that Sandy was a good pilot, as if it had been a test. He never flew with her again. Her mother never flew with her.

In mid-July Sandy moved into a one bedroom furnished apartment and started shopping for a condo. She gave the excuse of keeping the house clean and open for the realtor to show. In fact, she hated being in it alone. Bob had settled into her parents' house during her trip and kept his things there even though he spent week nights on Daryl's boat. On weekends, and when he had a date, he spent the night with his grandparents in order to avoid his father's teasing. The house sold in early August to a GM Exec with a young family. Sandy bought a three bedroom condo in Grosse Point Park. She and Daryl split most of the furniture between them. They gave some things to her mother, and stored the rest in her parents' attic. They had met one other time that summer, at his lawyer's office, to sign the necessary documents for their divorce. It was still not final, but they had proceeded with the property division in accordance with their agreement. After meeting at the house to divide up the furniture, they drove in separate cars to a restaurant near the Jefferson Beach marinas. Neither was comfortable, and their conversation was strained. She would have her instrument rating within a few weeks. His practice was fine. He found he was more efficient sober, which gave him more time for Bob and his boat. They talked mostly of Bob, his job, his education, and his future.

Bob left for Boston two weeks later. He took a week long cruise with his father before he left. Sandy wanted to fly him to Boston, but he declined, saying that he already had an airline ticket. He did not. The Sunday morning he left, Sandy showed up at the family's regular Mass. She sat next to her mother at the opposite end of the pew from Daryl. She went with them to The Club for brunch. Again the only topic of easy conversation was Bob. She said good-bye to Bob there because she was flying up to Traverse City with her instructor that afternoon to look at a plane. Her mother looked away and frowned.

The plane was an older Debonair/F33. It had a factory remanufactured engine with low hours, a new paint job, and an IFR panel with new digital avionics. It belonged to a local doctor who had run out the engine, and been talked into putting a new engine in it just to sell it. When buyers didn't come running, he'd been talked into the paint job; then the avionics. At this point, he was tired of showing it and left the keys with the local FBO. They flew it for over an hour. Sandy was instantly smitten. Her instructor did his best to calm her down. The $55,000 asking price was a fortune to him. He could not appreciate Sandy's perspective, and he did not know that she could write a check for the amount. He told her he would do the dickering and only begin that after getting a prepurchase inspection report from a mechanic. The next day back in Detroit Sandy went into action. She called one of the ads she saw in the aviation magazines about setting up a Delaware corporation to own her airplane. She had no business experience and law school was many years back, but it did make sense to her. If nothing else, having the plane in a corporation might help limit her personal liability. The business about depreciation made less sense to her, especially if she had to go to the trouble of writing a lease and paying a fair rent for each hour she rented her own airplane from herself. On the other hand, she knew it would cost a lot to operate the plane, and whether she paid the costs directly or paid rent to a corporation that paid the bills was only a paperchase. Besides, everyone did it. Pressed for a corporate name she stammered, then came up with Bonair Aircraft Corporation, by truncating the name of the Beech model. She gave a credit card number and was told that her corporation would be formed before the end of the day.

Three days later a box with a minute book and corporate seal arrived. Sandy signed all the prepared documents. As incorporator she issued herself a stock certificate. As sole shareholder she elected herself as the sole member and chairperson of the Board of Directors. As Board of Directors, she elected herself President, Secretary, and Treasurer. She went back to the bank and opened a bank account in the name of Bonair Aircraft Corporation and transferred $50,000 in cash and $50,000 in certificates of deposit into it. The mechanic's report of his inspection of the aircraft and logbooks came back clean, nevertheless, her instructor was able to get 10% off the asking price. He felt that the plane should be delivered, but the doctor refused. As is, where is. He got another 5% off the price. Sandy wrote the first check ever issued by Bonair Aircraft to the doctor for $5,000 as a deposit, pending a title search of the FAA records in Oklahoma City. If her instructor had not told her, Sandy would not have thought to get insurance on the plane. That was another hassle. She spent an afternoon at an insurance agency near the airport filling out forms and checking her logbook to get the answers they wanted. She gave them Bonair's second check. Reading another ad in the back of an aviation magazine, she sent away for leasing forms to rent her plane from Bonair Aircraft. She wrote the third check.

One week later she and her instructor flew back to Traverse City. The doctor came to the airport. He was impatient that he had to wait for their arrival. Sandy had planned to write him a check for the balance, she assumed he would then pay the Beech dealer its commission. He told the instructor that he did not want to write a check to them until Sandy's check cleared. He was adamant, even when it was pointed out that he was signing over the title, and they were flying away the aircraft before the check cleared. At that point he called his bank to see how he could secure Sandy's check. Sandy had been oblivious to the details in her excitement over the plane, but his delays were now annoying her. When he started demanding a cashier's check, the instructor came unglued and demanded he pay the cost of their useless flight. An airport bum looking on suggested that Sandy could wire the money into the doctor's account. Sandy called the branch manager of her bank, and moments later was reading her the account number off the doctor's checkbook. She transferred the purchase price, less the commission. She wrote a check for the commission directly to her instructor. The doctor disappeared into a small room for an hour while he made several calls. Ultimately, he came out saying that his bank had confirmed the wire. He signed the Bill of Sale, turned, and left without another word. As he drove away everyone made a game out of comparing epithets to describe him. Sandy and her instructor had a sandwich at the counter, then left. She took off first, and he caught up with her. She wanted to fly in formation, but he radioed her that was an art for professionals. They kept each other in sight the entire trip back.

She completed her instrument training in the new plane. Her last several lessons were in actual IFR conditions. It was more work than fun, and Sandy perspired heavily. She also took her check ride in the Debonair. She passed. At home that night, she decided that she would go visit Bob. She spent the evening studying aeronautical charts and airport directories. She planned to leave Friday, she could easily make it there in one day. Now that she was IFR, weather was not part of her initial planning. She could spend Saturday with Bob and come home Sunday. The trip went well. It was a beautiful autumn day, and she flew VFR all the way.

She landed at Hanscom field in Bedford, Massachusetts having made one intermediate fuel stop in Schenectady, New York. The hotel in Lexington sent a van. She swam in its indoor pool before she called Bob. She took a cab to Harvard the next morning. They toured the campus and had lunch in a small restaurant off Cambridge Square. After lunch, he came back to Lexington with her. They did the tourist walk, then went to the airport. She showed off her plane, but he didn't want to fly. They had dinner together at the hotel. She told him the divorce was final. He said he liked his studies and Boston. He wasn't sure if he would come home to Detroit the following summer. She saw him to a cab after dinner. The next morning she retraced her trip home. There was some weather in western New York. She filed IFR from her fuel stop in Schenetady. Everything went strictly by the book. On the other side of the front, it was clear again. She landed at Detroit City mid-afternoon. Rather that go home, Sandy went into the Beech operation and got two things going. She wanted to get rated to fly twins as soon as possible, and she wanted to move ahead on the commercial license.

The multi training went more quickly than Sandy had been told. It was expensive to rent a twin engine, and her instructor took pity even though more than once he had done the arithmetic to tally up how much Sandy had spent on aviation in the last year without showing any concern for the cost. She got the rating just before Thanksgiving, and forged ahead into the commercial work. Her routine was the same, early Mass, flight and the airport through most of the day, exercise in the late afternoon, and study in the evenings. Her study for the commercial license was more rigorous than for her private license. She often spent four or five hours a night. Bob's return home for the Christmas - New Year's break was a diversion, but she got back to the books in January 1991. She successfully took the written exam at the end of the month. The practical examination was an ordeal in February, but she made it. There was little fanfare for her afterwards. She went back home, organized her aviation books on a shelf and watched TV. There was a strong measure of anticlimax in her disposition. She was proud of her achievement, but looking back it did not seem that difficult. She distinguished herself from others mostly by the fact that she had taken the time to do something they had not. She fell asleep in a chair wondering if this is how Daryl felt when he passed the bar. She needed to get together with him. She had been wrong to avoid him at Christmas again. She woke in the chair after midnight. As she put herself to bed she resolved that tomorrow would be the first day of her new career.

CHAPTER 36

By 10:00 A.M. the morning after Sandy had gotten her commercial pilot license, much of the romance she saw in the profession was gone. She started the morning at the Beech operation with a "now what" conversation with her instructor. They had nothing for her, unless she would like to continue on to get certified as a flight instructor. It would only be part-time. Most used CFI work to build hours towards commercial. She was ahead of the curve on that. He suggested she make the rounds of the cargo and charter taxi operators. She talked to two that morning at Detroit City. Their candor left her glum. She had intended to go flying, but instead decided to go home. There she made a dozen calls to operators at Metro, Pontiac-Oakland, and Willow Run. All were pleasant, welcomed her to the business, but offered nothing. There were plenty of pilots with experience sitting on their hands. She got tired of hearing about 1,000 hours as pilot in command. It made no difference that she owned a plane. She would have to get licensed as an operator to fly her own plane. She might find an operator who would trip lease her plane and then contract with her to fly it. No one had anything. Sandy skipped her exercise. She spent most of the evening on her sofa reading a romance novel. She had started reading them on her trip. Halfway through the evening, she put the book down without marking the page. She'd had enough. She knew where it was going. Life wasn't like that. You had to make things happen.

The following morning Sandy went to a print shop instead of the airport. She spent several hours pouring through books of clip art and settled on two images, a stylized low wing single engine plane for Bonair Aircraft Corporation, and a propeller for Sandra L.C. Dobbins, Commercial Pilot. She ordered stationery and business cards for both. She paid for the corporate stationery with a Bonair check, and for her pilot stationery with a personal check. Next she went to an office supply store and bought a typewriter and other supplies. Back at home she reorganized the one bedroom she had made into a personal office into a business office. She moved the desk away from the window into the center of the room. She put two chairs in front of it. She put a small table under the window behind the desk and put her typewriter and answering machine on it. She spent the early afternoon typing address cards for all the operators she had called. When the stationery came in later in the week she would type letters to each offering her pilot services, her plane on lease, or preferably both, and enclose her cards. After the letters, she would start calling on them in person. After finishing the addresses, she felt exhilarated. She went flying and then jogged. That night she combed through the classifieds in Trade-A-Plane for opportunities. She found a few more names for her address file.

Later as she sat in front of the TV, she studied through the various forms that had come in the leasing kit. She decided on one that seemed to fit the operator trip lease. She typed it up on Bonair Aircraft stationery. She also prepared a rate sheet with various price options, wet or dry (fuel included or extra), by the hour, by the mile, or by the day. She knew what she had paid to rent Debonairs before she bought her's, she had used that price less ten percent in her own lease-back from Bonair Aircraft. She decided to use that price less five percent for her commercial leases. Then she started calculating her costs: fuel, insurance, maintenance, ramp fees, reserves for avionics, engine, and propeller replacement. She estimated usage, and saw that she needed thirty-five hours a month, better fifty, to make money on her plane. She resolved to include her rate sheet and specimen lease with her proposal letters. Instead of going to bed, she went out to a 24 hour copy shop and had a gross of the documents printed. Coming in at midnight, Sandy felt the excitement that she might have felt the day she got her commercial license. For the first time, Sandy felt the independence of being a businesswomen. Though she had not made the first penny, she liked it.

Daryl called in early May to invite her to lunch. She accepted. They agreed to meet at the restaurant near the Jefferson Beach Marina because it was mutually convenient. Sandy drove out of her way there to pass their old house. There were children playing in the front yard. She reported that to Daryl the first thing after they greeted each other. They agreed it was a good house for raising children.

"Have you heard when Bob's coming home?" Daryl asked.

"I don't think he is. He's trying to get a research job for some professor."

"Your father says he's thinking about majoring in international relations, wants to be a diplomat. I can't get him to talk to me about those things."

"Don't feel alone. We're lucky he's close to his grandfather."

"Your father is working on him to go to law school. He says that is the best preparation for the foreign service. I would have thought languages and political science, but not law school."

"Bob will make a good diplomat."

"Why do you say that?"

"We trained him for it."

"I don't understand."

"Only child, mediating the disputes of his warring parents."

"I wouldn't call it war."

"Cold war then."

"I suppose. Maybe we did plant the seed. I often wonder what it was, what little thing I might have overheard when I was a kid, that got me started toward law school. Your father was a lawyer. I really can't say what inspired me. It would be interesting to know what Muses control our destinies."

"Have you made peace with your parents?"

"Won't you ever let go of that?"

"It is Christian to forgive."

"Even the Church requires confession and penance before forgiveness."

"Daryl, they're the only parents you will ever have."

"I did nothing wrong. They abandoned their child. That's what Hell is for."

"I'm sorry. You deserve better."

"How's the flying?"

"I'm making money, not much, but I'm in business." She handed him the two business cards. "Bonair owns my plane. I lease it to myself, I also lease it to a taxi operator. I fly checks for them most of the time, cargo on occasion."

"Checks?"

"Yes checks. It's big business. Keeps the little guys going against the likes of all the giant courier companies. With the kind of planes they fly, their pilots have to be Airline Transport Pilots, which is a high end rating, 2,000 hours. Checks get flown all over the country every night in small planes by the banking system. Its a really amazing and efficient delivery system that no one knows about. You would appreciate it. Anyway, people like me stand in line for the work. I usually work towns in Michigan, Indiana, and Ohio. It's night work, but at least I get to come home to my own bed."

"Don't you get afraid?"

"Flying, no! I love it."

"No, coming home alone in the middle of the night."

"Sometimes. I'm careful." She showed him a tear gas canister fastened to her purse. "I have an office at home. I try to spend one hour a day marketing, calls, letters and the like; but it seems that I spend most of my time any more writing checks and paying bills."

"What kind of computer do you have?"

"Computer? I'm just a little business. I'm too little to be a small business. I have a hundred dollar typewriter, and I keep my books by hand."

"That's silly. You need a computer. It will give you more time for what's important. I suggest a laptop and a laser printer. I could take you computer shopping."

"Maybe, someday. For now I"m just trying to keep my nose out of the water."

"Takes money to make money."

"You're right about that."

"You've come a long way. It is wonderful to see you excited about your work."

"Thanks. So how is life at Campbell Short? Are you ever going to break away and set up your own shop?"

"Whether its their overhead or my overhead, it's still overhead."

"But you could cut their bloated overhead to next to nothing if you ran your own operation."

"You have become quite the business woman. I think its great!"

"Well, are you going to do it?"

"No. I'll die at Campbell Short. It's not bad there. I'm used to the bullshit. I get along just fine."

"You could make a lot more."

"I make enough. Besides, I owe them. I owe the firm a lot."

"What do you mean? They have profited off you since the day you walked through their door."

"You seem to forget that they were the only ones who would take me in. Without them, without the opportunity, who knows? I doubt if we would have made it to Grosse Pointe; no Sandy Shores, no Bonair Aircraft."

"You would have made it. You might have been Senator by now. They need you. You don't need them."

"I owe them."

"Loyal to a fault. That's just like you. I mean that as a compliment."

"Bob told me last summer that if I wanted to change the name of the boat, he'd clear it with you. I told him I liked the name. I think he wanted me to change it."

"He is not happy with me. I know that. It's just something he has to resolve for himself."

"It is your name. Do you mind?"

"Of course not. I'm honored. If you ever want to change it though, you don't have to ask."

"If I do change it, I will ask."

"I love you."

"Don't say that unless you mean it."

"You know what I mean."

"That's the problem. Listen, there is something I want to ask. It's why I called."

"Yes?"

"Do you think that there is any hope for us?" His eyes teared.

"Daryl, honey, we're divorced."

"That does not answer my question."

"We can't go back."

"That still doesn't answer my question."

"Why can't you just let go? Why would you ask such a question?"

"Will you answer me? I need to know."

"Why?"

"Why! Because I'm lonely. I hate my life. I can't stand living alone. There is this woman that I'm interested in. She doesn't know it. I love you, but I can't live like this. I can't be alone. I'm a simple guy. I won't get involved with someone else if I have any hope at all that you...."

"Daryl...." Sandy stopped to wipe a tear, but then broke down and sobbed. "I'm sorry. I'm so sorry." When she regained her composure, she looked directly into his eyes. "Ask her out. Get on with your life." He started trembling, then covered his face with his hand and looked down into his lap to hide his crying. Sandy stood, smoothed back his hair, then left.

When she got home she had a message on her machine from the operator for whom she flew. There was a parts flight for a marina in Ohio. It was today or never. If the people could get their yacht fixed that night, they would stay. If not, they would leave the boat and come back after it was fixed. Sandy called immediately, it was not too late, the part would be waiting on her at the airport. Within minutes she was on her way to Detroit City.

Two hours after she left Daryl, she touched down at Griffing Field in Sandusky, Ohio. On the way in she circled Perry's Monument at Put-In-Bay just for old time's sake. She left her plane at the fuel pump and went inside the small block building to call the number she had been given. Fifteen minutes later a new Corvette rolled into the parking lot carrying a handsome, well-groomed man, approximately her age. He signed for the package. She thought he was attracted to her, for he made more than the usual small talk. Sandy did not like his artificial tan and all the jewelry he wore. They exchanged business cards. He said he flew parts all the time and might be able to use her services. Sandy resolved to send him a letter and literature from her operator.

After he left, Sandy had a cup of coffee at the counter inside. She could easily get home before sunset, but the encounter with Daryl still hurt. She did not want to go home alone. She asked about local motels. They had brochures on several, but the lady behind the counter recommended The Maples, which was just east of the field, and was clean and quiet. For $3.00 they would take Sandy anywhere she wanted to go in their mini-van. Sandy started to call the motel, but the lady told her not to bother, there would be rooms. Sandy finished the coffee, got her plane topped off, and taxied it to a tie-down.

The counter lady also took her credit card for the fuel, tie-down, and taxi; then she escorted Sandy outside to the van. Sandy had not anticipated staying overnight, and asked the woman if she would mind taking her by a convenience store. The woman agreed and drove Sandy west toward town. In the convenience store Sandy bought a tooth brush, tooth paste, other toiletries, a sandwich, some potato chips, and a large bottle of pop. She made a mental note never to fly again without an overnight bag. She knew better. At the counter she noticed the covers of several skin magazines behind the cashier who was busy making change. One promised live couples in action. As the cashier started to give Sandy her change, Sandy stopped her and asked for the magazine. The cashier matter of factly reached for the magazine, rang up the price, and corrected Sandy's change. Another customer came up to the counter, and Sandy's face flushed while the cashier put the magazine in a brown bag. She wondered if the lady in the mini-van had seen.

Sandy's face cooled during the brief ride to the motel. The motel sat alone on the side of Route 6 surrounded by flat farm fields. By a car parked in front of one of the units, Sandy concluded that the small motel had only one other quest. There was a small pool and large shade trees, but it was too early in the year for swimming, and the pool wasn't opened anyway. The airport mini-van left before she entered the office to check-in. In her room, Sandy pulled the drape, sat on the bed, and immediately opened the cellophane wrapped magazine. Her faced flushed again. At first she was surprised at the photographs, then aroused. She quickly skimmed through the features from front to back and settled on one series that particularly stimulated her. Afterwards, she drifted off to sleep on the bed. She woke an hour later. The magazine was still open beside her. She closed it, got up and walked to the window. It was dark outside, but she could still see a red glow in the southwest. She turned on the TV and ate her sandwich. She idly picked up the magazine and studied it, this time noting clinical details. She felt herself quite naive. Later she drew a hot bath and took the magazine with her into the tub.

CHAPTER 37

I called Daryl in the summer of 1991. I'd had lunch with one of my subcontractor clients who had just gotten a target letter from the U.S. Attorney's Office. That was his big problem. He also showed me some bankruptcy papers he'd just received on a general contractor from Flint, Michigan, that owed him some money. He'd never filed a mechanic's lien, so he knew he was twisting out in the breeze. Normally, I wouldn't touch a civil case, but I caught Daryl's name on the document. I told my guy that he may as well forget his money, but that I'd call the other lawyer because I knew him from law school.

Daryl answered his own phone. That struck me because he's part of a big firm. You know how it goes. I used to ignore those guys, but lately they've really started bugging me. They make so damn much money, and they aren't any better or any worse than anyone else. Anyway, I told Daryl why I was calling. He told me to save my client's money and not bother to actively pursue its unsecured claim. I asked about Sandy. In one breath he told me that they were divorced and that she had become a commercial pilot. I didn't know how to react. It's kind of awkward to ask someone about their ex, but I had the flying bug myself. I'd owned a Cessna 172 for a couple of years that I used to fly my kids around on weekends. I really wanted to say something, to ask how in the world she ever got from an honors law student to a commercial pilot. Also, I frankly couldn't picture a seriously obese woman in a small plane. In any event, I didn't ask. I said something stupid, I don't remember what, and got off the phone. Worse, I completely spaced the conversation. It was only later that I remembered about her flying, but I'm getting ahead of myself.

III.

Their Story

CHAPTER 1

"I can't imagine anything that I'd ever want more." Sandy smiled her answer while she studied the oil on the dipstick and rubbed it between her finger and thumb.

Joe had asked if she liked flying. Pete Falloni sent Joe to meet her at Griffing Field to pick up a part on a rush job. It was April, 1992, and like every spring, there was a rush to get the yachts in the water. When he pulled into the parking lot, he saw her on the ramp near the fuel pump. Pete had described her as a beautiful blond. She was going over the plane while the lineboy topped off the tanks. Joe introduced himself and mentioned the package. Sandy asked why Falloni didn't come. He always met her himself. Joe shrugged. She nodded toward a cardboard box sitting next to the grass in front of the red block building, and told him she'd get the receipt in just a moment. Ignoring Joe, she squatted to inspect the retractable gear and tires. She opened the cowling hatches on both of the twin engines and studied the internals before checking the oil. Joe, standing off to the side, made small talk. When she stepped away from the engine to look at the dipstick, Joe leaned over and looked in through the cowling to inspect the engine. He noticed a single drop of oil on the engine from the dipstick and casually wiped it up with the red shop rag he kept in his hip pocket.

"This is my kind of engine. I'd love to turn a wrench on something like this."

"So, do you like what you do?"

"I don't know. I've been at the same place doing the same thing for twenty-five years."

"What do you do?"

"I work on boats for Falloni Marine."

"I should have known. Twenty-five years with Falloni, someone ought to give you a medal."

"Pete's not one of your favorite people?"

"I do business with him. Business is business, but I have to watch my backside."

"Well, Pete always had an eye for the ladies."

"I can handle that. What gets me is the chiseling. He constantly tries to find ways to beat me out of my fee. I have a business to run too. He's just cheap, that's all."

"Sounds like Pete. His father hired me. The place is much better run now, but its different. When his father was alive, he preached service. Said the money would follow. Pete preaches profit. He cuts every corner to make more profit. He's a percentage guy, tracks everything on his computer. Once a week he comes up with some new statistic to show us what a lousy job we're doing. I'll tell you, Pete is great at keeping the paperwork straight, but I know what you're saying."

"Paperwork, let me tell you my paperwork story. I'd been bringing packages in here for about a year when I finally got my own 135 Cargo and Passenger license. He called me at 10:00 P.M. on a Sunday night. It was my first job. He gave me a verbal purchase order number over the phone. I scurried around and met him here at 2:00 A.M. I go home and send a bill. Anyway, a month, then six weeks, go by. No payment. I call him. He acts like he doesn't remember the flight, says he can't find any paperwork. Tells me to send him a copy of the P.O. I don't have one, but I give him the number. He laughs and says no written purchase order, no payment. Then he tells me that number isn't anything like his purchase order numbers, that it sounded like his social security number. He even had the nerve to tell me I should pay him for the business lesson."

"That would be Pete. You're flying for him now. He must have paid."

"Not voluntarily. A few weeks later he called again. Another drop everything and fly deal. I told him where to go. He promised he'd bring a check for both flights to the airport. I still wouldn't do it. He offered to wire the money before I took off. Turns out we have the same bank, so he transferred the money into my account with a phone call. That's how I do business with Mr. Pete Falloni. Cash in the bank before I depart."

"What exactly do you do for Falloni?"

"Well, a little of everything. I'm in charge of service and storage. He keeps me out of the show room and office."

He closed the cowling hatch for her when she finished with the second dipstick. "I'd think you'd like your work."

"Oh I do. I'm a tinkerer. I just naturally got involved with engines. I'd like to spend more time on electronic gadgets, but I get to work on both fixing boats for Falloni. I have nothing to complain about. It's the years not the mileage. Sometimes I think I'd like to get something of my own going. I really admire people like you."

"I think I know you. Years ago did you ever go out to Put-In-Bay to fix a boat from Detroit?"

"Ma'am, I've been fixing boats everyday all year long for over twenty years. I get out to Put-In-Bay on a regular basis." He did not recognize her.

Sandy persisted. She prodded his memory. She set the time in the middle 1980's. They had limped in from Detroit on one engine. They couldn't get the other to start. They couldn't get a mechanic. She described running into her friend from law school who was out on South Bass camping with his son. He was a lawyer from Columbus. He had called a mechanic. She would swear it was Joe that came and fixed the boat. He had a few drinks with them on the boat. Joe remembered the day, the boys swimming, and her husband. He could not remember her, but he did not say that. They shared stories about their mutual friend, laughing about the same foibles and eccentrics from their different perspectives. Both wished that they kept up with him, and each confessed that they did not.

"So you're a lawyer and a pilot?"

"No, no. I never finished law school. My ex-husband is the lawyer. I got the money to go in business from my divorce. Law school was two lifetimes ago." She got Joe's signature. "Make sure Falloni gets his paperwork. Maybe I'll see you the next time. If you see that renegade lawyer, give him my best."

Heading back to town, Joe pulled off on the berm of Route 6 just at the end of Runway 9. She waved to him as she taxied her twin onto the run-up pad. He watched her take off and turn left to depart the pattern to the north across the East Bay and the Cedar Point Peninsula. As she disappeared out over Lake Erie, the fat woman on the boat at Put-In-Bay flashed through his mind. There was no possible way! He had to have her confused with someone else. Pete had accurately described her. Joe had become something of a connoisseur of women's bodies over the years. He imagined exactly what she must look like under her loose fitting clothes. What chance did he have? She was so far above him it wasn't funny; a lawyer's wife, a pilot, a business owner. He was just a mechanic that took the trouble to keep his fingernails clean. Besides, he didn't remember her name, he had no idea how to reach her, and he would probably never see her again. If only. If only he could meet someone like her. Back at Falloni's, Joe left the paperwork on the counter and took the part directly to the shop where he helped one of the mechanics install it. While he did, he planned another trip to Cleveland. It had been more than a month. There was a time when he never let a week pass. It was hell to get old.

CHAPTER 2

Pete Falloni joined his father in the family business in 1973. He and Sarah moved directly back to Sandusky when he finished his classes at the prestigious Wharton School of Finance and Commerce. He did not stay for graduation. He got his diploma in the mail. Both Sarah and Pete had both been in a hurry to get home, to get to work. Over the years, however, they both remembered their two years in Philadelphia as the best in their marriage. They rented the upstairs apartment in a hundred and fifty year old row house. Sarah got a job as a bank teller downtown. He studied. They had graduated from college in 1971. He from Notre Dame and she from St. Marys. Both graduated with honors. They were married in Norwalk that June. It was a gigantic affair. Her father was a car dealer and knew everyone, and the Falloni crowd from Sandusky was a minor invasion. Joe was invited, but did not go because of Molly's death. The reception was held at the country club southeast of Sandusky where both their families belonged. They honeymooned in the Pocono's on their way to Philadelphia. He had narrowly dodged the bullet of the draft with a lottery number just high enough to exempt him. His father offered to pay for graduate school, but Pete accepted only the tuition. They would live off Sarah's salary.

Pete never spoke with his father about his own salary before coming back. The first he knew of his wage was his first pay check. His face flushed and his ears burned when he realized that he would make $15,000 per year. What could he say? It was more than anyone else in the business made, except his father. Considering the business, it was fair. Still it was less than half the average of his M.B.A. class. His father would never understand that. He knew better than to bring it up. He and Sarah argued. They could barely afford a nice apartment and car payments. She wanted a house, soon; before they had children. She pushed him to demand more. Pete simply could not bring himself to challenge his father. He couldn't bring up alternative wages unless he was prepared for the alternatives. It was a family business. He could not remember a time when his father wasn't preparing him. He heard his voice talking to a child, "When you join the business..." He had no alternatives. He was trapped. He saw his only way out was to build the business. He did not expect that his father would be an obstacle.

Falloni Marine occupied a portion of an old factory on the waterfront. It was a three story red brick structure, with a fourth floor running along the shore side. Rising out of the center of the factory was a black water tower on four legs. The water tower itself was cylindrical, with a cone top and hemispherical bottom. There was a ladder up one of the legs, a catwalk around the base, and another ladder up the side of the tank to a hatch in the conical top. The pipe extending down from the center was cut fifteen feet above the little red brick block house that sat straddled by the tower's legs on the roof of the fourth floor. There was a twin to the block house below the tower on the other end of the roof. It housed the equipment above the old freight elevator. From the First Street side it looked like another gloomy, abandoned factory. Grass and weeds grew unattended. From the bay side, the gravel yard was a busy conglomeration of yachts in cradles criss-crossed by a traveling lift that hoisted the boats out at the old wharf. The black water tower was a landmark for boaters seeking the marina.

Falloni rented the high bay on the ground level of the factory and used it for inside storage and a shop. The office extended from the shop towards the street side. Every office was used, so before Pete returned, Mr. Falloni had an office built especially for him. It was located beside the parts room and extended out into the shop. It was bigger and nicer than his own office. Pete might complain about some things, but he could not complain about his office.

Pete took the location of his office as a signal that his father wanted him to oversee the shop. His first plans to paint the dark interior of the factory and install heat and lights were dashed because of the cost. His father gently reminded him that money spent on the building meant less money to take home, and besides, they did not own the building. Pete next turned to the organization of the shop, boats were brought in at random and wedged into whatever space was available. Pete drew up a floor plan in which he designated specific areas for specific types of work, for example, a body shop area for fiberglass work and painting. The old system was simply to bring the tools to the boats. When Mr.

Falloni caught Pete having yellow lines painted on the floor, the project came to a stop. It was silliness. They had to be flexible. Who knew from one day to the next what they would be working on. What if a boat didn't fit in the lines? Would they turn the work away? Keep the men working on the boats, that's where the money came from, not lines on the floor. The only thing that survived Pete's project was a magnetic board in his office. It reflected the floor plan and numbered magnets marked the location of the individual boats being worked on or in storage. His father took it into his office because he liked the idea. He didn't keep it current. Later he hung it in the hall outside his office, and gave Lynette the assignment of keeping it up to date.

Pete turned his attention to the parts room. When his father caught him at it, he congratulated him. They sold the parts to their customers at heavy mark-ups. Anything Pete could do to save them money in connection with parts would increase their margins and make more money. Pete ended the old practice of any mechanic wandering into the parts room for whatever part he needed. Pete had the room emptied and painted. When they reinstalled the shelving, he organized the parts by supplier and catalog number. Next he set up a card file with a card for each individual part in inventory. He had a lock installed on the door. Only he could pull parts. He could tell from his card file if a part was in stock and when it was time to reorder. The mechanics grumbled, but the controls made sense. They soon realized that they could get a part quicker from Pete than the old search-and-maybe-you'll-find-it method.

After a few months of working with the parts, Pete learned what parts turned and what didn't. He tried to get their wholesaler to take the dead inventory back, but they wouldn't. Then it occurred to Pete that there were other wholesalers. His father had used the same wholesaler for thirty years, and Pete used that fact with his father to make the lack of a concession seem callous. With his father's permission, Pete started shopping. He found wholesalers who would deliver on twenty-four hours notice. Unless they were high demand parts, Pete quit stocking them. He also found some manufacturers that would sell direct. He spent hours everyday on the telephone. He got a head set with a twenty-five foot cord so that he could do paperwork with his hands or pace his office while he dickered. The guys in the shop got a kick out of watching him through the window into his office. They made jokes, but they knew whatever he was doing was good for the business.

Eventually, he cut the inventory and its cost in half. When they paid shipping charges, they simply added them as a line item addition to the marked-up parts price. He tapped into the air cargo market for emergency deliveries. They always passed that cost through to their customers. He learned that the idea of having a part flown in just for them stroked the egos of most of the yacht owners, and he got proficient at presenting the cost to them in a way that made them feel special. His father bragged to anyone who would listen about Pete's success in their parts operation. Pete understood why his father had ignored parts; he hated paperwork and assumed that when he doubled the price he paid for parts, he had to make money.

Pete got his first look at the books the following spring. His father gathered him up and took him downtown to see their accountant. Actually, there were no books or financial statements as such. The meeting with the accountant was for the purpose of going over tax returns before they were signed and filed. At that meeting Pete realized that the tax returns were the only thing close to a financial statement that his father had. The business had two bank accounts, a checking and a savings account. His father ran all income and expenses through the checking account. When he had any surplus, he moved it into savings. When savings got above a point, he transferred the surplus into his personal savings account. The accountant pulled income and expenses from the check register. The account captured the cost of assets in the same fashion and calculated tax depreciation from that.

Until that day, Pete assumed that the business was a corporation. The checks said Falloni Marine Company, but Pete learned it was a sole proprietorship. There was really no difference between his father and the company. He wondered how much his father had slipped out of the savings account over the years. He wondered how much his father was worth. Riding back to the office, Pete tried to impress upon his father that financial statements could give them valuable information about running the business. His father protested that the tax returns were enough and scolded that any businessman who had to look at a piece of paper to know if his business was healthy didn't deserve to be called a businessman. Pete used the parts operation as an example. Financial statements that showed costs would also show what needed improvement and how much improvement they were making. Pete knew he lost his father when he tried to explain the difference between depreciation under the tax laws and generally accepted accounting principles.

A few weeks later, Pete happened to see the bill from the accountant lying on his father's desk. It was more than the annual wages of two mechanics, and that was exactly how Pete presented it to his father. Pete could hire a bookkeeping clerk and do 98% of the work for a third of the cost. All the accountant had to do was take the numbers and prepare a tax return. His father suggested Lynette do the bookkeeping, but Pete reminded him that she was busy full time with the phones, the billings, and the payroll. The first employee Pete ever hired was the bookkeeper. He gave her the assignment of pulling the numbers from the check records, just as the accountant did. She did, but grumbled that if they bought a package accounting system like her former employer had, her job could be done in half the time. She finally brought samples of the one-write manual system she previously used. Pete immediately saw its value. Together they convinced Lynette. Lynette liked the idea that her entries drove the system, and that would make life easier for everyone. With Lynette on board, his father agreed. When they implemented the new accounting system, the bookkeeper joked and welcomed them to the 19th century. His father didn't like the remark and later told Pete to reduce her to part-time status. Pete resisted and assigned her to run the parts room. He still did all the buying.

One Friday afternoon that May, Mr. Falloni took Pete to the country club for lunch and presented him with a $10,000 check in recognition of the improvements he had made to the business. Now that the accounting system kept Pete abreast of the money, he knew that his father had likely scooped three times that amount out of savings for himself. Still, he was relieved. His work was recognized. It would be a down payment for a house. He thanked his father and told him that. If they moved fast, they might find a house before Sarah had the baby. Sarah was much relieved at the news of the bonus. She missed Philadelphia, dressing for work, and the generally higher level of sophistication in the city; but she also liked being local gentry. Despite the discomfort of the pregnancy, she enjoyed the recognition of driving about town in a Corvette. They had two from her father's dealership. Pete drove the newer one. She was active in several church and civics groups. She was also on the planning committee for the Monte Carlo night at the country club. She had worried that they might have to leave Sandusky if the only way Pete could make any money was to take a corporate job.

They found a house on the 1100 block of Wayne street. It was smaller than most of the other homes in the Cable Park Historic District just south of downtown Sandusky. It was built in the late 1930's and wedged in between two larger homes built just after the turn of the century. The house was half the size of its neighbors, but still had three bedrooms. It's red brick construction, limestone window framing, Tudor lines, and gable actually distinguished it from the other homes on the block. It was a house on a boulevard in one of Sandusky's nicest neighborhood's that most of its working class would have aspired to own. Both Sarah and Pete were satisfied with it for a starter house. They both knew that in Philadelphia the same house would cost five times as much. Pete and two of the guys from the marina moved their furniture into the house while Sarah was still in the hospital after giving birth to their first daughter, Maria. Sarah and the baby came home to it.

That fall after laying up most of the boats for the season, there was a fire in the old factory. It apparently started from an extension cord or blower that they used to heat the shrink wrap on the boats. The cord had been left plugged in out and the blower left lying on the floor. The fire totally destroyed the 26 foot boat adjacent to the ignition source, burned a large hole through the second, third, and fourth floors. The tar roof burned entirely across the fourth floor level. It also did heavy smoke damage to all the boats inside and the offices. In the days succeeding the fire, Mr. Falloni was livid and spent most of his time yelling at employees, or into the phone at insurance people and his landlord. He could handle the employees, but the double talk from the insurance adjusters and his landlord stymied him. He gave Pete the assignment of making sense out of the fine print.

The lease promised that the landlord would carry certain insurance coverages, and required other coverages from the tenant. They had the type of coverage required, but not the amount specified in the lease, and not enough to cover the damage to the contents. The landlord had dropped its coverage altogether. They also learned that the landlord had not paid taxes on the building for two years and had no intention of repairing the damage to the structure. Finally, the boat owner's individual policies excluded coverage. As could be expected, Mr. Falloni reached into his own pocket and paid for the gap in coverage. Without financial statements, he would have fluffed it off as business; but it was a large number that jumped out from the balance sheet, additional capital contribution. Every time he looked at the statements he got mad all over again. The accountant got a little relief in the taxes for the casualty loss, but the statements made Mr. Falloni seethe.

Pete urged his father to set up a corporation. If the worst had happened, his father might have lost everything he had worked a lifetime to build. A corporation would limit his liability to the assets of the corporation, and shield his personal wealth. The accountant agreed. Mr. Falloni muttered that he would never leave a customer hanging, but acquiesced. He told Pete to handle it. Pete hired a young lawyer in one of the firms downtown. He was Jewish, but had gone to law school at Notre Dame. Pete knew him from the country club. Initially, Pete told him to put 100% of the stock in his father's name, but when they sat down with the lawyer for the organizational meeting, his father wanted 10% of the stock to go to Pete. Mr. and Mrs. Falloni and Pete would be the Board of Directors. Mr. Falloni would be Chairman of the Board and President. Pete would be Secretary and Treasurer. The lawyer explained that if they wanted to gain the benefit of the corporate shield, they would have to abide by all the corporate formalities. They would have to hold meetings, keep a minute book, keep all bank accounts in the corporate name, and never take money out of the business except as compensation or dividends. Either had to be approved by the Directors and entered in the minute book. At this point, it occurred to Mr. Falloni that his taxes would double, the corporation would pay taxes on its income, and then he would have to pay taxes on his salary and dividends. His face flushed and voice elevated. The lawyer immediately calmed him, telling him that it was a closely held corporation, a Subchapter S Corporation, and that for tax purposes there was only one tax. Mr. Falloni liked that, all the benefits, no burdens. Two more things came out of the fire. The Falloni's bought the building, and Joe's stature in the organization increased.

When Mr. Falloni learned that the building owner had no insurance, was in breach of the lease, had not paid the taxes, and was doing nothing to repair the building; he stopped paying rent and started looking for a new facility. He authorized Pete to sue their landlord, and Pete and the lawyer got a lawsuit filed. It did not take them long to figure out that they had been spoiled by the convenience and low cost of the space. The cost of constructing anything remotely equivalent was prohibitive, and there were no similar properties available. Moving all the boats would be an incredible expense. Pete hatched the plan to buy the property. The lawyer started aggressive discovery in the lawsuit to get the corporation's attention. During breaks in every deposition, he dropped hints that the absentee landlord, a large solvent corporation with other priorities, should settle before the cost of defense got out of hand, and especially before a local jury got ahold of it. A few words from the young lawyer during a friendly chat with the Erie County Auditor in the hallway of the courthouse got a tax foreclosure started. Finally, a meeting was arranged with the vice president of the corporation's real property department. He flew into Sandusky in a charter. Mr. Falloni and Pete picked him up at Griffing Field, gave him a tour of the plant, and met with him in Pete's smoke flavored office. Mr. Falloni did most of the talking. Pete admired the graceful way he handled it. In the end, their visitor agreed that Mr. Falloni could help him solve all his problems. The Falloni's would drop their suit, pay the back taxes, pay for all repairs to the building, and prepay the remaining rent on their ten year lease. In return, the corporation would deed the building to them.

Joe's advancement came with the reconstruction of the building. Mr. Falloni spent a lot of time blustering at Red and the mechanics for their sloppiness and neglect which started the fire, but all along they knew his ire would pass; and he knew that they worked just as he encouraged them to, putting everything into their work and nothing into their surroundings. After signing the contract with the owner, he called Red into his office, and they stayed there until midnight getting drunk. They had built quite a business together, but their day was passing. Now that they were buying the factory, he was going to let Pete use the repair work to rebuild the shop the way he wanted. Red got the message loud and clear and suggested that Pete work with Joe. Joe had been dropping hints since the day he arrived about how things could be improved; but he had to work through Red, and Red knew Falloni's will. Joe always kept his own work area and tools in meticulous order, but beyond that the shop was in happy disarray. Mr. Falloni had long recognized Joe's quality, and had often told Red they were lucky to have him. Falloni made it clear that Red would still be in charge of all the work on the boats, but that Joe would handle the rebuilding for Pete. After that, Joe would handle the "organization" out back. Red would still be responsible for the boats and quality. Organization, that's all. Red knew and understood. It was easier to accept because Falloni was taking a step back with him. Both of the old friends assumed that Pete and Joe were of like mind. The possibility of any friction between the young men was completely outside their thinking.

CHAPTER 3

Joe took Route 2 to Cleveland. He thought it was quicker than the Ohio Turnpike. He had the time to his destination down to ninety minutes. During most of the drive he thought of nothing. He simply noted the passing of familiar bridges, farms, and intersections. On the outskirts of Cleveland he made his regular stop at a fast food restaurant to relieve himself and comb his hair. He bought a soft drink and got back on the road. After that he started feeling his nerves. He took one of his hands off the steering wheel and looked at it tremble. He felt calm. He thought he looked calm. His chest was tight. His breathing shallow. He chided himself for not being accustomed to these sessions. He supposed that this excitement was programmed into men to insure the species would reproduce. He drove by one studio whose neon sign promised live lingerie models and private viewing rooms. He had gone there the last time. He liked to move around. He pulled into the parking lot of another studio down the street. At that point he was no longer excited, but felt curiously obligated to enter.

Twenty minutes later he was on his way back to Sandusky. Things had gone as they always did. In the waiting room he found three girls watching TV in negligees. Each introduced herself with a first name. He nodded to one. She led him to a small mirrored room with a large stuffed chair in the center. She took $50.00 and left him there for a few minutes. When she returned, she turned on a cheap stereo sitting on the floor and started dancing in front of him. After a few minutes she told him that he could make himself as comfortable as he wanted. He pulled the $20 bill he had waiting from his shirt pocket and gave it to her. She put it in her shoe and continued to dance as she slipped out of the flimsy clothing. When Joe unzipped his pants, she reminded him that there was no touching. Things had not always been that way, he mused as he got to the edge of the suburbs. He pulled back into the fast food restaurant, this time he got a soft drink from the drive through.

There was a time when this trip would have started with a twelve pack from a beer dock in Sandusky. He would have knocked back at least four on the way to Cleveland. There, he would have chosen a massage parlor and gone through a very similar drill, except the fees were higher and included a shower before and after. Back then, it also required a significant tip to get what he wanted. He had experimented with higher and lower tips until he concluded that a tip equaling the parlor fee was what it took to maximize service. He rarely chose the same parlor or same girl twice in a row, although there was one time when he had gone back to the same girl four times. There was a reason. She did not look like Molly, but she did many of the same things in the same order. When she wanted to know his name and if he was married, he lied and never returned. AIDS and law enforcement had closed down the massage parlors in the mid-1980's. After that he experimented with the escort services.

That required renting a hotel room, losing anonymity, waiting, paying higher fees, and more often than not, getting less than the type of contact he wanted. Even with condoms, the girls had new standards. He did find the escorts to be of a higher sort than the girls in the massage parlors. Sometimes he felt a twinge of regret for all of them. He wondered about their lives. He always, however, stopped himself short any moral conclusions. He had not invented the world. They would be doing their work with or without him. He had not been part of whatever brought them there. He was polite and paid. He never once felt any guilt. When he quit drinking, he quit using escorts. Sober, yet still driven by urges, one night he had driven back to Cleveland to check out the old massage parlors. They were opened again, now as modeling studios. He went in expecting the past. He quickly learned the new drill, and it was enough for him. It was not what he wished, but it was safe and filled a need.

To the extent that Joe reflected on his failings, whoring was not one of them. He considered drinking his problem. He and Molly drank too much. After her death, he drank every day. He drank every day for eighteen years. The first year after losing his wife and baby, he drank with Molly's father several times a week. They drank at the Brennan's house, in the Brennan's garage, at neighborhood bars, and at Joe's house. Joe had stayed in the small rental house for four years. For the first year, he touched nothing, including the nursery. Then, on a Saturday when he drank a case by himself, he cleaned house. He sat up an electronics shop in the second bedroom. He had occupied himself that first winter by building a kit stereo. In his new shop he built a HAM radio. He strung an antennae between two trees and spent evenings listening and drinking. Once in a rare while he would broadcast. Most of the time, he listened. He continued to ride his bike through the mid-1970's, but he also continued to gain weight. He helped officiate at races, but he could not do a century and knew better than to try. He bought a new bike thinking that it would shame him into riding. Shortly after that, he stopped biking altogether. Molly's sister Maggie visited Joe from time to time for the first couple of years. Joe worried that she was interested in him. If she was, it would be an incredible problem. He made a point of asking her about her boyfriends and giving her fatherly advice. He would never drink in her presence, or even finish the beer he was drinking when she arrived. He went to her wedding and visited her in the hospital after she delivered her first child. After that, he lost touch with the Brennan's. After losing Mr. Brennan for a drinking buddy, Joe drank alone.

For years, every night on the way home from work, he went through a beer dock. He usually bought a twelve pack and finished it before passing out in front of the TV or in his radio shack. If he was particularly busy at work, he would limit himself to a six pack. He never drank less than a six pack. By the early 1980's radios had become so compact and inexpensive that it was easier and cheaper for Joe to buy new units than to build them himself. To satisfy his electronics bug, he bought a personal computer that by subsequent standards was little more than a toy. He learned how to use it, then he took it apart. He subscribed to several more electronics magazines and built his own computer with components he ordered through the mail. He kept his personal finances in the machine, but had few other immediate uses. That lead him into on-line services and bulletin boards. He often monitored the HAM radio while he explored the on-line world. In the same fashion as with his radio, he received but rarely sent. He did make a few modest stock purchases through an on-line service, and he followed the stock market for entertainment. About once a week he bought a new girlie magazine. He never read the stories, but he studied the photographs. He kept two, no more than three, hidden under the clothes in his dresser. When he threw old issues away, he would put them in a brown paper bag and go by a trash dumpster in one of the strip shopping centers where, after making sure there were no witnesses, he casually tossed the bag inside. Joe was truly fascinated with the female body and never tired of looking, not only at the magazines, but also about town. Still, he never spoke to a strange female. He never asked anyone he met for a date. Occasionally, but rarely, he would think about someone he knew in the shower. He felt content with the magazines.

That was until he discovered massage parlors. That came quite by coincidence in Columbus in 1979. He had gone down to be in his friend's wedding. After an evening of drinking, he returned to his hotel room and fell on the bed. After a time, he opened his eyes, intending to get up and get out of his clothes. Lying there with his eyes opened, he noticed a marker had been left in the yellow pages of the telephone book next to the bed. He got up and opened it. It marked the section on massage parlors. Prices had been handwritten into most of the box ads. Joe scanned them for a downtown address. He did not find any. He did recognize one major thoroughfare on the north side, and he called the number. Yes, they were open. No, he did not need an appointment. The parlor fee was the same as written in the phone book. He would have his choice of three lovely attendants. They did accept tips. Joe showered, brushed his teeth, and went for a late night drive. His heart raced, his face flushed, and his hands trembled all the way there. The staff was experienced with novices and treated him cordially with indirect explanations about sharing an adult conversation that left no room for doubt. Afterwards, he came back to the hotel and drank at the hotel bar until it closed. He had hoped to find another woman there. It had been a long time. The magazines would never be enough again. Cleveland was closer than Columbus. He started going there every few weeks, usually on a week night in the hope of avoiding a crowd.

When the massage parlors started disappearing, Joe was truly perplexed. He made decent money and had few expenses, but the cost of a motel in Cleveland, the escort services, and the tips gnawed at his thrifty side. He tried a national service listed in the Cleveland yellow pages to see if they could provide an escort in Sandusky. They could. They described the agency fee and that the girls expected additional tips. He rented a motel room in Sandusky under a fictitious name and called again. Soon after that, the phone rang in his room. Later when the girl arrived, she insisted on seeing his driver's license. She did not mind that the name was different from the one he had given on the phone. She did mind the local address and the fact he had no luggage. She asked if he was a cop. He denied it, but she left in a huff. A few weeks later he called again, this time from home. After the fire and his promotion under Pete Falloni, he had bought a small house very much like the rental he had lived in before that. He gave the national number his proper name and home phone. When a girl called back, he gave her his home address, told her to pull into the driveway and come to the side door. Joe was satisfied with that arrangement for a time, however, he eventually got to know the girls working Sandusky. He did not enjoy seeing the same ones, and more than once declined when familiar voices called back. He worried that his neighbors might notice. Finally, one of the girls recognized him at the mall and approached him with light conversation. He stopped using the local girls altogether.

He liked to go to the farm on weekends. His father and Dieter saved any mechanical problems that did not require immediate attention for him. A week after getting an ag degree from Bowling Green, Dieter had married his high school sweetheart. She was a local girl of German extraction who not only shared Dieter's short stocky build, but also his carefree disposition. When Joe could get away with it, he would study her physique for any sign of feminine grace. Dieter's attraction to and fondness for her mystified Joe, but he enjoyed them together, and he loved their children. They had five, three boys and two girls. The kids all looked like their parents. The kids loved to wrestle with Joe, and as the boys got older, Dieter ordered them to work with Joe to learn about equipment. Joe's mother worried over his bloat and dissipation, and never once forgot to ask if he had met any women. She often snuck off by herself and cried when he left to go back to Sandusky. Somehow, in all the years of his drinking and driving he was never stopped, and he never so much as dented a fender.

Joe knew his mother did not like his drinking, but that did not stop him from drinking at the farm. In fact, it was his custom to bring a case along to share with his father and Dieter. When he planned to stay overnight, he brought two cases. He had converted Thanksgiving and Christmas into family binges. Then during a visit home for Thanksgiving in 1988, Joe noticed a framed picture his mother kept on the mantel. It was of himself standing between his parents the night he graduated from high school. He was struck by how much he and his father had looked alike. Then his father was only a few years older than

Joe was now. Joe took the picture and went to a curio cabinet that had a mirror behind his mother's collection. He looked back and forth from his father's face to his own. He weighed forty pounds more than he did when he graduated and no longer looked anything like his father. He resolved he had to get healthy, but that did not include cutting out the booze.

Joe continued to drink over the next few weeks. His one concession to his resolve was that he started jogging. Actually, his return to exercise was more humble than that. It was winter in northern Ohio, and he knew that he would not enjoy cycling, even if he could. After work, he bundled up and started to jog. The first night, he vomitted two blocks away from his house, but proceeded to walk the mile he had planned to jog. Back at home, he had eight beers and convinced himself he had made a good beginning. Over the next month he did increase his activity until he could jog two miles without stopping, and he did decrease his drinking to a six pack a day. He planned to spend New Year's Day at his parents, and New Year's Eve alone. Falloni's was on its holiday shut down, so after a morning jog, Joe started drinking with his lunch. In the early afternoon, he cleaned and tuned the best of his bikes that hadn't been ridden in thirteen years. He kept drinking. He listened to his Ham radio, now a small unit no bigger than half a loaf of bread. He kept drinking. He got on his computer, checked his stocks, then down-loaded a game. He kept drinking. He sent for a pizza and ate it in front of the TV. He kept drinking. About 9:00 P.M. he realized that he was not drunk. He counted his empties to learn that he had consumed fifteen beers. He walked a line, touched his nose, recited lines from poems he remembered. He was sober. He wanted to be drunk. He quickly gulped three more beers. His stomach hurt, it could hold no more. He went into his bathroom and stared at the mirror. This was it. He was going to stop.

He went to bed before midnight and slept in the next morning. His father and Dieter were surprised when he showed up empty handed, and offered him beer from their stocks. They laughed at his resolution, but his mother took him aside and kissed and encouraged him. Quitting proved not to be easy. Every day, all day long, he craved beer. He diverted himself by working late, exercising more, fiddling with his bikes, with his radio, and with his computer. He was surprised to find that he could go to sleep without passing out from booze, and he liked waking without a hang-over. He lost weight and people at work complimented him on his diet. The evenings were the worst part. He never seriously considered meetings. There was no way he could stand up in front of strangers and confess. He had no use for their problems. He knew his own. On one particularly trying evening, he decided to see what had become of Cleveland's massage parlors. Things changed. His needs weren't what they once were. The modeling studios were adequate. Driving back to Sandusky, he thought about the lady pilot. He mused about her body. If only.

CHAPTER 4

Years earlier, Mr. Falloni called Pete and Joe into his office late one afternoon. After a few beers, Mr. Falloni told Joe the open secret, that they were buying the building. Joe probably knew that Pete had a lot of ideas about improving the place. He sent Pete to get his sketches. Mr. Falloni knew that Joe had a lot of ideas of his own. He also knew that refitting the old factory was a big project during which he still had to run a business. Since they were laying the groundwork for another generation in the business, he was putting Pete in charge of the building. He and Paul would keep the business going. Joe would do whatever legwork and oversight that Pete wanted. They spent the next several hours studying and discussing Pete's initial sketches. The Falloni's were pleased to discover that Joe had thought through in much more detail improvements that were only rough concepts in Pete's plans.

Joe had years in the shop to think through his ideas. For example, Joe had long wanted rack storage for the boats inside the factory. Now that the fire had burned through the upper floors, Joe suggested it was the perfect time to install such racks. They would quadruple their inside storage capacity and save their customers the expense of shrink wrapping. They could also offer inside storage heated and unheated if they zoned off parts of the factory. Joe also suggested a showroom behind the office where Pete proposed a body shop. Pete lit up. Mr. Falloni could see Pete's mind at work. Mr. Falloni objected because they weren't boat dealers. Then he looked more closely at Pete and said that it was up to them, they had to set the course of the future. He left them in the office. The two young men drank and planned until late into the night.

Pete also negotiated the financing for the purchase and reconstruction of the factory. As it turned out, the budget for the building improvements got almost as large as the purchase price. Pete had hired an engineering firm to prepare drawings and specifications of their concepts and to handle the bidding. He would manage the contracts. Joe would be the project superintendent. Mr. Falloni interceded when he realized the magnitude of the undertaking. This occurred to him not from the total amount of the construction budget, but rather from the projected payment schedules on the debt. He finally issued an edict that the monthly payments on the permanent financing could be no more than 20% higher than their prior rent. They had been able to live with the rent, and he was willing to bite off 20% for ownership.

At first Pete was dejected, but the engineer was used to squeezing a project into budgets. Pete simply could not be convinced to lessen his plans, so the solution was to cut the improvements into phases. Phase I would modernize the shop with designated work bays, a paint and body shop, and a machine shop, and also add multi-level racks for unheated inside storage. Joe was most excited about having his own machine shop. They rebuilt engines, but he was tired of waiting for the parts they sent out. With the machine shop he had in mind, they could rebore engine blocks, balance shafts and overhaul propellers. He thought much of the rest was fluff. The show room, the marina, the ship's store, the restaurant, the health club, and the hostel were all left for subsequent phases.

The bank never expressed any problem with the amount of the loan, even when it was twice the amount that Mr. Falloni ultimately approved. As long as they could get his personal guarantee, they were ready to proceed. The lawyer came up with the idea that the building ownership be kept separate from the operating business. If there were ever some catastrophe, it would be another way to insulate the family's wealth from claims. The marine business would simply rent the building from another family business. As long as they were in debt, they could keep the rent equal to the debt service. Later, when they got out of debt, they could use the rental agreement to get money out of the business for the family. Pete was immediately attracted to the idea and told the lawyer to pursue it.

A few weeks later, the lawyer proposed to form a limited partnership, Falloni Properties, Ltd., to buy the building. The general partner would take on the purchase mortgage, the construction loan, and the permanent financing. Mr. Falloni would be general partner, would guarantee the mortgage, and have total control. Pete and his sisters would be the limited partners. All appreciation in the value of the building over the purchase price and initial improvements would accrue to them. Thus, Mr. Falloni would pass value outside his estate, and nick Uncle Sam out of some estate taxes. Focusing on the general partnership interest of Mr. Falloni, the lawyer suggested the formation of another closely held corporation, Falloni Properties, Inc., to act as general partner. That would cover Mr. Falloni for any personal liability exposure beyond the bank guarantees.

Pete liked that too, but suggested that the corporation be organized along the same 90% / 10% ownership lines as the marine business. In the back of Pete's mind, that would give him the leg up he wanted on his sisters. When his father died, he assumed his 10 % of the controlling general partnership would become 100 %. The lawyer told him that depended upon what his father did with his stock in his will. Without a will, it would go equally to Pete and his sisters. After a moment's pause, Pete told him to draft the corporate documents so that it took an 80 % shareholder vote to do anything. That way, his sisters and their husbands could never do anything unless he agreed. With his 10% and whatever he inherited, he would surely have more than 20% control. There could be no 80% without him. He would have an absolute veto, total control.

The lawyer smiled and complimented Pete's ingenuity. He suggested that they make it 85 % just to be safe. He also suggested that Pete offer to personally guarantee the debt. That would look good to the bank, it could be used to justify Pete's 10 % interest in the corporate general partner, and it further distinguished Pete from his sisters. Who dare criticize Pete when he dedicated his own financial future to the health of the family business.

Later, Pete and the lawyer presented the proposed documents to Mr. Falloni in his office. The lawyer did the talking. Both were surprised. Mr. Falloni knew much more about limited partnerships than they expected. He professed to being a limited partner in a restaurant and motel. That was news to Pete. Also, from the incorporation of the operating business, he quickly grasped the concept of using an S corporation to be general partner. He listened carefully as the lawyer explained that both he and Pete would personally guarantee the debt. He presented the 85% requirement on shareholder votes as a way to insure family harmony and order in the business after his death. Mr. Falloni nodded in thought.

After a moment, he stood and walked around behind Pete. He spoke to the lawyer over Pete's head. He talked about his concern for his daughters. Someday they would all marry, who knew what kind of men. He liked the 85% provision. It assured Pete control of the business. He wanted the provision added to the by-laws of Falloni Marine, Inc. He also wanted a will. He wanted his wife provided for so long as she lived, and he wanted to divide his property equally among his children, but he wanted to do that in a way that gave Pete total control over the business. He asked the lawyer if that was possible. The lawyer assured him it could be done in a number of ways, with Pete as trustee of a trust, by leaving Pete the voting rights to any stock no matter who got the beneficial interest, both, and other ways he had not yet thought through.

Mr. Falloni moved to pat the lawyer on the shoulder. He told him that it all sounded very jewish and that he liked it. He told Pete to make sure the paperwork was done the way he said. He told Pete that he had gone from no books to three sets of books, the operating business, the limited partnership, and the corporate general partner. He didn't like the bookkeeper's nose in family business. He told Pete to have Lynette handle all the books. Pete agreed that there were plenty of other things for his bookkeeper to do. She could take over billings for Lynette. Lynette would need the time. He told the two of them to get to work and politely chased them out of his office.

Mr. Falloni and everyone who worked for him was pleased as the work progressed. Virtually all of it was to the interior of the building. The original plan included painting the dirty red brick tan and the black water tower neon green. The exterior renovations had been postponed for cost, but Pete planned to proceed with the painting of the water tower. He regarded it as a major asset, a ready landmark to draw customers from the other marine operators around the bay. Mr. Falloni agreed and for that reason forbade the painting. They were already known by the black water tower, and he didn't want to risk the prospect of anyone on the lake making jokes of a new color. Good work was still the core business. Fixing up the shop and storage was one thing. Squandering money on the exterior was another. It signalled a business more interested in image than substance. Pete hated the dreary exterior, but told himself he had more important battles to fight.

With the expenses of the fire, the corporate reorganization, the building purchase, reconstruction and debt; they were happy to break even the first year after the fire. They made a handsome profit the second year. The third year, they exceeded anything in Mr. Falloni's memory. Pete used the financial statements to show that margins had increased from operating efficiencies; but Mr. Falloni never gave up his suspicion that it resulted from the corporate and tax finagling by their lawyer and accountant. Pete seemed to spend as much time with them as he did on matters concerning the shop. The fourth year Mr. Falloni finally relented to the show room.

His entire career he had refused to sell boats because he felt it would taint his reputation as an independent and reputable shop. Also, the manufacturers required their dealers to carry a minimum inventory, which he never wanted to buy nor finance. He frequently told disparaging stories about car dealers and their lawsuits, likening them to boat dealers. Pete knew all this and had charts and graphs to persuade him. Mr. Falloni was convinced only by one of Pete's small points, that his father considered a stroke of genius. Pete proposed putting Red in charge of boat sales because of his life long experience working on them. Pete's real reason was that he considered Red an obstructionist in the shop. Even though Joe was officially over Red, Joe still deferred to Red, and Red clung to the old ways. Pete knew that Joe, if unencumbered, would tune the shop like a well-oiled machine. Joe knew that there was very little Pete would refuse him. Pete may not understand exactly what all the equipment they bought did, but he loved to give tours of the facility.

Mr. Falloni became enamored with moving Red and personally took charge of setting up the sales operation. They became dealers for two lines, one power boat line, and one sail boat line. They cleaned out an empty portion of the ground floor for the used boats that they took on trade. They also started an active yacht brokerage business. Whenever Mr. Falloni saw Red showing a boat, he would interrupt and tell the customers that they were talking to the dean, the statesmen of boat sales. Everyone loved the interruptions, and fairly quickly, his boasts became true.

In 1983 Pete noticed Joe working on a hand held radio during his lunch break, and he asked him where he learned about electronics. That led to Joe inviting Pete over to his house that evening to see his radio shack and computer room. They got drunk together, listened to the BBC, and later some HAM conversations. Joe also showed him his computer tinkering. He displayed his personal checkbook and an amortization schedule for his mortgage on the CRT. Pete was more animated that Joe had ever seen him. Joe had never known Pete to be mechanically inclined, but he demonstrated an interest and aptitude for the radios. Pete resolved to build his own HAM set. Joe discouraged him, telling him that he could buy a better set cheaper. He did give Pete a stack of magazines and told him to study the ads. Pete told Joe that they should start a marine electronics shop. Joe thought it was drunk talk, but within a week, Pete had him cleaning out a room in the factory for that purpose.

Pete was equally excited about the computer. His father-in-law's car dealership was heavily computerized. They had a large system that handled everything, including their parts inventory, their work in progress, their billings, their receivables, their payables, and it also spit out financial statements. It was big and expensive, and his father would never agree. Joe told him that desk tops were coming, and that they could do a lot to improve the business with free standing units in each department, if they couldn't afford a main frame. Joe promised Pete that he could reproduce Pete's parts card file system in the computer, and make it a hundred times easier to use and maintain. When Pete stumbled out late that night, Joe stayed up and started programming a data base manager for their parts department.

When Joe finished his parts system he had Pete over for another evening of beer and a demonstration. By that time, Pete had also purchased a HAM radio kit. He kept the components on a side table in his office and regularly worked on it there in the evenings. He consulted with Joe a few times, but after a point got proud. He wanted to make it work on his own. Joe understood. Pete immediately saw the value of Joe's parts program, particularly its ability to sort by supplier name, parts number, and descriptive word. He had learned enough about electronics to know that any decent desk top cost over $5,000 and there was no way he could spend that much without a major confrontation with his father over the expense. He discussed building a system with Joe. They resolved to go to Cleveland together and make the rounds of the used component outlets, however, the next morning Pete did all that by phone. Pete called Joe in and estimated they could get the hardware for $2,000. Joe suggested they buy a new 64K system that had been pushed for kids over Christmas. They could get it on sale for $750. He could load his software. Pete knew his father wouldn't notice that expenditure, and so Falloni Marine began its computerization with a child's toy.

About the same time Joe got the parts system on-line, Pete finished his HAM. It worked. He was hooked. The collection of electronic gadgets lying around his office grew. He loved to show them off. Soon his Corvette had as many antennas as Joe's pick-up.

CHAPTER 5

By 1985 the Falloni operation was thoroughly computerized. Pete Falloni had four personal computers in place to run the business. The small computer and parts program that Joe initially set up was successful as a demonstration project. Pete soon replaced it with a more powerful PC and package software designed for an automobile dealership. With it, they controlled their parts inventory, entered work orders, and generated bills. That computer was kept in the shop office. Pete's former bookkeeper was now the shop clerk and did most of the entry. Joe knew enough of the system to use it himself when she wasn't around. Pete also got a unit for the sales department. It used a portion of the dealership software package. Of all the computers, it got the least use. His father and Red were intimidated by it, but they never tired of playing with it on rainy days. Lynette used her unit the most. She did all the accounting for the three business entities and generated all the checks, including the payroll. Finally, Pete had a unit in his office. All the programs that the other computers used were loaded into his machine. The individual units were not networked, but Pete had standing orders that each department give him a weekly backup disk with their current data. Thus he could monitor everything from his computer, and produce his own reports and financial statements as he wished. He had the capability that no one else had, to put all the pieces together.

Pete ran the business, but had grown progressively disenchanted. It was not because of his father's interference; indeed, within broad limits, his father gave him a free hand. His father did keep the titles, but that did not bother Pete. Pete had operating control. In fact, Mr. Falloni only came to work in the mornings, and then spent most of his time hanging out with Red and Lynette. Pete was dissatisfied simply because of money. He wanted more, and he couldn't see where it would come from. Sandusky was only so big, and there was a limit to the

Falloni's market share. Pete's income had grown steadily with the business, but it had plateaued a few years earlier when the income of the business peaked after they got the dealership established. Pete and Sarah were pillars of Sandusky society, they had a beautiful young family, and from all out outward appearances were living a life worthy of envy. At home alone, however, they shared their frustration. Sarah wanted a bigger house. Pete wanted a bigger, faster boat. He grumbled that he couldn't afford most of the boats his company sold and serviced. He bragged to his wife that he had completely restructured the business. She told him that he deserved more, at least what her brothers were getting at her father's dealership.

Pete still personally handled all the purchasing. He still used a headset rather than a conventional telephone. He had rigged up his own wireless set that he wore on his belt to link him with the telephone system years before they were commercially available. He paced his office dickering with suppliers for an hour to an hour and a half each morning. It was a ritual he loved. When he found out that some of the suppliers had billed more than their verbal commitments, he set up a process by which all packing lists and invoices passed across his desk, so that he could cross check them against his deals. Inevitably, he set up a computerized purchase order system. Only Pete could issue purchase orders. Sitting at his computer, he could match the suppliers paperwork against his orders. He used this system to create a parts list as they were received. He simply gave the shop clerk a disk and she added the information into her parts inventory. Likewise, he used the system to authorize payment of purchase orders. Lynette's check writing program was constrained so that she could not pay a bill unless there was a matching purchase order, and until Pete authorized payment by a clearance code that only Pete knew, and he changed it weekly. Once a week he gave Lynette a disk which freed payments.

Pete also used his computer to generate all sorts of management reports. Most of the software they used had their own standard report series, but Pete often generated his own from a spread sheet program that was only in his computer. Using that program, he quantified and verified many business concerns that he suspected but could not otherwise prove. Whenever he came out of his office with an excited look and a fist full on papers, everyone groaned, but they all had to agree with the numbers. Eventually, Pete turned the system on himself, and did an analysis of his purchasing and parts system. He felt he had increased the margin on parts about twenty percent. He quickly confirmed that percentage spread, and that it had consistently held for more than a decade. It was the hard numbers, however, that shocked him. He thought he was doing a good job, but he found the results so good as to be almost absurd. It gnawed at him. He laid awake at night unable to sleep because of the numbers. In the twelve years that he had been with the business, he had brought an additional million and one half dollars into the marine operation by his cost savings on parts.

Those were hard numbers with no adjustment for inflation. He couldn't believe his own numbers. He sat in front of his terminal for hours, coming at the same numbers several different ways. They still charged their customers double the wholesale list price. Since his father had historically paid list with no questions asked, he simply cut the annual parts sales number in half to establish a base line against which to judge the actual discounted prices he negotiated. He used sales tax payments to double check the annual parts sales figures. He used the payables system to capture the amount that they actually spent on parts. He went to the public library on the square downtown and got the consumer price index numbers back to 1973. He applied inflation to the annual savings, and convinced himself that he had personally been responsible for millions.

Where did it go? No wonder the bank never set a debt limit so long as they had his father's personal guarantee. His current $70,000 annual salary, even with the occasional surprise checks from his father, was paltry in return for what he had done. They were an insult. He felt like a chump for not seeing this before. All the books were open to him. He knew what his father took, and when he took it. He had simply never totalled the numbers before, never reflected upon them before. He compared it to his own total salary. Adding up his salary and bonuses, he had earned a grand total of $510,000 in twelve years. Over the same years, his father had taken home $2,618,000. That's where it went.

The 1985 year-to-date savings at the margin was already $156,238. He had increased the margins. He alone. No one else in the business even thought about this margin. His father enjoyed the benefit, only Pete carried the burden. If the margin changed, no one would know. They wouldn't have a clue. Profits would be down. His father would grumble about the economy. He wouldn't start chasing nickels. He didn't think like that. The business, his father, got 100% of the benefit of Pete's labor. He could not remember so much as a thank you.

Half of what he saved the company each year was as much as his salary. If he were sick, if he were only half as tough in his dickering, those savings would disappear. He should at least share in the fruits of his labor. He should be a partner in the benefits. After all the business wasn't a charity. Why should he be making donations? He didn't dare tell Sarah about these numbers. She would go crazy. He couldn't confront his father. His father may not know financial statements, but he had to know when the money started flowing. He had to know where it came from. The fact that he chose to keep, not share, told Pete all he had to know about his father. Pete had to do something. He laid awake night after night. Slowly, a little each night, he pieced his plan together.

Pete resolved to set up his own wholesale operation. He would continue, as he always had, to do the purchasing and haggle the prices down. The purchases, however, would be funneled through a new company, one which he alone owned, not Falloni Marine. The parts could still be shipped directly to Falloni Marine, but the bills would be sent to his company. He would bill Falloni Marine ten percent more than his company paid. Falloni Marine would still be paying ten percent less than wholesale list. The family business would still be better off than it would be without him. They were going to share. They would be partners at the margin. It was only fair. And though Pete had no trouble convincing himself of the fundamental fairness of this scheme, it never once occurred to him to reflect upon why he instinctively did this in secret.

He began to look forward to the quiet time for thought as his wife slept beside him. The insomnia was no longer a solitary agony. It was a time of uninterrupted concentration. Sometimes he even got up to make lists so that he would not forget the details of his scheme. The key to it all was control. He had to retain complete control. Whenever another touched his operation, even in the most casual manner, he had to be covered. He would set up a legitimate corporation, but not through the family lawyer. Sandusky was too small a town to risk a leak. In fact, he resolved to go out of state. That would add to the appearance of legitimacy. Michigan was only ninety minutes down the road. He'd set up a Michigan corporation. He cast about for a corporate name. He knew that it must not disclose anything about ownership, so any variation of his name was out. He rolled his initials "PF" about and came up with the generic sounding Preferred Wholesale, Inc. He would get stationery and invoices printed, also in Michigan. No direct links. He would open a bank account in Michigan. He would get a post office box. He might even rent an office. No, that would get him noticed. He must have anonymity. He could easily find an excuse to be out of the office for a few hours every week or two. He would run over to Michigan, pick up his mail, his bills. He would mail his own bills to Falloni Marine. He could do everything out of his computer at the office, but that would risk exposure, someone might stumble across a printed form or a strange disk. He'd get a PC and keep it at home. All Falloni Marine's purchase orders originated from him. All bills came across his desk. All payments were cleared by him. It was going to be easy. The only conceivable risk was that Lynette might notice an unusual amount going to a new supplier. He could explain that, if she ever ask.

Pete decided to base Preferred Wholesale in Monroe, Michigan. It was right on Lake Erie half way between Toledo and Detroit. He knew the town well. It was a third the size of Sandusky, but it was big enough that his comings and goings should not be noticed. On a clear day you could see the stacks in Monroe from the Marblehead Light House or Perry's Monument on South Bass Island. He could drive to Monroe in an hour and a half or two hours. He could even go by boat. His twenty-one foot runabout could make it in about two hours. He paid another visit to the library to look up lawyers in Monroe in the Martindale Hubbell directory. He chose a solo practitioner with a high numbered street address. He decided that a small office meant less people with access to his file. Also, he thought the solo lawyer was less likely to hang around talking to other lawyers. Finally, with an address away from the rest of the local lawyers whose offices clustered around the courthouse, the lawyer would have less opportunity to chat.

Pete called, and the lawyer answered his own phone. Pete tersely described his desire to incorporate and asked for an appointment. The lawyer asked several questions, then said it could be done over the phone. Pete liked that. They would never meet. Pete gave him the proposed corporate name, that it would be engaged in the business of the wholesale trade, that it would be an S corporation in which he would own 100% of the stock. When the lawyer sought his address, Pete told him he was in the process of moving and would call back with the new address. The lawyer promised it would be done within a week. When asked for his telephone, Pete explained that he could be reached at an Ohio number for the next few days, and Pete gave the number of the private line that rang only in his office.

The next afternoon, Pete drove over to Monroe. His first stop was the Post Office. There he rented a large box. He used the business name and did not put down a street address, only Monroe and the Zip code. The clerk did not notice. He paid cash for a month, and was told they'd leave a bill in his box in the future. Then he went to the largest bank downtown. He opened a checking account in the name of the business with $500 cash. The bank clerk wanted an Internal Revenue Service identification number for the corporation. He said he didn't know it offhand. She said she could use his social security number temporarily. He laughed and said he didn't like doing that, that he'd call back with the number. She agreed and opened the account. She gave him a starter set of checks, and he selected the check style he wanted for the computer printer checks. He gave her the post office box number for the address on the checks, but no phone number. His next stop was a local printer. He ordered purchase orders, invoices, letterhead, envelopes, and business cards, all in the business name. He persuaded the printer that it was a rush and agreed to pay 50% more than list. He went out for a cup of coffee and returned an hour later to pick up the business forms.

He was excited all the way home. When he got to Sandusky, he went directly to the office. Everyone else was gone. He went into his office and typed a letter to the lawyer using the new letterhead. In the letter he asked the lawyer to apply for an I.R.S. identification number for the corporation. Pete did not want to put his name on anything that he could avoid. The following week he bought a personal computer for his home office. He loaded all the software from work and set up the accounting, billing, and checking systems for the new business. The day after he was satisfied that everything was working, he started placing orders in the name of Preferred Wholesale. He cut his deals as always and casually told each supplier to change the name of the buyer to the new company in Monroe. He reminded them to be sure to continue to ship directly to Falloni Marine in Sandusky.

Pete could not believe how easy it was to get the system going and how smoothly it operated. There was a package that was too large for his post office box waiting for him when he made his second trip to Monroe. It was all the corporate documents, a minutebook, and a corporate seal. There was a letter from the lawyer instructing him how to fill in various forms, and implying that the lawyer would handle the formality of minutes for an annual meeting each year. Pete recognized the documents as nearly identical to those used in their Ohio businesses, so he resolved to take care of the formalities himself. When the lawyer's bill came, Pete sent a letter along with a Preferred Wholesale check stating that no future services would be required. Pete continued to enter orders into the purchase order system at the office, except that they were issued to Preferred Wholesale for ten percent more than the price he had negotiated with the supplier. Lynette printed and sent the orders to Monroe. She never asked.

Once or twice a week he took a disk home with the P.O. data and copied it into Preferred's system. Even at home he kept all the Preferred Wholesale forms in a locked file. Anything that left his home office, he carried in a locked brief case. He kept the only keys to both the filing cabinet and his brief case with his car keys. He printed purchase orders from Preferred to the suppliers at the lower negotiated prices. He printed invoices from Preferred to Falloni Marine at the higher prices which matched Falloni's purchase orders to Preferred. He mailed these from Monroe during his quick visits there. When the goods were received by Falloni Marine, the packing lists continued to flow across his desk. He used his computer to enter the goods received into inventory. He took the matching Preferred invoices from his brief case, stapled them to the receiving documents, and authorized payment on the paper and in his computer. He gave the paperwork and disk to Lynette. Falloni checks were issued and sent to the post office box in Monroe in the ordinary course. When he went to Monroe, he deposited them in the local bank. At home in the evening, Pete issued payment checks from Preferred Wholesale's Michigan bank to its suppliers in the same fashion. He sent them from Monroe on his next visit.

Much to Pete's satisfaction, money quickly piled up in the Michigan bank account. In one month he recovered all his start-up costs. He religiously kept computerized accounts on the new corporation and never tired of inspecting its financial statements on the screen. The company had one asset, his computer. It's only expenses were the initial legal fees, and the continuing stationery expense and post office box rental. Preferred made $6,000 a month, on average. He was careful never to print these statements. It was great to run a profitable business, especially when all the profits accrued to him. He loved the Income Statement more than anything. He studied it trying to determine where he could make improvements. The statements were so clean that they indicated little room for improvement.

In fact, as time passed, Pete did make improvements. He found ways to make his computer work even easier. Through the bank, he set up a lockbox with a different post office box number just for receiving payment checks. Falloni Marine's payment checks were sent to it. A bank clerk opened that mail and automatically deposited the payments into Preferred's checking account. That cut out his need to carry checks from the post office to the banking lobby, it also cut down the float. He also set up a personal account at the bank. With a telephone call, he could transfer money from the corporate account into his personal account. He still had to go to Monroe to send invoices to Falloni Marine, and pick up the invoices from and send payments to the suppliers. Later, and again with help from the bank, he began making direct electronic funds transfers. This way he could pay his suppliers without issuing checks. He had a modem installed in his home computer. Through it, he could tap into his account at the bank and transfer payments into any other bank account in the United States. All he needed was the routing number and account number that is printed on the bottom of every check. Not one supplier resisted in giving that information when they realized that they would get paid more quickly and with less float. Pete also transferred money into his own account through the modem. He toyed with the idea of EFT for Falloni Marine, but his father already complained that they paid their bills too quickly. Pete shelved that improvement for another day.

Pete still had to go to Monroe to send invoices to Falloni Marine; but he cut his trips back, sometimes going only once a month. He deliberately went on different days and at different times so that no one would notice a pattern. He simply disappeared for a few hours on the excuse of meeting someone to look at a boat, meeting a supplier, playing golf, or boating. In the summer, he often shot across the lake in his boat, cruising up River Raisin to the marina in downtown Monroe. He doubled his personal income. He deserved it. He reported it all on his tax return. In his way of thinking, that made it all legitimate. After all, he earned it.

In 1986, Pete and Sarah bought their dream house. It was one of the large stately homes along Columbus Street about a mile south of the downtown waterfront. It was over one hundred and thirty years old. Unlike most of its wood frame neighbors, this house was built from solid limestone blocks harvested from local quarries. The main body of the house was perfectly square with two massive square cut pillars supporting the roof over the main entrance, which also served as a balcony off the master bedroom. Around the top were stone battlements which made the house look like a small castle, as its designer intended. Inside, the house was equally solid and massive. The only improvement they made was the addition of storm windows. Mr. Falloni never asked Pete about the cost of the house. He seemed to take for granted that Pete could afford it. That silence irritated Pete. His father must have become callous to his wealth, thinking everyone had as much. Pete had struggled to earn this house. The mortgage was a stretch, even with his higher income. He deserved it. The most Mr. Falloni said was that it was a good place to raise children. It was not lost on Pete that his father and mother still lived in a house more modest than the one Pete and Sarah were leaving behind, and in which they had raised a bigger family. Pete could not have been more pleased with any other home in the city. Sarah finally felt she had reached her station.

CHAPTER 6

Pete Falloni found the cigar on the dash of his father's car. His father's teeth marks were still in it. The cigar was wedged between the windshield and dash, tip first. It had been Pete's task to get the car. Just before noon his father had been driving southeast out of town on Perkins. He was headed for the country club, lunch, a game of golf, and a late afternoon drunk. That had become his routine. Mornings at business, afternoons at the country club. They said it was a heart attack. They said he never knew what hit him. They said it was a massive heart attack. They said he was dead before he swerved off the road, dead before he bounced across the ditch, dead before the car stopped in the wheat field. The emergency squad had taken him to the hospital, but they knew he was dead. He was dead when they got there. A lady in a car coming up Perkins saw the whole thing. She knew the Falloni's. She stopped, ran to find him dead, called, then returned to watch over the dead.

She also came by the house that afternoon. His mother was in no condition, so Pete talked to her. She was eager to tell him the details. She saw the look on his face just before he jerked forward then fell over. She seemed driven by a belief that they would be better off knowing. Pete was polite, listened, then thanked her as he escorted her to her car. She said she thought they would want to know. When Pete came back inside, a policeman was on the phone. His sister gave it to him. They wanted to know about the car. Would the family be getting it, or should he make arrangements to have it towed. Pete told him that he would take care of it.

Pete was glad to have an excuse to get out of his parents' small house. He and his sisters had been there all afternoon with his mother. It wasn't the wailing. It wasn't the rosaries. It wasn't the eating. It was the gathering that drove Pete away. In the last year or two, Pete had become quite solitary, keeping his own counsel in all things. He needed to be alone to think things through. He needed to think about what this meant to the business. Pete called Joe and asked him to come by the house with his truck. Together, they would pull his Dad's car out of the field.

Pete was waiting just inside the front door when Joe pulled up and jogged out to the curb. As Pete settled into the pick-up, Joe expressed his shock. He tried to say how much Mr. Falloni had meant to him, how he had helped him land on his feet after Molly, but Pete cut him short. Pete thanked him for his kind thoughts. A moment later Pete caught a glimpse of Joe wiping a tear out of the corner of his eye. Joe noticed, and said that Pete's father was a great guy, cut without a pattern. It was his personality, nothing else that had made the business. He had built the business on the force of his personality. Pete looked out the window and did not respond.

Pete had never truly thought through the consequences of his father's death to the business. He analyzed and calculated every other move. He prided himself that he considered every contingency. He had even helped draft his father's estate plan, but that had been an intellectual exercise. He never thought about it as if it might really happen. Somehow, this one escaped him. He felt more alone than he ever had in his life. He did not just feel alone, he felt lonely. He tried to force himself to think about business, but he could not get beyond his pain. Mostly, he stared off at nothing, his mind blank.

When he could think, he considered his grief. That, more than anything else about the process of death and grieving surprised him. He could not concentrate on business matters, and he would not let himself consider his pain, but he did let himself focus on the process. Death and grief were new to him. He analyzed it. First, he was shocked; that was normal. Now he felt alone, adrift. He would never have guessed that would be his reaction. The last few years, he had focused all his frustration into resenting his father, his money, his indifference to Pete's finances. From this anger, he had constructed an elaborate fraud. Now his father was gone. Pete had simply never considered how that would leave him alone. He was amazed. So amazed, that despite his reflection, it did not occur to him that he had defined himself in terms of his father, even if that were by opposition and treachery. Now the defining essence of his career, his own life was gone. He ached from the loneliness. He knew what he felt, and he tried to understand it, but he never did. He simply wanted it to pass. He wanted it all to pass.

They got the car out with little difficulty. Pete was able to drive across the field. It was dry. He backed the car out the same tracks his father had made. He tried to minimize the damage to the crop. He needed to remember to call the farmer and offer compensation. He got hung up in the ditch. Joe tied a long line they used to tow boats between his truck and the car. With slightly more than a nudge from the truck, Pete overcame the ditch and parked the car along the berm of the road. Pete jumped out of the car and helped Joe disconnect the line. He told Joe they hadn't made funeral plans yet, but he'd let him know. He told him to make sure that whatever had to get done, did get done; and that beyond that, they could take it easy. They'd close the business the day of the funeral. Joe left him there.

Pete sat alone in the car for a moment. The radio was still on. It was the station his father always listened to. His father had turned the radio on. He wanted to turn it off, to at least change the station. He couldn't bring himself to do it. He drove, slowly at first, then with the traffic. His eyes came to rest on the cigar. A spasm gripped his body. He clenched the steering wheel with both hands and fought back with a groan. Coming up to the first stop light on the edge of town, he relaxed, but tears started rolling down his cheeks. Waiting at the light, he leaned forward and gently removed the cigar. He smelled it. He held it out and inspected the teeth marks. He resisted an urge to put it in his mouth. He laid it carefully on the seat. He drove to his own home. Sarah wasn't there. He found a note that she had taken the kids to her parents and would meet him at his mother's. He found a zip-lock bag in the kitchen. He put the cigar in it. Then he took it to their bedroom, and put it under the clothes in one of his dresser drawers.

Joe was a pallbearer. So were Red, Pete, and the husbands of Pete's sisters. Joe had not talked to Pete since the ride to pick up the car. Red had come up to Joe the night before at the viewing and asked him. Red said that Mrs. Falloni wanted Joe, that Mr. Falloni had thought the world of him. The morning of the funeral promised a beautiful early summer day. It was May, 1987. Joe stayed outside the funeral home as long as he could, pulling in the crisp smell of the season. Inside, the family was up front. He hung back, taking a seat in the rear. There was a brief prayer. As the people filed out and the casket was closed, Red caught his eye and summoned him. The pall bearers watched as the funeral director wheeled the casket to the side door. There they helped place it in the hearse for the ride downtown to St. Mary's. He hadn't been in this church since Molly died. He forced himself to keep his thoughts in the present. Joe was struck at how small the crowd seemed in the large church. He counted heads. He studied the stained glass. He looked up at the ceiling for signs of leaks. He satisfied himself that they took good care of the building. It was the incense that brought him back. It brought him back to this funeral and funerals long before. He felt as if he were suffocating. He gripped the pew in front of him, to keep from running out. The priest seemed to be finishing up. He would make it. At the cemetery, Joe paid his respects to Mrs. Falloni. She invited him to the house for lunch. As the cars pulled away, Joe stayed behind to visit the graves of his wife and daughter. He couldn't find Mrs. Oleschewski's grave. On the way to Falloni's, he thought about taking the afternoon to drive down to Attica to visit his parents. Memorial Day was coming. There was too much to be done at work, especially with the day lost for this funeral. After lunch he'd go to work and try to keep some things moving.

About dusk, Joe was surprised to hear voices coming from the office. Actually, it wasn't the voices that caught his attention as much as their tone. When he came to work after the funeral, he had been the only one there. There were no cars parked by the office entrance and the lights were off. He drove around to the back and came in through the shop. He went first into the shop office and got on the computer. He booted up the project management software Pete had recently added, and checked the status of the work-in-progress and the backlog. It was a great system. It was the kind of thing that Mr. Falloni would have grumbled about, but he would have appreciated it. Joe used it everyday, first thing.

The system always greeted Joe with a list of reminders of items that were scheduled for that day. After that he studied the bar charts that showed the percentage of completion on each boat. The system was organized by boat number, but he had the capability to get in by owner's name if he wished. He typed out daily work lists for the guys, and printed them out. Each morning Joe had a brief meeting with the men to make the assignments. When they finished the assignments and returned the sheets, Joe inspected the work, then entered the completion into the system. The management system was linked with the billing system, to the extent that the shop clerk could not issue a bill until Joe entered its completion.

That day, studying the screens, Joe noted that the electronic's shop was slightly behind schedule. He scrolled through the individual orders, and picked a few to work on. He printed them, shut the computer down, and spent the afternoon in the marine electronic's shop. It shared a wall with Pete's office. Had Joe not come into work, he might have spent the afternoon in a very similar fashion tinkering with gadgets in his own radio shack at home. The afternoon slipped away before he knew it. He was about to pack up when he heard the argument. He immediately recognized Pete's voice. It took him a few minutes to conclude from the substance of the conversation that the other was the lawyer. His first reaction was to see if there were trouble. He stopped himself when he realized that it was just Pete on another tirade. Then he was about to continue closing up, but he thought that Pete might turn the venom his way. He resolved to wait them out. He went back to work on a radio. He tried not to listen, but the factory was quiet and the voices were clear.

"This is a problem. This is a serious problem! How could you let this happen?"

"I don't understand you. You were there. You were more involved in writing the will and trust than he was for Christ's sake. You knew the terms of the estate plan. We've taken full advantage of the marital deduction and qualified terminal interest provisions to minimize death taxes. Under the trust, his assets are split equally among you and your sisters, but all income goes to your mother during her life. You cannot touch the assets or get any income until she passes."

"My mother does not need income from this business. He had millions salted away. You'll find out when you inventory his estate. I don't know the total or what it's invested in, but I know what he took out of here. It was millions. My mother's income might be over $300,000 a year without another penny from this business. She doesn't need the money. She won't know what to do with it when she gets it. It's ridiculous! We can use the money in the business."

"I don't know what to tell you. It's not like any of this was a big secret. If you didn't like it, you should have spoken up. The man's dead. We can't rewrite his will."

"You've got to find a way out of this. I cannot tolerate this. You know how my mother lives. She truly does not need the money. I do!"

"Well, let's think. Everything that flows into the trust for her comes in the form of a dividend from the corporations. It would be possible to reduce the dividends, provided the board of directors approves. There always should be a business interest to support their action, you know, investing in the business, building the business."

"Now you're thinking. The board was my Dad and I. Now, I'll just...."

"Not quite so fast. You and your father held all the stock. The by-laws required three directors, but since we only had two shareholders, we ignored it. We can't do that any more. Now its you and your sisters, of course, you have more stock than them because you started with 10%, and you've got the veto; but the shareholders have to elect directors, and the directors have to approve things like dividends, even if all the dividends flow to your mother."

"This is impossible. My sisters will do whatever their husbands tell them. None of them know shit about this business. I can't operate like this."

"Pete, you do not have a choice."

"Bullshit! You better get me out of this or I will get a lawyer who will."

"I think you are over-reacting. You sit down with your sisters once a year, go over a financial statement, and elect directors."

"No fucking way."

"It won't be that bad. I'm in these family meetings all the time. They will do whatever you want."

"They will do what their husbands tell them. Maybe not right away, but they will eventually. I cannot have this."

"Remember the 85% provision. They may oppose you, but they cannot do anything without you."

"I cannot operate a business under the constant threat of deadlock."

"The by-laws require three directors. Pick out two of your sisters who are the least likely to give you trouble, maybe the one's with the least sophisticated husbands. Maybe rotate them all through by letting them serve one year terms, that way they won't follow things too closely. All you have to do is present the numbers in a way to show a bona fide business reason for what you want. Any board action exercising business judgment can never be challenged. There's always a reason to investment in the business, to set up a reserve."

"What about my salary? Am I going to have to have them

approve my salary?"

"Shareholders elect directors. Directors elect officers and establish their compensation."

"One of their husbands pumps gas. How is she ever going to understand what the president of a corporation makes?"

"Two corporations, but that's not the point. Start with your father's salary. They won't argue with that. They know he was basically retired. You become president and bump up to his salary. Tell them the businesses will actually be saving money by one less salary."

"Sounds good, but that's more profit. More profit means more dividend. I am not about to pay dividends to an old lady who does not need nor want more money."

"Accounting, Pete. It's all accounting. You're ten times the accountant I am. The money can go to dividends, but it can also go into business expenses or capital investments. Get creative."

"Yeah." Pete drifted off in thought. After a moment he nodded agreement. "OK for now, but I want rid of them."

"Who?"

"My sisters, goddamn it."

"You mean you want to buy them out?"

"No! Why should I pay them? They didn't do anything to earn the stock. I work here. I built this up."

"Pete, it was your father's property. He had every right to dispose of it as he saw fit. He chose to leave it to his wife and children. He did not choose to leave it all to you."

"Jesus Christ, do I have to do all your thinking for you? I read the Wall Street Journal. Classify their stock and we'll squeeze them out, freeze them out, whatever the hell you bastards call it."

"Pete, you can buy their stock, if they agree to sell. If 85% of the shareholders approve, you could convert them to preferred stock. They would no longer have a vote, but they would have a guaranteed dividend."

"You are not listening. I am not going to pay a dividend to my mother or to them. They do not deserve it. I do. I want all the common stock. I have to have absolute control. I cannot work with nit-wits. We'll give them non-voting, common stock; no preference, no dividend."

"You can't take someone's property without paying for it."

"Bullshit! Read the paper. You figure out how to do it, or...."

"Pete, you listen to me. I have done a good job for you, and you have paid me well. I hope to continue to represent you and this business. I will do as good a job for you as any lawyer I know. I will not, however, be threatened. You lay down one more ultimatum, and it will be the last. I know what the fuck you want, and I know how to get there. It will take time and care. You do it any other way, and you might find your ass in jail. You just need to be patient."

"I'm sorry. You're right. Sorry. The funeral today. A lot of things are piling up on me. Sorry."

"Just be patient. Good things come to those who wait."

Moments later, Joe heard a car drive out. It was not Pete's Corvette. Pete sat alone in his office staring at his knees. To the extent he thought about anything, it was in anger at having to work through the lawyer. Just wait! He had waited too long already. He hated collaboration. He worked better alone. That way he could control all of the variables. He could handle his mother. The lawyer and his sisters were problems. He was not sure of his control. He was not about to wait. He kept losing track of his thoughts and started through them over again. Finally, he quit trying to concentrate and simply stared into space.

Later, when Pete backed out of his parking space, he noticed a light in one of the shop windows. For an instant he had an impulse to check on it. He let it go. It was Joe. It had to be Joe. He was weird. He had no life. He was smart. He knew as much about the computers as anyone at work, but there was no way he could ever get anything serious out of the shop computer. He would never network the computers. That was too much of a risk. There was a limit to Joe's intelligence. Why else would he work for someone else? He worked his ass off for the Falloni's, but for a wage. He was a simple minded wage-slave. Joe may be smart, but he was flawed. He did not have a clue about business, money, the things that really mattered. What a chump!

CHAPTER 7

I got a telephone call from Joe a couple of years after we ran into each other out on South Bass Island. I hadn't seen him since then. His call would have been in the summer of '87, maybe '88. I remember it was summer because I tried to talk to him about my plane, about maybe flying up to see him. I usually flew up to the islands several times each summer.

Joe never called, and he didn't call to chit-chat. He said he needed some legal advice. It was one of those tentative calls that lawyers get all the time. I don't even bother to make notes of them anymore. Most of the time, nothing ever comes of them. The way I see it, there will be plenty of time for me to dig in if things get serious, and I get hired. I just listen and shoot from the hip. Maybe a quick thought will solve their problem. I make it a point never to ask too many questions in these calls, because I know where it's going, nowhere. I get enough to give a quick response and tell them to call back if they think they need a lawyer. I'm sure I wouldn't even remember this call, except it was from Joe.

Joe said it involved an estate and corporations. He said he wasn't personally involved. It was people that he knew. He wanted to know if it was legal for a corporation not to pay a dividend. Naturally, I told him I wasn't a corporate or estate lawyer, covering my rear, but I did say I saw a lot of white collar shenanigans in the criminal cases I handled. I told him that corporations did not have to pay a dividends, especially if they were losing money. Profit usually meant dividends. He changed the question. Was it legal for a profitable business not to pay dividends? I said I thought so, as long as the board of directors approved. Corporations, just like people, can save money for a rainy day or maybe invest in something.

Then he wanted to know about stocks. Was it legal to take

someone's stock without paying for it? Stealing was stealing, I said; but in corporate securities, there were all kinds wrinkles. There were federal laws, state laws, and also whatever by-laws the corporation had. In general, you couldn't take someone's stock without paying, but that didn't have to be in cash. A lot of times majorities squeezed out minorities by printing a different class of stock and forcing an exchange. It was difficult to say what was legal or illegal. It depended. Again he changed the question. Could a minority squeeze the majority into non-voting common stock with no dividend? I laughed and tried to wiggle out by telling him that I was struggling to remember things I hadn't thought about since law school. I told him the key was "fair value" whatever that meant. To me giving up voting for non-voting common stock without getting something else, like a cash payment, preference, or dividend was not fair; but securities questions are not that simple.

On the subject of the minority getting rid of the majority, I told him that was done all the time. I told him it was usually the management of the company, the insiders, getting rid of the outside shareholders. I told him the typical scenario is that the insiders make the financial statements look bad so the price of the stock goes down, then they buy out the shareholders for a little premium over the depressed market price with the company's cash reserves. The shareholders are usually happy to get out. Joe caught on quickly. You mean you can buy somebody out with their own money? I congratulated him and told him it was done everyday. He wanted to know how that could be legal especially if the financial statements had been fudged and the price rigged?

Now, I told him, he was getting into something I knew about. If the numbers were fudged, then any of the decisions based upon them could be undone. People could even go to jail. Most of the time, however, the numbers were somewhere in the middle; not right, but not really wrong. Shareholders usually took the money and ran. Dissenters could sue, but usually settled for a little more money and their legal fees. I told him I didn't do that kind of work, except the criminal side of it.

Joe said he thought he overheard a scheme to do just what I described. He wanted to know if he should report it. I asked if he owned stock in the company. He didn't. I told him that the best place to start was with a shareholder. They were the ones with a stake in the action. They could take it up with the company's management, vote for new management, or if not satisfied, sue. He thought he should call the police or the FBI I told him that he could, but he really might be getting ahead of the action and stepping into something that he simply misunderstood. I told him the feds would probably not be interested unless it was a public corporation and there was some serious funny business like embezzling, extortion, or tax evasion going on. The local constabulary would probably take the view that it was an internal corporate problem. In most cases, criminal prosecutions came after civil suits by shareholders who got the ball rolling. I told him that if it were me, I'd start by informing a shareholder.

I could tell that he didn't like my answers. I tried to lighten it up a little by giving him the old one about steal from a bank and you get your picture on a wanted poster, steal the bank and you get your picture on the cover of a magazine. That didn't work. I could tell that there was nothing in it for me, so I didn't pursue it any further. I represented the kind of people he was complaining about, the real slick thieves, but I didn't tell him that.

I had a hard time keeping Joe on the phone after that. There was nothing unusual in that. He was never one for small talk. We promised to get together, maybe in Attica, maybe the next time I flew up to the Islands with my kids. I remember that he didn't ask about my plane, even though I volunteered. That was Joe. He would think he was prying. Well, we never did get together. The time just slipped on by. I had no contact with Joe after that until I got another phone call last year.

CHAPTER 8

Sandy did not expect that her new career would bring her home each day. In fact, she expected just the opposite. To some degree the gypsy life had attracted her, especially after her initial tour of the heartland. By its very nature, however, her cargo and charter flights were usually day hops. Even when she flew checks or urgent cargo runs at night, she eventually ended up in her own bed. When she got her twin, which she did just before Christmas in 1991, the increased airspeed not only attracted business, it also got her home earlier. She traveled so much that sometimes she would struggle to remember where she had flown that day as she drifted off to sleep at night. It was not the way she had envisioned it, and because of that, she deliberately found excuses to stay out overnight at least once a week.

Actually, she did not have to look far for an excuse. She regularly ferried her planes to small airports for service and waited overnight for it to be done. Bonair Aircraft now had two planes. The original Debonair/F33, which she now had on lease to a flight school as an IFR trainer; and a light twin Beech Duchess, which she leased to Bonair Aviation, Inc., her new Part 135 cargo and taxi operation. Federal inspection and maintenance requirements on the two planes was a time consuming task in itself. Each plane averaged over 50 engine hours a month, so she faced the required 100 hour inspection every six weeks or so. That meant she was getting a major inspection on one of the planes every three weeks. In addition, something, usually the avionics, was constantly breaking down or at least malfunctioning. There were FBO's at Detroit City that could provide all the services she needed, however, in a large city they naturally charged more than operators in remote airports. Sandy used her maintenance requirements to shop for bargains. The truth was, the cost of the ferry flights and overnight stays more than offset the price savings, but they were business expenses and Sandy enjoyed the getaways.

Sandy wasted no time establishing her own cargo/taxi service. She set up a second corporation, Bonair Aviation, Inc. just as she had the first. She did that and started wading through the stack of Federal Aviation Administration forms required to license her own operation even while she was still flying for other operators and learning the business from them. By comparison, she considered tax forms less onerous than those required by the FAA. She erred on the side of providing too much explanation and caused unnecessary delays in the process. She finally called and was lucky enough to speak with the examiner who was processing her application. After a little friendly advise, Sandy withdrew the initial application and resubmitted. There were printed forms for everything, forms to further supplement supplemental forms. As she encountered these she would have to call the FAA and ask for the next form. Weeks passed, but it all finally came together. Sandy eventually grasped the central concept, demonstrating her responsibility; and thereafter, all the documentation of experience, insurance, and inspections seemed less burdensome. When she got her certificate, she quickly forgot the burdens.

She also spent much of her free time in 1991 shopping for a twin. She was in less of a hurry than with her first plane. She continued to work through the Beech dealer at Detroit City, but as is usually the case with planes, the prospective planes were scattered across the country. Sandy learned the truth of the hanger talk, you need a plane to buy a plane. The only practical way to get to most of the planes that fit her profile was to fly into a small field. She had no intention of attempting to circumvent the Beech broker, and he trusted her, so she often went alone. She frequently took the long way home from a charter to test fly the candidates. By the end of the process, Sandy knew as much as the Beech broker, and could easily have done it without him. He did handle the price negotiations, which was a relief to her.

Along the way Sandy had acquired a stack of books on how to buy airplanes. She photocopied a checklist of the ultimate prepurchase inspection from one, and filled it out on each plane she considered. In addition to Trade-A-Plane, she also subscribed to a service that provided market values for used planes. She got to the point where she could work the formula and price a plane in her head. Like anything, prices were based on standards. The book values were based upon average total hours on the airframe, mid-time engines and propellers, and average avionics packages. Since the engines have fixed hours between rebuilds, and rebuilt engines have known prices, she could quickly adjust the book price by the actual hours on the engines. So long as there was no visible corrosion on the airframe and no damage history, she accepted that part of average price. She wouldn't even look at a plane that did not have a fully operational IFR package, however, her shopping inevitably got down to the avionics and the paint job. High end avionics and a fresh paint job were not usually reflected in the price, and that is where Sandy and every other sophisticated aircraft purchaser looked for the deals, not price but value.

The broker did get the price down, but then everyone knew where it had to go. Sandy didn't mind, for that was a part of the game she didn't want to play anyway. The price concessions slightly exceeded the amount of the brokerage commission, so it looked like they earned their keep. The plane sold within a hair's breath of the formula price at $75,000, and she got a new paint job and top of the line avionics. She also had a soft spot for the T-tail. It was like the Skipper in which she had initially trained. This time the paperwork was done in advance. They exchanged documents by telecopier and approved everything for form before she left to get the plane. She transferred money into her Bonair Aircraft account, and got a cashier's check which she carried with her to the closing. She and her former instructor, the Beech broker, flew into Decatur, Illinois to close the deal and take delivery. The plane was owned by a contractor whose business could no longer justify the aircraft. The owner of the business loved airplanes, had taken good care of this one, and knew what it took to sell it. They met in a hanger where he kept the plane. He was going to lose the hanger also. Sandy felt bad for him, but resolved that she needed to get a hanger of her own. The broker flew her Debonair back to Detroit with his commission check. Since they closed on a Friday and Sandy wanted to spend some time in her new plane, she flew to Muscatine, Iowa.

She chose Muscatine, Iowa, for no particular reason. She had landed at Muscatine Municipal once on a parts flight but had only been there long enough to refuel and have a soft drink in the pilots' lounge. She remembered it as a nice place, so she went back. Enroute she decided that she'd stay someplace nicer than the usual, which was whatever Mom & Pop motel was closest to the field. She would stay in a nice place and have a nice meal. It wasn't everyday she bought a new plane and launched a new business. It was close to Christmas. She would treat herself to a gift. She was a little impatient with the twelve mile ride in the motel courtesy van, but the young man driving pointed out the sites and gave her a feel for local history.

When she checked into the motel, she cast a quick look into the gift shop off the lobby to see if they carried skin magazines. Although they did, she decided to wait. In the room, she checked the cable TV. They carried adult movies. She'd do that instead. She called her voice mail service for messages, there were none. She showered and got back into the same clothes. She no longer felt like going out to a restaurant, so she gathered her papers and went to the motel restaurant. There she double checked the purchase documents while she waited for her meal. Back in the room, she tuned in the X-rated channel before she put her papers down. She came back to sit on the edge of the bed in front of the TV. After a few moments she got up, hung her clothes, and laid back on the bed with the lotion she had gotten from her toiletry bag. She woke when another feature started. She left the TV on, drew a hot bath, and listened from the tub. Feeling stimulated and cramped in the tub, she dried quickly and climbed under the covers. She propped herself up on two pillows, reached for the lotion and turned off the light. When she checked out the next morning, she was relieved to find that they had only charged her for one movie.

The flight home was uneventful. There was a solid layer of overcast at 6,000 feet. Sandy initially planned to return IFR, and looked forward to penetrating the cloud layer and getting up into the sunshine. After taking off, however, she saw she had good fifteen mile visibility. Even though it was a cold winter day, there was something warm and comfortable about staying below the cloud cover. When she radioed to open her flight plan, she amended to VFR. She broke out her sectional charts and worked her way home at 4,500 feet. She tied down next to her Debonair in Detroit City. After going home to unpack and check the mail, she went back to the airport with her camera. She took several pictures of each plane and both of them together. Later that afternoon she tried to reach Bob. She hoped to convince him to let her come pick him up from school in her new plane.

Saturday night at home alone was no fun. She caught up on her mail, paid bills, and attended to her accounts. She ran the TV in her living room for companionship, but she also had the radio in her office playing soft music. She spent most of the evening drafting an announcement that Bonair Aviation now had two aircraft at its disposal and updating her rate sheets. She hoped the photos she had taken would be good enough to include in the announcement. She decided that she couldn't afford to wait on the printer, so she proceeded to draft a less formal announcement in the form of a letter to be sent to all the local operators and also their customers whom she had flown for previously. Some of them had starting calling her direct, even before she got her Part 135 Certificate. About 10:00 P.M. she called it a day. She raided the refrigerator and settled in front of the TV. She did not like TV, but she watched it on nights like this. She had a VCR, but she did not like the inconvenience of renting videos. She curled up on her sofa and watched a show that bored her.

Once she had rented an X-rated video, but only once. It embarrassed her to take it to the clerk. She found it was not the same thrill at home that it was in a motel room. She worried that someone might come to visit and notice the tape. She even worried when she took it back, that she might get in an automobile wreck and the tape would be listed among her personal effects. She did regularly enjoy the videos in the larger motels. More often, when she stayed in the smaller motels, she bought a magazine and used it. She was also careful not to leave the magazines behind in her room. She put them back in the brown bag and threw them in whatever trash bin she could find. She never ran the risk of carrying a magazine in her flight bag or luggage.

On occasion she took the time on long flights to think through this aspect of her life, her secret life. To her way of thinking, it should be secret, for the excitement of being naughty, if nothing else. She was not ashamed. She had learned much from the magazines and the movies that she wished she had known twenty years before. Maybe things might be different. It was too late to be thinking like that. She was content. She wondered how she would be with a man now. Better, she was sure of that. Better for both of them. She had learned. It was an education. She pondered the dilemma of a secret life that was satisfying primarily because it was kept secret, but could be enjoyed only if it was open enough to be studied and learned. She never got beyond this point. She had not invented the world. She just lived in it. She thought of the men who inhabited the motel bars. They seemed so lonely, as lonely as her. No, she wouldn't do that.

Sunday was routine. She went to church with her parents. Daryl sat down the pew from her. At brunch they talked about Bob. She mentioned her new plane, but no one pursued the topic. She spent the afternoon at the airport. She sat in the Duchess and read the pilot's operating manual. She brought a label maker. She numbered the radios and made labels for the V speeds. She put labels wherever she thought it was appropriate. She swept the carpeting and cleaned the windows. She bought Chinese carry-out on the way home and ate it in front of the TV. She resisted the weight of the evening alone by getting out her flight planning chart to see where she might go for an overnight the following weekend. She could pick Bob up in Boston. As she hunched over the chart on her kitchen table, her phone rang. It was Pete Falloni from Sandusky, Ohio. He claimed to have an emergency.

She explained to him that she was no longer flying for others, but was now operating her own company. That was fine with him. He wanted to talk price. She held firm. She hated price negotiations. Without saying it, she wondered if the likes of Pete Falloni let people haggle their prices down. She was sure that he would be highly insulted if anyone questioned the prices he charged. Oh well, it was part of business. She was really in business now. This was her first order. She did not want to spend Sunday night at home alone anyway. This was why she did what she did. This was great. While others sat home in front of the boob tube, she would be overhead looking down on them. She started getting excited about the night ahead, even while she talked to him. She told him where her plane was parked and gave him the N number of the twin. He described the man who would meet her. She asked about size and weight. He estimated that the shipment could not possibly weigh more than one hundred pounds. Everything went as planned.

A station wagon pulled up on the other side of the fence just as she finished preflighting the plane. She casually took her tear gas canister off her purse and walked over to the fence. Before Sandy said anything, the man said her name and that he had a delivery for Falloni. She acknowledged that he was in the right place. He went to the back of the station wagon and pulled out a dozen white foam packages. Each was about the size of a lunch box. Each was sealed in clear shrink-wrap. The only labeling on any of them were identification numbers and bar codes. He carried them through the gate and over to the plane. Sandy took them from him two at a time and laid them in the back of the aircraft. She thought to herself that there wasn't even enough to worry with weight and balance. He quickly said good night and walked away before she got a good look at his face.

When she taxied out, she remembered that he had not had her sign anything. That was unusual. Oh well, it was not her problem. It was a crisp, star-filled night. They were calling twenty mile visibility, but it was unlimited. On take off, she could feel the additional lift of the cold night air under the wings. The plane seemed to jump off the ground. She saw the glow from Toledo as she climbed out of Detroit City. She loved nights like this. She flew VFR down the Detroit River, taking care to stay out of Canadian airspace. That was no big deal, but she'd rather enjoy the flight than do radio work. Cutting southeast across Lake Erie, she watched the lights along the southern shore. Within what seemed to her to be only a few minutes, she was over the Lake Erie Islands. When she put in the frequency for Griffing Field, she wondered what could be so urgent that the fellow couldn't have driven the couple of hours to Sandusky. That much time had passed since Falloni called. Whatever, it was money for her. Falloni was waiting when she got there. On the way back to Detroit, it dawned on her that he didn't have any paperwork for her to sign either.

CHAPTER 9

The instant Joe saw her, he recognized her. She was sitting in a lawn chair beside the pool of The Maples Motel reading a book. She was sunning herself in a one piece swimming suit. He was tired and was cruise cranking the last few miles of his ride back into Sandusky. He was well on the way to getting back into shape, finishing a fifty miler. He had started early that morning, heading south along the county roads. Ten miles out, he turned east and rode another twenty miles. Just outside Vermillion, he picked up Route 6 west to Sandusky. He rode on past the motel, wanting, but afraid to stop. A plane taking off from Griffing caught his attention, and he slowed to look up at it. When he looked back to the road, he gathered up his nerve and turned back to the motel. Sandy watched as he rode in, she did not recognize him until he took off his helmet.

"Hi." She smiled.

"Hi. Joe Altznauer. We seem to keep running into each other."

"Sandy Dobbins. You ride?"

"I used to be serious about it, now I'm just trying to get in shape."

"How far do you go?"

"I'm just finishing a fifty."

"Fifty miles?"

"Yes. That's really not much, not for a serious rider."

"You fly in?"

"Yes. I brought Falloni a shipment from Missouri; got here just after dawn; decided I'd give myself the day off."

Joe smiled but did not immediately speak. He wondered what the shipment might be. He knew of no rush work. Memorial Day was behind them. When he left work the night before, there had been nothing urgent. If something had come in overnight, he would have been called. He knew she did not like Falloni, and he thought it unbecoming to engage in a conversation in which he might be disloyal to his employer. Still, he wondered about the flight. He would check at work. "Seems like you fly in here pretty regular."

"Yeah, I guess about once a month, mostly for Falloni."

"C.O.D.?"

"No, cash in advance."

"You fly a lot at night?"

"Oh, yeah. It's just part of the business. I started flying checks. That was all night work. Once in awhile I pick up a contract to gather packages from the smaller towns for the major overnight air couriers. That's night work. Falloni, that's nearly all at night. I guess that's why the boss always comes to meet me, trying to be considerate of the help."

"Now come on, I've worked for the Falloni's almost since I got out of high school. They've been good to me." Joe filed away the information that she met Pete at night once a month. Sandy noted his loyalty and thought of Daryl. "So you live in motels between flights?"

"Actually, I live in Detroit. I get home almost every night, even when I'm flying. Sometimes I deliberately stay out. I could have easily flown home this morning. Sometimes, I deliberately go out. I like it here. I've stayed here before."

"That's the way it is around here. Some people just keep coming back. The locals call them pilgrims. Others hate it. OK with me either way, those that come make work for me, those that don't keep it peaceful."

"I was thinking about flying out to the islands this afternoon. Would you like to go for a ride."

"Me? I've never been in a plane."

"Never?"

"Never."

"Not even commercial?"

"No, ma'am."

"Then you have to come. I know you'll love it. Once you've been in the air, boats will seem ridiculous. They're nice to be on, but it's no way to travel. Come on. Even if you hate it, you'll learn that you do. What have you got to lose?"

"Well, OK. Do you have a car here?"

"No, I call the airport. They send their van."

"I'll ride on home and get cleaned up. I'll come back and pick you up. How's that sound?"

"OK. It's almost noon now. If you can hold off lunch, we can find a place to eat out on the islands."

"I'll be back within half an hour."

Sandy stood as Joe put on his helmet. She watched as he rode away. They both had their tight stomachs and flushed faces in common. Neither had been on a date in two decades.

Sandy was amazed by the gadgetry in Joe's pick-up. He had a stack of radios reminiscent of an airplane, and a master box so that he could choose among them with a push of a button. He had an easy listening station playing through the quadraphonic speakers. He explained that electronics were something of a hobby. She asked if he had a VHF radio for aviation frequencies. He did. She dialed in Sandusky's Unicom. They caught the end of a blind broadcast from a Cessna rolling on Runway 36. She pointed to the plane lifting off as they came up to the parking lot of Griffing Field.

Joe was impressed by the confident manner in which she approached the aircraft. She crouched on the wing and reached in through the open left door. She unlocked and pushed the right door open. As she hopped off the wing, she handed Joe a set of laminated pages on a metal ring, and told him that it was his job to call the checklists. As he looked them over, she told him it was the quickest way for him to learn. She said for him to read each numbered item and not to go to the next until she said "check" in response. He read and watched her complete each item.

It had never occurred to him that flying involved such preparation. They inspected the control surfaces for freedom and security. He was not sure if there were some problem when she touched each nut that held the cables to the rudder, so when she walked around the tail, he paused to look at them and touch them for himself. When he called it, she drew fuel in a clear plastic cup. She muttered something he didn't catch, and drew several more cups, discarding the contents of each across the grass. Finally, she was satisfied. She opened each gas cap and looked into the tanks. She ran her painted finger nail along the edges of the propellers. She squatted and stared into the openings behind each propeller, explaining that there were a lot of birds around who could build a nest in only a few hours. She checked the dipsticks and put her face inside the cowling, again looking for nests. When they disconnected the tie-downs, she smiled and said, "Let's go fly."

They climbed into the plane from opposite sides. She told him to leave his door open until they got settled. In the narrow cockpit, the full length of Joe's left arm pushed up against her. His face flushed. For the first time, he noticed the scent of her perfume. He looked at the side of her face as she put on her headset. She was even prettier than he remembered. She handed him a headset. As he put it on, her fingers walked across the panel touching circuit breakers and switches like a piano player warming up. He heard the head phones go live. He heard her tell him to continue the list. He adjusted the mouthpiece to his head set and continued the list. When he called seat belts, she reached down and pulled on the one buckled across his lap. They shut the doors. She primed and started each engine. She touched the face of each engine instrument when he called them. That made sense to him. The dual controls were much like those on boats. He called the navigation lights and rotating beacon, she pulled the switches. He called radios, she flipped the avionics master. As the radios lit up, she checked the frequency against those listed in a little brown book of airports which she laid back on the floor between them. He studied the radio stack. It was different from what he was accustomed to, but the Loran was familiar. She made a motion with her hand to gesture how the VOR's and glide slope worked. He nodded although he did not understand. She taxied off the grass and onto the ramp in front of the terminal. She leaned to look by him to the windsock at the end of Runway 36. She broadcast her taxi intentions blind, and they moved away from the terminal. She asked him to call the run-up checklist on the taxiway where she stopped, holding short of the runway.

That was when Joe fell in love with aviation. These engines were treated the way engines should be treated. He couldn't think of anyone he knew who treated engines with such respect. In his experience, power boaters seem to regard blown engines as a badge of honor. She was not about to take off unless everything was perfect. He took note of the intensity in her face when she studied the tachometer on each engine as they cycled through each magneto. She understood. This was his kind of woman. They were finally at the end of the before-takeoff checklists. Then she gave him three more instructions. She told him to watch the engine instruments until she called V-1. V meant velocity. If the oil pressure or RPM's were down, he was to sing out, and they would abort the takeoff. When they were airborne, he was not to assume anything. If a gauge looked funny, if he saw another aircraft, sing out. Finally, she told him to familiarize himself with the organization of the in flight emergency checklists so that if they had one, he could call the procedures. He loved it. He simply loved it. He wasn't even off the ground yet, and he loved it. It couldn't be the flying. It was the discipline. Everything had a place. Everything fit.

When Sandy broadcast that she was rolling, Joe had a flash of terror that he might find the same fear in flight that he experienced when on the water. Sandy called V-1 bringing his attention back to the instruments. Before he could read them, he heard her voice in his headsets saying everything was OK. They were at V-2. Lift-off. She retracted the gear while they were still over the runway. The East Bay, Cedar Point Peninsula, the amusement park, the roller coasters, Sandusky Bay, Marblehead, the Islands all unfolded below them. He glanced to his right to see the harbor at Huron and the perennial white plume from the stack. West across the lake he could make out the stacks in Monroe, Michigan. He felt as if he were looking down on a road map. He had never seen any of it before. He knew it all. He wasn't afraid.

When he pulled his attention back into the aircraft, he saw Sandy flipping through the little brown book. She put in the frequency for Kelleys Island Municipal and broadcast their approach. He couldn't believe they were at Kelleys already, it was only a few moments since they took off. She asked if he knew any good places to eat on Kelleys. He hesitated, said there were one or two places in town, then said most of the action was on South Bass. She flew up the east end of Kelleys, staying out of the traffic pattern, then circled the island, coming back east just off the southern coast. They flew along the row of mansions that face the mainland. She said she was hungry and that town looked too far from the airport to walk. She broke back to the left before they got to the airport and headed west across Kelleys for South Bass.

She consulted the little book again, changed the frequency, and broadcast to Put-In-Bay traffic that they were inbound for landing. They flew past Perry's Monument and over the town. The harbor was full of boats, the square full of people. Joe heard her in his headsets, speaking in a soft voice to herself, reciting the preparation for landing checklist. He found the laminated version. She had it down word for word. She broadcast they were downwind for Runway 4 full stop; then base; then final. The runway at Put-In-Bay had both a dip and dogleg. They were so pronounced that even Joe noticed them on short final. He looked for concern in Sandy, but could see none. He wondered if he should sing out, but he didn't. She did complain about the loose gravel as they came to a stop, saying she had a new paint job. Joe looked at his watch. It was barely ten minutes since they took off. He couldn't have driven to the ferry dock that fast. A young man in a golf cart taxied them to a tie-down.

Lunch was not as awkward as either expected. Joe rented bikes while Sandy paid for the tie-down. They rode into town. It was just after 1:00 P.M. and the tables were turning, so they were quickly seated in the Round House. Sandy declined a drink because she was flying. Joe said that he'd had enough to drink. Sandy knew exactly what that meant. She'd heard Daryl say it to the waiter at The Club in Grosse Pointe. She did not pursue it with Joe. He looked across the park to the boats, and asked if she had been in the restaurant before. Many times. They used to come to the islands several times a summer on her ex-husband's boat. She had never flown in before. He asked how long she had been flying. She gave him a quick history of her aviation activities. She skipped backwards through the divorce, her son, law school, her lawyer father, hierarchy within the automakers, Detroit society, her high society/former aircraft worker mother, her grandparents from Kansas. She spoke uninterrupted until their food arrived. Joe was happy that she took the burden of carrying the conversation. He concentrated on his table manners. She asked about him. He gave a terse answer that she had just flown over most of his life. He was a local boy who left the farm to find work in town. He'd never left. Never been out of Ohio, except on his honeymoon. She asked about his wife. He said she died. Before Sandy could respond, Joe said he loved flying, wished he had discovered it years before. He thanked her. She smiled.

When they were both finished eating, they agreed to spend the afternoon exploring the island. They biked around the park and over to Perry's Monument. They went up on top. Joe pointed out all the local sites, and explained the battle, gesturing west towards Rattlesnake Island. Whoever crosses the T first, wins. She mentioned having seen men in suits who wore sunglasses and appeared to be standing guard on Rattlesnake Island back in her boating days. She asked what went on there. He laughed. It was privately owned. No one knew for sure. Everyone agreed upon the same suspicions with a wink and a nod, but didn't say anything outloud. They biked back through town, then south towards the state park. There was an old cemetery just before the park entrance. They leaned their bikes up against its iron fence and went inside to inspect the headstones.

Sandy noticed an infant grave and said it tore at her heart. She noticed that the parents died within a year of each other forty years after losing their child. She wondered if they ever got over losing their child. Joe said probably not. He still thought about his daughter, even more as the years went by. He'd notice kids standing at a street corner waiting for a light and think that she would be about that age. He'd hear about a high school game, and see her as a cheerleader. Her mother had been in the marching band. She might have followed her into that. He'd see engagement pictures in the local paper and remember that she would now be older than her mother when they were married. He might have been a grandfather. No, the parents never got over it. He visited her grave; but the random thoughts, the flash what-might-have-beens were worse. Sandy was sorry, she hadn't known. Was it a car accident that took them both? No. Cancer. Joe paused and looked across the cemetery into the woods. Suicide. His voice cracked. He wiped a tear. Sandy put her hand on his shoulder and leaned into him. He told her he had only been a kid himself at the time. He hadn't gotten over it. He didn't think the people whose names they stared at did either. You just don't get over those things.

As they came back to town, Sandy noticed people going into Our Mother of Sorrows, a small but elegant limestone church. She asked Joe if he minded her taking the time to go to Mass. They leaned their bikes against a tree in the church yard and entered together. Joe naturally took a step back to let her get holy water to bless herself. He started to, then stopped. He touched Sandy's arm and whispered that he'd wait outside. He sat on his haunches under the tree near the bikes. He tossed nuts to the squirrels who played nearby. They ran when he moved to throw, but when he stayed still for a moment, they ran to collect what he had thrown. When Sandy came out, she smiled at him. She looked different, more familiar. She came close enough that he smelled her perfume again. It was dinner time, so they agreed to get a sandwich before they flew back. They got hot dogs in town across from the tram station. They didn't talk then, nor during the bike ride to the airport. They did the preflight together as if they had done it a thousand times.

She flew back south over Catawba Island and over Sandusky Bay. Joe was looking at downtown Sandusky when she asked where the family farm was. He pointed south to Route 4 cutting through the green to the horizon. She followed it. Ten minutes later they circled Attica. He pointed to the few buildings in the center of town, telling her that he spent much of his youth at the drug store soda counter. He pointed to the high school. She playfully asked if he kissed his first girl behind the high school gym. He didn't answer, but instead pointed toward the farm. He could already see it. They circled the farm buildings several times. He recognized Dieter's truck in the driveway. They must be visiting. Dieter's two girls came out and pointed, but they were too high for Joe to recognize which one was which. The sun was just above the horizon when they headed north to Sandusky. Joe watched it set, not paying the slightest attention to Sandy's landing. She greased it. By the time they tied down and Sandy paid the fee, it was dark.

They sat talking in Joe's truck in front of Sandy's motel room for nearly an hour. As they pulled in, she asked about local Catholic Churches. She wanted to go to Mass in the morning before she left. He kidded that she'd just done Mass for the week. She explained that she went daily. She had left a lot out of the story she had told him. She had made a mess of her life. She had been spoiled and demanding, self-indulgent and self-defeating. Now she went to church and flew. Life could be simple, if you let it. It could be good. Joe didn't think life was simple at all. He didn't have any answers. He didn't understand most things. He just took what life dealt him, tried to handle the stress without strain. She asked him how long it had been since he'd had a drink. He never answered the question, except to ask if it showed. She assured him life was simple. She used to know that it was complex, and she had not been up to the challenge she placed on herself. She had deceived herself. None of it was true. Life was simple. If he stopped drinking, he knew that. Why didn't he go to Mass? Joe told her his wife had been a devout Catholic who lit candles, said the rosary, went to Mass, and prayed fervently; but she did not believe in God. He believed in God. Beyond that, he didn't see much any room full of people could offer him. He would take her to Mass in the morning if she wanted. He said he'd call when he got home to arrange the time. Sandy thanked him and went inside. She pushed the curtain back and waved to him from the room.

It was Saturday night in the summer and Sandusky was hopping. Coming back into town along Route 6 from The Maples Motel, was like coming upon a carnival from a woods. The parking lots at the hotel and restaurant adjacent to The Harbour condominiums were full. As Joe passed them, he saw the young couples standing shoulder to shoulder on the decks shouting to each other over their drinks and over the music. He thought of Sandy back at the quiet motel. He had been so lucky to find her. He could never go to a bar like that. He decided to swing by work just to check on the building. You never could tell when some kids might break in, or if some boater was waiting for help. Coming along First Street he noticed something unusual on the water tower. He looked up. It was a silhouette of a person. The shadowy figure was coming out of the hatch on the top of the tower. What the hell! Kids! He punched in the police frequency on his radio and was about to broadcast, when he noticed Pete Falloni's Corvette in the lot. He drove by. He went two blocks down the street and turned around. He pulled off to the side of the street and turned off his headlights. He squinted to recognize the shadow climbing down the ladder on the leg of the tower. He couldn't tell who it was, except that it was a man in dark clothes. The figure disappeared into the block house. A few minutes later, Pete Falloni in the same clothes got into his Corvette and drove off. What the hell? Joe wanted to go into the tower, but he remembered Sandy.

Joe's heart pounded when he called the motel. When he heard Sandy's voice, it pounded even faster. He had the phone book before him open to the churches. He gave her several choices. She had checked her voice mail, and had no work, so she was in no hurry to get back to Detroit. They settled upon the 9:30 A.M. Mass at St. Mary's. He'd pick her up at 9:00 A.M. He liked to sit in the park downtown. They could have breakfast after. She could get out of town before noon. Later that night when they separately dealt with their tensions and urges, they thought of each other.

CHAPTER 10

Sandy climbed into Joe's truck, first putting her bag on the seat between them. It was a small bag. He wondered if she was wearing the same clothes from the day before. They looked similar. The big difference was the silk scarf draped around her shoulders. No, the blouse was lighter. The jewelry different. She had already checked out and was waiting on a lawn chair when he arrived. It was a hazy morning. The dew was heavy. The sun was just getting high enough to start burning it off. A teenager on a tractor was mowing the wet grass at the airport. They could smell the cut grass as they drove into town. As they drove, Sandy pinned a small lace to the top of her hair. He hadn't seen that in a long time. Joe dropped Sandy in front of St. Mary's and pointed across to the courthouse. He told her she would find him on the benches near the flower clock.

Joe settled onto a bench on the courthouse side of Washington across from the clock. He had found a parking space just around the corner. He bought the Cleveland newspaper from a dispenser chained to a light pole. He chose the bench because Sandy ought to be able to see both his truck and him when she came down the steps of the church. He laid his arms out along the back of the bench, and looked over his shoulder to the church. He saw a family climbing up the steps, three generations teens, parents, grandparents. He looked closer, the Brennan's. He hadn't seen them in years. Maggie's kids looked older than she was when Joe met her. Mr. Brennan looked older, but the same, red-faced and bloated. He must have retired by now. Joe watched until they disappeared inside. He looked down to the waterfront. The ferry from Pelee Island was docking. Pelee Island lies just north of the Bass Islands across the line in Canada. It is larger than any other of the lake islands, but sparsely populated. There is a small town, but the island is mostly farms. The ferries to the Bass Islands are faster than the one to Pelee. They also leave more frequently from several different locations in the rush to get the pilgrims out and back. The ferry to Pelee plied its route for more practical purposes than tourism. It carried supplies to the island. It brought islanders into Sandusky for church, dinner out, and shopping; sometimes, medical care. Joe opened the paper and turned the pages. Finishing one section, he was reaching for another when he saw Pete Falloni turn the corner in his Corvette and head down to the waterfront.

Joe couldn't stop himself. He was nervous, just short of afraid. He gathered his paper, crossed the street, and hurried down the sidewalk. He deliberately stayed close to the buildings. Coming up the last block, he saw Pete's car parked in the ferry lot. He saw Pete talking to one of the deck hands on the ferry. The man opened the can Pete handed him and pulled out a cookie. Joe was familiar with the cookies. Pete's daughters made them. Pete was always bringing cookies out in the shop. It was about the only endearing thing he did. When he would leave the shop after one of his tirades, someone was sure to say they would rather have had cookies. Joe stopped short at the corner a half block away. He leaned against the side of the old hotel and started to feel guilty about the sneaking and the suspicions. What in the hell could Pete be up to anyway? This was Sandusky, Ohio. How much trouble could anyone get into in Sandusky? The guy on the ferry might be a relative, a friend. Cookies, he was just giving a friend some cookies. Maybe they went to high school together. Pete broke away from the conversation and walked back to the Corvette.

Joe was about to turn and leave, when he saw Pete pulling several packages from the passenger seat of the sports car. Each was plain white, about the size of a shoe box. He couldn't tell anything more than that. Pete took them to the ferryman. Pete put them down on the ground, and they continued to talk. Joe counted six packages. Pete pulled something from his pocket and pressed it into the man's hand. Money. A tip. Joe thought it was probably a tip for delivering the boxes to someone after they got to the island. The ferry charged for packages. Joe scolded himself for being a sneak, but wondered about the water tower all the way back up the street to the courthouse.

Joe got back to his truck just as church was letting out. Sandy saw him. She smiled and walked briskly towards him. He smiled also. He was anxious to get her in the truck. He hoped that the Brennan's would not see him. He deliberately did not look to the crowd coming from the church for that reason. He felt relieved when they were both in the truck. He couldn't believe his good fortune. He wondered what she saw in a guy like him. She liked the church. She suggested they eat at the airport. Joe had planned to take her somewhere nicer for breakfast, maybe the hotel at The Harbour, but Sandy said she liked to leave whatever money she could at the airport. They were good people. Joe had been driving past the airport for twenty years, but had never eaten there. Sandy introduced Joe to the counter lady in the terminal at Griffing Field. The counter lady in the terminal knew Falloni's and asked Joe about different people. They traded the names of mutual acquaintances for several minutes.

While they did, Sandy took her coffee cup and went up to a table of airport bums. Joe did not hear what she said to them, but turned toward them when he heard them start laughing. A few minutes later when they were eating their eggs at the counter, the venerable Harry Griffing shuffled over and stood between them to tell Sandy a knock-knock joke. He winked at Sandy and left them alone. She told Joe what she knew of the family history, how Harry and his wife had got it started, how their kids kept it going, and how the grandkids were coming up. She said she'd love to run an FBO somewhere. Joe nodded. He was tired of working for others. He asked if it took something special to work on aircraft. Sandy told him they that mechanics were licensed by the FAA, just like pilots. She jumped up and went across to a stack of magazines on a coffee table. She flipped through one she picked from the top and spread it open on the counter before Joe, showing him advertisements for classes and promises of success on the first exam. It was the first time Joe ever saw the terms airframe and power plant.

When they went outside to preflight Sandy's plane, several people called out to her, asking when she'd be back, saying good-bye, wishing her a good flight. Joe felt like a stranger in his home town. When they finished the preflight inspection, Joe handed Sandy the checklist. She took it and without the slightest hesitation raised up on her toes and kissed his cheek. He blushed. He asked when he might see her again. She smiled but did not answer. She told him to wait. She stepped up on the wing and tossed the checklists on her seat. She leaned in and routed through her flight bag. A moment later she hopped off the wing and presented Joe her business card. She told him she kept strange hours, but that she could always be reached at the number on her card. She had voice mail. He could leave a message anytime. She'd get it within a few hours. He gave her his home and work numbers. She thanked him for the good time. He thanked her for the flight. He could still feel her softness on his face. He could smell her perfume. He wanted to kiss her, but he stood back and watched as she climbed into the plane.

They waved to each other, then she taxied out toward the runways. He pulled her card from his pocket and studied it. He went inside the terminal hoping to hear her voice on the Unicom. While he waited, he flipped through one of the magazines. He heard her broadcast that she was rolling on Runway 9. He went up to the window. He watched her rotate, retract the gear, and bank left off the end of the runway. He visualized what she was seeing. He wished he were with her. He missed her. Then he reminded himself that he had only really met her about this time the day before. He went to the counter and asked if they minded if he tore a couple of ads out of one of the magazines.

Joe went directly to Falloni's and got on the computer in the shop office. When the project management software popped up, it quickly confirmed his memory. There were no urgent projects, no projects awaiting parts deliveries. He got out of the project software and booted up the billing system. He scrolled through every work order in the last three months. The only air freight charge was the package he'd picked up the first time he met Sandy at the airport. He got out of the billing system and went into the parts inventory. Pete had always been concerned about good controls on the inventory. He wanted to know it turned, that it did not age. Every part was dated when it entered inventory. Joe sorted the inventory by date and looked for a pattern. He looked for expensive parts to show up about once a month. He went back two years and found nothing. He shouldn't have expected to find anything. Pete didn't inventory expensive parts, and when they went to the additional expense of air freight, it was for parts that were immediately installed. The extra cost of the freight was immediately billed out to their customers. Joe went back into the billing system. He found only three instances in the last two years of charging a customer air freight for a part. He remembered each one.

Joe double checked the office, shop and showroom to make sure he was the only one in the building before he went up to the tower. His heart raced, even though he walked slowly. He deliberately tried to walk as quietly as he could. He stopped short at the sounds the empty building made. They used all the first three floors of the main building, but only a portion of the fourth floor for rack storage. Joe hadn't been in the unused part of the fourth floor for years. He hadn't been in the block house under the water tower since they rebuilt the factory. He could see a path in the dusty floor of the unused portion of the fourth floor. Someone had been there regularly. He stopped to look back to see if he had made separate tracks. He hadn't. He stayed within the path and followed it up the steps into the block house. The path ended at the door onto the roof. Joe instinctively put his hand on the knob to open it, but then jerked back. Through the dirty window of the door he saw two TV cameras on the roof.

One camera pointed directly at the door. The other was cocked up at the tower. Things were getting downright strange. The only security to the building were door keys that a dozen people had. Pete, Joe, and the shop clerk had keys to the parts room. Only Pete had the key to his office, but he rarely locked the door. Only Pete had the code for his computer. He had it programmed so it even took a code to get to the main menu. What in the hell were cameras doing on the roof? Joe's heart was in his throat. He tried to swallow. His mouth was dry. He was getting into something that was none of his business. He ought to just leave it alone.

Joe stood at the door and studied the cameras through the window. It looked like a pretty simple set up and a sloppy job at that. Each camera was anchored to a concrete block with nylon ties holding it in place. One wire snaked across the gravel roof towards the door. Joe looked down and saw it enter the building through a hole drilled at near the base of the door. There was still dust left from the drilling. Whoever did it had not even bothered to clean up. The wire ran up around the door jam to a magnetic lead on the door. It was that simple. Home security systems were more sophisticated. Whoever opened the door would trigger the cameras.

Two cables and a power line ran the opposite direction towards the other block house. It was the abandoned motor house for the old factory elevator. Like the blockhouse under the water tower, it protruded from the fourth floor roof. The only way into the motor house was either up the elevator shaft or across the roof. Joe went back down and got a ladder. He opened the fourth floor gate to the elevator shaft and laid the ladder diagonally across the shaft up to the motor house. When he was half way up the ladder, it slipped. He swore spontaneously. After a moment when he was sure it was secure, he admitted that heights terrified him. No, flying hadn't bothered him. He was afraid of falling. Who wasn't? When he got off the ladder in the motor house, his knees were trembling. He'd never realized there was a factual basis for that expression. There he found two inexpensive video cassette recorders stacked on a plastic crate. They were connected to the cables that ran from the cameras. Red LED's indicated that both had power. He followed the power cords to an old receptacle on the wall. He shook his head. The entire system could be disabled by simply pulling the plugs. He looked for any indication that the motor house had previously been accessed through the shaft. He saw none. He saw a familiar track in the dust by the door.

He supposed that Pete came in through the door. He supposed that Pete would simply open the block house door triggering the system, then come into the motor house to turn the recorders off before he went up the tower. That assumed that the purpose of the system was to catch someone else going up the tower. It also assumed that whoever came through the door was stupid enough to ignore two cameras staring them in the face on the otherwise empty gravel roof. Bad guys could simply rip out the wires and go on about their business. Smart guys could circumvent the system. They could pull the plug. No, the VCR might have a time stamp. If someone pulled the plug that would throw the clock off and indicate tampering; that or a power outage. It was a stupid system. Joe concluded that the best way to beat the system was to just go out a window and leave the door closed. The door threw the switch. It was such a stupid system that it could have only one purpose, Pete wanted trespassers to see it. The tower was an attractive nuisance for every kid in town. If they saw the cameras, maybe they'd think twice. That had to be it. Pete was covering the down side, trying to keep the insurance premiums low. Why didn't he let Joe in on it? It was Joe's responsibility to take care of the building. Joe was better at electronics than Pete. Maybe Pete didn't think so. What the hell was Pete doing climbing out of the tower late on a Saturday night? There had to be more. Pete wasn't stupid. The cameras were intended to stand guard for whatever Pete was doing in the tower, and they were intentionally conspicuous so that they could be explained away as cheap security. Two birds, one stone. Pete was not stupid. Joe reminded himself to watch his step. He double checked to make sure he had left no footprints in the dust.

Joe called Sandy about 9:00 P.M. that night. He had hoped all evening that she would call. He asked about her flight. She asked about his day. He'd gone into work. She'd spent the afternoon washing and waxing her plane. She'd hoped to see her son, but he had gone boating for the weekend with his father. After a pause Joe asked where all she went to pick up freight for Falloni. She said she'd gone to Missouri a few times, but added that someone usually met her at the Detroit City field. She said that she'd often wondered why they wanted her to fly things that could be driven almost as quickly. She wondered why Falloni always met her himself. She got paid up front, so she didn't wonder about it too much. Joe asked what the cargo usually was. She didn't know. Parts. They were light. They were usually styrofoam packages, shrink wrapped in clear plastic. She had no idea what they might be. She guessed they were electronics, because of the packaging. She asked Joe why he wanted to know. Joe said he was just curious. He had never been able to understand the expense of air freight either. They assured each other that they had each had a good time that weekend. He asked what she had going the coming week. She was waiting for the phone to ring. She asked him the same. He told her the same old same old. They said good night. As soon as they hung up, each had the urge to call the other back.

Instead, Joe put on a pair of his black bicycling shorts and a dark T shirt. He got a small flashlight from his work room, and put in the red lens glass that was stored in the screw cap. Outside, he jogged along the sidewalks in the quiet neighborhoods of closely spaced wood frame houses. Most people were inside watching TV. A few were on their front porches. They said hello as he jogged past. He did not jog to the shop directly, he started in the opposite direction and worked his way there. He jogged east on Second Street, studying the old factory across a vacant lot as he ran its full length. A few blocks further, he cut over to First and ran back directly in front of the factory. He ran passed without stopping, looking for cars and lights. It appeared to be empty. He went two blocks further, then looped back. He cut back in the parking lot and stopped in a shadow alongside the building to catch his breath and to retrieve his key from his shorts.

The building was like Joe's second home, still he bumped into boats and tripped over tools as he picked his way through its darkness with only the red glow of a penlight. He could hear his heart pounding in his ears. He had no trouble with the first window he tried in the blockhouse. He scratched his knee climbing out, but that was not serious. He stood at the base of the tower looking up one leg to the catwalk around the bottom of the tank. To him, it looked much higher than the forty feet it was. He watched for cars, then started up the ladder. Half way up, he looked down and froze. Until that point, he had been climbing briskly, his body a foot out from the ladder. In his fear, he pulled himself close into the ladder so that he had to turn his feet sideways for his knees to clear each rung. He even closed his eyes, and felt his way up.

When he made the catwalk, he sat on it and held the railing so tightly his hands hurt. He still had to climb up the side of the cylindrical tank. He told himself going down would be worse, however, the worst part was the transition from the side of the cylinder to the rolling ladder on the conical roof. That ladder rotated about a fixed point on the top of the cone. He supposed it was for maintaining the roof. He rolled over to the hatch. The handles turned easily. The hatch cover opened out. He felt a rush of air coming up through the tank, he reminded himself of the chimney effect. He could hear the wind whistling up through the pipe which hung broken below the tower. The air smelt musty, but not significantly different that the usual tinge of mildew in the local air. He turned his flashlight back on. He climbed off the slanted ladder and through the hatch. The ladder inside, just like the outside, was half inch metal bar welded to the side of the tank. He started down it, but stopped to look around. His light barely shown across the width of the empty tank. He looked down. He thought he could make out stacks of boxes.

When he got to the bottom of the tank, he found neatly organized rows of shrink wrapped white styrofoam packages. They were stacked on 2 x 6 boards that had been brought in to level the rounded base of the tank. Joe marvelled at how much was in the tank and how much work it must have been to get everything in here in the first place. He studied the stacks of packages. The largest were the size of a small TV set, the smallest were no bigger than the size of a fist. Most were somewhere in between, the size of a shoe box or small loaf of bread. Joe looked for labels, and found none. All had numbers and bar codes, nothing more. They appeared to be arranged by size. Looking more closely, he saw that they were arranged by number. It was organized exactly as was the parts room seventy feet below. He thought about opening something, but Pete would certainly have a count and know if he were short. They had to be electronics of some kind. He was sure of that much from the packaging. They were not consumer electronics. He didn't know what to think.

He got claustrophobic and scampered out. His fear of height did not return until he closed and locked the hatch. He was startled by screams. They were from a roller coaster at Cedar Point. He looked across the water to its lights. He realized where he was and got dizzy from the height. He forced himself to get on the ladder. Each step his toe searched the darkness for the next rung below. He left teeth marks in the side of his small flashlight, but eventually got back down to the roof. He closed the window, and inspected the ledge for any telltale sign. He retraced his steps through the plant and the shadows along the side of the building. He waited there for several minutes studying all he could see, looking for someone looking back at him. When he made his break, he ran as fast as he could. He ran the entire way home. He felt as if he were being chased. He locked his door and immediately put on his police scanner. He stood in the shower extra long, replaying every step to make sure he'd left no sign of his entry. What in the hell had he gotten himself into?

CHAPTER 11

Pete Falloni's lifestyle changed quickly after his father's death. It wasn't from any inheritance, the estate was tied up in probate and an IRS audit for two years. Pete's prosperity came from his new salary. When he started taking the salary his father had, which he did the week after his death, his income from the family businesses jumped to two and a half times to $175,000 per year. The following winter he bought a three bedroom condominium with a boathouse large enough to accommodate a fifty foot yacht at The Harbour. The Harbour is a condominium complex for power boaters that is tucked in the shallows of the east end of Sandusky Bay, behind the Cedar Point Causeway and municipal water plant, on a channel dredged out of Pipe Creek and canals from Heron Creek, about a mile north of the business end of Runway 18 at Griffing Field. Most of its inhabitants are prosperous pilgrims from elsewhere in Ohio who rush to the lake each weekend. Pete's family could have lived comfortably in the condo, but they did not move into it. They kept the big home on South Columbus, and used the condo for weekends. Pete came by several times a week to sauna in the club house, and in the summer his kids were in and out of the tennis courts and pools. Pete's speedboat seemed lost among the yachts that idled up the canals to the condos and lonely hanging from the cranes in the boathouse that would lift a boat many times its size. Even with his new found wealth, Pete could not afford the boat he wanted.

Pete solved that problem late in the summer following his father's death. It was the end of the season, and boats were starting to be sold by owners who wanted to avoid the cost of laying them up for the winter. Through Red's brokerage activities, he got word that the owner of a 2 year old 40' cigarette with twin V-8's that normally retailed for $385,000 wanted a survey. That was the first step in the process of marketing yachts, an inspection and appraisal by a marine surveyor. Red was one. Sometimes it meant someone was refinancing their boat. Most often, it meant they were getting ready to sell. Pete contacted the owner immediately, before Red could do his survey. Eventually, he got them to sign a sales contract for $225,000. They would get $50,000 immediately and continue to use the boat through the end of September, when they would close, and he would pay the balance.

Pete's angle was that Falloni Marine, Inc. bought the boat, not him. He considered it a business expense. Advertising. He had the company name painted on the side of the boat so that it would be seen as he plowed across the Lake at 70 M.P.H. With this boat he could be in Cleveland, Toledo, or Monroe, Michigan faster by water than by car. He also intended to start racing. He was investing in name recognition, good-will. It was not the type of investment that his father would have made. He could hear his father saying that you could build a reputation, not buy it. His father was limited, however, he had failed to grow with the business. Big business required sophistication. Image had to match expectations. Expectations were created by imagery. Also his father did not have the problem of an extended family with their palms out. Pete had no intention of letting the business profits find their way to his mother and sisters. The new boat was often at Falloni Marine to be serviced. Pete was brutal on its engines. His boat always took precedence over any other work in the shop. Pete put all his incidental expenses incurred while travelling in the boat, dining out and the like, on a company credit card. They were ultimately charged to the advertising expense account. For his convenience, and of course, the better protection of the company's investment, Pete kept the boat in his boathouse at The Harbour. He did, however, make sure that Falloni Marine paid him rent for storing the boat at slightly above market rates for rack storage. After all, it got personal attention in a private boathouse.

Pete also instituted a third set of books shortly after his father's death. He had long kept two sets. The first set of books were the result of the daily business operations of Falloni Marine. Money came in, money went out. The shop issued bills, collected payment. The sales floor issued bills, collected payments. All the accounting information followed through Lynette who made sure all entries were posted to the correct accounts. Most of the posting was coded into to the point of entry computers so that Lynette's posting activity was limited to collecting backup disks from their computers and loading them into her own. She had become savvy enough about computers to advocate networking them to allow for direct data transfer and eliminate the step of importing data from backup disks. Pete listened, but would never agree. He said that he was worried about the risk of inadvertent file corruption by people getting into things they didn't know how to use. Networking was an additional expense, passing disks was not that inconvenient. In fact, security, not cost, was his central concern. Lynette reviewed accounts and issued financial statements on Falloni Marine. In the early days of the system, under Joe's father, she had also done the financial accounting for the limited partnership that owned the building and its corporate general partner. Since the activity of both those entities was limited to transferring money between bank accounts and paying a few bills, Pete soon took them over himself.

Pete also took personal responsibility for the second set of books, the tax books. Again, when the system was first established, Lynette held that responsibility. It was new to Falloni Marine to have one set of books, much less two; but there was nothing out of the order in business to keep two sets of books, one for the financial management of the company, the other for compliance with the tax laws. The two are profoundly different. Just as an example, under the tax regulations, the IRS has a thick volume which schedules the lives of assets for depreciation purposes; that is, the number of years over which the business can write down the value of the asset to nothing. In them, the IRS considers office furniture to have a seven year life, and allows the business to deduct 1/7 of the value each year. In reality, a desk might last twenty or thirty years. A business person who wants financial statements that accurately reflect the health of business wants depreciation to reflect reality, not arbitrary tax tables. Another area of difference, not totally separate from depreciation, is whether or not to classify an expenditure as a current expense, which for tax purposes is fully deducted in the current year, or to capitalize it as an asset that is depreciated over a number of years. Small expenditures are a good example, even they may be for a tool that will last many years, and small amounts accumulate into big numbers.

Businesses commonly capitalize expenditures for goods that are not immediately consumed in the business for their financial accounting, but expense those same expenditures in their tax accounting systems. It is an old game of which both business and the IRS are well aware, and is the center of the playing field in most IRS business audits. The accounting software Falloni used, provided for wholesale reclassification of accounting entries from the financial accounting system for use in the tax accounting system. Lynette could simply never get it right. Pete did not want to get crossways with the IRS, so he simply took it over himself. In one to two hours a month at his computer, he could prepare all the tax accounting income and expense statements, depreciation schedules, and other supporting detail that their accountant needed for preparing their tax returns. No one else needed to see the tax books anyway.

The third set of books came after his father's death. The reason for starting them was simple enough, it was the lawyer's suggestion to avoid dividends by spending the profits in the business. Pete quickly found that spending was limited by its conspicuous results. He bought the condo with his own money, and the boat was advertising, but even after the fixing, and painting and redecoration of the office and shop, he was still dissatisfied with the picture that the financial statements painted for his sisters. They showed a very profitable business. Spending the profits in the business was not going to be enough. Pete took it a step further. He set upon getting rid of the profits. He got busy on his computer and set upon the wholesale reclassification of assets purchases. In short, he wrote down the asset value of the business and increased the current expenses. The result was exactly what he wanted to portray, an old business with a declining asset base, high expenses to maintain the old assets, and low profits. Once he got the third set of books up and running, with the reclassification of certain types of expenditures programmed into the system, he could generate these in little more than an hour a month. These were the only statements that anyone in his family ever saw.

A funny thing happened to Pete. The more he got, the more he wanted. There was never enough. Even with the jump in his salary that bought the condo, he wasn't satisfied with his cash income. That cash income included his parts skimming operation, not enough; included the rent he charged for his boathouse, not enough. One month when preparing the financial statements on Falloni Property, Inc., Pete realized that although he was President and Chairman of its Board of that corporation, the only salary he drew was from Falloni Marine, the operating company. He rectified that in short order. He gave himself the old salary that he used to earn from Falloni Marine. Now he was drawing the combined total of what both he and his father previously took from the business. That was good. It would increase expenses and decrease profits. Soon, that was not enough.

Once he started looking for more ways to increase his wealth, they came easily. After a party at the condo, he had the lady who cleaned the offices for two hours each night, clean the condo. He considered the party business related, indeed, the business had paid for the caterer and bartender. The business could also pay for the cleaning lady. When he saw how easily he could issue a check to her, and how only Lynette might see it, he soon had her cleaning both the condo and his home. Sarah was always redecorating, painting and papering. There was so much painting going on in the old factory, that Pete simply had the same contractor put a couple of men in his house. No one would ever know, nothing in the paperwork indicated where the men were working. The operating company paid the bills. From that point forward, any little repairs to either the home or the condo were simply slipped into the repair and maintenance expense accounts of the business. It got to the point that Pete would not even attempt to repair a leaky faucet. Sarah was part of the routine. She picked up the phone and called carpenters, plumbers, painters. They sent non-specific bills to Falloni Marine. All the local businessmen did it. So the government got shorted a few tax dollars, they squandered it anyway. Pete worked hard to get where he had. He deserved it. Pete, and Sarah also, were quickly beyond reflecting on the legal intricacies of the situation, or even considering it a perk or privilege of position. To them, it was an entitlement.

They were not so indifferent to their actions as to lose sight of certain boundaries. Sarah, without being told, knew never to discuss the fact at the country club that the company was paying their personal expenses, even when she heard other women bragging about their husbands doing it. She also knew never to say anything to any of Pete's family. Pete had learned that he had to stop short of using employees from the shop. He had slipped into that easily enough from the fellows working on the big boat. That, of course, was company owned and within the bounds of common understanding. Pete had, however, started bringing his cars in for the mechanics to fix. Over the years they had taken them to Sarah's father's dealership where he had them pay only cost with no mark-up. It was an inconvenience to drive to Norwalk, especially when Pete could have his company absorb the cost. Since under the cost accounting system that Pete had established, the men in the shop had to charge all their time to a customer or some other account, and since the repair and maintenance accounts were getting a little too full for the size of the business, Pete gave them a new account number to charge the time they spent on his cars. What no one knew was that account was programmed to automatically charge its balance out to whatever customer orders were in progress at the time. Usually, it simply increased the charges to a customer a tenth of an hour on individual line items. If there wasn't much work in process at the time, however, the individual line item charges got higher. Under this system, Pete not only got his work for free from his company's employees, but he had their customers pay for it. He was proud of his cleverness. It worked well, until Joe, who reviewed every bill before it was issued, caught time charges he couldn't justify. He had the ability to adjust time charges, and he found himself doing it with increasing frequency. Finally, he complained to Pete that the time charges they put in the system were not always the ones that came out on the bills. Pete said he would investigate. Later Pete came back with an explanation that there was a glitch in the system that was bumping up time charges. He had fixed it. Pete and Sarah started taking their cars back to Norwalk. That damned Joe was getting to be a problem. Still, Pete felt he had learned a valuable lesson. He had to keep others out of his loop.

The cumulative effect of Pete's actions were making the business look much worse than even he intended. Now his problem was finding ways to improve the business. As he undertook that, it never occurred to him to undo any of what he had done. He had gotten so completely absorbed in manipulating the books, that he looked only to more manipulation for solutions. Historically, Pete had kept their tax books pristine. He had instinctively avoided anything that would cross the IRS. He had been scrupulously honest with them and had never once been audited. The more he saw how easily he could maneuver numbers about, the more he felt like a chump for paying taxes, for all taxes were nothing other than the result of numbers that he voluntarily produced for the IRS. Pete stopped thinking of taxes as the government's share of profits after expenses. To him taxes became just another expense of doing business. If he could cut that expense, it could bolster profit, and he could spend that money elsewhere. Pete followed that logic into the aggressive reclassification of asset purchases into current expenses. He also reclassified assets into shorter term depreciation schedules. Immediately, the taxable income of the business decreased as did its taxes. Paying less taxes had the desired effect he wanted over in the financial statements that his sisters saw. The business was profitable, but barely.

Two years after his father's death, the lawyer proposed a plan for dealing with his sisters that Pete accepted. It was far from the first plan. Pete had rejected a dozen. Pete felt he was caving in on this one merely because they were about to close out his father's estate, and it was an appropriate time to present it to the girls. The lawyer felt he had obtained the perfect middle ground, for his plan froze out the sisters, but did so with compensation for what was being taken from them. Pete had adamantly opposed any compensation, but this payout was through a formula that Pete could control. Pete balked at the lawyer presenting the plan to the girls out of Pete's presence, but finally agreed to that when the lawyer pointed out that it would make their ultimate agreement to the plan look free of any personal pressure. Pete would listen over an intercom from the next room.

The lawyer began the meeting with the girls in his office by speaking highly of their father and telling them how successful he had been. Like many successful men, his affairs were tangled, but could be broken into two parts, the family business and personal investments. Ultimately, each of them owned equal portions, but that was after their mother died. Until then, the property was in trust for her. The personal investments alone were generating over $300,000 per year in income for their mother. Naturally, that would be split among them down the road. The family business was a little more involved. Each of them and also Pete would inherit an equal share, but their father had given Pete ten percent of each business while he was alive. It had been his plan that Pete would always have more stock that the girls, since Pete had dedicated his life to running the business. Also, he had set up an 85% vote provision, so that even if all the girls agreed on something, Pete would also have to agree, or it couldn't pass. It was their father's plan, to provide for the girls but to make sure Pete could control the business, since he was there every day running it.

He interrupted with a few stories of how he had seen several family businesses disintegrate as they passed from one generation to the next and gave local examples that they recognized. He said that for the last two years as he probated the estate, he had struggled with the prospect of Falloni Marine going down the drain. Would everything their father worked for be lost in family squabbles, maybe not now but years from now? He had helped their father incorporate the marine business, and then separate the building ownership into the limited partnership and corporate general partner. It all made sense when they did it. Now that their father was gone, they faced new problems. Unlike their father, they were owners of a business in which they were not active. He had to be frank, as the years passed, if Pete was successful, they would be jealous; if he failed, they would blame him. That was only human. They could see it around town. In his opinion, if you cut through all the paperwork, their father's goal had been to provide for his family. He wanted to establish his son in business and pass value to his wife and daughters. He had taken it upon himself to come up with a plan to do that, and hopefully, eliminate the risks of a family business, that might years from now jeopardize family harmony. He had even proposed several ways that the business could be restructured to Pete, but Pete had rejected each one. He felt this one was the best, and for that reason was coming to them directly without Pete. Pete smiled in the next room.

The plan was this. He would set up a new corporation. The trust, which currently held each of the girl's stock in Falloni Marine, Inc., their limited partnership shares in Falloni Properties, Ltd., and their stock in Falloni Properties, Inc., would trade those for stock in the new corporation. Thus, ultimately, each of them would hold stock in only the one corporation. Pete would be left with all the ownership of the operating business and real estate holding companies. Pete would have no part of the new corporation. Now to achieve their father's goal of transferring value to them, the operating and real estate companies would enter a long term agreement to pay the fair value of the stock and partnership holdings they traded to the new corporation. The new corporation could then invest the money or distribute the money out to them. To also achieve their father's goal of putting Pete in business, the payments would be spread over a number of years and come only out of its profits. Too many family business were broken up in sales to divide their assets, or bankrupted by debt to achieve the same objective. In his opinion, this plan passed value to them, preserved the business their father built, and did so early enough and in a way that maintained family harmony. The only question was asked by the oldest, who wanted to know how they would establish value for the purchase price and value for the payments. He assured them that both would be standard formulas that used numbers right off the company financial statements. He assured them the formulas would be fair. He told them that he thought it was a good plan, fair to all. If they would agree, he would go back to Pete with it. He wouldn't let them agree that day. He told them to think it over. They could meet again before he went to Pete.

When they left, the lawyer was surprised to find Pete ecstatic. He had expected another struggle with Pete over the valuation of the girls' interests and the terms of the payments now that they were getting down to the point of drafting the fine print. He assumed it would be a huge debt load for the businesses and was prepared to defend it by the linking of its payment to profitability. The businesses would only have to pay in the good times. Pete could weather the bad times by the automatic payment moratoriums. The lawyer was caught off guard by Pete's glee. Maybe Pete was finally realizing that he would have immediate and total ownership of all the family businesses, and his sisters would only have a promise to pay from paper corporations, with those promises held by another paper corporation, and that corporation held in a trust. He could not know, what Pete did, that equity values and profits reflected in financial statements were little more than putty in Pete's hands. Numbers were what Pete wanted them to be. Pete was in total control. It was so easy. Pete had been a chump. Well, it had taken him years to learn how to play the game. He was not that old. It really was easy. He was in control, total control. He even had this lawyer placing offerings on his altar. The chump did not even realize what he was doing for Pete. He could come up with whatever formulas he thought fair, so long as Pete controlled the numbers plugged into the formulas. He could stay in the outer loop for now.

The plan came to pass, and still it was not enough for Pete. Pete turned his attention to Preferred Wholesale. If he could profit wholesaling parts to his own company, why not to others. Pete spent increasing amounts of time on the phone, wheeling and dealing.

CHAPTER 12

Joe was jumpy all Monday at work. He felt he was being watched. Pete had brought cookies in that morning and spent half an hour chatting with the men in the shop. He rarely did that anymore, almost never. Afterwards, he had pulled Joe aside and then taken him up to his office. Joe was convinced that he'd been discovered. In Pete's office, he produced his new cellular phone. He opened it, and the two electronics buffs commented as they inspected the internals. Pete attributed the small antennae to the wave length, Joe to the addition of power. Pete showed Joe his latest project spread on his credenza. Joe was about to make a suggestion, when Pete looked at his watch and swore. He had forgotten to make an important call. He was polite to Joe, but explained that it was time for him to get to work. Pete put on his headset even as Joe left. Walking back to the shop, Joe's ears were ringing. He hated the intrigue. He wanted out, yet he needed to learn more before he jumped.

Throughout the day, Joe could think about nothing other than the tower. He worked his suspicions over and over. Always he came to the same theory. Pete was involved in black market electronics of the highest order. They were not consumer electronics. Those had become too cheap. Even if they were stolen goods, he did not have enough volume to justify the hassle of sneaking them in and out of the tower a few at a time. They were not marine electronics. Joe did not recognize the generic packaging, and if they were, Pete could easily slip them into their own inventory without the hassle of the tower. It had to be extremely expensive merchandise. Why else the tower? It was absolutely the last place anyone would ever look. There were any number of places in the old factory he could have kept a stash, but any might be discovered. Still, the tower carried the risk of being seen on the way in and out. Maybe not, the tower was taken for granted.

People did not look up. The risk of being seen was minimal if he only climbed it at night, but then Joe had seen him at night. Maybe that motivated the video system. He'd already concluded it was to discourage climbers and record anyone who happened onto the roof. Yes, Pete was into something very shady and very big. That was Joes's theory.

When not worrying with his theory, Joe worried that he might be discovered. All day he wanted to return to the top floor and make sure he left no trace. He could not to that. Someone might notice. He never went up there. No one ever went up there. Hell, maybe it wasn't even Pete. He had seen a shadowy figure and a few minutes later he saw Pete. Maybe it was a coincidence. Maybe it was someone else in the tower. He thought that he could verify that by the tapes. If his analysis of the system was correct, Pete would trigger it every time he opened the door. He would then walk across the roof to the elevator motor house, rewind the tapes, turn off the cameras, climb the tower, then turn the cameras back on when he left. If that was so, Joe would find Pete on the tape, at least his most recent visit. It was time to verify his theories. He could easily buy the same type of video tape. He recognized it and knew exactly what discount store carried it. He would buy clean tapes and switch them for the tape in the cameras. He could do that through the elevator shaft without ever going out on the roof or up the tower. He ran out at lunch and bought two blank tapes. That afternoon, he hung back as everyone else left. When he was sure that he was alone in the building, he got the tapes from his truck, and scurried up to the fourth floor. As he went he looked for traces of his presence, and made sure to leave no new ones. He braced the ladder extra tightly across the elevator shaft. He climbed up into the motor house, switched the tapes, and was back downstairs in minutes. When he came down, however, he heard a radio playing in the front office. He hoped that it was the cleaning lady, but when he looked out the shop window, his heart sank when he saw Pete's car. He put the tapes in the drawer of his shop desk. The stress was killing him. He would go to Pete. If Pete was on to him, he was on to Pete. He had done nothing wrong. He was not afraid of confrontation. So he told himself.

"Hi, Joe. I saw your truck when I came in. I yelled out in the shop for you."

"I didn't hear you."

"You working on something? You've got to learn that you're the boss. Let the men do the work."

"Well, I was just doing some checking. You know me."

"I know better than to believe that you stop at checking. You just can't keep out things that are best left to others."

"Well, I was just about to leave. I thought I was here alone when I heard you. I'll be closing up."

"Yeah. Go ahead. Lock me in. I've got to put in a couple hours on the computer."

Joe could not tell if he had been made or not. Maybe Pete was playing cat and mouse with him. Maybe Pete was so wrapped up in his cloak and dagger game that he couldn't see what was there to be seen. Maybe Pete was innocent. He had to get a look at the tapes. Joe got the tapes, and watched them immediately when he got home. Joe was impressed at how well the cameras did with available light at night. The tape from the camera aimed at the block house showed Pete walking directly at it, then passed it. He was clearly recognizable when he got close to the camera and passed it. It was Pete wearing dark clothes, the dark blue overalls that hung in his office and a backpack. A few seconds later, the recorded tape stopped and went to snow. The tower tape showed only the tower, but both tapes were date and time stamped. Both showed they had been triggered at the same time. Pete had triggered the tapes last Saturday night shortly before Joe saw the shadowy figure coming down the tower. OK. He had proof that Pete was the one behind the tower stash. That dumb Pete, all he had to do was put the VCR's on an infrared remote to turn them off before he opened the door. He had left tracks he could have avoided, but why should he expect Pete to be clever. The whole system was stupid. Now he needed to verify that what was in the tower was what he suspected.

Tuesday Joe tried to be casual as he set up his plan to sample the tower stock. He assumed that Pete would have a detailed inventory, probably in his computer, so he couldn't take anything without replacing it. He would take one package of something that was in high volume and not so likely to be noticed. He would carefully open the package, inspect it, then return it, hopefully all in the same evening. That meant two trips to the tower. He hated the thought of climbing the tower. He focused instead on his plan to open and reseal the package. All the packages were sealed in clear shrink-wrap. They had all the equipment for shrink wrapping boats, which they still did on occasion if someone specifically asked. That involved large gas flame blowers, and large specially tailored covers with zippered doors that were shrunk around the boats. They also had rolls of clear wrap and electric blowers that they used to seal small items, like radios, that might be damaged by condensation and mold inside the sealed boats. There was always a little. Once or twice in the past, Joe had shrink wrapped components taken from their own parts room, that turned out not to be the right part. He recalled having done a fair job, and he wasn't even trying to impress anyone with his work. He was only trying to seal up the part and return it to their own stock. He was convinced that with a little time and care, he could reseal one of the tower packages so that Pete would never notice. He got a small box, a small roll of clear shrink wrap, an X-acto knife, and the blow gun, and started practicing on a bench in the shop. Everyone was busy working. No one paid attention to him. He was the boss.

Joe jumped when Pete came up behind him and asked him what he was doing. Pete apologized for scaring him. Joe flushed and stammered. He had noticed a little rust on a part from the supply room. He thought he might have one of the guys shrink wrap the parts. They had all the supplies just lying around. He was experimenting with the shrink wrap. Pete immediately wanted to see the box of the part that had rusted. New parts shouldn't rust. The manufacturer ought to wrap them so they didn't. Joe said it was no big deal, they had used the part. Pete told him to bring any parts like that to him in the future. He'd send them back and get credit. They shouldn't be wasting their time doing other people's work for them. They shouldn't have anything in inventory long enough for it to rust anyway. He wrote down the number off the box and said he was going to check the inventory system to see how long the part had been in their stock room. As he walked off, Joe told him that rust could form overnight, he was just trying to protect the inventory. Pete mumbled a response that Joe did not catch. Joe told himself that he had done enough for now, he was going to cool it for awhile.

Sandy called him at 10:00 P.M. Tuesday night. He was just in from a ride and just out of the shower. She was at Capital City field in Frankfort, Kentucky, picking up a new die for a stamping machine. It was for a small manufacturing company in Detroit. It was the same old story, a little company that could not afford to inventory spare parts. When their die cracked, they had to stop production. They had people waiting on her return. She explained the reason for her call was Pete Falloni. She had been thinking about what Joe asked her the other night about how many times and where she went for Falloni. She had spent the morning checking her records. Each time he paid her by EFT, she always called her bank to confirm the transfer, but she also got a written confirmation in the mail a few days later. Those slips showed not only her name and account number, but the account name and number of where the money came from. She had never noticed before, but of all her flights for him, only three had been paid for by Falloni Marine, Inc. All the rest were paid for by Preferred Wholesale, Inc. Joe told her not to lose those records. He couldn't say what, but he was sure something was going on. He didn't tell her about the tower or cameras. He thought he heard a helicopter in the background and asked her about it. She said it was the military. They came out to play at night and on weekends. If he flew with her, he'd get to know them. She ran into the same guys all over the place. She had to get going. She missed him. They promised to get together soon.

At work the next day, Joe was distracted by thoughts of Sandy, and for the first time, guilt over his past activities. He had not exactly been celibate. He wondered if using prostitutes was considered promiscuous. He did not think of himself as promiscuous. In any event, the consequences had never mattered before. He hadn't been concerned for himself, and he had no one else. Now he worried. He had stumbled into someone worth worry. He would never forgive himself if he passed some disease to Sandy. He had to know. He had to find out before he got to that point, before he got as serious as he knew he could. He left work again at lunch. From a telephone booth he called a urologist's office and asked for an appointment. He hesitated when asked the reason, but cleared his throat and said it was just a check-up. He'd like to be checked for any sexually transmitted diseases. The voice on the phone gave him a time late that Friday afternoon. On the way back from lunch, he stopped in the discount store and bought two more tapes. It had occurred to him that he might start to catch the comings and goings of Mr. Falloni.

Sandy had spent most of the flight home from Frankfort thinking of Joe. She recognized that she was quickly passing through her fondness for him to something much more serious. She smiled and thought of him in his biking shorts. She brought herself back to the objective facts. They could talk easily to each other. They seemed to be compatible. They seemed to have many things in common. They were the same age. Both had histories of pain. Both had found a way to get beyond it. Both seemed to have similar values. He didn't go to church, but she found him religious. As religious as Daryl was, she couldn't imagine a conversation with Daryl that had a truly theological content like Joe; maybe when Daryl was younger, not now. Daryl had been seduced by the secure routine of ritual. Maybe she had been also. Not Joe. She couldn't even imagine talking to a priest about God as openly and easily as she talked to Joe. Then she remembered that she and Joe had barely talked on the subject. That only bolstered her musing. He had communicated much in a few words. She understood. He had talked simply about belief, about faith. She could fall in love with him. She stopped herself with the image of her mother. She could see her mother having a fit. Her mother had groomed her for the first tier of automaker executives. A prominent lawyer had been a grudging alternative. Now she was about to get involved with a middle-aged mechanic.

Sandy slept in Wednesday morning and went grocery shopping after Mass. She stopped in front of the condom display. She knew nothing about them. Without a uterus, she had not needed them with Daryl. Birth control was no longer an issue for her. She did not think about other sins associated with passion. She only thought about the health issue. What would Joe think about her if she produced a condom? What would he conclude? Would he wonder about her health, her morals? If he had his own, she wouldn't have to produce anything. If he produced one, should she worry about his health, his morals? Would he be signaling his concern for her past? It was all very complicated. She grabbed one of the boxes. Better safe than sorry. Maybe he would see that she cared enough for him to think about these things in advance of the moment.

That Wednesday after work Joe stayed late. Once again he retraced his steps up through the elevator shaft to the VCR's. Again, he switched the tapes. At home on his VCR he saw Pete in action, dark clothes, backpack. Pete had gone up Monday night, a couple of hours after Joe locked him in the building. Joe resolved to change the tapes three times a week. He might not catch every time Pete went up into the tower but he'd catch enough to establish a pattern. Joe also resolved to check one of the packages, sooner than later. He would do it Friday night. Pete usually left early on Friday in the summertime, to get a jump on the weekend partying. Joe had his own doctor's appointment Friday afternoon. He would go jogging late Friday night, and after clearing the building, slip in and go up to the tower.

Joe's second trip up the tower was no less scary than the first. At least it went more quickly. He knew what to expect. He chose one small package from a section that contained two dozen stacked in two columns of twelve each. He watched for traffic before he came out of the hatch, and worked his way down the ladder without hesitation. When he got back into the shop, he worked holding the red light in his teeth. He had difficulty swallowing. More than once, his saliva drooled out the side of his mouth. He had hoped he might be able to open and reseal the same wrapper. There was no way to do that. Still, he opened it with the X-acto knife along its seam. He would use it as a model for the resealing. He carefully opened the styrofoam, making sure not to leave any marks or indentations. There was more plastic and foam sheets inside the box, but they were not sealed. When he finally got below them, he found the contents supported on a pedestal molded into the foam.

He knew what it was immediately. It was a chip. It was not a little chip, not like the timing circuitry in a wrist watch or automotive controls. It was a big chip. It could be the mother board for a computer. It could be....he'd been watching too much TV. It was a chip, that was all he knew for sure. He repacked it. His first effort to shrink wrap it was a failure. Some dirt had gotten between the wrap and the white foam. His hands were trembling. His seams were sloppy. He cut it off, blew the bench top clear, shook his arms and hands to limber them, and started over. The second effort was better but not good enough. He was satisfied that his third attempt was as good as he could get it. He put the shrink wrap and blow gun away. He took the package back up into the tower. On the way down, he did not think about the height, rather his mind raced through things he had half-heard in the news. He should have paid more attention. Pete was in the computer black market. That much was sure. This was the big time. This wasn't hacker gear. This was the really big time. Who knew what the components were for. Joe got so caught up in thoughts of missile guidance systems, nuclear triggers, and terrorists that he was back in the shop before he realized where he was.

Joe laid awake that night. He wanted to call Sandy, but stopped himself. He wondered about her roll in this. She acted innocent enough, but maybe she was part of it. Maybe she was out to trap him for Pete. After all, she had been meeting Pete late at night for a couple of years. No, she was a good woman. He took her to church. He hated this. He hated Pete for creating the mess in which he found himself. He hated Pete for making him suspicious of a woman for whom he cared. It wasn't the first time around on that score. Damn Pete! The next morning, Joe rode a century. He tried to ride faster than the demons that haunted him, but with no success. Afterwards, he laid in a hot bath soaking his aches away. There he concluded, it was time to get help. This was much bigger than him.

CHAPTER 13

I knew that frantic edge in the tone of Joe's voice. I knew it all too well. I had heard it creep up on and overtake my country cluber clients when they finally heard what I always told them. The massive resources of the federal government had been mobilized against them. Worse, it was highly likely that someone close to them had turned and would be an eyewitness to their misdeeds. They should expect resentment, not sympathy from the jury. They were more likely to be convicted than acquitted. Yes, there was a shrillness in their voice when they first realized they might actually go to jail. Later, they would get calm, accept their fate, and start to work with me on the legal aspects of their cases as if it were nothing other than another business problem. In a perverse way, I kind of like that moment of realization. Even though they are my clients, I confess I enjoy seeing the powerful humbled. I guess that's why I'm a Democrat. But they always bounce back quickly, almost too quickly. I guess that's why the Republicans win more often. Anyway, I know the tone. I have also heard it in the voices of witnesses who fear for their lives. Most have good reason, and still come forward. I know the tone. I have to say I respect those witnesses. Even when they are testifying against my clients. I heard that tone in Joe's voice.

I had a difficult time listening to what Joe was saying. He had called me at home on a Saturday. Usually, I let my wife or one of the boys answer. I just happened to be near the phone. That edge in his voice put me in mind of all the years I had known him. I had been around him in the best and worst of times, as boys, as teens, at his wedding, through his daughter's illness, at her funeral, then Molly's. He was talking quickly. I stopped him. I asked where he was. He told me at home. I took a minute to tell him about my practice. I was not sure if he appreciated the type of people I dealt with on a regular basis. If one one-hundredth of what he was saying was true, he was in deep, his well-being might be at risk. Nothing, no one was to be trusted. I told him to go to a phone booth and call me back collect. While I waited for the second call, I thought about Joe. I wondered how well I really knew him. Well enough. I knew him well enough, and if I had any doubt, that tone eliminated it. I picked up the phone on the first ring.

After the operator got off the line and before Joe could say anything, I gave him a little speech. It was a compendium of many things I used on different occasions. Unless he was personally part of the undertaking, he was a fact witness. He should limit his statements to his observations of facts. He should not make assumptions nor draw conclusions. If he limited his statements to only facts, then we could sort out the truth. Many times, people who were sure they witnessed a crime would ultimately come to conclude that what they actually saw was different from their recollection that they had worked over many times, each time getting more colored by their own suppositions and conclusions, and those of their friends. He listened impatiently, then started laying it out. The first time through, he included his worst fears, but with each pass, we cut more and more of that out. After the last time, I laid out what I had heard. A long term employee, hired and promoted by the owner of a business who ultimately forces the employee to work with his son whom he does not like, starts piecing together bits of suspicious behavior. Those include corporate shenanigans, padded bills, and a mysterious inventory. There are late night flights coming in, storage in a highly unusual location, behavior tending to keep the storage location secret, one observation of a shipment to Canada, and one inspection of one package.

Joe waited for me to continue. I could almost feel his anger. Finally, I said it was not what he had, but how it was being done that worried me most. He said, no kidding, like I just heard him for the first time. I told him that he was not just in deep, he was way over his head. It was not a matter of staying on top of the water, it was a matter of struggling up to the surface for a desperate breath. I told him not to do anything. Not talk to anyone, absolutely no one. He should not automatically trust cops, especially not the local constabulary. I told him I would make some discreet inquiries and get him to the right Federale. It would take a few days. In the meantime, I warned him not to do anything to compromise his position. I told him that virtually all these cases started when someone like him on the inside turned. I laid down a stern warning. He was to lay low. No more snooping. He should sit tight. The big boys might want him to play a roll, hopefully not. He did not need that kind of grief. If there was a case for them to make, he might blow it. I re-emphasized that his continuing health was a factor. I specifically told him not to ask questions. I warned him that questions often tell more about the questioner than is learned from the answers. I told him if he wanted to think about anything, he should think about the money. He should follow the money. That always made these cases. He told me about the compartmentalized computer system. There was no way he could follow the money, except he had heard the pilot was paid by bank transfers. I told him to leave the money trail to the Federales.

I really didn't know where to start. I thought about making calls to Washington, but I didn't know anyone there. I thought about calling some of my old cronies who were still in the U.S. Attorney's office. Then I remembered my own advice. My questions might disclose more than their answers. Almost in frustration, I decided on the head of the FBI office in Columbus. I didn't know him as well as a couple other of the agents, but I had cross- examined him a couple of times. I knew his name. It wasn't in the phone book, so I called the FBI office. I said I could only talk to him and it was urgent. The lady would not give me his home number, but dialed it, and patched me through. He cut me short when I started to identify myself. He knew who I was. I told him I had been contacted by a person who strongly felt he had witnessed illicit traffic in computer components that might involve national security. I immediately chided myself for disclosing that the witness was a male. At least I had not identified him as a friend. His response was matter of fact. If I thought it could wait until tomorrow, he was coming into Columbus Sunday morning. He could meet us at his office, my office, or wherever. I told him that it would only be me for now. I suggested the banister overlooking the Scioto River across from the federal court house. I kidded that I didn't want to be seen going into the FBI office, I had a reputation to protect. He did not respond. At least I had learned something. He didn't live in Columbus.

He was sitting on the stone wall waiting when I drove up the next morning. It was a beautiful summer morning. Downtown Columbus was empty. I parked illegally, a few feet from him and right behind his car. We chatted about the weather. He mentioned that he enjoyed the drive up from Lancaster, but had to get serious and get down to work. It was a shame on such a beautiful day. Responding to his mention of Lancaster, I told him I lived in Pickerington, and flew out of Fairfield County. He was surprised that I was a pilot. He had flown in the military, but not since. Suddenly, he asked me what I had. I told them that I really didn't know. I told him the prospective witness had initiated contact with me. I told him only the facts, not the suppositions and conclusions. He was intrigued at the storage in an abandoned water tower, and joked that it wasn't a typical lair. He wanted to meet my witness. I told him the witness was not local, and that I had warned him to lay low and do nothing suspicious. I didn't think the fellow should draw attention to himself by taking a day off work. Unless he wanted to travel for a night meeting, I thought I might be able to fly him in the following Saturday. I suggested we rendezvous on Mt. Pleasant, a sandstone cliff that dominates Lancaster. He shrugged and told me to call. He paused as he walked away and accused me of liking the cloak and dagger business. He turned back a second time to say that he had checked with others in the office before coming this morning. They said I was OK. Personally, he never liked me. He warned me that it better be good. I scolded myself again for disclosing that I would fly Joe in, I didn't need to disclose that. As for the rest, I was used to taking shots from law enforcement types. That was just another day in the life at the defense bar.

I started for my office to call Joe, but thought better of it. Now that the Feds were on notice, who knew? Who knew how fast they would move? At this point, I was the only one they knew about. I had made myself the focal point. I pulled over to a phone booth. Joe was not home. It was nearly noon, so I tried his parents. I still knew the number after all the years. His mother answered. Yes, he was there. I warned him not to talk to his family. I asked him if he liked to fly. He said he did. I told him I had arranged a meeting with a federal agent at a park in Lancaster, Ohio the following Saturday. I would fly up to Sandusky and take him to the meeting. He should be waiting for me at the airport in Sandusky at 8:30 A.M. Saturday. He should not call my home or my office. If he had to talk to me, he should leave a message at my office to call my friend and give me the number of a phone booth and a time to call him there. I also would call from a phone booth. I did not trust anyone, not even the Federales. He must not talk to anyone or do anything more during the week. He agreed.

I picked Joe up as scheduled that Saturday morning. He was waiting with a cup of coffee on a bench outside the terminal at Griffing when I taxied up. I had deliberately not filed a flight plan that morning. They might be watching for that. I doubted that they would tail my flight, although it would not be difficult. The FAA did it all the time in pilot enforcement cases. I have handled a few of those. They always trotted out these computer plots of flight paths, made from radar hits that were stored on their computer tapes. They could track me, but at least I wasn't going to make it easy on them by filing a flight plan. Joe and I did not talk about the situation on the way down. We talked about flying. He liked it. A friend had taken him up for the first time recently. He was thinking about taking some courses and getting certified as an A&P mechanic. I smiled at the same old Joe. We landed at Fairfield County and returned to my tie-down without ceremony. I drove him into Lancaster, and we walked up the back of Mt. Pleasant together. We found my man leaning on the old pipe railing along the rim. I introduced them and gave a quick profile of my life-long friendship with Joe. I was surprised when the agent told Joe that when I vouched for someone, he took it seriously. Joe nodded, then commented on the view. It was a picturesque town from this vantage, with the county fairgrounds and its racetrack at the base of the cliff, tightly packed houses on checkerboard squares, old glass plants at the edge of town, and the Hocking Hills to the south. The agent pointed out Beck's Knob and gave a thumb nail geological history of the area. He had grown up here. Joe wasn't used to the topography. Where he came from the land was flat. I excused myself and went to the south end of the rim while they talked. I watched them talking, but I could not hear what was said. Twenty minutes later, they came up to me. The agent called me "Counselor" I remember that, it's funny the little things you remember. Anyway, he said, "Counselor, your friend has agreed to give a statement. Want to come?" I was Joe's ride home, so I went.

When we got to the Holiday Inn on the northwest edge of Lancaster, my concern for how quickly the FBI could move was validated. The agent made a call from a phone in his car in the parking lot. We followed him to a drive-through where we all bought burgers and fries. When we got to the motel, another agent I knew was waiting in the lobby. He took us to a conference room. There, a video camera was perched on a tripod at one end of the table. A tape recorder and microphone sat in the center of the table. A court reporter sat to the side of the table. While we ate the lunches, Joe produced a half dozen video tapes from the bag he was carrying. The reporter marked each one and put evidence stickers on them. She had Joe put his initials on each one, and then she sealed each in a separate plastic evidence bag. I had been through the chain of custody many times, but this was the first time I saw it first hand.

When the statement started, I deliberately stayed off camera. First, the court reporter swore Joe. Then the agent read Joe his rights. He got Joe to confirm that it was the second time he had received his rights that day. He asked if Joe was represented by counsel. I asked if Joe was the target of an investigation. The agent said no. Joe looked to me. I shook my head no, so Joe answered that he was not represented and did not want an attorney. Then the agent asked if Joe had been made any promises or given any inducements in connection with his testimony. Joe said he had come forward on his own. Then the agent asked if Joe was aware of the serious nature of his statement, that the information would be used in a criminal investigation, and that there were criminal penalties for perjury. When Joe acknowledged, the agent simply asked Joe to tell his story. Joe did so in a calm and measured fashion. He stuck to the facts. After that, the agent had him identify and describe each of the tapes. Later, they went over the details again and again. From the questioning it was clear they were focused on two things, the identification of the cargo pilot and the contents of the tower. I could see the point of both. Obviously the pilot expanded their information base. Joe, however, refused to identify the pilot. On the contents of the tower, he was adamant it was all computer components, even though he could only describe the contents of one package. No, he had not photographed the inside of the tower, any of the packages or even the one he claimed to have opened. Towards the end of the session, with the audio and video tapes still recording and with the court reporter taking down every word, they asked Joe to sign consents to a telephone tap and a search of his home. Again he looked to me. I nodded yes, and he signed.

I motioned for Joe not to speak on the way to the airport. I was still concerned about our friends and their electronic gadgetry. While we preflighted the plane, I reviewed my thoughts of the afternoon. I warned him not to say anything he didn't want others to hear and record on his home phone. I told him that once an investigation got started, there was no telling where it would go. He would have to work at keeping his private life private. I smiled and told him they had gotten more than enough for a search warrant of the tower. They would probably wait until they had more, but they had enough. He was a reliable informant. Joe said he had never thought of himself as an informant. He didn't like the word. I asked why he was protecting the pilot. He had to know that they would find the pilot and set up surveillance on that end. Joe's holding back drew suspicion toward himself and the pilot. He seemed shocked. He didn't want to make trouble for her. Her, I asked. He said that I knew her. I had gone to law school with her. I rolled my eyes and groaned.

CHAPTER 14

"Sandy, Joe. Sorry I missed you. Listen, I don't know how to start this. Things are getting crazy. I'm not cut out for this. I need to talk to you. Whatever you do, do not call my house. Please. Do not call my house. I will keep trying until I get you. You can call work, but only leave a message for me to call my friend from Detroit. Do not leave your name. Please. I'm making my calls from telephone booths these days. You won't believe this."

Joe got back in his car. He cruised around Sandusky for an hour, afraid to go home. His friend had flown him back to Sandusky after the session with the FBI. They hadn't talked much on the flight. When they did, their talk was about the plane. Joe didn't say it, but he knew he could take the plane apart and put it back together without taking any classes. The plane would be better than when he started. He couldn't see Sandy in a plane like this. It was old and ill kept. The vinyl interior was discolored and cracked. The paint job was blistered and faded. His friend claimed the airframe and power plant were all that mattered. There were low hours on the engine, no corrosion, and no damage history. He didn't bother with the cosmetics because he stored it outside. It was late afternoon. The shadows from the trees and fence line were long. Lancaster-Fairfield County is directly south of Griffing-Sandusky. His friend told him it was the easiest flight he'd ever navigated. He simply took off, turned north, and followed the fence lines and county roads to Lake Erie. He seemed glad to be getting the hours. Joe was impatient. He wanted to talk to Sandy. It was a long hour and a half for Joe; made even longer as they had another round of hamburgers at the counter at Griffing-Sandusky. He had to put up with another round of stern warnings from his friend as they watched the line boy fuel the plane. He stayed until his friend took off. The message had been received. He was scared as hell. He had to warn Sandy.

Joe stayed out until after 9:00 P.M. He drove west to Port Clinton to kill time. He called Sandy from a pay phone there. He left a shorter message on her voice mail. Do not call his house. Leave only messages at work, no names, no numbers. He drove east to Huron and called again. He drove back to Sandusky. He slowed when he passed The Maples Motel. He surveyed the pool, the room where Sandy had stayed. He was falling in love with her. He admitted it. He had to warn her. He drove along the Cedar Point Peninsula then took the Causeway across the bay into town. He stopped at a phone booth near The Harbour to call one last time. This time he said he was going home. Do not call the house. He would call tomorrow. If their mutual friend called for a flight, go ahead. Everything had to stay normal. Proceed as usual. Joe laid awake until the wee hours cursing Pete Falloni. Unknown to Joe, Sandy landed at Griffing field at 11:30 P.M. She brought another shipment from Missouri. Pete was waiting when she landed. They chatted. She decided not to call Joe because of the hour. She departed just before midnight. She got home at 2:00 A.M. She wanted to call Joe, just to hear his voice, but she restrained herself. Instead, she checked her voice mail. After that, she couldn't sleep either.

Joe worried all Monday morning at work that a team of FBI agents were going to storm into the building, arrest Pete, and climb the tower. He should have told them not to do that. He should have insisted. He could do that. Pete might be a little piece in a much bigger puzzle. He had to be. The important thing was to trace where it was coming from and where it was going. The money trail would help, but he couldn't get into that. He only knew about the parts. He could deal with them. At noon he went out for lunch. As he left, Lynette gave him a phone message and teased him about his mysterious female friend from Detroit. He tried to reach Sandy, but got the voice mail again. She had changed her message. She was out and would return after 7:00 P.M. He called the FBI in Columbus. He had the calling cards of two agents, the one with whom he initially spoke and the second one from the motel. The first agent was not in, the second agent took his call. Joe urged them not to search the tower. It was too early, they needed more if they were going to do something other than bust little Pete Falloni. The agent perceived that Joe was jumpy. He tried to calm and reassure him. He promised they would do nothing without telling Joe first. They would not put Joe at risk. Joe did not believe it. He told him he was already at risk. The agent told him to go back to work, business as usual. Joe went by the discount store and bought more video tapes. Now he was angry and determined to get the little bastard.

Joe changed the tapes Monday evening after work. At home he was surprised to see that Pete had paid a visit to the tower early that morning. He looked around his house trying to determine if it had been searched. He couldn't tell. He went out to call Sandy. He finally reached her. She had a short hop that afternoon that she couldn't cancel. She had flown for their friend Saturday night. What in the hell was going on. Joe stopped her. He started to give her the number of the phone booth he was at, but then realized that if he did, someone might be listening. It would make no point for her to go to a phone booth and call this booth if they had the number. He noticed a twenty-four hour print shop across the street with a fax sign in the window. He asked her if she had a fax. She said yes, she had to turn it on. It was on her telephone line. Joe told her he would send a fax in fifteen minutes. She was to go to a telephone booth and call the fifth number on the fax. Number five. Joe frantically drove from telephone booth to telephone booth writing down the numbers and the locations until he had ten. Then he went back to the print shop and paid to telecopy the list to Sandy. When he got back to the fifth pay phone, it was ringing.

Sandy kidded at first, then listened to everything Joe had to say without responding. He told her about contacting their Columbus friend, the flight to Lancaster, the meeting in the park, the sworn statement in the motel. They wanted her name. He had not given it. They knew that a pilot was flying the goods in, that was all. She was stunned. Why did he think he had to shield her? Did he think she was in on it? Why would he keep calling if he thought she was part of it? She tried to find words but in her confusion could not. He asked her about the most recent flight. She told him it was just like any of a dozen others. It had been arranged Friday afternoon. The money had been transferred into her account. She flew to Missouri then back to Sandusky with a few packages. Falloni met her. Nothing out of the ordinary. Joe did not tell her about the video tapes.

He wanted to, and it hurt him not to, but he was learning the game. Why wasn't she saying more, asking more? Why didn't she sound as upset as he felt? Joe told her that since the flight was after his meeting with the FBI, that they should assume Falloni was followed and that the Feds now knew who she was. He knew his home phone was tapped. He had agreed to it. If she had to call, call work. He would tell her which item on the list to call and a time to call it. She should only call from a phone booth. At this point her line might be tapped also. He waited for a response, but heard only silence. He wanted her to offer to come forward, to cooperate like he had. Nothing. He told her not to call unless she absolutely had too. He hung up and stared at the phone. Now he couldn't trust her either. On the other end, Sandy stared at the receiver with tears streaming down her face. He didn't trust her.

As the week progressed, Joe actually relaxed. Business returned to the usual. They were busy at work, it was a comfortable distraction. Wednesday evening, he changed the tapes. At home, he found them blank. Friday afternoon, he got a telephone message at work. He hoped it was Sandy, but it was the urologist's office. Please call, was checked on the pink form. Instantly, he was loaded with stress again. Red was not in, so he went to his office off the sales floor to return the call. It was like walking to the gallows. He called the number, identified himself, and was told to hold. He felt his ears burning. His face was flushed, his hands trembled. If he could get through this, he could get through anything. A nurse came on and gave her name. She said she had his file in front of her. All of the tests were back. They were positive; no, she meant to say the tests were clear. Everything was fine. There was nothing wrong with him. She meant to say positive in the good sense. There was no need for another appointment. She was sorry about the confusion. She was so sorry. Joe remained tense for the balance of the afternoon. What difference did it make anyway? He must have been dreaming. That bastard Falloni! He went to change the tapes after work as usual.

Joe's chest tightened. He couldn't breathe when he saw the tapes had been changed. There was a different brand of tape in each recorder. Falloni knew. The son of a bitch was on to him. How? Where had he slipped up? He hadn't told Sandy about the tapes. It couldn't be her. Yes it could. She could have told him about me going to the FBI. That would be enough. If he knew that, why would he change the tapes? To destroy the evidence, that's why. What evidence? A glimpse of Pete and a date and time stamp. It meant nothing unless there were more to connect it up. He was overreacting. He had to calm down. The tapes in the machine were new. There were no marks or writing on them. He could match them also. Maybe Pete just decided the other tapes were old. After all, he triggers them and then rewinds them all the time. Maybe Pete reasoned that he was wearing out the beginning of each tape and simply decided to change them out.

When Joe pulled up in front of his house, he saw a solid color, no chrome, no hub cap car with two extra antennas. Inside it, two men in suits were waiting. They got out as Joe walked up to them. They suggested that they talk inside. Inside, they produced identification. They were from the FBI office in Cleveland. They were here to search his house on the basis of his previous consent. They asked if he wanted to withdraw the consent. When he said he did not, one kidded that they had a warrant just in case he refused. Joe asked if he could verify their identities before they started. He was nervous, but he was learning. He called the Columbus office on his phone. He supposed that it would not matter, unless Falloni was also listening. He could do that. Falloni wasn't as good of a radio bug as he thought, but he could do it. Joe put the phone down. He asked if he could use the cellular phone in their car. They agreed, and one of them called the Columbus office for him. The call was transferred through to the first agent's home. A child answered. Joe heard a TV in the background. Joe fought to overcome his embarrassment, but proceeded. He apologized for disturbing the man at home. He was scared, and all this was new to him. He wanted to verify identities. The other two men handed him their cases containing their ID and badges. Joe read the names and described the men. The Columbus agent vouched for them, then asked Joe how he was doing. Joe grumbled. He did have another tower tape. Falloni had received a flight Saturday night and gone up the tower afterward. The agent asked about the flight. Joe said he couldn't answer how he knew. The agent asked him to give the new tape to the men from Cleveland.

The search took two hours. The men worked together. They photographed each room. They filled out forms. They inventoried the entire house. They even checked the crawl space overhead and each air duct. They spent most of the time in Joe's radio shack. Again they inventoried all the equipment. Of the few things that were factory built, they took model names and serial numbers. They had him operate each piece of equipment. They had him turn on his computer and one made a list of the software names that came up on the main menu. The other went up to the keyboard and got into DOS. He pulled up a directory list and sent it to Joe's printer. They asked a lot of questions about the modem. The same agent got into Joe's communication software and printed a list of the last thirty phone calls on the system. They wanted to know if Joe did any banking through the computer. He didn't directly, but he did keep all his finances in the machine. He could pull up bank account numbers and balances if they wanted them. They did. Joe printed them out. He told them he had a few stocks that he bought and sold through the computer. He volunteered that also. He told them that all the phone calls were to an on-line service through which he connected with a discount brokerage house. He printed a copy of his portfolio. The agents didn't say anything to Joe, but they looked back and forth to each other when they saw he had over a quarter of a million dollars in stocks. Joe noticed and shrugged it off. He was an old bachelor with no one to spend his money on. He'd been lucky. He could account for every penny. His tax returns were in the computer too. Did they want them? They did. Before they left, they searched and inventoried his truck. They had him operate all its radios.

After they left, Joe went out to call Sandy. He drove around for a half hour before deciding he was not followed. He went into the Mall and found a pay phone there. It was number seven on his list. Sandy answered. He told her to call number seven as soon as she could.

CHAPTER 15

"Joe?"

"Yes."

"How are you?"

"Fine. Crazy. Stress not strain, so far. How are you doing?"

"The usual. Punching holes in the sky. Lonely."

"Yeah, me too. Listen, I don't know how to deal with this."

"You? Me either."

"I'd better get off the line. Don't call my house, ever. Things have heated up. I'll call when I can."

"Joe...."

He hung up. Both ached after the call. Back in her condo Sandy put the most recent bank confirmation with the stack of others. Another flight for Preferred Wholesale, Inc. She had already called the bank about it. They would not give any information other than Monroe, Michigan. It did not have a telephone listing there. She resolved to call the Secretary of State's office Monday and find out who was behind the corporation.

Driving home Joe realized that Saturday and Sunday nights seemed to be common times for Pete to climb the tower. He'd stake it out. He'd buy a video camera and stake out the tower. At home, he watched TV and thought of Sandy. She wasn't doing a damn thing to build confidence. It would be so easy. All she had to do was to offer to call the FBI. She was making them both look bad. He woke on the sofa, turned off the TV and went to bed. The next morning he went to the Mall and bought a camcorder.

Saturday night, Joe waited until it was pitch black before he went out. He knew that if Pete was going to climb the tower, it would be late. It was summer, and the sun set late. At 9:30 P.M. Joe drove slowly toward work. He drove by once, but did not see Pete's car. He circled around and parked in front of a small empty church on Third Street. There was a vacant lot between him and the old factory. Once, that lot too held a factory as did most of the lots several blocks along the waterfront in any direction. Now, at least half were gone. In some instances only the concrete floors remained. The rest had been completely raised. Some of the locals had gardens in the vacant lots. A few new buildings had gone up in the last ten years. A few of the old buildings had been restored. Most were occupied. Joe left his windows down. He had brought a pillow. He laid down across the seat, leaning up against the passenger door. He tested the camera. He focused it on the tower and checked the date and time stamp. He turned it on and spoke out loud so that the tape would record his commentary. He reviewed the tape in the view finder. It didn't look good, the tower was little more than a shadow against the glow from Cedar Point, but it might be better on a full size color screen. He listened to some neighborhood kids playing in the distance and fought back the frequent reflection that plagued him about that lost part of his own life. He listened to the sounds of the amusement park drifting across the bay. At 10:30 P.M. he saw Pete pull into the parking lot. Moments later, Joe taped him crossing the roof and climbing the tower.

Pete put his head through the hatch and surveyed the area before he climbed out of the tower. He thought he recognized Joe's truck across the lot in front of the building. There were a couple of small houses there. Maybe Joe was visiting friends, if he had friends. What a weird duck he had become. He really didn't know much about him, other than the electronics hobby. He knew that he'd quit drinking. He'd lost weight. He looked better. His work was the same. His work had never suffered. It was going to be difficult to do, but the day was coming. Joe made too much, he was too bright for his position, he knew too much. He had to go. The truck was in front of that little church. Maybe Joe had found Jesus. Seeing no traffic along First Street, he climbed out and down the tower. Joe taped it all. He stayed for several minutes after Pete drove away. He taped his departure also.

At home, Joe was elated at the quality of the tape. With the zoom you could tell it was Pete coming and going. You couldn't recognize him on the roof and tower, but you could clearly see a figure. The tower tapes would fill that gap. He was so excited he planned to switch the tower tapes Sunday night and climb the tower himself. Pete wasn't likely to go up two nights in a row. He would take his camera into the tower and tape it for the FBI. He changed tapes in his camcorder and experimented in his house. He zoomed in on magazines and envelopes. Then he played it on his TV. He could read the larger text. He learned he had to hold the camera still and count to ten to get a good enough image to read. He was going to get the FBI pictures of the tower and an inventory of its contents complete with serial numbers. They should like that. Joe found his four cell flashlight and checked its operation. He would use it for a light source for the camcorder.

When he woke Sunday morning, Joe's first thought was of the Pelee Island ferry. If Pete had gotten some packages the night before, maybe he would make a delivery. He couldn't be sure if Pete had carried things into or out of the tower. He put his Falloni tape back in the camera and drove downtown. He parked several blocks from the waterfront. He kept the camcorder in a nylon duffle bag. He didn't want to be too obvious. Sure enough, he saw Pete's car in the lot. It was the same, exactly the same. Pete was talking to the ferryman. Pete walked over to the Corvette and came back with an arm load of white packages. He pressed something into the man's hand. Joe put the camcorder back in the bag and hurried home. There he watched his handiwork several times. He was going to nail the bastard.

Sunday night, Joe was on a high. He was not scared. He was trembling from exhilaration. He compared it to the edge he got just before entering the parlors in Cleveland. Pete had turned him into an adrenalin junkie. He went out the window of the block house and crossed the roof to the motor house. Inside, he double checked the new tapes he bought to make sure they matched the ones in the recorders. They did. He went up the tower leg without hesitation. He laid on the catwalk for a moment to catch his breath, then went on up the side of the tank and into the hatch. Inside, he held the large flashlight along the edge of the camcorder. He took pictures down on the entire storage area from the inside ladder. He took long slow pictures of each stack. He focused on one of the serial numbers in each stack and held the camera on it. He read each number out loud in a muted voice for the camera to record. His heart skipped when he couldn't find the package that he had shrink wrapped. Maybe he had done such a good job that he couldn't tell it himself. No, he could tell. He had put it on the bottom of one of the stacks. It was gone. He was had. No, maybe Pete just took it in the ordinary course. Pete was an inventory fanatic. First in, first out. Pete would have taken the next package from the bottom of the stack.

Joe should have thought of that. Well, he was either known, or he wasn't. It was time to get the hell out.

Just as Joe was about to start down the tower leg from the catwalk, he saw the block house door open. Shit. He watched Pete cross the roof to the motor house. He knew he only had seconds. His heart pounded. He scampered back up on the catwalk. With his back up against the tower, he sidestepped along until he was on the bay side of the tower. He fought to control his breathing. He wished he could stop his heart from pounding. He could hear Pete climbing up the leg, even over the ringing in his ears. His initial plan was to wait Pete out. He'd stay until Pete left. He could hear Pete humming. The son of a bitch was humming! He had to get out. As soon as he heard Pete inside the tower, he hurriedly slipped around the edge and down the leg. About half way down, he heard the humming even more clearly through the broken off stand pipe that hung below the tower. The arrogant bastard! Pete had left the door to the block house open. Joe slipped in, then put his head out to see if Pete were following. No. Down in the shop, he climbed into a forty footer that was in a cradle for hull repairs. In the captain's stateroom under the fan tail, he opened a porthole and listened for Pete. Again he struggled to control his breathing. Moments later he taped Pete in the dark coveralls with a backpack. Later, Joe's jog home calmed him. He played the tape. It was perfect. He wanted to call the FBI right away, but did not because of the hour. He wished he could call Sandy. He needed to talk. He had twenty years to get off his chest.

CHAPTER 16

Joe was startled when his phone rang Monday morning. He was standing in his kitchen eating breakfast. It was the FBI agent from Columbus. Joe interrupted and said that he suspected there might be more than one set of ears listening. There was a long silence, then the agent told him his friends from Friday night would be there in a few minutes. Joe gulped his meal. He put his dishes in the sink and walked across his living room. When he looked outside, they were there. He grabbed the most recent tape. As Joe climbed into the back seat, one of them handed him a cellular phone.

"Listen, Buckaroo, you are not exactly ingratiating yourself with me."

"I'm sorry, I don't understand. Excuse me a minute." Joe asked the two men to drive, he didn't want his neighbors to notice.

"The guys you are riding with have some interesting observations of you. One of them thinks you're part of it. The other is convinced you are pure. It's my call. You know what I think. I think you have a pure heart and empty head. Do you have anything to say for yourself?"

"I got tape of Falloni climbing the tower Saturday night; more Sunday morning at the ferry. Last night I went into the tower and taped everything. I got you the serial numbers off everything there." Joe leaned forward and handed the agent in the passenger seat his latest tape.

"The guys are camping at the Radisson. They have a direct view of the tower. The lens they're using has superior light gathering capability. Right now I'm looking at a picture of you on the tower. It's a telecopy, but you should see the look on your face. I'd hate to be doing your laundry. You listen to me, this shit stops now. We are on the case. You are going to get yourself hurt. They tell me you are also in the foreground of their tape of the transhipment on the ferry. The cowboy shit stops now."

"Understood."

"So who do you think is listening?"

"I assume you guys are, but it occurred to me that Falloni could do it. He's fiddles with electronics. He could do it if he wanted."

"We'll sweep this morning. By the way, does Falloni use a cordless phone at work?"

"Yes. He has for years. He made it himself."

"We thought it was him. Picked it up Friday. He sure has the power on that thing cranked up. In my opinion the radio waves are public, and we're free to listen. Mr. Falloni is too clever by half. We're on his frequency. Just in case his lawyer is a little more cleaver, we're getting a warrant for a wire this morning. You understand. We are listening. He'll hang himself. You've done enough. Cool it. Anything else I should know?"

"It's all on the tape."

"You going to tell me about the pilot?"

"No. That's not my decision."

"Joe, it's my call. I believe you're with us. I have to be honest, we do have a scenario that you're the kingpin and you're using us to grab everyone else before the house of cards collapses on you. Now listen carefully. You are not a target. That means a lot legally. You are not a target. I want you with us. No more cowboy shit, no more sneaking around to pay phones. I need the pilot."

"Sorry. I can't."

"We'll have the pilot before the end of the day, a couple of days at most."

"Do what you have to do."

"Taxpayer's money, Joe. Hey, your buddy took me and my kid flying yesterday in his sorry excuse for a plane. He's worried that he hasn't heard from you. I told him everything was fine. I told him not to call you. I'd prefer you not call him. We need to contain this investigation until we get it focused. You're lucky to have a friend like him."

"Thanks."

"He let me fly a little. I learned in a 172 at the Academy. It's been a lot of years. It comes back, just like riding a bike."

"They teach you to fly at the FBI Academy?"

"No, Air Force. I just may start flying again. Listen, you'll be late for work. The guys will give you their number at the Radisson. You start talking to them. They are your friends. They may be your only friends."

"Yes sir. Thank you. I'm with you."

The field agents dropped Joe down the street from his house. He gave them permission to enter during the day to check his phone and sweep for bugs. He said he would leave the door unlocked. The Columbus agent had been speaking from his home office in Lancaster. Driving up Route 33 to Columbus he decided it was about time for the inter-agency inquiries and notices. He'd wait for the serial numbers from Joe's video and confirmation of what the goods were, but he'd draft the notice first thing when he got to the office. One thing was for sure, he was going to take it right out of the manual. He would tell who he had to, what he had to, but not one damn thing more. He hated sharing information. He hated electronic mail. It always seemed like he gave more than he ever got. It was just more bureaucratic crap. It was a security risk.

The rest of the drive he ran through the alphabet soup of agencies that he would have to notice and make inquiry: CIA, just in case; Defense, just in case; DEA, they seemed to think everything starts with drugs; the IRS, perhaps a stand-up citizen like Mr. Falloni got so busy he neglected his taxes; Commerce because of the export to Canada, certainly without an export license; and State, so they could notify the Canadians. Christ, here come Canadian Customs and the Mounties. How in the hell could they seriously preach information compartments at Agency seminars with all this mandatory inter-agency cooperation? Well, maybe they'd get lucky and find someone else working Mr. Falloni. Not likely. He wished that they still did the inquiries and notices from D.C. That's the way it goes. He and his peers around the country had complained en masse about information leaking out through other agencies, so they got put in charge of deciding which agencies to notify. Well, that was one way to handle it. He'd do anything to be drinking coffee with the guys at the Radisson in Sandusky.

Mid-morning, Pete came out into the shop and asked Joe to come into his office. Pete followed him, the stress loading. Pete stopped by the door and motioned Joe inside. Joe stepped inside while Pete closed the door. Pete motioned him to take a chair. Pete sat down behind his desk. Joe flashed back across the years to a similar encounter with Pete's father. He thought he was getting fired, but got a raise. Nothing would surprise him now.

"Joe, we go back a lot of years. My Dad thought the world of you. He used to tell me I could build a business on you. I think that you and I have completely rebuilt this business. It's not the business my Dad ran. Everything has changed." Joe nodded his agreement. "Lately, I get the feeling that you're not happy. Am I right?"

"You and your father have been good to me. This is home."

"Hell, Joe. You could have made a lot more working union in one of the plants."

"I tried that. I'm not a union man."

"Don't be too hard on the unions. They aren't so bad. Their members just want a better life. The leaders, hell, they're just businessmen. You ought to figure up what the take of union dues is at any of these places around here. Then when you consider the pension funds, now that's really big business. It makes us look like pikers."

"Not for me. I admit I have thought about my own business."

"That's what I'm talking about. I can tell that you're not happy. I don't know what to do. I used to consider you my strong right arm. Now I think of you as a problem."

"I'm sorry you feel that way. I know our business ethics are different. I may not agree with everything you do, but I know whose name is on the water tower."

"Joe, loyalty is not a simple thing. I know the guys look up to you. That's fine, but you hit it on the nose. It is my business. I have to run it my way. I know you would do most things different from me. Can't have two bosses. My problem is that I can't stand you looking over my shoulder. I can feel it. You have become a distraction."

"I just come to work and try to do a good job. Like your Dad used to say, that way, at the end of the day neither one of us owes the other anything."

"You know, when I started, I worked hard because I thought I should. Then I worked to make money. We all work for money. Anymore, I think, I really do it just to do a good job. You know, to stand back at the end of the day and look it over and say it's good. Everybody else would do it different. Somebody else might do it better. I did it good. It's my home, Joe, not your's. You are the hired help."

"Sorry you feel that way."

"Joe, if it's any consolation, there isn't another person in this company that I could talk to like this. You are a cut above the rest."

"Yeah, thanks."

"The Old Man was much better with people than me. I'm no good at this. Here's my thinking. You would like a place of your own. I can't have you around here anymore, but I don't want another competitor. What say, I give you a year's salary and you sign a one year confidentiality and non-competition agreement. That gives you a year to get something going. Hopefully, it won't be in the marine business, even after the year."

"That's it?"

"Not quite. Our lawyer will have to write it up. There's always fine print. I am very serious about it. I've got to get something for that kind of money. You couldn't take any of the software or customer lists. I can't have you hiring away people. You know a great deal about my business. I can't have you giving information about me to anyone. That's what the confidentiality part is about. You'll have to keep your mouth shut. Understand?"

"I think I do. Yes, I understand?"

"Let's make it two years. That better? I'll get the legal beagle started on the paperwork. You think it over. It's for the best. We'll both be better off. I can do things my way without looking over my shoulder for you. You can get your own business going." Pete stood, signaling Joe to stand also. "For now, just keep this between us. No one needs to know."

Soon after Joe left Pete's office, Pete had on his headset and was calling to place a parts order. There were several boat manufacturers in Missouri. One of them had clued Joe in on the very special source of components he was calling. The agents were just returning to their room at the Radisson. They had found Joe's house and phone clean. When they entered the room, one of their tape recorders was turning. The voice activated recorder was attached to a radio. The radio was wired to a collapsible gathering dish aimed at the old factory. They had stumbled across the cordless phone frequency Friday afternoon a couple of blocks from the building. It wasn't an FCC approved band, which is why they noticed the frequency on the scanner when it hit. They were used to seeing the authorized frequencies. They also took note of it because of its clarity. The substance of the conversations matched their boy. Both were amazed, even more amazed that they could pick it from the hotel. It was at least a mile. They did have line of sight, but this was highly unusual. The bozo was spoon feeding them. One of the men turned on the audio as the other settled into a padded chair. A man's voice was reading off a list of parts numbers and demanding to know when he could expect delivery. They took it to be Falloni.

"Pete, buddy, you're not listening. I'm not writing orders. I can't. You're not our only customer. Everybody is screaming. I just spent an hour on the horn with Brother Carrolla in San Jose. He's moth balling the operation for awhile. Apparently, the company has an audit team in the factory, logisticians, he called them. They are trying to figure out why their material purchases don't match their production." He laughed. "The assholes. What did they expect with no security? Brother C says there are suits all over the plant scratching their heads about inventory shrinkage. Our members on the line have stopped lifting. Them's the facts. I got no supply. You're just going to have to operate out of inventory for as long as you can. What the hell is a logistician anyway?"

"You can't do this to me. I have people expecting deliveries. My inventory won't cover it. I can't believe this! You must have an inventory. I relied on your pitch, '...steady stream of only the best made in the USA components, union made.' What bullshit! I have spent a fortune in time and money developing customers, putting together a delivery system. You just can't say you're not taking orders. That's bullshit. You people are in business. Where the hell are your ethics?"

"You're breaking my heart. Listen, I don't have time for this shit. I told you the way it is. Our members are under a spotlight. If we don't cool it, the whole operation could go down permanently. Just stay cool. A couple of weeks, a month or two, we'll get back in touch."

"Bullshit! Two months? Let me tell you something Brother O'Malley, you fill my orders or I'll personally come out to St. Louis and throw your fat ass out of that union hall."

"Pete, Pete. Calm down. I will overlook that last remark. I have to consider your inexperience. If I didn't, I'd have to consider it a threat. We don't take threats well, Pete. Stay calm, buddy. We'll get back to you. Remember, Pete, you don't fuck with us. We stick together." He laughed and sang, "You can't get me, I'm sticking with the union." Then his voice went flat. "Fuck with us, and your rotting carcass with be part of that sweet Lake Erie breeze."

The two agents danced around the room cheering and giving each other high fives. The whole operation was unbelievable. The bozos must really think they were untouchable. What incredible arrogance!

Don't they think anyone listens? The bigger they are, the harder they fall. They called Columbus. The agent there wanted to know exactly when the conversation took place. The hard wire under the warrant should have been activated at 10:00 A.M. They should have a full recording there too, plus phone numbers. He would follow up on that. It was moving fast. He laughed with them. He told them to enjoy it while they could. Investigations like this were few and far between. It made the years of boredom worth it. He congratulated them and told them to get back to it. He told them to pamper Joe. They had the outline, now it was time to start filling in the blanks. They might need Joe for that. After he hung up, he decided it was time for the inter-agency inquiries and notices to hit the E-mail. He'd better add the Department of Labor to the list. Joe called the men in the Radisson at noon. Falloni had tried to buy his silence.

CHAPTER 17

After work, as he had agreed with the agents at noon, Joe went home, changed into his biking clothes, and stopped in at the Radisson. They offered to share some of their pizza with him. He declined because he was riding. They made audio and video tapes of his recollection of his conversation with Falloni that morning. When they finished, they chatted about cycling. Joe offered to help one who professed an interest in fitness try on bikes. On his way out and knowing that they were still in their room, he called Sandy from a pay phone in the lobby. He caught her at home. He told her to go out and call number three on the list. Then he biked back to the McDonald's on the opposite side of the lagoon from hotel. While he waited for the phone to ring, he studied the front of the hotel, looking for the agents' room.

"Sandy, I hate talking to you like this. I don't have much time. I'll lay it out as quickly as I can. There is big trouble here. I'm in the middle of it. The FBI is on to Falloni. I am cooperating with them. Falloni even tried to bribe me today. This is big. It involves your flights. They have been pressuring me to identify you. I have not done that. Except for identifying you, I am cooperating. I will stop if you want me to."

"What are you saying? I can't stand Falloni. You think I'm part of this, don't you? Am I supposed to be impressed that you would cover for me because you think I'm a crook? Great! What kind of person am I supposed to think you are. Why wouldn't you identify me?"

"I don't know. I have no idea what I'm doing anymore. I just stumble along and do what seems right."

"I was dumb enough to think we had something in common, something like values."

"Look, I didn't see you rushing to step forward. I got out here alone. I didn't create this situation. God, I wish you were with me."

"That's rich. It won't work."

"I will do whatever you want. If you want me to identify you, I will. If you want me to stop cooperating, I will."

"You bastard." She started crying. "Do you think I'm part of it? Answer me."

"Of course not." Joe's voice cracked, he sniffled. "No. I just want this to be over. I'm tired of being alone."

"I'll talk to the FBI. Who do I call?"

"Just go home, we'll call in a few minutes."

Joe went back to the Radisson. The first thing he told the agents was that the pilot would talk. He gave no further explanation. He asked if it was OK to use their phone. The agent attached a mike and recorder to the phone. Joe called. He told Sandy that he was with two FBI agents. The conversation was being recorded. They gave him their identification and he read their names and badge numbers to her. He said if she was ready to talk they were ready to listen. She agreed. Joe handed the phone to one of the agents. He spoke with Sandy for over an hour. He began with the entire litany of warnings that Joe had received before his statement in Lancaster. She understood her rights, she did not want a lawyer, she knew it was serious, she knew about perjury, she had not been promised anything, she was coming forward voluntarily. She described her business and her history with Falloni, including the first purchase order and the bank transfers. She went to get her pilot's log and the bank confirmations. On her own, she had checked with the Michigan Secretary of State's office. Falloni was behind Preferred Wholesale. Using her logbooks and bank records, she went through her recollection of each flight. Some she remembered in vivid detail, some not at all, most vaguely. Except for the one time Joe met her, Falloni always personally came to the airport in Sandusky. It was the same in Detroit and Missouri. It was always the same men. Yes, she could identify them. She gave descriptions. Yes, she was willing to testify in court. She agreed to a tap on her phone and a search of her condo. They told her they were particularly interested in her business records. It would help if she got everything organized for them. She told them they could have whatever they wanted. They asked if she could stay home in the morning to meet two agents from the Detroit office. She agreed. Why had she delayed in coming forward? They could ask Mr. Altznauer about that.

Joe didn't get back to his house until after 11:00 P.M. After the telephone interview with Sandy, he went ahead with his bike ride. He rode east to Vermillion and back along Route 6. Afterwards he limped. He had pushed it too hard and pulled his right calf muscle. He showered, then massaged liniment into his calf. Then, he called Sandy. He got her voice mail. She wasn't answering. The only message he left was that he was sorry.

Wednesday Joe got another early morning call from the Columbus agent. Sandy had agreed to give a formal statement, like Joe had, on one condition. She wanted Joe there. She was going to fly into Fairfield County that evening. They would have a room at the Holiday Inn just like the last time. They didn't want her flying into Sandusky, just in case someone was watching. She suggested that she pick Joe up at Keller Field near Port Clinton at 5:30 P.M. Was he willing to come? Could he make it after work? Joe agreed. The agent asked how things were going at work. Joe had nothing to report. Business as usual.

Sandy did not speak to Joe the entire flight south to Lancaster. In her twin Beech the trip went much more quickly than in his friend's single engine Cessna. Joe watched the sun out his side of the aircraft most of the way down. When not doing that, he studied the small towns. Joe spoke with the agent while Sandy got the plane fueled and secured. Then they drove to the motel. At the motel, Joe recognized the second agent and court reporter. They greeted him like old friends. They shared a few good natured barbs about his misguided friend from the defense bar. Sandy was all business.

She took the seat at the end of the table and the session began. They used photocopies from her logbook but the original bank confirmations. All were marked as exhibits. She identified and described each one. They also had her bank statements. They traced the payments into them. They asked her if any other funds came from Falloni, directly or indirectly. They produced her telephone bills and had her recall various calls she had made, including recent credit card calls to phone booths around Sandusky. The telecopy of Joe's list was also marked as an exhibit. They had her review her last three years of tax returns and asked if there was any income not included on them. They spread out two dozen photographs and asked her to identify anyone she could. She identified Joe, Falloni, the man from Detroit, and the man in Missouri. The picture of Joe was of him plastering himself up against the side of the water tower at night. She studied it longer than the others. Throughout the session Sandy stared at Joe. It made him uncomfortable. He frequently stood and went to peek out the window through the curtains. He was careful to stay off camera.

When they finished, the agent offered to put Joe and Sandy up for the night in the motel. Sandy wanted to get back. Joe didn't want to miss work. He drove them back to the airport. It was just before 1:00 A.M. when they landed at Port Clinton. There was no one attending the field that late. Sandy taxied to an empty tie-down. Joe had thought she would simply drop him off and keep going. He watched while she secured the plane. She was not making any explanations. Finally, she said she wanted to see where he lived. She pulled a small bag from the plane before she locked it. During the ride to Sandusky, there was no conversation. Joe wanted to let his excitement about the prospect of the night with her run its natural course, but he contained it because of her stern demeanor. She spent the ride looking out the passenger window and down at the line on the side of the highway. He looked to her from time to time, but could never find the right words to say.

He let her in the front door. She left her bag in the living room and went immediately to the kitchen. Searching the refrigerator she asked if he had any wine, then answered her own question. She supposed not. She took a soft drink, and went into the bath room. When she came out, Joe took his turn. While he was in there, she inspected his bedroom. When he came out, he found her in his radio shack. She went from one radio to the next, turning them on, dialing through the frequencies, then turning them off. The only time she spoke was to ask about his computer. He explained he did his finances and a little investing on it. She seemed to approve of the laser printer. She inspected the clutter of magazines on the coffee table in the modest living room. Most were radio and electronics magazines. She picked up one of the two aviation magazines on top of the stack, then tossed it down. She looked about the room at the four stereo speakers. Two were as tall as her. She went up to the shelves, but did not look at the stereo equipment. Instead she inspected a bi-fold frame. On one side was a young Joe and his bride on their wedding day. On the other was a smiling pudgy infant with a pink bow in her hair.

Sandy turned and told Joe that she was totally exhausted. If he didn't mind, she'd like to sleep in a bed. If he did, the sofa would do. He told her that he would take the sofa. He got clothes and bedding from the closet in his bedroom while she stood in the doorway. When he came out, she went in with her bag and closed the door. With a remote, he turned on his FM radio that was tuned to a Cleveland jazz station. He quickly turned the volume down, then back up just high enough to mask Sandy's rustling in the next room. He woke to the sound of her in the shower. He waited until he heard the bedroom door close, then he took his clothes into the bath. She was eating when he came out. She asked if he could drive her to the airport. He didn't have time. He picked up the phone and called the Radisson. The agents agreed to take her. Joe left before they got there.

CHAPTER 18

With surprising speed the investigation faded from Joe and Sandy's foremost thoughts. They thought mostly about each other. Still, neither called the other. Friday, Sandy had a charter carrying three executives from Detroit to Erie, Pennsylvania and back. For Joe, it was another day in the shop, up until a half hour before closing. Then, Pete called him into his office. Pete presented a five page single spaced document styled "Confidentiality and Non-Competition Agreement". He told Joe it should be consistent with their earlier discussion. Two years salary for two years of no competition and silence. Joe seemed a little befuddled flipping through it. Pete told him they didn't need to sign it right away. He could study it over the weekend. Monday, if everything was satisfactory, they could sign it and see about getting the money. Joe mostly nodded. He did not agree. That night he made a photocopy on a machine in a grocery store, called the agents in the Radisson, and took it to them. One of them complimented Joe's good fortune, saying that Sandy was one classy woman. Joe made long rides both Saturday and Sunday. Sandy washed her twin Saturday and went to Mass and brunch with her family on Sunday. Both resisted the temptation to call the other Sunday night.

Monday morning the Columbus agent called Joe at home as had become something of a custom. He said he'd read a telecopy of the proposed document. It was up to Joe, but it was his advice for Joe to sign, take the money, and get the hell out of the loop. He'd done enough for God and country. He couldn't say when they would move on Falloni. They planned to work the case upstream and downstream as long as they could. Joe thanked him for the advice and said he would take the offer. The conversation ended with the agent saying he'd be in touch. Joe left for work with an unusual sense of calm and relief. In fact, he spent the entire ride to work trying to recollect when he had ever felt so relaxed. He could not recall a similar feeling. Even when Pete called him into his office, he was oddly at ease.

"So, have you read it? Are you satisfied?"

"It's fine. Should we sign now?"

"Joe, perk up. This is a big day for both of us. We'll both make a new start today, a clean break."

"Things have just been happening very quickly. A couple of weeks ago I wouldn't have imagined any of this in my wildest dream."

"We live in an ever changing world, good buddy. Listen, my primary bank is in Michigan. Why don't we take the cigarette over to Monroe. I'll get you a cashier's check. We can sign up in the bank. I've been having trouble with one of the engines. You can bring your tools and tweak it along the way."

"No thanks. You know me and boats."

"Oh, come on. It's my last chance to take advantage of your talents. This is a red letter day. We'll go to the bank, I'll buy you lunch. We'll be back mid-afternoon."

"Can't you just make a call and wire the money into my account. Isn't that how business is done?"

Pete paused, then forced a smile. "Come on. Old times' sake."

"OK. I'll get my tools."

Just after 11:00 A.M. a nineteen year old typist who had only been on the job six weeks told a co-worker that she couldn't believe what she was hearing. She was transcribing wire tap tapes in the federal building in Toledo. The more experienced one motioned to the shift supervisor. The supervisor listened to the tape. She listened a second time comparing it to the transcript appearing on the color monitor. She printed a copy and hurried from the room. Ten minutes later the head agent of the Toledo FBI office was reading the transcript to the head agent in the Columbus FBI office. The transcript was recorded at 10:15 P.M. Sunday evening. It originated in St. Louis, Missouri, he read the phone number; the call went to Sandusky, Ohio, the Columbus agent copied the second phone number and checked his file. It was Falloni's home.

Male Voice No. 1: Pete?
Male Voice No. 2: Yes.
Male Voice No. 1: It's me.
Male Voice No. 2: That was a quick two months. Have things opened up?

Male Voice No. 1:	Sorry. Pete, we've got a problem, a very serious problem.
Male Voice No. 2:	Yes?
Male Voice No. 1:	Friends in high places have let us know that outsiders are looking in on our private lives. You can imagine how offensive we find this invasion of our privacy.
Male Voice No. 2:	What does that have to do with me?
Male Voice No. 1:	The curtains were pulled open for the peeping toms by someone who works for you. Do you have any idea who that might be, Pete?
Male Voice No. 2:	There's only one person it could be. I'm on top of that. I came to terms with him last week. I'm paying him tomorrow. He won't talk to anyone.
Male Voice No. 1:	Pete, terms, agreements, and understandings are not acceptable. You are to terminate this person's ability to exercise any options under your agreement. Do you understand me, Pete? This comes from on high.
Male Voice No. 2:	You can't mean....
Male Voice No. 1:	You wanted to play with the big boys, Pete. It goes with the territory.
Male Voice No. 2:	I'm a businessman, not....
Male Voice No. 1:	Pete, I'm trying to be your friend. You know that any chain is only as strong as its weakest link. Better a short chain with strong links, than a long chain with weak links. This link is in your company. If you can't take care of that, then we will have no choice but to cut the chain at your level.
Male Voice No. 2:	This is unbelievable. You just can't call my house on a Sunday night and...."
Male Voice No. 1:	Did you have a nice Sunday, Pete? I did too. You know, church with the

	wife and kids. Did you go to church today, Pete? Are you at peace with God? Did you kiss your kids good-night?
Male Voice No. 2:	I need time.
Male Voice No. 1:	Twenty-four hours, Pete. We're making it easy on you. We're going to take care of the other part of the problem in Detroit.
Male Voice No. 2:	I don't need this.
Male Voice No. 1:	Twenty-four hours, Pete. It's from on high. Be sure to kiss your kids."

Pete laid awake all night working through ways he could kill Joe. He never considered any other option. He did not waste one moment on whether or not, he only considered how. He laid next to his sleeping wife, stared at the ceiling, and worked through possible solutions to his problem. He did not own a gun. Guns and knives were out. That would look like murder. There would be an investigation. He visualized being on top of Perry's Monument with Joe, then Joe going over the side. Joe was weird. Suicidal? Who knew? Who ever does? How would he get him up there? How would he get him over the side? He visualized using a bomb. He could put it in the old Victory Hotel pool, lure Joe in, then blow it with a remote. The pool would contain the explosion, protect by-standers. He didn't have access to explosives. How would he get Joe to South Bass? There was no time. A bomb looks like murder. Who would murder Joe? It should be an accident. He could rig a cradle and have one of the big boats fall on him. That had possibilities. He could rig an electrical igniter in a fuel filler port and blow it with a remote. Boats exploded all the time. By the middle of the night, he was actually getting excited. He would solve this problem. He always did. Joe could drown. He knew Joe hated the water and didn't swim. That had possibilities.

The Columbus agent immediately called the team in the Radisson. He demanded Joe's location. The overnight transcripts showed that the night before Falloni had gotten orders to kill their witness. They reported that Joe had left with Falloni on a fast boat about an hour and a half ago. They checked their logs, the men left on Falloni's Pride at 10:12 A.M. They had considered renting a boat, but they would never catch up. They thought about a chopper, but figured he was just going for a final spin with the boss. The agent who said "final spin" apologized instantly. The Columbus agent told them to muster the Coast Guard, and whatever air support they could get out of the Cleveland office. He would contact Detroit and Toledo. His office had a mission support agreement with the local Air National Guard unit. He'd try to get a plane or helicopter. He didn't know how quickly they could react. He would be up as soon as he could. It was time to haul ass.

When Sandy pre-flighted her twin before a cargo flight Monday morning, she found the oil filler caps missing from both engines. At first she took it to be vandalism, then she thought it was someone after cheap parts. The more she reflected on the possibly fatal implications of the missing caps, she started on a slow burn. While a mechanic who occasionally did work for her called around for replacement caps, Sandy walked along the flight line asking everyone she met if they had seen anyone tampering with her plane. One line boy said he did, early that morning. The description he gave was close enough to Sandy's memory of the man who brought her parts for Falloni, that she immediately went to an outside pay phone and called the Columbus agent. He professed that he was happy to hear her voice. They had tried to catch her at home. She was to sit tight. Two agents were on their way to the airport. They had reason to believe that an attempt might be made on her life. She told him about the oil caps. He told her to wait for the agents. She had caught him on his way out the door. He was on his way to Sandusky. She asked about Joe. He said that Joe had the same problem. Joe was somewhere on Lake Erie with Falloni in his fast boat. They were scrambling every available Coast Guard and military aircraft. He told her to stay put and wait for the agents.

Sandy stood at the pay phone holding the receiver until she recognized the mechanic walking up with the new caps. She hurried him to the plane. They both went over it twice. They studied the fuel samples and the oil on the dipstick for contamination. She had him sit in the plane while she ran up the engines. When they were both satisfied that the plane was airworthy, she thanked him, and told him to tell two men who would be looking for her that she had joined the search. When the ground controller gave her taxi instructions to Runway 33, Sandy asked if they could get her the control frequency for a Coast Guard search on Lake Erie. She labeled it an urgent request. She was number one for the runway, so she switched to the tower frequency and requested clearance to take off VFR southeast. When she got the clearance, she renewed her previous request while she was rolling down the runway. The tower controller told her to stand-by, they were working on it. She was over the Detroit River when Detroit City Tower came back. He gave her the frequency, told her the winds were 340 at 12 and the altimeter 30.33, wished her well, and told her the frequency change was approved. She thanked him. The tailwind and clear sky would help. Sandy looked at her watch. It was just before noon.

Sandusky Bay seemed calm to Joe, but after they passed Cedar Point and got to the mouth of the bay channel, the full force of the lake waves hit them. It was a beautiful clear day, but the strong winds from the northwest had whipped up the lake. Joe complained and asked if they should go back. Pete gestured at the clear sky, but turned on the NOAA weather channel for a report. They were calling three to five foot waves and small craft advisories. Pete said they weren't small and assured Joe that when he opened it up, their ride would smoothen out. They rounded Marblehead and turned west cutting across the South Passage between Catawba and South Bass Islands.

Pete ran the engines at full throttle. Joe had himself braced into the left seat. They bounced across the tops of the waves. The pounding was giving him a headache. He studied the gauges. The left engine was consistently running at a hundred RPM's lower than the right. Pete could back off on the right, but that would be too easy. He had no respect for engines. He shouldn't cruise above 75% full power. About ten miles north of Port Clinton and an equal distance west of the Bass Islands, Pete pulled the throttles back to idle. The waves started rolling the boat. Pete asked Joe to do something to his left engine. He suggested the timing. Joe thought if he couldn't get the left engine up, he'd retard the right. They went to the back together, bracing themselves along the way. They lifted the engine cover, and Joe opened his tool box. As Joe leaned over the engine, Pete slipped back up to the controls. He gunned both engines, sending Joe flying smoothly and quietly over the stern. Joe hit the water at 10:40 A.M. He never called out. Pete never looked back.

When Joe struggled to the surface, Pete and Falloni's Pride were nowhere to be seen. Pete smiled as he sped toward Monroe Harbor twenty-five miles ahead. Planning was everything. It was so easy with the right plan. He would go the bank, get carry-out lunch for two in a small restaurant where they would remember him, and return in two hours. When he got back in the vicinity, he'd make a distress call. Joe and he were working on the engines when suddenly they reved, and Joe went overboard. One of them must have bumped something. Pete circled frantically looking. Joe simply disappeared. Joe's tools were still scattered in the back of the boat. He was an old friend, a valued employee.

CHAPTER 19

The agreed inter-agency protocol was that Coast Guard would direct the mission as a search and rescue operation so long as the FBI considered law enforcement issues secondary. In the event law enforcement became primary, the FBI would assume command. Control would remain on the same frequency. In the event of a marine rescue, the Coast Guard would move in first. In the event of interdiction, the FBI would move first, followed by Customs, then the Coast Guard. This was agreed on the SAR control frequency. The Columbus agent spoke for the FBI. He spoke from a National Guard helicopter flying due north out of Rickenbacker A.N.G.B., south of Columbus. He spoke through a headset as he hung in a gunner's harness at the open side door of an old Huey, long since handed down to the Guard. Under Bureau policy, he was agent-in-charge. He agreed to the protocol with the Coast Guard Commander speaking from the helicopter. Any change in command was his call. If things started popping before he got to the lake, he was prepared to pass field command to the head of the Toledo office who was also airborne working the southern shore east of Toledo.

After quick mental calculations of the speed and range of Falloni's boat, the Coast Guard divided the search into three sectors, Sandusky Bay and the Lake Erie Islands, the West End, and Huron to Cleveland. All were searched with equal priority. The Coast Guard had two amphibian helicopters and six boats, only two of the boats were fast. Customs had four boats, all fast. The FBI was riding in three National Guard helicopters and one charter. An hour into the operation TV traffic helicopters from Toledo and Cleveland volunteered to join the search. The Columbus agent gritted his teeth when he listened to the Coast Guard Commander welcome their help. He was over Bucyrus when he thought he recognized a female voice from a Beech volunteering and asking for an assignment. He broke in before the Coast Guard

Commander could respond. After determining it was Sandy, he passed her back to the Coast Guard. She was told they were searching for a forty foot high speed boat, bright red with white lettering, carrying one or two men. If sighted she was to report the position and break off. She was assigned grids over the northwest corner of the lake.

At 12:30 P.M. Sandy was convinced that her area was clear, and she asked for a new assignment. They moved her fifteen miles east along the Canadian shore. She did not acknowledge the assignment. She asked if the Columbus agent was on frequency. He was. On instinct, he had not joined the lake search, but rather was over the west end of Sandusky Bay, searching along the banks of the Sandusky River. He was following a foul play scenario. Sandy told him she wanted to check Monroe, Michigan. The agent knew the basis of her suspicion. He told the Coast Guard Commander she had a good idea. He gave her the assignment but told her to stay at or above 3,500 feet, clear of their search traffic. Ten minutes later, Sandy reported she had a red boat in sight. It was docked in Monroe. She began a two minute circle around downtown Monroe, hoping it was wide enough not to give her away.

At 12:45 P.M. Sandy reported one man boarding the boat. The Columbus agent, now skimming across the lake towards Monroe, told the Coast Guard Commander that the FBI was assuming command. He told them to stand-by for further instruction. He asked Sandy if she could identify the man. She could not. She reported the boat was underway, proceeding east out River Raisin. The Columbus agent ordered all boats and aircraft to clear a five mile corridor on a direct line southeast from Monroe through the South Passage into Sandusky Bay. He reminded everyone of the right of way rules, FBI, Customs, Coast Guard, in that order. He told the FBI aircraft to get their cameras rolling. He told the TV helicopters their help was no longer necessary. Sandy updated position reports as the red boat passed under the Freeway, then by the water treatment plant, Ford, then Detroit Edison at the mouth of the channel. The Columbus agent asked again if she could identify the number of people on the boat. She said one. She could not identify the person. She asked if anyone knew what Joe was wearing. One of the field agents from the Radisson came on with one word "khakis". There was a long pause. Sandy came back after she regained her composure and said the man on the boat was wearing dark pants, probably black, and a yellow shirt. There was another pause, then she heard the same agent broadcast "Falloni." The hearts of all the FBI men

on frequency sank. Sandy broke off and climbed up to 7,500 feet. She kept the red boat in sight, but it was little more than a speck. For the next twenty minutes,
she listened to periodic position reports on the frequency. Suddenly the Coast Guard Commander came on in an excited voice. They were getting a distress call on Channel 16, he was patching it through to the control frequency.

"Mayday, Mayday, Mayday. Falloni's Pride, Falloni's Pride, Falloni's Pride. Man overboard. No life jacket. No sighting. Man overboard. No life jacket. No sighting. Man overboard. No life jacket. No sighting. Mayday. Mayday. Mayday."

Everyone listened to it twice more. Then the Coast Guard Commander responded in standard fashion. Everyone listened in as the Coast Guard Commander acknowledged the distress call and requested more information. Falloni seemed frantic as he scrambled out the story. They stopped to tune an engine, the boat lurched, his friend went overboard. He had searched. He was gone. He didn't think he could swim. He didn't have a life jacket. The Coast Guard Commander asked if he had Loran or GPS. He had Loran. He read the coordinates, slowly and calmly in a tone that was inconsistent with his first report. He guessed he was five miles due north of West Sister Island. He did not say that he was five miles north northwest of where he dumped Joe. The Coast Guard Commander told Falloni to hold his position, help was on the way. Only then did Pete slow the boat to idle. The Columbus Agent asked if communications on their SAR control frequency could be heard on Channel 16. The Coast Guard Commander responded that was negative. The Columbus agent ordered all aircraft to converge to a half mile radius. He and the agent with him would board. They would proceed with an arrest. FBI units were to prepare to assist. Customs units were to prepare to back-up. In his mind he chanted, you son of a bitch, you're mine. You son of a bitch, you're mine.

Sandy numbly followed the pack of aircraft converging in the middle of the lake. She was in the god position, 7,000 feet over the operation. She watched one green helicopter advance ahead of the rest and hover over the boat. She reduced her power and put in some flaps for slow flight. She held a one minute turn. She started counting aircraft and boats, it was amazing. A few moments later a new voice came on frequency, she took it to be the chopper pilot. He said that the suspect appeared to be in custody. In fact, Pete Falloni was lying face down in his boat with his hands cuffed behind his back and his ankles cuffed together. The second agent read him his rights. The first waited, watching the wild trapped look in Falloni's eyes. He had seen it before. Not that often, but enough. The pros never had the look. It was the smart alecks who thought they were better than everyone else, the ones who never thought they might get caught. When the rights were concluded, the questioning over the whereabouts of Joe Altznauer began in earnest. Sandy looked out at the horizon. A few fracto-cumulus clouds were forming with tops below her at 6,500. Indeed, the layer of mild haze seemed to stop there also. She was up above it, up in the clear blue. That is when she heard the transmission. Coast Guard Two had a body in the water at Niagara Reef. The pilot read the coordinates off his GPS.

Sandy's stomach tightened and pulled her forward in a spasm. Her reaction from that was to push back into her seat. She brought the yoke back with her as she moaned. She did not notice the change in attitude, nor the shudder of the aircraft when it stalled. She did heard the engine whine come up, and that brought her eyes back into focus over the nose. She was headed straight down, but she wasn't spinning yet. She recovered from the stall. It was a sloppy recovery with too much right rudder. She almost spun the plane out of the recovery. She saw two large white Coast Guard helicopters moving away from the rest of the activity, so she flew towards them. She pulled her carburetor heat and started a descending spiral above them.

When Joe went overboard he had a screwdriver in one hand and a wrench in the other. His first reaction had been to hold tightly onto his tools. He held them while he thrashed at the surface. He did not swim. For a moment he thought only that it was an accident. This was exactly why he hated going on boats. He always knew that someday he would go overboard. He held his tools and cut at the water with them. Falloni would come back in a moment. He was probably hard to spot among the waves. Gradually, he tired. As his thrashing relaxed in his exhaustion, he realized that he was more buoyant. He thought of cycling, his long steady strokes when he was cruising. He couldn't sprint for long. He knew that. He needed to relax. He slipped the tools into his hip pocket. Later, he felt his work boots were pulling him down. He held his breath and struggled to get them off. For a time he fussed with tying them to his belt. He hated to lose them. They had steel toes. He remembered several times when they had saved his toes.

Reluctantly, he let them go. He looked for boats, but never saw any. He looked for land, but never saw shore. After an hour he took a chill. It came and went. When he got very cold, he tried to swim. It was little more than a dog paddle. Most of the time he treaded in place, or so he thought. The winds were strong. They moved him with the waves. He got colder and colder. His hands trembled. He looked at his fingernails. They were blue. The palms of his hands were wrinkled. Something touched his foot. His terror ended that chill. He told himself over and over that there were no sharks in Lake Erie.

Sandy leveled out at 3,500 feet in accordance with her last clearance. She couldn't see anything in the water and really didn't try. She spent most of the time staring down on the rotors of the large choppers. At this point most of the boats were converging on Niagara Reef below the hovering choppers. Lake Erie boaters, at least those in the West End know about Niagara Reef. It claimed many a prop and rudder. It is marked with a channel marker buoy, but boaters regularly hit that also. At the shallowest point, it is less than three feet deep. Falloni knew that and gave it wide berth, passing well north to dump Joe in thirty foot water. Once Joe thought he saw a green can buoy, but it was during a chill. In a later lucid moment, he passed it off as an hallucination. "Correction, Coast Guard Two has a swimmer. Negative body. Coast Guard Two has a swimmer."

The second time Joe's foot hit something, he realized it was a rock. He struggled to find it again but couldn't. It was then that he saw the can clearly. He paddled to it, and grabbed on to its cable. He tried to keep his body close to the surface for the sun and the warmer water. It was several minutes before he lowered his legs and found bottom. He could stand. The water was little more than waist deep. Standing, the sun was warmer than the water, but he occasionally took another chill from the breeze. When he did, he would paddle about the buoy. It warmed him a little. He felt he was getting a sunburn through his thinning blond hair. He tied the corners of the red shop rag in his hip pocket and made a hat. He still had his tools. He also worried about what might be below his feet in the mucky bottom. That was another reason to swim. He wished he had kept his boots. Over the next hour, he started giving himself swimming lessons. He found he could float better on his stomach than his back. Floating on his stomach exposed his back to the sun. It took no effort whatsoever. He would raise his face every few seconds for a breath. He wished he'd discovered this a couple of hours ago. He was face down in this position when the Coast Guard spotted him. When he heard their jet engines and rotors, he jumped to his feet and splashed greetings.

CHAPTER 20

Over Joe's protest, the Coast Guard helio took him to the Firelands Community Hospital in Sandusky. He admitted he was chilled, sunburned, and water logged; but nothing beyond that. During the flight to the hospital, one of the Cleveland agents from the Radisson got the Coast Guard pilot to get a headset to Joe. Joe spoke wrapped in a blanket. They changed frequencies, and he took Joe's spontaneous declaration of the day's events. Tape recorders operated by agents in three of the four FBI helicopters captured his recollections. The Huey that had carried the Columbus agents orbited Falloni's Pride flanked by two other fast boats, one Customs and one Coast Guard. Neither of the Columbus agents had piloted such a boat, but with radio instructions from the boats accompanying them, they quickly learned. They took turns at the helm during the trip back to Sandusky, playing and ignoring Pete Falloni who was still face down on the floor of the boat. The rest of the task force broke apart and went separate directions, except for the two TV helicopters. They followed at a distance. The helicopter carrying the two Cleveland agents who had been staying in the Radisson orbited Firelands while the Coast Guard helio delivered Joe. When it departed, their Huey moved in to drop them.

The agents waited outside the emergency room while Joe was given a cursory exam. Sandy landed at Griffing-Sandusky and got the van to take her to the hospital. Coming south down the channel into Sandusky Bay, there was an extended conversation between the three fast boats over what should become of Falloni's Pride. After a call to the Coast Guard Commander, it was agreed that Customs could impound the boat. The Coast Guard had enough paperwork. The Columbus agents pulled into the ferry docks in downtown Sandusky. The local police had been alerted and were waiting. The agents removed the ankle cuffs so Pete Falloni could walk to the police car. Most of the by-standers knew him and whispered to each other. Another police car took the agents to the hospital. Sandy arrived just before the two Columbus agents. When Joe, wearing a hospital gown, came to the entrance of the emergency room with a young doctor, Sandy rushed ahead of the agents and brushed passed the doctor to embrace Joe. She wrapped her arms around him and laid her cheek against his shoulder. Joe was uncomfortable with the public affection and particularly his garment. He held the back of the gown together with his left hand and nervously touched the small of Sandy's back with his right. He deeply inhaled the scent of her perfume. The agents wanted another statement from Joe. After discussion, all agreed they would take it at the hospital while Sandy went to get Joe's truck and some dry clothes. One agent called for a police car while Sandy went with Joe to retrieve his wet clothes and his keys from his pants pocket.

Sandy was surprised to find Falloni Marine surrounded by local police cars. When she questioned the policeman who drove her over, he told her they were treating the business as a crime scene. They were simply holding a lid on the place until the Feds moved it. They had chased out all the employees. They were making sure that no one operated the computers or touched any papers. He walked her to a man in a suit and explained that she was to pick up Joe Altznauer's truck. He nodded without ever looking at Sandy. Sandy was self-conscious as the employees and locals idling about watched her drive it away.

Sandy was both hungry and thirsty, so the first thing she did at Joe's house was go to his refrigerator. She smiled when she found a bottle of wine with a ribbon on its neck and note that said, "For Sandy". She took a can of pop and piece of lunch meat. In Joe's bedroom, she inspected the half dozen sets of khaki work clothes hanging in his closet. She was determined not to take them. He only had two pair of casual slacks. In his dresser she found a colored knit shirt and a pair of touring shorts with a padded crotch and balloon pockets. They were khaki, but they would do. She grabbed some underwear, socks, and his running shoes and hurried back to the hospital. She found the agents in a small room with Joe. They had finished his statement and were casually talking about electronic ignition systems.

They waited outside while Joe dressed. In the hall, the head agent from Columbus said they had a lot to do that afternoon, but that he'd like both Joe and Sandy to come by the Radisson later so they could video tape their recollections, just to be sure. He told Sandy that her testimony of sighting Falloni alone in Monroe, and following him all the way up through his distress call would be a nice touch for a jury. He wondered outloud if the prosecutors would use that first or last. Either way, he liked it. He asked them to come by the hotel late in the afternoon. After the statements, they could have dinner together.

Joe and Sandy stood outside the hospital on a sidewalk. Joe deliberately positioned himself to stay in the sunshine and out of the shade from a nearby tree. He asked Sandy what she wanted to do, if she wanted lunch. She didn't answer. He looked up and down the streets, saying that he never appreciated what a peaceful place Sandusky could be. It was an entirely different town now that he did not have a schedule, that he did not have to rush back to work. She told him about the police cordon around Falloni Marine. He shrugged, said he guessed he was out of a job, and laughed that he and Falloni never did have a chance to sign the agreement. The agents had taken the mushy remnants of his water logged copy as evidence. He supposed that would be another nice touch. Sandusky seemed entirely different during the day than he had ever seen it before. He kind of liked it.

Sandy suggested that he go home and take a shower to get off the lake smell. He agreed. When they came into his living room, Sandy thanked him for the bottle of wine. He smiled, realizing her earlier discovery. She opened it and poured herself a glass while he went into the bathroom. Joe was soaking in the warmth trying to rid the last of his chill. She listened to the shower running and started thinking about how clammy she felt from the excitement. Joe heard the bathroom door open. He held his breath as he watched Sandy's silhouette through the steamy glass. She slipped out of her clothes and into the shower. Not long after, he fumbled with the new box of condoms he pulled from the stand next to his bed. When Sandy had stayed overnight the week before, she had gone through his drawers and not found any.

Afterwards, they napped. They woke and showered together again. Sandy put her same clothes back on, she had left her bag in her plane. Joe put on a pair of his dress slacks and a knit shirt. Before he dressed, he had suggested they bike ride around town. He had extra bikes, he could adjust one to fit her. She declined. Maybe another time. They decided to go check her plane and get a bite to eat at the airport. They found an FBI crew working on her plane. They watched for a few minutes while the technicians vacuumed the inside and fingerprinted the outside. Inside the small terminal, a group of airport bums circled around them. They avoided straight answers, bought drinks from the pop machine, and left. Sandy wanted to drive.

Joe liked watching her from the passenger's side. In town, they drove down Third Street and stopped across the vacant lot from Falloni Marine. There were a couple of dozen bystanders watching along First Street. Most were kids who stood next to their bikes. The building was swarming with people. There were a half dozen on the tower alone. They were using nets and ropes to lower its contents from the catwalk to the roof. Joe and Sandy watched without talking. It was getting so late that they didn't want to spoil their dinners. They went to the Radisson and waited in the lobby for the agents. Shortly after 5:00 P.M. the agents returned.

Joe and Sandy followed them to their rooms on the fourth floor. One of the agents had a grocery bag. Joe looked in it after he put it down. Inside Joe saw four sealed evidence bags. He recognized the contents to be hard drives out of personal computers. In response to Joe's question, the agent explained that after years of fussing, their current procedure was to simply pull the hard drives. They would copy the programs and data onto compatible units and return the new units so that business could continue, but the originals were now evidence. Joe said that if they wanted, he could help them figure out the systems. The Columbus agent told Sandy that Detroit had her friend in custody. They had found the oil caps in a trash can at the airport. They had his fingerprints on them, and they hoped to find his prints on her plane. He wished they'd had more time to push the investigation further before it broke, but that is how things went.

After chatting, they took Joe's statement a third time, this time on audio and video. While they did, Sandy stood on the balcony, looking down on the marina at The Harbour, and across the lagoon to the old factory and its black tower. Occasionally, a large boat would idle back into the lagoon, turn and idle out. When it was Sandy's turn, Joe traded places.

Joe and Sandy had dinner with the four FBI agents at a restaurant on the lagoon adjacent to the hotel. They sat outside on a deck overlooking the water. Taking the lead of the head agent from Columbus, none of the FBI men drank. They were looking forward to a long night, indeed, perhaps even a long week in Sandusky. Joe didn't drink, and Sandy did not want to drink alone. Around them, the restaurant and bar started to fill with an odd combination of boaters, families up for the amusement park, and well-dressed professionals getting a quick buzz on the way home. Sandy offered to fly the Columbus men home, but they declined. The one who lived in Lancaster said he had talked to his wife, and she was coming up with the kids for a couple of days at Cedar Point. He hoped that as taxpayers they didn't mind him combining a little pleasure with work.

After a pause, they started working backwards through the unraveled fortunes of Pete Falloni. Joe said he should have known, all the signs were there, now so many little things made sense. The biggest changes came a few years earlier, after his father died. Sandy compared dates. She had checked out Preferred Wholesale. It was incorporated years before his father died. The agent spoke knowingly. He was sure it had been a progression. He said that every normal person had watched a bank teller count money or looked into a cash register at one time or another and fantasized, if only. Even the bad guys fantasized about one big heist. It never went that way. Those who crossed the line could never be satisfied. They took more and more, thinking they deserved it, until they thought they deserved it all.

He laughed when he recalled the first contact from Joe's friend. He thought he was being set up for some elaborate practical joke. Joe told stories about his friend; of working together on his Olds as teenagers, of how he thought of himself as a Romeo in high school. Sandy told stories about him in law school. The two Columbus agents grumbled about his cross-examination, to them it was never on point. Sandy said that maybe with his clients, confusion was the most he could muster. They laughed and agreed. The head agent admitted that it wasn't Joe's friend, it was his clientele that bothered him. He raised his water glsss in a toast, any friend of Joe's couldn't be that bad. Sandy joined saying that if he was a pilot, he couldn't be that bad. Joe raised his glass with a smile. On the excuse of work, the agents left quickly after dinner. Joe and Sandy stayed to watch the boats.

"I was never much for bars, even when I was drinking."

"Me either. We usually went to private clubs or dinner parties."

"It's nice here."

"Yes. Thanks again for getting the wine. I appreciate the thought."

"I'm sorry about last week. I don't know what to say."

"It was a hellish way to get to know someone."

"After the Lancaster trip, after that night, I really didn't think I'd ever see you again."

"Then why the wine, the condoms? They weren't there last week."

"You notice a lot."

"I take that as a compliment. You haven't answered. Why?"

"I couldn't stop thinking about you. I guess it was just wishful thinking."

"I bought some condoms a couple of weeks ago. I was worried what you would think."

"I went to the doctor. Got all the tests."

"You're kidding?"

"This is a nice place. My wife liked bars. I never did. I could sit here all night."

They looked up and watched a light plane turn downwind to base for Runway 9. Sandy asked about his wife, she couldn't imagine what it was like to lose someone, especially a baby. At least time was the great healer of wounds. Joe disagreed. He said it was like the day before yesterday. All the years in between were a blur, but that time in his life was still vivid. It still hurt. They shifted to Sandy's marriage. She was very apologetic. She said that she had disappointed everyone in her family, especially Daryl and her son. Joe disagreed again.

"No, really. If you were there, you would have hated me. I hate to think of the person I became."

"I know something about that."

"Daryl did not deserve what I became. He really deserved better."

"Maybe. Who decides who deserves what, and what is better than something else. Molly deserved everything. In the end she got nothing. I couldn't even give her...."

"It's not the same. You can't compare your life to mine. Neither of you chose for your baby to get sick, to die. I had choices. I let him down in the end."

"Choices. They are the haunting memories. I had choices. Molly had.... Maybe your husband chose to let you down somewhere along the way."

"Not so much down, he simply let go."

"I never will."

"Joe, do you think we deserve each other?"

"I hope so."

"So, Joe, now that this is over, what do you want?"

"You."

"No, really. What do you want? Half your life is ahead of you. What do you want?"

"I don't know."

"I know what I want. I want to find a town like this somewhere. A town big enough to have the finer things like my mother loves, some culture and refinement; but a town small enough to be like the world my grandparents lived in. I want a little airport like the Griffings have. Instead of being a gypsy, I'd run the airport, sell gas, give a few lessons, be a short order cook. I'd like to be part of the community. I'd like to hobble into the airport as an old lady and tell lies to the airport bums. That's what I want. I know exactly what I want."

"Any man in this dream?"

"I want it to be you."

"Sounds nice. I don't know. I've been thinking about working on airplanes. I sent for some literature on getting my A & P license. Looks like I'm going to have the time to do it. I don't know. It's just an idea."

Sandy leaned forward and took his hand. Later they went out to the airport to get her bag. Standing beside her plane, they looked up at the stars then kissed. Sandy said it was a nice night to fly and urged him into the plane. They flew out over the islands, then west to Monroe. Joe said he'd like to see where she lived. They landed in Detroit City at 10:45 P.M. She told him over and over how everything along the way was a typical night for her. They found her car where she left it. After entering her condo development, she stopped to get the day's mail from her box. Inside the unit, she went immediately to the phone to check her voice mail. They each opened a can of pop. Joe teased her, asking if it were part of her routine to fly in gentlemen guests. She refused to answer. Before they finished their drinks, they were in Sandy's bed making love.

Sunday morning, they ate on the way to Detroit City, then flew back towards Sandusky. Over the west end of Sandusky Bay, Sandy asked if Joe would like to fly down to Attica. Joe asked if she would like to meet his family. She flushed. She didn't answer. Joe urged her. They always had chicken on Sundays. He told her his father drank beer and plucked a couple of chickens every Saturday night. It was a ritual. They wouldn't be imposing. Sandy studied her sectional. The nearest airport was Willard, at least ten miles east of Attica. Joe said they could call for a ride; better, they could hitch. It would be an adventure. He had hitch-hiked out of Attica when he left home. They had all morning. It would be fun. Their second ride dropped them on Route 4 at the county road running west past his parent's farm. Joe and Sandy walked the last half mile holding hands. Joe stopped at the sound of a coal train heading north. He turned to watch it pass, not speaking until it was out of sight.

"You know, it doesn't look any different than the day I left here over twenty-five years ago. Nothing changes."

"Everything changes."

"I love you."

"I love you."

They embraced.

CHAPTER 21

I used to have a standard part of every closing argument in which I told the jurors that the most difficult part of their work was to pick the truth out of the contrary testimony of the various witnesses and opposing exhibits. I always ended that section by warning them it wasn't like TV or the movies, no cameras were rolling to record the action. They would have to reconstruct the events from the evidence that they alone chose to believe; and then, and only then, base their verdict upon it. It was a standard. I did not invent it. I heard it at the bar and incorporated it into my repertoire.

I don't use that one any more. No one does. Now it is an exception to have any kind of case without some video involved, even if it is specially produced just for the trial. Now we talk about camera angles and lighting, acoustic footprints and echos. Now I remind the jurors of that old expression about it all being done with mirrors. I'm not old enough to start grumbling about the way it used to be when I started trying cases, but things have sure changed as near as I can tell. Maybe the system is getting closer to the truth. Maybe not. I ought to see if there are some statistics linking the tapes to the conviction rates. There was a belly full of government surveillance tapes in the Falloni case, but not to the point of being unusual. Not even the home videos made the case unusual.

I have lunch with the head of the Columbus FBI office every few weeks. I took him and his kids up a few times, then he started lessons to get his ticket back. It seems like the way is paved with gold for ex-military pilots. I've been trying to sell him my plane so I can step up. I guess you could say we've become buddies, at least fellow airport bums. He teases and says I should join the side of righteousness and virtue and become an FBI agent, or even a prosecutor. I tell him that I've been there and done that. I'd like him to become my law partner.

He won't hear of it. He keeps me posted on the progress of the Falloni case.

Falloni went through three lawyers in rapid succession. He kept trying to cut deals with the prosecution behind his lawyers' backs. He wanted to get off in return for testifying against a couple of union officials. The prosecution laughed it off, and his lawyers cut him loose. Union corruption is passe'. The government decided to make an example of the small town tycoon, mostly because of the tax aspects of the case.

There were one hundred and thirty-eight counts in the federal indictment, including everything from wire fraud, tax evasion, and racketeering to interferring with a witness. As they say, everything but the kitchen sink. When the forensic accountants moved in, they really opened a Pandora's box. What Joe and Sandy were involved in turned out to be just the tip of the iceberg. On the state side, the Erie County Prosecutor held back until the federal charges were filed. A few weeks later the county Grand Jury came back with an equally impressive array of charges. There was every flavor of theft by deception that I've ever tasted coming out of the business and corporate shenanigans; and, of course, the attempted murder. Falloni was really unbelievable! I would have loved to defend him. I can just see the cocky overconfidence of the county prosecutors. They always think that having an FBI agent as a witness in a state trial locks the case. I don't think so. I think that jurors are fair. I'll tell you, it was my kind of case.

You know, they even found out that Falloni was part of a fuel scam. He started by buying fuel for his marina from that Russian crowd on the east coast. They had established a beach head in Cleveland and started selling fuel to the marinas around the lake at prices too good to be true. The Russians take gas right off tankers and then market it to independent dealers, like Falloni, who buy out of their own self-interest. The racket is that the Russians create a phony paper trail showing the fuel being sold by the tankers to wholesalers, who in turn sell it to the independents. The paperwork shows that federal and state taxes are paid on the fuel, but they aren't. They collapse the wholesaler corporations every few months and set up new ones, just to disguise the trail. The paperwork that the independents see make it look like the taxes have been paid; but they know better from the price they pay. Falloni knew better and wiggled himself into the action. He started setting up some of the paper burn companies for the Russians and also generated phony invoices on his personal computer showing that the burn companies paid taxes.

It was good while it lasted, but it popped up in the investigation of the parts scam. By the way, all those components were not missile guidance systems nor nuclear triggers. I guess we had watched too much TV. It was awfully easy to convince ourselves. They were just garden variety guts for personal computers. Falloni's start in procuring moonlight parts involved electronic ignition systems for the boat engines serviced at Falloni Marine and progressed from there. Falloni tapped into the black market for computer parts, mostly in Toronto. The whole Pelee Island business turned out to be plain stupid. He had initially shipped the hot goods into Canada by truck with all the appropriate paperwork and paid a duty at the border. Falloni couldn't stand losing those few percentage points, so he set up an elaborate transhipment network to sneak them in. While he was putting the system in place, the new treaty eliminated the tariffs. Apparently, he never knew that. As for why he had the parts flown, the only explanation on that came from the union witnesses. They delivered most of the stolen components to their distributors by car. Falloni was willing to pay for the air freight, so they didn't care. It was easier and cleaner for them. When these guys get so disconnected from reality that they think they're above the law, no one should be surprised if what they do doesn't make a lot of sense. I can't imagine how the man could reconcile air freight and the Pelee Island Ferry. I guess that old tariff at the border really bothered him.

I went to the Preliminary Hearing at the federal courthouse in Toledo. I could never take the time to observe a trial like that, but from my perspective the Prelim is more interesting anyway. The ostensible purpose is to determine if there is enough evidence to justify holding the defendant for trial, but usually it quickly dissolves into the defense lawyers doing discovery into all the things their clients have withheld from them or lied about to them. Prosecutors know that. They sit back and learn about the status of the defense from the type of questions asked. Of course, defense lawyers say they are about the business of rubbing the government's nose in the weaknesses of their cases to get better deals. It's a tough call. I hate to turn over any of my cards before the game starts. That's why I like to watch how others handle Prelims. Anyway, I was going to fly up for the hearing, but I'm VFR only, and it started on an overcast day.

I drove up and got there late. Sandy and Joe were sitting together in the court room. I had never seen them together before. Cute is the only way I can describe them together. They were like a couple of teenagers. They constantly held hands. We visited during the breaks and at lunch. I guess most the adjusting was mine. Sandy testified before Joe. Her testimony was relatively brief. When Joe testified, Falloni went out of control. His face flushed. He was noticeably angry. He kept giving his lawyer orders to object to something. The judge gave him several warnings. I know what his poor lawyer was going through.

At the end of the day, I was standing in the hall with Sandy and Joe, when they brought Falloni out of the court room. They cuffed him there in the hall. That's when our boy Falloni lost it. He started yelling at us, "What do you think you're looking at? What makes you think you're so special?" Then he zeroed in on Joe. He kept calling him St. Joe and told him it was all his fault. "Everything you have came from me. You just couldn't keep your mouth shut. You don't understand anything about business. I could have made you a rich man. I built it up, no one else. I paid you. No one paid me. I deserved the money. I earned it. No one else could have done what I did. I deserved more than I ever took." The guards took Falloni by each arm and started moving him down the hall. I moved in front of Joe, facing him, hoping to shield him from that crap. Then Falloni got completely out of control, he yelled back to Joe over his shoulder, "What are you going to do now, St. Joe? Who's going to pay you now? People like you need people like me. I even had to train your wife for you!" I ended up tackling Joe and wrestling around on the floor with him. That son of a bitch Falloni. It was almost enough to make me want to go back to prosecuting. I stayed in Toledo for the next couple of days. I felt obliged to do it for Joe. He didn't deserve that kind of grief.

I don't know if Falloni knew it or not, but the family lawyer had put the businesses in receivership and approached Joe to run them for his mother and sisters. I'm sure Joe was tempted. That's not the right word. I'm sure Joe felt obliged. He did stay on for a few months, just to get them through the summer. An older fellow who had been tight with Falloni's father ultimately took over and liquidated the businesses for the family. I think he bought the dealership for himself. I guess Joe just had enough of the water. He and Sandy got hold of an FBO in southern Indiana. He works on the planes. She gives lessons. I fly in about once a month. Sometimes they fly into Fairfield County. A couple of times a year we rendezvous up in the Lake Erie Islands. I always camp overnight out in the islands with one of my sons. They usually fly back to Sandusky and stay in some little motel near Griffing field. I suppose its because they met there. Maybe it's just the Firelands. Some people just can't stay away. Who knows why. I have learned one thing out of this. I now make it a point to stay in touch with my friends. By the way, did I mention that Joe and Sandy had my wife and I stand up for them at their wedding.